CW00418516

SPACE WOLF
THE SECOND OMNIBUS

THE NOBLE SPACE Wolves are legendary among the Imperium's elite defenders, the Space Marines. Noble of heart and ruthless in combat, the Chapter is nonetheless forced to fight their own feral nature and the curse of the Wulfen. Renowned among their ranks is Ragnar Blackmane, and *Space Wolf: The Second Omnibus* continues his epic journey...

Wolfblade: Ragnar Blackmane is sent to Terra to provide an honour guard to the Navigator House of Belisarius. Much more used to the brutal nature of the battlefield, will Ragnar be able to see through the subtleties of Terran politics and foil an assassination attempt?

Sons of Fenris: When Chaos attacks are reported on Hyades, the Space Wolves are sent to investigate. The jungle world holds many obvious dangers, but the biggest threat emerges in the shape of Chaos Space Marines. Can Ragnar discover the secrets buried on Hyades and triumph against the Ruinous Powers?

Wolf's Honour: In the conclusion to the saga, Ragnar and Space Wolves find themselves fighting their most-hated enemies: the Thousand Sons. Ragnar has the chance for redemption, but will he be able to overcome the sorceror Madox and his traitorous forces to reclaim the Spear of Russ?

In the same series

SPACE WOLF: THE FIRST OMNIBUS
(Contains books 1-3 in the series: *Space Wolf,
Ragnar's Claw* and *Grey Hunter*)
William King

More Space Marine action from the Black Library

THE ULTRAMARINES OMNIBUS
(Contains books 1-3 in the series: *Nightbringer, Warriors of Ultramar*
and *Dead Sky Black Sun*)
Graham McNeill

THE BLOOD ANGELS OMNIBUS
(Contains books 1 and 2 in the series: *Deus Encarmine*
and *Deus Sanguinius*)
James Swallow

HEROES OF THE SPACE MARINES
Edited by Nick Kyme and Lindsey Priestley

LEGENDS OF THE SPACE MARINES
Edited by Christian Dunn

SOUL HUNTER
Aaron Dembski-Bowden

SALAMANDER
Nick Kyme

· SPACE MARINE BATTLES ·

RYNN'S WORLD
by Steve Parker

HELSREACH
by Aaron Dembski-Bowden

A WARHAMMER 40,000 OMNIBUS

SPACE WOLF
THE SECOND OMNIBUS

By William King
& Lee Lightner

BLACK LIBRARY

A Black Library Publication

Wolfblade copyright © 2003, Games Workshop Ltd.
Sons of Fenris copyright © 2007, Games Workshop Ltd.
Wolf's Honour copyright © 2008, Games Workshop Ltd.
All rights reserved.

This omnibus edition published in Great Britain in 2009 by
BL Publishing,
Games Workshop Ltd.,
Willow Road,
Nottingham, NG7 2WS, UK.

10 9 8 7 6 5 4

Cover illustration by Adrian Smith.

A CIP record for this book is available from the British Library.

UK ISBN: 978 1 84416 774 6
US ISBN: 978 1 84416 775 3

Distributed in the US by Simon & Schuster
1230 Avenue of the Americas, New York, NY 10020, US.

See the Black Library on the Internet at
www.blacklibrary.com

Find out more about Games Workshop
and the world of Warhammer 40,000 at
www.games-workshop.com

Printed and bound by CPI Group (UK) Ltd, Croydon, CR0 4YY

IT IS THE 41st millennium. For more than a hundred centuries the Emperor has sat immobile on the Golden Throne of Earth. He is the master of mankind by the will of the gods, and master of a million worlds by the might of his inexhaustible armies. He is a rotting carcass writhing invisibly with power from the Dark Age of Technology. He is the Carrion Lord of the Imperium for whom a thousand souls are sacrificed every day, so that he may never truly die.

YET EVEN IN his deathless state, the Emperor continues his eternal vigilance. Mighty battlefleets cross the daemon-infested miasma of the warp, the only route between distant stars, their way lit by the Astronomican, the psychic manifestation of the Emperor's will. Vast armies give battle in his name on uncounted worlds. Greatest amongst His soldiers are the Adeptus Astartes, the space marines, bio-engineered super-warriors. Their comrades in arms are legion: the Imperial Guard and countless planetary defence forces, the ever-vigilant Inquisition and the tech-priests of the Adeptus Mechanicus to name only a few. But for all their multitudes, they are barely enough to hold off the ever-present threat from aliens, heretics, mutants – and worse.

TO BE A man in such times is to be one amongst untold billions. It is to live in the cruellest and most bloody regime imaginable. These are the tales of those times. Forget the power of technology and science, for so much has been forgotten, never to be re-learned. Forget the promise of progress and understanding, for in the grim dark future there is only war. There is no peace amongst the stars, only an eternity of carnage and slaughter, and the laughter of thirsting gods.

CONTENTS

INTRODUCTION

OK, I'M GOING to go out on a limb here.

The Space Wolves are the coolest heroes in the Warhammer 40,000 universe. They are the fiercest, the loudest, and the most likely to kick back and have a damn good feast after a hard day's slaying. Space Wolves like fine ale, red meat and bawdy songs, but most of all they love the glory of battle. These are men who have fought to survive every day of their lives, warriors forged in the fire of volcanic isles and quenched in the haunted oceans of Fenris. Frankly, they are well worth reading about.

There are no doubt plenty of people out there that disagree with my rather broad opening statement, so let's look at the evidence. It is widely known that Space Wolves are recruited from the tribes of Fenris, one of the three deadliest worlds in the entire Imperium. That's pretty hardcore from the start. Because Fenris has an elliptical orbit around its sun, its climate alternates between deadly cold and searing, punishing heat. No scholariums, chapels or training facilities here – as infants, Fenrisian males are given an axe as their first possession, and those that do not grasp it firmly are thrown out to die in the ocean. Land is scarce, and competition for resources leads to constant war between tribes. Death is something to be embraced rather than feared, for beyond the veil lies an afterlife of eternal war. Only the strongest prosper.

The very best of this warrior culture may attract the gaze of the Wolf Priests, earning through hard-fought valour the chance to ascend to the mythical continent of Asaheim. It is from this hardy stock, this bloodline of heroes that reaches back across the aeons, that the sons of Russ are chosen. Because of their unique character, it is easy for those familiar with the Space Marines to concentrate on the superficial qualities that make the Space Wolves different – their trophies and totems, their elongated fangs, their extreme facial hair. But underneath the beards and topknots the Space Wolves are Adeptus Astartes through and through. Each is tall and strong beyond mortal comprehension, able to crush a man's bones in his fist, survive in a vacuum, spit acid or sniff out their prey in a snowstorm. Space Wolves carry a portion of the Emperor's greatness in their blood, but they are far fiercer and more headstrong than their fellow Space Marines. Remember, these were barbarian warriors to start with. Though they have undergone the apotheosis from man to superhuman Astartes, they still carry the same sense of loyalty and martial honour that they grew up with. That's a whole lot more coolness right there.

And then we have the Canis Helix. Unique to the Space Wolves Chapter, the Canis Helix is introduced into every aspirant as he undergoes the frequently lethal trials of initiation. Having been abandoned in the arctic wastes after drinking from the Cup of the Wulfen, the aspirant's body will warp and twist, bulking out massively and becoming covered with hair. A primal lust to hunt and kill seethes in his mind, and he becomes something inhuman, a predator supreme. Unless the aspirant can overcome the monster inside him and return to the Fang he will haunt the wastes of Fenris as a creature of madness and horror. Most make it back, but some carry the shadow of the wolf in their souls forever more. Though the Space Wolves do not talk about it openly, there is strength in the Canis Helix that lurks within them, a berserk rage that can mean the difference between victory and defeat.

Despite the fact these warriors are infamous for their savagery and battle-lust, they remain true and noble to the core. Space Wolves are weatherbeaten and grizzled but they are still heroes through and through. They have an inherent, dogged loyalty to their leaders and to the Imperium itself. This sense of decency and justice has more to do with the heart than the mind, and as a result Space Wolves always fight the good fight, plunging straight in even when commanded to desist by the higher authorities of the Imperium. They are not interested in the traditional doctrine of the Codex Astartes; obeying the dictates of a dusty, ten-millennia old treatise on the art of war is just not their style. Their tactics revolve around separate packs of hunters rather than squads of soldiers. Each pack is a resourceful and cunning combat unit in its own right, and each member has a bond with his pack brothers that is stronger than adamantium. The Fenrisians are used to harsh decisions, constant war and selfless sacrifice; they know what is right and they will fight to the death to make it happen.

These factors make for great characters, warrior kings from a long line of heroes that stretches back into our own history. So where do they really come from, these gods of war? It'd be an outright lie to say that the Norse myths and sagas weren't part of the inspiration for Space Wolves. Ripping yarns one and all, the Norse myths are big on warrior champions, sea monsters, beautiful blonde goddesses, blood and guts, and wolves big enough to eat the sun. They are full of divine heroes fighting, shouting, striding about the place and smiting monsters, giants, and anyone else who gets on their hairy man-chests. These tales have lasted over a thousand years, not because of the beer, the women and the fighting (though that probably helps) but because they deal with seriously meaty subject matter. Concepts of life, death, victory, betrayal, survival, brotherhood and war – powerful themes whether they occur in Midgard, Asaheim or the unforgiving galaxy of the 41st Millennium.

These ingredients, in the right hands, make for really great stories. Especially when they've got Space Marines in them.

Phil Kelly
Author of Codex: Space Wolves, 2009

WOLFBLADE

PROLOGUE

ALL AROUND WAS deathly still. The old trees, with grey bark, and leaves long since killed by pollution, loomed out of the shadows like tormented ghosts. In the darkness around him, Ragnar could sense armed men on the move. He was not afraid. They were his men, sworn to follow him, and die at his command if need be. He wondered where the thought had sprung from. There would be no deaths among his men this night – at least not if he could help it.

He looked to the soft ground underfoot. Although he was moving quietly there was no way he could avoid leaving tracks. The weight of his armour ensured it. After weeks of fighting amid the wreckage of the hives of Hesperida, he was almost among nature again. Almost. The area must once have been a park or forestry dome, before the cultists had begun their uprising. It would have been a place of pleasure where the wealthy came to experience what the surface of their world had once been like. Now it was an area of death, the great geodesic dome was shattered, and the foul air of the tortured planet could now enter. Everywhere there were splinters of armour glass from the collapse, some of them almost as large as a man.

The night air was a peculiar mixture of stenches: the rot from the dead trees, the spores of the fast growing fungi that blotched their sides, industrial toxins, the faint scent of animals that had passed by not so long ago. And everywhere and always there was the faint insidious stench that Chaos left when it inhabited a world's surface for any time; it was the smell of corruption, rich, sweet and sickly.

Abruptly it came to Ragnar that he knew the source. Some of the trees were still alive – the blotched ones, the palest, the greyest, the most degenerate looking. They were not being killed by some parasite, he realised. They were being changed by it, or into it. It was the only way any living thing could survive in an environment so rapidly altered.

For some reason, he thought of Gabriella, and the Navigators, and he smiled grimly. It was the first time such thoughts had entered his mind in decades. He shook his head; he needed to concentrate on the task at hand. There were enemies out there in this tainted night, enemies who badly wanted him and his men dead. And right now their only defence was stealth.

Ragnar was not sure what had gone wrong up in orbit, but something had. The last he had heard was a brief scrambled burst on the comm-net that told of the arrival of a massive enemy fleet. Then everything had been lost in static. It was almost as if it were a signal informing them that the enemy offensive had begun. The cultists had attacked en masse supported by heavy weapon fire, and strange sorceries. Ragnar had made his men hold their posts as long as possible, but he had known from the very beginning they were fighting a rearguard action, and that eventually their position would have to be abandoned.

Several times he had tried raising central command, but something had shut down the whole net. Whether it was sorcery or some freak climatic effect, it did not matter. There was no way his superiors could know what had happened, and there was no means of attracting support. In any case, he did not need access to the comm system to know that none would be forthcoming.

The roars of Chaos Titan weaponry and the sounds of battle drifting on the wind told him all he needed to know. The enemy were mounting a massive offensive all along the front. His Blood Claw scouts had brought back word that the two adjacent sections of the line, held by Imperial Guard and Planetary units, had already crumbled. His men and the local levies supporting them were now a salient pushed into the body of the main enemy advance. And they would soon be cut off.

In the face of the sledgehammer falling on them, there had been no choice but to give the order to retreat. It had not been a popular one. For Space Wolves the most honourable death was in battle, and it was not in their nature to give way before the enemy.

Ragnar grinned. A Wolf Lord did not need to be popular, he needed to be obeyed, and Ragnar was. It was not his duty to throw lives away needlessly. It was his duty to defeat the enemy. However, if that was not possible, he would preserve as much of his force as he could so that they could return and overcome the foe another day. They had held out as long as they could, giving their men a chance to find their way back through the ruins of the great dome while they still had the chance. In fact, they had done the work of ten times their number in throwing back the enemy assaults.

It had not been easy. They had spent most of the time in deep bunkers amid the rubble, riding out the storm of artillery fire, keeping their heads down, and knowing that the enemy would advance as soon as the barrage finished. Perhaps sooner, for the warlords of the Dark Gods of Chaos were careless with their followers' lives. They had emerged from their dens to throw back probing attacks, and one massive wave assault that had been repulsed by the thinnest of margins. When night fell, Ragnar knew it was time to leave. He had given orders to arm the booby traps that filled their position, and he watched as the first squads began to melt away into the night. Even now, somewhere behind him in the darkness, the rearguard waited, keeping up sporadic fire on their enemies so that they would think the position was still held.

He wondered how much the noose had tightened around their necks. If the encirclement was complete the scouts would soon encounter enemy pickets and patrols. They had orders to report back without engaging, but it was always possible that the sons of Fenris would somehow manage to start a fight.

He had done his best to impress on the Blood Claws in particular that now was not the time for violence. A mistake could lead to the death of their entire company. At the time, they had appeared to recognise the gravity of the situation, but who could know what they might do out in the field?

Ragnar pushed these thoughts to one side. He had done all he could, and matters were out of his hands. He should focus on things he could influence. He sniffed the air. He caught the scents of his comrades, along with something that made his hackles rise – the taint of madness and murder that he was so familiar with. Deep within him something stirred. He felt the urge to snarl and rend. His worries about the scouts returned. If the stink of Chaos could still affect him after all these years, what about those youths...

No point worrying, he reminded himself. They were as well trained as he had been. They knew what to do. He just had to trust in that.

The ground shook under his feet as more high impact shells slammed home. He froze, instinctively, seeking to blend in with cover. Those hits had come from close by. Had the enemy spotted and targeted them? It was hard to see how they could have done so by conventional means, but then Chaos did not have to use conventional means. They had sorcerers and daemons and all manner of divinatory enchantments to call on. Ragnar had seen evidence enough of that in his career never to doubt it.

Their own position was supposedly warded by the spells of the Rune Priests, but they had been cast days ago, and such things had a way of untangling when most needed. Ragnar breathed a prayer to Russ and forced himself to start moving again. All around him his warriors did the same. With the pack mentality of the Wolves, they had instinctively waited for his response. Now they loped into action again.

Step by tortuous step, they progressed through the shadow of the great warped trees, grey ghosts in a grey landscape, towards fleeting sanctuary. Ragnar was not even sure that there was a sanctuary any more. What the scouts had reported earlier might no longer stand. Battle was a fluid situation; lines that seemed solid had a way of melting like tracks in sand before the tide. Perhaps the men behind them had been over-run by the advancing tide of evil. He would not know until he was much closer. Once again he cursed the battle that raged overhead. Without access to the comm-net and the divinatory orbital sensors, they were blind as well as deaf. At least, he hoped battle still raged overhead. If the Imperial Fleet had been defeated, then they were cut off, and they were all dead men who did not know it yet.

He glanced skywards at the strange stars through a break in the clouds. They glittered and twinkled oddly, their light filtered by pollution. Some of those lights might be ships, he thought, and some might even now be firing weapons of unimaginable power at foes shielded by titanic energies. There was no way to tell. All he could do was watch and hope.

How quickly the situations change, he thought. A week ago everything had seemed well in hand. His forces had cleared most of the surrounding blocks of territory and were poised to strike at the heart of the enemy – the great citadel where the rebellion had its headquarters.

The appearance of the enemy fleet and an unexpectedly large number of enemy forces had thrown all careful calculations out of kilter. Ragnar told himself not to despair. He had been in worse situations. He had been in such tight spots that this seemed a mere feast day revel. It was strange though, how faded memories of long past dangers never compared with feelings engendered by current threats. He had seen enough men die to know how long the odds were. No matter how well trained or experienced, there was always the chance that a stray bullet would find you. Even odds of a thousand to one did not seem long when you had been in a thousand fights.

Where were these thoughts coming from, he asked himself? They should not normally occur to a commander with an Imperial field force at his beck and call. He was not normally like this. And he felt worse than a normal commander would, because his scent transmitted his mood back to his pack, and they in turn reflected this.

Was he under some sort of attack, he wondered? Was there some chemical in the air, too subtle for his detectors and his nose to pick out? Or was some daemon-worshipping sorcerer at work? Not all spells involved bolts of fire or the summoning of hell-spawned fiends. He was shielded against obvious attacks, and knew how to resist a direct probe at his mind. But this could be something more subtle, he thought, a flank attack on the citadel of his mind. He began to recite a litany of protection, softly, under his breath.

Immediately he felt better, although he was not sure whether it was from the comfort he took in his words, or the potency of prayer itself. Sergeant Urlec moved up beside him. There was acrimony in his scent. The sergeant had taken to questioning many of Ragnar's decisions in private. There was friction between them, and Ragnar recognised its source. It was the tension that rose between the younger Wolf and the older one, as to who would lead the pack. This friction was grafted into every Wolf's geneseed from the ancient days of the First Founding.

Ragnar had been like this once, and he wondered when the challenge would come. It was strange to think of himself as the elder in this situation. He had come early to his lordship and was probably younger in years than Urlec although that had no bearing on the way either of them viewed the situation.

'Scouts report enemy up ahead,' said Urlec. 'Looks like we are cut off!'

'Did they say that, sergeant?' said Ragnar. Both of them spoke so quietly that only another Space Wolf could have picked up their words, and only then if they were very close. Urlec's scent became more acrid.

'No, Lord Ragnar,' he said grudgingly. 'They only said the enemy were present.'

'Then there's no evidence of encirclement yet, sergeant,' said Ragnar, his hackles rising as he spoke the contrary words. 'Just because there are enemy there, we are not necessarily cut off. Send the scouts forward and tell them to feel out the enemy position. In the meantime, tell the rest of the packs to slow their advance. We don't want to blunder into a fire-fight in the dark.'

'It's already done,' said Urlec, with some satisfaction. Ragnar fought an urge to growl. Of course Urlec had done it. He was competent. That was why Ragnar had promoted him when Vitulv had died. He only wished the man was not so smug. He did not need this contest of wills and wit with his senior sergeant right now. There were more important things to worry about.

Ragnar forced his breathing to slow. The problem here was his. The folly of Urlec was just one more obstacle to overcome in order to preserve his company. The man would be dealt with later, but right now, Ragnar had to live with with his presence and his attitude.

'Very good,' he said, knowing that Urlec could read his mood from his scent. Briefly he considered once more the possibility of psychic attack. Perhaps this was more than instinctive hostility, perhaps it was some form of sorcerous assault. Ragnar wished Brother Hrothgar were present to perform a divination. But that was like wishing for a fleet to carry him to the moon. Hrothgar had been summoned to command days ago and had not been heard of since. It was a pity. Perhaps a sending would have been able to find out what was going on back there.

Ragnar slowed his pace, as he and the sergeant began to encounter groups of Wolves hunkered down in cover. They were taking things seriously at least. They knew that potential disaster lay ahead of them, as well as behind. He threaded his way through them, silent as a shadow. He made less noise than Urlec although he was the larger of the two. He wanted to get as close to the frontline as possible, and get the word direct from the mouths of the scouts as they returned.

He reviewed his options. One good thing about fighting on this ground was that he was familiar with it. Over the past few weeks he had scouted it himself several times, getting to know the terrain. He had wanted to be prepared for any eventuality, no matter how remote a retreat had seemed at the time. He knew that the dome was full of rolling downs, depressions and ridgelines that could provide cover for defence and attacks. That the hills were sculpted and artificial did not matter – they looked as natural as anything on his home world of Fenris. He knew there were two winding valleys, like canyons that snaked through the park and many sculpted streams and waterfalls.

Right now they were moving along the inside of those valleys, using the cover. On the other side of the elevation, flanking troops of scouts could make sure no ambushers took them by surprise from the ridge tops. This was the easiest line of retreat but also the most obvious for an enemy familiar with the terrain. He had chosen it because they needed to be swift as well as stealthy, and he trusted the ability of his men to keep out of sight of their opponents. He hoped that his trust would prove justified.

Why the constant doubts, he asked himself? He knew the answer. They were not the objects of some psychic attack. They were the products of what was happening. It was easy to have complete confidence in yourself and your men when you were winning. It was a lot harder when things were against you. He did not think it was a coincidence that Urlec's subtle challenges had begun when things started to go against them. He supposed it was only natural, but he did not like it.

Get used to it, he told himself, you cannot always be on the winning side. Not unless you were the Imperium anyway. It was a joke among the human military that the Imperium always won, even if it took a thousand years. Individuals, regiments, armies might be lost in meat-grinder campaigns but in the end the forces of the Emperor were always triumphant – they had to be, they were just too numerous for it to be any other way.

Part of him knew this was mere conceit. In the great cosmic scale of things, the Imperium was relatively young, despite its ten thousand year history. There were races out there that had been old when humanity had just begun to look up at the stars from the caves of a single world. Ragnar himself had seen the remains of civilisations that had once covered as many worlds as humanity did today, and perhaps had been even more powerful. 'Look upon my works ye mighty and despair', as he had observed once on the plinth of a toppled statue on a far off desert world. It had been erected by humans during the long gone Dark Age of Technology, but the sentiment could have been directed at any of the extinct races of the times before man.

He forced his attention back to the task at hand, pushing forward to the best cover at the front of his retreating force. He waited for the scouts to return. Urlec hunkered down beside him and waited too. There was still a look of challenge about him, but he said nothing. Ragnar wondered whether the man was right to doubt him. He doubted himself, and Urlec would sense that weakness and pounce on it. It was the Wolves' way.

He caught the scent of the scouts returning. They caught his and moved towards him, sure-footed in the darkness. Swift, confident and full of the blood lust of the Space Wolves.

'What have you seen?' he asked.

'The enemy are there, lord. They have moved to encircle us with at least two companies of heretics. Some of the accursed Thousand Sons are there too, at their head. They have set up wards, and work evil sorceries. The place stinks of them.'

That did not sound good, Ragnar thought. Ordinary infantry men would be easy to overcome with speed and surprise, but the Thousand Sons were Space Marines like his own men. No – that was not true, they were very different in important ways. They were Space Marines who had betrayed the Imperium at the dawn of its history and sworn themselves to the service of the Dark Gods of Chaos. They were ensnared by the subtle sorceries of the daemon god Tzeentch and were given over to the study of his dark spells. They were ancient, inimical and steeped in the most profound and subtle evil. And they were deadly fighters. Ragnar had fought them on dozens of occasions, and it seemed that he was destined to cross their paths throughout his career. Some of those encounters had changed the course of his life.

'Anything else?' he asked.

'There are gaps in their line. I do not know if they are aware of them, or whether it's a trap,' said the scout. He sketched out a map in the dirt, perceptible by the scent trace of his finger more than by the lines drawn. 'Here and here are gaps where their patrols have no line of sight. I could crawl between them and not be noticed.'

'Unless they have some spell waiting to be triggered by our presence.'

'Such was my thought, Wolf Lord,' said the scout, squatting.

Ragnar considered his words. It did not matter if it was a trap. They were caught between hammer and anvil. They could not wait where they were, for the dawn would reveal them to their foes. They could not go back, for soon their old position would be over-run. They needed to push through the gap and try to make it back to the safety of their own lines.

'The slaves of Horus,' Ragnar asked. 'Do they look towards us, or towards the Guard regiments behind?'

'They seemed to be mostly concerned with us, milord.'

Not surprising, Ragnar thought. They would not want to leave a fortification full of Space Wolves behind them when they moved on. That would leave the chance of a break out, or having their supply lines harassed. They would want their foe dead if they could achieve it.

'It was odd, my lord. I know nothing of such things, but I sensed that they were concentrating their spell energies in our direction. Certainly their witch lights flickered towards us.'

'I think if they were targeting us, we would have known it by now,' said Ragnar. He was surprised when both Urlec and the scout nodded agreement. 'Whatever evil they work, no doubt it is aimed at our former position.' Which we abandoned just in the nick of time, thought Ragnar. He offered up a prayer to Russ that the rearguard had already vacated the strongpoints. Whatever the Thousand Sons were planning it would not be pleasant, he was sure.

He thought about the darkness in his thoughts. He recognised it now: it was the effect of an evil spell cast in the vicinity, the seepage of wicked energies filtered into the sane and normal world by the forces of dark magic. It affected the mood of any living thing around it, sometimes so subtly it was not noticed until it was too late. The realisation raised Ragnar's mood. If you knew what you were fighting, you could resist it much better.

Another thought occurred to him. If the feeling was intense here, what would things be like in the abandoned strongpoint? Far more intense, no doubt.

'How many Thousand Sons?' he asked.

'I counted a dozen, Wolf Lord, but there may be more.'

'Not many,' said Ragnar. 'For a full company of Wolves.'

If the mages were wrapped up in their ritual and did not even know they were there, there was a chance they could strike a heavy blow before the enemy was aware of it.

How swiftly things change indeed, thought Ragnar. One moment feeling beaten, and the next considering swift attack. Such were the fortunes of war.

'I need to know where every one of those bastard offspring of Magnus are,' said Ragnar. He sensed he had the full and undivided attention of the scout and Urlec now. 'I want them all dead before dawn.'

Approval radiated from them now, albeit reluctantly from the sergeant. 'Pinpoint them all. Urlec, spread the word among the men. When I give the signal we're going to remind the Chaos-loving scum of the Scouring of Prospero.'

Both men nodded and set about their business. Ragnar considered his options. If the Thousand Sons were lost in evil rituals, his men could have the upper hand. What they needed was to destroy the mages, and then cut through the enemy along the line of least resistance. If things went well, they could interrupt the ritual and make it back to their own lines. If things went badly, they would at least drag some worthy foes down to hell with them.

Was he doing the right thing? Perhaps it would be best to try and find a gap in the enemy lines and go through it. He shook his head. No, this was the bold way – the Space Wolf way. The enemy obviously did not know they were here. Surprise was too great an advantage to throw away. The wait for the scouts to return seemed interminable. Every minute brought dawn closer. Every heartbeat increased the chance of discovery. Ragnar forced himself to relax, to wait, and let go of things he had no control over. He checked his weapons lovingly, a ritual that never failed to ease his mind. He fingered the pommel of his frostblade, which brought back memories of Gabriella and the Navigators and his long ago stay on the heart world of Terra.

He let his mind drift towards those ancient events for a moment, and then he snapped back. The scouts were returning. 'A dozen, Wolf Lord,

I am sure of it. They seem to be standing in some evil arcane pattern unless I am mistaken. Lines of witchfire leap between them, and they chant in some foul tongue.'

Ragnar nodded, and spoke swiftly, giving orders to the scouts to pass to the squad leaders. No sense in using the comm-net, even locally, at the moment. It might well be compromised. Word would have to ripple through the dark in the ancient ways, carried by sight, sound and smell. He sniffed the air, testing it. He could catch the change in the pack's scent. Word was being passed, men were readying themselves for the advance. In his mind's eye, Ragnar could picture them moving closer to all those thirteen points. Suddenly there was a flicker of light overhead, not as bright as a flare but intense nonetheless. Ragnar recognised it as a starship's shields going into overload and its power core going nova. High above them a ship full of men had died. He would have given a lot to know which side they belonged to. Irrelevant, he told himself. Keep your mind in the here and now.

The warriors of his bodyguard were close around him now. They were the best of the best. He had put himself at the spearhead of the attack for he knew it would make little difference now whether he lived or died. He had done all he could with the plan. Now it was a matter of fight or die.

Swiftly and silently, they slithered through the dark, bypassing sentry devices, stepping over tripwires. Most men would not have spotted them, but for Ragnar and his warriors, the stench of Chaos gave away their position. Suddenly up ahead, through a gap in the undergrowth, he caught sight of a glowing object. He paused and raised his hand. Immediately his men halted.

He studied what he could see, taking it all in with a quick glance. There was a tall, pale staff of yellowed bones, fused together at the joints. At its tip was a skull like that of a horse, only it was horned and had a faint suggestion of the humanoid about it. The skull glowed faintly and lines of fire sprang from it, speeding off to other places where no doubt similar staffs stood. On the bones, crimson runes glowed. The staff radiated an aura of power but what stood beside it commanded most of Ragnar's attention.

He could see a tall man, garbed in glowing armour that was like an ancient baroque copy of Ragnar's own. Every centimetre of the armour was either etched with runes like those of the staff or sprouted tiny cast metal daemon heads which leered and moved with a will of their own. The warrior's arms were spread wide, and Ragnar's keen ears caught the words of some ancient spell being chanted in the tongue of daemons.

All around the man stood Chaos cultists. They were normal men, though some were marked with the stigmata of mutation. All wore the patched uniforms that indicated they had once, in a better day, belonged to the Planetary levies. They looked gaunt and filled with fear and exaltation, but their weapons were serviceable. Their leader, wearing the shoulder markings of a lieutenant, looked as if he wanted to say something to the Chaos Space Marine but did not dare. The wicked warrior dwarfed normal humans just as Ragnar or any of his men would have done. The mage's voice droned on, almost imperceptibly rising, the words tumbling out faster now, as if nearing a dark climax. The air was charged with alien presence and a feeling of dread began to fill Ragnar.

He had no idea what foul ritual was being worked here, but the time had come to stop it. He sprang up and aimed a shot at the sorcerer. The bolter shell smashed into his armour sending him tumbling headlong into the dirt. Ragnar thought he caught sight of a faint flicker of chain lightning along the armour after he pulled the trigger, but did not let it bother him.

'Charge!' he bellowed, gesturing with his unsheathed frostblade. The men of his guard rushed forward. All along the line he could hear the sporadic sound of bolter fire as other squads engaged the enemy.

Ragnar let out a howling war cry that echoed in the woods around them, magnified a hundred-fold. He emerged from the bushes, cleaving at the nearest enemy and separating him from his head with one mighty blow. Moments later he was among the cultists, hacking and chopping, sending another soul to greet its dark masters in hell with every blow.

His men all did the same. They emerged from the tree-line like a thunderbolt, and cut through the enemy as if they were mere children armed with wooden swords. The initial engagement was not a battle; it was a massacre. Ragnar could see their lieutenant frantically demanding that his troops stand their ground. He put a bolter shell through the man's brain, and his attempts to rally his men ended forever.

'Ah, I might have known the fabled Wolves would show up and spoil everything,' mocked a beautiful voice that carried across the field of battle. 'It has always been your way.'

Ragnar glanced around to see that the Chaos warrior had risen from the ground and had unsheathed a darkly glowing runeblade. When he lashed out Ragnar saw Red Eric, one of his bodyguard, go down. The Chaos blade had cut right through his armour as if it were not there.

It was an impressive feat, for Eric had been a seasoned warrior of no little skill. The Chaos warrior's next strike cleaved through Urlec's chainsword, and then, with a blow from his armoured fist, he managed to knock the sergeant from his feet. Now the Chaos warrior stood over him, aiming a downward thrust. 'I suppose I should thank you for interrupting the tedium of the ritual, and for letting me offer up some half-way worthy souls to my patron. You are certainly more worthy than the mewling, puking defenders of this paltry planet, although if truth be told that is hardly a recommendation.'

Ragnar turned and raced towards the Chaos warrior, intercepting his downward arcing blade with his own. 'I don't care what you think,' he said. 'I don't care what your patron thinks. I just want you dead.'

'Spoken with all the arrogance of a Wolf! But you are no match for the High Mage Karamanthos,' said the Chaos warrior. He spoke with a dramatic flourish, like an actor, and appeared to expect recognition. Even if Ragnar had known him, he would not have given the daemon worshipper the satisfaction.

'It's a pity you don't have the strength to match your overbearing ego.' Sparks flared as their blades clashed. The red runes brightened. They fought over the prone body of the dazed sergeant.

'Don't I?' said Karamanthos mockingly. 'Perhaps it is you who doesn't.'

Ragnar's weapon grated down the runesword with a terrible scream of tortured metal. As it reached the guard of the Chaos warrior's blade it stopped, locked in place. The two mighty warriors stood breast to breast, their strength equally matched for a moment. Ragnar noticed the strange reek of ozone and hot metal coming from the visor of the Chaos Space Marine. Who knew what lay within that armour, he thought, but he was willing to bet it wasn't anything remotely human anymore. His muscles ached from holding his opponent in place. Perhaps this creature of sorcery had no sinews left to tire. Perhaps it did not feel fatigue. Perhaps it had the unfailing strength of a daemon.

'No, dear boy, you don't,' the Chaos warrior said and made to move its weapon. Ragnar held it in place. His breath was coming in gasps now. The sorcerer seemed to change his mind and began chanting something – a spell no doubt. With an effort of will, Ragnar extruded the claws in his boots. He stepped back and lashed out with his foot, catching the Chaos warrior behind the exposed knee, where the armour's thigh and calfguards met. He felt the blades bite home and saw Karamanthos begin to tip over. Seizing his opportunity he sprang forward, avoiding the Chaos warrior's desperately flailing blade, and buried his own weapon deep in his foe's throat. The chant cut off completely.

Sparks flared at the point of impact and rose into the night sky, accompanied by a dreadful smell of molten metal, corrosion and rot.

Vapour, hot as steam, but far more corrupt, rose too. It was as if the spirit of the ancient sorcerer was fleeing its host body. Ragnar lashed at it, but his blade passed through and the thing began to dissipate for a moment. Then it started to cohere and flowed towards the skull tipped staff.

Ragnar howled in defiance and struck the staff. For a moment the vitrified bone, product of alien sorcery, resisted his blade, but then it snapped. The glow faded. The lines of fire winked out as if they had never been. From various points in the distance Ragnar heard screams like those of lost souls in torment. He guessed that disrupting the focal point of this dark ritual had had no good effect on the sorcerers weaving it. He felt no sympathy. Those who trafficked with dark powers deserved what they got.

He brought his boot down on the glowing skull, and smashed it to smithereens. Immediately the sense of dark presence vanished. He howled triumphantly and his men echoed his call. Then he dived forward into the roiling mass of Chaos cultists, cleaving them asunder with renewed vigour. He drove them from him like a hero from some primitive saga unleashed once more into the world. His men followed him forward to victory. Howls of triumph along the line told him that the Wolves had overcome.

RAGNAR SAT IN the main camp of the Imperial forces. The walls had taken a pounding but he could see fresh troops gathering, ready to drive back the Chaos worshippers. The comm-net had been restored. It seemed the Chaos fleet had been driven off and the reinforcements they had been sending down to the planetary surface had let up. His men were encamped below, talking softly among themselves. Casualties had been mercifully light but they did not know about the rearguard, who had yet to report in.

Ragnar knew he would have to send out a search party for them, but now was not the time. The support barrage from the Imperial artillery was already pounding the earth around them. Soon, he would requisition some Thunderhawks and begin the search. He would either find the men, or collect their geneseed to be returned to the Chapter. Such was the way of the Wolves.

Ragnar stretched his legs and relaxed while he could. Soon it would be time for battle again. He caught the scent of Urlec approaching, and looked up, wondering what the sergeant wanted this time. Urlec gave him a shame-faced smile and said, 'I wish to thank you for saving my life, Wolf Lord.'

'It was nothing, sergeant. You would have done the same for me.'

'I doubt it, Wolf Lord. I doubt that I could have overcome the Chaos sorcerer.'

'Perhaps not today, Urlec, but you will learn.'

'I doubt that on the best day of my life I could. He was the chief of the Chaos lovers. None of the others gave our men such problems. I have never seen anybody so fast or strong as you, my lord. And his blade was stepped in evil magic! No normal weapon would stand against it. I am surprised that even yours could.'

Ragnar inspected the blade. 'I am not,' he said.

Urlec stared at the blade as if seeing it for the first time. Of course, he knew of the weapon, but knowing of it and seeing it in action were two different things.

'That is a fell weapon,' he said eventually. 'And no forge on Fenris produced it.'

'You are right,' Ragnar replied.

'How did you come by it then?' The sergeant asked.

'It was a gift,' he said.

'A gift worthy of a primarch then,' said Urlec.

'And yet it came from no primarch.'

'From whom then, lord? And why would someone make such a gift?'

'From a woman whose life I saved, although there was a price. It is a long story,' said Ragnar studying the position of the sun. 'And now is not the time to tell it.'

But as Urlec moved away, he could not help but recall it.

CHAPTER ONE

'BY Russ, I cannot believe that they are bloody well doing this to you,' said Sven. His blunt, honest, but ugly face was angry. He slammed his new prosthetic fist against the palm of his still-human hand. 'There are a million reasons for sticking your head on a spear shaft: vanity, ugliness, brute stupidity and your sheer lack of heroism and charisma, but this is daft!'

'Thank you, wolf brother,' said Ragnar. 'Your support overwhelms me.'

Ragnar tried to smile. He was glad to see his old friend, and more glad still to see he had recovered from the hellblade wound he had taken in the battle against the Thousand Sons. But he could not maintain his usual jocular tone – this was too serious. He was in deep, deep trouble. The assembled Convocation of Wolf Lords had made that perfectly plain. That all of the Wolf Lords present on Garm had met to discuss his fate was a sign of just how serious things were.

As was the business of confining him to his cell while the rest of his battle-brothers scoured the world of the remaining heretics. Sven was his first visitor in days, and he had snuck in during a brief respite in the campaign. There had been no guards, but visitors to this part of the shrine complex had not been encouraged.

'I mean, so what if you lost the Spear of Russ,' said Sven. 'You did it with the best of bloody intentions, I'm sure.'

'It is not something to joke about, Sven.' That was something of an understatement, Ragnar thought. The Spear of Russ was perhaps the most sacred of all the Space Wolves' holy relics. It was the mystical weapon that the legendary founder of the Chapter had carried into battle at the dawn of the Imperium. With it, the primarch had slain monsters and daemons, and had saved whole worlds. It was said that his first act on his return would be to claim his Spear from this very shrine. He was going to find that a little difficult now, Ragnar thought, all things considered. 'What you are saying is very close to blasphemy.'

'I am sure if good old Leman Russ is eavesdropping on our conversation he would agree with me.'

'And how would you know that, Brother Sven?' asked a stern voice from the back of the chamber. 'Does the spirit of the primarch consult with you in secret when he needs a particularly stupid opinion? If such is the case, perhaps you should share it with your battle-brothers? They will be pleased to learn that they have such an oracle among them.'

Both Ragnar and Sven looked around. They were startled to see that Ranek, the Wolf Priest, had entered the great chamber. It spoke something of the old man's stealth that he had managed to approach them unnoticed despite their supernaturally keen senses. He must have come from down-wind, Ragnar thought. He checked the direction from which the recycled air was coming. Either that or we were both simply too preoccupied to notice him. That is a more likely explanation, he decided.

Ragnar studied the old man. He was huge and grim and grey looking. The fangs protruding from his upper lip had an almost tusk-like quality. His hair was so grey it was almost white. But his eyes were keen and piercing, like the cold blue of glacial water off the coast of Asaheim. His eyebrows were enormously bushy, whereas his beard was long and fine. How long had it been since Ragnar first set eyes on him on the long voyage to the Islands of the Iron Masters?

A lifetime ago was the simple answer, no matter how you measured it in Imperial Standard years. In those days his father had still been alive and captain of his own dragonship. His people – the Thunderfists – were still one united clan. They had not yet been killed or become the enslaved thralls and bondswomen of the Grimskulls. It was before he had died and been reborn, when the limits of his universe were the grey, stormy skies and leaden seas of his home world, Fenris. It was before he had learned how big the universe really was, how strange and dangerous.

It was before he had become a Space Wolf, one of the legion of genetically re-engineered warriors who served the Imperium of humanity in its galaxy spanning wars. It was before he had fought with men and monsters and the daemon-worshipping servants of Chaos. Even before he had known what a green-skinned ork was.

'Well, Sven? Do you want to induct me into the mysteries of your new theology? As a Wolf Priest, I would be honoured to share in your wisdom.'

Sven looked abashed. There were very few things in this universe that could make him so, but this old man was one.

'I am sure Sven meant nothing by his words,' said Ragnar.

'Ah,' said Ranek. 'So you are the prophet's chosen interpreter, are you, Ragnar? He speaks only through you now, does he? He is too far above the rest of us mere mortals to deign to talk with us.'

'That is not what I meant,' said Ragnar.

'Then pray keep your mouth shut!' said Ranek. 'You are in enough trouble already without using your tongue to dig yourself deeper. Now, get out of here, Sven!'

Sven slunk off towards the chamber exit. Just as he was about to pass through the door, Ranek spoke once more, in a kinder tone. 'It does you credit that you came here, lad. But it will do you no good if the Wolf Lords find out.'

Sven nodded, as if he understood. Then he simply departed. Ragnar immediately regretted his going. He was now alone under the stern eye of the priest. The old man walked around him, studying him from every angle, as if he were a puzzle that could be deciphered with enough contemplation. Ragnar stood stock still, determined to show no nervousness under this chilly examination, even if Ranek could smell it coming from him, which he most likely could.

'Well, laddie,' said Ranek, 'you've caused quite an uproar, and no mistake.'

'That was not my intention,' said Ragnar.

'And what was your intention, when you cast the Spear of Russ into the realm of Chaos?'

'I was trying to prevent the arrival of the Primarch Magnus through the infernal gateway he had created in his temple on this world. I was trying to stop the resurrection of the Thousand Sons and the destruction of our Chapter. I believe I succeeded.'

'Aye, laddie, and I know you believe that. The question is whether it is the truth. Magnus is a powerful sorcerer, perhaps the most powerful who ever lived. He could have put that thought in your mind. He could have put others there too.'

'Is that why the Rune Priests have kept me segregated from the Chapter until today, and chanted their spells over me day and night?' Ragnar asked.

'It was. That and other reasons.'

'Which were?'

'You will be told them in good time, if you need to know, and if the Wolf Lords decide to let you live.'

'To let me live?' Ragnar was shocked. He had known things were serious but not this serious. He had imagined imprisonment, exile, even banishment to the nether regions of Fenris or some isolated asteroid. He had not imagined death.

'Aye – a fallen Space Wolf would be a terrible thing to let loose on the Imperium, laddie, and one who has been tainted by Chaos could not be allowed to live. Too much of a threat.'

Ragnar considered this and understood it. The Chapters were small, but their strength came from their ability to fight as a unit. Every man relied implicitly on those he fought alongside. To have a traitor within the Chapter was unthinkable. He knew he was not one but...

Of course, that is what he would think if he had come under some sort of spell. He might well believe himself to be completely loyal until some moment of Magnus's choosing and then...

He knew such things were possible. Psykers could read minds, alter memories, and change people's thoughts and emotions. He had been trained to resist such things but Magnus was a primarch of the Fallen, a being only marginally less powerful than the God-Emperor himself. Furthermore, of all the primarchs, Magnus was the one most deeply immersed in sorcery. So if anyone was capable of such a feat it was he.

Ragnar briefly considered that he might have been corrupted without his knowledge. What now? Could he live with himself if he was a threat to Sven and all his other friends and comrades, and to the Chapter that had become his home?

'You don't think I have been corrupted, do you?' Ragnar uttered, proud of the fact he had kept a plaintive note from his voice. Ranek shrugged.

'For what it's worth, laddie, I do not. From what I have seen of you, not even Red Magnus could power a spell through that thick skull of yours. But we will know for sure. You have been tested as thoroughly by the Rune Priests as Logan Grimnar was before he took the Wolf Throne. The probes they have used are deeper and more subtle than those you encountered at the Gate of Morkai. The Rune Priests will speak their findings before the Convocation at your trial. Only they know what they think, and they will speak first to the Great Wolf and his lords. That is the way it has always been, and that is the way it will always be.'

Ragnar was not at all reassured. His whole life, and the fate of his soul hung in the balance. Ranek looked at him. He stared back.

'Why are you here?'

'I am here to counsel you and speak on your behalf. After all, I am the one who chose you to join the Wolves.'

'You were assigned to this?'

'I asked to do it.'

Ragnar felt himself profoundly touched by the old man's faith in him. 'When will the Convocation reach its decision?'

A bell tolled distantly through the corridors of the temple.

'Perhaps it already has. Come laddie, let us go and hear what they have to say.'

Ranek led him into the chamber where the Wolf Lords sat in judgement. Great carved wolfs' heads glared down from the walls above. All the lords were seated in a semi circle on a raised dais. In the centre was Logan Grimnar, the Great Wolf himself, firmly ensconced in his floating throne. He looked as old as the roots of mountains, and as hard as the armour of an Imperial battleship. His face was bleak as he studied Ragnar. The others all looked equally impassive.

Before the dais stood three robed and masked rune priests. Their glances settled on Ragnar as he entered. Ragnar stood as straight as he could and met their stares. He did not want to appear daunted. Whatever their judgement and whatever his eventual fate, he would meet it like a Space Wolf. He thought he sensed approval coming from Ranek, but he was not entirely sure.

He strode directly in front of the Great Wolf's throne and looked up defiantly. The Great Wolf stared back unmoved and then spoke in his deep gravelly voice. 'Rune Priests of Russ, you have examined this Wolf Brother for the taint of Chaos? What have you found?'

Ragnar could not help but turn his head to look at them. The moment seemed to stretch into eternity as the Rune Priest glanced at him. Then he banged his staff three times on the stone floor. 'We have examined this youth to the very depths of his soul and we have found...'

Ragnar leaned forward. He was holding his breath.

'...that he is untainted by the Powers of Darkness and loyal to his Chapter. The decision he made, he made in all honesty and with only the good of his battle-brothers in mind.'

Ragnar allowed himself to breathe again. So he was not a traitor and a heretic. Nothing had been laid upon his soul. He saw some of the Wolf Lords nod. Others shook their heads and looked angry. Berek Thunderfist, his company commander, gave him a broad wink. Logan

Grimnar smiled gravely. Ragnar sensed the old Wolf Priest's relief beside him.

Sigrid Trollbane stood up. 'But, as you all know, there is another matter.' He had a surprisingly deep and cutting voice. 'No matter how pure his motives, this youth has lost us the Spear of Russ! Unless it is recovered and returned to this shrine, Russ cannot return to claim it in the last days. By losing it we have betrayed our sacred trust and forfeited all claims to be the true sons of Russ. Ragnar has betrayed a sacred trust.'

Ragnar considered this. He knew that all was not quite as it seemed. Berek had already explained this more than once. The politics of the Wolf Lords were at least as important as their religious beliefs. He doubted that there was any man among them who did not aspire to sit in Logan Grimnar's place on the Wolf Throne. The only difference was in the timing.

This was more than a simple attack on himself, deserving as it might be. Ragnar could *smell* the hunger and ambition of Sigrid and those who sided with him. Others merely watched, waiting to see how a leadership challenge would go. And others, like Berek, were siding with the Great Wolf for their own purposes. In Berek's case the motivation was clear. One of his men was the accused. Ragnar's misdeeds reflected on him, and undermined his prestige, and Berek was not a man to allow that to happen without a fight.

Berek rose to his feet, every inch a heroic commander. The lamplight turned his hair and beard golden. He moved and spoke with perfect poise and confidence. 'Ragnar performed a heroic action, single-handedly attacking a primarch in a bold attempt to save his battle-brothers. Who here can criticise him for such heroism?'

Ragnar saw some nods, and heard some muted murmurs of approval. Heroism was something that played well among the Space Wolves. They were proud warriors, with a respect for courage. Ragnar saw the ancient head of Egil Ironwolf nod grimly. Nonetheless, Ragnar could not help noticing that most of those who approved were of Berek's faction. Like Sigrid, Thunderfist was positioning himself as the natural successor to Logan Grimnar.

Sigrid smiled coldly. Compared to Berek he was pale. His face was thin and sallow. His eyes were cold, and his long moustaches drooped sadly down his face. Yet there was steel in him, Ragnar knew. No man became a Wolf Lord without it. He also had a chilly intelligence that was lacking in many of his fellows. His voice was mocking as it normally was when he was not bellowing commands on a battlefield.

'Ragnar is brave. Of that there can be no doubt. I salute his heroism. What I question is his intelligence. I also question our ability as a

Chapter to prove ourselves worthy heirs to our predecessors. And no matter what his motives, this is Ragnar's fault. It may be that there is a way for the youth to atone for his deeds but some sanction must be taken against him.'

Ranek stood and strode forward to confront the council of Wolf Lords. He fixed Sigrid with his gaze and spoke clearly and calmly. 'A prophesy is a prophesy. It will be fulfilled in its own time, and in its own way, or it is no true prophesy. Russ will return. Russ will reclaim his Spear. Russ will lead this Chapter into the final conflict with the Evil One. Of that there can be no doubt.'

Sigrid was not daunted. If anything, his smile became mocking. 'You are suggesting then, Brother Ranek, that it was somehow Russ's will that this callow youth cast his sacred weapon into the void?'

'I am suggesting that if the prophesy be true prophesy that is irrelevant. In its own good time the Spear will return to us.'

'I can see why you are a great priest, Ranek. I wish I shared the strength of your faith.' Laughter, this time from Sigrid's supporters, greeted this sally. Most of the assembled Wolf Lords looked shocked. Sigrid's mockery of a priest did not play well with them.

'Perhaps you ought to,' said Ranek.

The flash of emotion across the Wolf Lord's face showed he realised his mistake. When next he spoke his voice was more conciliatory.

'You protect the boy because you were his chooser, Ranek, and your loyalty is to your credit. But still I say he must be punished for his actions.'

Sigrid paused and let the implications of the statement hang in the air for a moment. He wanted all present to see the connection between Ranek and Ragnar and Berek. The fault of the one was a reflection on all three. 'And I do not think it sits well for a priest of Russ to claim that all will be well and that the Spear will find its way back to us of its own accord. I doubt that the warp will give up its prize so easily. I agree it would be wonderful, miraculous even, if it did. But what are we to do if the Spear does not come back of its own free will? What are we to do when the Last Days come? All the signs say they are almost upon us. What then?

'And whether or not the Spear returns to us or not avoids the question. Do we really want a warrior in our midst that could so easily cast it aside? We do not need one so careless. Who knows what his next exploit might lead to?'

Logan Grimnar and the others considered this. Ragnar could not help but feel that Sigrid had a point. He had not thought through his actions; he had acted without any thought as to the consequences. He had taken it upon himself to lose the Sacred Spear. He felt like stepping forward and saying so when he noticed a messenger had entered the council chamber. He spoke briefly in the Great Wolf's ear.

Sigrid stopped and all eyes focused on Grimnar expectantly. Nor were they disappointed. Grimnar knuckled his eyes wearily and said, 'Grave news, brothers. Adrian Belisarius is dead and so is our old comrade, Skander.'

Howls of grief echoed around the chamber from some of the older Wolf Lords. 'It gets worse,' continued Grimnar. 'Both were assassinated on the sacred soil of Holy Terra itself. This is a grave matter indeed. I move that we adjourn to consider our response to this.'

All present gave their assent, save Sigrid. Ranek led Ragnar back to his cell, wondering exactly what was going on.

CHAPTER TWO

ALL AROUND THE shrine was silent. In the mighty hall, banners of mourning flew at half mast. Ragnar wondered why he had been summoned to the chambers of the Great Wolf in the quiet watches of the night. It did not bode well. He was even less reassured when Berek and Sigrid emerged from the throne hall together.

Neither looked happy. Sigrid glared at him as they passed. Berek looked melancholic. Neither spoke to him.

Moments later, Lars Helltongue, Grimnar's stone-faced herald, beckoned Ragnar forward. He found himself in the long hall, which was covered in banners and trophies of ancient battles, under the eyes of the Great Wolf's bodyguard. At the far end of the chamber sat the lord of all the Wolves, ensconced on his floating throne, with a scroll in his hands.

He looked up as the young Wolf entered and was beckoned to stand before his throne.

Ragnar knelt briefly and then rose, as a warrior does before his lord. Grimnar studied him, not unkindly, half amused, half annoyed. Then he grinned.

'Well, Ragnar Blackmane, you have set us a pretty problem, haven't you?' He gestured with the scroll. 'You can speak freely here.'

Grimnar was obviously waiting for some response, so Ragnar spoke. 'And what problem is that, Great Wolf?'

Grimnar laughed. 'I would have thought it was explained with commendable clarity at the conclave today, pup.'

Ragnar was not stung by the address, as he would have been had it come from almost any other man. Grimnar was centuries old, compared to him Ragnar was still but a child. 'I would do what I did again, Great Wolf, under similar circumstances.'

'I am glad to hear it. Under the same circumstances I might have done what you did, Ragnar. On the other hand I might not. To take it upon yourself to use the weapon of Russ himself might be considered presumptuous. Some think you should be punished for doing so, others believe that it marks you for great things.'

'What do you think, Great Wolf?'

'I think you are a youth of great promise, Ragnar. Beyond that, I do not know. I do not wish to waste that promise, but at the same time you are a source of dissension among the Wolves. And at this moment in time we can afford no dissension. I fear that if I take no action against you, others might.'

Ragnar knew what he meant. Cold-blooded killings were rare among the Wolves, but other things could happen. In the heat of battle a stray bullet might find him. Comrades might be slow to come to his aid at a moment of deadly peril. Such things were never talked about, even though they happened. And if he was thought to be a blasphemer, or a traitor, they might happen to him.

'What would you have me do, Great Wolf?'

'I would put you out of harm's way, in a place where you might do some good.'

'Exile, Great Wolf?'

'That would be one way of looking at it. Tell me Ragnar, what do you know of the Wolfblades?'

Ragnar sifted through the memories that had been implanted by the training engines when he was an aspirant.

'They are Space Wolves sent to Holy Terra to fulfil our treaty obligations with the House of Belisarius. We provide them with bodyguards in return for the Navigators they provide us.'

'That is true insofar as it goes, Ragnar, but Wolfblades are much more. They train the Celestarch of Belisarius's House troops and lead them into battle. They act as his strong right arm when there is need. They slay his enemies in open battle and by stealth if need be.'

Ragnar could see where this was going.

'You wish me to go to Blessed Terra, Great Wolf?'

'There is need. Adrian Belisarius, the Celestarch, and a good friend to our Chapter, is dead. One of our battle-brothers died with him,

Skander Bloody-axe, an old comrade of mine from my Blood Claw pack.'

Ragnar could see sadness in the old warrior's face. There were few left from that generation in the Chapter now, and Grimnar and this Skander must have been among the last. There were no closer comrades in the Chapter than those who had gone through their initiation and basic training together, and who had been part of the same initial unit. They were almost siblings in a very real sense.

'Yes, Ragnar, I want you to go to Earth. And I want you to keep your ears open. One of the Wolves has died on holy soil, and I want to know what happened. What really happened! I have had reports. I want to know if they are true.'

'Do you seek vengeance, Great Wolf?' It was a presumptuous question, but Ragnar felt compelled to ask it. Grimnar shook his head slowly.

'If it is in the interests of the Chapter, Ragnar, I will take vengeance. If not, I would still like to know what happened.'

Ragnar considered the Great Wolf's words. Obviously, he could not commit the Chapter to wholesale bloodletting on the sacred soil of Terra. Nor could he simply order the assassination of some powerful man there without consequences.

He also knew that whatever the old man said, Logan Grimnar had a long memory, and he would find a way, if need be, to claim the blood price for his old comrade. It was the Fenrisian way.

'I will do my best,' said Ragnar.

'Do so, Ragnar, and let no one know that you are about this business.'

'How will I let you know my findings?'

'There are ways, Ragnar, channels of communication between Fenris and Belisarius. You will be told them before your departure. Also, Adrian Belisarius was assassinated. His daughter is with us on Garm but must return to swear allegiance to his successor. You will see that nothing untoward happens to her on her journey to Earth.'

'You think something might, Great Wolf?'

'If someone could assassinate the ruler of House Belisarius when he is surrounded by guards, then they have a very long arm and a very powerful one.'

'Yes, Great Wolf.'

'You may go, Ragnar.'

Ragnar knelt before departing, leaving the old man deep in thought over his scrolls.

* * *

'It's NOT BLOODY fair,' said Sven. 'You lose the Spear of Russ and they send you to Terra. What would they do if you had managed to destroy it? Make you Great Wolf?'

'That is not something to joke about, Sven,' said Ragnar.

'Who is bloody joking?' Sven gestured around his meditation cell with its sleeping mat, armour stand and weapon racks for furnishing. 'I get this! You get the fleshpots at the heart of the Imperium!'

'Earth is a holy planet, Sven.'

'Earth is as holy as a hornweed addict's visions. It's the capital of the Imperium. All the nobs are there and I don't think *they* spend their time fasting and meditating.'

'You might be surprised.'

'I bloody well would be if they did! I can't believe they are sending *you*. What is needed is a man of tact, diplomacy and vision, a man with enough sense not to have lost the Spear of Russ. A man like me! You think if I asked Grimnar he would let me go along?'

'I think if you asked Grimnar he would lock you up. The last thing we need is a brainless ape running amok in the streets of Holy Terra!'

'Then why are they sending you?'

'Because it suits them,' said Ragnar seriously. 'Anyway, I just came to say farewell. It seems the ship is outward bound in six standard hours, and I have to get ready.'

There was a long silence. In the years since they had been aspirants together, Ragnar and Sven had become fast friends. More than once they had saved each other's lives. But now Sven was a Grey Hunter, and Ragnar was something else, destined for a life in limbo as a Wolfblade, perhaps for the rest of his life.

A great gap had opened between them, and it was not just distance. Both of them knew it, despite the banter. Sven would be going to war and battle with the Chapter, while Ragnar was going to be stuck guarding the spoiled aristocrats of the Navigator Houses. Any dreams he might have had for a glorious destiny, of inscribing his name in the annals of the Chapter, would have to be given up. He would probably be remembered as the man who had lost the Spear of Russ. He would be the butt of jokes and maledictions of every new generation of aspirants.

Briefly he considered going to Grimnar and asking to be allowed to stay on, but he knew he could not. His fate was sealed. It was his duty to go to Earth. In a way, it was a punishment for his deeds, and a way to atone for his mistake. But I would do the same thing again, he thought defiantly.

Sven had stuck out his hand, and they clasped wrists. 'Watch your back,' he said. 'Without me to pull you out of the fire, you're going to have plenty of trouble.'

'Most of my troubles came from your blundering attempts to help,' said Ragnar half-heartedly.

'By the time you get back I will have blundered my way to Wolf Lord,' said Sven. 'They'll be singing my praises in the sagas.'

'Why bother with sagas singing your praises when you do it so well yourself!'

'Go on, get out of here! You have a ship to catch.'

Ragnar was surprised to find there was a lump in his throat as he turned to go, but he did not look back.

RAGNAR REPORTED TO Ranek's chamber. His personal possessions had already been sent to the shuttle. He bore only his weapons and such gear as a Space Wolf was expected to carry into battle.

'A Wolfblade, eh?' said the old priest. 'You've found an interesting trail to follow.'

'What do you mean?' said Ragnar.

The old man laughed savagely. 'Earth,' he said. 'Holy Terra. The Blessed Planet. The Seat of the Emperor. The Hub of the Imperium. The biggest snake pit in the galaxy.'

'It can't be that bad,' said Ragnar.

'Can't it? What do you know about such things, lad?'

'Not much but–'

'Earth is the hub of the Imperium. It's the centre of government, the setting of mankind's greatest temples, the home of our wealthiest and most powerful merchant houses. And the most corrupt.'

'What do you mean?'

'I mean, where there is government and where there is money, there is corruption. And there is no place in this universe that has more government and more money than Old Earth. You be careful there, laddie.'

'I will just be a bodyguard,' said Ragnar.

'Is that what you think? Don't be so naïve. You will be seen, quite rightly, as a representative of our Chapter. They will judge us by you, read things into your actions that you would never expect. You will be a living symbol of who and what we are, and don't you ever forget it.'

'I will try not to.'

'You will do more than try, lad. Remember these words and obey them, or I will personally come to Earth and rip your lungs from your chest.'

'Very well, Rune Priest.'

The old man's voice was gentler now. 'There's no need to be huffy, laddie. Just remember what I have said, and do your best. It will be more than enough.'

'What will my duties be?'

'You will be a soldier of the Celestarch. You will obey him as you would your own Wolf Lord. You will fight at his command, and you will die if need be. What else would you expect?'

'What if I am ordered to fight against the Imperium, or my battle-brothers? If Earth is so corrupt?' Ragnar realised he sounded sullen, and that he only asked the question to be contrary. But the reply surprised him.

'What would you do if your Wolf Lord ordered you to commit heresy?'

'I would depose him.'

'If he turned out to be a traitor sworn to Chaos?'

'I would kill him.'

'Having a bodyguard can be a two-edged sword, can't it, young Ragnar?'

Ragnar considered what he was being told. If he understood the Wolf Priest correctly, he was being given leave to assassinate the Celestarch of Belisarius should he prove disloyal to the Imperium. Ranek appeared to read his thoughts.

'Our pact with House Belisarius predates the Imperium itself. Some members of the Administratum dislike it, but they have to accept it. They know that we keep this Navigator House honest. The Celestarchs of Belisarius have been good men and women, Ragnar. They are loyal to us and to the Imperium and we have always been part of the reason for that. No matter what you see or hear on Terra you should remember that, before passing judgement.'

'The Great Wolf said Adrian Belisarius was assassinated, and so was our brother Skander. Who would do such a thing? Heretics?'

Ranek laughed. 'The reports say they were fanatics of some new cult, but many people would do such a thing, Ragnar. It might have been these supposed fanatics. It might have been a rival House, or a faction in the Administratum that supports those rivals. It might even have been an ambitious relative of the Celestarch himself.'

'What?'

'Not everyone follows our code, Ragnar. As I said, Earth is the locus of the greatest concentration of power and wealth in our universe. These things have a way of distorting morality. I repeat: watch yourself.'

Ragnar did not quite know whether the priest meant he should keep a close eye on those around him or on his own morals. Perhaps he meant both. It appeared that he was to face other perils than those of battle.

'Aside from assassins, what other dangers might there be?'

'You may be called upon to lead House troops or perform clandestine actions in support of the Celestarch's wishes. You will be briefed on your arrival by your fellow Wolfblades. Pay attention to them. Some of them have been on Terra longer than you have lived and know of its pitfalls and hazards.'

Ragnar felt his heart sink. It appeared he was in for a long exile. Ranek seemed to read his thoughts.

'Space Wolves can live for centuries, Ragnar. In the great scheme of things a few decades is not much to lose.'

'I would rather be here with Berek's company than playing nursemaid to Navigators.'

'Your wishes do not enter into this, Ragnar. And keep those thoughts about your duties to yourself. We expect your performance and behaviour to be exemplary. Never forget, some of the folk you meet, many of them very powerful, will judge us by you. And some of them may use your failures against us. We have many enemies among the factions of the Administratum as well as many allies. Imperial politics are a vast and complex web.'

Ragnar did not quite follow what the old man was saying. His training had been in battle and warfare, not politics. It looked like his duties were going to be more complicated than he had expected.

'The Great Wolf said there would be ways of communicating with Fenris should the need arise. He said I would be told them before I departed.'

Ranek gave a grim smile. 'Did he now? I wonder why he would do that... No, don't tell me. Should the need arise, go to Brother Valkoth of the Wolfblades. He will know what needs to be done. But be circumspect. And Ragnar, one more thing...'

'Yes?'

'Many great Space Wolf leaders have been Wolfblades. It does us no harm to have warriors who know how the Imperium works and who have personal contacts within its hierarchy. Use your time on Earth well. Logan Grimnar does nothing without purpose. Remember that!'

Ragnar felt his spirits rise. Perhaps in a roundabout way he was being groomed for leadership. Or perhaps this was just Ranek's way of raising his morale. Whatever the case, it was working.

'Now, en route to Terra, keep a careful eye on Gabriella. She is Adrian Belisarius's daughter, and she may be the target of an assassination attempt herself.'

Ragnar looked at the Wolf Priest's lined and chiselled face. 'You think some of our people might kill her?'

'You are not travelling on one of our ships, Ragnar. We cannot spare them. You will be returning on the courier that brought us the news from Terra. *The Herald of Belisarius* will not be secure. Stay close to the girl and see that nothing happens to her. You may go now.'

Ragnar walked towards the door of the chamber. 'And Ragnar...'

'Yes?'

'See that nothing happens to yourself either. Farewell.'

'Farewell.' Ragnar felt another lump in his throat. He liked Ranek, and trusted him. And he realised he might never see the old man again. Old age or battle might claim either of them. Such were the realities of a Wolf's life, he told himself.

AS RAGNAR STRODE down the quiet corridors, he realised how isolated he was. He would be on his own, far from his battle-brothers, for an incalculable distance for an unspecified amount of time, and for the first time since he had joined the Chapter. He felt a pang of loneliness, almost like pain.

Then unaccountably his heart lightened. He would also be free, in a way that he had not been in years. He was setting out on a great adventure, to the holiest and deadliest world of the Imperium. He would look upon the temples and palaces of Terra, and their glittering inhabitants. And it sounded like there would be danger and intrigue enough to occupy him.

Slowly his step lengthened, and he found that he was trotting and then running towards the loading bays where the shuttles waited.

CHAPTER THREE

RAGNAR STRODE THROUGH *The Herald of Belisarius* beside Gabriella Belisarius. Sailors and retainers greeted her formally and respectfully. Many of them flinched when they saw the massive Space Wolf standing at her shoulder. He could tell from their scents that he made some uneasy and others downright afraid.

'Your crew seems scared of me,' he murmured.

Gabriella turned and smiled up at him. She was a severe looking woman: tall, slender, with very long black hair and a face that was all angles. She was beautiful in an inhuman way, and the black dress uniform somehow enhanced that beauty.

Now that she was on the ship – her home territory as it were – she had removed the scarf from her forehead to reveal her third, pineal eye. 'They are a trading crew. They are not used to having one of the fabled Space Wolves aboard. The folk of Terra are a little more cosmopolitan, I think you will find.'

It was obvious that she did not share her crew's nervousness, but then again why should she? She had just spent a decade among the men of the Fang. He wished he could read her moods better. The Navigators smelled different from other humans. There was something alien about their scent. Alien and well nigh unreadable.

Ragnar knew they had been bred for countless generations to guide starships across the interstellar void. They had done so since before the

45

founding of the Imperium. Somewhere, their gene line and that of normal humanity had parted company. Ragnar knew that they were no longer human but they were tolerated by the Imperium because they were necessary. Without Navigators interstellar voyages would take years or decades, if they could be made at all. Travel through the warp was treacherous even with a Navigator. Without one, it could be deadly.

Ragnar considered this, as he considered the woman before him. Their skills had brought the Navigator Houses wealth beyond measure. Belisarius had sent a ship to bring the news of Gabriella's father's death to the Wolves. Granted it had also brought trade goods and a request for a new Wolfblade, but even so the thought was staggering. Ships were enormously expensive. Belisarius had its own fleet, one considerably larger than that owned by the Space Wolves. Ragnar knew this from the histories. They had leased ships to the Wolves on very favourable terms when they were needed. It was one aspect of the ancient alliance between the two.

'What are you thinking?' Gabriella asked, as they made their way to the command deck. She was going to guide the ship home to Terra. The Navigator who had brought it, a cousin, was to stay on with the Wolf fleet as her replacement.

'I was thinking about the alliance between our Houses.'

'It's one of the bedrocks of my family's power,' she said.

'How so?'

'It helps keep our rivals in check. Few would move openly against us for fear of reprisals from the Space Wolves.'

'Few would move openly against you on Terra anyway. It is sacred ground. Bloodshed is not permitted there.'

Gabriella laughed. 'Blood is shed on Earth as it is everywhere else. It is merely done more circumspectly. And we do not have holdings only on Earth.'

Ragnar thought about this. 'The Wolves have come to your aid in the past.'

'Aye, they have, and would do so again, if need be. Who knows, they might even fight on Terra if the need arose. Your Chapter is known to be wild and uncontrollable, a law unto itself.'

'All Space Marine Chapters are. Their privileges and prerogatives date back to before the Imperium itself.'

'Aye, but your brethren have a reputation for being more erratic than the other Chapters.'

'It has never stopped us from fighting well, or from being loyal to the Emperor.'

'I did not mean it as a criticism. Indeed from the point of view of my House it is praise. Our enemies might have swallowed us up millennia ago, had they not thought your Chapter would avenge us.'

'I thought Belisarius was one of the most powerful of the Navigator Houses?'

'It is now, and has been at many times in its history. But these things are cyclical. All Houses suffer setbacks. Such is the nature of trade and competition. In our history there have been many periods where we have suffered reversals, and we have been eclipsed. Leading a House is like guiding a ship: sometimes all it takes is one bad or unlucky decision for you to founder.'

'It has not happened to Belisarius yet. For more than ten millennia we have been your allies.'

'And let us hope that we are for another. Although I have a foreboding that events are taking a turn for the worse for House Belisarius.'

Ragnar wanted to contradict her, but he could see the sadness written on her face. He realised this was a woman who had just lost her father, a father who had been the leader of his House, the Celestarch, a Navigator of Navigators.

They passed more sailors in the wide corridor. Almost automatically Ragnar put himself in a position where he could interpose himself if they proved to be a threat. The humans sensed this and gave him a wide berth.

'There is no need to terrify the crew,' said Gabriella.

'I am here to ensure your safety. Those were my orders.'

She glanced at him. 'Fair enough, but there is no need to glower while you do your duty.'

'I had not realised I was glowering.'

'You Fenrisians never seem to realise. You are so feral. What you think is always written on your face, and what you think about is mostly violence.'

'Before this voyage is out you may be glad of that.'

'Perhaps. I am glad you are here anyway.'

'Why?'

'Because if there is a threat to my life, I think you will deal with it.'

'You think it a serious possibility?'

'Yes. These are troubled times. My father has just been assassinated. Anyone who could get to him could get to me.'

'You seem to take it very calmly.'

'It happens. It happens even within the Houses themselves. Siblings have been known to remove those they think of as rivals.'

'You think they would kill you to remove a contender to the throne?'

'Now you are thinking like a Fenrisian, Ragnar. I am not a contender for the throne. Not at this time anyway. The Celestarchy does not pass from parent to child. Our rulers are selected from a short list of available candidates by the Council of Elders.'

'They are the oldest and wisest of your tribe?'

'Something like that.'

The door slid open and they arrived on the command deck. Tech adepts hovered over command altars, linked to the ancient devices by cables that ran to occipital sockets. The smell of ozone and technical incense filled the air. Officers in the House uniform of Belisarius stood to attention as Gabriella entered.

'Navigator on deck!' snapped someone and the others bowed their heads reverently.

'Be at ease,' said Gabriella. 'May fortune smile on us and prosperity wash over us.'

'May fortune smile on us,' responded the crew. Gabriella strode forward to the centre of the command deck and began communing with the crew. They spoke a technical argot of their trade, which was less than gibberish to Ragnar so he took the opportunity to study his surroundings.

The command deck was large and circular. It occupied a blister on top of the massive hull of *The Herald of Belisarius*. There were several large circular armourglass windows. Through the starboard side the vast white and blue sphere that was Garm was visible. Swift moving dots told of other sub-orbital craft going about their business.

Various technical altars were arranged around a central holo-pit. Something like a huge throne occupied its own dais on the balcony overlooking the pit. Ragnar recognised this as the Navigator's command chair.

Various personnel presented reports for Gabriella's approval. She listened and nodded before beckoning Ragnar over.

'When we leave orbit, we will be about twelve hours away from our insertion point. The captain will handle the steering of the vessel until then. I am going to get something to eat and have some rest.'

'Very well,' Ragnar said. 'I will accompany you.'

She gave him an amused look. 'I have asked for you to be given the stateroom adjoining mine. Your gear has already been stowed there.'

'Very good.'

THE NAVIGATORS OF Belisarius did well for themselves, Ragnar thought. He was used to the bare cells of military starships. This chamber was more like something from the hookah dream of a Slaaneshi cultist.

The massive bed was bolted to the floor. The mattress was soft. There were chairs carved from single pieces of Leviathan tooth ivory, desks and furnishings from precious scented woods. Faintly narcotic incense perfumed the air. A vast mirror dominated one wall. The controls beneath it indicated that it doubled as a televisor. He had already dismissed the body servants who had hovered around waiting to satisfy his whims. He had told them that all he wanted was something to eat.

A bell announced that the food had arrived. 'Enter,' he called. A row of liveried servants entered bearing silver trays. On each was a collection of enamelled porcelain, which his enhanced senses told him bore all manner of highly spiced delicacies. The servants bustled around the room, arranging a table, spreading tablecloths, and setting heating elements in place to keep the food warm.

An elderly white-haired man, the possessor of a superlatively supercilious expression, uncovered each dish with a flourish.

'Pickled slime eels,' he said proudly. Ragnar nodded.

'Roast haunch of dragonbird in a venomberry sauce. I think this one will tickle your palate, sir,' he said with an ingratiating smile.

'Really,' said Ragnar.

'Boiled naga-goat tripes in leper brandy.' The dish looked as if someone had been sick in it, Ragnar thought. He ignored the rest of the descriptions until the old man tried to move into a position behind him. Without thinking, the young Space Wolf whirled ready to strike.

The servant blanched. 'Your napkin, sir,' he said, displaying a serviette almost the size of a small sheet.

Ragnar glared at him. 'Do not attempt to get behind me again,' he said.

'But how will I prepare you for feasting, sir?'

'I require no help to sit down to table,' said Ragnar. The servant looked affronted.

'But sir, proper etiquette at the Court of Belisarius dictates that…'

'Proper etiquette in the halls of Fenris dictates that a man is left alone to eat when he wishes. Breaches of etiquette require duels to settle them.'

'Duels, sir?'

'Personal insults require the challenge,' said Ragnar.

'I meant no insult, sir. We must all make allowances when two cultures meet.'

Ragnar grinned, showing his fangs. 'Indeed we must. Now I would be obliged if you would leave me to my food and my meditations. Else…'

'Quite, sir, quite.' The elderly servant clapped his hands, and they all fled the room. Ragnar was left alone in his chamber. He surveyed the food and realised that it must have cost a small fortune to bring it all this distance. The selection of wines, brandies and cheeses that had been provided had been brought all the way from Terra. Given the cost of transportation the Navigators charged, it seemed almost a sin.

Nonetheless he sat himself down to eat. The tastes were interesting but he would have preferred plain old Fenrisian seal or caribou meat. Perhaps he would ask about getting some. Just at that moment, he heard a faint panicked call from the adjoining door.

Without pausing to think, he snatched up his bolter and threw the heavy airlock door open. Fortunately it was unlocked or he might have had some trouble. He could see Gabriella on the far side of the chamber. Something glinting and metallic scuttled over the bed towards her.

The situation was dangerous. In this small heavily armoured chamber, bolter shells would ricochet. Ragnar's armour would shield him, but there was every chance they might harm the woman he was supposed to protect. He focused his attention on the thing that stalked her.

To normal humans it would have been moving with blinding speed, but Ragnar was a Space Wolf, and his perceptions and reflexes were superhuman. For him, in combat mode now, it moved in slow motion. The scent gave it away. It was a compound of metal and oil and subtle toxins: a form of robotic spider created by the black arts of some degenerate alien race. Two long needle-like fangs protruded from its front. Picter eyes glittered high on its back.

An assassination device obviously, probably controlled by someone nearby.

Ragnar sprang forward onto the bed, slamming the butt of his weapon down on it. He was taking a chance. If the thing contained an explosive device he might well detonate it, but he was counting on this thing being more subtle: you did not equip such a device with poisoned fangs, if you intended to detonate it. The spider cracked open. Blue sparks shot everywhere. A strong stench of ozone wafted into the air.

Ragnar picked it up in a gauntleted hand and crushed it again.

He glanced around to see if there were any other threats in the vicinity and detected none. He gestured for Gabriella to follow him into his own stateroom where he tossed the mechanical spider into a flagon of water, hoping to short it out permanently.

'Are you all right?' he asked. 'Did the thing sting you?'

The Navigator appeared perfectly composed but her face was white and her pupils dilated. The pineal eye on her forehead had opened. It was much smaller and less disturbing than he had expected it to be.

'If it had, I would be dead now. That is a jokaero death spider. An assassination device that contains zarthax, one of the deadliest poisons in the galaxy.'

Ragnar cursed. He had expected many things but not this use of foul deviant alien technology. Another thought struck him.

'You seem very well informed about such things,' said Ragnar.

'Every child of the Navigator Houses knows about such things. They are commonly used devices. Small enough to crawl through ventilator shafts, stealthy enough to infiltrate a mansion. I was lucky. I had gone to wash my face when I heard it thump down on the bed. I froze and shouted for help. Its camera eyes would have tracked movement. The operator could not have seen me or I would be dead now.'

Ragnar kept his manner all business, but part of his mind reeled. They were *commonly* used assassination devices? Such vile alien works were forbidden throughout most of the Imperium. He supposed that the Navigator Houses would naturally have access to these things but still... 'Whoever unleashed and guided that thing must be on the ship.'

'Yes.'

'We will find him.'

'Perhaps.'

'You do not seem very confident.'

'How could you tell who, on a ship as large as this, could have done it?'

'As long as they are human, I have my ways,' said Ragnar, knowing that the stink of guilt would be on someone, and his nose would pick it out. Another thought occurred to him.

'The attack was well timed: you were in your chamber, and I was supposed to be eating.'

'Yes.'

'Who would know about such things?'

'The ship's quartermaster, the major domo, and many of the serving men. A host of people, in fact.'

'In future, we will share the same chamber.' She considered this for a moment.

'As you wish.'

'Now let us call your security people, and see if we can get to the bottom of this.'

RAGNAR CURSED. A body had been found in an equipment locker near to the stateroom. Controls for the spider were with it. The man had taken poison, from a hollow tooth. It appeared he had been prepared for failure. Ragnar was surprised. This spoke of a level of preparation and fanaticism he had not expected.

'It does not surprise me,' said Gabriella when he told her. 'This sort of thing has happened before.'

'The man must have been a fanatic,' said Ragnar. To his surprise, she laughed.

'What is so funny?'

'That a Space Marine should accuse someone else of fanaticism.' Her face was suddenly serious. 'But maybe you are right.'

'The man must have been one, to give his life up so easily.'

'Perhaps he hated my family. Perhaps he belonged to one of the cults that hate Navigators. Or perhaps he had no motive at all.'

'What do you mean?'

'Perhaps he was hypno-conditioned or psychically brainwashed to perform this action. There are many ways it can be done.'

'We should check the body for marks. Sometimes cultists have tattoos or the stigmata of Chaos on them.'

'I doubt you will find anything,' said Gabriella, 'but go ahead. I must go now to guide the ship. We are less than an hour away from warp insertion.'

'I will come with you to the command deck.' As he spoke, Ragnar stripped the corpse.

'I doubt anyone would attack me while we are in the warp. You know as well as I do that the ship would founder and all of us would be lost.'

The girl was right. There were no tattoos, no stigmata of any sort. Even the scent was perfectly normal for a corpse, save for the faint acrid hint of poison.

'If the assassin is under some sort of mind control why should he care?'

'A fair point. But once we are warp-bound, I will be sealed in a life support throne, alone in the command blister. The place is secure as a fortress. It has to be.'

'Why?'

'It must be able to shield me from anything we might encounter in the warp. I can say no more than that.'

'There is no need to say more.' He gestured for the security men to take the body away and dispose of it. They obeyed. Some of them stuck close by. They seemed embarrassed and ashamed that a Navigator had almost been assassinated while she was in their care. Ragnar understood how they felt.

'How difficult would it be for an enemy to place an agent on one of your ships?' he asked as they strode towards the command deck.

'All our people are carefully screened, particularly those who serve on House ships like this one. Still, no system is foolproof. I would imagine that a truly determined enemy could get someone aboard. Or could corrupt someone who was already screened.'

'That's a worrying thought,' said Ragnar. He was a taken aback by how calmly the Navigator was taking this. She seemed to be treating it as part of every day life.

'It is also possible that someone in my own House wants me dead,' she said. 'It would be much easier for an insider to achieve, than an outsider.'

Someone had already got to the head of the House, Ragnar thought. And he was presumably more securely guarded than Gabriella would ever be. As they entered the command deck, he reflected that this assignment was turning out to be a lot more interesting than he had anticipated, and they had not even reached Terra yet.

CHAPTER FOUR

RAGNAR LOOKED DOWN upon the strange globe beneath him. The hemisphere glittered metallic silver in the daylight. There were patches of red upon it that might have been seas of rust. The lines of the ancient continents were gone. All that was left to suggest them were vague outlines where the density of buildings became even more intense along what had once been shorelines. Now the world wore metallic armour over its entire surface. It seemed fitting somehow.

Ragnar smiled; it was an astonishing feeling. The image was a familiar one. This was the birth world of humanity. He had seen the likeness so often that it was strange knowing that the planet was actually below him now, a glittering jewel set against the black velvet of space. Ragnar felt excitement build up in him.

This was where humanity had first reached for the stars, where the Emperor of Mankind was born and from where he had launched his great crusade. Where Horus had besieged the Imperial Palace and the future history of the galaxy had been decided. This was the hub of the greatest Empire that had ever existed, a seat of government of incalculable power.

Somewhere down there the Lords of the Administratum decided the fate of countless billions. Somewhere down there the Emperor lay half-alive within his Golden Throne. The primarchs had walked there amid the gardens and plasteel starscrapers. Russ had led the distant forebearers of the Chapter into battle on its soil. This was Earth, old and weighted with millennia of history. Soon he would join the countless trillions who had made the pilgrimage to its surface. Soon he would be part of everyday life down there.

He considered their approach. He knew that they had passed countless fortresses and fleets as they had swung in from the ultra-solar jump points. They had passed the armoured moons of Jupiter and the forge world of Mars. They had been subjected to hundreds of challenges and scans and they had been boarded twice. It had been a long drawn out process but it was only to be expected.

The world down there was better protected than any other planet in human history. There would not be a Second Battle of Earth if the terrible lords of the Imperium could help it. Even now, the sky was filled with satellite fortresses: great weapon installations with enough firepower to destroy battle fleets. The whole of sublunar space was crowded with warships. For once in his life, Ragnar felt insignificant.

Gabriella appeared by his side. She was wearing the full formal regalia of her House, a black tunic with the eye and wolf symbol of Belisarius was embossed on every button. Its epaulettes bore the mark of her status as a master Navigator. On the braided jacket were medals and emblems which doubtless told of her lineage and status. Some of them also contained powerful sensors. She had a dress sword and pistol on her belt.

Despite his polished armour and well maintained weapons, Ragnar felt almost slovenly beside her.

'It's time,' she said. 'The shuttle has docked with *The Herald of Belisarius*. We have been given permission to descend to the surface of the Earth.'

Ragnar felt almost nervous as he strode with her to the airlock. It slid open and a file of House troops garbed in uniforms only slightly less elaborate than Gabriella's emerged. Their weapons looked serviceable and they moved with a precision that would not have shamed an elite unit of Imperial Guard. Their commander moved up to Gabriella and gave her a formal salute. He surprised Ragnar by giving him one too.

'Lady Gabriella, welcome home,' he said. 'The Celestarch Elect sent my men to provide an honour guard. I would just like to say the honour is mine.'

Ragnar suppressed a smile. The officer was young with a wafer thin moustache that crept like a caterpillar along his upper lip. His hair was long. His features sharp, his lips thin. He was exactly the sort of soldier the Space Wolves were not.

'And you are?' Gabriella asked.

'Lieutenant Kyle, milady, at your service, now and always.'

'Well, lieutenant, I would be grateful if you could escort us the twenty steps from this airlock to the shuttle. I am keen to set foot on my home world again.'

'At once, milady.' The two rows of guards clicked their heels and swivelled, forming a corridor along which Ragnar and Gabriella walked into the airlock. Ragnar was about to strap himself into one of the military style bucket seats but Gabriella gestured for him to follow her. He passed through a second airlock into an infinitely more luxurious salon, decorated with the House insignia on the walls. The acceleration couches resembled huge, padded leather armchairs, far more plush than the military gear Ragnar was used to. The airlock swished closed behind them. Ragnar made sure it was sealed before strapping himself in.

'That was very formal,' he said eventually.

'Far more formal than most arrivals, I can assure you. But my father is dead and my aunt must be seen to make every effort to protect me. It was a message that protection is the order of the day.'

'I think the jokaero spider proves that she was right.'

'Indeed. What do you think of our House troopers?'

'They were very well dressed.'

'You do not think much of them as warriors then? You can speak as frankly as you like.'

'I think they would not last twenty seconds against a company of orks. They seem to have spent more time practising marching than fighting. Of course, that is just my opinion. I have not seen them fight.'

'They are merely security guards. You will meet the real warriors later. Perhaps they will impress you more.'

'You do not appear to think so.'

'I find my time at the Fang has changed me, Ragnar. Once I was impressed by men like them. That was before I spent time among Wolves. By the way, we will be met by some of your brethren on arrival.'

'I look forward to it,' said Ragnar. Through the porthole he could see the shuttle had already broken away from *The Herald of Belisarius* and had begun its descent to the surface of the glittering world below.

As they broke through the clouds, he saw they were heading towards what looked like a vast island separated from the rest of the world by barriers and towers at least a kilometre high. A fortress within a fortress, he thought – the fabled island enclave that was the Ghetto of the Navigators.

RAGNAR STEPPED OUT into the light of a new day on a new world. He squinted in the bright sunlight. The air had a faint acrid chemical taint:

partially from the exhausts of the shuttle but partially contained within the air itself. A faint shimmer rose from the plascrete. He strode down the exit ramp, in front of Gabriella. Then, he glanced around to make sure all was clear before signalling for her to follow. The honour guard had already begun to line up before them.

Ragnar noticed several small armoured vehicles nearby. An armoured figure, a head and shoulders taller than the locals, lounged against one of them. There was something about his posture that conveyed both an amused disdain, as well as a complete watchfulness of what went on around him. When he spotted Ragnar, he stood upright and strode purposefully forward. Ragnar was not in the least surprised to see that he was a Space Wolf, although many things about his appearance conveyed an impression of difference from the average battle-brother.

As he came closer, Ragnar could see that his hair was short but not cropped, and his moustache had been shaved pencil thin, in the style of the young officer who had greeted them on the ship. A faint smell of perfumed pomade surrounded him. Many strange amulets and pieces of jewellery were attached to his armour.

He smiled affably as Ragnar looked him over. Ragnar did not doubt that despite the man's languid expression, he was studying him too.

'Greetings, son of Fenris,' said the stranger in the tongue of Ragnar's home world. 'Welcome to Holy Terra.'

The troopers had begun to hustle Gabriella into the largest and most heavily armoured of the waiting vehicles. Ragnar was about to follow when the stranger spoke. 'Your duties as escort are done, Ragnar. You are to accompany me to the Belisarian Palace.'

The man was obviously a Space Wolf, but Ragnar felt a reluctance to part from Gabriella. Having seen her safely over such a great distance he wanted to escort her for the last small segment of her journey.

'She is safe now,' said the stranger. 'Or at least as safe as any of her kind can ever be on the surface of this world.' He gestured at the sky. Sleek air vehicles hovered above them, doubtless part of the ongoing security operation.

'Her father was not safe,' said Ragnar. A pained expression passed over the other Space Marine's face. 'Was he?'

'Do you think your presence would have made any difference there, brother?'

'Perhaps.'

The stranger smiled. 'I like to think mine might have as well, but alas duty called me elsewhere on that fatal day.'

There was a brief pause.

'I am Torin the Wayfarer,' he said.

'Ragnar Blackmane.'

'These are not matters that should be discussed openly. There are many with televisors who can read lips.'

'Can they also speak the tongue of Fenris?'

'Ragnar, you would be amazed at what a variety of skills can be found on ancient Terra. I have lived here almost twelve standard years and it still astonishes me.'

Gabriella had disappeared into the armoured car. Ragnar found he had fallen into step beside Torin as they headed for the smaller machine. Up close it looked like a smaller, sleeker version of an ork buggy. Although far more streamlined it had the same rugged look.

Torin vaulted into the open cockpit and Ragnar jumped in beside him. With a flick of a switch, a tinted bubble hood rose into place. Moments later he was pressed flat into his seat by the acceleration as they set off in pursuit of Gabriella's vehicle. It took a few moments for Ragnar to realise that they were following just far enough away to be out of the blast radius of a rocket attack, but close enough to act if there was an attack. For all his easy manner, Torin appeared to be competent enough. In fact, Ragnar had begun to suspect that he was more than competent. Instinctively Ragnar picked up on the deadliness of the man; it was a lethalness that was all the more effective for being partially concealed by his manner.

'That's a little better,' said Torin. 'The hood should protect us from casual snooping and this car has its own share of divinatory wards. We can speak a little more freely now.'

'Do you greet every ship that comes in?' Ragnar said, speaking loudly over the roar of the engine.

'Only the ones with new Wolfblades on them.'

'There must be few enough of those.'

'You are the first in five years. Any trouble on your way in?'

Ragnar told him of the jokaero spider. Torin did not seem in the least surprised. He simply cocked his head to one side without taking his attention away from his driving.

'Do you have any thoughts about it?' Ragnar asked eventually.

'Could have been anything from a jealous rival in the House to outsiders trying to destabilise a newly chosen Celestarch. Given Adrian Belisarius's assassination, I think it would be best to assume the latter, but who can tell?'

Ragnar could tell from his scent and his manner that he did not want to say more under the present circumstances.

'What's it like here?' said Ragnar. He had begun to study the massive buildings around them. They were far more ornate than anything he had seen on Fenris, or anywhere else for that matter. Great spires prodded the sky. Every centimetre of their ancient facades seemed to have been carved into elaborate patterns. Hundreds of statues lined the arches in their sides. Stone gargoyles and angel-winged saints stood sentry on the roofs. Lush vegetation was everywhere but it had none of the riotous uncontrolled life of the jungles Ragnar had seen. It appeared to have been tamed and cultivated, designed to add one more element to the carefully contrived beauty that surrounded them.

'It's rather like what you see,' said Torin, guiding the buggy around a massive fountain with a flick of the control bars. Water spouted from a dragon's mouth. Some trick of the light made it look like liquid fire. 'Beautiful on the surface, but rotten underneath. Don't ever, even for a second, doubt that this is the most dangerous world in the galaxy.'

'It does not look very dangerous. It appears quite peaceful compared to some of the worlds I have been.'

'Danger does not always come in the shape of orks with bolters, Ragnar. This world is where the elite of the Imperium have gathered. We are talking now of the most ruthless, ambitious, unscrupulous collection of rogues ever culled from a million planets. This is the place they have come to realise their ambitions, and on Terra they can, and will not let anything stand in their way. Not me, not you, not their own kin if need be.'

'I would have thought that on such a world, loyalty would be at a premium.'

'No one is loyal here, Ragnar. Trust no one save your battle-brothers.'

'Not even the Celestarch?'

'Particularly not her.'

'Why?'

'We are just another tool to her. One to be used when cunning, diplomacy and money fail. She feels no loyalty to us as individuals. As we are a link to the Space Wolves, we are an important ally. But we are disposable here, Ragnar.'

'You think?'

'I know. Don't get me wrong, that does not mean she would sell our lives cheaply, or be glad to see us die. But if the circumstances were right, we would be sacrificed.'

'That does not sound right!'

'It's exactly as it should be.'

'In what way?'

'The Celestarch is not responsible to us. She is responsible for House Belisarius and to its Elders. It is her duty to guard and protect the interests of her House, just as it is Logan Grimnar's to do the same for the Wolves.'

'Surely it is Grimnar's primary duty to be loyal to the Emperor?'

To Ragnar's surprise, Torin laughed. 'Ah, it does me good talking to you, lad. I was like you once, fresh from Fenris and the Fang. There are times when I think I have been too long on Terra. Of course, Grimnar's first loyalty is to the Emperor, just as it is the Celestarch's. Just as it is everybody's here on Earth and in the Imperium. But you'd be surprised to see how often people use loyalty in a way that promotes their own interests.'

Ragnar was starting to feel a little uncomfortable with Torin's attitude. It was not unlike some of the behaviour he had seen exhibited by the Wolf Lords. He did not doubt that Sigrid and Berek, for instance, both believed they acted in the best interests of the Chapter, and that their eventual ascension to the Wolf Throne would be assured. 'You are a very cynical man, Brother Torin,' he said.

'Maybe, Brother Ragnar,' said Torin smiling, 'or maybe I am just a realistic one. Keep an open mind until you have seen more.'

'I always try to.' They fell silent for a few minutes. Ragnar watched the magnificent buildings flow past. Generations of craftsmen seemed to have spent their entire working lives carving small sections of those walls. Even to Ragnar's untrained eye, it was evident that the sculpture and fresco were masterpieces.

'When will we reach the Belisarius Palace?' Ragnar asked.

'Soon. You're already inside the Belisarius estate. They own everything in this sector, from the spacefield to the shops to the residential buildings. It's a measure of their wealth.'

'In what way?'

'Land on Terra is the most expensive in the Imperium. For the price of one square metre of any of this, you could buy a palace on a Hive World, or on most worlds of the Imperium if truth be told.'

'The sacred soil of Terra,' said Ragnar.

'The sacred and very expensive soil of Terra, Brother Ragnar. Thousands of lives have been lost for areas the size of a small farm on one of the islands on Fenris.'

'I thought wars were outlawed on Terra.'

Torin grinned. 'Ragnar, look at this car, tell me what you see?'

'A fast manoeuvrable vehicle of more or less standard design.'

'Of more or less standard military design. It's armoured against anything short of a krak grenade. It contains every form of protective counter-measure the Adeptus Mechanicus have at their disposal. It has a beacon for summoning aid from the palace. If Terra were peaceful do you think all of this would be necessary?'

Ragnar considered the point. 'My briefing has begun, has it?'

'Good boy, Brother Ragnar, I knew you were quick.'

'I am not a boy, Brother Torin,' said Ragnar dangerously. Again, Torin grinned.

'No. I can see you are not. Even if you lack a Grey Hunter's colours. I shall not forget that in the future. How did that come about anyway? You are not a Blood Claw, and you are not a Grey Hunter…'

Ragnar felt sure that the man beside him already knew the answers, and was taunting him. 'You must know,' he said grimly.

'Let us assume for a moment that I do,' said Torin guiding the vehicle down a broad highway towards a massive building rising before them. They were on a flyover bridge that passed over a deep chasm surrounding the structure. Looking down, Ragnar could see that things were a little deceptive. The building appeared to recede into the depths below them. He could see lights burning in thousands of windows, and more bridges with traffic on them.

'Not everything makes it into the reports we get, believe me. Let's assume I simply want to hear your own side of the story in your own words.'

'I will tell you when I am good and ready.'

'That is fair enough, brother. We have plenty of time. You and I will be seeing a lot of each other over the next few decades.'

The words had all the finality of a prison sentence. Ragnar realised that his fate was indeed sealed. Like it or not, he was stuck on Earth with this man and less than two dozen of his compatriots. The realisation settled on him with all the weight of the great armoured plasteel gateway that had dropped into place behind the buggy.

CHAPTER FIVE

'WE ARE IN the palace now, Ragnar. Be discreet. Choose every word with care unless you are certain you cannot be overheard,' said Torin. The buggy rolled to a halt in the courtyard beyond the gate. He could see that the guards had already emerged from the large armoured car, and were hustling Gabriella through an arched doorway.

Torin hit the button. The control levers slid into the dash and the tinted bubble roof retracted. Both Wolves pulled themselves out. Ragnar studied his surroundings carefully. They were in a massive atrium. Far overhead, an armour glass ceiling allowed natural light to play down into the hall. From where he stood he could see countless balconies rising up the inside of the building. In each wall was a massive translucent elevator shaft. Although Ragnar knew this place could not be nearly so massive as the Fang, it felt as if it was, and it was disorientating to a newcomer.

While the Fang felt like a base of battle-brothers, this felt more like a bazaar. Humans from all over the civilised galaxy thronged the place. He could see Catachans in green silk and pale Boreans in robes of whale fur. There were metal armoured men from the forge worlds of the Talean Rim. One incredibly obese man reclined on a suspensor palanquin while two beautiful naked girls fanned his shaved head, and sweating servants pulled him through the crush. Retainers in the elaborate uniform of Belisarius passed everywhere on their errands. Many possessed bionic eyes and prosthetic limbs. Some were armed.

The building was the product of a great artistic endeavour. The walls were carved with frescos. Gargoyles clutched glow-globes in their talons. Saints radiated light from their halos as they perched on platforms above the throng. Closer inspection told Ragnar that some of the statues had televisor eyes.

He could see that a great deal of business was being conducted here. Niches in the walls led into halls from which came the sound of haggling and bargains being struck. Goods were traded for other wares. Future contacts were being exchanged. Agreements about the use of ships and fleets and Navigators were being made.

Thousands of scents filled the air: of man and beast, of spice, silk and animal pelt. Machine oil mingled with technical unguent and hallucinogenic incense. To a man with senses as keen as Ragnar's it was a little overwhelming until he started to catalogue the stimuli and get a grip on his surroundings. He followed Torin across the mosaic floor, through one of the archways and into an elevator. Moments later, without experiencing the sensation of motion, they were a hundred floors below, surrounded by walls of armoured reinforced plascrete.

Torin led him through the suddenly quiet corridors. The smell of Space Wolves was much stronger here. This was obviously an area frequented by the battle-brothers. Ahead of them a door slid open and they entered another chamber. This had walls of panelled wood. Furs of the great Fenrisian wolf were strewn across the floor. Alcoves in the walls held scrolls and books. What looked like a real log fire, but which was, in fact, a cunningly wrought hologramic simulation, warmed the room. All of this Ragnar took in at a glance before his eyes came to rest on the man behind the desk who dominated the room.

In his own way, he was as impressive as Berek Thunderfist or any of the Wolf Lords. He was thin for a Space Wolf, almost cadaverous. His face was long and sad and seemed unaccountably mournful. There were dark bags under his eyes, and deep lines in his face. His hair was long and grey. His beard was clipped short and streaked black. His eyes were cold, blue and calculating. They seemed to measure him in a moment, and file their conclusion away deep within a chilly brain. When he spoke, his voice was deeper and more resonant than Ragnar had been expecting.

'Welcome to Terra, Ragnar Blackmane. And welcome to our small band of brothers. I am Valkoth, and I am in charge of the Wolfblade contingent here.'

Ragnar felt no urge to challenge him. 'I have asked Torin to begin your briefing. He will take you to your quarters and see that you are settled in. If you have any questions do not hesitate to ask him. The

Celestarch is busy at the moment, but as soon as she has time you will be taken to her to swear your oath of loyalty. Until then you should act at all times as if the oath were already sworn and in force. Behave as if the reputation of the Space Wolves rests on it – for it does.'

'Aye,' said Ragnar.

'I believe there was an attempt on the life of Gabriella Belisarius,' said Valkoth. 'Tell me about it.'

Ragnar did so, and the older man listened carefully, without interruption. After Ragnar had finished, he said, 'Be vigilant. There will be more attempts on Gabriella's life and the life of everyone in our charge.'

Ragnar nodded and Valkoth turned his attention back to the open book in front of him and began to make marks on it with a stylo. It was clear that they were dismissed.

Torin led Ragnar back into the hallway and deeper into a labyrinth of corridors. There were far fewer servants and retainers here and no sign of any Space Wolves, save himself and Torin.

'That was the old man,' said Torin. 'He's something of a scholar but don't let that fool you. He is as fell-handed a warrior as ever lifted a chainsword and as cunning as Logan Grimnar himself.'

Ragnar did not share the common Fenrisian prejudice against scholars. It was obvious to him that what Torin was saying was true. 'Where is everybody else then?'

'You were expecting a welcoming feast, perhaps?'

'No. I just thought there might be more of us about.'

'Actually there are more Wolves in the palace than at any time I can remember, what with the new Celestarch taking her throne, but that is quite unusual. Normally we are scattered hither and yon about the Imperium.'

'Why?'

'Various assignments. Some train Belisarian troops. Some have covert missions to perform. Some are bodyguards to Navigators going into particularly dangerous situations.'

'People keep telling me about training Belisarian troops. As I understood it, the Navigators have no troops.'

'Yes, and no. They have no formal soldiery but they have security guards who perform the same function. And they have mercenary companies under permanent contract who have served them so long that they might as well be part of the House. They are House soldiers in all but a legal sense.'

Ragnar felt like spitting. 'What is the point in having laws if people find ways of getting around them? Civilisation!'

'You sound just like Haegr. You two should get along.'

Ragnar was not entirely sure that he was as righteous as he sounded. At the moment, he felt completely out of his depth and he was retreating into the code of his home world. Once again Torin read his mood. 'It's not entirely a bad way to be!'

Just at that moment a huge figure emerged from an archway. He had a double-sized ale tankard stuck on one foot and a massive hambone that had been gnawed clean in one hand. He was quite the largest man Ragnar had ever seen, gigantic even by Space Wolf standards, and the only one who might conceivably be called fat. His tiny eyes were sunk deep above huge rosy cheeks. His armour seemed to have been modified to contain a massive belly, which made it something of a triumph of the smith's art.

'Did I hear someone taking my name in vain?' He bellowed, in a voice that reminded Ragnar of an enraged bull moose. 'Was it you, little man?'

Torin grinned at the giant. 'I see you are trying to start a new fashion in boots.'

The hulking stranger looked down and blinked. 'I left my tankard by the bed when I lay down for a nap. I must have stood in it when I sprang manfully into action to challenge any who mock my good name.'

Ragnar realised that the newcomer reeked of ale. Spots of food had settled in his beard. 'You know I would not do that, Haegr,' said Torin. 'I was merely remarking to our latest recruit that you and he have something in common.'

Haegr blinked owlishly, as if noticing Ragnar for the first time. 'A newcomer from the blessed world of Fenris, where the cold winds scour the rugged earth of all pollution and corruption. I fear you have come to the wrong place, lad. This foul festering sinkhole of iniquity is anathema to our kind, to the manly virtues of the mighty Space Wolves…'

'Haegr is as windy as the world that birthed him,' said Torin.

'Do you mock me, little man?'

'I would not dare. I was simply admiring your new honour badge.'

'I have no honour badge.'

'Is not that the order of the gravy stain, used to mark the armour of the mightiest of trenchermen?'

Haegr reached down and touched the gravy spot on his armour, then licked his finger. 'If I did not know better I would think you were taunting me, Torin. Only I know that no man would dare.'

'Your logic is impeccable as always, old friend. Now I must show Ragnar to his quarters and brief him on his duties.'

'Be sure you let him know that he will be surrounded by effete cowards without the least of the manly virtues. This world is not Fenris, lad. Don't you forget it!'

'I don't think I am likely to,' said Ragnar. 'Everyone keeps telling me about it one way or another.'

'I will see you later then, and we shall quaff ale in the heroic fashion of the Sons of Fenris. Now I must see about removing this tankard from my foot.' He turned and stamped back into his room.

'That was Haegr,' said Torin. 'He's not the brightest man who the Choosers of the Slain ever picked to join our ranks, but he is perhaps the bravest, particularly when it comes to the consumption of ale and meat.'

'I heard that!' bellowed a muffled voice from behind the closed door.

'It was a compliment to your heroic prowess!' shouted Torin, lengthening his step suddenly.

'I would not want to have to beat you again,' shouted Haegr, his head sticking out of the door. His enormous bushy whiskers reminded Ragnar of a walrus.

'I am still waiting for the first time,' said Torin.

'What was that?'

'Go and take the tankard off your foot,' said Torin, as they ducked around a corner.

'He would not really beat you?' Ragnar asked. Torin raised an eyebrow.

'He wishes he could. Haegr is very strong, but his bulk makes him fairly slow. I have yet to lose a bout to him in unarmed combat.'

There was a quiet confidence in Torin's manner that was utterly at odds with Haegr's bluster. Ragnar saw no reason to doubt his words.

'How did he get so heavy? I thought our bodies had been engineered to burn food efficiently. I don't think I have ever seen an overweight Space Wolf before.'

'There is more muscle than fat in there, as you will find if you ever arm wrestle with him. As to his fatness, something went slightly wrong when Haegr made his ascension to Space Marine. It did not show up for a long time; the Wolf Priests merely thought he had a huge appetite. It was only after he piled on the pounds that they realised there was some sort of flaw in him. Not enough to turn him into a Wulfen or get him exiled into the Cold Wastes but one that made him what he is. You will find most Wolfblades did not exactly fit in back at the Fang. That's how most of us ended up here.'

'What brought you here then?'

'I asked for it.'

'You wanted to see the Holy World?'

'Something like that. And here we have your new chambers. It's not much, but it's home,' he said.

Looking through the door, Ragnar could see that once again, Torin was mocking. The chambers were vast and singularly well appointed. They made his suite on *The Herald of Belisarius* look positively spartan. He could see that his gear had already been brought in and laid out for his inspection on a massive oaken table.

'It's not quite what I expected,' he said.

'It comes with the job. The Belisarians like to keep us happy. They do not want anyone buying our loyalty so we get the best of everything.'

'They think someone could buy the loyalty of a Space Wolf? They do not know us very well,' said Ragnar. He resented the implied slur on the honour of the Chapter.

'Perhaps they know us better than we know ourselves, Ragnar. Or perhaps they simply project themselves onto us. Make yourself comfortable. You will be summoned to your duties soon.'

Before Ragnar could say anything, Torin had retreated and the door was shut behind him.

Ragnar moved through the suite of rooms, and tried to drink in the unaccustomed luxury. The fittings were of the finest quality. There were armchairs, couches and desks, a suspensor bed where it was possible to float above the mattress on a repulsor field. There was a wash chamber with a sunken marble bath.

There was a hologramic window which changed views when you passed your hand over a rune. He cycled through views of Fenris, a desert world dominated by massive ruins, the hall of merchants above, a huge structure that might have been the Imperial Palace with an endless queue of pilgrims about it. The air was filled with relaxing scents, low thrilling martial music was piped in.

Ragnar continued to look around for concealed surveillance devices. He unplugged cameras set within the plasterwork of the ceilings. He sniffed out sub-auditors beneath the beds. He found a camera eye in the poison snooper above the table. He did not like being watched and wanted to make sure that the person who had planted these things got the message.

After he had finished going over the room, he lay on the bed and stared at the ceiling wondering what he was going to do. This place was not at all what he had expected. It reeked of suspicion and intrigue and everyone he met had warned him about it.

It seemed he was to assume everyone he met was treacherous, just as they would assume the same about him. It was no way to live, he thought, and then realised that he had no choice. Assassination was evidently a way of life here. People committed stealthy murder for their own advantage. And it appeared that anything could be bought.

Why was it so, he wondered? Surrounding him were riches beyond the wildest dreams of most of the subjects of the Imperium. All of the Lords of the Imperium, and all of the Navigators shared in that huge wealth. Why did they need more? Perhaps it was not riches they fought for. Perhaps it was power. He had seen what the desire for power could do even among the comparatively austere warriors of Fenris.

And what of his new companions? How trustworthy were they? Torin seemed a man of many secrets and his mocking manner was unlike any Space Wolf Ragnar had ever known. He seemed to have become more a Belisarian in his manner of dress, speech and thought. Haegr seemed simple, but Torin had spoken of some sort of flaw that had perhaps resulted in his exile to this place. Perhaps the flaw went deeper than that.

Ragnar forced himself to relax. He was in no position to judge his comrades. He was simply uneasy at having been torn from the routine of his life with the battle-brothers and thrust into the murky undercurrents of this place. He was like a fish out of water. He had been trained to deal with the hard realities of battle, where objectives and enemies were clearly defined. He hadn't been trained in palace intrigue. Perhaps that was why he had been sent here. Perhaps this was something he needed to master. He knew that whatever happened here, he was being presented with an opportunity.

He was in a position to study the dark underbelly of the Imperial political system close up. He was going to do his best to learn from this, and master it. At this moment, Ragnar was alone and ignorant and vulnerable, but it was his task to see that he did not remain that way. He would take his destiny into his own hands. He would learn what was necessary, and he would triumph over his circumstances. This was a test he was not going to fail.

Coming to this decision made Ragnar feel better. He realised that ever since he had lost the Spear of Russ and learned that he must face trial at the Council of Wolves, he had been drifting, uncertain and unsure. That time was over now. Whatever challenges lay ahead he would face them like a true Son of Russ.

There was a knock on the door. He opened it and found Torin and Haegr waiting for him. 'The Celestarch desires the pleasure of an audience with her newest Wolfblade,' said Torin, half-jokingly.

'She sent us to make sure you would not get lost,' said Haegr, licking his lips.

'Actually she sent me,' said Torin, 'to make sure you both did not get lost.'

'You know I know my way about the palace better than any newly arrived cub.'

Ragnar smiled at them. 'I am sorry. I did not recognise you, Haegr, without that bucket on your foot.'

'Are you mocking me, lad?'

'Would I do a thing like that?' said Ragnar.

'You'd better not,' said Haegr.

'I think you're going to fit right in around here,' said Torin, leading them through the maze of passageways towards the distant elevator.

CHAPTER SIX

THEY EMERGED FROM another elevator in a different part of the palace. Ragnar's head was spinning from all the new sights, sounds and stimuli as well as the sheer immensity of the place. But the process of adapting to the new environment had already begun. As they walked they were leaving a scent trail he could use to retrace his steps. The more ground they covered, the more marks they would leave. Even now, he could find his way back to his chamber blindfolded.

The people in this area were better dressed. There were more Navigators, and more ostentatious signs of wealth. Hologramic tapestries of spun golden thread covered the walls; the perspective on the scenes changing as you walked past in a manner that fooled the eye completely. Here were pictures of treaties, and ships against starry backgrounds, and landscapes of a hundred alien worlds. In each landscape the banner of Belisarius fluttered. On each ship the sigil of its power was painted. A Navigator in House uniform played a prominent part in every negotiation.

Most startling of all was the picture of a Belisarian walking beside three haloed figures. One was winged like an angel, one had the long fangs of a Space Wolf, and one had a blazing aura. Ragnar gave it more than a passing glance. Unless he was completely mistaken, the picture showed one of the precursors of the current Celestarch walking beside the Emperor, Leman Russ and Sanguinius, Primarch of the Blood Angels.

Ragnar flinched a little at the sight of the spear in Russ's hand. He flexed his fingers. They too had briefly held that holy weapon. Looking at the accuracy of the depiction, Ragnar had no doubt that the artist had seen the weapon. The painting was a none-too subtle reminder of the ancient lineage and the mighty connections of the House of Belisarius.

He took time to study the people around him. The humans looked at them with a mixture of respect and fear, as they passed. Their nervousness was evident in their scent. The Navigators, as always, were much more difficult to read. There was something about them that was as alien and inhuman as an ork. Torin and Haegr gave no sign of being upset by it, but he supposed that they had had many years to get used to it.

Ahead of them loomed a massive archway. The support columns were formed by two starships, surrounded by angels with the third eye of Navigators – an image that some would think came close to blasphemy. In the centre of the arch was embossed the sigil of Belisarius, an eye flanked by two rearing wolves. The guards at the entrance saluted them and allowed them to pass directly into the presence room.

Here too was evidence of power and wealth. The domed ceiling of the chamber was a jewelled representation of the night sky. It was reflected in the black marble of the floor. On a raised floating dais of polished black stone, the present Celestarch rested on a throne of true silver. She was a tall woman, with an ageless beauty, garbed in a long black gown, belted at the waist with a girdle of silver. The buckle of the belt bore the sign of the eye flanked by two wolves, as did the diadem on her brow. In its case, the metal eye was positioned exactly so that the Celestarch's own pineal eye was visible through it.

Two men stood beside the throne. One was tall but stooped, with long fine silver hair and beard. He wore robes similar to the Celestarch's but trimmed with white fur at the collar. The other was shorter and more intense looking with black hair shot with grey and a well-trimmed goatee beard. He wore the dress uniform of the House with panache and looked like he knew how to handle the sword and bolt pistol clipped to his belt. All three of them bore a distinct family resemblance both to each other and to Gabriella. They were all tall and slender, with fine boned hands and faces, slightly sunken cheeks and large eyes. The Navigators looked up as the three Wolfblades entered.

'Greetings, Torin of Fenris,' said the woman. Her voice was deeper than Ragnar expected. 'I see you have brought our latest recruit with you.'

'I have Lady Juliana. May I present to you, Ragnar Blackmane of Fenris and the Wolves.'

'We are pleased to make your acquaintance, Ragnar Blackmane. Advance so that we may recognise you.'

Ragnar did so. He strode forward with all the confidence he could muster, determined not to be intimidated by the wealth of his surroundings or the ancient lineage of the Celestarch. He realised the ostentatious display en route to the presence chamber was designed to impress and intimidate the visitor. He was not going to let it sway him. He would judge the Celestarch on her own merits, just as she must judge him. Such had been the way of the warriors of Fenris with their chieftains since time immemorial.

He stood before the dais and looked up at the Celestarch. If she was offended she gave no sign, nor did the elderly Navigator. The uniformed man scowled but said nothing as he witnessed Ragnar's swagger. Ragnar thought he sensed amusement radiate from Torin and approval from Haegr.

'I can see you are a true son of Fenris,' said the Lady Juliana, not unkindly. 'Step on to the dais.'

Ragnar did so, and noticed not the slightest tremor in the suspensor field, as his massively armoured form rested on it. The platform might look as if it floated like a raft in a swell, but it felt solid once you were on it.

'You have come to swear allegiance to us, Ragnar?'

'I have. You have my word as a warrior and Space Wolf that I will follow you and shield you and obey your commands as I would the Great Wolf himself.'

'I can ask for no more,' said the Celestarch. 'Be welcome in House Belisarius, Ragnar Blackmane.'

'I thank you, lady.' A nod told Ragnar he was dismissed, so he bowed and backed off the dais, easily retracing his steps to Torin and Haegr.

'You may go,' said Lady Juliana. All three Wolfblades saluted and withdrew through the archway.

'I think she likes you,' said Torin.

'How can you tell?'

'She kept the formalities short.'

'Who were the other two?'

'The old man was Alarik, the chamberlain, also head of security. The dandy was Skorpeus. He is the Celestarch's cousin and he thinks he is her advisor.'

'Who cares?' said Haegr. 'Let us go and consume vast quantities of beer in a manner suitable for heroes of Fenris.'

'An excellent suggestion,' said Torin. 'Come, Ragnar, let us introduce you to one of the delights of Terra – the taverns of the merchants quarter.'

Ragnar felt like saying he was tired and wished to recover from his journey, but there was a challenge in the gaze of both his companions. Torin appeared to be judging him, and Haegr's manner made it clear that no true son of Fenris would miss such an opportunity. On reflection, Ragnar thought it would not be such a bad thing to do. He was keen to see more of his new homeworld and once his duties had started he might not get an opportunity. It occurred to him that this might be the case for the other two as well. Perhaps they had been assigned to show him around and would be assigned to something else if he left. That being the case…

'Lead on,' said Ragnar. At that moment, the uniformed Navigator Skorpeus emerged from the presence chamber. He was greeted by a hulking figure with a scarred face. The two of them exchanged a few words and then strode over towards the three companions.

'Welcome to Terra, Ragnar Blackmane,' said the Navigator. His manner was smooth and easy, perhaps overly so, thought Ragnar. 'I wish you better fortune than your predecessor.'

'Skander died performing his duty. No Wolf could ask for a better death.'

'Perhaps it would have been better for us all if he had succeeded in his duty which was, after all, to keep Adrian Belisarius alive. It would certainly have been better for my cousin.'

Haegr grunted and spat. Torin said, 'In his place I am sure you would have found a way to preserve both your lives, noble Skorpeus. Doubtless the stars would have warned you to stay away. Perhaps they did… which is why you were not around when the attack came.'

'The stars did indeed smile on me. Although, of course, it saddens me that my cousin did not heed my warnings.'

Ragnar turned to the Navigator's hulking companion. He was listening to the exchange intently and showing no sign of emotion. There was a hard competence in his manner that reminded Ragnar of the elite units of the Imperial Guard.

'Did the stars not also predict that you would become Celestarch?' said Torin smoothly. Skorpeus cast him a patronising smile.

'You think that the Elders' selection of Cousin Juliana invalidates that prediction, do you, Wolfblade?'

'To an untutored barbarian such as me it would look that way.'

Skorpeus's smile widened. He resembled a gambler who holds a trump card and is about to produce it. 'The stars did not predict when

I would become Celestarch. Only that I would. It's something you should keep in mind. I will be your master someday.'

'I think you misunderstand the relationship between Fenris and Belisarius,' said Torin. Ragnar noticed a faint hint of anger in his scent. Although he concealed it well, the Space Wolf clearly disliked Skorpeus.

'Perhaps once I take the throne I shall redefine it,' said the Navigator. He strode off with the jaunty air of a man who knows he has had the last word.

'What was that about?' Ragnar asked, when Skorpeus had disappeared out of earshot.

'That fine specimen of Navigator pride and self-love thinks the stars predicted him being on the throne,' said Torin, swiftly walking in the other direction. 'In case you missed it, he is convinced that he should and will be Celestarch. His lackey there, the ape Beltharys, agrees with him.'

'You think Skorpeus would do something to help the process along?'

Torin shook his head. 'He would if he could, but there is no way he could influence the selection of the Elders.'

'Who are they?'

'Don't ask,' said Haegr. 'Drink beer instead.'

'I am curious,' said Ragnar.

'They are very mysterious,' said Haegr. 'And really you don't want to know.'

'For once my vast friend is right,' said Torin.

'In what way mysterious?' said Ragnar.

'Most people never see them. To most of the people in this palace they are as invisible as Haegr's common sense.'

'I hope I am not going to have to thrash you again, Torin.'

'All know that common sense is a quality, Haegr, and therefore noticeable if not perceptible.'

'That's all right then.'

'You mean no one sees the people who select the ruler of House Belisarius.'

'There are couriers who venture into the Vaults below. They are blind. And the Navigators sometimes go down there too. And I think Valkoth has been. Skander had too.'

'Down there? Vaults?'

'Below this palace is a maze, Ragnar. It is fortified, and sealed off from the rest of the underworld by a ten metre thick moat of reinforced plascrete. It fills every corridor and is riddled with sensors and traps and detectors. The Elders dwell in these Vaults.'

'Perhaps they fear assassination,' said Ragnar.

'You're very quick, young Blackmane,' said Haegr sarcastically.

'And perhaps they fear something else,' said Torin.

'What do you mean?'

'Now is neither the time nor place to discuss it.'

'It's one of the Navigators' guilty secrets, is it?'

'Don't mock, Ragnar. It may be.'

'Are we going to talk or drink?' demanded Haegr.

'Doubtless you have noticed that our steps are taking us in the direction of the flitter bays, friend Haegr,' said Torin. 'And doubtless your mighty brain will have deduced that one of those vehicles will carry us to the tavern quarter. Many of us can perform two tasks, such as walking and talking at once.'

'Are you suggesting that I can't?'

'You have proven many times your capacity in those arenas. Even as we speak you perform both with diligence. Why then would I suggest otherwise?'

'There is a slipperiness in your manner, Torin, that I like not. A beating may be necessary.'

'Save your energy for the drinking, my friend.'

'I will consider your advice.'

Torin led them to a vast hangar somewhere high on the side of the palace. From its cavernous interior, there was a panoramic view of the skyline of the city. A number of enormous structures glowed in the distance, every window like a small beacon. The running lights formed streams across the skies. Gigantic trains wended their way between buildings and the endless tide of tens of thousands of people. The taste of pollution tainted the air. Ragnar felt a very long way from the cold wilderness of Fenris.

Torin led them over to a small four-man flitter. It bore the markings of Belisarius, a sleek streamlined insect like vessel painted in black and silver. They clambered in and Torin took the controls, handling them as expertly as a Thunderhawk pilot. He quickly ran through the pre-flight invocations, and the engines hummed to life. Moments later the vehicle slid swiftly out into the night.

Ragnar felt a moment's disorientation as he looked down at the metal and plascrete sliding away below. They were a thousand metres up and rising. Torin was giving his attention to their surroundings and the holosphere gauges. The Belisarius Palace receded behind them. From this vantage point Ragnar could see it was a massive black and silver lozenge with the logo of the House embossed on the side. He knew now that the skyscraper was but the tip of an iceberg: the real domains of the House extended far below the surface to the mysterious Vaults. What could possibly go on down there, he wondered? Why were the Navigators so secretive? What were they hiding?

Another glance showed him that the flitters were all following routes through the sky as distinct as the roadways beneath them. There were vast open spaces occupied by solitary structures that were avoided. He asked why.

'Those are the homes of the other Houses. No one violates their airspace without invitation and clearance. To do so is to risk being shot down.'

Ragnar understood that. Such cordons would be the easiest way to prevent a surface attack and would allow any gunner on the building a clear line of fire at any target – a thing that would not be possible if vehicles crowded the skies above them. It had been what he expected, but he was glad to have his thinking confirmed.

'I thought the Inquisition and the Arbites maintained tight security on Terra.'

'They do, but not everywhere. You are in the navigators quarter now. The whole island is a free zone. The families are left alone and maintain their own security. The Inquisition cannot enter here unless invited or unless there is some flagrant violation of the laws. There is little love lost between the families and the Inquisition.'

'Aye,' said Haegr. 'The black-cloaked bastards hate the three eyed devils. None of them are worth a fart, except one or two of the Belisarians, of course.'

'You don't like it here?' said Ragnar.

'The place disgusts me. I wish I were back on the icefields of Fenris with a herd of elk before me and a spear in my hand.'

'It's funny,' said Torin. 'That time when you saved old Adrian from those fanatics I thought I heard him offer you your heart's desire. He would have sent you home if you asked. Instead you asked for a meat pie.'

'It was a big pie,' said Haegr. He sounded almost embarrassed.

'It was indeed,' said Torin. 'They killed a bull and wrapped it in pastry. Haegr ate it all himself too.'

'It was my reward. I didn't notice you stepping in the way of any bullets.'

'Is it true you trampled several servants to death as you rushed the table?' said Torin.

'No. None would dare stand between me and such a prize.'

Ragnar was amused listening to them. Their banter reminded him of the cheery insults he had often traded with Sven. But he still felt out of place here. He noticed that the flitter had started to descend towards a tightly packed cluster of buildings. The sky above them blazed with light.

'You said the Inquisition does not come here.'

'It would take little short of open war between the Houses to give them reason,' said Torin. 'The Navigators spend enough in bribes to buy a small planet. It ensures their privacy.'

Ragnar was a little shocked by all this talk of bribery. That the heart of the Empire should be so corrupt disappointed him and left him feeling naïve. The others seemed to take it in their stride. Perhaps he would too when he had been here as long as they had.

'Are you saying the Inquisition takes bribes?'

'Nothing as blatant as that,' said Torin. 'You have to understand how the Imperium works, Ragnar. All the High Lords of Terra spend their time intriguing against each other, jockeying for position, prestige and power. That takes money. The Navigators have a great deal of money. The High Lords and many ranking bureaucrats ensure that the trusted allies who provide them with money are not bothered.'

'The whole planet would be better off if we virus bombed it,' said Haegr. 'Except the Emperor's Palace.'

Torin looked at him.

'And the Belisarians, of course,' Haegr added as an afterthought.

'Only you would suggest virus bombing Holy Terra,' said Torin.

'It would improve the place,' said Haegr.

'Don't say that too loudly where someone might hear.'

'What will you do if I do?'

'I will attend your funeral after the zealots incinerate you.'

'Bring them on. I do not fear them or the Inquisition. Haegr fears nothing in this galaxy.'

'Zealots?' asked Ragnar.

'Religious fanatics. Terra abounds with them, as you might expect. It's not all corruption and luxury. Not everyone can afford them. There are billions of people here on the holy soil who have no comfort but their faith. A certain percentage of them take comfort in killing anyone who does not measure up to their idea of virtue.'

'That's one of the reasons why the Navigators prefer to be isolated in the middle of this sludge sea,' said Haegr. 'The zealots hate them, they call them mutants.'

'They would kill Navigators?' said Ragnar.

'Who do you think killed Adrian Belisarius?' demanded Torin.

CHAPTER SEVEN

THE TAVERN WAS packed with hundreds of people. Sailors, soldiers, merchants and their bodyguards from a thousand worlds had congregated here. Music pulsed loudly. Semi-naked women danced on tables, while others brought food and drink to the customers. The interior had been built to resemble a wooden tavern on some frontier world, but Ragnar's senses told him that this was an illusion. The beams overhead were in fact painted plascrete, not wood. The walls were panels overlaid on stone. The fire, strangely enough, was real and roaring.

Many animal heads had been mounted on the wall. Ragnar recognised wolf and elk. Strange how some variant of these creatures could be found on thousands of worlds. Ragnar supposed they must have been borne outwards with the original migration from Earth. This idea brought him back to the realisation that this was where it had all started. This was the home world of the Emperor – this was where humanity had originally come from. It was an awesome thought, although he doubted it was passing through the minds of any of the revellers who surrounded them.

It was a testimony to the cosmopolitanism of the crowd that surrounded them that when Torin and Haegr made their way towards a table, no one paid them the slightest attention. It was not something Ragnar was used to. On any world save Fenris a Space Wolf could expect to be greeted with awe and not a little reverence. Of course, it was entirely possible, looking at this crowd, that the revellers were simply too drunk to have noticed three armoured giants moving through their midst.

Haegr had already bellowed orders for food and drink. The landlord greeted him as if he were a long lost brother. 'The usual?' he asked.

'The usual!' Haegr bellowed.

Moments later a massive tankard of ale splashed down in front of Ragnar. 'Skal!' roared Haegr and raised his stein.

'Welcome to Terra, Ragnar,' said Torin.

'Glad to be here,' said Ragnar, and found to his surprise that it was true. The ale was cold and went down well.

'Not as good as Fenrisian ale, but it will do,' said Haegr. He had already finished one tankard and was proceeding to another. It took a lot of ale to get through a Space Marine's ability to metabolise poison, and Haegr was obviously helping it along with a beaker of whisky. A few moments later what looked like two whole roasted sheep were set on the table in front of him.

'Are we going to eat all of this?' asked Ragnar.

'This is mine,' said Haegr. 'Here's yours now!' His gesture indicated that another dead and roasted animal was about to be delivered to their table.

'This is just a starter for Haegr,' said Torin, and seeing Ragnar's look added, 'I am not joking. Dig in, or he'll eat yours before you can have a mouthful.'

From the other side of the table came a noise like a chainsword going through a side of beef. Ragnar was astonished to notice how much of the meat on one of Haegr's sheep was already gone. Two loaves and a slathering of butter had gone with it. He tore off a haunch of his own and bit into it. It tasted good. The juices flowed over his tongue and down his throat. He washed them down with more ale, some whisky and then some bread.

He looked up and was surprised to see that Torin was using a knife and fork in the local manner, and was carefully cutting his food into small bite sized portions before chewing on it. A translucent goblet the size of bucket contained wine. It was his only concession to the Fenrisian style of feasting.

He smiled at Ragnar. 'Sensorin dreamwine. It contains some powerful hallucinogenic mushrooms. They have quite a kick. I like to test myself on such things.'

Haegr let out a belch like a thunderclap. 'Torin has gone all decadent. I blame the influence of all these effete earthlings. Only my regular thrashings give him any semblance of true Fenrisian hardihood.'

'Watch your arm, Ragnar,' said Torin. 'Haegr almost grabbed it by mistake. Several men have needed prosthetics after dining with him.'

'A scurrilous rumour spread by my enemies,' said Haegr, shredding the second sheep with his teeth. 'I am no ork.'

'Sometimes it's difficult to tell,' said Torin. 'Did your mother know your father well? I am sure I detect a greenish tint to your skin sometimes.'

'The only greenish tint around here is on your skin and it comes from your envy of my manly prowess.'

'Actually, as I recall, you did look a little green after our last drinking session. You claimed that you should not have had that last alligator curry, although I suspect it was the two barrels of firewine that disagreed with you?'

'How could you tell?' asked Haegr complacently. 'You were unconscious at the time. Which reminds me – you still owe me for that bet.'

Ragnar glanced around the room. The whisky had warmed his belly, and the food was going down well, but something made him uneasy. There was a faint prickling of the hairs on the back of his neck. He sensed that he was under hostile observation and tried to identify the source. Many people were looking at them now, but that could be because they were betting how much Haegr could eat. He could hear wagers being made at the other tables if he listened hard.

There was other talk too, about politics mixed in with the usual bar room gossip. Some of the strangers were talking about the death of Adrian Belisarius, and their discussion was becoming quite animated. It appeared the former Celestarch was not the only highly ranked Navigator to have died recently. Evidently there had been attempts on others too. Again and again, Ragnar picked up the word *Brotherhood*. He was about to go over and enquire about it, but a warning glance from Torin told him it would not be a good idea.

'It seems the death of Adrian Belisarius is common gossip,' said Ragnar. Torin shrugged.

'Men will talk about what men talk about.'

Ragnar considered what he had heard. 'Did he really die in a flitter crash?'

'You could say that.'

Haegr grunted something but his words were incomprehensible through his huge mouthful of food.

Despite the friendly hustle and bustle, Ragnar began to feel more and more uneasy. A couple of people eyed him with hostile intent. When he cast his mind back, he recalled that several of those men's friends had rushed out of the tavern earlier.

'It seems we are not popular here.'

'Space Wolves never are on Terra,' said Torin.

'Why?'

'Ask the locals, not me! You'd think they would be grateful after all we have done for them.'

Ragnar swigged the ale and considered this. He could just go over and challenge the strangers. Seeing his look the men got up and ducked for the door. Maybe he had been wrong, Ragnar thought. Maybe they were simply curious or disliked off-worlders. On the other hand they could be zealots though they certainly had not shown any zeal for sticking around when he looked like he was about to talk to them.

More and more food was being heaped on the table but Haegr and Torin appeared to be having a drinking match, in order to warm up. Goblets of whisky and massive steins of ale filled their table, and both contestants appeared to be able to consume them with little trouble.

Ragnar slowed his own drinking to sips. The atmosphere of incipient danger had not changed – if anything it had increased. A glance told him that Torin, while appearing to drink as heartily as Haegr, was also covertly studying their surroundings. He was subtle about it, and if Ragnar had not been doing the same he would not have noticed it. When their eyes met, Torin winked surreptitiously. Ragnar felt reassured. If there was going to be trouble, he was not the only one expecting it.

A mountain of food appeared in front of Haegr. He smacked his lips and gestured for the waitresses to keep it coming. Loaves, sides of beef, and fish the size of small sharks continued to disappear along with a small mountain of butter and cheese. More men had entered. Some of them brought with them an odd stink of hatred and menace. It was sharp as a knife and as bitter as the soul of a miser who had lost a gold coin. The hackles on the back of Ragnar's neck rose further, but aside from Torin he was the only one in the place who did not give off the odd scent or who showed any sign of unease.

All eyes were focused on Haegr now. Gasps of disbelief and cries of awe filled the chamber as the orgy of consumption continued. Haegr was chewing through whole bones now, grinding them in his teeth and swallowing them down. Torin had risen now to clap Haegr on the shoulder and congratulate him, but Ragnar caught him leaning forward and whispering in his comrade's ear.

Haegr's cheeks were red, and sweat dotted his brow. Although his whole concentration appeared to be focused on his eating orgy, he nodded imperceptibly and quaffed a huge mouthful of ale. Torin did not sit back down, instead he glanced around to seek the source of impending danger.

A man bumped into Ragnar. There was an angry expression on his face as if he resented being jostled. The anger was real, but the cause was not. Ragnar knew from his stink that he had already been on the verge of berserk fury before they had made contact. The man's pupils were the size of pinpricks and a faint trail of drool dribbled from his mouth. Close up, Ragnar caught the acrid unhealthy chemical scent of his sweat. A vein pulsed in the man's forehead. His lips were drawn back in a snarl revealing yellowing teeth.

'Out of my way, off-world pig,' he slurred. Most would have assumed the slurring was caused by alcohol, but Ragnar knew better. This was one of the many side effects of Fury, an alchemical concoction designed to goad men to berserker fits in battle. It had been banned by the Imperial military centuries ago because it made troops unreliable and increased their susceptibility to the influence of Chaos. Still, it had been used by heretics in several of the planetary rebellions that Ragnar had helped quash. He was shocked to discover it being used here on Earth.

He was not intimidated. A man in the grip of Fury could be erratic, incredibly strong and almost immune to pain but that would not make him a threat to a Space Wolf. The man obviously did not see things this way. He slipped something over his hand, and said, 'I said, out of my way off-world pig. Don't make me repeat myself again.'

Ragnar scented more men closing in on him. They all had the same tainted sweat. Ragnar grinned, showing his teeth. If the man was too far gone to back off after that, the consequences would be on his own head. The stranger swung at him.

The blow came in faster than it would have from a normal man but Ragnar blocked it with ease. He caught the man's wrist in his hand. There was a stinging sensation in his arm as a blue electrical arc jumped from the band on the man's fingers to Ragnar's arm.

The man was wearing electric cestii, designed to enhance the power of a punch with an electric shock. If set to maximum, the blast of power could stun or even kill a man if his heart were weak. Ragnar smiled and casually backhanded his attacker. Teeth flew everywhere and bones broke as his foe was thrown across the room. He landed on a table, but immediately struggled to his feet, his resilience obviously enhanced by the drugs in his system.

One of the people at the table was annoyed to have a stranger suddenly strewn across his food. He showed his displeasure by breaking a wine bottle over the attacker's head. That was a mistake – the berserker turned and lurched for his throat. Red wine and blood mingled as they ran down his face. Shouts, screams and warnings rang out as chaos spread and the brawl became general.

Ragnar made out more attackers closing in on him. They were a villainous looking bunch. Many had bionic hands or eyes. Some of their prosthetics had been enhanced with retractable daggers that emerged like nails from their finger tips. Some wore electric cestii, and others carried weighted truncheons. All of them threw themselves at Ragnar with an unhesitating fury that told of the drugs in their system. Ragnar caught the first by the throat, raised him high and then tossed him onto his friends, knocking three of them over.

Another came on in a rush, his claws extended to pierce Ragnar's eyes. Ragnar caught him by his prosthetic arm, twisted for leverage, and pulled. He ripped the mechanical limb clean out of its socket in a shower of sparks, and used it as a bludgeon to knock his assailant from his feet. Then he kicked him in the head.

More blows rained down on him now. Electric cestii sparked against his armour. Sparks flashed and the scent of ozone filled the air as they connected. Ragnar's armour was designed to take far heavier punishment than this, so he ignored it and concentrated instead on smiting his foes.

He lashed out around him with his fists. Each blow dropped a man but a surprisingly large number of them got back up again and instantly came back on the offensive. It seemed obvious that these men had been sent specifically to start this brawl and they were pulling no punches. The drugs left them incapable of hesitating. They would have killed him if they could. In fact, the treatment he had received would have killed a normal man ten times over. Fortunately, Ragnar was a Space Marine. His armour was almost part of his body and his bone structure and musculature had been heavily modified so he could absorb enormous amounts of damage. Still, he had collected a few bruises and cuts. He could feel his skin sting where his ultra-coagulant blood had congealed on them.

He glanced around to see what had become of his companions. Torin was swinging from one of the suspensor chandeliers. He planted his boot in the face of one assailant before letting go and flying into a mass of others. His every movement was swift and certain, every blow decisive. If anything he had less to worry about than Ragnar. He was moving so fast it would be difficult even for a man with a gun to draw a bead on him, and this was clearly his intention.

Then it happened. Up to this point Haegr had ignored the carnage about him as he concentrated on stuffing his face. One of the berserkers dived onto the table, scattering food everywhere, sending wine and whisky and ale splashing all over the place. Haegr looked at him for a moment as if he could not quite understand what had happened. A

look of confusion passed over his face as he reached for food that was
no longer there. Then his piggy eyes narrowed and he let out an enormous roar.

A sweep of his arm cleared the berserker from the table. Haegr reared
to his feet, like a mammoth rising from a mudhole. He had the same
mass and power, but suddenly he was even larger and more threatening. He picked up the metal table. The bolts holding it to the floor
snapped as he lifted it free and tossed it into the oncoming mass of
drugged fanatics. It bowled them over and left them sprawling beneath
its weight. Haegr reached forward and picked two up, one in each
hand, and then used them as clubs to batter their companions senseless. He raced through them like an out-of-control behemoth,
unstoppable as a charging rhino. Within seconds he had left a trail of
maimed and battered foes behind him. Any that tried to get to their
feet were stamped on. Their hands and legs shattered along with bion-
ics and bones.

Ragnar threw himself back into the fray, lashing out at his opponents,
careful to select only those who stank of combat drugs. He found himself face to face with Torin. He was smashing a couple of berserkers'
heads together, until not even the drug could keep them awake. 'Best
grab Haegr and get out of here,' he shouted.

'Why?'

'It might embarrass the Celestarch if we thrash any of the Arbites who
come to investigate this.'

'Fair enough,' said Ragnar, glancing at Haegr. He had picked up a side
of beef on a spit and was bludgeoning those around him with it. Occasionally, he paused to tear some meat from its flanks, and gnaw at it.
'But getting him out of here might be easier said than done.'

Torin nodded. 'He's enjoying himself, but this is for his own good.
You get one arm. I'll take the other.'

Ragnar nodded and they rushed at Haegr. Ragnar grabbed his left
arm, Torin the right, and together they began dragging him to the door.

Distracted as he was by the side of beef, it was like trying to tow a
bull. It took several attempts. Occasionally, they were interrupted by
Haegr's blows at the surviving berserkers. But they dragged him out
into the night air and began to calm him down.

'Let me go,' said Haegr. 'There are still foes to thrash!'

'We'd best be going. Those sirens you hear are the Arbites.'

'So? We can take them all out. You know we can.'

'Aye, but it might cause the Lady Juliana some problems if we
leave the streets of the merchants quarter filled with dead or dying
judges.'

Haegr was not convinced. Ragnar could see the running lights of many flitters coming closer. Ground cars too. 'They are not our enemies,' he said. 'They are merely doing their duty as they see fit. Besides, we will have to come back here anyway. We have a mystery to solve.'

'And what would that be?' Haegr asked.

'Why those men attacked us and who sent them anyway. The Arbites won't help us do that if we put any of them in the healing tanks.'

'Very well. I can see that you and Torin have made up your minds. I will go with you and keep you out of trouble.'

Something moving on a nearby rooftop caught Ragnar's eye. He glanced up and caught sight of a shadowy figure receding from view. He could not be sure that it was not a trick of the light.

CHAPTER EIGHT

THE TOLL OF a distant bell dragged Ragnar from dreams of Fenris. He woke instantly and rose from his bed. As if summoned by his motion, servants appeared with bowls of elk stew and fish porridge – traditional Fenrisian food, or as close to it as he was going to get on Terra. He was more than a little startled by the way they had entered without being asked. 'Who sent you?' he asked the eldest looking, a lean aquiline man with cold calm features and fine silver hair. He wore the uniform of Belisarius more like a soldier than a thrall.

'No one, sir. We assumed you would want breakfast as soon as you rose. Have we erred?'

'No.' The servant waited politely to see if he had anything else to say. Ragnar did not. It seemed like servants were invisible here, coming and going about their duties unbidden, changing their routines only if asked. They seemed to have access to most places as well. He realised the servants were still waiting. 'Carry on,' he said, and they promptly resumed their duties.

Ragnar recalled the events of the previous evening. After they had dragged Haegr to the flitter, Torin had taken them over the nearest roofs. If there had been someone there, he had vanished in the few moments it had taken them to get aloft. Either that or he was camouflaged enough to baffle even the Space Wolves' keen night vision. Ragnar knew that was not impossible, but they would have to be using military issue wargear. That was not impossible either, he had decided.

'Master Ragnar, I have a message for you, from Master Valkoth.'

'Yes?' said Ragnar.

'When you have finished your breakfast, you should report to him to have your duties assigned to you. It is not urgent, but he would appreciate it if you could be there before the ninth bell. That is in forty-five minutes and twenty-two seconds, sir.'

'Thank you,' said Ragnar, snatching up his food. 'Plenty of time then.'

'Yes, sir.'

As HE STRODE through the crowded section of the palace, Ragnar again pondered last night's events. He was certain that it had been no mere tavern brawl. Not unless men went out drinking here with Fury in their pockets and a desire to do violence. He supposed that scenario was not impossible. From what he gathered, the merchants quarter had a reputation as a wild place, at least by Terra's standards. Many went there to blow off steam. Perhaps that was one way of doing it.

And perhaps Haegr would grow wings and learn to fly, Ragnar thought. He was surprised to find Torin had fallen into step beside him. He must have approached from a side corridor downwind.

'Morning,' he said. 'Looking forward to today's duties, are we?'

'I don't even know what they are.'

'Well, you'll find out soon enough. How did you enjoy last night's little adventure?'

'It was interesting. Although I still wonder why those men chose to attack us.'

'Doubtless the Arbites report will be on Valkoth's table by now. He'll tell us if anything important has shown up, though I rather doubt it will.'

'Why? Who do you think those men were?'

'Could have been any number of people: zealot bully boys who don't like off-worlders; agents of another House seeking to test us and embarrass the Belisarians; or young nobs trying to spice up a dull night.'

'Are they really stupid enough to attack three Space Wolves?'

'You'd be surprised what a man will do if he's drunk enough or high enough on Fury.'

'I would be very surprised if he chose to attack three of us.'

'To be honest, I would too. It felt more planned than that, didn't it?'

'Yes.' They passed a golden pleasure girl garbed only in diaphanous robes. She strode along as if she was not semi-naked. A whiff of pheromone attractants sailed on the air behind her and she was gone.

'What do you think?' Ragnar asked, as Torin's eyes followed the girl.

'She's very attractive.'

'I mean about the attackers.'

'Agents of some kind, although I am not sure whose. Or why, for that matter. You never can tell these things on Terra. Although things are getting a little tense at the moment.'

'In what way?'

'Politically. There is a lot of manoeuvring going on between the Houses.'

'I thought there always was.'

'More so even than usual.'

'Why?'

'Old Sarius, the Navigator representative to the High Lords of Terra, is dying.'

'Why should that affect anything?'

'Everybody wants to have a say in who elects his successor.'

'Is he that powerful?'

Torin laughed and smiled at a couple of serving girls who went past carrying bowls of some perfumed liquid. 'Quite the contrary. The Navigators' representative among the High Lords has always been little more than a figurehead.'

'Then why do people care who succeeds him?'

'Because potentially the Navigator's voice has power. All of the High Lords do. Sarius is powerless because he comes from a relatively minor House with very little support from the more powerful ones. None of the great Houses would allow any of their rivals to take that position. At least none of them has managed it in the past two thousand years. It would signal their pre-eminence among the Houses. The rest have tended to gang up on anyone who looks like they might swing it. A weak man from a weak House can be influenced by anyone. And he can be counted on not to do anything that would upset the balance of power.'

'It all sounds rather foolish to me. Leaders should be strong, not weak.'

'Spoken like a true Fenrisian warrior, Ragnar, old son. But no Navigator wants a strong leader for the Houses, unless it's them, of course.'

'But this time it's different?'

'Maybe. It's always a tense time. Every great House is scared that the others will try and steal a march on them. They watch each other like hawks. There's a lot of horse trading and influence peddling.'

'Fascinating,' said Ragnar. He did not want to seem overly interested. All of this seemed somehow beneath a Space Wolf. Torin chuckled.

'You remind me of me when I first came here,' he said. 'Study these things, Ragnar, learn them. They are important. They may determine who we fight tomorrow, or next month or next year – and how. It never hurts to understand the political situation.'

'A Space Wolf fights where he is told.'

'One day, Ragnar, you may be the one doing the telling.'

They had reached Valkoth's chamber. The older Space Marine was already enthroned behind his desk. It was almost as if he had never left it. A stack of papers was scattered around. Ragnar wondered whether he and Torin were mentioned in any of them.

'Good morning, brothers,' said Valkoth, as they entered. His manner was more melancholy than usual. 'You have a busy day ahead of you and an interesting one. You are going to see a place few Wolfblades have, at least not without heading a strike force.'

'Where is that?' said Ragnar. Torin grinned.

'The Feracci Palace. You are to escort the Lady Gabriella on a visit to her aunt. Do try and make sure she comes home in one piece, won't you? Go to her chambers now and await her pleasure.'

His words and manner were casual, but it was clear they were dismissed.

IF RAGNAR HAD thought his own rooms were opulent, he now felt like a pauper. The smallest room in Gabriella's suite was larger than his entire living space. Antique furniture filled it. Bookcases full of ancient musty tomes covered the walls. A massive desk dominated the chamber.

Looking out of the huge arched windows, Ragnar realised that even her balcony was larger than his chamber. Everything was monogrammed with the House emblem. Serving maids came and went at will. Ragnar waited. Torin studied the paintings on the wall. They were scenes of alien landscapes.

'Celebasio,' he said.

'What?' said Ragnar.

'The painter. Quite a famous one. He did the murals in the northern audience halls. The Belisarians were his last and richest patrons. Each of these paintings is worth a potentate's ransom.'

Ragnar thought they were beautiful, but hardly functional. 'On Fenris we would use them as kindling for the fire.'

'You are not on Fenris now, Ragnar, and stop trying to pretend you're Haegr. You would need to put on a hundred kilos and grow a moustache like a walrus before you could carry it off.'

Ragnar laughed in spite of himself. 'Who are the Feraccis?'

'One of the other great Navigator Houses – perhaps the greatest. They are the Belisarians' most deadly rivals.'

'I thought Gabriella was going to visit her aunt.'

'The thing about Navigators, old son, is that they are all related: they only marry other Navigators. They do this to preserve the bloodlines that give them their gift. But no Navigator can marry within their own House, for reasons you can well imagine – although I have heard it has happened anyway.'

'So they marry their enemies?'

'They marry who they are told. All marriages are arranged with a view to keeping the bloodlines strong. There are great books of genealogy detailing each bloodline's strengths and weaknesses. The Navigators procreate in the same way people breed dogs or horses.'

Ragnar reflected on this. He had known these things, of course, or at least the teaching machines had left the knowledge in his head. But having knowledge buried in the deep recesses of his mind was not the same as learning about it first hand. Before it had been simply a bit of lore – interesting but seemingly useless. Now that he was familiar with the people involved, it all seemed a little inhuman. Torin noticed his expression.

'It is their way,' he said. 'And the Navigator Houses predate even the Space Marine Chapters, so it must work.' He gestured at their lush surroundings. 'Some would say it has served them well.'

'I sometimes wonder why, when someone has all this wealth, they could want more,' Ragnar said.

'Ask Haegr. He can eat a hundred sweetmeats and still want more. Horus was the most powerful man in the Imperium after the Emperor. Something drove him to rebel.'

'Evil,' said Ragnar, shocked that Torin would use such an example.

'Ambition,' said Torin. 'At first, anyway.'

'I do not think the Rune Priests would like to hear you talk this way,' said Ragnar.

'I agree with you there, old son. But stay on this planet long enough and you will understand why I think the way I do.'

Ragnar considered Berek and Sigrid and the other Wolf Lords, with their thirst for glory, and their hearts all set on the Wolf Throne. You did not need to go all the way to Terra to find ambition.

'For some people, the more they have, the more they want. And the lords of the Navigator Houses are among the richest and most powerful people in the Imperium. Indeed, some claim they are the most powerful.'

Ragnar had heard that view before too. Without Navigators trade would be reduced to a mere trickle and Imperial fleets would only make short crawls between nearby stars. The Space Marine Chapters would be in a similar position. Huge expanses of the Imperium would fall out of contact and revert to barbarism or be conquered by alien powers. The Navigator Houses had an effective monopoly on long haul interstellar travel. If someone could mould those fragmented Houses into a single combine, he would effectively control the Imperium, so great would be his political leverage.

Perhaps that was why the Emperor had encouraged the creation of so many rival Houses, Ragnar thought. Perhaps he had foreseen the consequences of having one united guild of Navigators. Or perhaps he was letting his imagination take him too far. He resolved to wait until he had a better grasp of the facts before jumping to conclusions.

'What are the Feraccis like?' he asked.

'Ruthless, driven, manipulative, more so than most Navigators. Their lord, Cezare, is thought by many to be the most ambitious man in the Imperium, and the most ruthless and cruel.'

'He has a lot of competition for those three titles, or so it would seem.'

'The fact he has that reputation should tell you something.'

'He can't be as bad as all that.'

'Playing the devil's advocate to draw me out, eh? Very clever, old son.'

Ragnar felt a little embarrassed for being so transparent. Torin continued speaking regardless.

'Oh, he is a smooth devil, all right, and a great patron of the arts – all the great lords are. I suppose they have to do something with their money, but beneath the facade, he's a plotter and weaver of webs. Clever too. Obvious schemes conceal devious ones, feints within feints within feints.'

'You sound as if you almost admire him.'

'I do have a certain respect for him.'

'You've studied him too, I can tell.'

'Ragnar, old son, he is the enemy. No matter what he says, no matter what you hear, no matter what anybody tells you, never lose sight of that fact. The Feraccis would love to see the Belisarians destroyed or at the very least humbled. There is a long-standing enmity between the two Houses. House Belisarius is a major obstacle in Cezare's way. He has a habit of removing such things.'

'And yet, the Lady Gabriella is about to pay him a social call.'

'Rivals, partners, relatives, that's the way it is here. Business must carry on regardless. Just because you are planning to slit a man's throat, it doesn't mean you can't both profit from a deal in the meantime.'

'It all sounds very complicated.'

'Keep it up, Ragnar. You play the simple Fenrisian very well. You'll fit in around here.'

'And what part are you playing, Torin?'

'Perhaps I am more of the simple Fenrisian than I look.' Ragnar found that very hard to believe.

At that moment the Lady Gabriella emerged from her chamber. She was garbed in the formal dress uniform of a Navigator once more with the badge of her House on her jacket and belt buckle. A sword in its scabbard and a holstered pistol hung from her belt.

'Shall we go?' she said. There was a slightly sour expression on her face. Ragnar wondered if she had been listening. He was starting to suspect that every chamber in these palaces contained hidden eavesdropping devices.

'TASTEFULLY UNDERSTATED, IS it not?' murmured Torin as he brought the flitter into a holding pattern over the Feracci tower. Gabriella laughed loudly. Ragnar held back a smile. The Feracci tower looked as if its kilometre-high spire had been gilded. Statues and gargoyles occupied thousands of niches in its walls, flanking every arched stained glass window. It would have made an Imperial temple from the High Decadent period look tasteful. And yet there was no denying it was impressive. It was taller by far than the Belisarius Palace and was easily the highest structure visible to the furthest horizon.

Ragnar's keen eyes made out weapons emplacements concealed within the gilt work. He had no doubt that the walls were thick and heavily armoured. Even before they landed, they were intercepted and escorted by two very heavily armoured gunships each bearing the rampant golden lion insignia of the Feracci, the lion encased within an eye. It fluttered on the thousands of flags that adorned the building.

Armed men waited for them on the rooftop landing pad. They were accompanied by a tall, thin young Navigator. He was good looking in a gaunt way, his hair black as a raven's wing and flowing down to his shoulders.

Torin emerged from the craft on one side, Ragnar on the other. Only once they had both looked around to check for obvious threats did they signal for Gabriella to emerge.

'Greetings, cousin Gabriella,' said the young man, bowing formally. He smiled at her warmly as he rose. He treated the two Space Wolves as if they were not there. Ragnar was not used to being ignored. It spoke a lot of the youth's self possession that he was capable of it. Not many mortals were.

'Greetings, cousin Misha.' Gabriella returned the bow with one just as courtly. She smiled. Ragnar was surprised to note that this pair seemed to genuinely like each other. Either that or they were both impossibly good dissimulators. As they were Navigators, their scents were too alien for him to read.

'My father would be grateful if you would join him in his chambers,' said Misha. 'He will not take up much of your time. He knows you are keen to visit your aunt.'

'I would be honoured,' she responded.

'This was not on the agenda,' said Torin, so low that only a Space Wolf could have heard him. 'Let's see what we shall see.'

Moments later an elevator carried them into the bowels of the Feracci tower. The closing of the doors was like a trap snapping shut.

CHAPTER NINE

RAGNAR WAS SURPRISED by the setting where Cezare Feracci greeted them. It was a garden, a huge hothouse geodesic set atop one of the lower wings that thrust out of the tower's side. The air was hot and humid and smelled of all manner of exotic off-world blooms. They were led along a dozen twisting paths to the very centre of the place. It was all part of a pattern he told himself, along with the seemingly endless security and surveillance equipment they had passed through en route.

In the middle of a grove of beautiful orchid like plants stood a tall man. He resembled Misha, although run slightly to fat. He had a small double chin and slightly puffy cheeks. The flowing robe he wore concealed his slight paunch, but for all that Cezare held himself well. It was obvious that there was hard muscle below the fat. His smile was pleasant, but his eyes were predatory. His face was very pale which contrasted with his very dark eyebrows and stubble. A circlet of pure platinum covered his pineal eye.

There was a definite family resemblance between him and Misha, more noticeable even than the one between Gabriella and the Lady Juliana. As the Wolves entered, Cezare looked up. He studied them with interest, and without fear. He was merely curious. There was a strange flatness in the man's scent that was different from any other Navigator's. If anything, he was even less readable than they. Ragnar felt as if he were in the presence of an alien being that happened to be wearing the flesh of a near-human. Reading Torin's scent, he could tell his fellow Wolfblade felt the same. There were other scents present that were partially concealed by those of the plants. They belonged to men – guards and observers within easy call.

Cezare smiled. There was a warmth and charm in his smile. His teeth were very white and square. 'Welcome, cousin. How do you like my garden?'

'It is very beautiful. It must take a considerable amount of work to keep it so.'

'All great and complex enterprises do,' said Cezare. 'Growing a garden is like running a House. You must know which plants to encourage and which weeds to prune out.'

Ragnar felt almost contemptuous of this man now, with his talk of gardens. Then he noticed what he was feeding the plants. He had extracted a small wriggling rodent from a sack and was pushing it still living and squirming into the bell of the orchid. After a few moments the animal's struggles ceased and its eyes took on a glazed and ecstatic look. Ragnar caught the whiff of narcotic perfume. His skin tingled faintly as his system analysed it and neutralised it. The plant had now swallowed the rat like a snake taking down its prey.

Seeing Ragnar's look, Cezare's smile widened. 'It's a prize this one, a Red Trapper Orchid, from Mako's World. Some of them can grow large enough to swallow a man.'

'I know,' said Torin. 'I have fought there.'

Ragnar realised there was a method to this madness. Thousands of subtle perfumes filled the air, and many of them were narcotic. The sheer profusion made it confusing, unless he concentrated. He felt like a man trying to hear a conversation in a room where very loud music was playing. Was Cezare aware of the Space Wolves' heightened senses? Almost certainly. Did he fear they might be able to read his emotions too, or was the meeting here for some other subtle purpose?

Cezare clapped his hands, and servants materialised from the forest of plants. Ragnar suspected there must be some concealed grav-tubes around here – so swift and smooth was their entrance. The sound of running water would easily cover the faint displacement of air. The men looked like servants, but Ragnar was sure they carried weapons.

He felt a little vulnerable. They were alone in the palace of one of Belisarius's greatest enemies, a man who had thousands of armed men on call. What would happen if they were to disappear here, he wondered? He dismissed the thought. If Cezare wanted them eliminated he would doubtless find a more subtle way to do it. He was simply off balance, confused by the unexpected surroundings and the scent.

Ragnar realised that it had been designed to make him feel that way. Without making an overt threat, Cezare had managed to make him uneasy and unbalanced. Torin was right. The man was subtle and dangerous. Still, even under these circumstances, Ragnar was sure he could snap his neck before a normal human could react. Cezare surely knew this and appeared completely at ease, even though Gabriella's bodyguards were far closer than his own.

He was brave then, and sure of himself. The servants produced a suspensor table and two floating chairs. Food and wine were swiftly placed on the cloth along with platinum cutlery. The food smelled highly spiced to Ragnar but that probably meant the Navigators found it a delicacy.

Ragnar moved around the clearing to cover one direction, while Torin moved in to cover the other. The thick vegetation concealed almost all lines of approach. A hundred men could have been hidden there.

Suddenly, and so subtly that Ragnar almost doubted it, he felt a feather-light touch of a strange energy brush against his mind. Pysker, he thought. Immediately, he was on guard, automatic wards clanging into place in his subconscious. He began reciting protective litanies under his breath. He knew he should be safe – this was not a very bold or potent attack. Briefly he considered what he should do. Should he seek out the psyker? Should he accuse Cezare Feracci of employing sorcery against him? Considered reflection told him the answer was no. There was no proof, only his suspicion. Cezare would deny it easily enough and leave Ragnar looking like a fool. He held his tongue.

'You wanted to talk to me, Lord Feracci,' said Gabriella, smiling pleasantly. 'I am curious to know why the master of this House wishes to speak with me.'

'Two things,' he said. 'My son Misha likes you. He has done since the first ball you both attended. I am a shamelessly indulgent father. I would know how you feel about him.'

Ragnar almost felt Torin stiffen. He had not expected this. Gabriella too seemed flustered and a little off balance. Doubtless that had been Cezare's intention. Perhaps the subtle psychic probe had been aimed at him for a similar reason. 'I like him well. Are you talking of trothplight here?'

'Let us say I would find out what you and your family think of him as a potential match.'

'You must take it up with my family.'

'Indeed. We must open channels of consultation on this matter.'

Ragnar immediately saw that such channels could be used for other things. While negotiating a wedding, the two Houses could negotiate other things. Subtle indeed.

'I will take word of your… suggestion to my family.'

Cezare laughed heartily, reminding Ragnar of a tiger purring. He reached for his food and dug into it with gusto. 'Eat! Eat!' he said.

'You spoke of another matter,' said Gabriella, spearing some small silver fish that were swimming in the soup with her fork.

'Indeed. A most important matter,' said Cezare genially. 'Someone is assassinating Navigators. Just as they assassinated your late father. There have been attempts on my life. Two of my sons have disappeared. Several other Houses have taken casualties as well.'

'It would be in both our Houses' interests to find out who it is,' said Gabriella, obviously choosing her words carefully.

'I believe I already know,' said Cezare. 'What do you know of the Brotherhood?'

'They are a secretive society of zealots, popular among the underclasses. They preach in the ancient warrens below Terra. They call us mutants. They hate Navigators but no more so than other cults.'

'I believe they are the pawns of our enemies. Their fanatics slew your father. Two of them almost managed to kill me when I visited the Shrine of St. Solstice two days ago. Their intelligence is uncanny. Few were informed of my visit, and all of them were trustworthy. I confess at first I thought Alarik might be behind it but, taking into account the fate of your father, I am no longer convinced.'

Ragnar pondered the conversation. Why was Cezare confessing to weakness before a representative of his greatest enemies? There was more going on here than met the eye. Clearly Gabriella thought the same. Why had he mentioned the Belisarius chamberlain and then dismissed him? Such an accusation could have meant a declaration of war between Space Marine Chapters. Be careful, Ragnar told himself. You are not dealing with Space Marines here but something infinitely more devious.

'I can assure you that Alarik has nothing to do with this,' said Gabriella. Ragnar realised that was all she could say.

'I believe you,' said Cezare, his smile unwavering, but his tone full of contradictory meaning.

'What would you have us do about this?'

'We could pool resources, influence and information. To this extent I am willing to provide dossiers of our intelligence to you. I will have them delivered to your flitter before you depart.'

'That is most generous.'

'No. It is in my self-interest. These are troubled times. Our enemies multiply. The Navigator Houses must stand together or we shall all be swallowed separately.'

'You have given me much to think on. Be assured I will carry your words back to the Celestarch.'

'I can ask no more. Now if you will forgive me, I must go. The tides of commerce wait for no man. Prosper and be free,' he said, rising. Gabriella rose too. 'Please finish your food,' he said, stretching out his hand palm forward.

'Delicious as it is, I am not so very hungry, and my aunt waits.'

'Your loyalty to your family is worthy. The major domo will take you to her. Rest assured she is getting the finest care available on Terra. It is the least I can do for the first wife of my late brother.'

Cezare bowed to Gabriella, and nodded pleasantly to the two Wolves before striding off. Within seconds he was out of sight among the plants. There was a mere heartbeat in which the three of them were alone. Ragnar caught Torin's warning look. However, he was well aware that this was not the place to discuss anything.

'I trust you had a pleasant meal, milady,' said Torin.

'Delicious,' she replied. It was obvious they were exchanging a code phrase that Ragnar was not yet privy to. Perhaps Torin was simply letting her know they were not alone for a moment later, an immaculately clad man garbed in a long flowing top-coat of red and black emerged. His hair was cropped short and his spry walk suggested that he was a soldier, not a servant. He bowed, and said, 'My master has requested that you be shown to your aunt's chambers, milady. If you would be so kind as to follow me?'

Gabriella nodded and the man turned. The more Ragnar studied him, the more he was convinced that he was no simple servant. His movements and scent suggested a hard competence, as well as many sub-dermal implants. A cautious glance revealed that the man's hands were bionic, encased in synthi-flesh. One of his eyes seemed mechanical as well, although it looked so natural that most men would not have spotted it.

He was reminded of the men who had attacked them last night in the tavern. Was there some connection, he wondered? His mind drifted back to the psychic probe. There was a great deal more going on here than met the eye.

Lady Elanor lay in a huge suspensor divan that floated over the marble floor. Through her arched window Ragnar caught a view of the hundreds of lesser towers of the merchants quarter sprawling below.

Enormous crowds of robed people flowed in endless tides along the roads. Ragnar had never seen so many, even on a hive world. But this was the navigators quarter of Terra, and a significant percentage of the trade of the entire Imperium probably passed through here.

Lady Elanor looked ill. One of her hands was cast in plaster. Her skin was sallow and jaundiced, the whites of her eyes were the colour of lemons. Her features were angular and gaunt, showing all the features of the Belisarius geneline. Gabriella set the small gift box she had brought on the table beside the bed and took her aunt's free hand.

'It is good to see you, child,' her aunt said, offering her cheek to be kissed. 'You have grown.'

'It is good to see you too, Lady Elanor. Although it pains me to see you so weak.'

'It will pass. It is the old ailment,' she said. 'So many of our clan have suffered.'

Gabriella paled a little. Ragnar heard her gasp sharply before she could suppress the reaction. 'How long do you have?'

'Months, perhaps weeks.'

'Have all the arrangements been taken care of?'

'Cezare is a very efficient man. He assures me I will be returned to the Belisarius Palace and the Vaults as soon as need be.'

Ragnar wondered if the woman was dying. Were the Vaults also some sort of necropolis? Perhaps that was why the Navigators were so secretive about them. Ragnar had seen many strange rites and rituals connected with death, and was aware of the tight security surrounding the protection of corpses.

The Lady Elanor certainly seemed ill enough. Her skin was so thin that it was translucent. A smell rose from the bed that was sickly sweet, like the corruption at the heart of an otherwise healthy plant.

'Anyway, I am glad you could visit. Come fill me in on all the details of your travels and the news of Belisarius. I understand you have been to Fenris.' She gave Ragnar and Torin an amused glance. There was a sly humour in it. Ragnar found himself warming to this frail, elderly-looking woman. 'Living among the Wolves.'

'Aye, that I have.' For the next few hours the two women exchanged seemingly inconsequential chatter, although, as Ragnar listened, he sensed concealed meanings beneath the surface like fish in a tidal pool. He wondered if he would ever understand the Navigators he had been sent to serve.

Two hours later, a man in the white and red uniform of a bonded physician entered the chamber. 'I am afraid that is all the talk I can allow for one day. The patient must conserve her strength.'

Gabriella nodded. The Lady Elanor clutched her hand once again. Ragnar could see that it was thin and all the veins were visible. 'Do come back and see me,' she said. There was a note of pleading in her voice.

'Of course, aunt,' said Gabriella, clasping the woman's hand with both of hers. 'But for now I had better go.'

Misha Feracci waited outside the chambers. A smile lit his handsome face. 'I thought I would escort you to your ship,' he said.

'I would like that,' said Gabriella.

RAGNAR WATCHED TORIN check out the flyer before they could climb in. A uniformed man presented them with a small folder before they departed. Gabriella placed it carefully within the internal storage compartment while Torin talked into the comm-net. Ragnar knew he was providing a record in case anything happened to them.

Misha stood on the ground below them and waved them off. The smile had not left his face during the whole trip back. The two of them walked along chatting amiably.

Ragnar did not like this development. It made him uneasy and he felt an instinctive dislike for the Feracci even as he found them impressive. Their tower was even more imposing than the Belisarius Palace and he had spent as much energy as he could memorising his way around it. It was unlikely he would be called upon to venture into the same places again, but you could never tell.

In any case, he had noticed incredibly dense surveillance. Televisor lenses and suspensor mounted floating eyes were everywhere, in far greater numbers than in Belisarius territory. But perhaps the Belisarians just kept them better hidden? Either way it spoke volumes about the nature of the House and its rulers.

No sooner had the bubble canopy slid into place than Torin said: 'Well, we're still alive.'

'That's hardly a surprise,' said Gabriella. 'Cezare Feracci would not have done anything to us while we were in his territory. It might provoke complaints to the Council of Navigators or draw unwelcome attention from the Inquisition.'

'We're not home yet,' said Ragnar. Torin had pulled the flitter into a steep climb and sent it arcing through the clouds towards the Belisarius Palace.

'What did you think of the place?' Gabriella asked.

'Security was very tight and very conspicuous,' said Ragnar.

'Don't be fooled,' said Torin. 'It was meant to be spotted. There are layers of more subtle sensors behind that.'

'How could you tell?'

'It's something of an area of expertise for me,' said Torin. 'I have studied it extensively since I came to Terra.'

'I believe my father spared no expense to see that you got a good education.'

'You believe correctly, milady.'

'Do you believe what he said about assassination attempts?' Ragnar asked.

'It's certainly possible. Religious zealots make no distinctions between the Navigator Houses. They want us all dead or at least off the sacred soil of Terra. "Suffer not a mutant to live", so they say.'

'Do you believe Cezare was serious about his offer of alliance?'

'It was not an offer of alliance, Ragnar. Far from it. He merely offered to share information. We shall see what his dossier contains. It might all be useless. Even if it contains useful information it might simply be a way of winning our trust or distracting us from Cezare's own plots.'

Wheels within wheels, plots within plots, thought Ragnar. 'No one here takes anything at face value, do they?'

'It would probably be a good idea for you to learn to do the same, Ragnar,' said Gabriella.

'He has already started, milady. Don't let Ragnar's barbarian act fool you. There is a mind at work there. I can almost see its wheels turning.' Ragnar did not know whether to be pleased or insulted by Torin's words, and he suspected that was his fellow Wolfblade's intention. 'A few years on Terra and Ragnar will be as smooth a plotter as old Cezare.'

That obviously was a joke, Ragnar thought. 'If he lives that long,' Torin added. Gabriella glanced over at Ragnar and smiled.

'What did you think of Misha?' she asked.

'I did not like him.'

'Why?'

'He reminded me too much of his father.'

'He seems pleasant enough.'

'Pleasant enough to marry?'

'I will never marry him unless I am ordered to.'

'Why?'

'I do not trust him either. And the Feracci bloodline has an odd, wild streak to it. It throws up many strange quirks – insanity and cruelty are common among them. They are brilliant but flawed, but then I suppose the same can be said of all the genelines.'

'Your aunt married into them.'

'Cezare's brother Lucio was one of the good Feraccis.'

'What happened to him?'

'He died mysteriously before Cezare came to the throne. Which is a pity since he would have made a better candidate.'

'How mysteriously?'

'A rare illness, or so it was said.'

'Like your aunt's?'

'No, that is something different.'

There was something in her tone that told Ragnar this was not a good subject to delve into. 'Some claim Cezare was behind Lucio's illness,' she said.

'And still he became lord,' said Ragnar disbelieving.

'They are strange ones, the Feraccis,' she said wistfully. 'It is said their Elders encourage the clan members to compete for the position of lord. They select the most ruthless and dangerous. If Cezare really was behind Lucio's death it would only serve in his favour.'

'That seems very wasteful,' said Ragnar. 'Killing a Navigator. You would think any House that did so would swiftly run out of members.'

'Only a very few are in the running to become Lord of Feracci and they know this from an early age. It would be wasteful and pointless to kill anyone who was not a rival. The Elders would not reward you for it.'

Ragnar considered this. It seemed that each House was as different from the others as the inhabitants of distant worlds were from each other. That was understandable. Over the millennia each House would have evolved its own culture and methods of survival. It was a big galaxy. There was room for numerous alternative and competing views. Indeed, he supposed it was better this way. If a weakness was revealed in one geneline's strategies, others would still survive. He guessed that any House that had managed to maintain its power and prestige since before the dawn of the Imperium must have evolved very efficient strategies indeed.

CEZARE LOUNGED BACKWARDS on the dais and considered the deadly man before him. He did not mind admitting that Xenothan made him nervous – more so than little Gabriella's precious bodyguards. The tall, slender, seemingly innocuous man was quite capable of killing everyone in this room – even Wanda, his pet psyker – and making it out of the Tower alive. Not for the first time, he found himself questioning the wisdom of the course he had charted. He smiled and shrugged. No great venture was ever undertaken without risks, and no great prize won without a gamble. His own career had proven this time and time again. The Elders had chosen him for his propensity for ruthlessness and cunning, and the fact he had eliminated all the other candidates including his own dear brother. He would not disappoint them.

'Well, what do you think?' he asked. His voice was clear, calm and commanding. It showed no trace of nervousness.

'The older of the two is a very dangerous man. The younger could become formidable given time. Both of them were aware of what was happening in the tavern.'

'We shall see he is not given time. You have them memorised?'

'Their look, their voices, their scents.'

'Can you kill them?'

'If you wish. When?'

'The time will be soon,' he said.

Xenothan smiled. There was no menace there, but it was chilling. Cezare told himself it was only because he knew what this man was – if 'man' was the term for a being so modified as he.

'You've decided, then?'

'Yes. Tell your master we will strike soon and eliminate our common enemies once and for all.'

A hint of menace entered Xenothan's manner. 'I have no master. Only patrons.'

'Then I should be obliged if you would inform your patron. We will move soon.'

He glanced over at Wanda. Soon she would need to send a message to her fellows in the Warrens below.

CHAPTER TEN

'WHAT DO YOU think?' asked Valkoth. 'What were your impressions? Tell me!'

Ragnar looked at the training area. The House guards of Belisarius were running the assault course under Valkoth's watchful eye. The soldiers were all Terrans. Many had long hair and drooping moustaches in the Fenrisian style.

They were trying hard but Ragnar knew that the youngest candidate for ascendancy on Fenris could have killed three of them easily. Then again, Fenris was a harder world than Terra. Men learned to survive there very early in the face of nightmarish elements, terrible monsters and even more terrible men. Those who did not learn quickly died.

He gathered his thoughts. It had been barely twenty minutes since the flitter had set down on the roof.

All three had been searched by a team of security retainers to ensure they had brought no long distance sensing devices into the palace. Gabriella handed the documents to the retainers for scanning and complete divination before heading off to present herself to the Celestarch. Torin had dispatched Ragnar to report to Valkoth, and had taken off on some mysterious mission.

'Cezare is a dangerous man.' Valkoth studied him carefully and Ragnar knew he was being measured and judged.

'In what way?'

'He is cunning, a schemer. He chose the location and the subject of the interview to throw us off balance. He conceals his emotions well. I find all Navigators difficult to read but he seemed even less human than normal.'

'I don't think you would find many people who would disagree with you, at least in private. People who speak out against the Lord Feracci in public tend to have short unpleasant lives.'

'That does not surprise me.'

'The Feracci are not sane in the way we define it, Ragnar. Most Navigators cannot be measured by any human standard, more so they. There is a streak of madness in them.'

'Why are they not put down like mad dogs?'

'Because that very streak of madness is what makes them superb Navigators. Feracci ships can travel further and faster than almost any others thanks to their Navigators' prowess. Only Belisarius, Helmsburg and True produce Navigators as good. The Imperium needs them. It needs all the Navigator Houses. It tolerates them as long as it goes on behind closed doors.'

On the training area, the men were engaged in mock skirmishes now. They had been divided into two sides and were armed with guns that fired pellets of dye. The dye contained an astringent which would cause pain but no permanent harm. They moved around obstacles that had been apparently set at random, towards goals at either end of the field.

'Anything else?'

'I have no doubt that we were observed with deep penetration scanners from the moment we entered the place. There was all manner of surveillance – from servants who followed us, to suspensor mounted televisors. I am equally sure our route was chosen so that we passed through sensor arches. I also believe there was some sort of psyker nearby.'

'It is rumoured that Cezare has a tame witch. A very powerful one. Perhaps several.'

'Bonded, of course.'

'Not even he would be mad enough to keep a potential heretic in his palace. Anything else?'

'The man intends harm to us all.'

'Of course he does. The two Houses are hereditary enemies. But they are also heads of the two largest and most powerful rival factions among the Navigators.'

'You do not think his offer of mutual aid was serious then?'

'Perhaps, but only if in the long run there is more advantage in it for him than us. We should be asking what he expects to gain from this.'

'All I know is he wants something,' said Ragnar. 'And I suspect he has planned something nasty for the very near future.'

'What makes you think that?'

'Instinct.'

'You would do very well to trust that instinct, Ragnar. I am certain that Cezare is setting a trap. We just need to make sure we do not set our heads in the noose.'

'What about the betrothal?'

'It might be serious. Gabriella is a superb Navigator which is why we got her. If her children receive her talent, they too will be great. Such children are a House's greatest resource.'

'So Cezare wants Gabriella then?'

'Maybe, or perhaps he wants to place his son within Belisarius. Who is taken in by whom would depend on the marriage contract.'

'Isn't that dangerous? It would be like having a spy within the House.'

'Perhaps. Adopted sons and daughters become members of their new House. They are supposed to be loyal to it. And they are closely monitored.'

'It sounds like madness.'

'It is their way. Some might consider them hostages. It depends on relations between parent and child.'

'From what I saw of Cezare I doubt he would hesitate to sacrifice a son.'

'He might surprise you, but I doubt it. Still, don't you think he must know that the Lady Juliana would be aware this?'

'I know that thinking about it is making my head spin.'

'Then I have something for you that will be more to your taste.'

'What?'

'We have a lead on the zealots who killed Adrian Belisarius.'

'How?'

'From the Lady Elanor.'

'What?'

'She passed her message on while you were with her.' Ragnar reflected on this. He had seen nothing change hands, but he knew there were ways. Dermal patches, microspores. The two women had probably been talking in a complex code as he had considered earlier. Alternatively, there could be a subtle psychic bond between kindred Navigators.

'How was that done?'

'They have their ways, and they choose not to share them with us. Nonetheless, the information was exchanged.'

'Under the very nose of Cezare! That seems rather too fortuitous.'

'Quite,' said Valkoth. 'Nonetheless, it corroborates information from Alarik's other sources.'

'How did she find this information? Why would she risk communicating it to us? I would take it all with a pinch of salt. It could easily be a false lead.'

'Indeed. The fact that she told us anything at all, means she is quite desperate. She appears to think that the survival of House Belisarius itself is at risk.'

'Could she not have waited for two weeks?'

'It's good to see that you use your brain more than Haegr. However, even if it were the case, the fact itself tells us something.'

Ragnar was intrigued now. 'Like what?'

'Like if the information is false we will have a chance to go over it in more depth when the Lady Elanor is returned to the Vaults in the next two weeks. Like the fact that she does not think we have two weeks.'

Ragnar turned this over in his mind briefly before saying, 'It sets a deadline. It tells us that if this is all part of some greater scheme, Cezare is expecting it to be done within the next couple of weeks.'

'Torin is right: you do have a brain. Also consider the fact that the information may be useful and true.'

'A sprat to catch a sea-dragon.'

'Precisely. The Feracci might be trying to suck us in to something bigger with useful information.'

'Is it really likely that Cezare would allow her to return to the Vaults when the time comes?'

'Yes.' There was absolute certainty in his voice.

'You seem very definite.'

'Ragnar, there are certain things that are sacred to the Navigators and limits that even Cezare will not transgress. The return of someone like Elanor is one of those things.'

'Why?'

'When you need to know, I will tell you.'

Ragnar was shocked. Valkoth appeared to be siding with Belisarius over his own Wolf brothers. What was the secret? What was so important about returning a sick woman to her family for burial? It seemed obvious that Valkoth was not going to share this with him, so he decided to try a different tack.

'What is this information?'

'There is a merchant, Pantheus, who fronts money for the various zealot Brotherhoods. There is a connection between him and House Feracci.'

'Which is?'

'Money. Power. Influence. We have had our eye on him for sometime. We believe he is the link between Feracci and certain zealot Brotherhoods.'

'If you have had your eye on him all this time, then Cezare must know he is compromised. He loses nothing by handing him to us.'

'Again, you are thinking, Ragnar. Pantheus disappeared some time ago. He went to ground just before the assassination of Adrian Belisarius. We believe we know where he is now. Elanor gave us the last piece of the puzzle.'

'Or some fine bait for a trap.'

'Once you close your jaws on something, you don't let go, do you, Ragnar? It's an admirable trait in a Space Wolf.'

'Where can we find this merchant?'

'He has what he believes to be a secure mansion in the asteroid belt. We are going to prove that it's not secure. We will take off this evening. You will be there.'

Ragnar nodded. Trap or no trap, this was more like it. He was suddenly excited. The prospect of combat was appealing. At least now the enemy was clear and the goals straightforward.

THE BRIEFING ROOM was small, which was hardly surprising, since it was located in a small, sleek courier ship belonging to the Belisarians. Present were Valkoth, Torin, Haegr and Ragnar along with a group of guards. Alarik, the House's Chief Intelligencer and chamberlain was also there. At the moment, he stood stage centre at the holo-pit, dressed the same as he had been when Ragnar had first seen him in the Celestarch's throne room.

'Pantheus is a rich man, because he fronts for various religious Brotherhoods on Earth. We have gained access to certain Inquisition reports that suggest some of these Brotherhoods are recruiting grounds for our enemies. All of them have access to clandestine funding networks that they use to buy arms and equipment for their missions. Some run a nice sideline in extortion.

'Pantheus also has a lot of dealings with the Feracci. He started out with them in Gellan system fifty years ago, before branching out on his own. We believe his initial seed money came from Feracci. Interestingly, he worked directly with Cezare when the Lord Feracci was senior House representative in the sector.'

'There is a direct connection between Cezare Feracci and the Brotherhoods?' Valkoth asked.

'Almost certainly he has infiltrated agents into them. Most of the Houses have.' By implication, Ragnar thought, so have the Belisarians. Power, money, religion, and politics. They made a strange mix.

'In any case, Pantheus is not a nice man. He also deals in a number of illicit substances: narcotics, combat alchemics, as well as weapons. Every man is entitled to make a living, but this is going too far. We are going to pay Pantheus a little visit and administer suitable chastisement. I will be responsible for the interrogation.' Ragnar sensed there was a real personal animosity between the chamberlain and this merchant. He appeared to be looking forward to the questioning.

'We shall forcibly board his asteroid mansion. We shall kill his guards, and then seize him and his records. On departure we shall destroy the asteroid and any evidence of our visit. The main security datacore must be seized before we go. Jammers will prevent any comm-net transmissions so, unless Pantheus has an astropath with him, no one will ever know what happened.'

'You are certain he is there?' said Valkoth.

'The Lady Elanor has confirmed our suspicions. We have had a shielded monitor at the asteroid itself for some time. His ship arrived a day after Adrian Belisarius's assassination. It appears logical to assume that Pantheus himself was on board. The Lady Elanor seems to indicate that we must find out what he knows quickly if it is to be useful to us.'

'Guards?' asked Torin.

'He has a security detail recruited from Brotherhood thugs. They are tough and well armed. Some have bionic enhancements. All have access to military weapons and a supply of proscribed alchemics. They are all fanatical. It may be hypno-conditioning but I doubt it. I believe they are the genuine article.'

'How many guards?' asked Ragnar.

'One hundred and five.'

'That's a lot of security.'

'This assignment is a reward for loyalty. Many pleasures are available on the asteroid. Not all of the men will be on duty, although all will be capable of fighting at a moment's notice.'

'Defensive systems?'

'The asteroid has the usual anti-piracy defences. They will be neutralised before you go in. This ship has the capability.'

Ragnar did not ask why they were so sure. Normally in a battle between a ship and a fortified asteroid there could be only one winner. It was possible to mount more firepower on a hollowed out rock than in most small ships. The others seemed certain though. Presumably Belisarius's sources must be reliable. Or this ship must be a lot better armed than it looked.

'Gravity?' asked Torin. It could be important.

'No artificial sources. It comes from spin.'

Ragnar considered this. It meant the deeper they went into the core of the asteroid the less centripetal force there would be. This could create sudden fluctuations in apparent weight. Such things could be important in zero G combat.

'What about survivors?' Ragnar asked.

'There will be none. When you leave it will look like there has been an unfortunate but catastrophic collision with a stray meteor. Such things happen.'

The other Wolves grinned. Ragnar considered the odds. There were just the four of them but, as the plan was outlined, he considered that it would most likely work. They would fly in from the shielded ship using jump packs. Once down, they would use thermal charges to blow out a large section of the wall and let themselves into the tunnels. There was no point in being subtle. Any opening of an airlock would be noticed, and airlocks could easily become deathtraps if you were sealed in one.

Explosive decompression would cause the mansion's safety systems to kick in. Under the circumstances there would be confusion inside as the cause of the system failure was tracked. The enemy would waste time suiting up and going through standard decompression drills. The closing of bulkheads would divide their foes and isolate them in portioned sections, so it would be easier to dispose of them. The Wolves would move inwards towards the central datacore killing anything that got in their way. They would secure the record core, acquire the data and depart.

It was a simple enough plan, which was good. But Ragnar had enough experience to know that no matter how simple, no plan ever went smoothly even when executed by Space Wolves.

RAGNAR GRASPED THE controls of the jump pack and applied power. A jet of compressed gas from the attachment pushed it away from the side of the shielded ship. He was on the long slow trajectory towards the distant asteroid. He could hear nothing but felt a slight tremor in the pack as he moved.

The gas jet would give out no heat signature. And no power was being used so it should not be traceable by sensor divination. They were carrying too little metal to show up on magnetics. A human being would be too small to set off a standard proximity detector designed to warn of collisions with ships and large asteroids.

There was a slight chance that if someone was looking closely, they would notice the occlusion of the stars but here in the asteroid belt that would happen often enough with tumbling rocks and space debris. The

William King

chances that objects of their size could be spotted were infinitesimal, but the chance remained. It was enough of a possibility to send little shivers of controlled fear through Ragnar. It was one thing to die in battle in the fury of hand to hand combat. It was another to be blasted into non-existence by a defence laser in the cold, silent void of space.

His helmet was down and in position. His recyclers were working perfectly. If need be he could live for weeks out here in the void. Like all of his battle-brothers he was virtually a small, self-contained space-ship. Not that it would make much difference if they got this wrong. There was no way to drift anywhere close to civilisation if they could not make it back to the ship. If anything went badly wrong he would become just another piece of tumbling debris in endless orbit around the sun.

He wondered how many others were out there already. When he considered all the battles that had been fought in this system since long before the Imperium and the Horus Heresy, he was sure it was not a few.

The asteroid grew larger in his field of vision. He could see lights winking on its side. He could make out the huge crystal geodesic dome of the gardens that provided the mansion with some of its atmosphere. At one end of the asteroid was a forest of antennae and dishes that connected the asteroid to the comm-net. In a few minutes they would be jammed and shot out by the Belisarius courier. He wondered if there was anyone down there looking at him now, unaware of how little time he had left to live.

It is amazing how old ideas stay with you, he thought. In the immense void of space, down was a meaningless concept. The asteroid's gravity was insufficient to draw him in. From the outside a man could leap into space, its escape velocity was so low. Any direction could just as easily be up or down. Yet his brain insisted on imposing a framework on it. The asteroid was down. The ship was up. He told himself such preconceptions could be dangerous because in space combat you had to be able to think in three dimensions. Limiting yourself with concepts like down and up could be fatal.

The asteroid swelled, becoming first the size of an apple, then a boulder, then a house. It was as large as the icebergs in the Sea of Dragons in winter. Tunnels extended below its surface. He had the plans the Belisarian spies had managed to provide him with locked in his suit's systems.

He wondered how accurate they were. Presumably they were good for the Navigators to be risking so much on this raid, but you could not always be certain. All it would take would be for the informant to have missed one section or one hidden defence and the outcome could be terrible. Still, these were the risks you took. Ragnar was confident that he could overcome anything thrown in his path. He was one of the Chosen of Russ, after all. Be careful, he told himself. Overconfidence has killed more men than bolter shells. This was a hellishly inhospitable environment, and any mistake could easily be your last.

He glanced over and saw his comrades making the long drop. Somehow each looked exactly as Ragnar had imagined they would. Torin had his arms folded across his chest, holding the demolition charges, and a heavy bolter dangled in a sling at stomach level. He suggested relaxed confidence.

Haegr looked odd with his helmet on and his custom armour. His bulky silhouette was nothing like that of a normal Space Wolf. A huge hammer was strapped to his chest. Valkoth looked stern and forbidding even in freefall. His back was straight, his hands firm on the controls.

Ragnar turned back to the asteroid. He knew that perfect timing would be called for. It would take a five second burst of gas to kill his velocity before he impacted. A hard landing might result in injury, armour breach or even death. It would not be a glorious way to go. Ragnar did not want to be inscribed in the annals of the Chapter as the man who lost the Spear of Russ and then killed himself by banging into a rock.

The proximity detector attached to his armour gave its alert. Ragnar piked and twisted the throttles on the flight pack. In his peripheral vision he could see his comrades do the same. A moment later he braced his knees for impact. His boots grated on the hard surface of the asteroid. They were down.

The easy part was over.

CHAPTER ELEVEN

THE ASTEROID ROTATED below him. Its motion threatened to throw Ragnar off. He lifted his feet as the surface moved smoothly underneath him. He used the jet pack to move with slow controlled bursts. The others did the same. They resembled fish cruising along the bottom of an ocean.

In seconds they reached the point they intended to breach – a large window above the observation deck. From inside it would probably look more like a glass floor. The asteroid's rotation would push people down towards the outside walls as it simulated gravity.

Torin slapped the thermal charge into place. They scooted away from the blast area, taking cover in the crevasses covering the asteroid's rocky side. A moment later, a brilliant flash lit the shadows of the small canyon. Ragnar looked up and saw a glittering trail of crystal debris erupt. Air crystallised as it streamed into space. Plants and paintings and small pieces of furniture followed it.

They headed in. Ragnar increased the power of the jets to compensate for the outward rush of the gas. They could have waited for the decompression to be complete but time was precious now. Glittering contrails and earthshaking explosions told him that the courier had struck, taking out the comm-dishes and external defences.

Disorientation struck Ragnar as he piked through the blast hole. Suddenly up seemed down and down seemed up. He had gone from being on the outside to the inside of this hollow world and the two directions were now reversed. He somersaulted through the air and landed on his feet, hitting the restraint release button on the pack's harness with one hand while drawing his bolt pistol with the other. Before it hit the ground, his chainsword was in his hand and he was moving along the corridor.

Men lay on the ground with blood pumping from their noses, ears and mouths. They writhed in agony as decompression ruptured lungs and eardrums. He swung his chainsword, not wanting to waste bolter shells to put enemies out of their misery. The temperature dropped rapidly. Warning runes flashed on the walls proclaiming danger to any survivors within.

Ragnar did not like this. The helmet constrained his senses. He had to rely on his eyes now. Hearing and scent, the Space Wolves' primary sources of information, were useless when they were suited up. All he could catch was the sound of his breathing and the recycled stink of his own body. He glanced around and saw his companions moving into position, weapons drawn. Torin slung his heavy bolter over his shoulder as he fingered his utility belt for tools. Haegr brandished his enormous hammer.

For now, they were comparatively safe. Any foes would not yet have had time to suit up. Doubtless they were confused, unsure of what had hit them. Torin had moved to one of the internal airlocks. This was the risky part. If they wanted to take Pantheus alive they needed to get into the air-filled interior of the mansion. This meant using an airlock. Hopefully the confusion would help them, but things were still tricky.

Torin knelt by the door. He had a tool-kit in his hand and was swiftly stripping the lock's external covering. At the point of decompression, all the doors had sealed automatically but they could still be manually over-ridden. In seconds there was another cloud of freezing air as the door slid open. Moments later they were inside and letting air cycle out. Now things were getting dangerous.

If anyone was monitoring the airlock system at that moment, their position would be given away. Hopefully, anybody at the control altars had other things on their mind. They might construe one airlock opening as some sort of system failure, but even if they did so, it would still attract their attention. An airlock malfunction in any sealed environment always would.

At least he could hear now, as air rushed in to fill the lock. There was little space for four huge Space Marines along with their weapons in this small space. Once again it was made graphically clear to him why airlocks had such a well-deserved reputation for being death traps in boarding actions. All it would take would be one well-placed grenade and the four of them would be sent to Russ's Iron Halls to await the Last Battle.

Ragnar found himself holding his breath, his eyes focused on the internal door. His weapon was at the ready. If someone was waiting to attack, he was certain he could snap off a shot before they could. His reflexes were far, far swifter than a normal human's, except if they were on combat drugs. This thought niggled at his mind.

Air filled the chamber now. Green indicator lights showed that pressure had equalised. Torin opened the internal door. They were in. There was air here too, and sound carried well enough. Ragnar could hear the warning klaxon's blare. Ahead of them lay a corridor and an elevator shaft leading upwards. Elevators were another death trap to be avoided. Ragnar unsealed his helmet and tasted the air. It was pure and breathable. His helmet would not have unlocked if it had not been.

A rush of unfamiliar scents hit him: purification essences, body odours, the never-quite extinguishable sewage smells of humans in a sealed environment. He greeted them all like old friends, taking in deep breaths, and orientating himself. He felt immediately more confident and capable, the master of his environment. He clipped his helmet to his belt. His comrades had done the same.

'Avoid the elevator. There should be a maintenance ramp around the corner,' said Valkoth. His dark lean face looked grim and more pensive than usual. He held his bolter steadily though, and there was no sign of tension in either his stance or scent.

They moved off past the elevator, Ragnar in front, Torin at the rear, and the other two in the middle. Ragnar felt adrenaline flood through him, bringing a peculiar sense of joy. He might die here, but he felt fully alive, knowing each minute could be his last. A wave of scent warned him before he turned the corner that he would find humans there.

There was a group of confused men, running to their emergency positions. One of them shouted into an intercom, demanding to know what had happened. They all carried sidearms. Ragnar did not wait for them to see him. He pumped bolter shells into the leader, and watched the man's head explode as if hit with a mallet. A second later Haegr stepped forward and reduced the rest of him to bloody shreds of red meat.

'What's going on? Report!' demanded a voice from the other end of the intercom. Torin strode past and bellowed, 'Hull breach, decompression, what the hell!' then he smashed the device with his gauntleted fist.

They raced up the ramp and entered a large open hallway. The wall hangings were luxurious. The lighting was dim and off centre. A great deal of religious imagery covered the walls: icons depicting the Golden Throne and the Emperor's Slaughter of the Mutants. One could almost have mistaken this place for the monastery of a particularly sybaritic religious sect. Perhaps that was what it was. Ragnar was not impressed by this outward show of piety. He had seen the followers of darkness wear the cloak of holiness far too often in the past.

Ragnar noticed that he felt lighter as they rose. More and more scents filled the air, criss-crossing and fading as the fans mingled the odour trails. There certainly were plenty of men in this mansion, he thought. One of them appeared in the arched doorway at the opposite end of the hall.

'Who the hell are you?' he asked. Ragnar shot him.

They proceeded towards another ramp. More men appeared behind the first and a volley of fire from the Wolves took them down. Ragnar heard footsteps receding. Obviously someone was trying to get away. He must not be allowed to sound the alarm.

Ragnar sprinted forward, and rolled through the archway, coming up in a crouch, hoping he would be below the line of fire of any enemy. A man dressed in brown stood at the far end of the corridor. He was shouting something into another intercom. Ragnar took aim and fired. The man went down with a huge sucking wound in his chest. Another shot smashed the intercom. Too late. The sound of the klaxon had become a jagged, rising wail. Ragnar surmised that this was a security alert.

'Looks like we've been spotted,' said Haegr from behind him.

'Really?' said Torin. 'I would never have guessed.'

'Good,' said Haegr. 'I never liked killing people who couldn't fight back.'

'You'll kill anybody necessary to get this job done,' said Valkoth. 'Don't you forget it!'

Haegr grunted. They moved onwards. All around them, Ragnar could sense the enemy mustering. The Wolves increased their pace. The faster they got away from the site where they had been spotted, the harder it would be for the enemy to use their superior numbers and their control of the facility against them.

As THEY ROSE towards the asteroid's core, the displays of piety grew more luxuriant and profuse. Glass cabinets in the walls held relics marked by golden placards. In swift succession they passed the finger bones of saints, prophets and scholars, the death masks of Imperial heroes, a bolter that had been borne by Commissar Richter. All the relics shared one thing in common: they were connected with famous men who had hated deviants with a passion.

It was not something of which Ragnar would normally have disapproved. His entire upbringing and all his training had drilled into him the idea that the mutant was mankind's greatest enemy. Strange, he thought, that now he was fighting in defence of those who many considered to be mutants. He pushed these thoughts to one side. He was coming dangerously close to the Sin of Relativism.

A wave of scent told him that doors had opened down the corridor. He whirled in time to see a group of armed and armoured men. Some had donned full-body armour, others were wearing military flak, and all carried lasrifles. Before any of them could fire, Ragnar opened up. His battle-brothers joined in. More men were cut down. Las-beams splashed off the walls behind Ragnar, and blistered his armour. He ducked and weaved, trying to make himself a difficult target. In this narrow space, with a sufficient concentration of firepower, the enemy could not avoid hitting them.

A small egg-shaped object flew overhead from behind Ragnar. It bounced and rolled down the corridor into the chamber where the cultists lurked. A moment later an explosion smashed through the men. Screams and the scent of blood told Ragnar that it had even got those out of sight. They moved on.

A crackle of static in Ragnar's earbead told him that the courier had managed to patch itself into the asteroid's internal comm-net. He could hear a dozen voices gabbling away now.

'There are dozens of them!'

'Hull breached in three places.'

'Enemy sighted in quadrant four.'

'Have found bodies. Signs of mutilation.'

'I swear I saw Space Marines.'

'What?'

'What is going on?'

'Wolves.'

'Belisarius. It must be Belisarius.'

'The Emperor watch over you!'

Ragnar muted the volume in the earbead so that it did not interfere with his concentration. It sounded like the defenders were reeling in shock and confusion. Hardly surprising: the runes on his chronometer told him that they were barely minutes into the mission. Until now, many of the survivors would still be busy suiting up and trying to deal with the hull breach.

So far, so good, he thought, wondering exactly when things would start to come unstuck.

THEY FOUND THE door of Pantheus's chamber sealed and locked down. He had obviously decided to barricade himself in until the source of the emergency was clear.

Ragnar looked at the portal. It was a heavy blast door with some sort of complex security lock. It would take heavy cutting gear to get through it. They did not have the gear. He patched into the comm-net. Voices told him that the enemy was starting to regroup and sweep the place for their foes. They obviously had not yet realised their comm-links had been breached so their progress could be monitored.

Valkoth looked at Torin. 'How long?' he said.

'It's an old design. Responds to digital code or eye-scan.'

'I did not ask what it was. I asked you how long to get through it.'

'Thirty seconds,' said Torin. He knelt with his tools and began to prod at the interior of the lock. Ragnar wondered where he had learned these skills. They had certainly not been taught during his training as a Wolf.

'Ragnar, stop gawping at Torin and cover the corridor. Haegr, you take the other direction. Maybe you could stow the hammer and use a ranged weapon for a change.'

'That's hardly sporting,' said Haegr, clipping the hammer onto straps on his back harness, and drawing a pair of bolt pistols. Ragnar swung his attention to the corridor, keeping his bolt pistol ready for any foe that should appear. An enormous belch told him that Haegr was bored.

Ragnar tuned back into the comm-net. Their foes were closing in. Some of them had broken out heavy weapons. The fight looked like it was going to be a lot more difficult now. The real problem would be taking Pantheus out through a firefight. That was where they were going to need all their skill.

A whoosh of air told him the lock had given way.

'That was forty-five seconds,' said Valkoth.

'The mechanism had a booby trap attached and activated. I thought it better to take the extra time than to have the lock melt and take my hand off.'

'He couldn't comb his moustache if he lost a hand,' said Haegr. 'A tragedy.'

Torin was already in the chamber and covering it with his bolter. The furnishings were fit for a Navigator Prince. A massive mirror dominated one wall.

'He must be as vain as you, Torin,' said Haegr.

'But not as handsome,' said Torin, admiring his reflection.

'Less jokes, more speed,' said Valkoth. 'Where is the bastard?'

He moved deeper into the chamber. A moment later he was reaching into a massive wardrobe and pushing aside a mass of heavy furred robes. Quickly he pulled out an enormously fat man. Ragnar recognised Pantheus from the intelligence briefings. He floated lightly in the low gravity of the core. Doubtless that was why he had chosen this place for his apartment.

'Not as handsome as me, but almost as fat as you,' said Torin.

'He lacks my rugged Fenrisian nobility,' said Haegr.

'Haegr cover the door,' said Valkoth.

'Good choice,' said Haegr. 'Torin would spend too much time admiring himself in the mirror.'

Valkoth pinned Pantheus to the wall and inserted the muzzle of his bolter into one nostril. It was a tight fit. 'Where do you keep your records?'

The man's fear was palpable but he controlled himself well. 'This is an outrage. I will lodge a complaint with...'

'You are exactly one heartbeat away from death,' said Valkoth. His cold smile revealed his fangs. There was nothing remotely human about his expression at that moment. Pantheus might well have been looking at some hideous legendary ogre. Valkoth's scent told Ragnar that he was not going to kill Pantheus, but there was no way the merchant could know that.

He reached down towards his chest. Valkoth's free hand caught his wrist. The merchant winced. 'I keep my records in a memory crystal locket. I am not reaching for a gun.'

'It would be the last thing you would ever do,' said Valkoth.

'Don't you think I know that?' Pantheus produced a glittering gem on a platinum necklace. Ragnar could sense the tension in his comrades ease slightly. They had been prepared to respond if the merchant had drawn a protective device. There was nothing threatening about him, particularly.

Valkoth took the gem and inspected it, dropping the crystal into a small scanner he produced from his utility belt. Runes showed it was safe and a datasource.

'And the rest,' said Valkoth. Pantheus nodded to the wall. It was a portrait of himself looking considerably younger and thinner. The apparition was so different it could have been another person.

'Open it,' said Valkoth. 'No tricks or you die.'

The fear smell intensified. Here was someone who obviously believed the worst about the Space Wolves.

Pantheus walked over to the portrait and passed his hand over a series of runes. He muttered an incantation of opening under his breath. The picture slid aside. Treasure glittered within. Not just memory crystals but jewels of all sorts. The merchant kept a small hoard here for emergencies. Judging from the way Torin was sweeping it into a rolled up pillowcase it would soon be swelling the coffers of the Belisarians.

Valkoth passed his scanner over the pillowcase. It bleeped, and runes told of datacrystals there. It looked like they had got what they came for. Now all they had to do was make their way to an escape pod and rendezvous with the courier. Easy, thought Ragnar sardonically. He knew better. Things had gone too smoothly. They were bound to take a turn for the worse soon.

The sound of Haegr's pistols blasting away told him he was right. Trouble had already found them.

CHAPTER TWELVE

'TAKE IT, TAKE it all,' said Pantheus. 'Just let me go.'

Valkoth smiled grimly. His drooping moustaches and long fangs made it look more like a snarl. 'You're coming with us.'

'What? Where?' The merchant looked ready to burst into tears. He hardly seemed like a deadly conspirator. Maybe he was just in shock. It was not every day four Space Wolves broke into your secure asteroid and abducted you from your sleeping chamber. It would be enough to unsettle most people.

'You're coming with us. That's all you need to know.'

'But my collection. I can't leave all my precious icons.'

'They will be leaving you soon enough.'

'What do you mean by that?'

Valkoth raised his bolter and aimed it directly at Pantheus's head. 'No more chatter. You're coming with us. Ragnar, watch his back.'

Valkoth turned on his heel and moved with Torin towards the door. Ragnar put his bolt pistol to Pantheus's spine. 'Move,' he said. 'Or you'll have a hole in your stomach big enough to put your head into.'

Pantheus moved.

HAEGR HAD ADVANCED down the corridor. Ragnar could tell by the sound of bolter blast. Las-fire splattered the walls. The surface had fused and run, and paintwork was blistering off to reveal the hard rock beneath. Torin and Valkoth moved out. Torin turned to cover behind them, while Valkoth bounced forward in the lowered gravity, adding his bolter fire to the blaze of Haegr's pistols. Nothing much remained alive in the corridor now. A pile of corpses smouldered slowly. Haegr and Valkoth moved through them.

Ragnar prodded Pantheus with his bolt pistol again. The merchant moved forward effortlessly, well adapted to the low-gravity. For the moment he did not appear to be having much difficulty in keeping up with the Wolves. They would see what happened soon when he felt the increased weight of his bulk on the lower levels.

COMM-NET communications told Ragnar that the crew of the asteroid had worked out what was happening. They knew Pantheus's chamber had been breached and that he was taken. It should be fairly easy for them to work out what would happen next, although so far no one had. If he had been in charge, he would have had all the external air-locks and escape pods covered.

Perhaps he was being unfair to the enemy commanders. They had other things on their minds and normal men simply were not capable of thinking and responding as fast as Space Marines. The walls of their asteroid had been breached and unless they were resealed, they would be dead. He doubted there were enough reserves of air to replace what was being lost. And then there was the courier, a formidable enemy craft that had sliced through their long range comm dishes and defensive emplacements. It looked like the element of surprise had been overwhelmingly successful. His chronometer told him that less than ten minutes had passed since the operation had begun.

As they progressed down the levels, resistance stiffened. Everyone was aware that there were enemies on board. They were watchful, and armed, mostly garbed in light space armour. Such was the speed of the Space Marines' advance that they swiftly overwhelmed anyone they encountered. They always fired the first shot, and often that was the last.

PANTHEUS'S BREATH CAME in gasps and he seemed in danger of founder-ing. Ragnar guessed he was feeling every extra kilo, although the gravity here was still far less than Earth's. He wondered what the man did when he was on the surface of Terra. Doubtless he used suspensors to lighten his weight.

Ahead of them lay the escape pod they had marked for their escape. Just as they entered the corridor a group of men in brown uniforms appeared at the other end. Haegr opened fire cutting them down. Rag-nar bundled Pantheus into the escape pod.

'Go with him, Ragnar,' said Valkoth. Despite feeling the urge to stay and fight, Ragnar did not. They could not take the chance that the merchant might activate the pod without them. Without their locator beacon, the pod would be destroyed by the courier. The Belisarians were not about to risk anyone escaping to tell the tale. Ragnar threw himself in beside the merchant, weapon at the ready.

Outside, the others continued to blast away. Ragnar understood why. Like elevators, escape pods could be death traps if attacked at the wrong moment. If someone tossed a grenade while the door was open, the blast could be catastrophic in a contained area. Las-fire bristled all around the Wolves now. Some of it hit. Ceramite armour blistered in several places. One by one, the others jumped in through the pod's doorway, until only Haegr was left.

'Come away now!' said Valkoth when it looked like he might want to blast away all day. Haegr growled. His beard bristled, and his piggy eyes squinted. It looked for a moment as if he might disobey. Valkoth growled and there was no mistaking the menace and command in his voice. It was like a wolf pack leader calling down a young and inexperienced challenger. Somewhat abashed, Haegr snapped off a couple more shots and then threw himself in.

'Strap yourself in,' Valkoth barked at the merchant. The rest of them were already fastening the restrainers, and slamming their helmets back into place.

Torin hit the quick release rune, and the escape pod blasted free of its restrainer bolts and headed down the launch slip into space. On the comm-net the Wolves finally broke silence as their beacons began to toll out. Acceleration pushed them flat into the padded couches. Pantheus's fat rippled like waves. The effect was particularly noticeable on his double chins.

'Well, we made it,' said Torin.

'Only if the Belisarians manage not to blow us to bits,' said Haegr.

Ragnar looked through the porthole and saw the asteroid recede behind them. Moments later an inferno of explosions bristled on its surface as the courier began to reduce it to rubble.

'So much for an asteroid impact,' said Torin.

'I don't think anyone will be coming to look soon. And once they finish with the devastator charges, there will be little enough to find.'

Pantheus gulped air. He was very pale. Ragnar was hardly surprised. He was watching billions of ducats worth of mansion being reduced to rubble. And he was in the grip of men who would not shrink from doing him serious personal harm. The merchant had doubtlessly known better times.

* * *

IT WAS ALMOST an hour before the courier picked them up, and waiting was uncomfortable for Ragnar. As always, there was the possibility of something going wrong. A stray rock or munition might hit them. The systems might fail and kill Pantheus. Such things had been known to happen. He was glad when the huge form of the courier appeared in the porthole and scooped them into its maw, like a whale gulping down krill.

Alarik awaited them in the landing bay. Sailors on the courier covered the escape pod with lasrifles, doubtless in case they had made a mistake and taken the wrong pod. Valkoth stepped out first, bolter pointed at the ceiling. Under the circumstances, when armed men were nervous, it was best to take no chances of there being any misunderstanding.

'I see that you got him,' said Alarik.

'Did you doubt it?' asked Haegr.

'Things sometimes go wrong,' said Alarik. 'No matter how good the troops are and how good the plan.'

'Well they didn't,' said Haegr. He sounded almost huffy. 'They never do when mighty Haegr is involved.'

'Haegr fights like two men,' said Torin. 'Which is easy for him since he has the bulk of four.'

'I see I have neglected your customary beating too long, Torin,' said Haegr. 'All here know that I have the valour of five men.'

'And vanity enough for ten.'

'I see you are determined to deny the truth and get the last word,' said Haegr. 'Fortunately I am not so base as you.'

Alarik's men took Pantheus off into custody. He looked defeated and shrunken, like an inflated bladder that has had the air let out of it. Ragnar noticed he was limping. He was obviously not used to bearing his own weight, and was well aware of what was waiting for him in the interrogation chambers.

'I would not feel too sorry for him, my friend,' said Torin. 'Pantheus has been responsible for the deaths of many good men.'

'I'm hungry,' said Haegr. 'Killing always works up my appetite.'

'Sleeping usually does that as well,' said Torin.

'Go, get something to eat. Take a rest,' said Valkoth beginning to stride away, adding, 'Well done.'

AFTER THE VIOLENCE of the attack on the asteroid, Ragnar felt unsettled. The moments of battle lived in his memory with peculiar intensity, and everything else seemed dull and colourless compared to it. He had heard it said that Space Wolves were made that way. Parts of their brains had been altered to respond precisely that way, so they were keen for combat. Ragnar was not sure this was the case. Perhaps it was simply a product of the process that had awakened the beast within him. Perhaps the heightened memories were simply a product of his heightened senses working to keep him alive.

He prowled around the ship, like a wolf coursing for the trail of deer. He did not want to sleep. He had no desire for wine or ale. He was not hungry. He was uneasy. It was partly due to the unfamiliar scents around him. Normally when he came back from a battle there would be the scent of many brothers around him. If they were on a ship, the air would be filled with the familiar scents of Fenris and the flesh of those who had served in the Chapter's fleets.

Now he was somewhere else. The incense in the recyclers, the icons on the duralloy walls, the uniforms of those around him were not what he was used to. All that reminded him of home were the faint scent trails of his fellow Wolfblades. But even these were different: they carried the effects of many years of living on Terra, consuming different food, being surrounded by different things.

He was a long way from home now. Get used to it, he told himself. It is your duty to serve the Emperor and the Chapter no matter where they send you. If you live long enough you will doubtless be sent to stranger and less hospitable places than this.

It was one thing to possess knowledge of the complex mix of Imperial politics. It was another thing to live through it, and learn it first hand, just as there was a world of difference between reading a tale of a battle in a scroll, and actually meeting a foe breast to breast, and sinew to sinew.

His footsteps had taken him to part of the ship he had avoided. He noticed there was an immediately recognisable taint to the air. Blood, he thought. And sweat, and pain all mingled with faint traces of ozone. He moved closer and his ears, keener than an ordinary man's, picked up what could only be screams from what was meant to be a sound-proof door. As he rounded a corner, two men in the uniforms of Belisarius's guard raised their weapons. Their movements seemed absurdly slow to Ragnar. Before they had brought their weapons to bear, he could have drawn his own, or sprung forward and snapped both their necks.

They recognised him and lowered their weapons once more. He could not help noticing that they both looked pale and there was a faint sheen of sweat on their brows. Clearly they knew what was going on beyond the sealed door. Ragnar did too. Pantheus was being questioned. He shook his head in disgust as he strode past. This was something he did not like.

It was one thing to kill your foes in clean combat, it was another to torture them for information. He shook his head again as he considered his softness. He knew that torture was one of the instruments of Imperial rule. The Inquisition used it. Planetary Governors used it when information was needed. He knew all the arguments in its favour. Better a dozen heretics should know agony than a single innocent suffer. Did heretics not deserve whatever punishment was heaped on them?

Maybe, he thought. He understood the logic of it, but once again, it was one of those things where knowledge and reality were two separate things. And he knew that no matter how long he lived, he could never approve of it.

The idea that Pantheus might not even be a heretic but a devout follower of the Emperor gnawed at him. What was going on here was nothing to do with the protection of the Imperium or the preservation of humanity. It was about one faction seeking political advantage over another. It was just another skirmish in the long struggle in which one immensely rich and powerful group within the Imperium sought to gain the upper hand.

The beast within him stirred. It understood cruelty and darkness and the compulsion to triumph over your rivals. It whispered that his life might depend on the knowledge gained here, along with his honour and the security of House Belisarius that his Chapter had pledged to uphold. And it might not, came the response. The man whimpering beyond that mass of sealed metal might know nothing. Only time would tell.

He strode down the corridor, wishing that he could leave his evil thoughts behind, but knowing that he could not.

'WHAT'S THE MATTER with you, Ragnar?' Valkoth asked as he strode into the chamber where the others meditated. 'You look like orks pissed in your ale.'

'There are some ales on Terra that would improve,' said Haegr knowledgeably.

'I passed the place where Pantheus is being questioned.'

'And?' Valkoth sounded genuinely interested, and his scent confirmed this. The others were giving him their full attention.

'It sounds like they were carving the blood eagle on his back.'

'I doubt the Navigators would do anything so unsophisticated,' said Torin. 'They are using machines. Neural induction coils, electrodes. Drugs as well, I would imagine.'

He sounded a little too knowledgeable for Ragnar's liking.

'The old ways are the best,' said Haegr. 'Though I doubt any of those effete Terrans would have the stomach for the eagle. They might get some blood on their nice uniforms.'

'Maybe you should go and show them how it's done,' said Valkoth sourly.

'Don't suggest it,' said Torin. 'Haegr would only forget what he was supposed to ask and try and learn where he kept all his food.'

Ragnar did not find the joke funny. He was shocked by their attitude. They obviously shared none of his qualms or queasiness about what was being done. He could tell from their manner, their voices and their scents. Was it possible that he was the only one who saw anything wrong here? If so, was it possible that he was the one who was wrong, who was out of step with his comrades and his world? Was all this just the sign of some weakness in himself?

He shook his head and stared bleakly out of the porthole. The steel-clad mass of Terra was visible once more. He was not glad to be back.

CHAPTER THIRTEEN

RAGNAR LAY IN his chamber in the palace and stared at the ceiling. He could not help but notice the elaborate plaster patterns there, complex swirls of leaves and coins forming what he thought was the star pattern over Fenris. He would have much preferred the actual stars himself, but it seemed no one was consulting him.

Gravity tugged at him again, and the air held the distinctive tang of Old Earth. He considered it. This was air that had been breathed a billion, billion, billion times. It was tainted with the dust of ages. The weight of the buildings around him appeared incredible and oppressive. He realised that this palace was older even than the Fang. Yet the Fang was a solitary miracle, a huge base hidden in a gigantic mountain that was one of the wonders of the galaxy. This palace was surrounded by buildings just as old and situated atop layers of buildings even more ancient. He had heard it said that all the ancient civilisations of Earth could be found here still, buried in layers. And if you dug deep enough you would find the remains of even such legendary ancient places as Atalantys and Nova Yoruk. It certainly seemed possible.

A strange languor filled him. The events of the previous day could have happened to someone else in a different lifetime. The thick pile carpet, the heavy wooden furniture, and the ancient works of art conspired to make his memory of the battle dream-like. Such things could not happen here, they whispered. Everything was too ancient, too civilised, too comfortable.

131

He forced himself upright. That was an illusion, he knew. Many many times, the streets and warrens of old Terra had run with blood. No doubt battles had been fought within the walls of this very palace. Certainly there must have been killings, and stealthy murders aplenty.

Someone knocked on the door. The scent told him who it was before he said: 'Enter.'

'Greetings, Ragnar of Fenris.'

'Greetings, Gabriella of Belisarius. What brings you here?'

She paused for a moment. 'I wanted to see how you were finding things here.' Ragnar rose from the pallet and moved across the room towards the food on the table. It was simple Fenrisian fare.

'Strange,' he answered truthfully. 'Not what I expected.'

'What did you expect?'

'Holiness. Sanctity. The radiant presence of the Emperor.'

'You will find all of those on Terra, though not in the Houses of the Navigators. Our religion is commerce. For us gold has a sanctity all of its own.'

Ragnar knew he should have been shocked to hear such words spoken but he was not. They echoed only too well what he thought himself. 'You sound as if you do not approve.'

It was her turn to smile. 'I fear I have spent too much time among the stalwart warriors of Fenris. It may take me a little time to get used to being back here.'

'You'd better not take too long,' said Ragnar. 'It might prove fatal.'

'Yes,' she said. 'That is the hard part. In all my time among the Wolves I have seen a great deal of action and faced no small amount of danger, and yet I was never threatened by those around me. I had no need to guard my words or thoughts. I knew who my enemies were. They did not smile or offer me wine or feign interest in my conversation. They fired weapons at me across the gulfs of space. I miss such simplicity. And I fear I shall miss it more in the days to come.'

He studied her closely, wondering if he should take her at face value. He thought about it from all angles, as he always did. It was a mark of how his few days on the holy soil of Terra had changed him, he thought. If he took them at face value, he could sympathise with her. He too felt out of place amid the murky waters of Navigator politics. But there were other things to be considered. If she was not speaking generally, and he doubted she was – for he had learned that Navigators rarely did anything without purpose – then she had talked with those she felt were her enemies. It was possible she did fear for her life.

'Why are you telling me this?'

'Because you are a familiar face from the time before I came back. You are a link to that simpler time.'

It could be, Ragnar thought. It made a certain emotional sense although he was hardly what she could call a close friend. And he had saved her life, so maybe she felt secure with him. Furthermore, she had every right to feel threatened: her father had just been assassinated and her clan was surrounded by potent enemies.

'Has someone threatened you?' he asked.

'Not specifically.'

'What do you mean by that?'

'I mean that I feel uneasy, and I sometimes see hidden meanings in the simplest things.'

'That I can understand,' said Ragnar.

'Perhaps, but I doubt you can understand precisely how complicated my life is.'

'Explain it to me.'

'Things are very simple for you, aren't they?'

'Are they?'

'I see you have not spent your time here without profit.'

'You have not explained your situation to me. Do you not wish to?'

She paused for a while and then spoke calmly and clearly. 'There are factions within Belisarius, just as there are among the other Navigator Houses. You know what they say: when two Navigators meet you get three conspiracies. Since I have been away I have not been part of any political camp. Now, several of them have approached me, to see if I will support them.'

'Is that such a bad thing?'

'No, it is to be expected. But there are the usual hints and veiled threats.'

'From whom?'

'From various people, Skorpeus included.'

'Do you take them seriously?'

'After what happened to my father and what happened on the ship? I take everything seriously. Things are in a state of flux now. The whole family teeters on the edge. There are those who would take advantage of this and they are not scrupulous.'

Ragnar thought perhaps things were exactly as she said. Perhaps she was merely talking to him because he was outside the family power structure and so was no threat to her. Perhaps. Then again she might have some ulterior motive. Was she trying to recruit him? He had saved her once. It might be convenient to have him do it again. He considered this and could see nothing wrong in it. He was here to protect the

Belisarians, even from each other. Still, he wanted to be sure that he understood exactly what was going on.

'Do you want me to be your bodyguard?'

'No. That is not your decision to make anyway. You must perform the duties the Lady Belisarius gives you.'

'True, but there is nothing to stop me from keeping my eyes and ears open. You of all people should know how keen they are.'

'Would you?' There was hope and gratitude in her voice, and a few days ago it would have stirred his heart. It did so now but it also excited his suspicions. He felt as if he was being drawn more tightly into a web. He knew that there would come a time when his personal loyalties and duties might come into conflict if he allowed this to continue. He drew back his fangs in a snarl. He would cross that bridge when he came to it.

'I am meeting with my cousin Skorpeus in an hour. I would be pleased if you would accompany me.'

'I doubt your cousin would talk freely with me present.'

'Perhaps that is my purpose.'

Ragnar shrugged. 'It would be my pleasure to accompany you.'

THE VIEW FROM the top of the Belisarius Palace was stunning. Ragnar could see as far as the horizon, through the polluted haze. Pollution diffused and refracted the sunlight creating a rainbow effect across the entire sky. He had a view of all the craggy old starscrapers and massive temples and palaces of the navigators quarter. Gabriella pointed out the various abodes of different Navigator families, and their own personal space fields.

She seemed happier now, and more pleasant to be with. Her cares had fallen from her. She seemed almost playful, although that was perhaps too strong a word given her Navigator's self-control. Behind the playful mask he sensed steely self-control.

All around them servants came and went constantly. She seemed no more aware of them than she was of the furniture. Ragnar was; he had to be. Every person who came within striking distance was a potential threat and had to be treated as such. There had been one attempt on Gabriella's life already, and her father had died even though he was surrounded by his own guards. He wondered how easy it would be to get another assassin into the palace. Easy enough, he supposed, with the right contacts.

It was as wearing as spending nights on patrol, constantly having to be on guard and concentrating on the conversation at the same time. He knew that he needed to pay attention. Navigators did not waste words. Indeed they believed in making one sentence carry as many meanings as possible, most of them ambiguous. Was it part of their mutation he wondered? Did their minds think in this mazy fashion because of the way they were born, or because of the society they were born into? Perhaps a little of both, he decided.

A servant came too close and Ragnar glared at him. The man backed away, startled. Ragnar could smell his fear and the sense of panic he inspired. It was a little galling, he thought. Here he was standing beside a known mutant, and he, one of the Emperor's chosen, was the person that normal people were afraid of. It did not make a whole lot of sense.

'What are you thinking about?' The Navigator asked.

'Why are the people here so afraid of me? Some of them hate me, and they do not even know me.'

'You are a Space Marine,' she said, as if that explained everything.

'So?'

'The people of Terra have bad memories of Space Marines.'

'Bad memories? The Chapters have defended humanity for ten thousand years. They should be grateful to us.' Ragnar was surprised by the strength of his avowal. Something had touched a nerve.

'The Warmaster tore this planet apart. He reduced areas with populations of hive worlds to molten slag. His people offered up millions to his dark gods.'

'Horus was not a Space Marine,' retorted Ragnar immediately, but even as the words left his mouth he regretted them.

'No. He was a primarch. His followers were Space Marines.'

'That is perilously close to being an insult.'

'It also happens to be the truth.'

Much as he would have liked to deny it, Ragnar could not. 'Surely the folk here know that the Wolves had no part in Horus's rebellion? We came here and fought against it.'

'Aye, and your forebears were not gentle either. They killed many people.'

'Many heretics.'

'That may be, but the people here remember them as their neighbours and friends and kin. They remember you as off-worlders who brought fire and death to the soil of Terra.'

Ragnar was silent. His training and indoctrination had not prepared him for this. He had always thought of his Chapter as heroes. He had imagined that those who knew them would at least respect them, while others would admire them. He had not expected to be hated. And this woman was telling him that the folk of the most sacred world of the Imperium feared and hated them.

'Fire and death are the shield maidens of war.'

'And you think that good. But people whose trade is not battle do not.'

'They are weak.'

'Such contempt will win you a great deal of friendship, I am sure.'

Ragnar could see that this was not an argument he was going to win, particularly as he suspected that Gabriella was telling an unpalatable truth. Did it change anything? Ragnar supposed not. The Wolves would do their duty regardless of whether the people they protected loved or hated them. In reality what they felt was irrelevant.

The Navigator smiled as if she could read his thoughts.

'You can see why my people and yours are natural allies,' she said. 'We are both powerful groups that the Lords of the Imperium have no reason to love.'

Perhaps it was true, but it was not the reason they were allies. 'The Wolves are bound to you by the word of Russ. That is why we are allies.'

'And do you think Russ did not see the reasons why such an alliance would be necessary? He too was a primarch and far sighted.'

Ragnar was not sure that was entirely correct. Most of the tales of Russ portrayed him as a bold warrior, a little reckless and heedless of the needs of politics when honour was involved. Still, he was a primarch, and who could say what visions such a mind could encompass? These thoughts brought him back to the Spear of Russ that he had so thoughtlessly lost. Was it possible that Russ had foreseen this, or was Ragnar thinking this because he wanted to believe it?

A faint whiff of perfume and the pheromone trace of the Navigator gene told Ragnar that someone approached. He turned his head and saw it was Skorpeus and his ever-present henchman. If the would-be inheritor of the throne of Belisarius was disconcerted to see him there, he gave no sign of it. He smiled smoothly and bowed to his cousin and then to Ragnar. Ragnar nodded back.

'Sweetest cousin, it is a pleasure to see you once again. Shall we walk?' He offered her his arm, and they linked arms and strode across the roof. Ragnar and Beltharys fell in behind. They were far enough behind that they could not hear anything but close enough so that Ragnar was aware of every word being said.

'I hear talk of marriage in the air, lovely Gabriella,' said Skorpeus.

'Whose?'

'Why, your own! There is no need to be coy. It is the talk of the palace. We all know the purpose of your visit to that old monster Cezare.'

'I visited the Feracci tower to see our aunt. She is sick.'

'Of course,' said Skorpeus, giving a sardonic little cough. 'But other things were talked about. They always are.'

'Other things were talked about, but why is this of interest to you?'

'A Feracci married to a Belisarius, a strengthening of the ties between our two Houses just as old Gorki lies on his death bed. Do you think this is a coincidence?'

'There have been many marriages between our Houses before. Two hundred and twelve to be precise.'

'I see you have been studying the Books of the Blood, sweet cousin, to know the figure so exactly.'

'Obviously I have an interest.'

'Obviously. Do you not think it… interesting that old Cezare has offered his son as a prize to our House while all the time he is twisting the arms of the lesser Houses right and left to get that same son elected to the High Council of the Administratum?'

Gabriella stopped short. She turned and looked directly into her cousin's face for the first time, laying her hand on top of his. He seemed to flinch from the contact for some reason. 'That is news to me.'

'It is news to most folk but nevertheless I assure you it is true. The Lady Juliana knows it as well as I.'

'How do you know? Was it written in the stars?'

'I have other sources than my charts. You have been away too long if you do not remember that.'

'The other Houses would never stand for it. To see a Feracci on the Navigators' throne. It would break the old compact and give Cezare too much power.'

'Nonetheless, Cezare obviously believes it possible, or he would not even make the attempt. He is too cunning to try and fail.'

'It is not possible. Every time one of the great Houses tries, it runs into the massed opposition of the others. That is why the likes of old Gorki are always picked – a non-entity from a lesser House, who could not do anything if he tried.'

Skorpeus gave a cruel little laugh. 'I fear it is a little crude of you to speak so ill of the dying, true though your words might be.'

'Crude or no, we both know it to be the truth. If Cezare Feracci intends to change that then he will be upsetting a pattern that has kept the peace among the Houses these past two millennia.'

'And you think that would trouble our dear kinsman by marriage? Do not be so naïve, sweet cousin. He is the most ruthless and ambitious man in this galaxy and he has friends in very high places. I tell you, Cezare means to put one of his brood on the throne and become *primus inter pares*.'

'No one has claimed that title since Jormela the Mad.'

'Just because no one has done so does not mean that many have not thought about it.'

'Perhaps including yourself.'

'How could I covet such a thing? I do not even occupy the throne of my own House.'

'No, but neither does Misha Feracci.'

'I am gratified that you take what I say so seriously.'

'Do you really believe it is possible?'

'Look around you. Cezare is spending his coin like water. The leaders of three of the great Houses are conveniently dead. New, inexperienced lords rule. Now he proposes a marriage alliance with us: between you and his young inexperienced and malleable son. Such a thing might be construed as an offer of power sharing.'

'But you do not believe it to be so.'

'Cezare will share power with no one. You must understand this as well as I.'

'Are you seriously suggesting he had a hand in the killing of three lords – in the death of my father?'

'I am merely saying it is a strange coincidence that they should all happen just as the Lord Feracci plans the greatest coup in two millennia.'

'Surely he knows he could not get away with it?'

'Dearest heart, you are repeating yourself. Cezare *is* getting away with it.'

'Surely he must know there will be reprisals?'

'Will there? If his chief rivals are dead and his son is seated on the Navigator throne, he will have shown himself to be the greatest power to arise among the Navigators since Tareno. The minor Houses will line up to do homage to him. The Lords of the Administratum will court him. The great Houses will do their best not to offend him.'

'It is not possible.'

'Sweet cousin, the great Houses have become fat, complacent and sure of their success. At such times, the predators always emerge from the undergrowth. Cezare Feracci is a predator.'

'Why are you telling me this?'

'It seems to me that we must either accommodate ourselves to a new order or we must strike before Cezare becomes too mighty to be brought down.'

'This is a conversation that should be had with the Lady Juliana.'

'It has, but she needs time to consider the matter.' The sneer was faint but audible.

'Then why tell me?'

'You are the one who may be married into the Feracci family.'

He did not need to say the rest. Even Ragnar could follow the chain of implications. Gabriella might be married into the Feracci family. Her father had been killed by Cezare, if what this subtle man said was true. Was he really hinting that she might consider the assassination of the lord of the Feraccis?

'I will think on what you have said, cousin,' said Gabriella, unhooking her arm from his and bowing formally with hand on heart.

'Do not take too long,' said Skorpeus, bowing to her and then to Ragnar before retiring. It seemed to Ragnar that the Navigator looked knowingly at him before departing.

CHAPTER FOURTEEN

TORIN SWEPT THE eavesdropping augur over the room once more, then relaxed and smiled. Ragnar was glad that he had come straight here after his meeting with Skorpeus and Gabriella. Torin seemed exactly the man to turn to for advice under these circumstances.

'Ah, Ragnar, old son,' he said. 'Here less than a week and already knee deep in conspiracies. That's the spirit.'

Ragnar heard the mockery in his voice, and felt the hackles on the back of his neck rise. Torin's smile widened as if he knew what Ragnar was feeling, and then just as suddenly it vanished.

'A subtle man, Skorpeus,' he said. There was disdain in his voice. Ragnar was not sure whether this was because Skorpeus imputed subtlety or because Torin thought the Navigator was not subtle enough.

He glanced at his battle-brother's chamber. It was the opposite of his own. There was a four poster suspensor bed and ancient paintings of distant landscapes. One showed a one-armed warrior mounted on a horse, shouting commands as he rode dramatically through the snow. Doubtless he had been a great warrior in his time.

'Is he correct?' Ragnar asked.

'Almost certainly. There has been talk about this for months among the Navigators. They are very good at avoiding eavesdroppers, but they sometimes forget how keen our ears are.'

'What would it mean for us if Cezare got his catspaw on the throne?'

'By "us" do you mean the Wolves?'

'What else could I mean?'

'You are a bondsman to Belisarius now, Ragnar.'

'Our interests in this matter are the same.'

'You are more subtle than you seem, young Wolf,' said Torin. He poured himself a glass of narcotic wine and sipped it delicately. The crystal glass and ornamental decanter looked incongruous in his gauntleted hand, and his expression was one that would not have been out of place on the face of a Navigator.

'You think he means to use Gabriella to assassinate Cezare?'

'Do you really think she could?'

'At the cost of her own life perhaps. Everyone is vulnerable if you get close enough.'

'The Lord Feracci will be extraordinarily well protected.'

'So you are saying no, then.'

'She could not do it, but there is one present who could.'

'You mean either Beltharys or myself?'

'Now you simulate obtuseness, Ragnar. What need would Skorpeus have of discussing this matter with her if he intended to use Beltharys?'

'He would not have known I was listening.'

'Men like Skorpeus never forget such things, old son.'

'Then why not approach me directly?'

'Because he could not deny doing that. But if a certain hot-headed young Space Wolf were to take it into his own head to do Skorpeus's killing for him he could honestly say, even under truth machines, that he had never talked about it with you.'

'It seems a subtle distinction.'

'You need to start thinking like a Navigator.'

'How could he have known that I would be accompanying her?'

'Perhaps they cooked it up between them.'

'What?'

'You heard me.'

'Are you saying the two of them are in league?'

'I am suggesting it is possible. A gallant, naïve young Space Wolf, fearing a threat to a young woman whose life he has already saved once, acts to save her from potential harm. It has a certain tragic romantic ring to it.'

'It seems very unlikely.'

'Ragnar, when you have been on Terra as long as I have, you will learn when it comes to Navigators' plots nothing is too far-fetched to escape consideration. If Skorpeus wants Cezare dead, and there is a slight chance that you would do it, why would he not take the opportunity? He has nothing to lose, and everything to gain.'

Ragnar could see a certain logic to this. The question was did he really believe Ragnar was stupid enough to fall for it? He supposed that was also possible. 'It seems to me that you are suggesting the Navigators think too highly of their own intelligence and too little of ours.'

'We are barbarians to them, Ragnar. Useful barbarians, but barbarians nonetheless. But do not underestimate them. The Navigators are, for the most part, as clever as they think they are. They would not survive otherwise. They are born and trained to conspiracy as we are born and trained to war.'

'That's an interesting thought.' Ragnar could see that it was true too. Wild dangerous worlds like Fenris bred hardy warriors. Rich ancient ones would shape something else. A new idea lodged itself in his mind. It occurred to him that if the Navigators saw only what they expected to see when they looked at him, they were likely to continue to underestimate him. Very few foes were ever likely to do so on the field of battle but this was another arena entirely, and he needed to seize any advantage he could.

'You are looking duplicitous, old son.'

'Am I so transparent?'

'Only to a brother Wolf.'

'I was thinking that it would be well for them to continue looking at me and seeing a barbarian.'

'Indeed. And there is another thing you should never forget.'

'What is that?'

'You *are* a barbarian.'

'As are you.'

'I make no claims to be otherwise.' Ragnar doubted this, but was not about to say so.

'We come from the same place, Ragnar. We passed the same tests. We serve the same Chapter. I have not lost sight of that.'

He sounded as if he were trying to convince himself. Perhaps he had been on Terra too long and it had seeped into his veins. It seemed unlikely to Ragnar but you could never tell. For all his cleverness and confidence, Torin did not seem entirely at ease in either of his two worlds.

'You really think Gabriella and Skorpeus might be in league?' he asked.

Torin's smile flashed again, as if someone had hit a switch, but there was a hard malicious edge to it. 'Perhaps. Or perhaps he wants to get rid of a rival.'

Ragnar met his gaze and felt the hair on the back of his neck begin to rise again. 'Kill her?'

'Kill her.'

'Then why go out of his way to recruit her?'

'Schemes within schemes, Ragnar. Perhaps he really does want to convince her to try and kill Cezare. Perhaps he wants to get her guard down. If one thing does not work, perhaps another one will. Also, the Navigators believe in keeping their friends close at hand and their enemies closer still.'

'A few minutes ago you were saying that she was in league with him. Now you are suggesting he might kill her.'

'One does not preclude either, Ragnar. Also, I did not say they were in league, I merely pointed out the possibility that they could be.'

'What do you suggest I do?'

'Is any of this really your business, brother?' His gaze was suddenly probing, and Ragnar sensed that all of Torin's attention was focused on him. He could see what the older Wolf was getting at. His loyalties should be to his Chapter and to the Celestarch. He had no business letting them stray. He considered his feelings and thoughts carefully. He had saved Gabriella's life, and he liked her. He was not about to stand by and let her be killed, if she was in any danger.

'I am making it my business,' he said eventually. Torin nodded as if he had expected nothing less.

'Well spoken,' he said. 'But all you can do is keep your eyes and ears open. Don't get too involved in any of this. Look at it like the Navigators do. Treat it as a game.'

Ragnar knew he was not capable of that. He was surprised that any Wolf could even suggest it. 'It's a game where the stakes are life and death.'

'Possibly,' said Torin, 'but that's the way it's played here, and no one would have it any other way. And here's one last piece of advice...'

'What's that?'

'Remember that on Terra, you never have the whole picture.'

Ragnar was still thinking of a reply when the comm-net summoned them to the presence of Valkoth.

'WE HAVE ANOTHER mission,' Valkoth said. His face was even more grim than usual, the lines on it even more pronounced.

'Pantheus talked?' Ragnar asked.

'They always talk eventually,' Valkoth said.

'What did he have to say?' Torin's voice drawled almost like a Navigator's.

'A lot of things. He says that money is being filtered from the Feraccis to the Brotherhood.'

'What?' asked Ragnar. 'That makes no sense. The cult would have Cezare's head on a spit if they could.'

'It does not make them any less useful to him, if they are killing his enemies,' said Torin. His words came out very quietly but they were perfectly audible.

'What else did he say? Was there any proof?' Torin asked.

'Nothing the Celestarch could take to a Tribunal of the Houses. Cezare could simply say the man would say anything under torture and he would be right.'

Ragnar thought of the inquisitors he had known. 'An inquisitor could find out the truth – one with psychic powers.'

'True, but the Houses would never let the Inquisition look at their business. There is no love lost between them and the Navigators. It would give the Inquisition too much leverage over them, and they still sniff the taint of heresy on the Navigators even after ten millennia.' There was something odd in Valkoth's scent, Ragnar realised. It was as if the man was concealing something.

'You did not bring us here just because the fat man squawked about Cezare,' said Haegr. It was a surprisingly intelligent statement coming from him. Then he spoiled the effect by gnawing on a whole shank of beef. Seconds later he was crunching the bones with his fangs.

'You are correct,' said Valkoth. 'I brought you here because the Celestarch has need of your services.'

'Good,' said Torin. 'I could use a little excitement.'

'I thought you got that trimming your moustache,' said Haegr from around a mouthful of beef. 'And admiring yourself in the mirror.'

'By Russ, a talking whale has snuck into your chamber while we were listening to you, Valkoth,' said Torin.

'A talking whale probably could creep in, given your level of alertness,' said Haegr. 'I am surprised you can smell anything over the scent of your pomade.'

'Enough,' said Valkoth. His voice was soft but the command carried weight. Torin snapped shut his mouth almost involuntarily, and the retort on the tip of his tongue vanished forever. 'There is work to be done.'

'What would you have us do?' Ragnar broke the sudden silence.

'Pantheus gave us the location of another nest of vipers,' said Valkoth. 'You will go there and clean it out.'

'Where is it?' said Torin.

'The under city,' said Valkoth. 'Deep down in the under city.'

The very tone of his voice made it sound ominous.

'You have scouted this out?' Torin asked. 'It could be a trap.'

Valkoth's lips twisted in what might have been a smile. 'I am not a Blood Claw, Torin. Our agents have already been through the area. The Brotherhood has been building up its forces there for weeks. We were going to have to do something about it eventually. They are too close now. They have a munitions dump and base camp right here beneath the navigators quarter.'

'I don't like this. Things are moving too fast,' said Torin. 'We are constantly reacting, not acting. It's like we are following a path set out for us by someone else, and I think we can all guess who that someone else is. This is a huge distraction coming conveniently as the Houses jockey for the Navigator throne.'

Valkoth nodded almost imperceptibly. Ragnar could tell from his scent that he agreed with Torin but there was not much he could do. 'Yes. But the threat is still there.'

'You two are being overcunning,' said Haegr. 'It ill befits two true sons of Fenris. How can this be some huge plot? How could Cezare know that old Gorki was about to shuffle off to hell?'

Even Ragnar could answer that. 'Perhaps he arranged that too.'

'There are many poisons that can simulate illness. If anyone can find a way of having them administered it is Cezare.'

'It's a huge risk though, isn't it?' said Ragnar.

'No one ever said Cezare lacked nerve,' said Torin.

'Whether you are right or wrong, Torin, you still have a mission to perform,' said Valkoth. 'Let's get to it.'

THE CORRIDOR WAS dark and gloomy. The crumbling walls looked like they had been here since the first cities were built on the ancient soil of Terra. The air was filled with the scent of fungus, rot, polluted water and rust. Huge rats scurried away from them into the dark.

'I've been in more cheerful places,' said Ragnar. 'This is a side of Terra the pilgrims never see.'

'I could have cheerfully lived out my life without seeing it myself,' said Torin fastidiously wiping a spot of muck from his shoulder-pad. He had been meticulously cleaning it ever since the water started to drip from the ceiling. Behind them a full company of House guards moved through the gloom. They were the best troops the House could muster. They would spearhead the attack. Valkoth remained above, guarding the Celestarch. Torin was their acting commander.

'This is not what I expected,' said Ragnar quietly as they moved along. The tainted water was ankle deep now. He wondered if anybody down here really drank it. Without the digestive system of a Space Marine they would most likely be poisoned or mutated within weeks. 'This is more like a hive world. A run down hive world in a sector that has suffered a hundred-year industrial decline.'

Torin moved along, bolter held casually at the ready. He had taken the lead ever since they had been dropped off at the entrance shaft that led down into the depths of the Earth. 'This is like no hive world you ever visited, Ragnar. There are hundreds of layers of buildings above us. Each of them represents a century of history or more. This part of Terra was built and overbuilt and then built on again. Parts of it were cannibalised to build the layers above, and what was left was slowly crushed down by the new stuff above. We're walking through history. Some of these walls around us were built before the Emperor entered his Golden Throne. Much of these corridors were the same when Russ walked this earth, ten thousand years ago.'

'You sound like one of those guides who show pilgrims round old temples,' said Haegr, belching thunderously. 'The ones who are always praising the wonders of Old Terra and trying to sell locks of the Emperor's hair.'

'If they tried to sell you a sausage made from the flesh of Horus you would buy it,' said Torin. 'Most likely eat it, too.'

'Hush,' said Haegr, raising his hand. At first Ragnar expected another joke, but the expression on Haegr's face told him differently. He strained his ears to catch whatever it was the huge Space Marine was listening for.

Ragnar thought he heard something up ahead. Voices. They were nearing the inhabited area of this eerily empty zone. Good, he thought. He did not like the feeling of those tens of thousands of tons of plascrete pressing down above his head. They should do what they had been sent to do and get out. They were to cleanse this nest of cultists and seize their leaders for questioning if they could. Mostly they were to make an example of them, and make them think twice about striking at the Navigator Houses.

Ragnar questioned the wisdom of this course of action. These were men driven by relentless hate. Killing a few of them would only give them more reason to hate, and deepen their sense of grievance. Still, it was not his job to question the strategy of the Celestarch. It was his job to see that it was carried out.

Once again the numbers would be against them. The thought did not trouble Ragnar very much. Ten or a hundred to one, the odds did not matter. They would be much better armed and armoured and far faster and stronger than those they attacked. And they had the element of surprise. That was why they were sending in such a small force.

Torin signalled for the House troops to remain where they were. He gestured for the other Wolfblades to advance and scout out their goal.

Ragnar's nostrils flared as he caught another scent. There were definitely people up ahead. His keen eyes picked out a disturbance in the surface of the water just ahead of Torin. His brother Wolfblade had already spotted it. He stepped over. There was something hidden just below the surface.

'Tripwire, Haegr,' he said. 'Just in case you were too busy thinking about food to notice it.'

'Since even you could notice it, there is no reason why the ever-vigilant Haegr could not,' replied Haegr.

'No reason other than not having a brain to notice things with,' murmured Torin – so low that only the ears of a Wolf could have caught it. His caution had increased considerably now that they were near their objective.

Slowly but surely they by-passed and disarmed the tripwires. Other men would have failed to notice them in the dark, but Space Wolves were not like other men. Ahead of them more lights were visible. There was a smell of recycled methane, which was hardly surprising. An area like this could not be connected to the great electrical furnaces that fed power to the surface.

So much the better, Ragnar thought. Normal human sight would be far less efficient in the gloom than the ears and noses of the Space Marines. He felt a tension in his stomach as he prepared for combat. He knew that the folk they would soon encounter would be desperate, hard-bitten men. From what Valkoth had said, they had fled the surface of the world, and the ancient privileges of job and caste to come here. He knew too that they would be armed with the best weapons that could be stolen from the well-stocked armouries of Terra.

They emerged above a wide open space. Water dripped from the access tunnel in a slow turgid waterfall down into a polluted pool below. Flickering gaslights lit the whole shady area. Ragnar took it all in with one long appalled glance. The ancient, crumbling caverns teemed with life. Here and there dozens of other tunnels entered the chamber. In their entrances were lean-tos made from salvaged steel and hardboard. A motley assortment of jerry built huts barnacled the walls and floor. Hundreds of armed men moved around. All of them wore cowled robes and the red and black armbands of the Brotherhood.

High atop a makeshift altar of welded pipes and plates of metal, a masked man bellowed a sermon of hatred to his avid listeners. He spoke of the evil mutants that lurked on the surface and sullied the sacred soil of Terra. He talked of the whore of commerce that was corrupting the values their ancestors had held dear. He talked of the evil that the Navigators concealed beneath the mask of loyalty and the robes of righteousness.

It was a fiery speech and passionate. Ragnar could see that it fanned the flames of hatred in the heart of every listener. The man was plainly telling his audience what they wanted to hear, he was playing on their fears and hatred and their resentment of the wealth and luxury enjoyed by the Navigators. It was easy to see that this was a spark that had found dry tinder. The men down here were exiles living the lives of rats in the walls of the world. They had nothing to lose. Their lives held little meaning even for themselves.

'Quite a little rat's nest down here,' murmured Torin. 'You'd think they were getting ready for a war.'

'Maybe they are,' said Ragnar. He'd seen enough rebellions and uprisings on other worlds to know that this was how they started. Heretics and fanatics had to have a hard core of warriors around which to build their insurgencies. They had to have weapons to provide to the dupes they conned into fighting with them, and to train the pitiful fools too. He had seen variants on the likes of this camp on a dozen worlds. It was a seed of disruption and heresy and it was his task to see that it never sprouted.

The little group down there might not look like much when you compared it to the massed forces that guarded this world, but there would be others like it. Even if there were not, such groups could so often be like the small pebbles that started avalanches. A world as densely populated as this one contained hordes of the poor, dispossessed and angry. Sometimes, it did not take much to turn that anger to rage, and then focus that rage on war. He had seen it happen many times before.

Even as the thought passed through his mind, the sheer audacity of the people below appalled him. This was Terra, the father world, the hub of the Imperium, the most sacred soil in the galaxy, and these men intended to profane it.

And why not? Most of them probably felt that they were doing nothing but cleansing the sacred soil of the unrighteous. He had heard that rhetoric countless times too. Without ever having heard his particular words, he could probably reconstruct the speech of the fanatical preacher down there. The alarming thing was that they were so close to the things he himself had been taught. It was one of the weaknesses of Imperial dogma, he thought, that the same words that could strengthen a community could also be used to undermine it. The robe of religion could conceal the form of the fanatic revolutionary just as easily as that of the loyal and devout citizen.

Now was not the time for philosophy. It was the time for action. He looked at Haegr and Torin. He knew they were thinking the same thing. It was time to summon the rest of the troops.

Just as the thought occurred to Ragnar, the preacher suddenly touched his ear and glanced up. It was not possible he could have seen them, Ragnar thought. But somehow he had detected them. He gestured with his right hand, and pointed an accusing finger towards the shadows in which the Wolves lurked.

Torin's finger tightened on the trigger of his heavy bolter. A hail of fire tore the preacher in two. It took his appalled followers a moment or two to realise what was happening. 'We're going to have to do this the hard way,' said Torin. 'Looks like the munitions are over there! Frag them!'

'Good, I like these odds,' said Haegr. In that moment, with surprising agility, he vaulted over the makeshift banister and landed on the corrugated roof of a hut below. Ragnar glanced at Torin, then shrugged and followed him. Doubtless the big man would need someone to watch his back as he carried out his insane assault.

Moments later, they advanced into the tight mass of fanatics. Ragnar's bolter kicked in his hand as he took out first one man and then another. His chainsword sliced through skin, muscle and bone, splattering those around him with blood. Haegr's monstrous hammer did even more damage as it pulped the flesh of anyone who got in his way. The big man raced through the crowd like a runaway mastodon. It was all Ragnar could do to keep up.

The fanatics had not realised how few attacked them. Many broke and ran for cover. Others snatched up weapons and let fly into the gloom. Muzzles flashed and lasbeams lit up the gloom, adding to the confusion. Before they knew it, groups were engaged in combat, each believing the other to be some deadly enemy. Others had fled unthinking into the darkness.

Ragnar proceeded forward, first giving cover to Haegr, then being covered in turn by Torin, as he advanced towards their goal. He rested for a moment in the shadow of one of the huts, when he heard a mighty voice bellowing orders. 'Stand firm! There are but three of them. Ready yourself for battle. The righteous shall prevail.'

Ragnar was astonished. How could this newcomer know the exact number of attackers? There was only one way. They had been betrayed.

CHAPTER FIFTEEN

'BONES OF RUSS,' Ragnar cursed. He glanced around. He could see enemies entering from all sides. They were heavily armed and obviously prepared. They must have been waiting outside the Wolves' line of approach. In their need for speed and surprise, they had not done a complete reconnaissance of the area. They were going to pay for that now.

'They knew there was going to be only three of us,' said Haegr.

Ragnar's keen hearing could make out his voice despite the background roar of heavy weapons. At that moment their foes were concentrating their fire on the balcony where Torin stood. A glance showed Ragnar that the Wolfblade had already dropped out of sight.

'They knew when we were going to attack. That means someone informed them – and recently.' Ragnar could see Haegr nod as he checked their foes' weapons. Those heavy flamers and bolters out there were capable of penetrating even their armour. This was not going to be easy. There was one consolation: in the maelstrom of conflict the enemy could not get an exact fix on them. They might still get away.

'They are over there, amid the bubble-water shanties,' bellowed the same commanding voice.

'He has good eyesight,' said Haegr.

'Or some other means of knowing we are here,' said Ragnar.

'The holy light of the Emperor's sanctity will smite the mutant lovers!' As the deep ranting voice spoke, a wave of white light flashed overhead. Ragnar's hiding place began to glow. 'Hear me, I, your prophet, the Prophet of Light, call upon you, blessed Lord, to smite these sons of Darkness.'

'Look out!' Ragnar shouted, throwing himself forward. Haegr moved, not a heartbeat too soon. Moments later their flimsy shelter exploded in a shower of shrapnel. It was like nothing Ragnar had ever seen, but that did not surprise him. He already had a good idea of what had caused it. A glance confirmed it – a halo of light surrounded a figure of glowing whiteness. It would have dazzled Ragnar had his protective second lid not dropped into place to protect his sight.

'Psyker!' he shouted, snapping off a shot as he continued to roll. The bolter shell flew true but was repelled by the aura around the cultist. It ricocheted off at right angles. Things are going from bad to worse, Ragnar thought.

'See how the light of the Emperor's holy brilliance smites his foes,' the psyker shouted. There was a thrilling undertone to his voice that Ragnar recognised as one of compulsion. No need to ask why these mutant haters helped the person they avowed to despise. Ragnar had seen and heard of a hundred instances like this. Doubtless the psyker claimed that his powers came directly from the Emperor, and they were proof of his holiness for his credulous followers. An aura of compulsion would aid their weak-willed credulity. Knowing how the trick was done would not help him survive it. They needed to find a way out of here, and fast.

Whips of blazing light smashed through the flimsy structures in which the Space Wolves had taken cover. Tendrils of whitish golden ectoplasm sought them like probing limbs of some giant beast. It was only a matter of time before they made contact.

As the tendrils moved like great oily serpents of brilliance through the wreckage, hundreds of bolter shells, bullets and lasbeams crisscrossed the air above his head. Ragnar hunkered low, knowing that their enemies believed them to be pinned in place by the crossfire. He glanced at Haegr, who nodded to show he understood. There was only one thing for them to do: attack.

Ragnar threw himself onto his belly and writhed forward towards the psyker. Ghastly, ghostly limbs passed overhead, seeking him out. They looped around, apparently knowing where he was.

Ragnar tapped his belt dispenser and caught the grenade that dropped into his gauntleted palm. A quick touch set the fuse, and he lobbed it at the psyker. A moment later the explosion smashed into the man.

Not even his powers could fully shield him. He was tossed backwards off his feet and the glow around him flickered. The ectoplasmic tentacles momentarily became misty. Acting on the instinct that allowed them to coordinate without even speaking, Haegr charged.

The enormous power hammer connected before his glowing shield could spring back entirely to full luminescence. The psyker let out a groan of pain but gained control once more. Ragnar smelled blood. The glow sprang into place once again although its brilliance varied and strange veinous seams of red ran through it. The tendrils returned and continued to loop down, fumbling for Haegr. It was as if their owner were no longer able to concentrate on two targets at once. So, thought Ragnar, they had managed to do some damage.

A second later the sorcerous limbs found their target, wrapping themselves around the giant Wolfblade. There was a strange sputtering sound as the ceramite of his armoured carapace began to bubble and melt. Haegr grunted and attempted to break free but even his massive strength was ineffective against the psyker's power. Snarling, he was pushed inexorably away from his foe. Ragnar wondered how he could help, but realised all he would do was get caught like a fish on a hook. However, if the psyker was killed, then his ectoplasmic tentacles would no longer be a problem.

Ragnar moved closer to study his target. He was in no doubt that the man was badly wounded. Another grenade would most likely do the trick. He lobbed it forward and it flew true to its target before detonating. This time, however, its effects were less than Ragnar had expected. The blast made the shield dim momentarily, but it had somehow adapted to protect its owner against this form of attack. The psyker did not even flinch this time.

So much for that idea, thought Ragnar. This heretic was powerful. 'There's more than one way to skin a dragon,' he said, and continued forward, springing from a crouch and launching himself directly at the psyker.

The man had bodyguards but they were all standing back from him as he used his unholy powers. They were concentrating their fire on the balcony where Torin had been. Ragnar suspected that the Wolfblade had most likely already slipped away.

Ragnar offered up his thanks to Russ for the distraction, as it enabled him to get a clear leap at his prey and to keep out of the line of fire. His chainsword was in one hand, his bolter in the other. As he flew forward, he fired, pumping shell after shell into the false prophet of the Brotherhood. The glowing shield repelled them all except one. They impacted where the glow was at its faintest, and where the red veins of light were at their thickest.

One of his shells passed into the glow. He heard a faint, muffled scream. It appeared that the Prophet of the Light was not used to pain.

Ragnar intended to show him a lot more of it. He aimed his chainsword at the darkest blotch on the shield and thrust. For a moment he thought it would pass right through, but it met resistance and the glow brightened once more. No matter, Ragnar thought, bringing his bolter to bear on the area of the glow where a human head should be. Even if the shield repelled the shells, he hoped the effect would be like a blow to the helmet. Perhaps the shock would stun and disorientate his target.

Once more he was rewarded with a groan. The tentacles snaking over him to hold Haegr began to pulse and flex. Ragnar sensed their approach behind him. He sprang to one side as a tendril of ectoplasm passed through the space where he had been. As an experiment he lashed out at the thing with his chainsword. The whirling blades passed through it, severing it, but moments later the thing had congealed together again. Ragnar abandoned this ploy and returned to smiting his original target. He smashed blow after blow into his prey.

Although their reflexes were mortal, the Prophet's bodyguards finally reacted. Some of them opened fire. Ragnar writhed. Even the most glancing impacts felt as though his armour had been struck with a heavy hammer. He had hoped the cultists would have withheld their fire for fear of hitting their leader, but he realised that they believed him to be protected by the glow. He sprang to one side, putting the body of the Prophet between himself and the rabble, and was rewarded with the impact of a dozen weapons on the glowing screen.

'Cease and desist, brethren!' said the Prophet, his voice like thunder. 'The power of the Emperor's light is all that is needed to slay this mutant-loving degenerate. See to it that his companions are cleansed from this area. I will deal with this one myself.' Ragnar could tell from the tone of the man's voice that he intended to make him pay for the pain he had inflicted. At that moment, the Prophet's followers swept past him, intent on reaching Haegr. The huge Wolfblade had slumped to the ground as the tentacles withdrew. Was this psyker really so confident of overcoming him, Ragnar wondered?

The glow around the man flickered, dimmed then intensified. This time the tendrils came straight at Ragnar with unbelievable speed. Not even Ragnar's superhuman reflexes could carry him out of the way. His armour sizzled where they hit him, and worse than that waves of pure agony passed through him from the points of contact. The pain was not the product of the heat, rather of the touch. He was amazed that Haegr had been able to endure it without shrieking. Ragnar resolved to do the same.

He clamped his lips shut and offered up a prayer to Russ. He sensed a far off, distant supernatural presence. Perhaps it was only a figment of his pain-wracked imagination but instantly his agony diminished. Furthermore he noticed that the glow surrounding the Prophet had dimmed and that a bright red area had appeared over his heart.

With his chainsword free he stabbed forward. The angle was awkward and he could not get much leverage, but this time his blade successfully passed right through the glow. He could feel it rip through flesh and grate on bone. A snarl of triumph twisted his lips as the glow faded to reveal a man in blood-spattered white robes. A sweep of Ragnar's blade separated the Prophet's cowled head from his shoulders and sent it bouncing and rolling into the nearest open sewer. Another sweep of the blade carved the carcass in two.

A heartbeat later he was amid the bodyguards, attacking them from behind as he came to Haegr's aid. His blade flickered with electric speed, killing and maiming with every blow. His bolter could not help but find targets amid the closely packed bodies. Step by step he carved a bloody path to his companion. Haegr looked bad. His armour was fused and rent in a dozen places, the ceramite cracked and blistered by the power of the Prophet's psychic onslaught. Worse still, he appeared tired and drained by the pain he had endured. Even so, he reared to his feet and began lashing about with his hammer. His speed and power were greatly reduced, but at least he was fighting.

Ragnar hewed his way forward, chainsword carving flesh from bone and severing tendons and veins. He felt a surge of glorious berserker rage begin to take hold of him. A fierce unholy joy in blood and battle surged through his veins. He fought it back. Now was not the time to give in to bloodlust. He needed to keep a clear mind to get out of this desperate situation. It was difficult, but he fought the beast within him, until it was under control.

He risked another glance up at where he thought Torin was. No sign. He hoped his battle-brother was not on the balcony awash in a pool of his own blood.

With a savage kick sideways, he collapsed one man's ribs like rotten twigs, sending him tumbling back into his friends, with blood pouring from his mouth. He drowned in his own blood. A vicious swipe of the butt of his bolt pistol smashed the skull of a man who was clinging to his legs into jelly. He lowered the gun and fired point-blank into the face of another, decorating the surrounding area with a splatter of blood and brain. He found himself back to back with the reeling Haegr, defending him from the onrushing horde.

All discipline seemed to have been lost by the mob now, which was to the Wolves' advantage. Had the heretics held their ground and maintained a steady stream of fire, they would have won, thanks to their sheer weight of firepower. However, their desperate desire to rescue their Prophet had undone them. They were engaging in a melee with two men who were physically superior and their casualties were immense. Still, thought Ragnar, it was only a matter of time before their greater numbers told, or someone realised that they should fall back into a firefight again. Meanwhile, before they had the chance to do so, he needed to think of a plan to extricate himself and Haegr from this trap.

A heavy built man slammed into his chest. He had barrelled through the fanatics and launched himself forward in a mighty bound. He was huge – at least as big as Ragnar and he was obviously used to over-bearing his foes through sheer bulk. But it was a mistake this time.

Ragnar absorbed the impact with a flex of his knees, his armour's internal gyros compensating for the force of the impact. The warrior reached for Ragnar's throat, but failed to find the windpipe and so he gripped his neck with both hands. He made a twisting motion obviously intending to snap the Space Marine's neck. Idiot, thought Ragnar, as he brought his bolt pistol up to the man's belly and pulled the trigger. The reinforced vertebrae of his neck could with-stand far more stress than any mere mortal man could bear. Ragnar realised there was no way the man could have known about this, just as he would not know that Ragnar's altered lungs could keep him alive far longer than a normal man, even with the air to his lungs cut off.

In a blinding flash of inspiration Ragnar knew how they could escape. It was obvious. 'Haegr,' he shouted. 'Head for the water.'

The giant Wolfblade nodded groggily, seeming to understand. Imme-diately he began to smash his way towards the smell of the polluted stream. Ragnar watched his back, all the while whirling and striking to left and right, constantly on the move to prevent anyone drawing a bead on him. Within seconds Haegr was at the bank. He paused, looked back and swung a blow that took down the men closest to Rag-nar. Then he tumbled backwards like a man shot into the water. The waves closed over his head and he disappeared from sight. So far, so good, Ragnar thought.

He angled towards the bank himself. A hail of las-fire was flashing out of the darkness now. Hundreds of tracer bullets seared across his line of sight. Overhead were men obviously intent on killing him at range. They no longer seemed to care whether they hit their fellows, because the fire pouring into the area took a terrible toll on the men around Ragnar. Las-fire splashed his armour. A heavy bolter shell smacked into his chestplate and he felt it crack. It was time to go.

Just then, two more men flung themselves forward, oblivious to the sleet of death about them. They grabbed Ragnar and attempted to restrain him, all the while howling curses and death threats at the man who had slain their prophet. Vengeance was the only thing on their minds.

Ragnar did not care. He continued to dive forward carrying them with him by sheer force of momentum. Instinctively, he took a huge lungful of air. Moments later wetness engulfed him and the horrid clammy waters closed above his head. He kept a grip on his weapons as he began to sink towards the bottom. The weight of his armour was pulling him down, while the force of the flow carried him away. His skin tingled from the pollutants and poisons. A trail of bubbles overhead guided his eye to where the two men he had grabbed were making their way towards the surface.

The membrane protecting his eye from chemical irritants allowed him to see fairly well in the murk and gloom. Unless they were using filters, the men above had lowered their life expectancy by drinking the foul water. Ragnar doubted that these death-seeking fanatics worried about such things.

He looked around for Haegr. There was no sign of him, but Ragnar was not concerned. Unless his armour was damaged to the utmost extremity, its locator beacon would enable Ragnar to find him if need be. It looked as if they had avoided the ambush after all.

Just as the thought swirled through his mind, there was an enormous tremor, and a wave of incredible force and violence drove him through the water. It took him a heartbeat to realise what was going on. The fanatics were lobbing grenades into the water. Unless he did something quickly, they would kill him.

CHAPTER SIXTEEN

ONCE MORE, ENORMOUS quakes set the water roiling. Contrails indicated where more munitions were going to fall. They had all been aimed at points from which he had disappeared. None had thought to blast towards where he might be going. But that would soon change. The concussions caused Ragnar a great deal of pain, as changes in pressure smashed into his sensitive eardrums. It affected a Space Wolf a great deal more than it would a normal man.

He fumbled his sword and bolt pistol back into their holsters. They were Space Marine weapons; continued immersion should do them no harm. He had to grit his teeth and keep swimming, and get as far away from the explosions as he could.

Charges were starting to fall near to him now. Ragnar considered making for the bank, but realised that would only make him more visible and more vulnerable. He needed to keep going and try to win his way free.

He swam on, glad that he had learned to do so in the turbulent waters of Fenris as a boy. Even so, this was bad, like trying to negotiate the maelstrom at the centre of a storm while all around giant monsters bellowed and sought your life.

Another tremor smashed through the water close by and sent Ragnar tumbling end over end. He became completely disorientated, unsure of which way was up and which way down. His head felt as if it was going to split. For some reason, the water tugged at him more strongly. The

invisible fingers of the current were like those of the hag maidens of
Fenrisian legend who were said to lie in wait for drowning mariners.
Ragnar kicked out with the current, letting the flow carry him towards
the far end of the chamber. As he did so, the impact of the quakes lessened as they travelled further through the water.

All around the water bubbled and boiled. Another blast boomed
through the water, and he felt himself suddenly hurled forward and out
into space. All around him the water thundered and yet he felt clear
patches of air around his flailing limbs.

He knew now what had happened. The underground river had carried him all the way through the chamber and out of the other side. He
was tumbling down some sort of exit sump, and falling towards incalculable depths below. As the water smashed against him Ragnar strove
to straighten his body into a diving position.

Vague terrors filled his mind. He had no idea how far he was going
to fall, or what awaited him at the bottom. There might be jagged rocks
or piles of broken metal waiting to impale him. There might be a
swampy morass that would suck him down forever.

Horror and doubt threatened to overwhelm him. Every moment
stretched until it felt like an hour. It was not his predicament that
scared him as much as the sheer impossibility of knowing what was
going to happen. He almost wished he had emerged from the water
and sold his life dearly in the slaughter that would have followed. That
would have been a man's death. Now he might fall far from where his
comrades could find him and recover his gene-seed. It was possible that
his remains might never be found.

In those brief moments, Ragnar came closer to despair than he ever
had in his whole life. The beast within him howled in rage and fear. His
monkey mind gibbered and rattled the cage of sanity. But suddenly his
long tumble ended and he smashed into blackened waters. The force of
the fall drove him still further down.

With powerful strokes, Ragnar swam out of the range of the current,
and headed in the direction that his armour told him was up. It was
possible that his sensors had been damaged and that they were malfunctioning but they were the only guide he had. Moments later his
head broke the surface. He saw a beam of light spearing towards him
and sensed splashing in the water near by. Haegr's pain-filled voice
called out: 'I see you made it as well, Ragnar.'

Relief filled him. He was still alive and had found his comrade. Or,
more correctly, his comrade had found him. They had escaped from
the deadly trap above and were alive. 'Aye, Haegr it is me.'

'I see Torin managed to avoid a bath once more.'

'Let us hope that he got away with his hide intact.'

'Do not worry about him. It will take more than a few hundred angry cultists and their pet wizard to put him down. If they wanted to lure him into a trap, they would have had to set up a corridor full of mirrors.'

'This is hardly the time to be talking like this,' said Ragnar, swimming closer. 'We need to find a way out of here ourselves.'

'That should not be too difficult. Just keep heading upwards and we will get there eventually.'

Ragnar did not bother to ask him why he had not suggested activating their beacons. Any enemy that knew they were coming would be able to locate them by it. It was only a matter of tuning in to the correct comm-net frequency and knowing the scrambled codes. A few hours earlier he would have said that was impossible. Now he was not so sure.

'I think we were betrayed,' he said. Judging by the echoes around them, they were within a large cave or tunnel. The walls could not be too far. The only question was whether there would be dry ground there. There was only one way to find out.

'Maybe,' said Haegr. 'The self-proclaimed prophet was a psyker. Maybe he foresaw our arrival.'

Ragnar considered this. It was possible, but he did not want to abandon his own theory. There was too much else that pointed to the presence of a traitor within the ranks of House Belisarius. 'Maybe.'

'You don't think so, do you?'

It must be written all over his scent, Ragnar thought. He began swimming towards the shore, with his head above water so they could talk. He did not fear the possibility of being followed down here. The Brotherhood members would have to be suicidal to cast themselves into the waterfall.

'It is possible.'

'But?'

'There's the assassination of Adrian Belisarius, and the attempt on Gabriella. Too much points to there being an insider.'

'There always are insiders among the Navigator Houses, Ragnar. You are not on Fenris any more. Every House is filled with spies. Every one of them is compromised.'

'But back there, you thought we had been betrayed.'

'It was my first thought until I saw that blasted sorcerer at work.'

There was something to what Haegr was saying. A psyker could predict their arrival and perhaps tell their number. Such feats were not beyond some of the Rune Priests of his Chapter. It beggared belief that other psykers would not also be capable of them. He did not know which idea he liked less: traitors in their midst or their enemies having recruited powerful psykers to fight for them.

'A rogue psyker, right here on the holy soil of Terra,' said Ragnar.

'Who says he is a rogue, Ragnar? There are many factions who might be pulling the strings of the Brotherhood. Some of them employ psykers.'

Ragnar could only think of two off the top of his head. It seemed ludicrous that the Astropaths would want to get rid of all the Navigators except one. 'Are you suggesting the Inquisition might be behind this?'

'No. This is not their way. But Ragnar you forget many of the High Lords of Terra, and the organisations they represent have access to psykers as well.'

The bank was ahead of them now. Ragnar could hear water lapping against rock. A moment later a sheer wall was picked out by the pen-beam on his shoulder-mounted light. He sensed a disturbance in the depths below him. Was there something living down there? Some mutated creature of the depths surfacing from below? Were hungry eyes watching him from the cold depths?

He swam to the edge of the water and studied the wall of plascrete ahead. It rose sheer about three metres and above it there appeared to be a ledge. He unhooked a grapnel from his belt and tossed it upwards. It caught the first time and he tested its hold with a few sharp tugs. Moments later he had swarmed up the wall and lay on the edge, Haegr right behind him. He flopped onto the bank like a beached walrus. And not a moment too soon. Something large and luminous was rising from the depths, but it did not quite reach the surface. Sensing its prey had gone, it slowly receded into the deep dark waters.

Ragnar listened carefully. All around he could hear the sound of falling water. Not just from the nearby falls, but from a great distance as well. It seemed as if there were other sources feeding this vast reservoir, or whatever it was. He could not see the far side of the lake – for that was how he was beginning to think of it.

He watched Haegr as the older Space Marine flopped down beside him. He was badly beaten up. His armour was cracked in many places and had been broken through completely around his left shoulder and forearm. His whole face was horribly burned. His beard and whiskers had been singed on one side of his face. It was nothing that competent healers could not repair, but they were far away from medical help. Perhaps Haegr had internal injuries as well, he appeared to be moving slowly and favouring his right side. Things were not looking good. Any time a Space Wolf did that, it spoke of an enormous amount of pain.

'You think one of the High Lords might be behind all of this? To what end?'

'Don't ask me, Ragnar. I am only a humble Space Wolf. Torin could doubtless tell you.'

'There is nothing humble about you, and I am sure you have some ideas.'

Haegr grinned wryly. 'Who can tell anyone's motives in the tangled weave of Imperial politics? A lord might be trying to curry favour with the Inquisition, or ride the wave of a jihad to supreme power. It's been tried before, even here on Terra, and it has succeeded too.'

Ragnar stood upright and almost offered to help his battle-brother to his feet, but a warning glance told him it would be unwise. A Space Wolf would have to be in his last throes before he would accept help of that sort.

He took in their damp and unwholesome surroundings. How old was this place, he wondered? So old that even the gargoyles had crumbled and even the so-called 'ever-burning' lights of the ancients had faded.

The air smelled damp and fusty. There were currents in it that spoke of a recycler in action somewhere far off. If he concentrated he could hear the distant hum of machinery muted by the sound of falling water.

They strode forward towards the direction of the air-currents. A few hundred strides brought them to a massive archway. A canal ran out through it, flanked on either side by a path. Hundreds of corroded metal pipes lined the walls. Water leaked from them and had discoloured the stone and brickwork. A gigantic mosaic depicting what might have been the Primarch Sanguinius, or one of the angels of the ancient's religion, decorated the wall above the arch. The figure stood so that his legs bestrode the entranceway. Ragnar could make out one huge wing, but more became visible as he traced them with his shoulder light. Did Sanguinius ever carry a huge horn? Ragnar did not think so. Or a flaming sword with which he smote daemons? There was much here the artist had got wrong, Ragnar thought, as he followed the limping Haegr along the canal bank.

'I sometimes wish I was back on Fenris. Life seemed much simpler there.'

'Perhaps, but if you went back now I doubt you would still think the same way.'

'What do you mean?'

'Terra changes men, Ragnar. Once you get used to seeing scheming behind everyone's actions it is very difficult to stop. You will take new eyes back to Fenris when you return.' There was a strange note in his voice and an odd glint in his eye. It was said that the closeness of death brought on the skill of foretelling in some men.

'You seem very certain that I will.'

'I am a good judge of men, Ragnar. I know you will. You have that look about you. You have been marked out for great things. That is your fate.'

Ragnar considered Haegr's words. 'I have been marked out for great calamity. I lost the Spear of Russ.'

'No, Ragnar. You used the Spear of Russ. You smote a primarch with it. It responded to you. Do you think that any man could cast such a weapon? Even a mighty hero such as I?'

Ragnar did not consider himself blessed, rather accursed. But there was something akin to envy in Haegr's voice. Ragnar wondered if there was any truth in his words. He couldn't think of a response. Instead, another thought struck him. He should try and contact his companions. He patched himself into the comm-net, but caught only static, which was unusual. Haegr gave him a knowing smile.

'The local relay must be down on this level.'

'They need relays down here?' Ragnar was astonished. He had never encountered such a thing before.

'Yes. Some of the levels were built with seals, or materials that somehow resist the net. You need to be near a relay to use the net and this one must be down.'

'Down! That is criminal incompetence.'

'But it happens. Maybe by accident, maybe by design. We'll need to find another level, or a relay station.'

'Come on then, we need to get back to the surface and see if we can smoke any conspirators out.'

AHEAD OF THEM were lights. Ragnar moved forward cautiously. He gestured for Haegr to stay where he was. He was worried about his companion – he appeared slow. His wounds were bad. Normally a Space Marine would have begun self-healing by now, if he were capable. His system must be overloaded trying to keep him alive. Judging by his pallor it might even fail. Despite this, Haegr managed to grumble about the lack of food.

All through the long weary trudge up from the reservoir, he had been uncharacteristically silent, moving slowly as if conserving his strength. The only time he had become animated was when some huge rats had scurried away from their lights. He had even made a half-hearted attempt to catch some.

Ahead of them lay a large empty chamber. It looked as if it had once been an open square surrounded by high buildings. There were still walls and windows and doorways enough to give the illusion an air of reality. If this place had once been open to the sky, now it was roofed over with plascrete. Doubtless that was where the next level began.

Ragnar could see many people. Some dwelled in what looked like huge over-turned metal barrels. Others were in translucent blisters that seemed stuck to the walls above. Some clambered up to the higher windows on towering metal ladders. A few seemed to have got into a vast metal pipe through holes in its side and had made their home there.

In the centre of the square was a small building. On the roof towered an armoured figure representing the Emperor from before the time he was entombed in the Golden Throne. It was an early archaic symbol of the Imperial cult. Perhaps it was the sign of some branch of the Adeptus Ministorum he did not know. Perhaps it actually dated from a time when the Emperor walked the streets of this world.

Ragnar wondered whether it would be best to skirt this community. After all, it might be allied with the Brotherhood. But if it were not, they might be able to find a healer. Haegr was in a very bad way. Any medical help, no matter how primitive, was critical now. Ragnar decided to risk it.

Many robed and cowled figures moved through the underways. Methane gas recycled from sewage was used to light the whole area. Ragnar could smell both both the gas and the processing works; neither was a treat to his sensitive nose.

Doorways lined the tunnel walls; some were blocked by pieces of corrugated metal, others were hung with drapes. The smell of roasting meat mingled with the methane burners over which it was cooked.

The people up ahead moved slowly. Every now and again, a skinny emaciated hand or face was visible. Whoever these people were, they were not thriving. Most of them were not armed either. This reassured Ragnar. This place had neither the look nor the smell of the Brotherhood camp.

He moved forward through the gloom, certain that no one would detect him until he was really close, unless he wished it. Ahead of him he could see a small skinny man, moving along. His walk was a crooked waddle, as if his legs were bowed. He was helped by a long staff carved from bone. Ragnar tapped him on the shoulder, and was surprised when the man leapt into the air and shrieked. He would have bolted had Ragnar not restrained him.

'Peace, stranger,' he said. 'I mean you no harm unless you try to harm me.'

The little man turned round to look at Ragnar. The light reflected on his round spectacles, turning his eyes briefly into circles of fire. 'In the Emperor's name, I doubt that is possible for the likes of me, sir.'

His voice was high-pitched and quivering, his manner shy and tentative. He sounded more like a scholar or a clerk than a member of the Brotherhood. 'And who are you?' Ragnar asked.

'I am Linus Serpico the third, junior clerk third class at the Imperial sprocket works number six, like my father, and his father before him.'

He paused for a moment and considered his words. 'At least I was. Until the sprocket works blew up.'

'Blew up?'

'An unfortunate industrial accident, sir. It does not reflect on the management in any way. Although I have heard it say that it would never have occurred if they hadn't spent the entire safety budget on a gold-plated statuette of Saint Theresius for the high foreman's retirement.'

Ragnar cocked his head to one side, baffled as much by the speed of the man's garbled speech as by his words.

Linus took Ragnar's silence the wrong way. 'Not that I place any credence in such scurrilous rumours, sir. You can always find people who will read the worst into anything. Just because the high foreman, his wife and the under-foremen retired to their own private gallery on sublevel 5, it does not mean that they were illegally appropriating funds for their own use.'

'If you say so,' said Ragnar. The little man let out a long sigh.

'I do not say so, unfortunately. As junior clerk third class it was my misfortune to have to scribe and blot the great account books, and if I may say so I suspect – although I do not firmly accuse anyone – I suspect that there were certain irregularities.'

'Do you indeed?' said Ragnar.

'I do. And in time, once the evidence was suitably corroborated I would have been in a position to put the evidence before the auditor general of sprockets. It would have been my duty to do so, sir, and it was a duty from which I would not have shirked. Unfortunately, the whole factory was reduced to rubble by the unfortunate aforementioned blast. Had I not been abroad on an errand for Supervisor Faktus, sir, I would most likely have been blown to high heavens with it.'

'Indeed. You are a resident here?'

'I am sir. At least I am temporary, although I pride myself on being a better class of person, sir, than most you will find here. I am not indigent, but alas there are few openings for a scribe of the third level these days.'

'You could always consider other work,' said Ragnar, a little taken aback.

'Other work, sir! Impossible! Why the very thought of it! My forefathers would turn in their graves if I accepted a position of lesser merit. I am a scribe of third class like my father before me, and his father before him.'

Ragnar was a little astonished by the ferocious intensity of the man's speech. He sounded almost as if he had been insulted by the Space Wolf's words.

Fascinated as he was by this encounter with a Terran, he had his plans and he needed to move closer to fulfilling them.

'Be that as it may, I need a healer.'

'If you don't mind me saying so, sir, you look the picture of health, although your canine teeth could use a little work by the look of them.'

Ragnar let out a long growl that made the little man cringe backward. 'It is not me that needs help. My companion is hurt.'

Linus seemed to notice Ragnar for the first time. He took in his size, his weapons, his dented armour and his threatening appearance. Then he shrugged. 'Why did you not say so immediately, sir? I am sure Brother Malburius will be able to help. Come let us seek him.'

'First I must bring my comrade.'

'Of course, sir, of course.' He acquiesced so quickly that Ragnar's suspicions were aroused. Was the little man preparing to lead them into a trap? With Haegr wounded and himself at less than one hundred per cent things might go ill if that were the case.

Slowly, partially supporting Haegr now, they made their way towards the temple in the middle of the square. By the time they reached the doorway, Haegr had all but collapsed.

CHAPTER SEVENTEEN

BROTHER MALBURIUS WAS a tall lean man with a grey, well kept goatee beard. His hair too was grey and his face was lined. He had a slight stoop. He wore the robes of the Adeptus Ministorum with a weary pride. He looked tired and not at all happy to see two battered Space Marines cluttering up the inside of his ministry.

'Space Wolves, eh?' he said. 'Attached to House Belisarius, no doubt.'

'How do you know that?' Ragnar asked. His suspicions were fully aroused. He glanced around the converted tunnel that was the temple. He noted nothing threatening – only some salvaged pews, worn Imperial saints that looked as if they had been scavenged from a dump and a massive Imperial eagle embossed altar. The temple looked as run down as its artefacts, but at least it was tidy.

Brother Malburius looked closely at Haegr and beckoned them to follow him into the depths of the temple. Behind the altar was an antechamber packed with run-down looking medical equipment. It smelled of blood, pain and antiseptic incense. As he walked, the priest talked. 'It was hardly difficult. One look at you tells me your Chapter, Brother Ragnar. The Wolfblades are the only Space Marines on Terra. Your kind has not been popular here since the Heresy.'

'Is that so?' said Haegr, grimacing. 'I would never have guessed from the reception we got.'

Malburius gestured for Haegr to lie down on an examination table. Much to Ragnar's surprise the big man obeyed, slumping down on top of it. The bronze and metal table, a mass of universal joints and moulded gargoyle heads, flexed under Haegr's weight, but held firm.

Malburius screwed a magnopticle into one eye, and bent to examine the Space Marine's wounds. He adjusted some dials on the control altar and invoked the Machine God. Two globes of light flickered to life on either end of the table. Malburius attached dermal divination sensors and lit two sticks of medical incense.

Ragnar was not sure what good those would do given the armour that covered Haegr and the changes that had been made to his physique when he became a Space Marine, but he did not say anything.

No sooner was the connection made than the sensors began to pulse wildly. Malburius banged the machinery with his fist and uttered an invocation to the tech-spirits but it made no difference. He thrust a thermal sensor into Haegr's mouth. Linus Serpico watched, eyes wide, saying nothing.

'Don't eat it,' said Ragnar. Haegr grimaced. The fact he did not speak indicated to Ragnar that the situation did not look promising. After a few moments, Malburius removed the sensor and shook his head.

'It does not look good,' he said. 'I have to assume there is internal damage. I will need to remove the carapace and take a look inside.'

'Are you sure you are qualified for this?' asked Haegr with a fixed grin. Brother Malburius looked at him.

'If truth be told, no. I received basic medical training in the seminary. I can perform basic battlefield work and anything necessary to treat my flock. I was never taught to deal with the likes of you. Judging by the readings of my old instruments, I expect to find all manner of alterations to the basic human bio-form. Will that not be so?'

There was disapproval in his voice. Ragnar was not used to this and resented it. Haegr nodded. Malburius had an aura of competence that commanded respect.

'I expect that your battle-brother here...' A gesture indicated Ragnar. 'Could most likely perform any surgery as competently as I.'

'This is not what I wanted to hear,' said Haegr. He looked at Ragnar as if expecting confirmation. Ragnar knew the basics of field medicine but he was not a trained chirurgeon. 'You have probably had more experience than me,' he said.

'I've had plenty of practice down here. There are always accidents and fights and there is no one else to patch people up.'

Haegr looked as if he was weakening rapidly. He concealed his pain from the priest but Ragnar could sense it. He also sensed that Malburius was nervous and was trying to delay the operation for as long as he could. Ragnar came to a swift decision. 'Do what you need to. I will assist you in any way I can.'

Malburius nodded and moved to the nearest cabinet. He spoke directly to Haegr. 'I have painkillers, somnabulium and surgical tools here. I can render you unconscious and...'

'That will not be necessary,' said Haegr. 'Begin at once. A hero as mighty as myself need not fear a little pain.'

'Ah, the famous Space Marine hardihood,' said Malburius. He glanced at Linus. 'Friend Serpico bring me boiled, purified water and lots of it.' He looked at Ragnar. 'There may well be a loss of blood. I doubt your blood type is common among people here. I may need to transfuse yours.'

Ragnar knew what he was talking about. Many types of blood were incompatible. Fortunately all Space Wolves shared the same type. It was part of the process that turned them into Wolves. 'You can use mine,' he said. Malburius nodded and headed over to a strange contraption of translucent tubes and accordion fan pumps. He wheeled it over to the long table. 'I don't get much call for this sort of thing usually. Normally it's appendectomies, or childbirths or amputations after roof-falls. You two have been in battle.' It was not a question, although he made it sound like one.

'We fought with some of the Brotherhood of Light and their prophet.' Ragnar wanted this out in the open. If Malburius had any sympathy for the heretics he wanted to know before the man stood over Haegr with a las-scalpel in his hand. Malburius only nodded.

'I wondered how long it would be before someone took action against them,' said the missionary. 'They have been building up their numbers in the area for a while. It was only a matter of time before someone did something.'

The man was sharp and fishing for information. Ragnar could see nothing to be gained either by contradicting him, or agreeing with him, so he kept his mouth shut.

Malburius slapped the table and looked at Haegr. 'We'll need to remove your chestplate,' he said.

Haegr muttered a curse and bit his lip as they did so. His massive tusks must have made it painful. Ragnar could see that the black filament layer was badly damaged. There were gaping holes in it through which pink flesh, clean white bone and glistening internal organs could be seen.

Linus entered bearing a bucket of steaming water and Malburius washed his hands and sprayed them with a chemical designed to kill disease spores. It came from a standard military dispenser marked with the Imperial eagle. Swiftly and competently he hooked Ragnar and Haegr up to the blood machine. 'There is no power grid near here, Brother Ragnar,' he said, 'so you must power the machine. If there is a need, you must work this pump with your foot. If the pain becomes too intense, say so, and friend Linus will take up the task.'

Linus did not look at all happy to be here.

'I am a scribe third class, not a medical auxiliary,' he said.

'Nonetheless,' said Malburius, 'you will help. This man's life may depend on it. And believe me, the Imperium places considerably more value on his life than it does on yours. Is that not so, Space Wolf?'

Ragnar growled. Linus swallowed deeply in a manner that did not inspire confidence, but he nodded. Malburius kneeled and offered up a prayer to the Emperor and then took up his las-scalpel. Ragnar leaned forward watching closely, ready for any contingency, and prepared to deal with any threat. If Malburius attempted treachery, he would die for it. This maze of thin pipework would not even slow Ragnar down.

Malburius gave no sign that he was aware of how close he was to violent death. He unscrewed the magnopticle and donned a pair of goggles of thick smoked glass. Ragnar could see that they contained some sort of optical magnification system. He lifted the las-scalpel and touched the activation rune. A beam of pure intense light sprang into being. It was about a hand-width long.

Malburius twisted the body of the scalpel and the beam shortened. He leaned forward and began slowly and carefully cutting away the carapace. Then he sliced the flesh to expose the internal organs beneath. Haegr flinched. The smell of seared flesh filled the air.

Malburius moved very carefully. The priest was obviously used to dealing with normal humans, and there was much about a Space Marine's anatomy and skeleton that apparently confused him. The bones were thicker and reinforced to be strong as steel. The ribs were much wider and flatter than a mortal's, designed to provide an extra layer of armour over the vital internal organs. Most of these were in different places, intermingled with grafts that had no place within a human's body.

'Are you sure you know what you're doing, priest?' asked Haegr, through gritted teeth. Sweat beaded his brow. 'I am very fond of my belly. It has taken a long time to bring it to the peak of perfection that it enjoys today. I would not have you reducing my manly girth.'

'Perhaps you would like to do this yourself,' said Brother Malburius. He shook his head and tutted. 'This is what comes from letting your patients remain conscious,' he added.

'Perhaps you could give me a sermon, priest. They usually put me to sleep quickly enough.'

'And blasphemy as well,' said Malburius. 'Little wonder the Emperor has seen fit to withdraw his favour from you.'

As he spoke, the missionary leaned forward and pushed aside the oolitic kidney. Ragnar could see that it was inflamed. Blood was flowing from several places. The wounds did not look good. He pointed this out to Malburius.

Swiftly the priest moved the las-scalpel over the perforations and with practiced skill, cauterised them closed. Haegr gritted his teeth. He was becoming paler, but emitted no gasp. Malburius looked at him, but the Wolf gestured for him to continue.

Sweat was dripping from Haegr's brow. Ragnar studied him closely, wondering whether his friend would remain conscious.

Haegr had lapsed into complete silence, as if he were concentrating on conserving all his strength for a superhuman effort to come. His breathing sounded strange until Ragnar realised it was the faint flexion of the lungs themselves. Malburius moved to them and attached suction cables. Blood pumped into the translucent plasmite as it drained away. Ragnar felt a faint sting as his own blood was drawn forth. Haegr was obviously losing the precious red stuff quickly. Still he gave no sign of complaint.

A faint dry retching indicated that Linus Serpico was finding it difficult to remain sanguine. He was obviously not used to dealing with situations like this.

Brother Malburius sucked in air, and leaned forward. It was obvious that he had found something amiss. He reached down and wafted some antiseptic incense onto an area. Haegr let out a stifled moan. Malburius again leaned forward and began making practiced careful movements with the scalpel. 'Artery sealed,' he muttered. 'Let's see what else we can find.'

He continued to explore the wound gently, probing with his fingers. Ragnar maintained his silence until the priest seemed satisfied. 'That is the best I can do,' he said eventually and began to close up, carefully cauterising the wounds and sealing them with synthi-flesh. 'I would recommend to most people that they spend the next few days abed, but you are Space Marines. I have heard much of your miraculous healing powers. I now begin to believe it. Much of the internal damage was healing itself even as I operated. Only the major perforations needed work although they needed it desperately. It is astonishing, and a testimony to the greatness and mercy of the Emperor.'

'If you say so,' said Haegr opening his eyes and belching. 'I rather think it a testimony to my heroic powers of recuperation.'

Ragnar shook his head. Weak as he was, Haegr was incorrigible.

'It's time to begin closing you up,' said Malburius. Only now did he permit himself to look nervous. Ragnar saw him swallow. Swiftly and precisely he began to set about the task.

'What do you know of the Brotherhood?' he asked Malburius as the man worked.

'They call themselves "The Righteous", and they are certainly filled with righteous hatred.'

'You agree with them?'

'They choose to interpret the Emperor's words in a way that suits their prejudices.'

'Suffer not a mutant to live?' asked Ragnar.

'Aye, but they spread their nets too widely.'

'What do you mean?'

'They hate those to whom the Emperor gave shelter, and to whom he extended the cloak of his protection.'

'The Navigators?'

'Aye, the Navigators.'

'You think they are wrong?'

'If the Emperor himself chose to spare the Navigators, who are they to contradict him? It seems to me that they combine the sins of wrath and pride. They are arrogant.'

'Yet they do not seem to lack supporters.'

'The layfolk are ever easy to lead into error. That is why my brothers and I must continue the great work here on the sacred soil of Terra. Even in this holding, despite all my efforts, they have sympathisers.' There was an obvious sincerity in the man's voice when he spoke of the holy nature of the home world. It commanded respect, even though Ragnar disagreed with him. As Ragnar listened he constantly watched the doors, as well as the priest who sutured and repaired his colleague's flesh. He would give any sympathisers of the Brotherhood of Light a warm welcome if they intruded.

'WE THANK YOU for your help, brother,' said Ragnar. He glanced at Haegr. The big man had regained some colour. 'Now we must find our way to the surface.'

'That will not be easy,' said Malburius. 'It is many days' march to the great access conduit and a long climb from there. I should know. I made the journey myself coming down.'

'It is something we must do,' said Ragnar. 'We have work to do up there.'

'I would show you myself, but I have duties here. Linus will show you, I am sure.'

'I am not a guide,' Linus retorted. 'My family would never stoop to such a function.'

'It seems to me that you no longer have employment as a scribe,' replied the priest. 'And it seems to me that these men are engaged in the Emperor's work. You must help them.'

Ragnar added. 'I am sure House Belisarius could find work for a reliable third class scribe,' he said. 'If you would help us.'

'I am not sure,' said Linus. 'My grade applied only to Imperial sprocket works number six. I do not know whether it is transferable to the upper levels.'

'Perhaps it might be worth finding out,' said Ragnar. 'You have nothing to lose and everything to gain.'

Linus appeared undecided. Ragnar was about to ask Brother Malburius for a less timorous guide when the bird-like little man spoke up. 'Very well, I shall do it.' He seemed to be addressing his proud ancestors as much as the Wolves. 'I will do all that needs must in order to regain my accustomed station in life.'

'And maybe improve it,' said Haegr, rising from the table. He had begun to apply repair cement to his chestplate, temporarily patching the holes until they could find an armourer. Linus looked a little shocked.

'Maybe even that,' he said eventually, in a tone that suggested he was appalled by his own daring.

'Rest here for a few hours,' said Brother Malburius. 'I will provide you with provisions for your journey.'

'We have no need of provisions,' said Ragnar.

'No, but Brother Linus has.'

'As have I,' reprimanded Haegr. 'After all, Ragnar, it has been hours since I have eaten, and I need to regain my mighty strength.'

'Please wait here,' said the priest. He seemed astonished that Haegr could even speak of food so soon after surgery. 'The fewer people who see you, the fewer tales will be told. No doubt, word of the strangers' arrival has gone round the whole holding by now.' He strode out.

Ragnar watched him go, uncertain of what to do. Doubts flickered into his mind. What if the priest were in league with the brothers? What if he had gone to summon them? He dismissed the thoughts immediately. Malburius did not seem that sort of man. His scent marked him as one who was trustworthy. He had shown no hint of duplicity. Even if he was treacherous, it did not matter. Ragnar felt sure that they could deal with any threat. He settled down to wait patiently, keeping watch on his companions.

Haegr complained about how hungry he was then he boasted about how many of the Brotherhood he had slain in hand to hand combat. Linus Serpico looked progressively more worried as the huge Space Marine rambled on. He was obviously having second thoughts about travelling in their company. To distract the little man, Ragnar asked, 'How long do you think it will take us to get to the conduit?'

'Two sleeps at most,' said Linus. 'If we walk fast and avoid the lurkers in the dark.'

'The lurkers in the dark?'

'There are many different sorts. Huge spiders. Giant rats. Cannibal men who are outside the Emperor's law.'

'Who would have thought it on Holy Terra?' said Haegr sardonically.

'We are deep beneath Holy Terra now, and far from those who enforce the Emperor's law.'

'We enforce it,' said Ragnar. 'And we shall protect you?'

'But how will I get back?' asked Linus.

'I thought you were coming to the surface with us, to seek employment with House Belisarius.'

Linus looked unsure once more. He seemed to be having profound misgivings. How could my destiny find itself entwined with a mouse like this, Ragnar thought, but dismissed the question. Linus Serpico was not a son of Fenris, he had not been bred for battle and war. It looked as if even a short march from this shabby holding was a major adventure.

Suddenly Ragnar realised that for Linus it would be. In his scheme of things, this was a mighty journey. It had been once for Ragnar too. There was a time, not that long ago, when he had never left the island of the Thunderfists. Then the very concept of an interstellar journey would have been incomprehensible. He smiled to himself, and oddly that seemed to reassure the little man.

'Of course, I will come with you,' he said. 'Of course, you will protect me.'

He sounded as if he needed reassurance, so Ragnar nodded. Perhaps he was right to be worried, despite the relatively short distance. Doubtless this vast underground world was packed with dangers. Perhaps Ragnar was wrong to be overconfident. After all, the Brotherhood of Light was looking for them. And there may be others. He shrugged. All he could do was be prepared for the worst and, as a Space Marine, he always was.

CHAPTER EIGHTEEN

BROTHER MALBURIUS RETURNED with food. There was a thoughtful expression on his lean bearded face. Ragnar could tell from his scent that he was uneasy. He could sense Haegr responding to that as well. In the brief time the priest had been away, he had already started to recover. Malburius inspected Haegr. 'Astonishing,' he muttered, 'you are up and about already.'

'You should expect no less from a great hero of Fenris,' said Haegr. 'Do you have anything to eat?'

'What is going on, Brother Malburius?' Ragnar asked. 'You seem a little nervous.'

'Some of the men have disappeared. It may be nothing. They may have just gone spider hunting.'

'But they may not…'

'The ones who are missing – Burke, Smits, Tobin and the others are all the ones who listened most closely to Brotherhood doctrines.'

'You think they may have gone to contact the zealots?'

'Let us say I don't rule out the possibility.'

'Will you be safe if you stay here?'

'It will not do the Brotherhood's reputation for piety much good if they start killing priests, will it?' His voice was steady but Ragnar could tell that he was not quite as certain as he appeared. Nevertheless, he was determined to stay with his charges. Malburius was certainly a brave man. 'You had best get going! It is a long way to the surface.'

'Are you sure you will not come with us?'

'My work is here. My folk are here. I must continue to deliver the Emperor's word to them.'

'Then may the Emperor watch over you,' said Ragnar.

'And you too, Space Wolf.'

'What about food?' demanded Haegr? 'A man could starve around here.'

'I am not sure you should be eating,' said Malburius with humour.

'So the torture is to continue,' said Haegr.

But the priest produced loaves and a bunch of mysterious meat that smelled like giant rat. Haegr did not care. He dug in with gusto. 'You should save some for your journey,' said Malburius. 'This was all I could collect from the holding.'

Ragnar nodded and began to check his weapons. It never hurt to know they were in perfect working order before entering potentially hostile territory. Haegr continued to eat while Linus Serpico watched appalled. At least, Haegr was less troubled by his wounds.

'What do you think has happened to Torin?' Ragnar asked.

'He probably found a mirror somewhere and is busy admiring himself,' said Haegr. 'The man's vanity is overwhelming.'

Ragnar could tell from his scent that Haegr was more worried about his friend than he let on. 'Unlike your own,' he said.

'My pride in my manly prowess is entirely justified,' said Haegr as he let out a thunderous belch. He paused for a moment for a reply, but when none came he carried on eating.

'We'd best get going,' said Ragnar.

THE NARROW CORRIDORS of the holding were empty and very quiet. Ragnar could hear furtive movements all around him. He knew people were trying to watch them unobserved. There was nothing menacing about the noises or the scents. The people were merely nervous around strangers, and Ragnar could understand why. They were poor, ill-fed and unarmed. And two massive Space Wolves must be very intimidating. He and Haegr would be like legendary daemons of the Horus Heresy to them. It was an odd thought that rankled deep within him.

'Look at the rats hiding in their holes,' jeered Haegr with his customary sensitivity. 'Don't worry, we won't hurt you!'

Your manner will certainly do nothing to improve their impression of us, thought Ragnar. Haegr sensed his disapproval and quietened down. He contented himself with rambling about what he would do if they encountered any of the Brotherhood of Light. He showed considerable imagination in his descriptions of mutilation. Linus Serpico began to look queasy. And the sicker he looked, the louder Haegr boomed. The huge Wolf was enjoying the little man's discomfort.

Despite his bombast, Ragnar remained concerned. It was still only a few hours since his surgery, and the big man was not at his fighting peak. He moved slowly although his long strides still matched Linus Serpico's,

Ragnar turned to their surroundings. They were down deep, and the air smelled dank and musty. Somewhere far off ancient systems must still be working to keep it in motion, but everything had a stale smell.

All around were ancient buried buildings, and fragments of defaced murals that spoke of a time when these streets might have been exposed to wind and sun. Judging by their depth that would have been when Terra had seas of open water and not toxic sludge. Some depicted a sort of sailing vessel that would not have been out of place on the waters of Fenris. It was hard to imagine that there was once such a time. It was all so incredibly ancient. Ragnar wondered how many feet had trodden these stones before him, wearing those smooth indentations into the very surface. Too many to count. The weight of history pressed down on him as much as the weight of the ground above his head. He felt trapped and claustrophobic, not for the first time in his life.

He noticed his unease had communicated itself to Haegr for he had raised his head and was glancing around. As they left the inhabited warren behind, Ragnar became aware that the place had begun to stir once more. The people seemed shy and timorous, so that even Linus Serpico looked bold. Ragnar wondered if they were hiding something, a stigma of mutation. But he caught none of the giveaway scent traces and he was sure Malburius would never have stood for it, despite his tolerance of the Navigators.

He pushed all thoughts of the people they were leaving from his head. It was better to concentrate on their surroundings, and their destination.

The corridors were becoming narrower and more oppressive. In some places they were merely tunnels, excavated and propped up with bits of broken girder and salvaged plasteel. These were traces of old roof-falls. It was testimony to the skill of the ancient builders that there were so few. Common sense indicated that no architect of Terra would have built anything that could not support the new structure. The real question was why they had done so. Why had all these layers accreted over the centuries? What had compelled them to build atop what must have been perfectly good houses and palaces and warehouses? He cursed. Curiosity was an affliction of his, just as hunger was Haegr's. He asked Linus Serpico.

The little man glanced at him, like a sparrow looking at a hawk. 'I know not,' he said. 'Most likely it was either population or economic pressure. Tales tell of how the structures beneath were still occupied even as new ones were built.'

'Economic pressure?' Ragnar asked. He understood population pressure. He had seen the worlds of the Imperium where billions were crammed into massive hive cities, but the concept of economic pressure was more difficult for him to grasp.

'Land is very valuable here,' said Linus, not without pride. 'The most expensive in the galaxy. Every square metre is titled and deeded to someone – a Navigator House, a great noble of the Adeptus, a religious order. Selling is rare. Rents are high. When you can't build outwards, you build upwards. New layers are constantly being added.'

Ragnar's grasp of economics was good enough to tell him one thing. 'Surely that would reduce the value of all the land beneath.'

'You would think! But no – it means they simply charge more for the new space above. Eventually, after millennia of this you end up with places like we have. The rent rolls must be fascinating. Some of them date back more than ten millennia.'

Ragnar had assumed that the area of warrens was abandoned and the people there were squatters who lived free. Linus soon corrected him.

'No, we pay rent. Not much by modern standards, but we pay according to the agreed schedule. The toll collectors still come and enter our payments in the book of records. Interesting work for a scribe – you get to see a bit of the world.'

'Not the most appealing bit,' said Haegr. 'Judging by this place.'

'I suppose not,' said Linus. 'But then you have lived on the surface.'

He made it sound as if he were talking about some distant and luxurious planet, not that which lay directly above his head. Another heavy impression imprinted itself on Ragnar's mind – there were countless generations that lived and died here without seeing the sun or the sky. He began to get a sense of how blessed he had been to be born on Fenris, despite its dangers.

'You will see the surface soon,' said Ragnar.

'Indeed,' said Linus. He sounded both hopeful and astonished at his own temerity.

They moved on through the gloom, the shoulder lights of the Wolves flickering on automatically as they entered pockets of darkness. Ragnar did not bother to suppress them by over-riding the automatic controls. He wanted some light to see by, and he was sure that his own eyes gained more advantage from the lights than a normal man's. Besides, in these twisting winding corridors, he would catch wind of anyone approaching in time to dowse the lamps if the need arose.

In some places the ceilings grew so low that Ragnar had to crouch and Haegr had to bend almost double to work their way through. Linus had no such problems. Ragnar wondered if his small size was some sort of adaptation to his surroundings rather than a product of a poor diet.

He smiled. There was a time when he would not have considered such things, but the strange knowledge the teaching engines of Fenris had placed in his brain chose the oddest moments to surface.

There were faint animal smells around them now, and he began to notice small holes in the walls; places where long feral things that looked more like weasels than rats emerged, with a baleful glitter in their eyes. They glanced at the three companions as if to see whether they were edible. Linus flinched, but the creatures recognised the threat the Wolves represented and did not attack. They probably sensed Haegr's hunger. The big man was more likely to eat them than they were to get a bite out of him. Ceramite probably did not smell particularly appetising to them either. A tasty bite of Linus Serpico would be different, though.

Ordinary men like Linus lived in a different world, where even these rodents might prove a threat. In his own diffident way the scribe was showing more courage by making this journey than either of the two Wolves. Linus was risking his life. It was not just the rats – it was the diseases they might carry, the poisons in the tainted water, things to which he was not immune. By making him come with them, they were putting their needs before his life. Ragnar wondered if Linus realised that, and how great his courage really was.

Everything is relative, thought Ragnar. He realised he was coming dangerously close to heresy. The Imperium was built on absolutes: the absolute truth of the Emperor's revealed word, the absolute supremacy of man in the universe, the absolute evil of Chaos and mutation that must be opposed by the defenders of order. These formed the bedrock of Imperial faith.

He did not need to start thinking in terms of relativity – that way leads to weakness and worse. The truth of it was that every man, woman and child had a place in the great scheme of things. It was up to Ragnar to stand between mankind and its enemies. It was Linus's place to write down facts and figures. They had simply been given gifts of strength and courage proportionate to their responsibilities. There was no need to look further than that.

The great edifice of the Imperium had lasted ten thousand years, and would last ten thousand more as long as men adhered to their sound beliefs. Anything worth settling had been done by the Emperor and the primarchs at the dawn of their history. That was the end to it. There was no need to start attributing more courage to Linus than he had, or to belittling himself and Haegr because of it. He and Haegr were worth more to the Imperium than Linus and a hundred like him.

And yet... part of him did think that way. It was a flaw in him that he must wrestle with ideas. Not all heresies were obvious; the most dangerous were the subtlest. Pride was the greatest of all sins, the one that had led the Warmaster astray. Pride in intellect was the worst of all, and Ragnar suffered from precisely that. He needed to talk it over with a Wolf Priest when he saw one. And he realised there would be penances.

Haegr possessed a simple acceptance of what went on around him, and a simple faith in the rightness of the old ways. But Ragnar was being hypocritical. He was not like Haegr, and would not be happy to be like him. Pride again, he thought. There is no escaping it.

His feelings were partly a reaction to being on holy Terra itself. He had been expecting something special, a glow of sanctity, the touch of the divine, such as he had experienced in the shrine of Russ on Garm. Instead he had found politics and corruption and crumbling corridors. A deep sense of disappointment had settled in.

'I think we should head left now,' said Linus. They had come to a fork. One path led up and to the left, the other down and to the right. From both emitted fusty air, dank and redolent of rust and the smell of ancient machines blew.

'You think,' said Haegr. 'That's reassuring.'

'It's been a long time since I came this way, and I was headed in the other direction.'

'You are an excellent guide,' said Haegr. He sounded peevish. Ragnar put it down to the pain.

'I am sure you are correct,' said Ragnar, striding confidently up the crumbling stairwell, much to Haegr's astonishment.

It became obvious that there were people all around them. These crumbling corridors were as full of them as rotting cheese was riddled with maggots. They were squeezed into nooks and crannies, shyly trying to avoid the sight of the Space Marines, but unaware of how great their failure was. There were women and children and old men. They sat beside traps that they inspected for rats and large insects to eat. They pumped dirty water from standpipes. They moved silent as shadows and ghostly as wraiths. They were the dispossessed poor of this ancient planet.

Now and then, Ragnar smelled alcohol in a raw state. It was always accompanied by the sounds of muted laughter and quiet discourse.

There were taverns down here of the most basic sort, where brewers fermented drinks from sugary waste and mixed it with tainted water. Everything echoed with the brighter world of the surface. These people might as well have been ghosts of ancient days, he thought, for all the life that was in them. The trip had taken on a strange quality. It was like a journey through some mythical afterlife, or a primitive civilisation on which the shades of the departed fed on dust and performed odd parodies of the tasks they had done in life.

They moved on through the spectral gloom and Ragnar was filled with a growing sense of unease. He wished he had more brothers with him. Where was Torin, he wondered? The shadows gave no reply.

CHAPTER NINETEEN

THE CORRIDORS GREW wider, more like avenues. Ancient statues, dull and dusty and crumbled with age lined what had once been a street. Ragnar's unease grew and he could smell that, despite his cheery demeanour, Haegr was growing tense too. The huge Wolf had started to favour his right side again. Not even the fabled healing powers of a Space Marine could make him entirely immune to the effects of his injuries. Ragnar raised his head and sniffed the air. Something was making him wary.

He padded forward cautiously and studied a statue. It was robed like a member of the Administratum, and doubtless represented some forgotten hero of an ancient struggle. It held a book in one hand and a bolter in its outstretched right arm. Who were you, Ragnar wondered? Did the citizens erect a statue in your honour, or did you erect it as a monument to your vanity? The whole place seemed like a storehouse of monuments to forgotten struggles and peoples.

'What is it?' asked Linus Serpico, in the tone of a man who has just been told he has a fatal disease by a chirurgeon.

'I don't know,' said Ragnar, 'but something's not right.'

'It's my stomach,' said Haegr. 'It thinks my throat's been cut.'

'It just might be, if you don't shut up.'

'I am not sure I like your tone, little man. I may have to give you a sound beating.'

Haegr was scanning their surroundings intently. Perhaps, thought Ragnar, a brain did lurk behind that ox-like façade after all.

'What is it?' repeated Linus. There was an increasing note of desperation in his voice. Ragnar noticed that he had produced a small clasp knife. It would have been as useful against a Space Wolf's armour as a child's toy. But maybe it could do some damage to an ordinary man if he got close enough. Ragnar could not picture the little scribe being able to use it. He had not liked the sight or the smell of blood.

'Gunmetal,' said Haegr. His nose was fantastically keen. It must be useful for sniffing out food. 'What do we do now?'

Ragnar was surprised to be asked. He shrugged and waited. He needed more information before he came to a decision. He could sense people in the distance, but there was a scuttling furtive quality to their movements. It was as if they were trying to move rapidly but with caution. It was the sound of troops on patrol in enemy territory.

Ragnar sniffed again. Faint and far away he caught something.

'Must be twenty or thirty of them,' said Haegr. Ragnar was surprised again. Whatever he thought of Haegr's brains there was nothing wrong with his senses. Few men were as keen as Ragnar and, if anything, Haegr was his superior in this area. He could hear Linus Serpico gulp. The stink of fear clung to the little man. 'Stand or fight?' Haegr asked.

Ragnar considered. There was nothing to be gained from standing and waiting. There was nothing to be gained from fighting. They might get wounded, or lose Linus and be back where they started. He did not consider the possibility that they might be killed. 'Neither,' said Ragnar. 'We run!'

'Run?' said Haegr. He sounded outraged.

'There's no time to argue,' said Ragnar. 'Let's go.'

He did not wait to see how Haegr responded. He had found it best when giving a command to behave as if it would be obeyed implicitly. He broke into a run, doing his best to keep ahead of his pursuers. He hoped they could reach their goal before they were overtaken. Linus needed no encouragement. A few seconds later he heard a curse, a grunt and heavy footfalls as Haegr did his best to sprint.

As the statues blurred past Ragnar wondered if he was doing the right thing. Any moment, he expected to feel a las-blast in his back. He half expected to hear Haegr stop running and turn to face their attackers. If that happened it would be bad. He would have no option but to do the same. A Space Wolf did not desert his battle-brothers.

'They know where we are going,' said Linus. His breath was coming in gasps but he was just managing to keep up with the Space Marines.

'What?'

'They know we are heading for the access conduit.'

'How?' asked Haegr, who did not sound much better than Linus.

'Where else would we go? It's the shortest route to the surface from here.'

Ragnar considered the possibilities. If he were the enemy leader he would have posted a force ahead of them to cut them off. There was no sense in assuming their enemy would do anything different. In which case the force behind them were not just pursuers, they were like beaters in a hunt, driving the prey into a deadly net. 'You're right,' said Ragnar. 'Is there any other way up?'

'None so easily accessible.'

'I say we fight our way through,' said Haegr. He was panting loudly. 'It beats all this running about.'

Ragnar glanced over his shoulder to see if anyone was following. He detected no one close. They had temporarily outdistanced those behind them. He ducked through an opening in the wall and found himself in an abandoned chamber. The others followed. Both looked at him as if he were mad.

'First it's run, now it's hide,' said Haegr. 'Make up your mind.'

Ragnar shook his head and smiled bleakly. There was no point in running blindly forward. They were foolishly doing what their enemies wanted.

'You said there were other ways, although not so easily accessible,' said Ragnar to Linus Serpico.

'There is a place traders come down by. I have only been there once for supplies.'

'Can you get us there now?'

'Maybe.'

Ragnar assumed the main escape route would be covered by their foes. Was he willing to take a chance that Linus could find this other one? Or would it be best to proceed? There were too many variables here, and he did not have enough information. He supposed they could spring an ambush on their pursuers, who were closing in fast.

'Think you can take them?' Ragnar asked Haegr.

'You jest? A couple of dozen of these earthlings against the mighty Haegr – perhaps I should tie one hand behind my back.'

'I don't think that will be necessary.'

Ragnar could hear their pursuers coming closer. They were moving fast, confident that their prey was in full flight ahead of them. That was a very dangerous assumption. 'We stay,' said Ragnar.

'But of course,' said Haegr. He was outraged that Ragnar might think anything different.

'I want a prisoner.'

'Why?'

'Information. We need intelligence.'

'Speak for yourself,' said Haegr, and then added, 'that sounds like something Torin always says about me.'

Ragnar knew the big man was wondering where his battle-brother was. 'We wait here. We let them pass. I will take a prisoner. You will guard Linus.'

'Why do you get to take the prisoner?'

'I am the stealthiest.'

'My heroic form is not best suited to skulking,' said Haegr. ''Tis true.'

'And they might hear your wheezing kilometres away.'

'I do not wheeze,' said Haegr. 'I merely take bigger breaths than you midgets. My mighty frame needs more oxygen.'

'Your boasting certainly does,' said Ragnar. 'Now be quiet and let them pass.'

Haegr quietened. His stentorian breathing quietened too, after a while.

They did not have long to wait. The sound of jogging feet echoed outside the doorway. Both Ragnar and Haegr waited with weapons ready in case they had been spotted and needed to fight. Ragnar would not have minded. The beast within him was keen to start bloodletting. He was almost disappointed the pursuers went by.

'How long to the access conduit we originally headed for?'

'Perhaps twenty minutes,' said Linus.

'It will not be long before they realise they have missed us and double back,' said Haegr exhibiting a certain amount of thought. Ragnar nodded. He needed to be swift and sure. He made a sign to tell Haegr to wait and be silent, and moved to the doorway. He concentrated but could sense nothing close. He ducked out and loped swiftly but silently in the direction of their pursuers' scent.

He did not have far to go until he overtook them. They were the same sort of warriors they had fought earlier in the presence of the prophet. They were armed with lasrifles with bayonets attached. There was no sign of any psyker for which Ragnar was profoundly grateful. He held back in the gloom trusting that his eyes were better than the men's and his senses keener. Now all he needed was a little luck.

He got some immediately – but it was bad luck. As if warned by some sixth sense, one of the men glanced over his shoulder. Ragnar barely had time to duck into a narrow doorway. He held his breath and counted silently to ten but could detect no sign he had been noticed. He risked a quick sidelong glance and saw that the man was standing waiting. In fact the telltale smell and a faint glowing point showed that the man had lit some form of narcotic bac-stick. Were they really so confident, Ragnar wondered, or was this man very addicted? If so, he was going to regret it. Ragnar stalked closer, bolter held lightly in his hand. He could hear the man's companions recede and as he came closer he could smell sweat and stale bac-stick fumes. He could hear the man's gasping breath. He was obviously tired and resting. He did not seem to be in such good condition as his fellow zealots, perhaps because of the drug he smoked.

Ragnar walked right up to him from behind, looped a hand over the man's mouth and placed the muzzle of his bolter against the man's spine. The man began to sputter and gasp and Ragnar realised that he had swallowed the bac-stick. Doubtless the flame was burning his tongue. It could not be helped.

Lifting the man effortlessly, hand clamped over his mouth, Ragnar turned and loped back in the direction of their shelter.

By the time they had arrived, the man's face had turned an interesting shade of purple. He had given up trying to free his sidearm from its holster.

'What have we here?' said Haegr as he entered. 'A new toy?'

Ragnar let the man go. He opened his mouth to shout and Haegr buffeted him to his knees with what for him was a gentle love-tap. 'I don't like zealots,' said Haegr. 'I think I am going to pull this one's arms off.'

He was very convincing. Even Ragnar wondered whether he meant it. Perhaps he did. He advanced on the man and jerked him to his feet as if he were a puppet. He held an arm in each massive fist. The zealot tried to scream but nothing came out. His face looked even paler. It was framed by long dark hair.

'What's your name?'

'Crawl back to your hellworld, offworld scum,' said the man. Haegr imprisoned the man's wrists in one hand and casually buffeted him with the other. 'Talk or I'll rip your nadgers off and eat them,' he said. He radiated uncompromising malice as he said it.

'Antoninus.' There was defiance in the man's voice, but it had a brittle quality. The man was very afraid although he was trying to hide it.

'How many of you are waiting at the access conduit?' Ragnar asked.

'Go to hell, mutant lover,' said the zealot. His voice was hoarse and rasping. Eating that burning bac-stick must have hurt. There was an odd grinding sound as Haegr closed his grip and the man screamed. It sounded like bones were about to break in the man's wrists.

'How many?' said Ragnar.

'Twenty,' said the man. His scent said he was lying.

'I smell a lie,' said Haegr sounding like an evil giant from old legend. The grinding continued. The man gasped in pain. 'Fifty.' It was obvious he had reached his threshold of tolerance. Ragnar was glad. He did not enjoy torture, no matter how much the Imperium claimed some people deserved it.

'Heavy weapons?' Ragnar asked.

'Yes – covering the main approaches. Heavy bolters.'

Ragnar looked at the man. That was military hardware. He did not know why it should gall him that these zealots have access to it here on Terra but it did. It niggled at him for a moment, and then he realised why. Unless they had their own armaments manufactories they had to be getting them from somewhere. Somewhere off planet most likely. Mars was the nearest forge world, but he could not see the Adeptus Mechanicus engaging in arms smuggling within the Holy System – although stranger things had been known to happen. More likely the weapons were being brought in from somewhere further. He wondered what he would find if he searched some of the Navigator's bonded warehouses. He doubted he would ever get permission to do so, but he might attempt to find out on his own.

All these thoughts flashed through his mind in an instant and he kept his full attention on the zealot. He needed to know more. 'Who is your commander?'

'Edrik – he… he reports direct to Pantheus.'

'The merchant!' said Haegr. It seemed the fat man had been high up within the hierarchy. Perhaps this had not been such a bad lead after all.

'You have heard of him?'

'Who has not? He is rich as Mithras and twice as pious. Always giving money to good causes.'

'And one of those is your Brotherhood?' Ragnar felt like they had stumbled over something very important, if only he could get to the bottom of it.

'It sounds like he is giving more than money,' said Haegr.

'Are you sure this is true?' Ragnar demanded. The man nodded. He certainly believed it to be so. Ragnar could tell from his scent. 'How can you be so certain?'

'Edrik was at his mansion. He has also been to his palace in the belt.'

'The asteroid belt?'

'He's so fat he prefers to live in low gravity,' said the prisoner. There was a note of contempt in his voice and it shone in his wild, wide eyes. 'He likes the world to think he's holy, but he has many secret vices.'

'Not unlike yourself,' said Ragnar, indicating the man's bac-sticks. If the man saw Ragnar's point he gave no sign. The certainty of the fanatic was starting to seep back into him, the longer they let him live.

'I quite like the sound of him,' said Haegr, not letting on that Pantheus had been captured. 'Certainly more than I like the sound of you.' Antoninus's certainty was shattered by another twist of his wrist. There was more than physical pain involved here. Haegr's strength was so overwhelming that it increased his sense of helplessness and eroded his confidence. Haegr gently bashed his head off the wall a couple of times, just to make sure he got the point.

'What is your connection with House Ferracci?' Ragnar asked on the off chance that the question might dislodge a tasty nugget of information. The expression of contempt on the man's face returned, hardened, and intensified a thousand fold. 'I have no connection with those mutant bastards,' he said. 'The sooner the sacred soil of Terra is cleansed of their worthless Chaos-be-damned lives the better… And yours too,' he added as after thought. 'Only the pure blood of humanity should set foot on the sacred soil.'

There was certainty and fervour here that went bone deep. 'Why do you work for a mutant then?' he asked. The man glanced at him as if he were mad. If Ragnar had spoken Fenrisian to him, he could not have received a more blank look of incomprehension.

'Your prophet was a psyker. We killed him.'

'The prophet was blessed by the light, granted his powers by the Emperor himself so that he might continue the Emperor's work. He will rise again! Or another will rise to lead us.'

'If there are more like him then the Inquisition will be down here to scoop out your warrens like a fishwife gutting a sea bass.'

'The Inquisition blessed his work.'

Ragnar somehow doubted this, but the man seemed certain. Ragnar wondered whether the Inquisition hated the Navigators so much that they would sponsor acts of terrorism and assassination against them?

He shook his head. His mistake was thinking in terms of organisations. Organisations had rules, guidelines, principles. They did not think or feel. Only people did that. All it would take would be one man high up in the Inquisition. It would not be the Inquisition itself. He filed the thought. They were sailing in waters that were deep and murky indeed.

'This is taking too long,' said Haegr. 'His comrades will be coming back this way soon. Who knows, they might even have missed him. I say we kill him and be done.'

Ragnar shook his head. This man might have more useful information. Ragnar wanted him alive so that the Belisarians might pick his brains. Doubtless they would be better at it than he and Haegr could ever be. Antoninus lifted his head and spat at Haegr. 'Do your worst. I am not afraid to die.'

Haegr laughed. 'On second thoughts, let him live so that I can cut the blood eagle in his back. I don't think I will even cut it, I might just break his ribs and pull his lungs out with my bare hands.'

Antoninus's glance shifted to Haegr's gauntlets. Both of them knew that it was no idle threat. The huge Space Marine was capable of doing exactly as he said. At that moment Haegr lifted his head and seemed to strain to hear something.

'I think his comrades are coming back now.'

Ragnar was once again astonished by the keenness of his senses. Only now could he make out the faint distant sounds.

'We must away!' he said.

CHAPTER TWENTY

ANTONINUS SMIRKED IN triumph. Haegr caught him and said, 'You will not live to greet your friends. You might say hello to them in hell though.'

'I am not afraid to die!' said the zealot.

'That's twice you've said that,' said Haegr. 'Third time is the charm. Just remember, not all deaths are easy.'

Antoninus paused for thought. Ragnar put the muzzle of his pistol to his head. 'You can make your choice now. You can come with us or we can decorate this wall with your brain.'

It was one thing to say you feared nothing when surrounded by friends, it was another when staring at your enemies. It was one thing to defy your enemy and tell yourself you were not scared, it was another to actually make the decision whether to live or die. When the moment of crisis came most people could find reasons why they wanted to live. This was not a heroic death in battle or a glamorous martyr's doom on the flames. This was an anonymous execution. It served no purpose. And Ragnar had sensed the brittle nature of Antoninus's courage.

Antoninus swallowed. Ragnar could almost see thoughts swimming across his face. If he lived he might help his companions to bring the Wolves down. If he lived he would be able to smoke another bac-stick, and see his family if he had one. Abruptly the bravado leaked out of the man, like wine from a pricked skin. He deflated visibly. The glow remained in his eyes but they had taken on a more furtive look.

There was an almost guilty expression on his face which mixed with
hatred when he looked at Ragnar. This was not a man who would
thank him for making him reveal the brittle truth about himself or
being there to witness it. Ragnar felt a moment of sympathy for him,
even though they were enemies pure and simple. And he felt shame
that was the mirror image of Antoninus's self-hate. This did not fit his
heroic self-image as a Space Wolf either. He forced a snarling grin onto
his lips. He would live with it.

'Shouldn't we gag him?' Linus asked.

'I could rip out his tongue,' offered Haegr hopefully.

'Gag him and bind his hands,' said Ragnar to Linus. 'Use his shirt.'

He turned to Antoninus. 'Make any sudden moves, or attempt to
betray us and I will give you to Haegr.' He could tell from the man's
scent, there would be no treachery, at least for the moment.

'What now?' Haegr asked. Ragnar considered their options. The men
could not wait by the access conduit forever. Or could they? He cursed
the lack of comm-net relays stations down here, and the shielding the
layers of buildings provided. Then it dawned on him. 'You must have
ways of communicating with the surface?' he said to Antoninus.

'Of course,' he said looking at Ragnar as if he were an idiot. 'There are
emergency comm-net relay flexors that go all the way up, they patch
into the surface grids.'

'Where is the nearest access point?'

'Anaconda Station. It's a sleep away from here. Up a level.'

'Guarded?'

'Of course. It's in our main shrine.'

'I suppose you're going to say storming it is out of the question,' said
Haegr in the petulant tone of a child who knows his parents are going
to deny him a treat.

Linus cleared his throat. 'There was a flexor in Imperial sprocket
works number six,' he said. 'Before it was destroyed.'

'We don't have time to clear away the rubble right now.'

'There was an emergency node five hundred metres away. It patches
into the grid as well.'

'How far?'

'The next level up.'

'Why didn't you say?'

'You never asked.' Ragnar suppressed his frustration. Linus was right.
Haegr was not so understanding.

'Anything else you forgot to mention? You didn't also happen to have
an emergency escape elevator all the way to the surface, or an aircar, or
a division of Imperial Guard based there or...'

'Of course not.' Linus's tone showed how absurd he considered the suggestions. He apparently did not see the joke.

'The flexor is still functioning then.'

'It ought to be. It has worked for the last ten millennia. I don't see why it should decide to stop now.'

'If we can patch into that we can contact the surface and get some support.'

'Then let us be on our way,' said Haegr.

Ragnar nodded. He led them back out into the street. 'Lead on, Linus,' he said.

The little man glanced nervously down the street to where he thought the zealots must be. Lacking the Space Wolves' keen senses he obviously thought them a lot closer than they were. He then risked a glance at Antoninus, obviously fearing the man would give away their position. He need not have worried. The zealot was still gagged, and Haegr had one hand over the man's mouth for good measure. They headed off in the direction that Linus indicated.

'What will your friends do now?' Ragnar asked Antoninus, removing the gag. It looked for a moment like the zealot was not going to answer. Haegr growled.

'Since they have not found you yet they will split up into search parties and scour the area. They will probably request back-up from our temple. You will not be allowed to escape alive.' Antoninus could not keep the satisfaction out of his voice.

Ragnar considered their surroundings. The further they moved from the main warrens, the more run down they looked and the lower the ceilings became. More vile animals surrounded them. And yet, according to Linus, they were getting closer to his former place of work.

It was hard to imagine humans living and working in these rat holes, but according to the little scribe hundreds had. Most had moved away from the cell-like dwellings when their employment failed, although a few still haunted the rubble, eking out a pitiful existence. According to Linus they knew nothing else. They had spent their whole lives in the area, and could not conceive of moving away.

Ragnar revised his opinion of the little man. He had thought him drab and unadventurous but he could see now that by the standards of his upbringing Linus had been more dynamic than many. He had at least moved away from the area, and now he was considering moving further still. Once again Ragnar was considering the sin of relativity. Antoninus glanced around him with disdain. The people around here were low on the social scale as far as he was concerned. That much was obvious.

He realised that they had come up at least one level of the warrens in their travels. The stairwell had been long and rusting in many places. Massive spider webs had blocked it, and those must have been recently woven because Linus claimed traders and travellers still occasionally used these paths. The thought of such huge creatures did nothing for Ragnar's peace of mind, although in his heart of hearts he did not truly fear them.

As they turned another corner Ragnar noticed that Haegr was grinning. A moment later he caught a familiar scent. He could not quite believe it. It was the smell of a Wolf. 'I believe Torin is looking for us,' said Haegr. 'We will be surprising him soon.'

'Your appetite constantly surprises me,' said a soft mocking voice from the shadows. Ragnar was surprised. The scent trail was quite old and this meant that Torin must have circled round and caught them from downwind. Ragnar wondered how deliberate that was. He doubted the Wolfblade would ever tell. 'I knew you would blunder up here sooner or later.'

They were on the same level which meant that over relatively short ranges their comm-links should work. 'Why did you not try to contact us?' Ragnar asked.

'Same reason as you don't have your beacons on. Security. If the mission has been compromised who knows whether the Belisarius channels or any others are safe? The relays may be monitored and short range pulse traffic can be picked up by people with the right divinatory apparatus.' Ragnar knew his comrade was right.

'Glad to see you're still alive.' said Torin. 'I thought Haegr had gobbled down his last ox, judging from the wounds I saw.'

'Hah! It will take more than a few scratches to impede Haegr's mighty form.'

'What happened to your escort of Belisarians?' Haegr asked.

'Ambushed. I fought my way clear with half a dozen of them, and ordered them to head to the surface while I looked for you. I knew you would need help since you had to look after Haegr.'

'Mighty Haegr needs no help from cubs.'

Suddenly they were all talking at once.

'Who are your friends?'

'How did you find us?'

'Easy, I followed the trail of empty food silos and knew Haegr would be there.'

'Linus here is our friend. Antoninus is a prisoner. He has information that we may find useful.'

'There has been no time to empty silos. Chance would be a fine thing.'

'Where were you headed?'

'An emergency relay station for the Imperial sprocket autofac. We were going to contact the surface on the emergency channel.'

'Smart thinking. I am sure Haegr had no part in that.'

'A beating, Torin. Within an inch of your life...'

Ragnar was glad that their companion had been found or had found them. Torin had been searching high and low for them, stalking zealot patrols looking for clues to their whereabouts. Of course, he could not track all of them but he had learned a few things.

The zealots were far stronger down here than anyone had supposed, but they were thrashing around headless at the moment without their prophet. It appeared the dead psyker had been their leader, in this sector at least. It also appeared that they extorted food and money out of the local inhabitants in return for protection.

It was an enterprise as old as life on Terra according to Torin.

'The surprising thing is how strong the Brotherhood is down here. I suspect some sort of military build-up. I fear we could be looking at rebellion and open warfare on the surface soon.'

That did not surprise Ragnar. It followed a pattern he had seen many times before. 'We need to assemble the guards and clear this place.'

'I fear it will take more than the might of Belisarius to do that,' said Torin. 'The fanatics are numerous and well armed. We may need to forge new alliances to deal with this and soon.'

'It's just as well we found this out then,' said Ragnar.

As they talked, they followed Linus, and prodded the zealot at gunpoint. Torin and Haegr bickered cheerfully. The presence of his old sparring partner seemed to have worked wonders for Haegr's health. The ceiling became lower; the smell of dust and crumbling brickwork filled the air. There were more rats and more large spiders. Linus nodded and said they were close now.

A few moments later they turned the corner and found themselves face to face with a duralloy panel in the wall, covered in warning runes and messages in the local alphabet.

'This is it,' said Linus. 'Although I am not sure how we are going to open it without the key.'

Haegr ripped it open with one hand.

'That's against the rules,' said Linus.

'I am sure the Arbites will be along any moment to arrest me,' said Haegr.

Torin studied the ancient engine of brass cables and ceramite panels. He reached forward to tap the runes. He was making a few adjustments to the settings to the tune of the basic engineering litanies. He ran a few test protocols on the link and moments later, was sending pulsed communications to the surface. Apparently he got a response. He had sealed the circuit so that not even Ragnar and Haegr could hear what was being said.

'A pick up team will be with us within hours,' said Torin, looking satisfied. 'And then we will be out of here.'

'Not before time,' said Haegr. 'We should have been gone a day ago.'

'Better late than never,' said Torin. He glanced at Antoninus. 'Now, what about telling us a few of your secrets?'

RAGNAR STUDIED HIS chronometer. The pick up team was running late. It had been three hours now and there was no sign of them. He looked at Torin who simply shrugged. 'Maybe they ran into some unexpected problems,' he said. 'They will be here. Valkoth himself is leading them.'

'That reassures me' said Haegr. 'If he sent out some of those fancy dressed Belisarian clowns on their own, they might have got lost.'

'Not everyone has your unerring sense of direction,' said Torin. 'Although I seem to recall even you have made a few errors in your time. There was that incident with the orks on Hera V.'

'I knew you would bring that up,' said Haegr. 'A man can be right a thousand times, as heroic Haegr usually is, but let him make one little mistake and...'

'Leading us into the ork boss's camp instead of the Imperial Palace was not a little mistake,' said Torin.

'I didn't notice you opening your mouth to tell me I was wrong,' said Haegr.

'I was unconscious at the time after you managed to accidentally connect with that flailing hammer of yours.'

'You always bring that up as well. One little accident and...'

'It is hard to forget such accidents when your skull is involved in them.'

At first Ragnar thought he was ignoring the remark, but then he noticed the giant was listening. So did Torin, for a cutting remark died unspoken on his lips.

'That's not Valkoth,' said Haegr. A few heartbeats later, Ragnar realised what he was talking about. He could hear stealthy sounds approaching, and could make out the faint but distinctive odour of men. The scent was a compound of meat, incense, bac-stick smoke and a dozen other things. It was not the smell of Valkoth or of any Belisarian.

'They found us again,' said Haegr. He did not sound disappointed. 'It seems an unlikely coincidence,' he murmured.

Ragnar wondered if they had been betrayed again. 'Perhaps the signal was traced,' he said.

'Perhaps,' said Torin.

Antoninus had started to grin again. Ragnar was filled with a desire to wipe the smirk off his face. Torin clearly felt the same way.

'We could set a trap. Knock their friend here unconscious and rig his body up with explosives. They could all become martyrs to their holy cause together.'

Antoninus's smile turned sickly. Linus looked shocked. 'You would not really do that, would you?' he asked.

Torin shrugged. Haegr said, 'Hardly seems worth the effort. I say we just go and kill them.'

'Showing off your tactical genius again, I see,' said Torin. 'Let's at least try and find out how many of them there are and what corridors they have covered.'

'And spoil all the fun!'

'You're right. What was I thinking? Oh yes, I remember – my duty to return and protect House Belisarius and uncover the traitor who set us up.'

'Well, when you put it that way...'

A glyph blinked in Ragnar's vision. A faint chime sounded in his comm-link earbead. A moment later Valkoth's voice spoke. 'We are on the same level as you now and picking up your signal. These corridors are a maze, so it may take some time to get to you.'

'It looks like the enemy found us first,' said Torin. 'Just head for the sounds of carnage.'

'We ran into some Brotherhood boys which is why we were not there sooner,' said Valkoth. 'Just hold them off until we get there. Praise Russ.'

Torin laughed as the link dropped. 'It's nice that the old man has faith in us. I like the way he casually informs us to hold out until he gets here.'

'He knows mighty Haegr's bravery,' said Haegr. 'He knows I will keep you alive until he gets here, with a little help from Ragnar of course.'

'Well, I suppose I could always use your great bloated mass of blubber as a shield. Better than sandbags.'

'I fear I am going to have to beat you again, Torin.'

'Later,' said Ragnar, as he noticed shadowy figures appearing in the distance. Antoninus followed the direction of his gaze, but he could obviously see nothing. He looked as if he was considering running

for it. Haegr flattened him with a blow of his ham-like fist. 'It would
be a shame if he got away now that we have brought him all this
way.'

He lifted the recumbent body and tossed it through a doorway
one handed. 'We can always come back and collect him later. You'd
better join him, little man. Things might get hot out here. Just
make sure he does not get away.' The last was a bit of needless cruelty, Ragnar thought. Linus looked and smelled nervous enough to
faint.

'Best get moving,' said Torin. Linus scuttled under cover leaving the
three Wolves ready to face their onrushing foes. There appeared to be a
fair number of the enemy coming in along all the approach corridors.
No doubt there were more making their way from chamber to chamber. He raised his bolt pistol and snapped off a few shots into the
distance. The shells could not miss the tightly packed bodies. He was
rewarded with a scream.

'Spearing blowfish in a barrel,' said Haegr, leaning on the shaft of his
hammer and meditating on the targets. The metal pole puffed his fat
cheeks out even more. 'I could have hit that man with my hammer
from here.'

Ragnar looked at him in astonishment. 'You doubt my word? The
word of mighty Haegr?'

Casually, he threw the hammer down the corridor. It carried a long
way, and Ragnar could smell blood and hear bones crack. 'I suppose I
shall have to go and get it back now,' said Haegr and lumbered off into
the distance before Ragnar could say anything. Ragnar exchanged
glances with Torin. 'He is a law unto himself,' said Torin. 'But don't
worry about him, somehow he always survives.'

Ragnar heard grenades going off. He could see the huge bulk of
Haegr limned in the flare of their detonations. His wild laughter
echoed down the corridor. He was obviously the one throwing them,
and it sounded like he was enjoying himself.

'Perhaps we should go and help him,' said Ragnai.

'No, he would only object to us spoiling his fun. Besides, someone
has to stay here and make sure no one gets behind us.' The two Wolves
had instinctively moved to cover separate lines of approach. More of
the zealots were coming both ways. Others were moving chamber to
chamber.

Ragnar crouched in a doorway to make himself a smaller target
and snapped off another shot. This time the response was a hail of
bolter and lasrifle fire. He doubted that any of his assailants could

see him. They were just firing at random, but that would make no difference if one of those shells was to connect with a vulnerable point in his armour.

How long would it take Valkoth to arrive?

CHAPTER TWENTY-ONE

THE CULTISTS KEPT coming on down the corridor and edging closer through the chambers. The bellowing of Haegr told Ragnar that the huge Space Marine had engaged the enemy. The cracking of skulls and splintering of bone indicated that he had regained his hammer. Bolter shells and autogun bullets chipped the plascrete around Ragnar while las-beams made it bubble and stink like hot asphalt. He considered ducking through the doorway, but it was a single chamber with no visible way out: a death trap if he were caught in it, and if the enemy had grenades or any reasonably heavy weapon. Of course, he could pick many of them off, but being pinned down was generally a recipe for disaster.

'I hate to say this, Torin, but maybe Haegr had the right idea!' said Ragnar.

'I am starting to think so myself,' bellowed Torin over the din of battle. 'Cover me!'

'I will do my best,' said Ragnar, ducking down and snapping off shots, first in one direction and then the other. As he did this Torin dived across the street and through another opening, oblivious to the hail of fire at his heels. A moment later, a hand emerged from the doorway that sent a grenade bouncing up the corridor towards their attackers. The screams told Ragnar that he had caught somebody.

It was Ragnar's turn now. Crouching low, he bounded into the corridor and moved upwards towards the attackers. Billowing smoke obscured him from sight and the hail of fire seemed to have lessened.

Ragnar felt confident that he could more than hold his own against their assailants. Once he was in their midst they would be unable to shoot at him without risking their fellows. All he would have to worry about was saving his own armoured hide. It appalled him to think that Haegr probably had done the right thing. But of course, the big man was an experienced tunnel fighter, so it was no great surprise.

Ragnar could hear the enemy babbling up ahead. A wounded man cursed and screamed alternately while his fellows told him to shut up. A commanding voice bellowed instructions. Ragnar lobbed a grenade in their direction, and the orders ceased, to be replaced by more screams and howls.

Ragnar drew his chainsword as he emerged from the smoke, and found himself face to face once again with the cowled members of the Brotherhood. He did not wait for them to recognise their peril. He leapt among them, striking right and left, slaying as he went. He showed the wounded no mercy, stamping on them as he passed, crushing hands, heads and ribs under his armoured boots. He had seen many wounded men pick up their weapons to kill again and he was not going to take any chances here.

The sheer fury of his sudden onslaught panicked the zealots. They did not know they were facing only one man. All they knew was that some furious daemon had emerged from the smoke of battle and was killing them. Ragnar passed through them like a whirlwind. Nothing withstood him. The chainsword cleaved through the barrels of lasrifles raised in hasty parries. It sent sparks scattering and made the screams of tortured metal mingle with the last wails of the dying.

He did not let up when his foes started to flee. He pursued them, despite being outnumbered scores to one. When his prey ran into their comrades from behind, he realised that he only faced the advance guard of his enemies. But that did not slow him down. As the cultists barged into each other, and tripped one another up, he followed, hacking with his chainsword, blasting with bolter shells at point-blank range, letting the wild ululating war cry of his Chapter reverberate down the corridor.

Bones broke, blood, meat and gristle got caught between the swiftly whirring blade of his chainsword. As the friction heated them, they sent up an awful stench. He kept chopping, severing limbs, opening the top of one man's skull with one blow. Once more he heard someone bellowing, telling the zealots to stand firm in the name of the Light. It said that they would prevail. He aimed himself towards the voice, knowing that if he slew the leader, he could create more panic and disarray.

One or two men tried to make a stand now. One of them had raised his autorifle to his shoulder and was aiming at point-blank range at Ragnar. The Space Wolf sprang to one side, as the autofire ripped past him. He brought up his own bolt pistol and slew the shooter with a single shot, silencing his weapon forever.

Someone tugged at his legs and he felt something sting the back of his knee. Looking down he saw that a wounded man had caught the weak joint at the back of his kneeguard with a combat knife. Instinct told Ragnar that the wound was neither serious nor likely to slow him down, but it was a warning to him to be more careful. He lashed out with his boot. The impact threw the wounded man's head backwards and his neck snapped. Ragnar could hear the crunch of vertebrae, but it seemed that he was losing the initiative now.

More and more fire impacted on his armour, the force of the bullets were like hammer blows. Something glanced off Ragnar's skull, drawing blood and sending waves of pain and blackness surging through his head. Perhaps he had been overconfident, he thought. There were too many of his foes for even a Space Wolf to overcome. As he reeled backwards, they continued to rally, raising weapons, drawing blades, making ready to carve him up and chop him down. Ragnar sprang back pulling the trigger of his bolt pistol repeatedly. He sent shells tearing through closely packed flesh. He howled as he fought. He was rewarded with a familiar war-cry echo close by.

Over the scent of blood and opened innards he caught the familiar smell of Fenrisian flesh and hardened ceramite. Valkoth's rescue party must be close. He need only hold on for a little longer.

He snarled defiance. He was not going to hold on, he was going to kill and kill again, dragging as many of his foes to hell as he could – like a true Fenrisian warrior. The beast within him was filled with killing lust, while the saner part of his mind turned it to his advantage. He knew that if he pressed on through his attackers he would link up with Valkoth and his force.

Guided partly by feral instinct and partly by cold calculation, he struck out again. Gathering all his strength he sprang forward, lashing left and right with his chainsword, taking off heads and limbs with every blow, leaving men to slip and fall on their own spilling intestines.

The fury of his renewed onslaught took his opponents off guard for a moment, and he hewed a bloody path through them in the direction of the oncoming Belisarians. But it did not take the fanatics long to regain their wits. Whatever their faults, a lack of desperate courage was not one of them. Some of the wounded grasped at his legs, trying to slow him. Others aimed their weapons. A wave of them threw themselves forward, trying to grapple with Ragnar, and to immobilise his arms and legs. It was a mistake; no two men were as strong as he. He threw them off, sending them flying through the air to smash into walls or into other zealots. He dashed out the brains of others with the butt of his bolt pistol. Trying to restrain his sword arm was like trying to grab the jaws of a hungry tiger.

Still they came on, and still their comrades fired. They did not care that their bullets thudded into the bodies of their fellows more often than smashing into Ragnar's armour. All were overcome by the madness and the chaos of battle. He realised that none of them had as clear a picture of what was going on as he did. The gloom and smoke confused them, as did the loud echo of their weapons. All they could see was a huge shadowy figure moving among them with almost supernatural speed. Even when they did not panic there was a natural urge to shoot, to do something – anything in the face of the threat.

Ragnar lashed out with his boot at the head of one man who was lying on his belly and shooting upward at him with a pistol. His foot connected with sickening force, sending teeth and splintered bone flying. A moment later he was through to Valkoth who was leading a line of black-garbed Belisarian guards towards him. Knowing what would come next Ragnar turned and faced the zealots. A moment later Valkoth and his men were at his side, and the fighting became close and deadly.

'By Russ, Ragnar, you might have left some for us,' said Valkoth. His gloomy aura seemed to deepen in the midst of battle. He moved his head fractionally and a lasbeam hissed by. He raised his bolter easily and fired back at his assailant. Only one shot, but it was enough. There was a precision about Valkoth's way of fighting that was very odd in a Space Wolf, but he was none-the-less deadly for it.

'I think there are a few,' said Ragnar, ducking the stab of a bayonet, then carving through weapon barrel and then man with his riposte.

'Glad to hear it,' said Valkoth, sending another man to hell with a single shot of his bolter, then laying open the forehead of an assailant closing with him with its barrel. Even as the man fell Valkoth pumped a shell into him and moved on.

They headed down the corridor towards Torin, who was holding off more zealots from behind a barrier built of corpses.

Ragnar wondered whether he really could have killed all those men on his own and then driven the others back. But when he thought of the number he had killed, he realised that it was more than possible.

'The situation here is under control. I think you should go and see what Haegr is up to,' Torin said. 'He's probably got his foot caught in a bucket.'

Even as he spoke, Valkoth was issuing a clipped order to the Belisarian guard who moved off in the direction of Torin's attackers.

'Let us all go together,' said Valkoth, leading them in the direction Haegr had taken. Within a hundred metres they found the first mauled bodies, and heard the receding sounds of slaughter. Somewhere further off they heard Haegr bellow: 'Come back and fight like men!'

'Doubtless he thinks that if he shouts loud enough they will obey him,' said Torin sardonically.

'No sign of any bucket,' said Valkoth.

'It's only a matter of time,' said Torin. 'You know that as well as I do. Well, we'd best get to him before he falls down a lift shaft trying to persuade those zealots to come back and be slaughtered.'

They advanced through scenes of awful carnage. Bruised and mangled corpses lay everywhere, their heads oddly indented or turned to jelly, broken ribs protruding through flesh. Ragnar had seen bodies run over by Land Raiders in better condition.

'I am surprised he did not stop for a snack,' said Torin, and catching the disgusted glances of his two companions, he raised an eyebrow. 'Well, he probably hasn't eaten more than a small killer whale in the past few hours.'

Ahead of them loomed the man himself. Gore covered him. Spatters of blood and brain and less recognisable substances decorated his armour and the head of his hammer. He looked around at them and said, 'You did not miss anything here. These worms were barely worth killing.'

'Your mission took a little longer than you expected,' said Valkoth sourly.

'That's the way these things go sometimes,' said Haegr, entirely unabashed. 'No plan survives contact with the enemy, as I have heard you say yourself.'

'Those are an ancient philosopher's words, not mine.'

'Well they are the first sensible words I have ever heard from any philosopher.'

'This is a first,' said Torin sardonically. 'Standing in the ruins under Earth discussing philosophy with Haegr. Whatever next?'

'We were not discussing philosophy,' said Haegr. His outraged tone made it sound as if Torin had accused him of molesting a sheep.

'Don't let me interrupt your intellectual debate,' said Torin wickedly.

Haegr lapsed into sulky silence, folded his huge arms across his chest, and snorted audibly. Valkoth looked at Torin. 'We should be going now,' he said. 'After all, I have rescued you and you have duties in the world above.'

'Rescued us!' said Torin and Haegr near simultaneously.

'The situation was under control,' said Torin.

'Mighty Haegr would have battled his way to the surface, carrying his two weak-stomached companions if need be,' said Haegr. Ragnar noticed that Valkoth's long drooping moustaches were oddly twisted around his mouth. Is he mocking us, Ragnar wondered? Was there a sense of humour at work there?

'We'd best fetch our prisoner and our guide,' said Ragnar.

'A guide?' said Valkoth. He sounded disbelieving.

'He has been of assistance,' said Ragnar innocently. 'And I believe he should be rewarded appropriately.'

RAGNAR GLANCED AROUND his chamber, glad to be back on the surface, all too aware of the comforts of the place, and the security. He lay down on the bed and stared at the ornately carved ceiling. No, that was wrong. There was no security on Earth. It was an illusion. There were traitors everywhere, even here, and soon they would need to smoke them out. There was no place in the Imperium that was truly secure, not as the ancients might have once understood the word. This was a place of intrigue and danger, of fanatics filled with burning religious hatred and self-righteous anger.

He smiled to himself. He had heard the Wolves described in those terms, and he knew that some Chapters and organisations prided themselves on zealotry and a fanatical devotion to their duty. Was there really so much difference between the Inquisition and the Brotherhood, Ragnar wondered? There was a great deal of similarity between them. Both were pledged to defend mankind from the mutant. Both were staffed by dedicated fanatics. Why single out the Inquisition, he thought? His own Chapter was as guilty of these things as the Brotherhood. Ah, but then his own Chapter was in the right. Ragnar could almost have laughed. Of course, that was what he had been taught, and that was what he believed, and in this he was no different from Antoninus.

He lay on the bed for a long time wrestling with the sin of relativity.

CHAPTER TWENTY-TWO

Two days later, Ragnar stalked through the halls of the Belisarius Palace. Outside it was night, but inside business went on. Over one of the doors was a sign that read 'commerce never sleeps,' and the men sitting in the booths, bidding and contracting in hand sign and pidgin Gothic proved that fact. He had no idea what they might be contracting for. It could be anything from the futures in Necromundan industrial production to the shipping of a million sides of grox from the steppes of Thunder Plain.

He suspected it would not matter to these men who gathered under the shadows of the Navigators either. Their business was business. They traded where they could find a profit. The Navigators got a cut for shipping it, and possibly financing it. He had been in the palace long enough now to know that the Houses bankrolled an enormous amount of trade even though they were supposedly above such things. There were fronts over fronts over fronts. The middlemen had middlemen. It was not as it was supposed to be, but Ragnar supposed sourly that this applied to a lot of things on Terra.

He saw Linus Serpico sitting at the side of one booth frantically making notes on vellum. He looked both tired and happy, as if his only purpose in life was writing things down.

As Ragnar approached, the negotiation came to an end and both richly garbed merchants rose and shook hands before affixing their seals to the document Linus had prepared. Linus stifled a yawn, bowed to them both and flitted over to Ragnar.

Ragnar smiled at him and he smiled back happily. The Belisarians had given him work and that seemed all he required. Then a troubled look flickered over his brow. A strange edge entered his scent too. 'Excuse me, master Ragnar, but I have heard the most disturbing rumours.'

Ragnar looked at him and waited for him to say more. He was not surprised. Linus had a quick mind, and good ears, and few people seemed to pay him much notice. It was for this reason that Ragnar suspected he heard everything. 'Rumours?' he prompted.

'They say there have been riots against the Navigator Houses, and that men are massing to sweep them from the face of the planet. I mean no offence, I merely repeat what I hear.'

'I take no offence, Linus,' said Ragnar, 'but where did you hear such things?'

'The merchants talk about it. They say such things are bad for business, and the Inquisition should do something about it.'

That would suit the Inquisition, Ragnar thought. They would love to get a foothold in the navigators quarter and all they needed was a reason. If the House troops could not quell the protests and riots, the Inquisition surely would, by whatever means necessary. Disturbances to the peace of Holy Terra would only be tolerated so far. It was worrying. Ragnar himself had been involved in the suppression of several minor riots. He had been called out along with the rest of the guard to keep the peace. The mere sight of him had been enough to send many of the protesters running for their lives, which had surely been Valkoth's intention.

Still, the memory disturbed him. He had not seen so much unreasoned hatred and fear for a long time. In addition, there was something about an agitated crowd he did not like at all. Its behaviour reminded him of a Space Wolf pack, but without the guiding intelligence, or the ability to think independently when called on to do so. The people had been armed with makeshift weapons, burning and looting the stores of those they thought did business with the Navigators. In truth Ragnar suspected it had been more of an excuse for looting than anything else. They had come nowhere near the palaces, and he doubted the shopkeepers had anything more or less to do with the Navigators than anyone else in the quarter.

'These are troubled times, sir,' said Linus.

'Indeed,' said Ragnar. The little man looked up at him nervously and licked his lips.

'Is it true that the Navigator throne is vacant?' he asked.

By the Emperor, news travels fast, thought Ragnar. The Celestarch herself had only had word of old Gorki's death an hour ago. Now it was the talk of the bazaar. He did not know why he was surprised. Fortunes could be won or lost on such information. Right now factions were manoeuvring to get their representative on the throne before it was barely cold. The status and power of entire Houses would be decided. People would try and back the winner.

'As far as I know that is correct,' said Ragnar.

Linus nodded as if this confirmed what he already knew. 'There will be trouble,' he said.

Ragnar did not ask him what drove him to that conclusion. When mastodons fight, grass gets trampled. Political awareness was a basic survival skill for people around here.

Linus fell into step beside him as they made their way through the halls. He smelled tired and hungry and doubtless was returning to his cell. Ragnar was strangely glad of his presence, because he was feeling uneasy. Something did not feel right. Perhaps it was his encounter with the howling fury of the mob earlier that day, but he doubted it. Such things had never made him uneasy and restless in the past. He felt as he often did when he was hiking through the frozen peaks of Fenris. The first signs of an avalanche were often not striking. They were small meaningless things. A slight vibration underfoot, a creak of ice in the distance, an odd tone carried on the wind. He felt he was hearing such things now.

The riots, the rise of the Brotherhood, the mazy intrigues of the House surrounding him were all small signs but they hinted at a large threat. Events were occurring somewhere that boded no good for House Belisarius and his battle-brothers, he was certain. They walked a deadly path during a thaw, he thought. None of the bustling commerce that surrounded him could make him feel differently.

They left the halls of commerce behind them, passing the guards who stood vigil at the entrance to the private quarters. Ragnar returned the fist to chest salute of the House warriors and strode through. Linus made his way towards the elevators that led down to the cramped chambers of the servants' levels.

He touched Linus on the shoulder. 'Come and tell me if you hear anything suspicious, anything at all.'

'That I shall do, master Ragnar,' said the scribe before flitting off down the corridor. Ragnar gave his attention back to his surroundings. He realised that he was checking for cover, and points of ambush. He was treating these hushed, carpeted halls as if they were a battlefield he was going to have to fight on. It was a measure of his worry that he should be thinking this way.

Superficially there was no reason to be nervous; everything seemed to be fine. The guards looked alert. The people coming and going gave no sign of treachery. It was just him, he guessed. He was on edge. Terra had done that to him. That there were traitors here, and they had not been smoked out, might have something to with it too, he thought sourly.

He strode towards his chamber. He needed rest. No need to be so worried yet, he told himself. No need at all.

'You WILL STRIKE tonight,' said Cezare, stroking his upper lip with one thick finger.

Xenothan regarded the head of House Feracci warily. In his heart of hearts he loathed the man. For all his power and pride in his ancient lineage, he was nothing more than a mutant. It was an abomination that his type should sully the sacred soil of Terra. He considered these thoughts with bitter amusement. If this man is a mutant, then what are you, he asked himself? The answer came back at once. Better. And despite all the implants and all the bio-surgery, he was at least human.

'Indeed, Lord Feracci. We will strike tonight. You need have no fears. After this evening you will have far fewer enemies.'

Cezare smirked in a way that irritated Xenothan. He would have liked nothing more than to take one of his most interesting toxins and inject Feracci with it. While the man died he could have regaled him with details of which excruciating agony would strike him next. Xenothan was not naturally a cruel man, but Cezare was a mad dog, and should be treated like one.

'The Brotherhood are in place?' Cezare asked.

'Their troops are ready.'

'Your agents?'

'They know what is happening. They know tonight is the night. The death of Gorki is their signal. The way into the Belisarius Palace will be clear.'

'See that you do not fail,' said Feracci, leaning forward to sniff one of the orchids that floated in a suspensor vase before him.

The arrogance of the man is breathtaking, Xenothan thought. Still, that would be dealt with soon enough. Once the Belisarians had been brought low, his patron would want this posturing buffoon ground into the dirt as well. Let me see, thought Xenothan, what would I use on you? Something slow, and something that would ensure that your pride suffered as well as the rest of you.

Borac would make you vomit, he thought, and you would taste again all those subtle foodstuffs you so love to indulge in on your tongue, although this time they would be laced with your own stomach acid. Childish, Xenothan told himself, and not nearly subtle enough. It would be like using avierel, the victims of which voided their bowels as they died in howling agony. Perhaps something that would make him mewl and beg? Scorse suppressed certain centres of the brain that allowed decision-making, thereby reducing its victims to mindless drones.

No, he thought, that was a drug for pleasure slaves. He shook his head slightly. It was a pretty dilemma.

'You are sure the Wolfblades will give you no problem?' It was almost laughable, Xenothan thought, the way Cezare looked around furtively as he said it. It was as if he thought the accursed Fenrisians could over-hear him. He felt like saying their senses are keen, but not that keen, milord. But he did not. He kept a carefully schooled look of rapt def-erential attention on his face as he said, 'None, milord. If any of them get in my way, they shall die.'

'It's those who get in *their* way who tend to die,' said Cezare, the way he smiled showed it was not entirely a jest.

'With all due respect, milord, none of those others had my talents.'

'Your talents,' said Cezare with soft mockery. 'It's about time you dis-played those highly lauded talents.'

Xenothan let the man's words slide off him. It would not do to let himself be baited, he thought, but he made a small note in the mental file he kept of all those upon whom he would avenge himself. The list of the living in that file was very short, the list of the dead very long. Someday soon, Cezare would make the transition from one side of the ledger to the other. Not today though, Xenothan thought. Today, he had other business. 'I believe you will find the results satisfactory, milord,' was all he allowed himself to say.

'I had better,' said Cezare. 'After all the money I have ploughed into your master's coffers.'

'Your financial arrangements are something best discussed with him,' said Xenothan smoothly. Take up that challenge if you dare, he thought. Not even Cezare Feracci would want to confront a High Lord of the Administratum without much a better reason than that. It was best to remind him that there were some things that even the head of one of the greatest of the Navigator Houses need fear. He saw Cezare pause to consider this. He knew that Xenothan's master could crush him just as easily as he was going to crush the Belisari-ans.

The nice thing about the Navigators was that there was always some House that wanted to do the dirty on its enemies. It was not hard to find allies among the factions, even against their own kin. It was a fact that Cezare was well aware of. Still, he was not going to allow Xenothan to get away with having scored a point.

'How do you propose to deal with the Wolfblades? They seem remarkably adept at avoiding mortal weapons.'

'They are men, like any others, a bit faster, a bit stronger, and a bit more fierce, but believe me there are things in this universe that make even Space Marines seem feeble.'

'And you are one of those, are you?' Cezare made no attempt to hide his mockery.

'I am one, yes,' said Xenothan, with absolute certainty. 'And I have weapons against which they cannot prevail.'

'What would those be?' said Cezare. His face was smooth, but his interest was obvious. Weapons that could prevail against Imperial Space Wolves would be worth a fortune on the open market, and Cezare, for all his pretensions of being an aristocrat and a connoisseur of art, was at heart a merchant. A mutant and a merchant, thought Xenothan with some contempt. It was hardly a happy combination.

'There are certain secrets it is best not to be privy to,' said Xenothan quite truthfully. 'Secrets men have been killed for knowing.'

Cezare nodded, able to take the hint, and yet Xenothan could see the wheels moving behind his eyes. Here was a man who would never rest until he had found out what Xenothan was talking about. Not that it truly mattered. He would be dealt with long before those plans came to fruition.

It would never do for him to know what only very few in the Administratum knew. That within certain dark and almost forgotten departments of the Inquisition, there were small units of scholars and alchemists who had been working on the Adeptus Astartes problem since the time of the Heresy. It was a problem having such powerful, uncontrollable and near invulnerable groups at large within the Imperium, particularly as they were under no man's direct control. These hidden inquisitors had for millennia been working on methods of controlling or even slaying the Space Marines, and their research had borne strange fruit.

Xenothan smiled, thinking of the vial of potent toxin he carried on his person. It acted directly on the gland that the Space Marines used to neutralise poisons, temporarily overloading and confusing it. Ultimately, it turned the gland itself into a weapon against its owner. When the poison entered a Space Marine's system, he would be paralysed for a short time – not enough for an ordinary man to take advantage of – but for someone like Xenothan, a heartbeat would be more than he needed.

Of course, the poison was rare, produced only from the first blossoms of the rare Mercurian Swamp Orchid, and it was very secret. It would never do for enemies of the Imperium to acquire it, or for the Astartes to find out about all of those black research programmes. But it did exist, and Xenothan possessed some. Soon he would use it. He had to confess that he was quite looking forward to it. It had been a long time since he killed a Space Marine. Tonight, he thought, he would kill many.

'You look pleased with yourself,' said Cezare.

Xenothan smiled, although he was inwardly shocked by his lapse. 'I am merely thinking of your impending victory. Tonight, at one stroke, all of your enemies will be removed and the Belisarians will be your puppets.'

'Why do I find it so hard to believe the prospect of my victory makes you so happy?'

'Because it is our victory. Tonight your enemies die. Tonight I get to kill them. Tomorrow you will be *primus inter pares* – first among equals – which we both know means you will be lord of all Navigators.'

'Very well. See to it that nothing goes wrong.'

'Nothing will go wrong from my end. See that your pawn keeps his part of the deal. If he does not, many people will have cause to regret it.' Not the least you, my over-ambitious friend, thought Xenothan. It was gratifying that he did not have to speak the threat aloud for Cezare to grasp it.

RAGNAR COULD NOT sleep. It would not come. Something was not right. He could feel it in the air. The beast within him snarled, and he understood its unease, if not its source. He rose from his bed and strode through the corridors. He passed Haegr's chambers but the big man was not there. Tonight he was on duty.

He took himself off to the library. He wanted to find a book, something that would distract him. He was surprised to meet Gabriella in the corridor. She was garbed in her dress uniform and smiled at him. 'You are up late,' she said. 'Or is it true that Space Wolves never sleep?' She smiled to show him she was joking.

'I could say the same for you.'

'I have been attending the Celestarch. We were all summoned to conclave. With Gorki's death will come a great deal of horse trading as the Houses seek to gain advantage in the negotiations for the throne.'

'You think Misha Feracci will get it?'

'Not if Lady Juliana has any say in the matter.'

'The conclave has ended?'

'The Celestarch has gone to the Vaults to consult with the Elders.'

Once more the mysterious Vaults, Ragnar thought. What is down there?

She fell into step beside him. 'Where are you going?'

'I thought I would visit the fabled library of Belisarius.'

'You have decided to become a scholar now?'

'I am hoping to find a history sufficiently tedious to bore me to sleep.'

'What is it? You look pensive.'

'I had not realised I was so easy to read.'

'You would not be had I not spent ten years in the service of Wolves. Now I can tell a thoughtful frown from an angry one.'

'I do not know. There is something in the air tonight that I do not like.'

'You sound like Valkoth. He was saying the same. He ordered the patrols redoubled before he escorted the Celestarch to the Vaults.'

'Did he now?' Ragnar was not reassured. If he were not the only Wolf to feel like this, perhaps there was something more to it than mere unease. Valkoth was a veteran. His instincts for danger would be keen.

'Yes. He has Torin and Haegr supervising the guards. He muttered something about wishing more of the Wolfblades were here but they were needed elsewhere.'

Ragnar nodded. There was a small pattern emerging here. This evening there were far fewer Wolfblades present than normal. If someone knew their schedules they could choose such a night to strike.

But it was a big if. Those were facts known to very few outside the inner circles of the Belisarius clan.

Still, he thought, what could possibly go wrong here, within the fortified stronghold of Belisarius?

SKORPEUS MOVED TOWARDS the lower entrance. The guards here were fewer and saluted him as he passed. He returned their salutes easily and nodded to those he knew. So far, so good, everything was going according to plan. He circled and stopped to speak to the two at the security console.

'Everything in order?' he asked. They nodded and saluted.

'Are you sure?'

'Yes, sir. Lord Valkoth has ordered a third order alert this evening.'

Inwardly Skorpeus cursed. The Wolves were wary indeed. Valkoth's instincts were sound. He hoped the Wolfblade had not picked up anything from his scent. No, it was impossible. They could not read him and the proof was that he was still here. If they could sense anything he would be in an interrogation cell, right now.

Calm down, he told himself. There will be no cell for you. One way or another. The poison capsule will see to that. There was no need for such thoughts. Had not the stars foretold he would become Lord of Belisarius? It would be so even if he required Cezare Feracci's help. There would be time enough afterwards to show Cezare that he would be no mere catspaw. Now all he had to do was let Cezare's tame assassin in.

He made a mental note to find out how the Lord Feracci had managed to corrupt one of the Imperium's most deadly killers. Such knowledge would be an invaluable tool.

'We know, sir, but still it's all clear.'

'Very good,' he said, striding behind the men at the console and studying the holosphere. Security in the area was indeed all clear. Except for one thing. He glanced left and right and saw no one. He slid the weapon from its holster and put it to one of the men's backs. He pulled the trigger. The man fell forward, coughing blood.

'What is going on?' he asked the other guard. The man looked at him confused. 'Is he sick?'

'I don't know, sir–' The man's words were cut off as the blast took him in the kidneys. The traitor pushed him aside and sat down in front of the holosphere. He passed his hands over the master control runes and began the cryptic invocations that would open the secured doors.

He knew that at best he would have only a few minutes. The tech-adepts would most likely assume that this was some sort of system error, and send someone to investigate. Unless those accursed Wolf-blades sensed something, he thought. Well, it was too late to worry about that now. Green lights changed to red as the security doors opened. There were several of them, and their locations were known to but a few. They were meant for evacuating the palace if things went terribly wrong. Tonight, though, they would be used for another purpose.

He rose from the command desk and moved to the security doors. They slid open to reveal a mass of black-clad masked figures led by the man he recognised as Xenothan.

'What is this?' he asked the assassin. 'You need help to kill one woman?'

'There's been a slight change of plan,' said Xenothan. Only then did Skorpeus realise that the gun in the assassin's hand was pointing directly at him. It was the last thing he ever saw.

CHAPTER TWENTY-THREE

XENOTHAN LOOKED DOWN the corridor. It was all clear, as he had expected. Already the Brotherhood men were fanning out, heading for their objectives. Some stripped off their coveralls to reveal the uniforms of Belisarius servitors, others moved towards the lower depths in full military gear. A few squads moved with feral grace into the vents overhead. Two men moved to the console and began patching themselves into the security systems.

It was amazing, Xenothan thought, just how much damage a well-motivated team could cause in a contained environment like this. The very self-sufficiency in air and water that made the palace a mighty fortress could turn into a dreadful weakness once the walls were breached. Contaminated water and air would see to that.

Don't be too sure, he told himself. There were backups for the backups and many, many layers of security. It never paid to be over-confident. Still, this mission had been planned for decades, and he was fairly sure they had accounted for all contingencies. He smiled and his facial muscles flexed, pulling his skin into a new configuration. He looked almost exactly like Skorpeus now, and he had the man's dress uniform and security talismans. There had been no blood. The poison dart had seen to that.

He doubted that anybody except another Navigator could tell that his implanted pineal eye was an artful fake, and if any Belisarian

Navigator got that close, he was a dead man. Then there were the four Wolfblades, Xenothan told himself with relish – they would see through the disguise in a moment. His scent would give him away if nothing else did. Still, the same thing applied to them as applied to the Navigators. If they got that close they would be dead.

'Let's get going,' he said. The fanatics moved on with gratifying swiftness.

SERGEANT HOPE WATCHED the new servants move down the corridor. One of them was very pretty, he thought, perhaps once he was off-duty he would seek her out for a chat. Just then he noticed something from the corner of his eye. He turned swiftly and saw a man he did not recognise wearing the uniform of the House. The man moved with a sense of urgency. A squad of troops followed behind him.

'What is it?' Hope asked.

'Security breach,' said the officer. 'Come with me.'

'We can't leave our posts,' said Hope. He tried not to sound as if he was keen to avoid work. He tried to sound like a man who was doing his duty. 'We have to guard the inner core.'

'Lot of precious books in that library,' said the officer. 'But the order comes straight from Valkoth.'

There was something in the man's tone Hope did not like. 'Show me the authorisation.'

'Certainly,' said the man, holding out his hand. There was something metallic in it. It was the last thing Hope noticed before his brains decorated the wall.

'WHAT WAS THAT?' Ragnar asked.

'I didn't hear anything,' said Gabriella. 'But then I do not have the keen senses of a Wolf.' There was a note of mockery in her voice and a challenging expression on her face. It vanished when she looked at Ragnar.

'Wait here,' he told her, moving down the corridor, his feet near silent on the ancient flagstones.

'I think not,' she said. 'I will be safer with you.'

Ragnar did not have time to argue. He rushed forward. There was a strange stench in the air, of death and something else. There were traces of strangers. He rounded the corner and saw that the guards who should have been there were not. He sniffed for scents and headed through a doorway into a storage chamber. There were corpses and a great deal of blood. The warmth of the scent trace told Ragnar that the killers had been here recently.

He patched himself into the comm-net. 'There are intruders within the palace,' he said. 'We have lost two warriors already, maybe more.' He added the coordinates of his position within the building. 'Inform Valkoth and the others.'

'I have already been informed,' came Valkoth's deep melancholy voice. 'I am dispatching reinforcements to your position.'

'The intruders were here very recently. I am going to investigate.'

'Be cautious, Ragnar. We do not know what we are dealing with.'

'Aye,' said Ragnar. His mind raced. This could be very big. They had no idea how these strangers got in. One thing was certain, murder had been committed here. The Belisarians had not drawn their weapons; they had been taken completely off-guard. Was this an attack? Who could be behind it? The Brotherhood, or someone else entirely. Surely it would be impossible for the fanatics to get in, he thought. Unless they had help...

'Stay here,' he told Gabriella. 'House troops will be here soon. You will be safe.'

'These men were House troops, Ragnar,' she said, pointing to the corpses. 'How safe were they?'

It was a fair point. 'Stick close and dive for cover if there is trouble. I cannot guarantee your safety.'

'I will take my chances.'

'That's what you will be doing.'

Ragnar moved swiftly and silently in the direction of the scent trace. They were coming perilously close to the entrance to the Vaults.

The scent trails became thicker. There were at least a dozen men here and they were certainly not from within the palace.

Ragnar drew his chainsword and bolt pistol. He felt his awareness expand as it always did when he approached combat. They came to one of the massive sealed doors. It was sealed no longer. Someone had over-ridden the controls, and let themselves into the Vault.

'That's not possible,' said Gabriella. 'Only the upper echelons of the family have access to these codes. And the senior Wolfblades.'

'I fear it is possible,' said Ragnar, sniffing the air. 'Someone has access to the treasures of Belisarius.'

It was then his nose caught another scent. It had the mad strangeness of Chaos. This was getting weird. Was this how the strangers had entered? Had they used Chaos sorcery to let themselves into the Vaults and then fanned out from there? That was not what the scent trails told him.

'This is worse than I thought,' he said. 'The stink of mutation is all over this place. Chaos has corrupted even the sacred soil of Terra it would seem.'

Gabriella gave him an odd look. 'Perhaps it is not Chaos you scent,' she said.

Ragnar did not have time to answer her. The sound of a weapon being fired echoed through the corridor, and there was a wild inhuman scream. At the same time, the lights flickered and failed. Total darkness. Ragnar shrugged. This was no hindrance to him. He could move by scent and touch and instinct if need be, but the girl would not be safe. He was surprised to sense her moving ahead of him.

'It is all right,' she said. 'I am a Navigator. My pineal eye can see through far worse gloom than this.' The scent of gunmetal coming from her became slightly stronger. He sensed that she too had drawn a weapon. A moment later the lights flickered once more and came on although much dimmer than before. He noticed that there was a still-ness in the air that had not been there before. The palace's ventilation systems were down.

As his eyes adjusted to the new conditions Ragnar saw that Gabriella was well ahead of him, a small laspistol in one hand, her dress sabre in the other. He moved swiftly in front of her. No harm would come to the daughter of Adrian Belisarius if he could help it.

He lengthened his stride towards the sound of violence, and emerged into a large chamber in which something bloated and white and huge lay on the floor. Its legs looked more like flippers, its arms like tentacles. But the face appeared human and it had three eyes, one in the middle of the forehead that looked suspiciously like that of a Navigator. Had this crea-ture somehow found its way in here during the attack, Ragnar wondered? Very unlikely. What then were the Navigators doing with the thing? Was it a prisoner, something they performed experiments on? Whatever it was no longer mattered. The creature was dead now. Someone had filled it full of bullets. They had taken the time to write 'Die mutant scum' on the walls in its blood as well. There was a lot of hatred there.

Gabriella entered and let out a small shriek. At first, he thought it was in horror at the sight of the monster but then he realised that she was weeping openly.

An awful suspicion entered his mind that was confirmed when she said, 'They are killing the Elders.'

'What?'

'You heard me – they are killing the Elders!'

'These things were Navigators?' said Ragnar, appalled.

'They are Navigators, very old ones, very wise ones.'

'They are mutants.'

'As are we all!'

'But you look…'

'I look more human. It makes no difference. If you live long enough and are exposed to the warp often enough, this is what happens. It's the price that we pay so that humanity can have star flight.'

Ragnar shook his head, struggling to comprehend. The logic of her words was inexorable, and he remembered the conversation he had with Ranek back on Fenris about the things he might learn on Terra. It all made more sense now. The old man must have known this, and in his own way he had tried to prepare him. But nothing could have prepared him for this reality.

'The Emperor...' he said.

'The Emperor knew, Ragnar. The Emperor knew and he granted the charters anyway.'

'But he told no one, said nothing.'

'He might have done had Horus not wounded him mortally and sentenced him to eternity in the Golden Throne. He was a great man, Ragnar, and he knew the truth. And while we stand here debating this, others of my kin are dying. You can hear it if you listen!'

Ragnar paused. He felt very unsettled and very unsure of himself. He was being called upon to defend mutants, real mutants. The Brotherhood was right. Was defending these mutants honourable?

'Are you going to do your sworn duty or aren't you?' Gabriella asked. 'Are you going to side with those mindless bigots or are you going to side with us?'

And there it was. It was not about the Navigators, it was about him. It was his choice. He could defend the Navigators or not. It would reflect on him. What was the difference between Gabriella whom he liked, and the corpse at his feet? Time. 'Will you...?'

'If I live long enough,' she said. 'I will look like that. Maybe not exactly but close enough. And I will still have done my duty to the Emperor. Will you?'

'It's not for you to question my loyalty to the Imperium, girl.' His decision made, he was already on the move. He had sworn to serve the Celestarch and he was going to protect her people. He would do his duty, the rest he would figure out later. The universe was more complex than he had been led to believe.

From up ahead came the butchering sounds of somebody using a chainsaw, followed by screams of pain, and then laughter.

'Hard to move without any legs, isn't it, mutant?' said a man garbed all in black, as he brandished a chainsword over the strangely altered body of someone who once surely must have been a woman.

'Yes, it is,' said Ragnar and put a bolter shell through both of the man's kneecaps. It was a cruel and unnecessary thing to do, but someone was going to feel the brunt of his anger. The man's companions turned to face him. They were quick and hyped on combat drugs and they brought their weapons to bear with astonishing speed. Ragnar did not care. He stepped to one side putting himself behind the shelter of the doorway and then snapped off shots. Every one of them was rewarded with a scream. A hail of shells answered him, tearing chunks out of the wall opposite the archway. He holstered his pistol and lobbed in a flash grenade. A moment after it exploded he stepped through the door and opened fire. He wasted no shots this time. He put a bullet through the head of every stunned man and then approached the Navigator they had been torturing.

She was skeletally thin and unnaturally tall. Her face was narrow like an eldar's, but her skin was scaled like a snake. Her stomach had been slit fully open and her innards had tumbled out. Not even the most advanced medicine would guarantee her survival, and judging by the look on her face she knew it. Terrible agony twisted her features. 'Kill me,' she said.

Ragnar turned to Gabriella who nodded. Ragnar put a bullet into the ancient woman's head, right through the pineal eye. He wished he had not felt a faint grim sense of satisfaction as he did so. He hoped for Gabriella's sake it had not shown on his face. His prejudices ran very deep.

From all around came the sounds of shooting now. It seemed that this was not the only team loose in the Vaults of the forbidden zone. There were others.

Gabriella looked very angry now. 'Navigators were behind this,' she said.

'How do you know?' he asked, ready to lunge off into the darkness once more.

'Only another Navigator House would know about these hidden Vaults and their significance.'

'Feracci?' Ragnar asked.

'The most likely candidate, don't you think?'

'If it is, he will pay.'

'Not if my House is wiped out. No one will avenge us.'

Ragnar moved on. 'The Inquisition might.'

'No. It might use this as an excuse to move against the other Navigators. But Cezare must know about this and be prepared to deal with it, or he would not have done it.'

'Then the Wolves will claim your bloodgeld for you.'

'Will they?'

'Indeed they will.' Ragnar wished he felt as sure as he sounded. Honour was one thing; the politics of the Imperium was another. Something occurred to him.

'If Cezare was behind this, then he was also behind the death of your father and Skander.'

'You could never prove that.'

Ragnar showed his fangs in a wolfish grin. 'What makes you think I require proof?'

XENOTHAN STRODE THROUGH the corridors doing his considerable best to look like the panicked folk around him. Terrible chaos had erupted right in the heart of House Belisarius. Long held plans raced to fruition. The fanatics were loose in the Navigator's precious Vaults. Assault teams were contaminating the water and air supplies. The main powercores were out.

Over the comm-net earbead he could sense panic. Word of the attack on the Vaults filtered back to the Belisarian command. They assumed that the Elders were the target of all of this and moved to defend them. Now was the time for Xenothan to strike. Misdirection was the key, he had to keep two steps ahead of his enemies. That counted for more than strength, or firepower, or wealth. It was something he was a master of. He marched on through the heart of Belisarius towards his goal.

Before this night was over the power of one of the oldest Navigator Houses would be broken, and his employer would have moved one step closer to his goal.

'How ARE you feeling?' Ragnar asked Gabriella. She looked pale and wan and filled with horror.

'I've been worse,' she said. She was bearing up well, given the number of her relatives she had seen butchered. But he could tell she was tired, scared and beginning to fray at the edges. He could not really blame her. This style of warfare was enough to test the nerves of the most seasoned warriors.

They stalked the gloomy Vaults. Massively outnumbered, their only chance was to strike from the shadows, and withdraw. If they were going to save the Elders there was no sense in courting a heroic death. Speed, savagery of attack and swiftness of flight would serve their purpose better.

Again and again, they came upon small groups of fanatics. Ragnar would open fire on the men and try to draw them away from their prey. If that failed, and it often did, he would return and snipe again, killing more and more. Overwhelmed by blood lust, the invaders brutally tortured the mutated Elders instead of proceeding with their mission. Ragnar suspected that it was only bloodlust that was preventing total eradication of the Navigators. If the Brotherhood's warriors had moved swiftly and killed quickly, they might have succeeded in their task.

Perhaps not. Here and there Ragnar came upon massive blast doors. Some had been shattered with thermal charges, but many had held. Ragnar knew that beyond them, an Elder perhaps survived. He could only hope so. At least time was on their side. More and more House troops were rushing down here, and soon they might begin to overwhelm their attackers.

The fanatics must have known this would happen, he thought. But still they came on. There was something almost admirable about the way they were prepared to throw away their lives for the cause they believed in.

Almost, he reminded himself. But they were throwing their lives away to slay people who could not fight back: crippled mutants who were incapable of holding a weapon, let alone using it.

Over the comm-net Ragnar was getting reports that they had used other weapons as well. Poisons had been introduced into the air-circulators and water supplies. The filters were being replaced and casualties were light, but it was obvious, even to Ragnar that they had come incredibly well prepared. They had staggeringly detailed knowledge of the place they were going to attack and all its weak points. Everything pointed to the presence of a traitor in their midst. It was the only way anyone could have acquired such a complete pool of intelligence data.

As he padded forward towards the scent of more fanatics, his mind continued to gnaw away at the problem. A traitor would explain how they got in too. He did not doubt that somewhere and sometime later investigators would find a security door that had been unsealed, as well as guards who had either been bribed or killed. It was the only way such a breach could be achieved.

He poked his head around the corridor and saw a group of black-garbed men. One of them was sawing the tentacles off an Elder with a chainsword, while another lay groaning and bleeding nearby. It seemed that they had encountered one mutant determined to fight back. While he was sighting the back of the chainsword wielder's head, another thought struck him.

What if the Elders were not the invaders' principle target? He was drawing conclusions from what he had seen, and in military terms that could be a dangerous and incorrect method of doing things.

Presumably with the intelligence they had they were capable of striking at anyone they wanted within the House.

Why would they pick on the Elders? They were politically powerful, but from what he understood, they were mostly retired or engaged in strange research.

He pulled the trigger and the back of his target's head exploded in a cloud of red mist. His brains decorating the intruder in front of him. Ragnar sprang forward, sweeping his chainsword down at another target, and decapitated him instantly.

Gabriella too closed with the enemies. He moved swiftly to put as much distance as he could between them. He did not want to strike her accidentally in the savagery of the fray.

He lashed out with his boot, sending one invader flying into his comrade behind them. As the men went down in a tangle of limbs he pounced like a tiger on a tethered goat. He broke one man's neck with a blow from his fist, the weight of the bolt pistol clutched in it adding power to the blow. He took the other's head from his shoulders with the sword. It rolled to the ground and blinked stupidly for a moment. There was a look of utter dismay on its face.

As his body went through the motions of combat, Ragnar asked himself, why now for this attack? Perhaps it had something to do with the guards' shifts, and the presence of traitors within the defence. But it could be more complicated. What had changed with the big picture? Why would an attacker choose to roll the dice on this evening, and not some other?

Ragnar threw himself flat as a fanatic opened fire on him with a laspistol. While the man struggled to bring his weapon to bear, Ragnar rolled and shot him, coming to his feet with a single lithe spring. Then it occurred to him: the vote for the new representative was tomorrow. This attack might well throw the Belisarians into confusion at a most critical moment. Or, he thought sombrely, it might bring a traitor to power if the Celestarch was killed. With the Elders gone or in disarray the House would have to find an alternate way of selecting its new ruler. That would take time.

But, he thought, as he lunged to put his blade through a man's heart, that could only happen if the present Celestarch was dead. A sudden dread filled Ragnar. He felt certain he had divined the enemy's plan.

CHAPTER TWENTY-FOUR

XENOTHAN PROCEEDED THROUGH the palace, following the guidance he received from the main datacore over the comm-net. In case of emergencies, he had memorised the layout from the plans the traitor had provided, but so far he had had no need to use it. Some of the area he knew from his own many trips in disguise, but these were the public places and the less secure sectors abutting them. Now he was right in the core of the palace. Behind his altered features he felt excitement, the excitement of the hunt. Tonight he stalked dangerous prey for the greatest prize of all. Tonight, he would alter the course of the Imperium for generations to come. It was a mission worthy of his talents.

A young servant strode up, with fear on her face. 'What is going on, sir?' she asked. In the stress of the moment, she had abandoned the usual protocols and spoke to him without being spoken to. 'Why the alert?'

'Intruders,' said Xenothan, injecting a note of panic into his voice. He knew that the more alarm and confusion he caused the better.

'The guards are all heading down into the Vaults,' she said. 'That is forbidden.'

Indeed it is, thought Xenothan, and we have set Belisarius a pretty conundrum. What will they tell the men who see the residents below? How will they deal with them? Perhaps they would be shipped out to some distant hellworld, and new guards would be brought in. Death was an obvious answer, but would the Celestarch have the stomach for it? Possibly. The Navigators were capable of anything when their survival depended on it.

Well, soon enough they would have other things to worry about. Xenothan headed on towards the throne room. His goal was finally within reach.

RAGNAR SPOKE QUICKLY into the comm-net. 'Is the Celestarch secure?' he asked.

'She is being guarded by Torin and a company of guards in the throne room. We never got her to the Vaults before the alert sounded.'

'Move her,' said Ragnar.

'What?' said Valkoth. Ragnar swiftly outlined his suspicions. They needed to ensure that she was not in an expected location. If there was a traitor and an attack came, they had to assume the killers would know where to strike. Ragnar had even considered suggesting she be put on a ship and lifted out into orbit, but it was likely that the invaders had considered this option and prepared for it. All around, troops had started to flow into the Vaults.

'Ragnar is right,' he heard Torin say. 'We cannot take the risk.'

Valkoth's voice returned. 'There are no signs of any breach up here.'

'That does not mean there has not been one.'

'Aye, you are correct. Explain to the Celestarch she has to move. I respectfully suggest taking her down to the Vaults.'

Very good, thought Ragnar. Not a place the enemy was likely to consider, and one already swarming with House troops. Of course, the situation down here had yet to stabilise, but it probably would before the Celestarch got here.

'Ragnar,' Valkoth continued crisply. 'Take over the fifth company and secure the nearest defensible area to the shaft nine entranceway. Let me know when you've done it. Immediately.'

'Immediately,' Ragnar agreed.

'Come with me,' he told Gabriella. 'We have work to do.'

EXPERIENCE TOLD XENOTHAN that something was wrong. There was not the density of security in the area that there should have been. He had been challenged several times but his appearance combined with the passes and rites the traitor had provided him meant that he had got through unscathed. Mostly. Those who had thought to challenge him had not lived for more than a few moments. He should now be challenged constantly but there were not many guards around.

Was it possible that the enemy had anticipated his coming and had changed their strategy? Had he been betrayed himself? Briefly he considered aborting the mission. Very briefly. His patron would not accept anything short of total success. Anyway, there was nothing so far to suggest that he had failed. He decided to push on. First, however, he needed to find a place to patch into the comm-net to let the fanatics know that there had been a change of plan. He needed to know if the Celestarch was being moved, and if she was, they were to slow that down, or stop it if possible.

He smiled. Small setbacks were part of the hunt. They would make his triumph all the sweeter once they were overcome.

RAGNAR FINISHED SUPERVISING the clearance of the holding bay. There had been more enemies than he had thought and they had fought with surprising deadliness. His force had taken more than a few casualties before they had overcome the enemy. Now he supervised the fortification of the area. He had set some of his men to guard all the approaches to their position, but held the bulk of his force in reserve, knowing that they could be attacked from any side.

Gabriella looked on. Her face was sooty and marked with scratches and blood. She had taken a few small wounds in their battles. A medic had hastily applied a synthi-flesh plaster to them, and it was swiftly being absorbed into the skin. 'I never expected to have to fight here,' she said.

'There are no safe places,' said Ragnar. 'You have to be prepared to fight anywhere.'

'Spoken like a true Space Wolf,' she said. 'But tell me, how would you feel about fighting in the place where you were born and grew up?'

'I have,' said Ragnar automatically, casting his mind back to that long ago time. 'I saw my father killed and my family enslaved.'

'Somehow that does not reassure me, Ragnar,' she said.

'I don't suppose it would,' he said, as the realisation of what he had said sunk in.

She smiled.

'It serves me right for asking the question in the first place.'

'No, it doesn't. This is your home. You have a right to be upset. You still have to fight though, if you want to keep it.'

'Those are the words of a Fenrisian.'

'The words are true no matter where they come from. In this universe there is little else we can do but fight for our place, if we want to keep it. There are plenty who would take it from us.'

'That's certainly true if you are a Navigator.'

'It's true for everybody, even a Space Marine.'

* * *

XENOTHAN MOVED THROUGH the palace, stalking his prey. Tonight, as things stood, he might not get a chance at his target, but he was not about to admit defeat. He could remain within the building, secrete himself in some hiding place and bide his time. No, that would never do. After tonight, the identity of the traitor would be revealed, and security would be redoubled. It was tonight or never, he thought. The only decision left to him was whether to abandon his mission and leave the tower or push on.

He grinned. There had never been any chance of him aborting the plan. This was the high spot of his career, a thing that would be talked about amid his secret brethren for centuries to come, if he was successful. No, he told himself, *when* he was successful.

He spoke more orders in code into the comm-net. His followers were closing in on what they thought was the Celestarch's bodyguard. He did some quick calculations. They could achieve a temporary superiority at this point, two levels down. The Belisarians were mobilising by the ramps, which was sensible. They did not want to be trapped in an elevator or dropshaft. There was far too great a possibility of something going wrong.

He gave orders for the intercept, knowing it was only a matter of time before they worked out that he and his followers were using scrambled transmissions piggy-backed onto the Belisarian net. There was plenty of time to do what was needed; all the time in the world.

TORIN KEPT HIMSELF beside the robed woman at all times, ready to interpose himself between her and danger. He sniffed the air, taking in the conflicting scents. He caught the faint traces of strangers on the recycled air, and hints of subtle toxins that had been released in miniscule amounts. He wondered what the casualties were. How many had died before that particular attack had been neutralised? Stick to your task, he told himself. He would know the worst soon enough.

He was still astonished by the boldness of this attack. Now they knew why there had been such a build-up of Brotherhood forces beneath the quarter. Every fanatic on Terra must be here. Who would have thought anyone would have dared to attack the Navigators within their own stronghold? It showed a boldness of planning and a competence of execution that he found almost admirable. But there would be hell to pay tomorrow. The Belisarians would spare no expense to find out who was behind this and avenge themselves.

Surely the attackers must have known that and planned for it too. They would have been fools not to, and this was not the work of fools. It was a chilling thought, that gave him pause even as he hustled the

Celestarch's crack bodyguard through the halls of the palace. Perhaps the enemy did not expect them to survive in any state to harm him. He would be proved wrong.

Be careful, Torin told himself. The night is not over yet. Who knows what other nasty surprises are in store? Perhaps there are other traitors. Torin felt certain that there was at least one: no one could have penetrated the palace without inside help from someone high up. It simply could not have happened any other way. The question was who? The Navigators had many flaws but loyalty to their clan was practically bred into them. It had to be. How could someone have got around that?

Assuming they survived, the list of suspects could be narrowed enormously. Very few people were in a position to do what had been done, so one of them was the traitor. It could not be himself, or Haegr or Valkoth, he was sure. It could not be Ragnar. He did not know the youth well but he had just arrived from Fenris, and he did not seem the corruptible type, although he had come with the wench Gabriella. Still, she had just spent ten years with the Wolves, so she would be in no position to be a traitor so soon. They needed to look among the high command of the House. Torin had a few ideas about where.

Just then he caught a strange scent on the air. There were enemies coming towards them, and lots of them. 'Ready yourselves to defend the Celestarch,' he told his men as their adversaries rounded the corner and opened fire. He let his wolfish howl ring out, knowing it would frighten the foe and give heart to his own men. Moments later he lunged headlong into the swirling maelstrom of battle.

He was happy. There were few things he loved more than feeling his blade bite into the flesh of his foes.

XENOTHAN HEARD THE wolf-cry and the sound of the Brotherhood men engaging the enemy. This is it, he thought, the time he had been waiting for. He moved around the bend and saw the halls filled with the wild swirl of combat at close quarters. War raged among the tapestries and statues as the Celestarch's guard were ambushed.

From the balcony he had chosen as vantage point, he watched the Space Wolf slash away at the fanatics who came within his reach. Xenothan allowed himself a fellow professional's appreciation of the man's deadliness and then gave his attention to the target. The Celestarch was firmly behind a wall of her elite guard. They refused to give ground even in the face of ferocious attacks. The presence of their ruler and the Wolfblade seemed to stiffen their spines remarkably.

In the natural course of events things would not go well for the Brotherhood. It was only a matter of time before House reinforcements got here and they would be swept away before the storm of blades. Fortunately, Xenothan thought, that was no concern of his. His mission was all but accomplished. He took a heartbeat to savour the moment, raised his customised bolt pistol and snapped off a single shot, almost without aiming. The shell sped directly into the Celestarch's head, causing it to explode. Only Xenothan and an observer close to her side would notice that he had put the bullet right through her third eye.

The Wolfblade gave a howl of rage, and his response almost caught Xenothan off-guard. He raised his pistol and launched a snapshot. It was pure chance that caused his shell to smash into Xenothan's gun, sending it broken and spinning over the banister.

Xenothan took no chances and lunged backwards, filled with a growing sense of triumph marred only by a faint niggling feeling that something was wrong.

He was down the stairs and almost into his extraction routine when he realised what it was. The image of the tumbling Celestarch had burned itself into his brain, and was taking its place in the gallery of his proud triumphs. It was one of those things he would savour as long as he lived. He could freeze the scene in his mind.

Replaying it now, he realised he had made a mistake. The woman had been a Navigator but she was too short and too broad to be the Celestarch. At a distance she was almost identical, and few people could have told the difference, but Xenothan was one of them. He had been made a fool of. The Wolfblades had used a decoy to distract the intruders while they hustled the real Celestarch to safety. It was a simple ploy but in the confusion of the invasion it had proven an effective one.

What to do now, Xenothan wondered? Time was running out.

RAGNAR WATCHED AS Haegr arrived. With him was a woman garbed in the dress uniform of an ordinary Navigator. Ragnar recognised her immediately as the Celestarch. Valkoth had taken a bold gamble and it had paid off. Haegr had managed to guard her all the way down into the Vaults. Somehow he had managed to stop off for food along the way. His lips and beard showed traces of fat and gravy. Ragnar could smell gammon on his breath.

'Hardly a real fight all the way here, just a few men in black to decorate my hammerhead with their brains.'

'For which I am profoundly grateful,' said the Celestarch.

'Indeed, lady,' said Ragnar leading her into the security chamber. There was only one way in and out of this place, but it was the best he could find at short notice. It might turn into a death trap if they were attacked in overwhelming numbers, but he was certain there was no other way in or out. Anyone seeking the death of the Celestarch would have to clamber over the dead bodies of Haegr, himself and a company of Belisarian guards to get her. Besides, more troops would be here as soon as they had finished clearing the Vaults of intruders. It looked like the situation was stable for the moment. The tone of the comm-net bead in his ear suddenly gave Ragnar a sense of foreboding.

'Ragnar. There is a problem,' said Torin. His voice sounded urgent.

'A problem?'

'The decoy is dead. They got to her. Is the Celestarch safe?'

'Haegr is here and so am I, and so are scores of guards. We have the Celestarch in the Vault. I don't see how he can get past us.'

The signal cut off abruptly with the sound of gunfire in the distance. A moment later a voice spoke over the comm-net. 'Ragnar, this is Torin. We have just been attacked and the decoy is dead.'

'I know, you just told me.'

'What? I have been busy killing our new guests.'

'You did not call me thirty seconds ago?'

'Thirty seconds ago I was removing my chainsword from somebody's guts.'

'Then who called me?'

'I don't know, it wasn't me. But I need to warn you about something. There is an assassin loose in the palace.'

'There are many of them but we seem to gaining the upper hand.'

'No, I mean a real Imperial assassin. He killed the decoy Valkoth sent with the Celestarch's bodyguard. When I shot at him he moved away so fast I almost could not see him. I am on his trail now, and I suspect he is heading your way.'

'An Imperial assassin? That does not seem possible. Has the Administratum turned against us?'

'I do not know, Ragnar, but I am certain that such a creature is here now. Be very careful. They are tricky and almost unstoppable once they are committed to a kill. He will try to find a way. Sit tight while I get him. Praise Russ!'

Ragnar's mind reeled. It seemed like the enemy had access to the secure codes of the Belisarian comm-net. Not only that, but he knew how to imitate Torin's voice.

How was that possible? Ragnar thought of their visit to the Feracci tower and all the machines that had been present along with all the servants. They certainly could have been eavesdropped on there.

He braced himself. It looked like the battle was not yet over. One of the deadliest creatures in the galaxy was on his way.

CHAPTER TWENTY-FIVE

XENOTHAN HURRIEDLY GAVE instructions to the last surviving Brotherhood warriors. He hoped that they would abandon their bloodletting in the Vaults long enough to converge on their great enemy, the Celestarch. By now they must realise that they were doomed, and hopefully they would be willing to give away their lives at the highest cost to the hated mutants. Killing the Celestarch would achieve that.

He quit broadcasting into the comm-net. He had to assume that by now his ruse had been discovered, and he was taking no chances of being located before his mission was complete. The Wolfblades had already proven that they were not fools. They would be doing their best to locate him. Keep moving, he told himself.

As he raced through the corridors, he checked his selection of special weapons. He had a few surprises up his sleeve. He still had the envenomed blades, the dart throwers and the grenades filled with poison gas. He had changed his appearance once more and now wore the stolen uniform of a House guard. His face was completely different – wide and flat. Sub-dermal pigmentation sacks had changed his skin colour from Navigator pale to dark brown. His scent meant he would not fool a Space Wolf, but it would fool any normal person looking for one of his previous appearance.

He was not sure the Space Wolf had caught enough of him to be able to circulate it, but again it never paid to take chances.

A guard called out to him to halt. Xenothan had no time to waste now; swiftness, not concealment was of the essence. He concentrated and his altered body responded. Time slowed as his chemically enhanced reflexes sped up. The man seemed to barely raise his weapon before Xenothan was upon him. He reached out and speared his fingers into the man's eyes, pushing them deep into their sockets. They punctured under the impact of his razor sharp fingernails.

As the guard fell, Xenothan caressed the edge of the man's throat with the edge of his hand, crushing the windpipe.

A moment later he was gone, speeding down the corridor towards his intended target. He was determined that she would not elude him a second time this night.

'THAT WAS MORE like it,' said Haegr, smacking his lips with satisfaction, as he contemplated the ruined bodies that lay everywhere on the battlefield. Ragnar rose up from behind the hastily improvised cover to survey the area in front of them. Bodies sprawled all over the entrance to the Vault. The smell of exotic woods burning filled his nostrils. The dead lay everywhere.

'I am sure you'll have plenty more entertainment in the next few minutes,' Ragnar said. 'I think I can hear more of those maniacs approaching now.'

'You can, young Ragnar. And I must admit, for feeble humans, they certainly know how to die. They fight like men possessed.'

'No doubt they will take that as a great compliment.'

'They ought to when it comes from the lips of mighty Haegr.'

Things had worsened over the past few minutes. Assembled en masse, the fanatics had attacked their position again and again. Most of the guards were wounded. None of the promised reinforcements had arrived. They were pinned down. The only consolation was that no enemies had penetrated the chamber where the Celestarch and Gabriella waited. So far they had held off all attempts to do so.

Haegr was right. The enemy did fight well. Ragnar was astonished at how well co-ordinated the fanatics were. He doubted that it was coincidence that they had suddenly started attacking this position in great numbers. A swift evil intelligence guided them. How high did the treachery within the House reach? Others would be thinking that too. Such thoughts would paralyse and demoralise their side while the enemy swept through them.

'I never thought I would have such a good fight in here of all places,' said Haegr. 'It seems these Vaults have served a useful function after all.'

Did he know about the mutants, Ragnar wondered? Did he care?

'Somebody put a lot of work into this,' said Haegr with uncharacter-istic astuteness. Right again, Ragnar thought. It had to be tonight, the meeting of the Navigator Council tomorrow ensured it. If the Celestarch died, House Belisarius would be disorganised and its allies thrown into confusion.

With the House in disarray and so many of the Elders dead, it would take weeks, if not months, to choose a new Celestarch. If Cezare was behind this, he could seize the moment, promise the Navigators strong leadership in the face of this new and ominous threat, and make his son one of the High Lords of Terra. He would score a victory such as none of the great Navigator Houses had in two millennia, and his power would become insuperable. Ragnar realised that he was making a huge leap of imagination, with absolutely no proof, but it fitted the facts well. The only problem with the theory was that the power behind the attack did not have to be the Feracci; it could be any of the great ambitious Navigator Houses. There would be no way to confirm or deny the thing until the election to the throne was held tomorrow.

'We'll just have to see that they don't succeed.'

'Well said, young Ragnar. Very well said indeed.' Haegr grinned, showing his enormous tusks, and Ragnar suddenly realised why Torin respected him so. Haegr might be coarse, brutal and a diplomatic lia-bility but, in a tight spot, the giant was just the man you wanted at your side. He showed no doubts, no fear and had no need for reassurance. He was entirely what he appeared to be – unafraid. He was quite pos-sibly insane, but he was a truly fine warrior.

'The only way they are going to get to the Celestarch is if they climb over my dead body,' said Ragnar.

'And they'll have to climb over mine to get to yours,' said Haegr. 'Can't be having any young pups stealing the glory that is rightfully mine.'

Ragnar laughed, then glanced around at the carnage, the dead and stinking bodies, the limbless corpses, the blast marks on the marble walls. He breathed in the tainted stench of close combat in the hallways of the palace. The stench of opened guts and las-seared flesh, splattered blood and excrement. He did not see much evidence of glory here. His theories were all very well but they had to survive until the morrow. It was imperative they keep the Celestarch alive, for if they could the plot would fail, and the Belisarians would be in a position to fight another day. Perhaps they would even be able to ferret out and take vengeance on those behind their attackers.

He was surprised by his desperation. He would never have suspected things could get so bad so fast. Until this evening he had thought the power of House Belisarius unassailable. The Navigators had seemed so rich and so powerful, but not even their alliance with the Wolves had kept them from teetering on the edge of oblivion before daybreak. He realised that in the vast machine of Imperial power, the House was but one tiny cog and, by extension, so was his Chapter. It was not a pleasant thought.

'Well, it looks like we have some more visitors,' growled Haegr. 'I suppose we had better get ready to welcome them.'

XENOTHAN BOUNDED DOWN the slope and heard the roar of battle ahead. It had been a long night, but it was almost over. One last push would see this thing finished. He checked his weapons one last time, and raced headlong towards his goal. From up ahead, he heard the howling of Wolves.

RAGNAR MET THE first of the fanatics breast to breast, and sent him reeling with a punch from the hilt of his blade. Unbelievably, he had run out of bolter shells for his pistol, and the fighting was so close now, it seemed pointless to snatch up any sort of ranged weapon. Instead he grabbed a sword from a fallen guard officer and used it left handed while he wielded his chainsword with his right.

They had been forced to come out from behind the barrier and enter the battle in the chamber beyond. Now he raced through the melee butchering foes while Haegr smashed his way through more of the enemy warriors like a blood-mad bull let loose in a crowded bazaar. All around them, the enemy fell, but now it was only the two Space Marines who kept them at bay. Most of the guard had fallen, and still the zealots came on, reckless and fanatical.

It may have been the proscribed combat drugs they chewed on, but Ragnar suspected they would have been as bold without them. They simply would not have been so untiring and fierce and strong. Haegr did not care. He laughed as he slew. His hammer smashed skulls as if they were eggshells and snapped ribs as though they were made from dry twigs. Gore splattered his beard and his chest plate. Blood dribbled down his face giving him a daemonic look.

For all his bulk he moved so quickly that no enemy was able to draw a bead on him and few managed to land a blow. Suddenly, out of nowhere, flew a dart. It impacted on the giant's forehead and stuck there. For a moment, nothing seemed to happen, and then a look of horror came into Haegr's eyes and he stiffened and fell forward like a great oak.

If Ragnar had not known it was impossible, he would have guessed his comrade to have been laid low by some vile poison. Something flashed in his peripheral vision and he threw himself forward, smashing into the enemy warriors ahead of him. A dart whizzed past his ear, missing him narrowly.

A shriek from just beyond his position told him that somebody else had not been so lucky. A glance to his left revealed a man writhing on the floor in dreadful agony, his face turning swiftly blue, muscles writhing beneath his skin like tortured serpents.

Ragnar kept moving and more darts rattled off his armour. He caught the hint of a smell, the faintest suggestion of an unbelievably revolting mix of toxins. Wildly, he glanced around. He had yet to catch sight of the man shooting at him. No human being should have been able to evade his perceptions. He guessed that the assassin had arrived.

XENOTHAN CURSED. HE had not expected the youth to respond so swiftly. Tracking his evasive action had expended too many of the assassin's precious poisoned darts and still he had not hit. All he had done was succeed in laying low half a dozen of his own side.

What now, he wondered? There was no more time to waste. If he was going to slay the Celestarch he needed to get over the barrier and into the Vault now. He headed for the doorway.

FROM THE CORNER of his eye, Ragnar caught sight of a tall, thin, black-garbed man moving with blurring speed. He vaulted the barrier and headed towards the entrance of the inner Vault.

The stranger moved far too fast for a normal human. There was something almost insect-like in his scuttling swiftness. This was the assassin, Ragnar surmised, and in a few moments, if he wasn't stopped, he would enter the Celestarch's chamber. Ragnar did not give much for the chances of the guard keeping him from his prey. It was time for him to do his duty.

Ragnar sprang forward over the barricade, aiming for his opponent's back, ignoring all the blows that flashed towards him from the fanatics, trusting his armour to keep him from harm. He lashed out with his chainsword, hoping to catch the assassin at the top of his spine. He almost succeeded, but at the last second, the assassin threw himself forward, stretching almost bonelessly to avoid the strike. More than that, he somehow writhed out of the way, rolled forward and caught Ragnar with his foot adding to the Wolf's momentum and propelling him head over heels into the chamber.

Ragnar had to let go of the chainsword in case he fell on his own blades. He tried to control the roll and bring himself to his feet. The chainsword skated away across the marble flagstones and came to rest against a far wall. Ragnar sprang upright but the killer was ready. His boot connected with Ragnar's chin with a piledriver force that would have broken the neck of anyone other than a Space Marine. Ragnar was once more hurled off-balance, while the assassin vaulted over him. He was amazed by the speed of his foe. Never before had he encountered someone so much quicker and apparently stronger than he. There were many stronger, but none so fast. This stranger was a lethal combination of the two.

Ignoring Ragnar the assassin moved towards his target. The guards were confused by the startling speed with which events were unfolding, and were not firing because of Ragnar's presence.

'Shoot,' he bellowed, reaching up to snag the man's ankle. He just managed to grab it and once more the stranger twisted, trying to break free. The first hail of bullets filled the air around them. Several smashed into Ragnar's armour but he held his grip.

Xenothan cursed. What did it take to put this youth down? So far he had absorbed enough punishment to kill a dozen normal men and he kept coming. Worse, he managed to thwart Xenothan's every effort to get to the Celestarch. The assassin realised he had made a mistake putting down Haegr first. The giant's ferocity was legendary, and Xenothan had assumed he was the greater threat. Only now he was not sure. Another mistake, he thought, and one he had very little time to put right.

Somehow, superlatively swiftly, the assassin avoided being hit and returned fire with a weapon he held in his left hand. More darts flew through the air and Ragnar feared the Celestarch was about to be killed. She would have died there and then had not several of her bodyguard intervened, interposing themselves between her and the assassin. They had become a human shield.

Ragnar heard the assassin curse in a strange tongue, then he bent from the waist and struck Ragnar with his hand. The blow was aimed at Ragnar's eyes. The young Space Wolf just had time to turn his head, while taloned nails sliced the skin of his forehead. He lashed out with the sword he had retained, but the man took the blow on his forearm. Ragnar expected to feel flesh slice open, but instead the blade rebounded as if it had hit solid metal. The stranger's slashed tunic was only cloth. Ragnar realised at once that he possessed some sort of sub-dermal armour.

The assassin brought his free foot down on the wrist of the hand with which Ragnar immobilised him. The force was irresistible and the stranger was free. A moment later the man was airborne almost as if gravity had no grip on him.

He performed an arcing backward somersault and continued to fire his darts of death into the bodies of the men protecting the ruler of Belisarius. Ragnar hoped for her sake that he did not find any chink in the wall of flesh. He assumed that the men would already be dead from the poison in their veins. He threw the sword with all his strength directly at the stranger's stomach, hoping it was not as well protected as his arms. The man twisted in the air, flailing his arm, and struck the blade away. It dropped directly into the guards, piercing one's throat. If that had been deliberate, and Ragnar had to assume it was, it was an astonishing feat of coordination.

Ragnar rolled and snatched a lasrifle from the hands of a guard. He brought it to bear on the stranger and pulled the trigger. Lacking anything to gain purchase on, and forced to follow the arc prescribed by gravity, the assassin, for once, made an easy target. Not even his reflexes were swift enough to avoid coherent light, and Ragnar hit him. The beam burned cloth and seared flesh, charring it black. Somehow the assassin managed to keep his arm in the way all the way down, and as soon as he hit the ground, he came straight at Ragnar, despite the sizzle of fat and muscle.

Too late, Ragnar noticed the knife in the killer's good hand. He caught the hint of faint deadly poison, like the stuff that had brought Haegr down. He desperately brought up his arm to try to deflect it but the stranger got the blade around it and punched it at his eye. Ragnar turned his head, and it caught him on the cheek just below the eye.

Searing agony passed through Ragnar instantly. All of his senses rearranged themselves. Sounds became colours, light became sound, touch blurred into taste, all in a way he would never be able to describe. For one who relied so much on his senses it was a sanity-blasting experience. The pain flared through him in bright red and yellow waves of agony. His gasps came out in clouds of grey and green. He tasted the acid sting of the poison in his veins. Everything became roaring madness to his tortured, overloaded senses.

Desperately wondering if he was even doing what he thought he was doing, he threw himself forward, biting and rending, feeling his jaws close on something, and thinking his arms encircled his foe. He kept attempting to crush it and bite it long after the waves of red madness overwhelmed him.

CHAPTER TWENTY-SIX

HE WOKE SUDDENLY and found himself looking into the face of Gabriella. Above him he could see the ceiling of his own chamber. He breathed deeply but there seemed to be something wrong with his sense of smell. It had not seemed so dull since he had become a Wolf.

'I must be alive then,' he said. 'Else you have somehow accidentally found your way into the halls of hell.'

'Yes,' she said. 'You are alive.'

'The Celestarch?'

'She is well too, all things considered, and she prepares for the great council. It looks like there will be much else to discuss along with the selection of the new throne.'

'What happened?'

'I think I can answer that,' said a familiar voice from close by. Ragnar caught the scent now as well. 'Torin?'

'Yes, old son, I am here. I came up just as you were fanging the assassin.'

'Haegr?'

'He's too stupid to die. He is even now engaged in single combat with all the pies in the kitchen.'

'That is exactly the sort of foul slur on mighty Haegr's honour I would expect from a jealous toad like you, Torin,' said Haegr. He and his collection of meat pies found their way into Ragnar's field of vision too. 'And one that will be richly rewarded with a beating later.'

'The poison did not kill you?'

'There is no poison strong enough to kill me,' said Haegr. 'Although I admit it did slow me down a touch. Seems to have blocked my nose for the moment as well.'

'He recovered before you, because he had not taken quite the beating you did.'

'I was in the chamber before you,' said Haegr outraged.

'By one step.'

'Between us we proved more than a match for the killer despite his noxious tricks.'

'Ignore this great fat liar, Ragnar, old son, he was almost dead from the beating you gave him.'

'He was very dead after the bolter shells mighty Haegr put in him.'

'I have never fought anybody so powerful,' Ragnar said. 'He was faster than me and stronger. I never expected that from anyone, except perhaps one of the slaves of darkness.'

'No doubt he would have said the same of you.'

'What happened?'

'When I entered you were holding him all but immobile and rending his flesh with your teeth. We finished him for you, then hustled the Celestarch to safety.'

'The traitor?'

'It was Skorpeus. Or so we surmise. His dead body was found near the breached security gate.'

'Why did he betray his own clan?'

'Why does anybody? Because he wanted power and prestige and he felt he had been passed over. Doubtless Feracci promised that he would see him installed as the new Celestarch. He would do. Skorpeus probably figured better to be a puppet than a servant.' There was something false in Torin's explanation but Ragnar could not quite put his finger on it. Yet.

'Can we can prove Feracci was behind this?' asked Ragnar.

'We don't know that it was. It would be our word against his. Cezare would simply say we were lying, and that it was a plot to discredit him. Even those who disbelieved him would admire him, and fear him for being able to corrupt one of the Belisarians. It would just enhance his prestige.'

'So he will get away with it then? All those people will have died in vain.'

'I would not say that, Ragnar,' said Torin. 'He will not get to control a High Lord since the Lady Juliana will block his son's appointment and that was his dream. He has been planning for this day for decades, that much is obvious. And he failed because of you. He will be seeking vengeance for that.'

'Let him,' said Ragnar.

'Spoken like a true son of Fenris,' said Haegr with almost paternal fondness.

'Ragnar, you will either have a short career or a glorious one, possibly both,' said Torin. 'In your very brief stay on Terra you have managed to make an enemy of one of the most powerful men in the Imperium. I shudder to think what you will do as an encore.'

'What about the Imperial assassin? How is that being dealt with?'

'What Imperial assassin?' said Torin. 'If you made any inquiries I am sure you would find he was some sort of renegade.'

'That's not what you said a few hours ago...'

'No, but it's what the Administratum would say were we foolish enough to lay this matter before them.'

'That is not fair.'

'Life is not fair, Ragnar, get used to it. But again, if it's any consolation to you, I think we have ruined somebody far higher placed than Cezare tonight as well. There will be repercussions there too.'

'I would wish for something more than that.'

'Don't worry, Ragnar,' said Haegr. 'I am sure something else will come up that you can get your teeth into.'

'If that was meant to be a joke,' said Torin, 'it was not very funny.'

Haegr roared with mirth and Ragnar was forced to join him.

Valkoth appeared in the doorway. 'Still lazing about, eh?' he said gruffly. 'Well, get up off that bed and get ready for duty. You are needed in the presence room.'

RAGNAR MARCHED INTO the presence room. He felt almost fully recovered now. His senses had started to return. The place was just as he remembered. The other Wolfblades flanked him. All of them looked smug as if they knew something he did not.

The Celestarch looked down gravely from her throne. She looked older somehow, and there was a sorrow and an anger in her eyes that had not been there during their first meeting. She stretched out her arms regally.

'We are only here because of you, Ragnar, and our House would be finished were it not for your bravery.'

'I only did my sworn duty,' Ragnar replied.

'Nonetheless, Belisarius owes you a debt of gratitude, and I am prepared to show our appreciation.'

Ragnar said nothing. To do anything else would have been presumptuous.

'You lost your blade while fighting to defend us. It is up to us to replace it.' She gestured and two of the guards brought forward a massive rune-encrusted weapon. It was ancient and very beautiful and its like could not have been forged in this age. 'Take it,' she said.

Ragnar reached out and gripped the weapon. It fitted his hand as if it was made for him, and its balance was perfect. An aura of strange coldness radiated from the runes.

'I thank you,' said Ragnar. It was all he could say.

'This blade was borne in the time of the Emperor, by one of the first Wolfblades. It belonged to Skander before it belonged to you. See that you prove worthy of it.'

'I will do my best.'

'Now,' she said, 'we have other business. We must go to council and see that a new throne is correctly chosen. Gentlemen, if you would be so good as to accompany us, we will leave at once.'

Flanking the ruler of Belisarius, they strode towards a meeting that would decide the fate of Navigators for generations to come.

EPILOGUE

THE STRANGE SCENT drew Ragnar from his reverie. He looked up. It was night once more and the sounds of distant carnage filled the darkness. It seemed to Ragnar that it was coming closer. All around, warriors moved, preparing for battle. Some rushed towards the front line positions. Nearby, Urlec and the rest of the Wolves checked their weapons. They looked ready to return to the fight at a moment's notice. His nose twitched. There was a faint odour there, one that set his hackles rising.

He looked down at the blade, reluctant to let go of his memories of those long gone events and comrades and enemies. Some were dead now. Some disgraced. Some had met stranger fates. He thought of the odd twist of fortune that led him to the secret truths about the assassin on that long ago night. There was a tale that would never find its way into the Chapter's annals. He shrugged and smiled, rising to his feet. It was good to remember the past, he thought, and where he had come from, and the long distance he had travelled but now he needed to live in the present. The smell he had caught spoke of the presence of enemies. Seeing him rise, the men rose too and made their weapons ready. He gestured for them to be wary. They responded instantly, throwing themselves into cover, leaping for foxholes, glaring out into the darkness.

The earth shook as a shell impacted nearby. The impact raised a huge cloud of earth and threw several men from their feet. Counter-battery fire blazed a trail through the night. Ragnar sniffed again. He sensed sorcery. Strange energies flowed all around. It looked like the followers of Chaos were not done yet.

He concentrated hard trying to find the source of his unease. Now that he was aware of it, it was easier to pinpoint. In the woods nearby, he now saw the massive armoured figures of Space Marines who did not belong to his Chapter and were not loyal to his Emperor. They must have cloaked their approach with magic, he thought. It looked like they were intent on repaying him for his earlier surprise assault. Ragnar felt he understood. This morning was merely one small skirmish in the unending war between the Imperium and Chaos, between the Space Wolves and the Thousand Sons. That was the way of the universe – countless warring factions and unending strife. He spoke softly into the comm-net telling his men to get ready. If they acted swiftly they could turn this sneak attack on itself.

'Fire!' he shouted, and the last vestiges of his memories were whirled away by the winds of violent actions. There was a war to win. There was always another war to win.

SONS OF FENRIS

PROLOGUE

Splashes of colour painted the clouds with a swirl of reds, oranges and yellows, silhouetting the black and grey towers of Saint Harman, the once great capital city of Corinthus V. Wolf Lord Ragnar Blackmane found a sense of satisfaction in the ability of instruments of Imperial justice to duplicate the dawn of a new day in the middle of the night. Every explosion from the Imperial artillery, every bombardment from the fleet above, left its own mark on the tapestry of the sky.

Ragnar took an extra moment to commit this battle to memory. So many wars on countless worlds could make a Space Marine forget. The wars never ended for humanity's defenders. They constantly went forth to do the will of the Emperor of Mankind and battle the enemies of the Imperium. The Imperial Guard had fought the Chaos incursion for almost a year. After only a month, Ragnar and his great company of Space Wolves had turned the tide of the campaign.

Once Corinthus V had produced munitions and vehicles for the Imperium's vast armies, and the populace took pride in their work, too much pride in fact, looking to the glory of the machine instead of keeping their faith in the Emperor. While the citizens had performed their duties making ammunition for the Space Marine Chapters and the Imperial Guard, including Ragnar's own Space Wolves, the taint of Chaos had slipped onto Corinthus V. Every one of the Space Marines, the ultimate warriors of the Imperium, knew the dangers of Chaos. Daemons from the warp whispered twisted thoughts, corrupting even the most dedicated. Only faith in the Emperor could protect one from Chaos. When Corinthus V lost its faith, Chaos gained its hold. Now, the Space Wolves had almost reached victory.

Ragnar made a point of trying to remember each campaign before its end, and it was time for the end. The time was right for his Space Wolves to make their final assault. The treacherous enemy, rebels and worshippers of the ruinous powers of Chaos, were all but destroyed. One last strike and this campaign was won.

RAGNAR STOOD ALONE on top of the rocky heights overlooking the city. He enjoyed this time the most. Just before battle, the world seemed different, quiet and tranquil. Moments of quiet were rare in a lifetime of constant warfare. He knew that the moment would not last. His job was not yet done. He caught a familiar scent on the air, and knew it was time.

Powerful strides brought Ranulf, a member of the Wolf Guard, Ragnar's own elite bodyguard, to the top of the hill to stand next to his Wolf Lord. Ranulf was the largest Space Wolf that he had ever known, gifted by the spirit of Leman Russ, primarch of their Chapter, with unparalleled strength. Ragnar thought that if Leman Russ returned to lead the Space Wolves, this Wolf Guard might be able to look the ancient primarch in the eye. More important than his size, Ranulf was one of Ragnar's oldest and dearest friends and the most trusted of his Wolf Guard, holding the title of battle leader, giving him command if the Wolf Lord should fall.

'Are the men assembled?' Ragnar asked.

'Yes, Lord Ragnar, your Wolf Guard awaits you,' Ranulf replied.

Ragnar turned and clapped Ranulf's shoulder. 'As well they should. I'd hate to have them finish the war without me. Ranulf, let's finally be rid of this Chaos filth.'

'What's the current status?' asked Ragnar.

'For the most part, the heretics are scattered and disorganised, but some of them have fortified small strong points within Saint Harman. The Imperial Guard has kept them at bay, but they need us to break the final strongholds.'

'Good. The Imperial Guard commander remembered my instructions from the beginning of the campaign. He's saved the last for us to face in the assaults. Starting a war is easy, finishing it is hard. We've got the hard part to do. These heretics have one last push in them.'

'M'lord?' asked Ranulf.

'My instincts tell me that they are luring us into a false sense of security. They haven't fought nearly as hard this time. We haven't even moved into the combat in Saint Harman. Our Space Wolves had to help the Imperial Guard to even gain a foothold in the other cities. On every other location on this planet, the Chaos worshippers fought tooth and nail, but here in the capital as their last stand, they are routed? I don't think so. They are in trouble, but a cornered animal is always dangerous. Of course, so are Wolves,' Ragnar grinned, exposing his long and sharpened canines. The gene-seed, which transformed Space Wolves from men to superhuman warriors, gave them many gifts. Besides their stature, standing half a metre taller than any man, the most outwardly visible sign was their extended canines. The older a Space Wolf was, the longer they grew. For a Wolf Lord, Ragnar was rather short in the tooth, but no one dared mention it to him.

The Wolf Guard stood ready. Three of Ragnar's finest warriors, Tor, Uller and Hrolf, awaited him. Unlike other packs, Ragnar's Wolf Guard each carried their own individual arms and weapons. The most experienced and reliable of all of his Space Wolves, they had proven themselves a hundred times over. Now, they would have to prove themselves once more, and each one relished the chance.

'You'll break up and go to the packs for this one. Each one of you will lead a pack. Ranulf, I want you and Tor to take Grey Hunter packs near my flanks. Uller, you'll move your men parallel to Tor. I'll be with the Blood Claws.'

Ragnar preferred to fight alongside the Blood Claws, the youngest and most restless warriors, newly initiated Space Wolves. They possessed a wild abandon, a raw desire for victory that required strong guidance.

Ragnar unfolded a map. 'Tor, your pack will flank my right. You will enter the city here and move north towards the Administratum sector. Ranulf you'll flank my left, on the edge of the merchant sector. We'll be spread thin, so stay alert.'

Ranulf, Tor and Uller took command of their Grey Hunters, the Space Wolves' tried and true veterans. Ragnar watched them leave. He had fought alongside all three countless times. However, Ragnar had just granted Tor the honour of joining the Wolf Guard. Ragnar knew he was ready for it. He just wondered if Tor knew it.

'What would you like me to do, milord Ragnar?' The sarcasm in Hrolf's voice was so thick that a frostaxe could cut it.

'Hrolf, I'm sorry, I thought you were dead,' Ragnar stated. The two men shared a long running joke, as Hrolf was by far the oldest member of the great company and Ragnar was the youngest of the Wolf Lords. Despite the difference in rank and age, Hrolf and Ragnar shared a strong bond of brotherhood.

'Haven't found the war big enough to kill me yet, Ragnar, and once I do, you'll have the Iron Priests wire me into the next available Dreadnought, because you hate going to war without me.' Both men burst into laughter.

One look at Hrolf's face said everything about the old Space Wolf. It was a map to his past, riddled with scars like landmarks from centuries of war, while his storm-grey eyes reminded Ragnar of the worst hurricanes on their home world of Fenris. Ragnar could see countless horrors and wonders reflected in those eyes. However, his huge smile stood out in contrast to his rough face.

Ragnar threw an arm around his oldest Wolf Guard. 'Old friend, once again I need you with your Long Fangs. Who else can best handle the heavy support? I'm assuming that you've scouted the best place to position your pack?'

'Aye sir, up on the ridge where you spent the morning admiring Saint Harman, and the ruins of the old spaceport shuttle pad there.' Hrolf pointed to the south-east ridge, which jutted from the tree canopy, and then to the south-west.

'Looks perfect, Hrolf, in fact you're in luck, someone positioned my Long Fangs at both locations.' Ragnar admired Hrolf's initiative. 'Should anything unexpected arise you'll have enough firepower to shift the balance back in our favour.'

THE SPACE WOLVES moved into the city on foot, making their way first through the burning industrial sector. The air held the scents of blood, decay, smoke and death, along with burning toxins from destroyed machinery. Beneath it all, Ragnar could separate one scent from the others: the sickly sweet taint of Chaos. The enemy was here. The hairs on his neck rose.

The Space Wolves spent the next few hours in silence, communicating through hand gestures and body language. The packs knew each other and each individual covered his battle-brothers. There was no resistance, even though the Imperial Guard had reported fire from several of the buildings that the Space Wolves cleared. Ragnar found access tunnels and entrances to sewer pipes large enough for a man. The enemy was moving. He suppressed a low growl. Stories of Commissar Yarrick's defeat of the orks on Armageddon came to mind. Surrounded and left for dead, the commissar had rallied a hive to hold out against the ork horde using pipes and tunnels to ambush the greenskins. If the heretics intended to defeat Ragnar that way, they'd learn that he was a wolf, not an ork.

The packs had spread out, seeking resistance. Ragnar worried that they had moved out too far. His Space Wolves had a little of their Wolf

Lord in them, and confidence was not something he lacked. He activated his comm.

'Ranulf, report your position and situation.'

'We've moved along the merchant sector and entered what looks from the ruins to be the workers' housing area. We're just to the north of you. Everything is quiet, Wolf Lord... too quiet.'

'Agreed. Stay cautious and hungry. We're in a bombed-out intersection on the western edge of the Administratum sector, near the library. If they are going to strike, it will be soon. Pass the word,' Ragnar replied.

The Administratum sector of Saint Harman was once the heart of the city. Holding elements of the vast bureaucracy meant to enforce the Emperor's will, the area dictated the ebb and flow of Corinthus V. Reports flowed freely on every aspect of the citizens' life. Like many worlds in the Imperium, freedoms were strictly controlled to protect humanity from outside influences. Administration buildings, mediator precincts, and Imperial chapels were everywhere, all designed in the architectural style of the same structures on Holy Terra, home of the Golden Throne, eternal resting place for the Holy Emperor. They served as a constant reminder that it was from Terra that the Emperor of Mankind launched his holy crusade to reunite humanity in the hopes of protecting them. They hoped to protect them from exactly what had happened on Corinthus V.

Ragnar turned to the Blood Claws around him. The pack was restless. Arik, one of the youngest, kept activating his chainsword, causing the blade to growl like a hungry beast. Ragnar shook his head. 'Steady lads. Keep your senses keen and your minds focused,' he said quietly.

Suddenly, Ragnar heard a crash from inside the ground floor of the Imperial library to the east. It was a tall monolithic building, which put Ragnar in mind of a colossal crypt. Before the war, servitors and aged scholars would have moved quietly through stacks of scrolls, books and datapads within its walls. The tall windows of the library were dark, giving no signs of life, but Ragnar and his pack had definitely heard a crash.

Arik broke into a run, waving his chainsword, and howling his desire for combat. 'There, Wolf Lord, in th–'

Those were the last words that Arik would ever speak. A bolter shell tore through the Blood Claw's head, spreading fragments of his skull in front of his body. To Ragnar's surprise, the shot had come from behind. It was an ambush.

A barrage of fire echoed from behind the pack, and Ragnar felt a bolter shell ricochet off his power armour.

'Ranulf, ambush, we're pinned in crossfire! Hold your ground and be ready for a rapid fire drill.' Ragnar growled in anticipation, feeling more like a Blood Claw than the Wolf Lord he was. 'It should be a full-scale counter-attack.'

Suddenly shards of reinforced rockcrete and ceramite exploded all around the pack. The hot wind of plasma fire vaporised stone and reinforcing steel. The Blood Claws howled, more like wolves than trained Space Marines, circling for a target, looking for someone to attack. 'Find cover,' ordered Ragnar, but the violent explosions drowned his words. The air was rank with smells, so much so that it was hard to isolate and identify them. They were surrounded. Quick glimpses of targets were all they could see, like smoke in a strong wind, almost visible for a second and then gone.

Then Ulrik, Bori and three others stopped. Ragnar knew they had a target, he also knew...

'Ulrik, Bori, stop,' Ragnar shouted. It was too late. They had committed themselves in the direction of the library. He had lost control and his pack was going to charge into that dark vault. Ragnar had no choice. 'In the Emperor's name...' he cursed.

'*Charge!*' Ragnar howled, drawing his frostblade and charging at the library.

The Blood Claws all heard their leader's command. Charging replaced confusion, as the rest of the pack joined Ragnar, screaming out their battle cries as one, 'For Fenris, for Russ, for the Emperor!'

The Space Wolves unleashed a hailstorm of bolt pistol shots into the library as they charged. Chainswords growled to life, and power weapons flashed with energy, hungering for the blood of their unseen foes. The huge Space Marines raced each other, each one hoping for the first strike.

Before the Blood Claws could reach the enemy the ground rippled and exploded as a missile strike stopped them short, shredding two of their number and sending Ragnar flying. Melta guns lashed out into the pack, instantly incinerating even the Space Marines' ancient power armour. Ragnar watched his own symbol melt away with the arm of one of his Blood Claws, and realised that he and his Wolf brothers were not facing a mere group of Imperial citizens corrupted by the foul powers of Chaos. Their hidden enemies were too well equipped and far too accurate. The Space Wolves were in trouble. Ragnar had only seconds to regain control. He moved through the cover, trying to get a better view. Taking up a position against a large section of collapsed wall, a cold chill enveloped Ragnar's hearts as he realised who they faced – Chaos Space Marines!

* * *

TEN THOUSAND YEARS ago, a terrible civil war nearly destroyed the Imperium. After the fall of the rebels' leader, Horus, the traitors fled into the warp, the nightmare realm beyond space and time. Living in a realm of daemons for ten thousand years, they had honed their skills and fuelled their hatred. Their armour and weapons had changed, fusing with the daemonic energies of Chaos. In all ways, they were better warriors than the Space Wolves, with age-old experience empowered by millennia-old hatred.

Chaos Space Marines lacked only one thing that the Space Wolves possessed: faith in the Emperor. For Ragnar's Space Wolves, they would have to hope that their belief in the Emperor was greater than the Chaos Space Marines' desire for revenge. That was their only advantage.

Ragnar saw one of the Chaos Space Marines stride forth from the swirling smoke of battle. The giant figure wore glittering dark armour that reflected the light as if it was wet with slime – a Night Lord. A halo of burning fire leapt between the traitor's mutant horns. He swung a black flail that howled like the winter winds of Fenris in one hand, while a skull covered bolter spat death from his other hand.

Ragnar felt the wave of hatred and anger lash out as the servant of Chaos fired his bolter, each shot striking a Space Wolf as if the ancient warrior willed his shells into his victims.

The Wolf Lord raised his gun to return fire, but the Night Lord stepped to the side, avoiding the shots instinctively. For a second, Ragnar thought the smoke of battle poured from the Chaos Space Marine's armour. If it did, then it served the traitor well. The veil enshrouded him once more. When it cleared a second later, Ragnar's giant enemy had moved. He felt the beast howl in rage within, eager to give chase and destroy his treacherous enemy.

Glancing around, he saw that not all of the buildings held enemies. 'Blood Claws to me,' Ragnar commanded as he leapt and rolled to the nearest shelter. The former Administratum building had never seen much excitement. Now, it might witness the last stand of a Wolf Lord. Nine Blood Claws joined him. Better numbers than he had expected.

They entered what looked like an office complex. The room spanned the length and depth of the entire building. Large rockcrete columns were spaced evenly throughout. Sections of the walls and floor had been destroyed, and remnants of desks and other furniture were strewn about. At the far end of the room was what looked like an old elevator shaft, filled with debris from the floors above. Next to it was a stairwell. It looked severely damaged, but it was intact.

'Sons of Russ, follow me. Our destiny awaits!' Ragnar crossed the room and vaulted up the stairs. They had to reach higher ground and get above the fray. He hoped that whatever spirits held old buildings together they'd keep this one from collapsing.

It was time for Ragnar to stop playing Blood Claw and be the Wolf Lord. He activated his comm.

'Hrolf, bring your Long Fangs to bear. Target the Imperial library and whatever building nearby has Chaos Havocs shooting from it. We've got real enemies.'

'Havocs? They're mine. You'll have new drinking vessels from their helms, if my men leave enough of their horns.'

The stairway shook as explosions rocked the building's foundations. Ragnar looked behind to check on his pack. Despite his concerns, the Blood Claws kept their balance as they clambered across rubble and broken stairs, moving ever higher. More tremors struck and Ragnar saw a bright orange flash through one of the cracks in the walls. This was what being a Space Wolf was all about, he thought. Ragnar and his Wolves were in their element, outnumbered and outgunned, but not outmatched. It was good to be a Wolf Lord.

Ragnar's comm crackled into life. 'Wolf Lord, this is Tor. I'm not going to let the enemy assassinate you. You have the only action, centred around the Imperial library. My Grey Hunters have not met resistance. I'm bringing my pack and having the others coordinate as well. Just give me the word.'

Ragnar didn't like this. He responded, 'Tor, hold your position,' but his only reply was a high-pitched buzz. They were being jammed. It wasn't a trap for Ragnar, he was the bait, and loyal Tor was about to put his foot in it.

Ragnar reached a reinforced metal door, sealing off the roof. Despite the seal, he could smell the stench of Chaos on the other side, a sickly odour somewhere between sulphur and rotting meat. This building wasn't abandoned. The enemy were waiting on the other side of the door, ready to cut Ragnar and his Blood Claws to ribbons the minute it opened. They had set another trap for him. If they smashed the door, they'd step out into a firing squad. Fortunately, the pack wasn't going through the door. Ragnar hoped that a Havoc squad held this roof, just to get them before Hrolf did.

Ragnar gestured to his Blood Claws. They had the scent as well. Stepping away from the door, Ragnar turned towards the right wall. Made of solid rockcrete, it still appeared less reinforced than the metal door. Years of experience had taught Ragnar that engineers often made their doors stronger than their walls. He took a couple of steps back from the wall, signalled and readied his Blood Claws. Lunging forwards into the wall, the force of Ragnar's impact reduced the rockcrete to micro-particles. Ragnar and his Space Wolves poured through the opening to find nothing. All that remained was the scent of the Chaos taint. The Chaos Space Marines had passed this way, but they weren't here any longer. Like spiders, they had lurked on the rooftops, and then lowered themselves down into positions near the library square for the ambush. Ragnar chided himself for a moment, but he knew that he couldn't take chances against these foes.

TOR AND HIS Grey Hunters closed the distance to the Imperial library. There had been no response from Wolf Lord Ragnar, so it was up to him as a Wolf Guard to make a decision. He needed to protect Ragnar. If the Wolf Lord was all right, he would have responded, and if something had happened to Ragnar, Tor would make sure that the heretics got to see their Chaos masters when they went screaming to hell.

The pack of Space Wolves came to a large pile of debris, where the upper floors of an unrecognisable building had come to rest at its foundations. The ruins provided a strong defensible position for Tor to get his bearings and formulate a strategy.

'Tor, are you sure about this?' asked the voice of Uller, one of the other Wolf Guard over the comm.

'I have no response from Ragnar. We need to get as many Space Wolves to his side as we can, right now! It's my decision,' answered Tor. 'Bring as many of the others as possible, and keep moving.'

'Tor, this is Ranulf. My last orders were to hold and stand ready for attack.'

'Ranulf, you're too far away to help. You should hold, but the rest of us need to be there.'

'You should wait for Lord Ragnar.'

'He may not have time.' Tor clicked off his comm.

Tor led his men out of cover and ran fast through the empty streets. Tall office buildings loomed all around them. Each one could contain dozens of enemies. The Grey Hunters were the only living things running through a deserted rockcrete canyon. The dark empty streets could become a kill zone at any second. For Tor, caution was no longer a concern. The pack would save their Wolf Lord, or their spirits would go back to Fenris covered in glory. They reached the library square, coming beneath the long shadow of the vaulted Imperial library. Across the square, Tor spied Uller's Grey Hunters hugging the edge of an Administratum building. The air was quiet. Tor scanned the rubble, catching glimpses of blue-grey ceramite, fragments of Space Wolf power armour, scattered among the debris. He moved his Grey Hunters forwards.

Night Lords burst from hiding places behind the Grey Hunters, leaving the Space Wolves pinned against the cover. Space Wolves were known across the galaxy for their superior senses, a fact the Chaos Space Marines were obviously aware of. Establishing their point of ambush down wind, they had been able to hide their presence from the Space Wolves.

Unlike Tor, the traitors did not hesitate. They fired their weapons with brutal accuracy. Nearly every shot found the armour of a Space Wolf. Tor caught a glimpse of the skulls and bones hanging as trophies from their belts, along with the heads of Imperial Guardsmen and even a Space Wolf helm. The young Wolf Guard looked to Uller's men, hoping for support. He saw three of Uller's Grey Hunters drop to their knees as blood poured from their armour. The Night Lords had got in behind Uller's pack as well.

Tor realised his mistake. The enemy had used the Wolf Lord as bait, and not only had Tor led his own pack into the deathtrap, he had led the others as well. Mere moments before, he had seen the square as the perfect cover to approach the large grey doors of the Imperial library. Now, it was a maze of debris, trapping his men. The Night Lords had closed off their exit routes and left them pinned. They were surrounded and outnumbered. They were going to die.

He tried the comm but it was jammed.

Bolter rounds came from all sides, but unlike normal bolter shells, these shrieked and exploded with burning flames. Inhuman laughter echoed across the library square as if the buildings themselves mocked the dying Space Wolves. A dark-armoured Chaos Space Marine stood up in the middle of the debris, less than three metres from Tor. With a war cry akin to the howl of a banshee, he raised a writhing metal gun, and fired a burst of blue-white plasma, not at Tor, but at a cluster of Grey Hunters, engulfing two, and leaving them melted piles of flesh and ceramite. An incendiary ignited within the debris all around the Grey Hunters. Even if the Space Wolves had found cover in the plaza, they were in danger of roasting alive.

There was only one chance. Tor's Space Wolves had to assault the enemy and break out. He yelled at Uller, while his men fell around him. 'We've got to charge.'

Uller nodded, although Tor could see the glare in his eyes. Uller blamed Tor for this disaster, and rightly so.

'For Russ!' howled Tor as he charged the Chaos forces. The Space Wolves had to break free and regroup. The inhuman laughter grew louder. The enemy wanted the packs to come closer. The Night Lords never hesitated in firing. A Grey Hunter twisted to the ground as a bolter round tore through his armour and his intestines. Tor felt the bolter rounds crunch on his armour, each a hammer-blow. He prayed to the Emperor that his armour would hold, even as he watched the Chaos Space Marines draw their spiked and rune-covered weapons, continuing to fire their bolters one-handed.

Tor swung his axe at a Night Lord, who hissed like a serpent. The Chaos Space Marine parried with a tendril coiled around the hilt of a chainsword, sending blue sparks flying from the frostaxe as the blade's teeth shattered one by one. The traitor's bolter slammed a round into Tor's chest plate.

Tor gritted his teeth and fired his plasma pistol, all the while trying to keep his eyes off the enemy's armour.

The plasma enveloped the chest plate of the Night Lord, burning its way through the ancient ceramite. The intense heat melted everything it came in contact with including the chest of the Space Marine encased within. Liquid remains oozed out of the opening as he collapsed to the ground.

There was no time to celebrate the death of his enemy. A black-clad giant, its armour covered in writhing green runes, drove a spiked blade into the joint of Tor's armour above the thigh. The Wolf Guard felt the end of the blade twist back and forth inside him as if it was alive. Another Night Lord, with horns twisting out through his armour like weeds through broken rockcrete, delivered a hard blow with a double-bladed axe, cracking Tor's helm.

'Tooorrr,' cried out one of the Grey Hunters as he dived to protect his Wolf Guard. A third Chaos Space Marine moved to intercept with preternatural speed, catching the Grey Hunter on a chainaxe in mid-air. The Grey Hunter's heroic dive proved his undoing, as the chainaxe carved through him, splattering Tor with his comrade's blood and insides. The Night Lord raised his chainaxe in triumph and inhuman laughter echoed round the square.

RAGNAR COULD SEE everything from the roof's edge. Chaos Space Marines surrounded his packs of Grey Hunters. Ragnar's insides curled in knots. He could make out Tor and Uller. Tor was on the ground, but still struggling. Uller swung his large power fist around in a deadly arc, heroically keeping three Night Lords at bay as he tried to force his way to Tor. A Grey Hunter sliced off the arm of a Chaos Space Marine, yet his inhuman foe didn't falter, redoubling his attacks with his remaining arm and thrusting a burning crimson power sword through the Space Wolf's chest. One Night Lord tore the helmet off another Grey Hunter, and spat acid across the Fenrisian's face. The Night Lords were more than a match for the Space Wolves, and they had the advantage of terrain and numbers. The enemy was toying with the Space Wolves, enjoying the slaughter of the Emperor's finest.

Ragnar wanted to leap down into the fray. The fall would kill any normal man, but he knew he could survive. However, it would only drop him into the trap. Even he wouldn't last long in the middle of the melee. He had to come from the side, from somewhere unexpected.

He spotted a neighbouring building that was leaning threateningly towards the one they stood on. Weeks of fighting had damaged it badly but somehow it hadn't completely fallen. However, it was close enough to their building to give Ragnar and his men a way out. 'Follow me,' he ordered then backed up and ran as fast as he could, leaping at the last moment. He flew across the chasm between the buildings, and for a moment, he wondered if Logan Grimnar, the Old Wolf and greatest of the Wolf Lords, would have tried this. He crashed into the roof of the other building, smashing through the rockcrete. He had made it, and his power armour had kept him going. The other Blood Claws landed around him, like a volley of missiles. 'Let's move,' Ragnar snarled.

They raced through the oddly angled building, running, crawling, and even jumping at times to reach the far side. If Ragnar needed evidence of Chaos infestation here in Saint Harman, he had found it. The facades of the buildings looked normal, but the insides held architectural madness. The builders had fallen away from Imperial standards and walked the edge of sanity. Corners jutted out into hallways, and strange rounded floors bulged upwards. Discoloured ceiling tiles seemed to form alien glyphs, and the height of the ceiling changed, sometimes reaching over three metres and other times forcing them to crouch.

Ragnar hoped that by travelling through the building his pack had crossed the Chaos lines. Now was the time to find out. There was no time for stairs. Ragnar tore his way out of the building through the wall and dropped, reaching out against the side of the building to slow his fall. He landed heavily in a shower of debris, followed by his loyal Blood Claws. They showed no hesitation. Power armour and myomer muscle had absorbed the impact, micro-servos contracting and releasing, transferring the energy of the landing. Ragnar's gambit had worked.

Ragnar leapt to his feet and broke into a run. He knew where Tor was trying his breakout, and knew they had little time. The sounds of warfare clearly guided them to the assault.

'This is Ragnar, if you aren't near the library, hold your positions and brace for possible attack,' he growled over the comm.

'Hold here,' he ordered the Blood Claws, raising a fist in the air and pointing to a ruined building that looked as if it might provide decent cover. 'Ulrik, take the four other Blood Claws with you, move through that building and take up firing positions on the other side. Wait for my command before you act. Is that clear?'

'Yes, Wolf Lord,' Ulrik replied. The Blood Claw showed signs of control. Perhaps he was on his way to being a Grey Hunter.

'The rest of you, come with me.' Ragnar waved them forwards.

Ragnar manoeuvred closer through the debris and rubble, keeping cover. He could see Chaos Space Marines surrounding Tor and his remaining Grey Hunters. The Night Lords were firing into the fray without regard for their own, killing Space Wolf and Chaos Space Marine alike. One of the Night Lords clutched a standard bearing the icon of their wretched god of Chaos, a mystical item not uncommon to their ilk. Laughter echoed from below, centring on the icon itself. The essences of daemons were often bound to such standards, allowing horrors from the warp to manifest and claim victims for the Dark Powers. However depraved the enemy's attacks seemed so far, daemons would do worse. As Ragnar watched, a ghostly green mist formed around the icon bearer. His heart pounded in his chest, the enemy was about to summon their daemonic allies. He had to destroy that icon.

'When I break cover shoot everything you have into the traitors.'

Ragnar tried his comm again, only to receive an earful of high pitched static. He'd have to do it on his own. He hurled himself over the wall and sprinted towards the cultists. Behind him, the Blood Claws unleashed the wrath of Fenris with their bolt pistols. Ragnar heard Ulrik's force following their lead. The traitors turned their attention away from the Grey Hunters, searching for their new attackers.

Ragnar crashed into the melee, snapping the neck of a Night Lord by twisting its horned helm. Bile, ichor and goo shot forth instead of the flesh and bone of a man.

The suddenness of the Wolf Lord's attack threw the Chaos Space Marines into confusion. Ragnar put his blade through the twisted faceplate of another traitor. Their enemies had let themselves become overconfident.

A gigantic Chaos Space Marine, nearly the size of Ranulf, threw Tor to the ground, and stood over him, gloating and carving through the Imperial eagle on his armour, trying to reach his heart. Ragnar could hear him speaking a strange chant as he prepared to sacrifice the Wolf Guard to the gods of Chaos. The traitor's depravity was his undoing, as Ragnar shot him point blank, never giving him a chance. Only Tor and two Grey Hunters were left alive, and one of the Space Marines was too wounded to fight on. Without hesitation, Ragnar hoisted the wounded Space Wolf over his shoulder and ran back towards the ruins where his Blood Claws continued firing. A bolter shell crashed into Ragnar's back-pack. The attack had startled the Chaos Space Marines, but they recovered quickly. 'Don't stop,' he shouted.

Behind Ragnar, the world exploded in a bright fireball. Then, a second blast erupted, and a third. The Night Lord holding the icon fell as a lascannon shot instantly vaporised him. The greenish mist dissolved with a high-pitched wail, and the laughter was cut short.

'Wolf Lord, didn't you promise me some Havocs?' came Hrolf's voice from the comm.

Thank Russ for that grizzled old warrior. The Long Fangs were giving them cover fire. They would escape.

The rest was a blur of smoke, debris and confusion as the Long Fangs pounded the Chaos position. A few more Grey Hunters found their way out of the trap, but they were too few, far too few.

WITHIN THE HOUR, Ragnar stood at the clamshell hatch of his Land Raider Crusader. He had established a command outpost just below the ridge in the industrial section of Saint Harman, where his men had entered the city hours before. The Chaos forces had forced the Space Wolves to withdraw and regroup. Fortunately the casualties were not as heavy as they could have been. Heaviest hit was his Blood Claws pack, and Tor and Uller's Grey Hunters.

Ragnar had no time for thoughts of remorse. His battle-brothers had met a worthy end in the service of Russ. He had to focus on how the enemy forces had reinforced on such a level. He had underestimated them.

Ranulf ran up to the Crusader, just ahead of two Space Wolf scouts. 'The scouts have returned, Lord Ragnar. They bring news.'

Scouts of the Space Wolf Chapter were an odd sort, shunning the standard organisational doctrine of the Space Wolves, serving Russ in a more solitary and isolated way. Like the Priests of Iron, the Great Wolf himself controlled them, dispatching and deploying them wherever he saw a need. In fact, it was the Wolf scouts who had identified the first signs of Chaos on Corinthus V. Ragnar was aware of their presence and had been receiving intelligence from them.

Two grizzled Wolf scouts walked up slowly, as if they were saving their energy for combat. The taller of the two looked to be several centuries old. Wolf pelts hung around his waist and over his right shoulder. He wore wolf teeth, more than could be counted, on a leather cord around his neck. His face was weathered, a scar running across it, starting just above his left eye and spreading down across his nose and through his lip, ending on his right lower jaw. The wound was so deep that when it had healed it had separated his lip, exposing his canines, making him appear to be constantly snarling. He was armed with a bolter, but there was nothing simple about the ice-blue edge of the axe that was strapped across his back. Ragnar knew his name was Hoskuld.

The second scout seemed more subdued, wearing a hooded wolf pelt that almost completely enveloped him. The hood hid his face so that Ragnar could only see the glow of a bionic eye. Across his back, he carried a sniper rifle.

Ragnar nodded to them both.

'Hoskuld, it is good to see you again. What have you discovered?' he asked.

'M'lord, as instructed we made our way deep into the city. It is as you feared. The traitors have significantly reinforced their numbers,' the scout reported. 'The enemy has a sorcerer who opened a portal to bring reinforcements through. We overheard them talking–'

'You overheard them talking?' Ranulf interrupted. 'Just how close were you?'

'Close enough to hear them talking,' replied Hoskuld, dryly.

'Ranulf!' Ragnar held a hand up to silence his battlebrother. 'Please continue.'

'They are too few to open a portal big enough to bring anything very large through, but they did say that by tomorrow night they would be strong enough to open a larger gate,' the scout concluded.

'We have to go in tonight, Ranulf,' said Ragnar.

Ragnar turned back to the scouts. 'Could you lead a small force back to the position where you witnessed this ritual?'

'A small force, yes milord,' the scout replied.

'Good. Ranulf, gather the Wolf Guard, and find Tor. I will need him for this.'

'M'lord, are you certain that you want Tor?' Ranulf inquired.

'He's going to lead the force,' stated Ragnar.

'Lead it?' Ranulf growled with surprise.

'Yes Ranulf, Tor will lead the incursion force to destroy the portal. We will launch our own attack to distract them.'

'But milord, Tor–'

'Needs an opportunity to redeem himself, Ranulf. Redemption requires two things, desire and opportunity. I know this better than most. Tor will get his chance for redemption.'

ONE
Service to Belisarius

WITH A QUICK strike, Ragnar splattered a large beetle. A yellow smear on his blue-grey power armour marked its passing, and finally he could focus and listen. He needed the full use of his ears, many times sharper than those of ordinary men. The jungle scents confused his acute sense of smell after he had spent so long on the industrialised surface of Terra, and his vision couldn't penetrate far in this endless thicket of greenery.

Hyades was a lush planet, many sectors from the Imperial capital of Holy Terra on the fringes of Space Wolf territory. Life had taken root on this world in quantity and variety at the high end of Imperial surveys. Colonists had quickly established strongholds on the planet, and although it was not a deathworld, the native fauna and flora did fight against the colonists. On Hyades, the men and women of the Imperium had turned the planet's promethium deposits to good use. The planetary law of survival was simple: if it moved, it burned. The first colonists had established their cities near promethium mines and burned the jungle to expand their territory. Citizens of Hyades destroyed the environment rather than adapting to it.

After years of political manoeuvrings, the Celestarch of House Belisarius had been granted custodianship of Hyades. Ragnar wondered what types of closed-door dealings had resulted in the acquisition of a planet but he had spent enough time on Terra not to let politics surprise him.

The Navigators of House Belisarius kept their power through their abilities to guide ships safely through the warp. The value of their gift to the Imperium could not be understated. Without Navigators to guide them safely through the immaterium, Imperial spaceships could never travel long distances between the stars. Even the custody of a planet was a side business interest compared to the House's true asset of Navigation.

Promethium production was one of House Belisarius's many benefits to the Imperium. Promethium, the white-hot fuel used in Imperial flame weapons, was found naturally in only a few places, including Hyades. In the last three years, production on the planet had fallen dramatically. The excuses given for the drop in production bordered on the ludicrous: reports of unusual equipment failure, coupled with narratives describing attacks from native predators unafraid of Imperial lasguns. The bureaucrats even blamed the weather for problems, claiming that they had faced an abundance of storms. Ragnar was all too familiar with bureaucrats from his time on Terra. They were spineless men who would blame anything for their failure. These people took the coward's path for their failures, instead of facing them with the responsibility of a true warrior.

The Celestarch had ordered Lady Gabriella to review the situation. She was one of the most promising of the young Navigators and it was generally agreed that she would rise to take the reins of leadership in House Belisarius. In addition, she had spent time on Fenris, home world of the Space Wolves, continuing to cement the centuries-old alliance between the Space Marine Chapter and her House. She had brought with her to Hyades living proof of this alliance, the House's most trusted defenders: the Wolfblade. Ragnar would have volunteered to escort her, but luckily Gabriella had selected him to accompany her anyway.

Ragnar wanted, as much as he wanted anything, to leave Terra and return to a galaxy where he could easily tell friend from foe instead of confronting the conspiracies and verbal sparring of the Imperial capital. Despite his desires, he accepted his duty and his responsibility. Once, he had served as a Blood Claw, a young hot-blooded member of the Space Wolves. Ragnar had battled on the front lines against the Imperium's deadliest enemies: the bloodthirsty orks, the enigmatic eldar and the heretical followers of Chaos. However, he had been responsible for the loss of a precious artefact, the Spear of Russ, a weapon that had belonged to his Chapter's primarch, the legendary Leman Russ. The cost of his failing had been his exile to the Wolfblade, in honour of an ancient pact to defend House Belisarius from its enemies.

And he had done his duty well, saving the Celestarch from an assassin, back on holy Terra. Still, he longed to return to the endless wars on the frontiers of Imperial space.

Gabriella's shuttle had arrived on Hyades, in its capital city of Lethe, earlier that day. She had been received with a formal celebration in the city's central palace, where she had met with the governor and dozens of other local dignitaries and functionaries.

Once Gabriella had been settled in, Ragnar had requested permission for the Wolfblade to inspect the city and review its defences, taking the opportunity to investigate the fall in promethium production. Gabriella had suggested the Space Wolves also search out the creatures that the locals were claiming were attacking them.

Ragnar's fellow Wolfblade members, especially Torin, a veteran of the civilised life on Terra, seemed less than pleased. Haegr had wanted to go, probably just to annoy Torin, Ragnar suspected.

Gabriella had assigned eight of the twelve Wolfblade escorting her to the patrol. Ragnar thought she sensed that he needed the adventure. The team was organised into a single pack of eight men, even though the Wolfblade was accustomed to smaller units. The unit was organised more for actual warfare than the skirmishing that the Wolfblade commonly participated in as the bodyguards of House Belisarius.

The members of the Wolfblade had quickly reviewed the city and its defences, although in truth, after spending so much time on Terra, Ragnar had had enough of cities. When they left the city walls to explore the surrounding wilderness, he could feel the excitement creeping in his blood.

The jungle was thick with closely placed trees coiling their roots together just below the soil and their branches together far above to create a dense canopy. Creeper vines hung between the tree trunks and bushes and ferns pushed through any spot of soil left by the roots. Little light penetrated to the jungle floor, and Ragnar wondered how so much life could survive without sunlight. He wondered if the heat of the promethium below the surface somehow sustained the jungle life.

The jungle wasn't uniformly dense. In places, spaces opened up beneath the canopy. The entire environment made Ragnar feel more like he was moving underground or through a cluttered building than outside. The jungle also held a constant hum from the beetles that the Space Wolves found everywhere. The team had remained silent and on alert but in the first four hours of their patrol, they had found nothing larger than a fist-sized crawling insect.

Finally, the silence was broken by the grumbles of Ragnar's fellow Space Wolves. 'Great idea Ragnar, coming out here,' said Haegr.

Although his friend's girth made him seem unfit, Ragnar had seen the speed and power that his massive comrade possessed. Haegr was probably half as dangerous as he boasted, and since he was a master at boasting, that made him formidable indeed.

'Come on, Haegr, don't you feel better now that we're away from civilisation?' replied Ragnar.

'Well, of course I do, but I would have chosen somewhere less hot and buggy.' Haegr flicked a beetle from the end of his boltgun.

Ragnar's ears picked a strange noise out of the buzz of the jungle's insects: a faint scratching sound, and then a click, coming from off to his left. A reptilian scent brushed against his nostrils. Another click answered to the right. Ragnar's blood warmed as he braced himself and held up a hand to his compatriots. To their credit, the other members of the Wolfblade kept up their bickering as they readied their weapons.

The attack came with a torrent of leaves, as the creatures tore through the jungle overgrowth. One of the beasts hurtled itself into Ragnar hard enough to send him sprawling. Ragnar's blade glowed with power as he fell back against a solid tree trunk. The sharp edge of the weapon sliced its way into the tree behind Ragnar as if it was paper, not wood. The tree tilted down, trapping the sword for the moment as it teetered on the verge of falling.

Ragnar's assailant reared over him. Covered in emerald scales, the alien creature blended perfectly into the jungle. Three rows of serrated teeth gnashed in its mouth, while its yellow eyes fixed on Ragnar and black diamond pupils narrowed. The creature's arms and legs reminded Ragnar more of an ape than a lizard, but the triangle-shaped head, forked tongue, lashing tail and reptile smell suggested it was mostly lizard.

Ragnar put three shells from his bolt pistol into the lizard thing's chest. Blood spurted out of its tattered torso and it twisted forwards, trying to attack, before something in its primitive brain realised that it was dead. It fell in a heap, and Ragnar moved on to his next foe.

A lizard-ape tore at Haegr in a frenzy, claws sparking as they failed again and again to penetrate the Space Wolf's ceramite armour. The creature increased its efforts, and the strength of the blows kept Ragnar's fellow Space Wolf pinned on the ground. Haegr was not hurt, but he was off-balance against the assault.

Ragnar hit the beast in the back of the head with his bolt pistol before putting a shot through its skull. With a roar, Haegr clambered to his feet, and leaving his weapons behind, he grabbed two lizard things by their necks and slammed them together with bone-crushing force. Ragnar thought of grenades exploding as their skulls burst.

The entire attack was over in less than a minute. The corpses of the beasts lay strewn around the blackened jungle. They certainly matched the description of the predators reported by the local people.

'Ragnar to Lady Gabriella, we've encountered some of the alien life forms,' he relayed on the comm.

'This is Gabriella. What is your status?'

'We're fine. They're dead. We'll find their trail and track it back to their lair. Ragnar out.'

The rush of excitement was intoxicating. Ragnar had missed it. He yanked his blade out of the jungle tree. 'Let's go,' he said, as he hacked his way along one of the creature's trails.

The team found a worn path in the dirt leading away from Lethe to the east. From the size of it, the Space Wolves agreed that it seemed to have been left by the lizard-ape life forms. The team couldn't be more than a few kilometres from the city itself, although Ragnar had lost exact track of their exact location. He suspected that his armour's locators needed some recalibration.

The slope of the ground indicated that the team had found a valley beneath the thick canopy of Hyades. Ragnar recalled from one of the briefings before arrival that in places the jungle canopy could reach over two hundred metres. As they continued, the sunlight faded. Ragnar was reminded of nothing so much as swimming into the depths of the sea.

After another quarter of an hour of travel, Ragnar caught the sickly smell of death and rot in his throat. He swallowed and shook his head. The stink was strong enough to make his eyes water. Considering a Space Wolf's superhuman resistance to toxins, Ragnar was impressed.

Just in front of the team, the tree trunks spread out, leaving a large clear space beneath the canopy. The space was big enough for the canopy above to be broken, and the size of it was comparable to the sanctuary hall in a cathedral. Sunlight filtered down from far above, shining down on the huge carcass of an enormous reptilian creature. The life form stretched almost twenty metres from tip to tail. Behind the dead beast, the far side of the clearing appeared to be a vine-covered rock face.

Ragnar quickly gestured for some of his team to secure the clearing, while he went to examine the corpse more closely. The men carefully readied their weapons and spread out to the edges of the clearing, checking for signs of movement or another ambush.

Ragnar deduced that the massive monster had fallen off the cliff to its doom, crushing trees and destroying vegetation on its way down. He could imagine that it had fallen in stages, catching on trees until its weight snapped them, sending it hurtling again until its final impact.

On further examination, Ragnar realised that his initial deduction might have been wrong. Cuts and tears marred the creature's mottled skin and long stakes jutted from its sides. Dried blood covered the beast. It appeared that the monster had been driven off the cliff to fall into a clearing filled with stakes. By the positioning of the stakes, the monster must have survived the fall and tried to stand, pulling up the stakes meant to impale it. Then, it had been attacked again.

A smashed emerald lizard-ape lay beneath the corpse's jaw. Three other bodies lay shattered near its tree trunk-sized tail. Ragnar wondered how many more might be underneath the corpse. He guessed the lizard creatures had driven the monster off the cliff, and then ambushed it.

'Those things killed this,' said Ragnar, voicing the thoughts of his fellow Space Wolves. In order to take down this behemoth, the lizard-apes must have hunted with patience and cunning. It appeared that they had stalked and wounded the beast using spears, and then driven it off the edge of the cliff. A group of them had lain in wait to finish it off once it had landed. They had coordinated their efforts to kill the rotting leviathan. Odd, then, that they had attacked the squad like frenzied animals.

Ragnar activated his comm. A healthy amount of static blared back at him. One of the complaints about production stated that something about Hyades caused problems with communications.

'At least they had hefty appetites,' remarked Haegr, 'a sure sign of deadly warriors.' Bite-sized holes showed in the behemoth's skin. Haegr looked like he was considering a taste.

Despite Haegr's jocularity, Ragnar stayed serious. 'Did any of the briefings say anything about intelligent alien creatures on this planet?' asked Ragnar.

The Space Wolves looked back and forth. They all knew that no one had reported intelligent native life on Hyades.

'Over here,' said Haegr, 'there's something that can't escape my keen senses.'

'Is it food?' asked Ragnar, trying to collect his sense of humour. Haegr's appetite was legendary.

Haegr shook his head. 'Just remember who saved you from that Imperial assassin.'

'All I remember is the way you fell down when he shot you,' said Ragnar. Cautiously, he pushed through the foliage in the direction Haegr pointed. A faint path between the trees marked the way. Haegr had found a path well traversed by the native fauna. Only a few hundred metres from the rotting corpse, a second immense space opened beneath the canopy.

The new space was extremely large, reaching a height of perhaps twenty-five metres and possibly having a diameter of ninety metres. This new opening looked unnatural, with an arched ceiling created by the twisting vines and trees, almost as if some alien gardener had created a cave out of plants. Strange flora shone with phosphorescence giving the setting an eerie blue and green glow. A large stone structure, wider than it was tall, sat shadowed in the centre of the space, perhaps half the height to the canopy, but at least thirty metres wide. It reminded Ragnar of a great toad lying in ambush for unwary insects.

Magni, a recent addition to the Wolfblade, pushed his way closer. The others followed, scanning for guards, feeling both compelled to investigate and an uneasy sense of horror. Ragnar was reminded of the feeling he had on a silent battlefield, covered with the wounded and the dying. It was that same sense of not wanting to see the carnage visited upon your battle-brothers, and yet having an inability to tear your eyes away.

Magni moved as if drawn by an invisible magnet. Ragnar felt his fellow Space Wolves' unease as they checked their weapons and scanned their surroundings. When Magni reached the base of the hidden structure, he activated his armour's luminators. The bright light revealed far more than the flora's phosphorescence.

The stones formed a great, tiered ziggurat. Ragnar couldn't tell if it was a great rock that had been carved into the shape of a ziggurat or if it was a carefully built structure. Faces leered out from the stone, grinning and laughing, some human, some insect, some animal and some completely unrecognisable.

Ragnar felt that this was the home of evil, an ancient evil. Though he had no reasons other than his old tribal superstitions, Ragnar suspected that this place was somehow tied to the gods of Chaos. Ragnar always suspected Chaos.

Other members of the team activated their luminators, combatting the dark and quiet atmosphere of the temple with bright light. Slowly, the Space Wolves circled the ziggurat, studying it, looking for openings and signs of age and use. Stone stairs led up the tiers while sculptures of flame marked the way. Ragnar thought the symbols were appropriate for a planet that produced so much promethium. He led a few members of his team in a climb of the stairs, while the others stood guard at the base of the structure.

On the third tier, the team found an opening. The outside of the passage was carved in the shape of a single eye. The hair rose on Ragnar's neck. He didn't like this, but he knew that if it was dangerous there was only one course of action.

'We should go inside,' said Ragnar.

'I agree,' said Magni. For a moment, Ragnar felt as if he was looking into a mirror of his past. Young Magni had all the fire of a new Blood Claw.

'Ho,' Haegr shouted up from below. The heavy Space Wolf had stayed on the ground to guard the stairs. Haegr directed his luminators to a section of soil.

Ragnar could make out tread marks. Alien creatures didn't use tracked vehicles. He gestured and took the team members who had made the climb back down with him to investigate.

The tracks that Haegr had seen were recent, but the Space Wolves soon found signs of older tracks beneath the fresh ones. The tracks belonged to a vehicle, probably a Chimera. The trail went off in the direction of the jungle back towards the east. Ragnar could make out where the trees parted, leaving only a sea of vines to cover the hole used by the vehicle.

Imperial troops had been here, and from the freshness of the tracks, within the last few days. They might even have been here just hours before Gabriella's shuttle had arrived. Why in the Emperor's name had they let such a foul place stand?

'Chimera tracks,' stated Magni, voicing the conclusion Ragnar had already reached. The Chimera was the standard transport vehicle of the Imperial Guard. Although troop carriers, Chimeras boasted an impressive amount of firepower. It could have easily burnt its way through the forest and survived the twists and turns of the hills beneath the canopy.

Ragnar said what the other members of the team were thinking. 'If they knew about this place, someone should have told us.'

Haegr clapped Ragnar on the shoulder with his meaty hand. 'Then why are we still standing here? Let's go.'

Ragnar paused, glancing back at the temple. 'I agree. We can study this place later,' he said, but he wondered if he'd regret not continuing their exploration. Besides, what if there were traitors in Lethe, possibly inciting these beasts to cover their own sabotage? Ragnar shook his head. It was best not to engage in unfounded speculation.

The squad moved as one, following the tracks through the undergrowth. The Chimera was a versatile vehicle, but even with terrain modifications, Ragnar found it surprising that one would force its way here to the temple. A tank driver couldn't have followed one of the narrow paths used by the reptile things, so they must have known where they were driving.

Unlike the slow hacking of before, the Chimera had burnt a hole through the jungle easily large enough for the Wolfblade squad. Insects smacked into the eye plates on Ragnar's helm as he took the lead over the others. Few Space Wolves could match Ragnar's speed, especially when his duty was at stake. He couldn't fail House Belisarius.

As his armoured boots crushed the remnants of foliage beneath them, he thought back. It wasn't House Belisarius he didn't want to fail, it was Logan Grimnar. He recalled that day on the Fang, standing in front of the Great Wolf himself, the leader of all the Space Wolves, when he had been assigned to the Wolfblade. He had seen it as a punishment. He was an exile from the Space Wolves. Since then, he had learned from Haegr, Torin and others about the glories of the Wolfblade, but still, he longed to return home to the Fang. He wanted to be back on Fenris, as a Space Wolf. Then, if he volunteered for the Wolfblade, that would be his choice, not something he had been forced to do. All he needed was a chance.

More light filtered through the jungle as the trail twisted and turned. The squad was surfacing from the jungle depths. Surprisingly, the further along the path they ran, the more the jungle had grown back. The entire jungle seemed accursed. The tracks couldn't have been more than a few hours old, yet vines crossed the trail and new saplings almost half a metre high thrust out of the ground.

Plants couldn't stop Ragnar. With his enhanced strength and the servo-motors in his armour, he tore the vines and snapped saplings. A group of blood thorn trees flung their deadly poison spines at the Space Wolf as he passed. An unprotected man would have died in seconds from the barrage, but the volley provided only a moment's distraction as it clattered off his power armour.

The team ran for over half an hour following the tracks. With their enhanced muscles, each Space Wolf moved faster than an ordinary man despite their armour. The pace was relentless. They were on the hunt.

Magni reached Ragnar and then passed him. The young Space Wolf gave the victorious howl of a Blood Claw. Ragnar remembered that Magni had been sent to the Wolfblade for disobeying orders in his zeal to fight. Although all Blood Claws were hard to control, when battle lust and excitement gripped Magni, he lost his head and had trouble regaining it. Ragnar considered ordering him back in line, but decided that he would simply meet the young one's challenge.

Ragnar saw the trees thinning and he knew that they were coming close to the capital. The city's defenders worked to keep a swathe of clear ground around the walls and would kill anything that ventured out of the jungle. The kill zone wasn't far away. He pushed himself to pass Magni, although he knew that such a breakneck pace was dangerous. Ragnar wasn't going to let anyone beat him.

The city of Lethe was a walled fortress in the jungle. Massive walls, reaching twenty metres high, loomed over a several hundred-metre kill zone. The citizens had poisoned the earth and kept the jungle away from the city with flame. Several gates allowed transports to move in and out to the mines along guarded roads maintained with more flame. Planetary Defence Force Sentinels with armoured cockpits patrolled the kill zone, armed with Hyades's signature heavy flamers and chainblades to fight the ever-encroaching vegetation. Hellhound tanks stayed ready to emerge and unleash their Inferno cannons on anything that threatened their city. The Planetary Defence Force manned the walls with large twin- and quad-linked heavy bolter turrets.

The amount of emphasis placed on defending Lethe from its surroundings seemed suspicious to Ragnar, but he had been around the galaxy enough to know that war would find the unprepared. Now, he wondered exactly who had done the preparing.

Ragnar dropped his pace as he reached the kill zone. The other Space Wolves behind him started catching up, although it appeared that giant Haegr was lagging a little behind the others. Magni surged forwards as Ragnar slowed.

Ragnar activated his comm. 'Magni, stop,' he ordered, but there was no stopping the young Space Wolf.

Magni looked up at the walls, and Ragnar knew that he could see the gun turrets. The men on the wall were trained to fire at anything entering the kill zone from the jungle. Still, the defenders knew that the Space Wolves were on patrol and surely, they would recognise power armour.

Ragnar heard the retort of the turrets from the wall. Heavy bolter shells pounded Magni. Dirt sprayed into the air as the blasts gouged holes in the earth. The large shells knocked Magni from his feet, cracking his power armour.

Ragnar watched in horror. He was in charge, and Magni was one of his men. The turrets had targeted the young Space Wolf, and Ragnar wasn't sure if the wall's defenders had recognised his fellow Space Marine as an ally.

Magni twisted backwards as another blast threw him into the air, instinctively seeking the shelter of the jungle. He came to rest at Ragnar's feet in a broken heap of blue-grey armour.

Ragnar shook with rage as he knelt to check Magni. Taking a deep breath to control his anger, he activated his comm. 'This is the Wolf-blade, we've arrived on the southern edge of the city. Stop firing the guns.'

No one answered. Were the city's defenders fools? Bolter shells ripped through the trees, tearing through bark and wood. They were still firing. Ragnar was furious, and the other Space Wolves started yelling. Despite the noise, Ragnar's ears caught the whirr of large servo-motors. The Sentinels were coming.

'We're under fire from our own side. Go defensive. Let's show them that we're Space Wolves, not animals,' Ragnar said, but in his heart, he wanted to teach the men a lesson.

'Ragnar, native predators attacking from the rear,' said one of the Space Wolves.

Ragnar heard Haegr yell a war cry, using the sound of snapping bones to punctuate his statement. The alien creatures had attacked the rear of the patrol. In his zeal, Ragnar had strung out his squad, and the creatures had ambushed them.

'Pull back and regroup,' Ragnar shouted to his men. 'If something comes at us from the jungle, kill it.'

Again, he tried to contact Lethe. 'By the tendrils of the kraken, some-one answer this comm. We're on your side.' More bolter shells tore through the jungle canopy. Ragnar realised that the comm wasn't work-ing. The men on the wall probably didn't know that they were firing on their own side.

The ground shook, and acidic sap sprayed from the side of the path as a chainblade ripped the jungle asunder. Like a giant of legend, a Sen-tinel towered over the Space Marines. The two-legged walker was armed with a chainblade mounted on a mechanical arm, and it had a heavy flamer attached on its side, just beneath the pilot's compartment.

Without even hesitating long enough to identify his targets, the pilot activated the Sentinel's heavy flamer. A bright fireball of promethium blew through the jungle, turning everything in its path to ash.

Ragnar's superhuman reflexes barely saved him as he dived towards the walker. He knew from countless battles that the flames spread out-wards in a cone, meaning that the safest place was right next to the Sentinel. Of course, most Sentinels weren't armed with chainblades.

The blade pivoted downwards, slicing towards Ragnar in a deadly arc. The blades blurred as they cried out for his head. Ragnar raised his glowing sword in an attempt to parry. The large chainblade struck the sword with enough force to make the Space Wolf's arm go numb. Grit-ting his teeth and straining his enhanced muscles, Ragnar kept his grip on the sword. The runes on the ancient blade glowed as it held against the Sentinel's chainweapon. The teeth of the chainblade snapped, flying in all directions. Then Ragnar's sword cut through the mechanism, sending sparks flying after the blade's teeth.

Ragnar could hear the rest of the squad fighting off their alien attackers. From the sounds of blades, bolters and breaking bones, he suspected that his men had the best of the enemy. One of them fired a bolter at the Sentinel, but the rounds bounced off its armour.

Not wanting his squad to endure another blast from the heavy flamer, Ragnar gripped his sword with both hands and swung it around at the two-legged walker's knee joint. The sword ripped through the servos and maimed the mechanical beast. The walker balanced on its sole remaining leg for a moment, and then fell forwards, driving the nozzle of the heavy flamer into the soil.

Haegr flung the body of an ape-lizard into the upper branches of the jungle. Bolter fire echoed as the other members of the Wolfblade dispatched the hissing lizard things. Even in an ambush, the creatures were no match for the Space Wolves.

The guns stopped. The ground shook. Another Sentinel was approaching. Then, Ragnar felt the earth vibrate. Years of warfare had taught the Space Wolf what an approaching tank felt like. From the engine noise, Ragnar could identify the vehicle. Lethe's Planetary Defence Force was sending a Hellhound to roast the entire section of jungle.

Several members of the squad shook themselves while their armour smoked from the heat. The Sentinel's heavy flamer had whitened the ceramite and discoloured the heraldry on every Space Marine caught in the blast. Besides Magni, two other members of the Wolfblade were down.

'Ragnar, what's going on?' yelled Haegr.

'No comms. They think we're the enemy and they are shooting at us.'

'Give me a moment, I'll do something,' said Haegr.

Ragnar looked out of the jungle to the kill zone. He had to think of something. The Space Wolves might be among the best warriors in the Imperium but they weren't ready to fight the defences of an entire city.

Haegr grabbed the hatch on the fallen Sentinel. In an impressive display of strength, the giant Space Marine ripped open the hatch to reveal the frightened man inside.

'Get out,' ordered the Space Wolf.

The pilot said something and leapt out of the hatch. Haegr reached inside with substantial effort and grunted before pulling out a comm. The vibration grew louder. 'Hurry,' said Ragnar.

'By the frozen hells of Fenris, this comm is jammed as well,' shouted Haegr, shaking his prize.

Ragnar knew what he had to do. 'Brothers, stay here.'

Ragnar charged out into the kill zone. The heavy bolters on the walls opened fire immediately, ripping gouts of soil from the earth. He changed direction, evading the shells, uttering a swift prayer to the Emperor that his armour would hold.

Bolter rounds clanged off Ragnar's shoulder pad, breaking his stride. To his left, another Sentinel charged forwards, although only armed with a heavy flamer, the walker remained out of range. To his right, he saw the source of the bolter fire, a Hellhound. He had hoped that the defenders would realise that a giant man in grey power armour wasn't a jungle beast.

The Sentinel slowed its advance. Perhaps the driver had some brains after all. The gunners on the wall kept firing, but fortunately their aim lacked accuracy. The Hellhound revved its engines and the front end of the tank leapt towards the Space Wolf.

Ragnar took in the situation and did the only thing that he knew the driver wouldn't expect: he charged. The turret of the tank's Inferno cannon swivelled in Ragnar's direction. This was going to hurt. Ragnar let out a howl and as the promethium flames splashed out of the Hellhound, he leapt at the tank, straining his legs and his armour's servo-motors. He only had one chance.

Flames sizzled against his leg guards as he flew through the air. The heat was overwhelming. Alarms screamed in his armour. He hoped that he had pushed himself enough. He wanted to land on the tank. If only the members of his original Claw could see him. The next time that he saw his old friend, Sven, from his Blood Claw days, he'd have to tell him about this, assuming that he lived.

Ragnar crashed heavily against the top of the Hellhound and pulled himself onto the turret of the Inferno cannon. His plan had worked. The guns had stopped firing. Lethe's defenders didn't want to risk blowing up their own tank.

A moment of silence and indecision followed from the walls and the lone Sentinel. Ragnar took a deep breath. His hearts felt like they wanted to pound out of his flesh. He stood and pulled off his helmet, letting it bounce off the Hellhound's armour.

'We're on your side,' he shouted. 'The comms aren't working.'

A flurry of activity broke out on the wall. Amid the shapes of defenders, Ragnar saw the familiar blue-grey of Space Wolf armour. He hoped that it might be Torin, his friend and Wolfblade veteran.

Ragnar's comm crackled to life. 'What do you mean your comms aren't working?' asked Torin. The grey-armoured figure on the wall waved down to Ragnar.

'I mean that this place isn't as different from Terra as I'd hoped. We've got a problem,' answered Ragnar on the comm, 'and we're at least one man down. Magni was wounded.'

'We wouldn't be Wolfblade if we didn't have problems, lad. Now, stop wrecking the paint on that Hellhound and get inside the city.'

Haegr came out of the jungle, leading the others. Two of the Space Wolves carried Magni. Haegr dragged part of the Sentinel's leg behind him. The large Space Wolf made an announcement to anyone who could hear.

'Let the Planetary Defence Force know that they need to repair one of their Sentinels,' said Haegr with a note of disgust in his voice.

The massive gates leading into Lethe shuddered open, and the squad shed one wilderness for another. Ragnar knew that he had felt safer with the beetles. At least in the jungle, he had known that everything was an enemy.

TWO
Unknown Enemies

AFTER ENTERING LETHE, Ragnar and his team had quickly made their way to the central palace complex and the med labs with Magni. Although he was a Space Marine, Magni had suffered serious injuries and had lost consciousness. Lady Gabriella had joined Ragnar after the medics and chirurgeons had begun their examination. She sent the other members of the Wolfblade off to continue their duties, but she had let Ragnar wait for a time to make sure Magni recovered.

Ragnar stood watching as the medical servitors and medics worked on Magni. The lab was up to Imperial standards with prosthetics, augmetics and surgical tables. Like all labs, it was a place of antiseptic smells mixed with blood and waste, unnatural scents that irritated Ragnar's inner beast.

Despite their knowledge, the strange anatomy of a genetically enhanced Space Marine defied the medics. They had cleaned Magni up and performed some healing rituals but in the end, Magni would have to heal himself naturally.

The young Space Wolf began to stir, starting to regain consciousness.

One of the medics left their patient to speak to Gabriella. 'Your servant should recover, my lady. We are unfamiliar with Space Marine physiology, but we have done our best.' The grey-haired man shook his head. 'I've heard of the Astartes' regenerative abilities but I was a sceptic until witnessing it myself, today. May the Emperor be praised.'

Gabriella nodded as she stood beside Ragnar. She was a tall, slender woman, more angled and severe than beautiful, yet in her black dress uniform she made a striking figure. A black scarf stayed tied over her forehead, covering her Navigator's third eye, and her long black hair flowed out below it.

One look at her pale skin made it apparent that she wasn't from Hyades. The natives of the planet all had a reddish tinge to their skin. Ragnar wondered if it was something in the air, an effect of exposure to the sun or a result of vapours from promethium leaking from the soil. Whatever it was, it made it easy to distinguish those who lived on the planet from most of its visitors.

Ragnar kept his eyes on Magni. Ragnar felt guilty about the young Blood Claw's wounds. He knew that he should have kept better control and not let Magni race him to the city. The young warrior lay across two tables, since one wasn't large enough to support the massive frame of a Space Marine. Magni grumbled and complained as the medics continued to examine him.

The sheer number of mechanical limbs in the room impressed Ragnar. Prosthetics of all sorts, some utilitarian and others covered in attachments, such as electro-blades and fusion torches, hung all along the walls. The men of Hyades apparently lost limbs on a regular basis.

Gabriella turned to look up at Ragnar. 'He's out of danger.'

'I wanted to make sure. We need to talk.'

'Come.' Gabriella walked out of the infirmary into a quiet hallway outside the examination room and sighed. 'Tell me why you think what happened outside the walls was not a mistake.'

Ragnar had given Gabriella a full briefing upon his arrival inside the city gates and she knew him well enough to tell that he sensed that something was wrong. 'We should talk somewhere more secluded.' Ragnar glanced up and down the hallway. He couldn't see anyone and yet he felt as if its walls might hold listeners.

Would you prefer we talk like this? Gabriella's voice echoed in Ragnar's mind.

The Space Wolf shuddered. He trusted Gabriella, indeed he was pledged to her protection and service, but there was something that bothered him about her psyker abilities. Although the Rune Priests of the Space Wolves had similar gifts, Ragnar still kept something of the superstitious warrior in his heart, and he clung to his old instincts.

'Let's go to the shuttle,' said Ragnar. 'It's shielded and secure.'

If you insist, but it's a good walk to the hangar. Gabriella's voice echoed in Ragnar's mind.

The Space Wolf shuddered ever so slightly, and Gabriella smiled, enjoying Ragnar's discomfort.

As THEY WALKED through the upper floors of the palace, Ragnar gazed out at the city. From above, it looked more like a series of mining structures and service buildings than a city. Since Lethe had been constructed atop tunnels connected to the mines and underground refineries, the architecture made sense, although it held all the style of a series of rockcrete bunkers. Many of the buildings were solidly constructed and were a constant reminder of the potential danger of explosions from storage tanks filled with the precious promethium.

The one exception to the uninspiring city was the palace, where the Wolfblade were getting settled alongside the dignitaries of Hyades. The building conveyed a regal image with architecture that included finely crafted columns, wooden floors, arched ceilings and courtyards with gardens of imported flora. The entire palace made Ragnar uneasy, as if the imposed sense of civilisation was a blasphemy against the constant struggles of the people of Hyades and the natural power of the jungle.

Where the rest of Lethe was built for function, the palace was built as a symbol. It felt out of place to Ragnar, but the citizens of Lethe respected and admired it. For them, the building represented the promise of wealth and luxury, a future in which humanity would tame Hyades.

As Ragnar and Gabriella walked down the carpeted corridors, they were joined by Torin. 'Ragnar, my lady, we need to talk,' he said.

'Join us, Torin. I think we all need to talk,' said Gabriella.

Torin was more at ease in these civilised surroundings than Ragnar, who preferred battlefields. A long-standing member of the Wolfblade, Torin had spent decades assigned to Holy Terra. He was the best-groomed Space Wolf that Ragnar had ever met. His hair was neat, unlike Ragnar's wild mane, and he wore a moustache that would be the envy of most overly powdered Imperial nobles. Torin wore jewelled amulets and medals from many worlds, rather than the typical wolf teeth and runes of his Chapter. He constantly smelled of perfumes and cologne, which to Ragnar carried the stench of civilisation.

Torin had mentored Ragnar upon his arrival on Terra as he adjusted to the Wolfblade, and had continued to do so, because despite his time in the Wolfblade, Ragnar still had to make necessary adjustments. The Wolfblade could take him off Fenris, but no one could take Fenris out of his heart.

Despite his friend's foppish tendencies, Ragnar respected Torin's skill as a warrior and a diplomat.

Gabriella led the two giant armoured warriors to the hangar and they escorted her inside the shuttle. There, she led them to a private cabin covered in the heraldry of House Belisarius. She crossed to a large chair and sat down, then pushed a button, and the door slid shut. 'We can talk safely now,' she said.

Torin started. 'I spoke with Cadmus, the planet's military commander, immediately after Ragnar returned from the jungle. He told me that sometimes promethium beneath the surface interferes with communications. The city guards were trying to maintain that kill zone. They've been working extra shifts to keep the entire area around the city clear, but with the increased activity in the jungle, they've only been able to protect about half of the walls. In the other places, the trees and vines come right to the city.

'They detected the movement before our men even broke cover and someone was trigger-happy. Once one of the men fired, the rest did as well. The officers on the walls were ordering everyone to stand down when Ragnar performed his acrobatics on the Hellhound. The planetary commander apologised for the incident.' Torin smiled as a thought crossed his mind. 'Although, I think he was a little disappointed. With all the guns on the wall, two Sentinels and a Hellhound, his men didn't manage to kill a single Space Wolf.' He looked at Ragnar. 'You should have seen yourself leap onto that Hellhound while it was firing. What made you think of that?'

'I just knew what I had to do. I thought the comms were being jammed,' said Ragnar. 'We found something out there in the jungle, a large ancient structure. The native life-forms killed some large behemoth near there, and there were Chimera tracks leading away from the temple.'

Gabriella raised her hand as she spoke. 'Perhaps Commander Cadmus and the governor are aware of this temple. The commander asked to speak to all of the Wolfblade after you returned from your excursion. These people are part of House Belisarius and they have asked for help. That is why we are here, to help them.'

'She's right,' said Torin. 'Let's go find Commander Cadmus, and see what you think, Ragnar.'

'I'm not going to like him,' said Ragnar.

'One day, Ragnar, I'm going to teach you how to act like something besides a barbarian,' said Torin.

'At least you can trust barbarians,' commented Ragnar.

THE TRIO FOUND Governor Pelias and Commander Cadmus sitting in a large stateroom, with windows open to the sun, and the colours of

Hyades and House Belisarius prominently displayed. A tech-priest stood facing their chairs, unable to sit with his extensive cybernetics and appearing remarkably out of place in the elegant chamber.

Governor Pelias was the least imposing of the three. A slight man with the burnished glow that marked him as native of Hyades, he had a thin ring of silver hair around a bare scalp. His dress uniform included a clasped cape, a number of medallions weighing heavily on the front, and polished long leather gloves and boots. He looked uncomfortable, even lounging, as if he was the sort of man who had had the burden of leadership thrust upon him, rather than desiring it.

The tech-priest wore a crimson hooded cloak, as was their custom. Ragnar's nostrils burned with the acrid scent of oils and smoke that clung to him. Faint whirring noises accompanied the priest's breathing.

At least one of his eyes was false, replaced by a red light burning within his skull. He had a massive musculature, and Ragnar could not tell how much of the man was flesh and how much machinery. A large bundle of wires and gears clung to his back, like a giant mechanical insect hiding under the cloak. The six appendages on the man's back were thick and short, suggesting that they weren't fully extended.

'Governor Pelias, Commander Cadmus, Tech-Priest Varnus, allow me to present my Wolfblade. I know you've met Torin, and this is Ragnar, who along with his men, was a victim of the friendly fire incident this morning,' said Gabriella.

The governor and commander stood to greet Gabriella.

Ragnar met Commander Cadmus's gaze. Something was missing. When Ragnar looked upon most men, he saw fear, no matter how well they hid it, but Cadmus showed no such emotion.

The commander was a massive man, although not quite the size of the towering Space Wolves. His eyes struck Ragnar: pale blue and very calm, watching everything. Ragnar felt the hair on his neck rise. Cadmus didn't have the typical Hyades skin colour, marking him as an offworlder. The commander wore a uniform jacket over mesh armour and his sidearm was a plasma pistol.

'My apologies for the earlier incident, Ragnar,' said Cadmus, returning to his seat. 'My guardsmen are trained to react to anything coming out of the jungle as if it were a threat. I must admit, I'm surprised that your men escaped the initial volley with so little damage. I hope Magni – that is his name, isn't it? – is recovering?'

'Wolves don't die easily.'

'Evidently,' said Cadmus.

'Lady Gabriella,' said the governor. 'I hope that you and the Wolfblade realise that the earlier incident was exactly what the commander said, an accident. I'm ordering a review of the defence procedures immediately, so nothing like this will ever happen again.'

'Sir,' said Cadmus, 'is that wise? It was a foolish error to be sure, and I'm already disciplining the men involved. If I have my men slow down operations to review the defences the jungle will reclaim sections of the kill zone. We've almost completely cleared it from around the city. If we don't, something might find a weakness in the wall and make its way inside.'

'By the way, commander, what sort of threat are you preparing for?' asked Torin.

'The ape-lizard creatures are the greatest danger. We call them the reptos, although I'm not sure that the Imperium has approved our choice of name,' said Cadmus, 'but I believe in being ready for anything. I've travelled from one end of this sector to the other, and I've seen a lot of fighting. An invasion could come at any moment. We need to be eternally vigilant.'

Cadmus nodded. 'I have security concerns. There are strange structures out in the jungle, buried deep under the canopy. We think that the reptos built them, but they could be remnants of a lost colony or, well, anything. I'm sure you can understand and respect that, as members of the Wolfblade.'

'Indeed, we can, commander,' said Torin.

'Has anyone contacted the Inquisition about these structures? What does the local Ecclesiarch have to say?' asked Gabriella.

The governor answered. 'Centuries ago, the Inquisition declared the structures abandoned and safe. We've been busy mining as opposed to worrying about such things, and I'm afraid the priesthood is poorly represented here on Hyades. It's a harsh world and we do dangerous work mining the promethium.'

'We ensure the wellbeing of the workers,' said Tech-Priest Varnus, his metallic voice hollow and echoing. 'If the Ecclesiarchy wishes to send representatives, we will do our best to accommodate them.'

Ragnar bristled. Before he had been part of the Wolfblade, he had learnt that the Space Wolves didn't trust outsiders, even members of the Inquisition. Some could be trusted, but others had their own agendas. He had learned on Terra that not all servants of the Imperium were on the same side.

'I want to know more about the structures and the behaviour of the reptos. I believe that such investigations may uncover the truth about the attacks and why the flora and fauna of this planet have decided to remove humans from their soil,' said Gabriella.

'Lady Gabriella, have you sensed any disturbances with your Navigator's gifts?' asked Cadmus.

Ragnar thought the question was unusual. Although it was no secret, indeed quite the opposite, that House Belisarius was a Navigators' House, and the abilities of the Navigators to guide ships through the horrors of the warp were the key to Belisarius's wealth, such a frank question seemed strange. It would not have been asked in mixed company on Terra. He reminded himself that everyone in the room was supposed to be supporting House Belisarius.

'No. I would have let the governor and you know if I had. Governor Pelias, I'd like Commander Cadmus to consult with my Wolfblade on the progress of the investigation of these structures and the activities of the reptos.'

'Of course, Lady Gabriella,' responded the governor.

'If you'll excuse us, governor, commander, I wish to check on the drop in production and review your records,' said Gabriella. She rose, as they did, and exited, flanked by Torin and Ragnar.

Haegr stood outside the doorway. 'My lady, mighty Haegr stands ready to protect you.'

'Thank you, Haegr.'

'Lady Gabriella, Ragnar and I will go and check on the shuttle,' said Torin. 'I want to make sure that the crews have resupplied it and the proper litanies have been chanted over its engines,'

'You have my leave. I'll be safe enough with Haegr,' she replied. 'We may go and inspect the promethium refining facilities. I'll contact you if I need you.'

'I assure you, you won't need them with me around,' said Haegr.

Torin guided Ragnar down a wood-floored hallway covered in tapestries depicting the history of House Belisarius. One of them showed Leman Russ holding his spear. It was a scene with which Ragnar was familiar, but it always painfully reminded him why he was a Wolfblade.

'Torin, why do we need to check the shuttle?' asked Ragnar.

Torin gave Ragnar a look that made him feel like an ignorant Blood Claw before realising that his friend simply wanted to talk to him in private.

'Brother,' started Torin, in a tone that was a sure sign that the older Space Wolf was irritated with him. 'Do you remember the lessons you learned on Terra, or has traipsing through the jungles of Hyades purged them from your mind?'

Ragnar sighed. 'Of course, I remember.'

'Well then,' said Torin, 'let me remind you of what I told you there. On Terra, you never have the whole picture. It's true here in Lethe as well. Be cautious.'

'I don't trust Cadmus and I'm not sure why,' replied Ragnar. 'He's dangerous. He carries himself like a man who isn't afraid of Space Marines. Outside of the Inquisition, I've never met a man who wasn't a little intimidated by us.'

'Brother, of course he's dangerous, he's the commander of the planetary defences. If he wasn't dangerous, we'd be standing in a jungle or dealing with a rebellion. The people here mine promethium. There are as many servitors as men in those mines. The citizens here have more in common with Terra than they do with other people from frontier worlds. They are a soft people. Cadmus is a hard man.'

'Torin, he's not from here. Why don't they have a leader from their own world commanding their military?'

'It should be obvious even to a young pup like you that he's seen his share of combat. Be careful about making assumptions about who your enemies are and who your friends are. If he wanted to harm Gabriella, then he threw away a fantastic opportunity to eliminate some of the Wolfblade this morning,' said Torin.

'He's not afraid of us, Torin,' stated Ragnar.

'I know, brother, but I also know that he's afraid of something,' said Torin, rubbing his moustache in thought. 'No one emphasises preparedness as much as he did without fearing something. It's probably his previous battle experiences. You'd be the best person to find out,' said Torin.

'Why me?'

'Because he knows you don't trust him,' said Torin.

'Do you trust him?' asked Ragnar.

'This isn't about me,' answered Torin. 'We'll talk more later. Go check back on Magni. I better make sure that the food supplies are stocked in our quarters. After all, Haegr will be looking for a good meal when Gabriella finishes with him.'

Ragnar tried to think of a reply as Torin walked away. He couldn't come up with anything worth saying, so he walked towards the infirmary.

Torin was right. Even though the planet of Hyades bore little resemblance to Holy Terra, the city of Lethe itself tried to emulate Terra and mask the fact that it was a frontier colony. The people stayed away from the world around them and insulated themselves, instead of learning how to survive in the jungles.

Ragnar had made it halfway back to the infirmary, when a voice came over his comm. 'Wolfblade Ragnar, please meet me at Tower 4 on the city's north wall.'

It was Cadmus.

Ragnar considered saying no, but he was sure Torin would tell him to meet with the commander. The summons was close enough to a request for Ragnar to decide to go along with it, despite his instincts.

'I'll be there,' was Ragnar's reply.

A CHIMERA MET Ragnar at the main entrance to the palace. He thought having an armoured vehicle drive him through the city seemed extreme, but Cadmus was in charge of the military. He sat alone in the back of the tank as it rumbled to the mighty wall protecting Lethe. Ragnar took note of the way, committing it to memory as a tactical lesson.

The tank stopped by the outer wall. Ragnar got out the tank and looked around. On one side, he could see nothing but the city wall and the buildings, mostly barracks and command centres built into its base. Back towards the centre of Lethe he saw nothing but uniform blocky rockcrete buildings. A few soldiers and a servitor with a bionic claw walked around atop the wall. The wall stretched skywards and given the choice between the lift and a set of rungs set into the wall in case of emergency, Ragnar chose to climb the rungs. He wasn't in that much of a hurry to see Cadmus and besides, it just felt right.

He paused mid-climb to look out over the city. The banners of House Belisarius flew from a number of buildings. Far off, he could see the gleaming palace rising from the centre of the city. The palace complex was at the heart of Lethe, where shuttles launched for the heavens, monuments rose to the glories of the people, and the only bit of green within the city wall was there. Despite the dramatic view, Ragnar felt unsettled, as if something was not right.

Cadmus was waiting for Ragnar at the top of the wall, staring out at the kill zone. Behind him, servitors and military men ran drills, checking and rechecking reports. Cadmus had his people ready, as if they were expecting a full-scale invasion. Ragnar thought they'd spend their time better worrying about the jungle.

The commander's uniform was immaculate: well-pressed, his boots polished to a reflective shine. He smiled as Ragnar walked over.

The Space Wolf took a moment to catch the commander's scent. He hoped that somehow he'd detect the taint of Chaos, anything to have an excuse to deal with this man he distrusted.

'Ragnar, once again, I want to offer my apologies for the earlier incident,' Cadmus said.

Ragnar nodded. 'Why did you want to see me?'

'I want us to understand one another, Ragnar. We seem to be very much alike, you and I. I've heard rumours that most of the Wolfblade receive their assignments due to some issue during their service as Space Wolves,' said Cadmus.

'How do you know about that?' asked Ragnar, surprised by the statement.

Cadmus nodded. 'I've studied the history of House Belisarius, and I understand a bit about how the Wolfblade are selected. Many great men do things that others don't understand. I have many such men with me. They serve in positions of authority here, helping ready the people of Hyades in case of attack.'

'Why did you need to bring your own men here? Why did they select you to lead them?' asked Ragnar.

'I lead these men because they know my skills. I've fought in many battles across the Imperium. The people of Hyades need protection from the wilderness of their own planet. They strive to change their world for the better. However, they do not have practical experience in dealing with the threats this galaxy has to offer. I do. They look inward, and I can see much more.'

Ragnar shook his head. This amount of talk was never to his liking, unless heavy amounts of Fenrisian ale and good stories were involved.

'Ragnar, I'm glad that you and your Wolfblade are here, and I want to make sure that you are ready to defend House Belisarius against all threats.'

'Commander, I'm ready.'

'Good. I'm glad to have you. What you did today against the Hellhound was remarkable, and I'll have some of my best men ready to go with you into the jungle in the morning. One reason that I've held off investigating those ruins more fully is because I didn't see them as a threat. Ages ago, the Inquisition declared them safe.'

Ragnar said nothing, not really knowing what to say. An uneasy moment passed. He wanted to make sure that he didn't insult Cadmus with his tone or his words. 'Tell me what you know about the ruins. I discovered signs of activity there, and I know that a Chimera made its way there recently.'

'I'll find the reports and have them sent to Lady Gabriella as soon as I can. I'll let you get back to your duties, Wolfblade,' said Cadmus.

'You can be sure of that,' said Ragnar.

Far below, Ragnar could see one of the Hellhounds belching promethium into a section of jungle. It looked as if Commander Cadmus had his men working hard.

'Are you able to maintain the integrity of the kill zone?' asked Ragnar.

'We have it encircling about seventy per cent of the city at the moment. Of course, it changes, but luckily we have an unlimited amount of promethium. All of the gates are constantly monitored and reinforced in the areas where the jungle touches the wall. Are you concerned about the reptos breaching the wall, Space Wolf?' asked Cadmus.

'No, but I do think the security of Lethe is important,' said Ragnar.

'Good, on that we agree.'

Ragnar walked over to the rungs and began his descent down the wall. Ragnar still didn't like Cadmus, but he didn't know why. His instincts told him that something was wrong. The Chimera was waiting for him at the bottom of the wall. He climbed in, ready for the ride back to the palace complex.

COMMANDER CADMUS watched Ragnar climb down the wall, admiring the power of the superhuman warrior. 'The Space Wolves will serve their purpose,' he whispered to himself, 'and wrongs will be made right.'

THREE
To Kill a Kill Team

HIGH ABOVE THE planet of Hyades dozens of transports, cargo barges and cruisers of various designs and sizes were going about their business, transporting supplies and promethium to and from the planet. The amount of activity within the orbital corridors above Hyades made it easy for a light cruiser to enter into high orbit without attracting any attention. Following the standard merchant flight path the cruiser slowly crossed the terminus into the night skies of the planet. To standard scans the ship's configuration was that of a light cruiser, no different from any other used by merchants to transport goods and cargo. However, the cargo on board this vessel was very different.

A solitary figure stood at the observation port watching as the transport slid into orbit around Hyades, his dark green power armour appearing black in the low light. His clean-shaven, almost youthful face hid his years well, however his deep piercing blue eyes did not. They reflected centuries of wisdom in service to his Chapter and the Imperium.

Watching as the transport took its place within the controlled orbital lanes he could not help but be concerned. His purpose on Hyades was of such importance that every detail must be conducted with flawless precision. Recognising his concern over the flight path of the transport he smiled inwardly, realising that he had much greater concerns to occupy his mind than that of piloting the transport into a stationary orbit.

However, Captain Jeremiah Gieyus was not just a Dark Angel, he was a member of the Deathwing, the elite Dark Angels First Company. He had reached this level of authority by controlling every detail of his assignments. It was with meticulous care that he inspected every weapon and each grenade, and supervised the Techspace Marines as they prepared the armour that his battle-brothers wore.

Jeremiah crossed the corridor and entered a large cargo bay, at the centre of which stood a teleport chamber. Cables ran across the floor to this structure, connecting it to ship's power, sensor and internal computer terminals. Servitors, cybernetic caretakers, moved around the outside of the device, confirming that everything was properly anointed, and that all the proper chants had been evoked, preparing the teleportation chamber for activation. As Jeremiah watched these servants of the Machine-God perform their rituals he could not help but feel a sense of profound pride.

Within moments Jeremiah was joined by five of his fellow Dark Angels. He watched as they entered the chamber, taking their assigned positions inside. Thirteen pillars circled the interior of the chamber, each covered with inscriptions of faith and devotion to the Emperor. Servitors made final anointings to the interior systems, couplings, conduits and power emitters. Everything had to be in order to ensure that no harm would come to the Sons of the Lion this day.

Jeremiah joined the rest of the kill team within the chamber. The Dark Angels green armour appeared almost black in the low light, and their weapons were in hand and at the ready. Combat deployment was needed, even though Jeremiah had picked a secluded position for the insertion, making detection almost impossible. However, when dealing with an objective of this nature one could never be too careful. Jeremiah did not intend to lead his brothers into a trap.

Several weeks ago the Dark Angels had received intelligence that a member of the Fallen had been detected on Lethe, capital city of Hyades. The information was vague and limited on details. All they knew was that one of their ancient brothers was in a position of authority within the governor's inner circle.

Jeremiah and his kill team had been sent to reconnoitre the situation and, if possible, capture and detain the member of the Fallen until an Interrogator-Chaplain and reinforcements could be dispatched.

Only the Dark Angels' most senior officers and the Deathwing were aware of the terrible shame the Chapter carried. For ten thousand years they had hunted down the Fallen, rooting them out wherever they hid and thrusting them into the cleansing light of the Emperor. So it would be with this new report of one of the Fallen being present on Hyades. He and his kill team would confirm his presence and then capture him, turning him over to the Interrogator-Chaplains. Then, if need be, reinforcements would descend and remove any additional Fallen and the contamination they may have left behind.

As the other members of the kill team were not aware of the existence of the Fallen, they had been told their mission was to locate and capture a heretic commander who had thrown in his lot with the Dark Powers.

Their preparations complete, Jeremiah finally signalled the Techspace Marine to begin the litanies of transport. Slowly the pillars began to glow until a searing white light filled the chamber.

THERE WAS A flash of light in the jungle as the Dark Angels kill team materialised on the surface. At night a flash of this nature would be visible several kilometres away, however Hyades's thick jungle canopy restricted the flash's visibility considerably.

Slowly, the kill team began to move, each member taking his position to secure the drop area, their dark green power armour virtually invisible against the night. Five of the Space Marines moved out from the teleport site enlarging the circle while one remained at its centre.

Releasing the auspex from its belt restraints, Elijah made several adjustments to the controls. Its screen blinked in and out, revealing only quick glimpses of what it detected in the area. He studied what information it did reveal very closely to ensure that his report would be as accurate as possible.

'Brother-captain, there is some kind of interference that is diminishing the auspex's effectiveness. However, I believe we have deployed approximately fifty metres off our original target point, which places us 1.5 kilometres from Lethe.' Elijah pointed in the direction of the city.

'Understood,' Jeremiah responded. 'Also Elijah, we all share the same risk and fate this night, so normal protocols are not required. Please refer to me as Jeremiah.'

'Yes, Jeremiah,' Elijah responded.

'Besides, my brother, it will hide from our foe the chain of command. Plus Jeremiah knows his rank, so we do not need to remind him.' Nathaniel's humour made the entire team chuckle.

Jeremiah looked at each member of his kill team in turn, then spoke.

'The Lion watches over us, his guiding hand leads us this day. Praise the Lion.' His words made a physical impact on his team. Evoking the name of their primarch sent a ripple of pride through his men, reminding them all of the importance of their mission.

'Who are we?'

'We are Sons of the Lion! We are Dark Angels.' Their response was in unison, a testament of their honour, an oath to right the sins of their brothers. Each in turn fell into line, taking up the position that he had been assigned.

Elijah was the most recent addition to Jeremiah's team, having proven himself on several campaigns before finally earning the honour of this placement. Although the youngest in age, his experience was equal to that of any of his battle-brothers, and his keen eye and attention to detail made him the perfect choice. Nathaniel was next, being the oldest and most experienced as indicated by the grey that gathered at the temples of his short-cropped black hair. He and Jeremiah had served together the longest and he felt it his duty to look after the younger Elijah. However, his constant reference to Elijah as 'young one' at times visibly annoyed his battle-brother.

Marius was always third. His plasma gun was best suited to supporting Nathaniel and Elijah should they run into unexpected trouble. As always, Jeremiah took the fourth spot, allowing him a tactical position should the need arise. He was followed very closely by Gilead, with Sebastian bringing up the rear.

Once again Elijah attempted to scan their surroundings. The soft almost imperceptible hum of static was the only reading that he could obtain. With ritualistic precision Elijah made a series of adjustments. A slight change in the hum's pitch was the only result.

'The interference seems to have worsened, brother-cap– Jeremiah. I'm uncertain as to the exact cause,' Elijah explained as he brushed away a large beetle that was crawling across his helmet visor.

'We could be picking up some kind of feedback or impulse from the promethium mines,' Nathaniel theorised. 'Intelligence reports indicated that the entire area was honeycombed with mine shafts and pipelines that feed to the many refineries on Hyades.'

Jeremiah nodded his acknowledgement and signalled that they keep moving. As the team moved through the dense brush the jungle seemed to engulf each member. It became so dense at times that Jeremiah would momentarily lose sight of his battle-brothers.

The foliage of Hyades was of a type that he had never seen before. Its shapes and colours all appeared similar, but it was dramatically different. Leaves like small combat knives scraped and scratched as they tore across Jeremiah's armour, and the vines and branches seemed to voluntarily constrict and contract around his arms and legs as if trying to capture or restrain him for some purpose. This feeling was reinforced by the many sounds that swirled around them. Most were similar to sounds he'd heard on other worlds, others however, seemed to be calling out to one another. Jeremiah was certain that they were being observed. His only concern was whether they were being stalked as well.

The team continued to make its way through the jungle. As they proceeded, Jeremiah noticed skeletal remains of small creatures ensnared in ivy-like foliage around the base of several trees. They continued to trudge through the thick jungle, receiving momentary respite from the native fauna of Hyades when the occasional clearing would appear. The jungle ceiling was not as generous. There were no breaks or openings, with the canopy allowing no light to penetrate its shielding of the jungle floor. The visual enhancements of their helmets coupled with the Lion's gift of genetically enhanced vision were all that allowed them to see.

They were moving through one of the few clearings when a fury of sound and movement erupted from beneath a thicket of tangled vine to Jeremiah's right. He unleashed his sword ready to meet whatever was coming for them. A small, fur- and feather-covered creature leapt up onto the exposed gnarled root of one of the trees. It turned, hissed and spat at Jeremiah, spraying the right flank of his helmet. The ceramite underneath the creature's spittle began to blister. The poisonous phlegm was not strong enough to actually penetrate his armour, but Jeremiah did consider that if the creatures were bigger they could pose a serious threat.

The rodent-like thing hissed again in defiance and leapt from the root. It had made two hops deeper into the woods when suddenly the ivy-like growth ensnared it. The creature instantly began to convulse and blue-white tendrils of electricity danced across the ivy and its now stunned victim.

'Stay vigilant brothers. It would appear that Hyades's reputation is well deserved.'

'I think we may have discovered where some of the interference is coming from,' Elijah stated.

'Small rodent things, electrically charged, carnivorous ivy; I think this place's reputation may be an understatement,' Nathaniel added.

'That may be,' said Jeremiah. 'However it will not deter us from our objective. Let's keep moving.'

THE DARK ANGELS had been travelling for almost two hours when Elijah's voice broke through the comm. 'I see light ahead.'

The team slowly began to spread out, taking great care to move quietly: detection at this point would be disastrous. Jeremiah crouched and crept up behind Elijah. Then he raised his right hand, making a closed fist, and the team stopped instantly, frozen in place like ancient statues.

A beam of light began to strike the leaves and trunks of the trees as it moved slowly across the jungle. The searchlight indicated that they had finally reached the capital city. Using hand signals, Jeremiah instructed Nathaniel to move forwards to the very edge of the jungle to retrieve better information on their current situation. Nathaniel slowly moved through the foliage while the other members of the team remained perfectly still awaiting his return.

'I would estimate the kill zone to be one hundred to one hundred and fifty metres across,' reported Nathaniel. 'Looks like a manned weapon emplacement every thirty metres, and two squads of Sentinels patrolling the kill zone in thirty-minute intervals.'

Jeremiah pulled the entire team back into the seclusion of the canopy, with the exception of Nathaniel, Gilead and Sebastian. Nathaniel was left to observe and report the activity of the Planetary Defence Forces while Gilead and Sebastian were dispatched to reconnoitre along the perimeter and report back any weakness or opportunity that the team could exploit. Upon his return Sebastian's report echoed Nathaniel's. Jeremiah awaited the final report. If Gilead's report mirrored the others then he would need to formulate a new insertion plan.

Prior to their departure, Jeremiah had been given a fairly detailed intelligence report of Hyades and its capital city of Lethe. Included in that report were troop strengths, defensive capabilities and a fairly detailed map of the city as well as a layout of the governor's palace and control compound.

Initially the plan was to reach the city walls, scale them and move through the city under the cover of night until they reached the compound. According to the reports, there was no known conflict or crisis in this area of space so Hyades's defences would be minimal. Something must have changed to cause this level of fortification. This heightened level of defence was not a coincidence, for in Jeremiah's experience coincidence did not exist. His thoughts were broken when Gilead's voice broke through the comm.

'Jerem… *hssssst*… the jungle I… *Hsst*…' The rest of the transmission was lost to static.

Jeremiah looked at the rest of the team, confirming that they had received the partial comm transmission as well. With a quick nod of his head he sent his battle-brothers into action. He had no idea of Gilead's location or condition; he only knew his direction. The team formed a skirmish line, moving as quickly and as quietly as possible. Stealth was not a skill that most Space Marines possessed, their sheer bulk making that difficult, but fortunately the jungle provided them with enough cover and background noise to make things a little easier.

'Gilead, respond please. Report your location and situation,' Elijah requested.

'Tra.... brea... p... Kil... alls,' was the only response.

The team had travelled through the jungle for three hundred metres when Jeremiah ordered them to stop. He then signalled to Elijah to try to make contact again.

'Gilead, respond please. Report your location and situation,' Elijah repeated.

Gilead did not respond. The Dark Angels waited, but there was no response.

Jeremiah's frustration grew. One of his team was lost, and he wanted to know why, but he could not jeopardise the mission by sending more men out to look for the missing Space Marine. He scanned the jungle in front of him looking for a sign, any indication at all of what could have happened to Gilead. The plants and trees here were not as dense as the area they had come from, and the strange electric ivy, which the team called the shocker vines, was much more prominent. That might account for the increased difficulty with the comm. He wondered just how large the ivy would grow and if it could become a threat to him or his battle-brothers.

'Transmission breakin... Ha... ound end to kill zon... making way back...' Gilead's voice broke through the comm.

'Understood Gilead. We have moved closer to your position. We will await your arrival,' Elijah responded.

Within minutes Gilead broke through the jungle, rejoining the team.

'What have you found out?' Jeremiah asked.

'There is a large section of the jungle that has not yet been cleared away,' said Gilead. 'And it goes right up to the city wall.'

'How wide is this area of jungle?' Jeremiah asked.

'At least one hundred and seventy-five metres, brother, if not wider,' Gilead responded. 'I managed to scout into it about one hundred and fifty metres before I realised that I had lost comms, and turned back to report.'

'Excellent work, Gilead.' Jeremiah stroked his chin while turning away from Gilead.

'You seem troubled, Jeremiah,' Elijah said.

'Our leader is curious as to why the details of the kill zone were not in our intelligence reports,' Nathaniel speculated.

'Exactly. What has occurred on Hyades that would require this heightened defensive posture? And why now?' Jeremiah's words silenced the team.

'The time for speculation is over brothers, whatever the cause it will not deter us from our holy mission. We move on.'

THE TEAM HAD moved to a point they estimated was the centre of the uncleared jungle area. Determining their position was now easier. The noise from the flamers and patrolling vehicles dominated the jungle orchestra, giving them a permanent reference point, as well as allowing them to travel more quickly, as they no longer needed to conceal their movement so much.

All that remained for Jeremiah was to determine how to gain entry to the city. Using charges to burn through the wall was out of the question. He considered scaling the wall, a task the Space Marines could accomplish with ease, but with the increased patrols and heightened security measures they would risk detection, and although the Hyades defence forces that manned the wall would be no match for them they could not take on the entire city, nor could they risk alerting the target to their presence. However, the latter was becoming less of a concern for Jeremiah, who was certain that their presence was already known to the Fallen.

Elijah looked up from his auspex, turning towards the others. 'Interference is still too intense. I cannot penetrate it.'

It had taken the team about three and a half hours to reach this point. Based on Hyades's rotation cycle, they had about eight more hours to breach the city walls and reach their objective. Although time was always a factor when on a mission of this nature, it was becoming increasingly more important. Their final obstacle was finding a way to gain entry.

Jeremiah had ordered the team to pause for a moment, allowing them a little rest. He was once again pondering the events of the last few hours when Nathaniel placed his hand on his forearm. Jeremiah looked up to see what his brother required, noticing that Nathaniel was not looking at him, but past him. He turned, slowly.

'We are not alone, brother,' Nathaniel stated. 'Something is moving through the jungle.' He pointed in the direction of the city wall.

At first Jeremiah did not see anything, but finally he caught a glimpse of something moving through the jungle past them. With the rest of the team alert and ready, he nodded and they all moved towards the disturbance. Each member of the team had slung his weapons and was wielding his combat knife. Even with the cover from the noise made by the clearing teams a firefight was not an option this close to the city's defence forces. Whatever this threat was it had to be dealt with by hand to hand means.

A hissing noise was the only warning any of them received as the jungle seemed to come to life around them. Several creatures erupted from the foliage. Jeremiah, raising his knife to ward off the unknown assailants' attack, suddenly found himself falling backwards as something entangled his legs and pulled them out from underneath him. Landing on his back his mind leapt back to the shocker vines and his thoughts of how large they could grow and whether they could attack a creature as large as a Space Marine. Before he could discover the answers, the real enemy landed squarely on his chest.

His genetically enhanced vision augmented by the helm of his cherished armour revealed a large creature that looked like an unholy combination of lizard and ape. Jeremiah struck the creature with his closed fist, in its ribs just under its arm, knocking the creature off him.

Rolling onto his side and bringing himself to one knee, he was ready for the next attack. The creature squared itself with the Space Marine, when its elongated tail lashed out wrapping itself around his arm at the wrist. The strength of the creature was staggering, catching him momentarily by surprise and almost pulling him off his feet once again. Jeremiah stepped in the direction of the creature, stabilising himself while raising his arm and pulling the creature towards him. Then in one quick motion he brought his combat knife down in a circular strike, slicing completely through the tail severing it, while the creature tumbled backwards into the jungle.

Blood sprayed from the severed appendage as the tail whipped back and forth and the creature screamed in pain as it clambered to its feet. Fear and panic ruled its primitive mind as it turned, leaping into the jungle, fleeing from the cause of its pain. Jeremiah leapt up and gave chase, realising that the creature was heading towards the clearing teams. He did not want the creature to be found. The clean cut of his combat knife would reveal that the wounded tail was not the result of a fight with another animal. He had to catch the thing before it reached the edge of the jungle.

Crashing through the jungle he realised that whatever this thing was it was fast, moving through the jungle with unbelievable agility. He could no longer see the creature, only the visible signs of where it had been. It was escaping.

Suddenly, several metres in front of him the jungle became engulfed in fire as flames roared amongst the trees. Rising above the roar of the flame came a horrific screaming. The clearing team had found the creature, or more correctly, it had found them. Jeremiah dived for the ground, coming to rest underneath several thickets of razor leaf bushes. He was in no danger from the flames. He was more concerned that he would be detected. As the screaming and the flames began to subside he could hear the sounds of a Chimera engine as well as several defence force personnel as they moved around the area of the burnt remains.

'Looks like one of those damn reptos again,' a man stated.

'That's just great! See any more?' another man responded.

The Chimera's engine roared and Jeremiah heard it begin to move, the sound of small trees snapping as they gave way to the greater strength of the transport. Slowly reaching down to his belt he retrieved a grenade, preparing for the coming engagement. Then the Chimera stopped and Jeremiah could see a searchlight piercing the jungle, silhouetting the trees as the light moved slowly over his position.

'I don't see any more,' the voice said, rising to overcome the noise of the Chimera.

'All right then, let's get back to work. We've got a lot of jungle to clear.'

Jeremiah sighed with relief. He waited for a few moments to ensure that the men had returned to their work before he slowly crawled away. Once clear he rose to his feet and moved towards his team.

WHEN JEREMIAH REJOINED the rest of the team he learned that the attack was short-lived, and there were seven of the lizard-ape creatures lying dead on the jungle floor.

'Everyone all right, no one injured?' he asked.

'We are all intact and unharmed, sir,' Nathaniel responded. 'We've found something of interest, though. After the attack had been dealt with, I dispatched Elijah and Sebastian to reconnoitre the area that these things had come from to determine if there were any more there and they've found something we should check out.'

Jeremiah followed as Elijah and Sebastian led him and the rest of the team through the jungle. Within just a few short minutes they reached the point where the jungle met with the city wall. Jeremiah could not believe what he saw before him. These ape creatures, which they had thought were mindless animals, had been removing chunks of the city wall. The area around the opening was strewn with chunks of rockcrete and primitive tools made from bones and tusks of other animals.

'They were creating a tunnel into the city,' Jeremiah stated in amazement.

'Not exactly,' Sebastian replied.

Elijah and Sebastian stepped towards the opening. Reaching in, they removed several pieces of foliage and rock, placed there by the ape creatures to conceal their work.

Behind the makeshift screen was what appeared to be an old metal maintenance hatch.

'Looks like these creatures discovered an area of the wall where they had sealed off an old maintenance hatch,' Elijah said.

'They were almost finished I would say. We must have gotten close enough to interrupt their work,' Sebastian added.

'It would appear brothers that we have found our access point. Praise the Lion!'

JEREMIAH STOOD IN an alley at the edge of the entrance to the street. Since gaining access to the maintenance hatch he and the team had crawled their way through several maintenance tunnels until finally reaching what appeared to be an abandoned sewage system. Then they had followed the sewers until they found a service shaft that would allow them to exit undetected. They had found other shafts, but upon inspection they opened up into areas that were not secluded enough to conceal their presence.

Once they were free of the sewers they were able to conceal their movements by using back alleys and side streets. The few citizens they encountered were either attempting to avoid detection themselves or were too intoxicated to care who was there.

At one point they passed a large vid panel mounted on the side of one of the buildings. A thin, pinch-faced woman was elaborating on the events of the day: production quotas from the mines, scores for athletic events, local magistrate activities, and how the curfew was a popular and necessary edict from the governor.

Now they were at the entrance to a light-filled street, illumination panels spaced along either side of the street ensured that. Personal ground craft were parked at various points along the street. Movement through the alleys had been fairly easy and the time of night made the streets of Lethe all but deserted. Six large men moving along a city street at night would be fairly easy to conceal, however six of the Emperor's Space Marines would be a much more difficult prospect. Jeremiah scanned each and every alcove looking for any sign of activity, or anything that could give away their presence.

'Spectral rotation scan.' Jeremiah sub-vocalised this command.

The optics in his helmet responded, switching through each wavelength of the light spectrum, giving Jeremiah a clear picture of what was on the street. However, Jeremiah was also aware that whatever the divine technology of the Emperor would allow him to see could also be thwarted by the insidious technologies of the Emperor's enemies.

Like all of his team, Jeremiah wore dark-coloured robes that covered most of his armour, but the sheer size of a Space Marine was hard to hide regardless of the time of day. They would have to risk moving down the street.

Jeremiah removed his helmet and clipped it to his belt. He indicated to his team that they follow suit. Should they be spotted, they had a slight chance to explain away their size, but their helmets were another matter. His curly blond hair was matted by sweat against his forehead, but his blue eyes held within them wisdom that belied his youthful appearance.

'Elijah, find the best path to approach the palace compound,' Jeremiah instructed.

Elijah silently activated the auspex and uploaded the city maps to the display. Even though the interference had played havoc with its sensors, it could still display the city maps they had acquired.

'The south-eastern entrance of the palace is the least protected,' he said. 'Only a few lightly armed palace guards are standing sentry, and it's the farthest away from any reinforcements that could be summoned should we be detected.'

'Good! Take the point and get us there. Remember we want to get in, locate and capture our target and then get out. We do not want to alert the entire city to our presence,' Jeremiah warned.

Once again Elijah took the point position and began moving through the shadows, followed by Jeremiah and the rest of the kill team.

As THE TEAM made its way down the street, a figure watched from the shadows atop one of the tall residential buildings that lined the streets. As if by sheer force of will he held the light at bay, hiding his features in the shadows, shrouded in an unnatural darkness. Once the team rounded the street corner he began to move, bringing his hand up to his mouth.

'The bait has been taken. They've arrived. They'll be at the palace in about ten minutes. Make sure everything is set. Let's be certain that we have a greeting befitting guests of their stature. I'll be joining you soon.' Having sent his message, the mysterious watcher turned and disappeared into the darkness.

THE SERVICE KITCHEN was efficient, making the best use of space. Three large refrigeration units stood to one side, while cabinets occupied the opposite wall. Although compact, there was room enough for several kitchen staff to work within its confines quite easily. The large bulk of the Space Marine on all fours with his head in a refrigeration unit made the room look abnormally small. Haegr made a growling sound as he looked through the chilled drawers. Actually, it was the massive Space Wolf's stomach that was making the noise at that moment.

He was searching through frozen concentrated food packs looking for something, anything, that was fit to eat. He had not had a decent meal since they had left Holy Terra; in fact it had been so long that earlier today while they were scouting outside the walls, he had considered eating one of the many beetles. It would not have been very satisfying, and it would have tasted fairly awful, but it would still have been better than the frozen food packs. This was the second refrigeration unit he had looked through, and so far his luck had not been good.

'How do these people live on this? I'm going to starve. Wait, that's it, that's been their plan all along!' Haegr was fond of talking to himself.

'Torin and Ragnar cannot take me in a fair fight so they brought me along on this mission knowing that food would be in short supply, weakening me.' Haegr began to put the pieces together.

'Well, there is food here. I can smell it. If it wasn't for this accursed planet with all its wildlife! I'm lucky to breathe.'

In frustration Haegr stood up, forgetting that he was halfway in the refrigeration unit. The upper two shelves came crashing down, spilling food packs all over the floor and making enough noise to wake the entire palace. Haegr was oblivious. He was on the hunt, and nothing could deter a wolf in search of food.

'What in the name of Russ is going on in here?' a voice asked.

Ragnar stood in the doorway, holding the leg of a large cooked bird, his other hand hidden behind his back. Taking another bite from the leg he asked again.

'Haegr, what are you doing?'

Haegr answered without even turning around. Nothing would stop him from reaching the third refrigeration unit.

'I'm onto your little scheme, Ragnar! You and Torin have your little laugh. I will find what I'm looking for, and then you will both pay.'

Ragnar swallowed. 'Hmm… What is it you are looking for my friend? Maybe I can help,' he said, taking another bite.

'Don't distract me, Ragnar, the scent is stronger now. I've nearly found it. It's so close I can almost taste it.'

Haegr finally made it to the door of the refrigeration unit. Grabbing the handle he yanked the door open, gazing inside to see more shelves full of food packs. Howling in frustration he slammed the door shut with so much force that his footing gave way and he spun and crashed to the floor. Haegr came to rest sitting on the floor with his back against the door of the refrigeration unit and his legs sprawled out in front of him.

'See what you've done, Ragnar. See what you and Torin have reduced me to,' said Haegr with frustration.

'Well, my old friend, I came here to ask your help with something,' Ragnar said as he walked across the room, bringing his other hand from behind his back, revealing a platter containing the rest of the roasted fowl.

'I seem to have found this meat and I can't possibly eat it all myself,' Ragnar finished.

Haegr looked up to see the huge roasted bird, and a smile stretched across his face. He grabbed the platter with one hand while ripping off the remaining leg with the other.

'You… *chomp*… and Torin… *gulp*… both have a… *chomp*… severe beating coming when I'm done here,' Haegr said.

'Well then you'd better take this as well,' Torin said, entering the room with a flagon of what appeared to be ale.

'I'd hate to see you smash both of us while you were parched and dehydrated,' Torin teased as Haegr grabbed the flagon.

'You show wisdom beyond your years, Torin,' Haegr said.

'Well, before you administer that beating, please be sure that you clean up in here. Let's not be too much trouble to our hosts,' Torin instructed.

Both Ragnar and Torin turned and left the kitchen.

'We'll be enjoying more of that fine ale on the atrium balcony. Why don't you join us when you've finished here,' Ragnar shouted over his shoulder. Haegr did not reply, at least not in a way that Ragnar could understand.

RAGNAR AND TORIN stood on the balcony overlooking the palace atrium. The hour was late. In fact it had rolled over into early morning. Maintenance personnel scurried around, watering the many plants that lined the space and cleaning and polishing the floors. These were tasks that were to be done in the late and early hours of the day. Ragnar had learned on Holy Terra that those who did the everyday drudgeries were not to be seen in the light of day where the palace or political officials could observe them at their work.

Ragnar was glad to be off Terra and back in the galaxy again. He had hoped that by getting away from Terra he would have seen an end to all the cloak-and-dagger mischief they always had to contend with. He longed for the black and white of the battlefield, the clear view of who the enemy was, but considering all he had witnessed he was beginning to believe that political intrigue was simply a part of life. Even his assignment, or one might say exile, to the Wolfblade was politically motivated. Perhaps it was just the way of things and Ragnar could no longer afford to view the galaxy through the eyes of an immature Blood Claw. Perhaps it was time that he grew up and stopped longing for how he wanted things to be and started accepting things the way they were.

'Ragnar!' Torin raised his voice to get Ragnar's attention.

'I swear sometimes you are the most brooding sort I've ever seen,' scolded Torin.

Ragnar looked up from his drink to see that Magni had joined them. Magni still had not regained his colour, and he appeared to have a slight limp, but other than that he seemed fine. His armour also showed signs of recent repair. The young Space Wolf could thank Russ that his armour had absorbed the brunt of the explosive rounds.

'My apologies, brother, I did not see you enter the balcony.' Ragnar still bore the guilt of Magni's wounds. Getting up from his seat he retrieved a chair for Magni and allowed him to sit before retaking his own seat.

'Yes, Magni, you'll have to forgive our honoured friend, he is sometimes a brooding sort,' Torin continued. 'However, tonight I decree will be a night of song and story, and of daring deeds and warriors of Fenris overcoming insurmountable odds. It will not be a night of brooding and analytical debate,' Torin concluded.

'Perhaps I should start with the story of how I defeated Torin in hand to hand combat back on Terra,' Haegr stated as he entered the balcony. He was carrying a new flagon of ale and there were enough particles of roast meat in his beard to feed a platoon of palace guards for a week.

The three Space Wolves lifted their tankards in salute of their battle-brother as he approached.

'Yes, yes, or perhaps we could discuss the time you were bested by a tankard that attached itself to your foot,' retorted Torin. Ragnar laughed so hard he almost snorted ale out his nostrils as he recalled his first day at House Belisarius. Magni was laughing as well, but it was an uncomfortable laugh. Noticing this, Ragnar elaborated on the story, only embellishing occasionally and only enough to make the story funnier.

'I would have loved to have seen that,' Magni continued, 'but what I would really like to hear is the story of Ragnar and the Spear of Russ.'

Silence instantly fell over the four Space Wolves as all eyes fell upon Ragnar.

'Why would you want to hear that story, pup?' queried Ragnar. 'Why would you want to hear about a young Blood Claw's foolish mistake?'

'I meant no offence, Ragnar, really, and it was not told to us as the mistake of a Blood Claw at all. Lord Ranek tells the story quite differently in fact. He tells of how you used Russ's own spear to thwart Magnus the Red, preventing his entry through the portal and saving the lives of your battle-brothers with quick decisiveness and courage,' Magni stated proudly.

'So the old man tells that story, eh?' Ragnar never realised how much he missed the council of Ranek until that moment. 'Perhaps some day I'll grace you with the tale, but not this night. There are far better things to talk about than that.' Ragnar looked at Torin who gave Ragnar a wink.

Torin knew all too well the anguish in Ragnar's heart and his desire to return to Fenris.

'Besides, why would we want to talk about that when I'm here? I've got much more entertaining stories,' Haegr began to elaborate.

Ragnar walked to the edge of the balcony and looked out over the atrium, its cathedral-like pillars, rising up into a vaulted ceiling. The ground level was clear glass all across the front and down both sides, so that passers-by could see in and enjoy the astounding collection of plant life, and a fine collection it was. Exotic offworld plants were painstakingly cared for and displayed here. Ragnar thought it was odd that anyone felt the need to transplant plant life onto a planet like Hyades. Just above the ground level several large stained glass windows lined both sides of the atrium, each one depicting some glorious part of Hyades's rich history: soldiers fighting back unspeakable creatures, and heroes protecting the masses from certain death. Ragnar understood these images. He, like all his Wolf brothers, was dedicated to the same calling, destined to defend those who could not defend themselves.

Laughter from behind Ragnar caused him to turn. Haegr had picked up the small table and was wielding it like a shield, no doubt acting out one of his greatest adventures. Ragnar knew that even here among the Wolfblade their calling was the same, it was no different here than on Fenris, within the Fang. The mission was the same, and he knew that it was here that he belonged.

Ragnar turned once again, but this time it was Haegr dropping the table that had caught his attention. As usual Haegr's story skills were no match for his imagination. Ragnar was heading back to rescue his outmatched comrade when a scent caught his attention. It was subtle, almost undetectable, but it was a scent that should not be there. During the maintenance of a Space Marine's armour, the Iron Priests were very careful during the rituals to utter every incantation exactly, and to anoint every part with the sacred oils. It was this attention to detail that allowed these ancient artefacts to serve the Emperor. The scent of anointing oil was on the air this night, and it was not coming from the Wolfblade.

It was Torin who noticed the change in Ragnar first. All Space Wolves were gifted with an enhanced sense of smell, it was one of the many gifts from Russ, but Ragnar's was the sharpest Torin had ever known. If Ragnar had a scent then there was something out there.

Torin crossed the balcony to stand beside his friend.

'What's got your attention, little brother?' Torin asked, referring more to their comparative ages than their sizes.

'As I've told you before, Torin, you've been on Terra too long,' Ragnar replied. 'The scent should not be here, and I definitely can't explain it, but there are Space Marines on the palace grounds.'

'Other than the Wolfblade there should be no other Space Marines here, Ragnar. Are you certain?' Torin asked.

'There are definitely other Space Marines here,' said Ragnar, trying to locate the direction of the scent so he could pick up the trail.

Haegr and Magni had noticed their two companions' movement and had joined them. Ragnar opened the exterior door that went outside onto a mezzanine outside the atrium. He was locked on the scent; it was strong and unmistakable. He held up his open hand, placed it in the air horizontally and slowly pulled it down. This signalled the others to slow their pace and move with stealth. Slowly, Ragnar moved along the mezzanine, following the olfactory trail.

Quietly, the Space Wolves readied their weapons, prepared for whatever they might encounter.

It was not common for servants of the Imperium to exchange fire, but it had been known to happen, so the Wolfblade could not afford to take any chances. Whoever the intruders were, they did not belong here, and he needed to know why they doing on Hyades.

As Ragnar approached the end of the mezzanine, he spotted six large cloaked figures moving along the opposite side of the garden, heading towards the parade ground. As one of the cloaked figures turned the wind pulled the edge of the cloak from his shoulder, revealing the shoulder pad of power armour. They were definitely Space Marines and Ragnar recognised the winged sword immediately, but why were there Dark Angels here on Hyades?

FOUR
Firefight

WHEN JEREMIAH WAS assigned the mission on Hyades he pored through every document on humanity's colonisation of the world that he could locate. The more he knew about the planet and its capital the better prepared he and his team would be. Unfortunately, as with most planetary histories, time and neglect made finding information difficult at best. However, while searching through the technical data from the Adeptus Mechanicus he found several historical schematics of the city of Lethe. This, combined with the other historical data, enabled him to piece together a basic construction record of the city.

Lethe was the capital city of Hyades, but it was also the original point of mankind's first presence in this harsh realm. Lethe was the location of the first promethium mines on the planet, mines that from every piece of information Jeremiah could find were still intact. Some were still in operation, while others were exhausted and no longer in use. In addition, the area of the city that was referred to as the governor's palace was in fact Hyades's first human settlement. The walls that surrounded the palace grounds were the walls of the original city.

Due to the hostile environment of the planet, as the settlement began to expand, the inhabitants left the original walls in place and built the new city around the old. Once complete, the citizens left the old city in favour of the new. Rather than destroy the old structures, subsequent governors had simply refurbished the original core of the city, using it to house the Administratum, the defence forces and any other offices they deemed important.

Jeremiah found the basic common sense of the city's previous governors fascinating and impressive. The palace compound was completely separate from the new city in almost every way: it was self-contained for power, waste reclamation, as well as water and food storage. This meant that during a siege the palace could hold out for an extended period of time.

JEREMIAH AND HIS men found themselves standing just outside the ancient city wall. From his vantage point in the alleyway, Jeremiah could see the main entrance. The palace compound was completely surrounded by a rockcrete wall about ten metres in height. Its facing had been modelled to appear like an ancient brick and mortar structure, giving it more of an artisan-built feel than most walls. This made it aesthetically pleasing to look at, but easy to breach. Surveillance skulls were placed at each corner and at the midpoints of the wall. Each skull panned back and forth scanning the conveyance road and pedestrian walkways that surrounded the compound, roads and walkways that were now clear due to the newly imposed curfew. Squads of sentries were posted at each of the four gates and at least a dozen two-man patrol teams moved along the top of the walkway. These teams patrolled in thirty-second spreads in counter rotating patterns. This made an undetected entry difficult, but not impossible.

Using hand gestures, Jeremiah signalled the team, and each man acknowledged with the all clear. With that the team went into action. Synchronising their actions with the patrols and surveillance skulls, each, at the appropriate time, crossed the street and scaled the palace wall. Using the seams and cracks of the decorated wall as foot- and hand-holds, the Dark Angels successfully traversed the wall and gained access to the palace in no time. Jeremiah was last to cross, waiting to ensure that each member of his team was safely over before he followed them.

Jeremiah quickly broke from cover and ran to the compound wall, as his team had done before him, and scaled the wall with relative ease. Grabbing the top, he swung his legs over and crouched on the surface walkway. From here, he could see the interior of the compound for the first time.

The governor's palace rose from the centre of the city. It was a beautiful structure of glass and ceramite steel, with stained glass windows depicting many aspects of the city's history. Fantastically lush gardens and small stands of trees populated the grounds surrounding the palace. It was surrounded by rows of buildings that all had a purpose in the day-to-day operation of the city, including the defence force's billets just behind the palace. The Dark Angels' intelligence reports were unclear on exactly where their target would be, however it was a good bet that the palace compound was the best place to start. Jeremiah quickly made a rough mental map of the area then dropped off the other side of the wall to join the rest of his team.

Once on the ground and in the cover of shadows, Jeremiah spoke.

'How does it look, Elijah?'

Elijah was focused on the auspex, studying the maps and intelligence reports of the palace compound.

'The interference is not as strong here, but the signal is still sporadic. According to the maps, we need to move in that direction,' Elijah explained.

Slowly, and with precision, the Dark Angels moved through the shadows towards their objective.

The parade ground was nestled in the centre of the palace grounds, where the planetary governor could inspect his troops. Over one hundred and fifty metres in length and nearly seventy-five metres wide, its flat grassy surface was used for the governor's military ceremonies. The entire grounds were bordered by a paved walkway, which was often used by palace guards as an exercise area or training track.

From the centre of the palace, a large two-storey stained glass atrium jutted out into the grounds. From here the governor could stand in the centre mezzanine as his troops passed by for his inspection. The outer edge of the parade ground was spotted with small areas of trees and shrubs landscaped around man-made brooks and streams with benches and tables positioned so that guests could enjoy the tranquillity of the gardens away from the hustle and bustle of the palace.

It was this tranquil environment that concealed the kill team. They would proceed from here without the use of the auspex as it was rendered useless, apparently by the palace's own internal defence systems.

Their optical scans revealed nothing in the vicinity. Jeremiah signalled the team to begin moving through the parade ground using the foliage for cover. Staying on the opposite side of the grounds from the atrium they should be able to move through undetected.

Elijah took point with Jeremiah bringing up the rear. They moved quickly, stopping occasionally to scan ahead to ensure that there were no visible threats. They were approaching the centre of the grounds.

'Elijah, do you see anything within the atrium itself?' Jeremiah asked.

'Full spectrum scan,' Elijah sub-vocalised the command. The optics within his helmet began to cycle through the visual spectrum. To his surprise the visual sensors were unable to penetrate the glass of the atrium.

'The atrium is shielded from my optical scan, my lord.' Elijah's voice came through the comm. 'I'm unable to detect anything within.'

'Very well, keep moving,' said Jeremiah. 'The living quarters are located on the other side of the grounds, we should locate our target there.'

The Space Marines spaced themselves out as they moved from shadow to shadow. Elijah led the way while Jeremiah assumed the rearguard position. They met no resistance at all. One by one they reached the opposite edge of the grounds, moving across the open area between the grounds and the palace. From there it was a mere fifty metres to the Planetary Defence Force barracks.

Jeremiah was the last one to cross. Using the foliage for cover he surveyed the area behind them one last time to ensure that they weren't being followed. There was no visible movement. He slowly broke cover and made his way across the opening to the corner of the palace. As he crossed, something caught his eye, and he turned to see four figures moving along the mezzanine of the upper floors of the palace. Judging by their size and bulk, they could not possibly be normal humans. There could only be one explanation; there were other Space Marines on Hyades.

THE SPACE WOLVES and the Dark Angels had a turbulent history that dated back to the time when Leman Russ, the Space Wolves primarch, and Lion El'Jonson, the primarch of the Dark Angels, still walked among the stars. The exact reason for the animosity between the two Chapters had long since been forgotten. All that was known was that a great rift grew between the brother primarchs over events that occurred during the Horus Heresy, events so great that Russ challenged Jonson to single combat. Ten thousand years later the Sons of Russ still bore this old grudge from those events and although they were not considered outright enemies, the Dark Angels were not to be trusted.

Ragnar knew that in the Spaces Wolves' long history there were times when the Great Wolf of the time refused to aid or assist the Dark Angels and there were even limited engagements between the Chapters.

He was not sure why there were Dark Angels on Hyades but he knew the Wolfblade had to act.

'Magni, I want you to alert Commander Cadmus. Inform him that we have uninvited guests in the grounds, let him know that Haegr, Torin and I are moving to engage,' Ragnar instructed.

'But Ragnar you're outnumbered you'll need my–' Magni pleaded.

'Do as you've been instructed, pup,' Haegr interrupted. 'There are only six of them, that's barely enough for me,' he boasted.

Magni knew not to argue any further, more from the look he was receiving from Ragnar than from Haegr's barking. He turned and ran back into the atrium.

Ragnar grabbed the handrail and leapt, swinging his legs over the railing and landing on the asphalt of the track, barely noticing the four-metre drop. Torin and Haegr followed immediately. Before they had hit the ground Ragnar was already at a full run across the parade ground.

The three Wolfblade crossed the parade ground in no time. Ragnar and Torin leapt over the foliage that a mere moment ago the Dark Angels intruders had been using for concealment.

Ragnar paused for an instant and took in the scent. From here it was no longer a faint hint, but a fully-fledged trail: one that he could easily follow. As Ragnar turned to Torin the foliage behind them erupted and Haegr crashed through.

'What are you standing here for? Let's get moving,' Haegr said.

Ragnar and Torin exchanged a grin and moved to the corner of the palace that the Dark Angels had just gone around. Slowly Torin looked around the corner, but seeing nothing he turned and signalled the all clear. As he and Ragnar stepped out onto the walkway, the side of the palace wall exploded as bolter rounds peppered the corner. Torin took a hit to his arm, which spun him around and back. Seeing where the shots had come from, Haegr instantly opened fire. Although the target was well out of his pistol's range, it gave Ragnar enough time to leap back behind the corner.

Torin was getting up from the ground.

'Are you all right, my friend?' Ragnar inquired.

'Armour stopped it cold, just caught me off guard. I won't make that mistake again,' Torin answered.

Haegr continued shooting at their unseen adversaries. As he leaned out to fire another burst, Ragnar and Torin broke from cover and ran across the small courtyard to the large statue of a former governor of Hyades. There was no return fire. Haegr quickly joined his fellow Wolf-blade battle-brothers.

Ragnar wasted no time. He rounded the base of the statue and sprinted towards the corner of the barracks. Flattening himself against the building wall, he quickly glanced around the corner just in time to see their Dark Angel assailant. Ragnar and the Dark Angel's eyes locked, and in that quick glance more information was exchanged between the two warriors than could be exchanged in hours of conversation.

Ragnar knew that giving chase would lead them into an ambush. He had to find a way to gain the advantage. Turning, he ran back along the Administratum building's wall, leapt up the entrance steps and crashed through the double doors. Torin and Haegr who were just behind him instantly adapted to the change in tactics and ran into the building after him.

Ragnar was in full combat mode. The Dark Angels should not be here. If they were here for legitimate reasons they would have observed standard Astartes protocol. The Chapter-wide distrust and hatred of these so-called Space Marines was proven. They had fired upon him and his brothers with no provocation. They were not the enemy, but they were not supposed to be here. They would live to regret their deceit.

Ragnar ran past the reception desk into a maze of corridors and hallways that had statues of long-dead city officials placed throughout. Using his genetically enhanced memory and intellect, he manoeuvred down several long corridors until he reached a door to a room that from his best estimate would lead to the opposite wall of the building. If he had got this right the Dark Angels would be on the other side.

Ragnar stopped at the door, grabbed the handle, and cautiously entered the room, trying to avoid being seen through the widows should the Dark Angels be where he suspected they were. Ragnar looked in upon what appeared to be a large conference room. A large table lined with high-backed chairs sat in the centre. There were three windows on the opposite wall, grand paintings adorning the walls between them. A large tapestry of the Holy Emperor hung from the wall at the end of the room. Skulls of previous adepts were stacked on shelves like books, while candles burned brightly from their corner holders, sending a wavering glow across the room. Ragnar spotted his adversaries through the middle window. They appeared to be setting up for an ambush.

Ragnar wasted no time. He leapt onto the table, took one additional step and then dived through the centre window. Glass and wood showered down onto the nearest Dark Angel. Landing on the Space Marine, Ragnar grappled him around the shoulders. Using Ragnar's momentum, the Dark Angel threw Ragnar from his back and then tumbled across the ground and came up on one knee. Ragnar landed on all fours, crouching low, ready to strike.

Ragnar sized up his opponent. He had recovered nicely from his initial attack. The Dark Angel, now on one knee, glared at him, flung his cloak aside and drew his sword. The remaining five members of the

Dark Angels squad were spread out behind his current prey, scrabbling to support their apparent leader. His attack had taken them all by surprise.

Now that he had accounted for them all, Ragnar once again returned his focus to his original foe. This Dark Angel appeared younger than he'd expected, but the service studs he wore indicated otherwise. The moment seemed like a lifetime as the two Astartes sized each other up, waiting for the right moment to strike. Tension built, stronger and stronger, and myomer muscles and tendons tightened and released. Finally the time came.

Thumbing the activation rune on his sword the Space Wolf leapt forward, his battle cry echoing through the courtyard. Raising his weapon high above his head, Ragnar brought it down in a swift killing blow towards the Dark Angel's neck. His adversary had barely enough time to bring his own weapon up to parry the blow. The two swords crashed together and locked. The warriors struggled against each other, and their weapons sparked as each man tried to gain the advantage. The blades were crossed and locked at the hilts.

Ragnar leaned in, trying to force his blade down, while the Dark Angel kneeling below pushed up with all his might trying to keep Ragnar's sword at bay. Ragnar knew that his opponent was determined and would not yield.

Torin leapt from the window that Ragnar had broken, followed closely by Haegr who made his own contribution to the remains of the wall as he forced his large frame through the makeshift opening.

Torin immediately assessed the situation. Ragnar had proven time and time again that he could take care of himself. However, there were at least five other Space Marines that needed to be dealt with.

Torin and Haegr flanked Ragnar on either side, protecting him should any of the Dark Angels try to overrun him. They would have to get through them first. Torin could make out five figures in the shadows. Suddenly one of the Dark Angels was bathed in a faint bluish green glow. Torin immediately leapt to his right, barely evading the ball of plasma flame. The wall of the Administratum building burst into flames as the plasma erupted against it.

Torin watched as the Dark Angel stepped closer, ensuring that he would not miss a second time. The Dark Angel raised the plasma gun for a second shot. Suddenly the plasma gun began to glow first red and then white hot. Waves of electrical energy danced across the surface of the weapon and up the arms of the Space Marine, who began to convulse from the sudden surge of energy that the plasma weapon was discharging.

The technology behind plasma weapons was ancient and their devastating power made them highly effective in combat. However, that effectiveness came at a price. Sometimes the massive energy was too much for the weapon to contain, and it would short circuit, overheat and then explode, sometimes taking the wielder with it.

This was not one of those times. The weapon exploded, engulfing its wielder in the blue-green flame of plasma fire and throwing him back and to the ground. His armour was scorched and melted in spots, but it was intact.

Haegr squared off against the remaining Dark Angels, bolt pistol and sword ready.

'You should feel honoured, for it is Haegr you face and it will be Haegr who ends your days,' the Space Wolf bragged as he closed on the Dark Angels.

Suddenly the entire courtyard was flooded with light, and the roar of military transports was deafening as several squads of the Planetary Defence Forces surrounded the Astartes warriors.

'This is Commander Cadmus of the Hyades Planetary Defence Forces. You are hereby ordered to lay down your weapons and surrender.' Cadmus's voice echoed around the courtyard.

Ragnar was distracted for only an instant, but an instant was all that his opponent needed. With a surge of strength, he pushed Ragnar away, rolling to one side and onto his feet.

The six Dark Angels stood together, their backs to the wall surrounded by dozens of the planetary defence troops and three members of the Wolfblade.

Ragnar stood up and walked over to join Torin and Haegr. It was over.

'It's time for some answers,' Ragnar stated as he walked towards the surrounded Dark Angels.

Suddenly the Wolfblade and the defence forces found themselves blinded by an intense white light. Then the ground shook so hard that Ragnar was knocked down, confused and disoriented.

'What in the name of the krakens of Fenris was that?' Ragnar heard Haegr shout.

'Blind grenades,' Torin shouted.

Blind grenades exploded with a blinding visible white flash. While the explosion did no physical damage, the bright burst of light could cause momentary or even permanent blindness to the unprotected eye. However, they also emitted an electronic pulse, designed to disrupt electrical and even neurological systems. This would cause even the optic in an Astartes helmet to temporarily cease to function.

* * *

It took several minutes for the effects of the blind grenade to wear off, and Ragnar could see again. He stood up and looked around. Even though the Wolfblade were not wearing their helmets for protection, they were Space Marines, and their genetic gifts allowed them to recover their faculties quickly. Unfortunately the defence forces were not quite as lucky and even those with eye protection were affected. Several had fallen to their knees, sobbing, succumbing to the panic of the loss of their sight. Many walked around, arms stretched out in front of them, trying in vain to find their friends. Ragnar knew that the effects would wear off soon, and he turned his attention back to the matter at hand.

Cadmus walked past Ragnar towards where the Dark Angels had been standing. All three of the Space Wolves turned and followed. As they approached the area, the smoke began to clear, and they discovered what had caused the ground to tremble with such force. There was a two metre-wide hole in the ground where the Dark Angels had been standing.

'Where are they? Where did they go?' Haegr asked.

'Down there it would appear,' Torin replied, pointing to the large hole.

'Lethe was the site of the first promethium mines on Hyades, and although the ones below the city are exhausted and no longer in use, they still exist, and as the city grew they built right on top of those old mines. It would appear that our intruders made their own escape route,' Cadmus explained.

Ragnar knelt down to examine the makeshift escape route. The dirt was scattered around the outside of the hole in a circular pattern, with most of it gathered around the hole's edge. Smoke still hung heavily in the air. The sick stench of promethium residue assaulted Ragnar's senses.

'This looks more like something erupted out of the ground,' Ragnar stated.

'I would imagine that some sort of directional explosive, possibly a melta-bomb charge was placed on the ground, it burnt through the dirt and bedrock until it reached the abandoned mine, igniting the promethium fumes,' Cadmus explained.

'You seem to know a lot about how these intruders were able to escape, commander.' Torin's tone was more interrogatory than curious.

'Not really, Space Wolf, it's merely what I would have done.'

'It doesn't matter how they got there, that's where they went and that's where we're going,' Ragnar stated.

'I think not, Wolfblade Ragnar. My men will handle this from here,' Cadmus countered.

'Fortunately we don't take our orders from you, Commander Cadmus,' Ragnar retorted.

'Of course, I would never dream of giving you or any of your fellow Wolfblade orders. I was merely assuming that you would wish to search the palace to ensure that no other kill teams were present to endanger the life of Lady Gabriella. She was undoubtedly their target. However, my men will endeavour to fill your shoes in your absence.'

Ragnar wanted nothing more than to simply reach out and remove the arrogant smirk from the commander's face, but the point he made was undeniable. The Wolfblade were honour-bound to serve House Belisarius, which only made the situation that much more frustrating.

'Of course commander, you are correct,' Ragnar agreed. 'The Wolfblade's place is beside Lady Gabriella.'

'We can't just let them go, Ragnar, we must follow them,' Haegr stated.

'My blood is up as well, my friend, and I too long to finish this fight, but our first duty is to see to Lady Gabriella's safety,' Ragnar replied.

Torin nodded his head in agreement. Haegr merely snorted his compliance.

Ragnar turned, looking back towards the defence forces, several of whom had started to recover and were leading those still affected to medical personnel. The Administratum building that had been set alight by the plasma fire raged on, fire teams working to bring the blaze under control. It was quite apparent that the Wolfblade was not needed here. Their duty was to locate Gabriella and to ensure that she was safe.

Ragnar moved to leave, heading in the direction of the palace. Torin walked beside him.

'You'll make a fine politician Ragnar,' Torin said with a grin.

'Great, now I've got to take your insults as well.'

'Well, that was a good bit of exercise,' Haegr commented.

'I'm glad you enjoyed yourself, Haegr,' Torin replied.

'Did you see how those Dark Angels ran when they realised that they faced the mighty Haegr of the Wolfblade?' Haegr continued.

'Yes, I did. You should be most proud of yourself,' Torin quipped.

'I've never driven a foe underground before! That's a first even for me. I can't wait to tell Magni.'

Ragnar stopped in his tracks. He had sent Magni to alert Commander Cadmus, but he had not been with the defence forces. Where was he?

'Torin...?'

'I'm thinking the same thing, Ragnar,' Torin replied.

Ragnar and Torin broke into a run, heading straight for the palace, both worried that the presence of the Dark Angels was just a distraction.

Ragnar activated his comm.

'Magni. Magni, respond!' There was no reply.

Earlier, Ragnar had felt as if he and the Wolfblade were being manipulated. What if he was right? The role of the Wolfblade was to serve and protect the members of House Belisarius. Although Ragnar always said he was in exile, he knew it was more than that. He knew that Logan Grimnar himself had sent him here. If he had been manipulated he would not only have failed the Wolfblade, he would be failing Logan Grimnar too.

Ragnar's stomach tightened as they entered the atrium, reaching the steps to the second level instantly. In two bounding leaps he had cleared the stairs, moving to the hall that led to the main conference chambers.

Just as they were about to reach the entrance to the hallway Magni and Gabriella emerged, bringing the trio to an abrupt halt.

'Magni, we sent you to alert Commander Cadmus. We expected you to come with him,' Ragnar scolded.

'The comms were down so I went to the command centre but he wasn't there. He was apparently on a night training mission with his elite regiment,' Magni replied. 'I was on my way back, when I ran into Lady Gabriella.'

'Once he had informed me of the situation, I instructed him to assist me,' Gabriella explained.

'Now, why don't you fill me in on the details to this point?'

Ragnar took a moment to gather his thoughts.

'As you are aware, we discovered a small team of Astartes attempting to move through the palace compound.'

'Dark Angels, Lady Gabriella,' Haegr interrupted.

Torin placed his hand on Haegr's shoulder.

'Sorry, Ragnar,' Haegr apologised.

Ragnar nodded his acceptance and continued.

'We began to stalk the Dark Angels through the parade ground when they fired upon us.'

'They opened fire on you!' Gabriella's shock was undeniable.

'Yes, it was after that that we moved to engage them. During this engagement Cadmus and the Planetary Defence Forces were able to surround our position, cutting off their escape route, or so we believed.' Ragnar paused.

'So they managed to escape?' Gabriella asked.

'Yes, Lady Gabriella. Using blind grenades, giving them just enough time to blow open an access point into the abandoned mines below the city,' Torin replied.

'That's one of the things I find odd about this whole situation,' Ragnar added.

'They ran away like the cowards they are,' Haegr scoffed.

'No, Ragnar is right,' said Torin. 'I'm puzzled by that and by the fact that they fired upon us without any provocation. The history between our Chapters is well-known; neither trusts the other. However, they are Astartes and nothing in that history justifies their actions tonight.'

Lady Gabriella stepped forwards, hands clasped behind her back as she mulled these events over in her mind. 'I agree. There is something bigger going on here, something beyond a simple production slow-down. I sense that the events of this evening are bigger than just promethium production. I'll inform the governor of the situation. Perhaps you should ensure that the palace is secure and then assist the commander in his search,' Gabriella instructed.

'Very good, my lady,' Ragnar replied.

'Magni, let me tell you about the time that my mere presence alone drove six Dark Angels into hiding underground,' said Haegr.

FIVE
Escalation

THE DARK ANGELS kill team had been moving through the abandoned mines since their escape from the Space Wolves and the Hyades defence forces. Jeremiah had kept them moving to ensure that their escape had been secured, in case there was anyone following them. He had also kept them going to give him time to prepare for the inevitable discussion that would take place. He and his brothers were Dark Angels, Adeptus Astartes, Space Marines. They had just retreated from a fight, and if that was not enough, their retreat had been from a pack of Space Wolves, ancient enemies of the Dark Angels Chapter. His brothers did not take kindly to retreat, and since he encouraged and valued their opinions he knew that they would have some thoughts on the recent events, thoughts that would need to be addressed.

A room off one of the tunnels provided a convenient stopping place.

'We'll stop here, brothers, and assess our next move,' said Jeremiah to his team. 'Elijah, Marius, stand watch at the door.'

The rest of the team took positions throughout the chamber. Empty barrels and crates were strewn about, and ancient lighting systems hung from the walls. Their internal power source was still intact, and generated minute amounts of light, casting the chamber in an eerie twilight glow.

Jeremiah watched as Sebastian paced back and forth across the room, a mix of anger and disappointment etched onto his face, looking up occasionally as if ready to speak, but changing his mind at the last minute. Nathaniel was standing next to a large metal vat against the opposite wall from Jeremiah, arms folded across his chest as he leaned back against the wall. His expression was one of composure and control. Jeremiah knew that he would never openly speak against him.

However, he also knew that he had some concerns. The rest looked at the other three, and feeling the tension that was building, they waited the inevitable confrontation.

'Sebastian, you wish to speak?' Jeremiah inquired.

'With respect, no,' Sebastian stated.

'Sebastian, we all have an equal voice within Lion's Pride. You know that. Jeremiah will hear your words,' Nathaniel prompted.

'I'm uncomfortable with retreating, regardless of the reason. There is no honour in such an action,' Sebastian stated.

'Do you share Sebastian's concerns, brothers?' Jeremiah made eye contact with each member of his team, and they all nodded their agreement until he reached Nathaniel.

'And you, Nathaniel?' Jeremiah asked.

'Let's just say I understand it, brother,' Nathaniel replied.

'As do I, Nathaniel, as do I. However, there are more important things than personal honour, Sebastian.' Jeremiah's words drew the air from the room. He again scanned the room gauging their reaction. 'Yes, we retreated, but we did not retreat in fear of defeat. We retreated to protect what we could not afford to lose.'

Jeremiah watched as his words began to take hold. Sebastian lifted his eyes from the floor and looked him squarely in the face. Nathaniel stood, unfolding his arms, looking like the warrior that he remembered.

'We sacrificed nothing. The honour was ours because we had to protect something much greater than ourselves: the honour of our Chapter. The success of our mission is paramount. We gain honour by keeping that oath, my brothers.'

With those words the team was whole again, ready to continue its mission. Jeremiah looked to Nathaniel his oldest and dearest friend. Nathaniel simply nodded his head, assuring him that he was right.

A DAGGER OF LIGHT ripped through the black canvas of stars, leaving a jagged tear in the fabric of space and time. Imperceptibly the tear expanded, until it became a hole filled with light. Time stood still, making mere moments last an eternity, until something emerged from the light.

The bow launch bay of the starship entered normal space first. A robed winged figure thrusting a sword upwards stood above the bay opening, challenging all that lay in her path. With a ripple, the remainder of the Space Marine battle-barge cleared the tear and completed its entry into real space. The hole of light shuddered to a close in the vessel's wake.

The starship's dark green colour made it almost invisible against the blackness of space. After a moment, running lights flickered on and off, outlining this monster of Imperial technology. Along its bow, the words 'Vinco Redemptor' became visible. The winged sword emblem of the Dark Angels was clearly displayed above them.

INTERROGATOR-CHAPLAIN VARGAS dominated the bridge of the battle-barge. His mere presence seemed to control every function of the vessel. His gaze panned from control station to control station, ensuring that all was in order. Any variance would be unacceptable. He was the master of all things aboard his vessel.

'Lord-Chaplain, we have successfully transferred from warp space into real space. We have now entered the Hyades system.' The adept's voice revealed his relief.

Vargas caressed the large tome that hung from his belt: an ancient book with a gold binding, on its cover the symbol of his Chapter. Its contents were for his eyes only. A gold rosarius hung from a gold chain around his neck. His robes covered almost all of his dark green power armour, partially obscuring the Imperial eagle emblazoned on his armour's chest plate. Although the hood of his robe shadowed his face, his bionic eye gave off a gentle red glow beneath it. His crozius arcanum, the ancient weapon of his order, hung from the left side of his belt.

The Chapter Master had dispatched Vargas to Hyades to retrieve one of the Fallen. He had inserted a kill team in secret, hoping to avoid unnecessary conflict and retrieve the traitor without incident. The kill team had instructions not only to capture their target, but also to assess the extent of the contamination.

Vargas studied the comms podium confirming that there had been no word from the kill team since insertion. His men could find no signal from the Thunderhawk that had been left for emergency withdrawal of the team. Vargas could only surmise that the kill team had been compromised or destroyed outright. Their fate would be determined in time.

Vargas turned, walking the length of the bridge until he stood just behind the helm station. The adept quickly glanced towards the

Interrogator-Chaplain in an effort to acknowledge his presence before turning his attention back to guiding the *Redemptor*.

'Distance to Hyades?' the Interrogator-Chaplain asked. His raspy voice had a metallic quality to it.

'Approximately twenty-five million kilometres, Lord-Chaplain,' replied the helmsmen.

Vargas nodded. 'Comms, contact our kill team on Hyades. See if they respond.'

Vargas strode over to the comms console. 'We have high levels of interference, Lord-Chaplain, but I think, yes, we have a signal,' the relieved communications officer stated.

Vargas took the main comm. 'Captain Jeremiah, this is Interrogator-Chaplain Vargas aboard the *Vinco Redemptor*. Respond.' Vargas paused for a moment.

'Captain Jeremiah Gieyus of Interrogator Kill Team Lion's Pride, respond.' Vargas's impatience was apparent through his metallic tones.

Static answered him.

'Comms, are you certain we have enough signal strength to get through?' asked Vargas.

'Yes, Lord-Chaplain we–' He was cut short by the response of the kill team.

'This is Captain Gieyus of the Kill Team Lion's Pride, reporting, Interrogator-Chaplain Vargas.' Jeremiah's voice burst through the comm speakers.

'Captain Gieyus, may I assume that you have subdued your target and are awaiting extraction?'

'Negative, Lord-Chaplain, we encountered unexpected obstacles in our mission,' Jeremiah stated.

'I am confused, Captain Gieyus. What "unexpected obstacles"?'

'We gained access to the governor's palace when we were engaged by a small force of Space Wolves. To avoid capture we escaped into the mines below the city,' Jeremiah explained.

'Space Wolves?'

'The Space Wolves are in the service of House Belisarius, administrators of Hyades. Their presence was unexpected,' Jeremiah said.

'The presence of the Space Wolves is unexpected but not a cause for great concern, considering the area of space we are in. Have you located the target?' Vargas tried to hide his frustration.

'No, Lord-Chaplain,' Jeremiah replied.

'Well then as with my original plan I will deploy several squads of Dark Angels to secure the city and we will root out our objective, street by street, building by building.'

Vargas sounded almost pleased. The interrogator was well known within the ranks of the Dark Angels. He had never failed when hunting down the Fallen. He ran them to ground each and every time. He was also known for using any and all means at his disposal to accomplish his task. The ancient secret of the Dark Angels could never be revealed. This above all else was his goal.

'The target must be captured and brought to justice, captain; everything else is secondary.' Vargas attempted to hide the annoyance in his voice.

'I understand that, my lord, but once again I respectfully submit that we do not need to secure the entire city for one heretic, no matter how dangerous. Lion's Pride will locate and subdue the Fallen. We simply need more time,' pleaded Jeremiah.

'Captain Gieyus, you have already failed in your mission. However, let it not be said that I am not a fair man. How much longer will you require?'

'We will only need another twelve hours to locate and secure our objective, Lord Vargas. We will not fail again,' Jeremiah replied.

'See to it that you do not, captain. You've had ample time. Another failure will not reflect well on you in my report.' Vargas's statement was clear.

'My Lord-Chap–' Jeremiah's reply was cut short as a high-pitched whine broke through the comms, forcing several adepts to quickly cup their hands over their ears.

'Things are dramatically different with the Sons of the Lion than I remember.' The strange augmented voice burst through. 'In my day failure such as this would not have been tolerated.'

'This is Interrogator-Chaplain Vargas of the Dark Angels. Identify yourself,' Vargas commanded.

'So I am addressing the great Interrogator-Chaplain Vargas. I am honoured, your reputation precedes you. However, you have disappointed me, Vargas, disappointed me greatly.' The unknown voice laughed.

'I say again, identify yourself,' Vargas repeated.

'I thought that would have been obvious to one of your reputation, again I am disappointed. Very well if I must: I am the one you seek.' Laughter once again filled the bridge.

'I will not bandy words with the likes of you! I will simply offer you this one chance to surrender to receive just punishment, or we will use ultimate force.' Vargas's voice was strained with anger and disdain.

'As I said, Vargas, you have disappointed me. Sending down a simple six-man kill team, delegating subordinates to do your job, I mean really

Vargas, I had hoped for better from you.' Venom dripped from the voice of their persecutor.

'You have an expanded perception of your own importance. A simple kill team is more than sufficient to apprehend you.' Anger grew to rage in Vargas's voice.

'Do you think I am some terrified refugee cowering in a corner?' The voice laughed. 'I am prepared for you and your fellow Astartes, but I do not think that you are prepared for me.' Again laughter filled the bridge.

Suddenly defensive alarms sounded throughout the ship drowning out the hideous laughter. Vargas quickly turned to the tactical screen. Adepts and servitors reacted furiously to identify the new threat.

'Lord-Chaplain, several orbital defence platforms just went active. I'm detecting laser batteries and torpedo bays.' The adept was shouting to overcome the alarm sirens.

'Lord-Chaplain, I'm detecting launch. We have an inbound torpedo salvo!'

'You see Vargas! Do you finally see what a great disappointment you are to me?' With its final assault the voice cut off.

Vargas felt his anger growing, but he was too experienced to allow that anger to completely take over. It was time to bring this to an end, to bring it to an end his way. He turned to give his instructions when a single voice came from the comm. It was the voice of Jeremiah Gieyus.

'Lord Vargas–' Vargas cut off Jeremiah in mid sentence.

'The target must be located, captured and brought to justice, captain. All other concerns are secondary. Do what you must to secure him. The threat of contamination is too great, and the time for covert operations is over. I will be sorting this my way.' Vargas gestured to the communications officer to close the channel.

'Guidance, bring us within assault range. Activate shields and all weapons batteries,' his metallic voice commanded.

Weapon and defensive system adepts repeated Vargas's words back to him as they accomplished each command with lightning precision. The bridge access doors sprang open as two Dark Angels entered the bridge, taking positions on either side of the door. Should the ship be boarded they along with the adepts, servitors and Vargas would defend the bridge.

Activating the inter-ship comms, Vargas continued, 'Forward launch bay prepare and launch Thunderhawk Squad Alpha for defensive cover. Drop-pods prepare for immediate launch.'

Returning his attention the bridge, he continued his commands, 'Tactical control, display the current position of the *Redemptor* and all other vessels in the system,'

Vargas turned to the tactical screen. A holographic image sprang to life. The planet Hyades was at the centre. Several ships floated at various orbits above the planet. The orbiters were mostly transports and cargo vessels in standard docking orbits. These ships posed no threat to the *Vinco Redemptor*. The defence platforms however were another matter.

'How is it you missed the platforms on your initial scans?' Vargas demanded, clenching his gauntleted hands.

'Their power grids must have been down as we approached, Lord Vargas, and we were too far away for visual confirmation,' the tactical officer replied, failing to hide the stress in his voice.

Vargas was troubled by the fact that the defence platforms were left powered down. Not to mention that these defences had not been included in the intelligence reports. It wasn't uncommon for planets like Hyades to have planetary defence platforms, but to leave them powered down to hide their presence was unheard of. Was it possible that the Fallen had set a trap for them? Well if it was a trap, the fools were about to catch far more than they could have imagined.

'It would appear that we are in for a bigger fight than we expected. So much the better,' said Vargas, the anticipation in his voice coming through the metallic tone.

Vargas stroked his rosarius and let his hand rest on the two black pearls hanging there. An Interrogator-Chaplain earned one black pearl for each Fallen who confessed his sins and sought redemption before his death. Today, he was determined to capture the Fallen that would bring him his third pearl.

The Interrogator-Chaplain stormed across to the bridge's observation deck. From his vantage point, the massive ship stretched out before him. He could see its weapon batteries spring to life, powerful weapons capable of punching through a ship's hull with ease. Planetary bombardment cannons rose from their enclosed bays, primarily used to soften a target prior to Space Marine deployment by orbital bombardment. However, that would not be their purpose this day, since there was no need to lay waste to the capital city... yet.

Doors covering the massive torpedo bays retracted in preparation of their impending salvo. Vargas knew that within his ship's hull, her crew moved to their assigned combat stations. Cybernetic servitors, half-man and half-machine, lumbered through their programmed duties, moving within areas of the ship where radiation, heat and the harsh bite of vacuum would not allow others to venture.

The Dark Angels commander looked out from the pulpit on the observation deck as the battle-barge closed on Hyades. Small pinholes of light flashed through space towards the great vessel. The incoming torpedo salvo was almost upon them. Subconsciously he grabbed either side of his pulpit, preparing for the inevitable engagement.

'It begins,' Vargas said to himself.

'Lord-Chaplain, impact with inbound torpedo salvo in twenty seconds,' the tactical adept declared.

Twenty-four torpedoes cut across the void on a collision course with the *Redemptor*. The civilian transports and cargo ships between the torpedoes and their target banked and turned, making dramatic course changes and showing manoeuvring abilities more akin to warships in avoiding the oncoming wall of destruction. Weapons turrets aboard the battle-barge vomited a hail of defensive fire against the unexpected onslaught. Several torpedoes unable to alter course exploded while others fell horribly off course as they passed through the *Redemptor's* defensive salvo. Four passed through the hail of defensive fire unscathed. Onboard klaxons trumpeted the impending collision.

'Four torpedoes remain inbound,' the adept shouted, attempting to be heard over the alarm klaxons.

'Launch torpedoes... brace for collision.' The chaplain's voice remained calm and precise.

Torpedoes erupted from their launch tubes on course for the defence platforms. The *Vinco Redemptor* banked hard to her port side in a sluggish attempt to position her heavier armoured side to the enemy torpedoes, protecting the open launch bays from the destructive force careening in her direction. Not designed for manoeuvrability, the *Redemptor* resisted the unnatural movement, but slowly she brought her bow around.

The first of the torpedoes struck amidships. Ripples of blue energy radiated in waves out from the point of impact as the *Redemptor's* defensive shielding absorbed most of the weapons' energy. The next two torpedoes sent waves of blue energy rippling across the ship as they also wasted themselves on the defensive shielding. The fourth torpedo struck home just outside the forward launch bay. The defensive shield, already strained by the previous strikes, was not able to withstand another direct hit.

The explosion ripped through the weaker sections of the armoured hull and flames engulfed the launch bay. Shards of metal, fragments of ceramite plating and other debris ripped through crewmen manning the launch craft. Secondary explosions from ammo lifts and fuel carriers enhanced the destruction. Automated fire suppression systems activated, working to extinguish the flames and contain the damage.

Servitors moved into the damaged bay, clearing debris and rubble. Techmarines took their places near the wounded deck, beginning the ritual anointing ceremonies, which would allow them to reroute damaged systems and control functions.

'Damage control reports minor damage to forward launch bay, Lord-Chaplain,' reported the tactical officer.

The *Vinco Redemptor* returned to her course. She was almost in range to launch the landing force. The transport and cargo ships appeared as small green images on the tactical display, scattering as they attempted to avoid the coming conflict.

Vargas turned his attention away from the observation deck, back to the tactical display. As Vargas watched, he noticed something odd. Though the civilian ships were in disarray, one of them was following an escape course dangerously close to the Dark Angels battle-barge.

Collision alarms sounded.

Vargas spun back to the observation deck. 'Report?' Vargas asked already knowing the answer.

'Proximity alarm, Lord-Chaplain. One of the transports is on a collision course with us.'

'I want that transport out of our flight path,' commanded Vargas.

'Lord-Chaplain?' asked the fire control officer.

'All port weapons, bombardment cannons two and four, target that ship and fire.'

The transport ship rocked as the *Redemptor* obeyed its master. Laser and plasma fire sliced through the transport's hull, cutting through the craft's bridge. Then, the dreaded bombardment cannons struck the transport's cargo bay. The ship listed, drifting lifelessly. Fire and electrical residue danced across her hull. Unexpectedly, the transport exploded.

The force of the blast was not like anything that the engines of a transport of her size should be capable of producing. The blast shot outwards, as if in dying, the ship had become a small star. The bridge of the *Vinco Redemptor* rocked violently as the shockwave crashed into the ship's port side. Flame and debris peppered the ship like shrapnel, causing secondary explosions to erupt across the ship.

JEREMIAH DEACTIVATED HIS comm and took a deep breath. His mind flew back to the moment when the intelligence report for this mission had been presented. Commander Azrael, Supreme Grand Master of the Dark Angels, had been there for its presentation. After its reading, a debate among several of the Interrogator-Chaplains had begun about who would pursue this member of the Fallen, and how his apprehension would be effected. After several days of deliberation Lord Vargas had been nominated and approved. He remembered this quite clearly because after the chaplains had agreed they had turned to Commander Azrael who simply nodded his approval.

Vargas very quickly began to discuss his plans for securing the Fallen.

'My plan is quite simple: I will dispatch a kill team to Hyades to locate and secure the Fallen. Once our objective has been achieved, the *Vinco Redemptor* will arrive to extract the team. Should something go wrong or the team fails in its mission then I will deploy troops to search and subdue the city until he is found.'

There were no objections to Vargas's plans, only a question from Commander Azrael. 'Hyades is in a sector that falls under the protection of the Space Wolves. How can we explain such action on one of their protectorate worlds?'

There was a long pause before Vargas spoke. 'Grand Master, the entire operation will not take long at all. In fact we should be in and out before they even know we are there. However, to ensure the highest possibility for success, I will deploy Kill Team Lion's Pride, led by Captain Jeremiah Gieyus.'

JEREMIAH KNEW THAT Chaplain Vargas had just absolved himself of any responsibility of failure. Everything rested squarely on the shoulders of him and his team.

He looked into the eyes of the members of his team. None of them knew the real reason why they had been assigned to this hunt. The path they were on would require more from them than he had ever asked before.

'My brothers, you are all aware of what's about to happen. Chaplain Vargas will be launching the assault force in a matter of minutes. Our target has infiltrated the Hyades defence forces. That means they will be used as cannon fodder so he can make good his escape. We cannot allow this to happen. It is imperative we locate him and bring this matter to a swift conclusion.' The passion in Jeremiah's voice rose.

'We are all with you, Brother-Captain Gieyus. You have but to lead.' Nathaniel spoke for the entire team.

Jeremiah drew his sword and held it out in front of him. Each Dark Angel in turn placed his mighty gauntleted hand on the blade and they spoke in unison.

'Repent! For tomorrow you die.'

VARGAS REACHED UP and grabbed the pulpit, pulling himself back up to his feet. As the bridge lighting returned, he checked the bridge and the crew for damage. Adepts and servitors were pulling themselves up and doing their best to assume their duty. Some lay still and twisted on the floor; these would not rise again.

Vargas had seen many ships burn in space. He'd witnessed reactor explosions, but this was different. The explosion was much more powerful than a ship of that size should have made. Had the transport been any closer, it could have severely damaged the *Redemptor*.

'What caused that explosion? It was too big to be a reactor overload,' Vargas asked.

'Lord-Chaplain, I've conducted a focused scan of the remaining transports. Most of them are empty, but four of them are loaded top to bottom with promethium fuel cells.' The tactical adept transferred the sensor information to the tactical screen. The holo images of the loaded transports glowed red to demonstrate their threat potential.

'Treacherous bastards! Damage report! How badly are we damaged?'

'Reports are coming in now, sir. We've lost our port weapons batteries, gravity generators on decks twelve through fifteen port side are down, and the port shields have been depleted to thirty per cent,' reported the tactical officer.

Vargas scanned the restored tactical display. The *Vinco Redemptor's* initial torpedo salvo had severely damaged several of the planetary defence platforms, but they still posed a threat. It was time to bring this to an end. Vargas activated his armour's internal comm system and patched directly into the ship's speakers.

'Brethren, prepare for ground assault. The Lion will be with us on this day. All drop-pods prepare for immediate launch.' Vargas resumed his place on the observation deck.

Dark Angels from the Fifth Company carrying support equipment reported to their assigned drop-pods. Space Marines passed by the Thunderhawks towards the drop-pod launch tubes. Each drop-pod could deliver a single squad of Space Marines amongst the enemy, hurtling through the atmosphere with incredible velocity, making them virtually impossible for enemy weapons teams to target. Just before impact, powerful engines would ignite, bringing the pod to a safe touchdown. Only the toughened bodies of the Astartes could survive the pressures involved in such a descent.

The *Redemptor* closed on Hyades. Starboard and forward weapons batteries opened fire. Torpedoes and missiles raced from their launch tubes. Wave after wave of Thunderhawks burst from the forward launch bay, forming a shield in front of the *Redemptor*. Smaller and more manoeuvrable than their mother ship, they provided the perfect screen for the much larger battle-barge.

Hyades's remaining defence platforms opened fire with everything they had, using torpedoes and lance batteries. Thunderhawks engaged the torpedoes, protecting the *Redemptor* until she was in range to launch her drop-pods.

Lasers from the defence platforms' lance batteries sliced through the Dark Angels Thunderhawk shield. A few Thunderhawks broke off to conduct strafing runs on the slower and less manoeuvrable suicide transports, destroying them far from the *Vinco Redemptor*.

The *Redemptor* turned slightly, attempting to protect her weaker port side. With the bombardment cannons in range, she opened fire on the defence platforms. Massive projectiles ripped through the remaining platforms, turning them into clouds of metal fragments. With the sky clear of enemy fire the drop-pods were clear to launch. In moments, the Dark Angels would be on the planet.

Vargas stood on the bridge observation deck, watching as his battle-brothers entered the atmosphere.

'The Fallen will be redeemed,' he murmured.

WITH THE ASSISTANCE of the governor's guard, the Wolfblade had just completed a search of the palace grounds. Ragnar and Torin had considered entering the mines to continue their search for the Dark Angels when they received a message from Gabriella.

'My Wolfblade, a Space Marine battle-barge has engaged Hyades's orbital defence forces. Report to me immediately at the governor's command centre,' she ordered.

Ragnar and the others were stunned by the news. Their encounter with a squad of Dark Angels in the capital was strange enough, but now a battle-barge had not only entered the system, but had actually begun an assault of the orbital defences. The foursome quickly broke into a run.

IT TOOK THE four Space Wolves several minutes to reach the command centre, but upon their arrival they found themselves in the middle of a torrent of activity. Two large circular tactical screens filled the far wall. Control podiums and communication pulpits stood directly in front of the tactical screens, where a number of adepts delicately ran their fingers across runes, constantly feeding new data to the screens. Several of them glanced towards the Space Marines. Many had never seen a warrior of the Astartes before, let alone a Space Wolf, and they were afraid. Ragnar could smell their fear, it hung on them like a cloud, but even filled with fear they were not distracted from their duties, which impressed him.

Governor Pelias stood next to the consoles surrounded by advisors, all of whom seemed to be talking at once. Gabriella stood beside the governor listening as the reports came in. Upon noticing the Wolf-blade, she immediately made for them.

'My lady, we've detected no signs of any other forces within the palace grounds,' Ragnar reported.

Gabriella swept her hand towards the tactical display. 'We have. Our uninvited guest is a Dark Angels battle-barge.'

'They brought a battle-barge?' Torin said, shaking his head. 'But why? Are they planning a planetary assault?'

'That appears to be their intent. What we don't know is why they are attacking. The governor has made several attempts to make contact with them, but they refuse to answer,' Gabriella responded.

Ragnar searched his memory for some grain of information, some insight into why the Dark Angels were here. Why were they invading Hyades? What could they possibly want?

He replayed the fight with the Dark Angels over and over again in his mind. He must have missed some detail. He had first spotted them moving through the parade grounds, but where had they been head-ing? Ragnar pictured the palace grounds, trying to map out where the Dark Angels might have been going.

Ragnar scanned the command centre, podium to pulpit, looking for the adept that could provide him with what he was searching for. Finally he saw what he needed: a young pale technician who looked confused.

Ragnar walked over to the man. 'I need you, now,' he said. The man nearly fell out of his chair as he stared up at the armoured Space Wolf. 'Can you bring up a map of the palace grounds?'

'Yes, sir, Lord Wolf, sir, I mean…' With a few simple keystrokes, his screen came to life with a topographical view of the palace grounds. Ragnar traced the path of the Dark Angels through the parade ground. Torin and Gabriella leaned over, flanking Ragnar on either side.

Haegr tried to push through to see for himself, but there wasn't enough room.

'Haegr, old friend,' said Torin, 'why don't you take Magni and gather the rest of the Wolfblade, I've a feeling that we are going to have need of our wolf brothers shortly.'

Haegr looked as if he wanted to protest, but he knew that planning and calculating were not among his strengths.

'Come, lad,' said Haegr, 'Torin's right, we'll be around for the fighting, don't worry.' Haegr realised what Torin was doing. There was a fight coming, and they needed to be ready for it. He and Magni would collect their brothers, and the Emperor help them when they met up with him.

Torin quietly asked Ragnar, 'Care to share with us what you're looking for, my friend?'

'A reason, something, anything that we may have missed during our engagement with the Dark Angels, anything that will give us some insight into why Hyades is so important to them. If we discover why they are here, we may be able to bring this conflict to a quick end.' Ragnar continued to analyse the map.

'You think that the answer is on this map?' Gabriella asked.

'I'm trying to work out where they were going before we engaged them,' replied Ragnar. 'We've assumed that it was somewhere in the palace, that they were trying to assassinate you, Gabriella, or maybe Governor Pelias.'

Ragnar stepped in closer to the display and continued. 'We detected them right here,' he said, pointing to the relative position on the map. 'They moved along the parade ground, beside the Administratum building, on the opposite side of the atrium, leaving the parade ground here.'

'Yes, but then they moved around to the front of the Administratum building,' said Torin. Circling the area with his finger, he continued, 'So you think they were searching for someone or something in the Administratum building?'

Gabriella leaned back, folding her arms across her chest. 'I cannot imagine what they could have been looking for there. Information on trade or weapons, possibly, although it would take weeks to work out what.'

Ragnar travelled back in his mind to the moment when he and his companions had encountered the Dark Angels. He remembered making eye contact with the leader of the kill team. 'They altered their path to engage us,' Ragnar said softly, not realising that he was speaking aloud.

'What's that, Ragnar?' Torin asked.

'The Administratum building had nothing to do with what they were looking for. They altered their plan to engage us. They realised that they had been detected and they reacted to that threat,' Ragnar concluded.

Gabriella folded her hands, obviously aware of more activity and shouts. 'So, if not to the Administratum building, then where were they heading?'

Torin turned back to the map. 'We can assume that if we had not detected them, they would have continued along in this direction.' Torin traced his finger along the map. 'So what lies in that direction?'

Gabriella stopped pacing. 'The armoury, the physical training facility, and the barracks for the elite palace guard,' she said.

'Maybe they were hoping for a decapitation strike before the invasion began.'

'I don't know,' Ragnar said, but he was certain there was something more.

The command centre suddenly exploded with a flurry of action, as alarms sounded. 'Excuse me for a moment,' Gabriella said, leaving to confer with Governor Pelias, who was speaking to someone on the comm; Ragnar guessed it was probably Cadmus.

Gabriella touched the governor reassuringly on the shoulder, and then left him to rejoin Ragnar and Torin.

'Come with me,' she said.

The Wolfblade joined her, flanking her on either side as she moved to the opposite side of the room and entered a lift. The doors closed behind them. Gabriella pressed a button on the control panel and the lift ascended.

'The time for speculation is over, my trusted Wolfblade. The Dark Angels have refused all our hails. They've destroyed our defence satellites, and right now several drop-pods are on course for Lethe.'

The doors slid open. Gabriella and the Wolfblade stepped out of the lift into a large, well-furnished office. Ragnar guessed it might belong to the governor or one of his aides. Gabriella walked over to a balcony on the far side of the room that overlooked the city.

The Space Wolves stood and watched the smoke trails from the drop-pods as they burned their way through the atmosphere. All three shared a moment of silence; this entire situation had rapidly spiralled out of control.

Gabriella placed both hands on the balcony rail. She leaned forwards, and for the first time, Ragnar could see the tremendous stress she was under. She was trembling ever so slightly. 'The answer we seek lies with the Dark Angels in the mines. The Dark Angels sent a kill team to infiltrate the palace looking for something or someone. You somehow stopped them from achieving their objective. I should have let you go after them when you wanted to, but I thought we should secure the palace grounds first.'

'Your decision was the correct one, Lady Gabriella. We needed to make sure that your and the governor's immediate safety were assured,' Torin explained.

Ragnar had never seen Gabriella like this before. She was afraid. Even in the most serious of situations on Terra, she had kept her composure. He remembered when they had come upon the dead elder Navigators of House Belisarius. She had wept, but stayed firm. He needed no other measure of the seriousness of this situation, although he wondered if she knew something more than she had told them. Had she seen some psychic vision?

'Ragnar, Torin, go into the mines and locate the Dark Angels. Find out what is going on. We have no other options at this point,' Gabriella sighed.

'Lady Gabriella, we cannot leave you unprotected,' protested Ragnar.

'Whatever is happening here is bigger than my safety, Ragnar. Warriors of the Astartes have engaged in combat. We must know why so that we can bring this to a halt before it expands beyond Hyades.' Gabriella's voice quivered as she spoke.

'Then I will remain by your side while the rest enter the mines,' Ragnar replied.

'A compromise then and I will speak no more of it, Ragnar. Torin and Haegr will need you, so you will go with them. Magni is still not fully recovered from his injuries so he will remain here with me.'

Ragnar knew that the time for debate was over and Lady Gabriella's wishes must be carried out. He and Torin straightened and bowed their heads in acknowledgment, then turned to leave the balcony. As Ragnar walked away he felt Gabriella touch his mind.

Ragnar, I cannot express how imperative it is for the Wolfblade to succeed. I feel that everything rests on you.

Ragnar made no acknowledgement of the words. They would find the Dark Angels, and they would tell him what they knew.

SIX
Capture

Ragnar knew that he could never live in a city like Lethe. As the Wolf-blade moved through the darkened tunnels and refinery that still existed beneath the city, he had a new appreciation of how tenuous human existence was on this planet. All around him, promethium flowed through cooled pipes to keep it from exploding in the hot air of Hyades. Though he trusted in the tech-priests, still it seemed to Ragnar that the danger of this underground complex dwarfed that of the jungle surrounding the city. He wondered just how much promethium flowed through those pipes.

Underground, Ragnar had hoped the temperature would fall, but the servants of the Machine-God had made minimal use of fans and vents. Keeping the oxygen content of this complex low probably made the promethium safer, Ragnar thought.

The corridors and tunnels were cramped and narrow, meant to be only large enough for the workforce to run the refinery and maintain the pipes. The walls were alternately reinforced with ceramite and rockcrete or left as bare rock. Everywhere, servitors meticulously performed their duties. They smelled more of oil and unguents than sweat as they ignored the Space Wolves stalking past them. Whirrs and whines of machinery accompanied by a low rumble from the pipes echoed through the tunnels. The refining equipment and gauges provided the only light sources, giving what little could be seen an artificial blood-red cast.

They had been searching for hours. Haegr panted as Ragnar led the Space Wolves as quickly as caution and stealth would allow through one of the bare rock sections of tunnel. He didn't want to fall into an ambush. The other Wolfblade followed, constantly scanning the area for signs of the Dark Angels. Ten men from the Planetary Defence Force trailed behind them.

They all had to be careful how they reacted to a sudden strike by the enemy. Ragnar was sure that a wrong move or weapon discharge could burst a pipe and set off large quantities of promethium, cooking all of them in their armour. Ragnar hoped that the Dark Angels would fight as true Space Marines and not resort to shooting a pipe to end things for both groups. Still, while the Space Wolves conducted themselves with honour, the Dark Angels had a reputation as fanatics in their pursuit of their own interpretation of the Emperor's will.

Despite his protests, Magni had stayed to protect Gabriella, along with two other Wolfblade. The young Space Wolf had recovered quickly from his wounds, and Ragnar recognised his potential and prowess. Torin had told him that Magni was one of the best young recruits he'd met, despite the offence that had led him to the Wolfblade. Magni had disobeyed orders in his zeal to defeat the enemy, a sentiment that Ragnar found understandable. However, Ragnar could see that Magni still hadn't learnt his lesson from the kill zone incident.

Ragnar still had trouble believing that the Wolfblade hunted fellow Space Marines. Like all Space Wolves, he was well-versed in the rivalry between the primarchs Leman Russ and Lion El'Jonson. Yet, like his initial experiences with the Wolfblade, he had never expected servants of the Emperor to battle each other on Holy Terra. Now, two groups of Space Marines would engage in combat for the second time on Hyades. Perhaps in battling the Dark Angels, Ragnar might gain a better understanding of his primarch. In his heart he believed that Leman Russ would have ordered him to use the Spear of Russ to defend the Imperium.

The mines shook, sending streams of rock down on the Wolfblade, making Ragnar suspect that a battle raged above their heads. He could imagine the PDF fighting the Dark Angels in the streets. He knew that Lethe's defenders didn't have much chance. Lasguns would be useless against the Dark Angels' power armour, while the human troops would be mown down by the Space Marines' bolter fire.

Despite their superior troops, the Dark Angels wouldn't have it easy. The city centre would hold out the longest with its strong defences and numbers of men, and the rest of Lethe was basically a series of rockcrete bunkers. He guessed Cadmus would have his troopers armed with flamers and heavy flamers. If the men stayed loyal to Cadmus and didn't lose their heart, the Dark Angels would have to fight building by building to defeat the men of Lethe. He hoped that the troopers of House Belisarius could continue to hold out long enough for reinforcements to arrive.

Though he distrusted the commander, Ragnar liked the leader of the PDF unit ordered to search with them. The man, an offworlder named Markham, had learned to fight in a unit of deathworld veterans. Ragnar's instincts and observations told him that Markham was a tested warrior who commanded respect from his men. He hadn't questioned the Wolfblade and had managed to keep pace, even though the stifling heat of the tunnels and the sounds of warfare from above weren't making it easy on his men.

The members of Markham's team were from Hyades, wearing carapace armour and rebreathers. They were some of the best-armed and armoured troops Ragnar had seen, virtually the equal of elite Imperial Guard stormtroopers in regard to their equipment. Ragnar had asked Torin to keep an eye on the man who carried the flamer, and had given orders for its tanks to be disconnected while they were underground. Ragnar knew that if the Dark Angels escaped into the city above or the jungle, then the weapon would be invaluable, but the sheer madness of anyone having a flamer in these tunnels made his guts churn.

The Wolfblade kept their assault weapons in hand. With the twists and turns of the tunnels, any corner could hide an enemy ambush, and they had to be ready to initiate hand-to-hand combat at a moment's notice. At extreme close quarters, the Space Wolves might not have a chance to shoot, even if the pipes would allow it. Ragnar gripped the hilt of his personal sword, his Wolfblade. It had been a gift for saving the Celestarch of House Belisarius, and it was at least the equal of a frostblade, a weapon only given to the greatest Space Wolves. Torin had his sword out, and Haegr hefted his hammer. They were ready.

Ragnar had an idea. He checked his comm, just as a precaution. He wouldn't take chances with communications on Hyades any longer. His armour's systems all appeared fully functional. He raised his hand, stopping the Wolfblade behind him and activated his comm. 'Markham, take your men and continue the search. The rest of you, go with them and give them support worthy of the Wolfblade. Torin and Haegr, stay here with me.'

'Wolfblade Ragnar, I have orders to assist you,' stated Markham. Even in the bad light, Ragnar could read enough of Markham's expression to know that the man wanted to make sure he had the opportunity to battle the Dark Angels.

'The best assistance you can give us is to press on with the search. I want to try something. If it doesn't work, we'll rejoin you. Go,' said Ragnar.

Markham saluted, 'Yes, sir.' He signalled his men and moved forwards along with the other members of the Wolfblade. They turned down an intersection of tunnels ten metres past Ragnar.

Torin and Haegr both gave Ragnar a hard look. 'Little brother, what kind of scheme have you come up with?' asked Haegr.

'Indeed, lad, what are you thinking?' asked Torin.

'By the bones of Russ, don't you trust my instincts yet, old friends?' asked Ragnar.

'I'm still thinking you haven't had a good thrashing in some time to keep the sense in you,' said Haegr.

'I'm thinking like our prey. They are hunters and Space Marines. They don't intend to go back as failures.' Ragnar activated his comm, pleased that it still worked. 'Tech-Priest Varnus, this is Ragnar of the Wolfblade.'

JEREMIAH'S KILL TEAM had outmanoeuvred the city militia. A Planetary Defence Force, even trained by one of the Fallen, was no match for the Dark Angels. He had not anticipated Space Wolves. Vaguely, he remembered some information about one of the Navigator Houses having an alliance with Space Wolves. Now, events had escalated to a full-scale assault on the city.

Of all the Chapters of Space Marines, none had the rivalry that existed between the Dark Angels and the Space Wolves. Jeremiah knew that the Space Wolves had a reputation as savage berserkers, relying on brute force and animal cunning to defeat their foes. Their devotion to their primarch and their homeworld of Fenris was legendary. Few foes could survive the fury unleashed by the Space Wolves.

For their part, Jeremiah believed that no Chapter inspired as much loyalty among its members as the Dark Angels. For thousands of years, the Dark Angels had kept their secrets, hunting down the Fallen and working to redeem themselves. They had an unwavering faith in the Emperor and in their primarch, Lion El'Jonson. Just as their primarch had before them, they used intelligence as well as power to defeat their foes. The mere presence of the Dark Angels was enough to send most enemies fleeing in terror.

Reputation would not defeat the Space Wolves. Furthermore, they were the Wolfblade. Unlike their brethren, nay, Wolf Brothers, they had experience on Terra. They would be cautious, balancing the wild tendencies of their Chapter with the acumen needed to survive the politics of mankind's homeworld.

When Jeremiah had fled to the mines, he had hoped to find a way out into the jungle, through another maintenance hatch or engineering tunnel. While parts of the refinery were well marked beneath the main city complex, the outer sections had fallen into disrepair. The servitors might not need signs or markers to navigate these corridors, but men certainly would.

Many of the tunnels appeared abandoned and in other places, the original engineers had made use of natural caverns. Jeremiah was accustomed to standard design patterns from Imperial engineers, but as his team passed through sections of the mines that curved back on themselves, he found himself disoriented. As yet, they hadn't found a way out, just endless underground facilities containing mindless servitors working the promethium. Originally, they had merely dropped down four metres to the tunnels, but now Jeremiah suspected they were much deeper. Elijah had few readings on his auspex.

What disturbed Jeremiah most was that the Fallen had known the attack was coming and had been able to prepare for it. The presence of the Space Wolves had to be his doing. The Fallen were clever and resourceful foes, with the skills to match the most dangerous members of his Chapter. Nonetheless, if the Fallen had known about the battle-barge in orbit and suspected the possibility of a planetary assault, then Jeremiah would have expected him to do his damage and make his escape. The Fallen had to have a contingency plan to deal with the assault, and it had to be something completely, incredibly dangerous. Their target had to have allies.

Could the Space Wolves be more involved than Jeremiah suspected? What if the Fallen had made a deal with the Space Wolves to expose the Dark Angels to the Imperium in exchange for their aid?

But from what Jeremiah knew of the barbaric Space Wolves, a deal with the Fallen made no sense. The Fallen would manipulate the Space Wolves, but he would have his own allies and his own resources. The Fallen's allies would have to be extremely powerful for him to risk being trapped in a city filled with the Dark Angels.

Ultimately, Jeremiah knew it made no difference. His faith told him that the Fallen would be redeemed. The Dark Angel shuddered when he thought of the redemption process. Few dared to gaze upon the Interrogator-Chaplains and they would stop at nothing to restore honour to the Fallen's soul.

'Jeremiah, the auspex is no longer functioning,' said Elijah. 'I do not know where the Space Wolves are.'

'The radiation of the machinery and promethium flows must be causing problems. Our adversaries will suffer the same difficulties. Even now, our brethren above attack, seeking to make certain our target does not escape. The time for flight has ended. The Sons of the Lion do not flee from wolves. Elijah, find a way back to the surface. Our target may send his dogs to hunt us, but we are the hunters. We have not failed in our mission. We will not return to our battle-barge without our prey,' said Jeremiah.

Jeremiah's battle-brothers nodded in unison.

A DARK ANGELS Thunderhawk roared between the rockcrete buildings of Lethe, using them to evade the anti-aircraft rounds of the city's Hydra platforms. From the ground and the upper floors of buildings, individual defenders targeted the low-flying landing craft with small-arms fire.

Dozens of lasgun shots glanced off the Thunderhawk's armoured hull, as ineffective as fireworks. As the Thunderhawk landed on a building halfway between the wall and the palace complex, its ramp was already lowered, and a squad of ten Space Marines opened fire on their unseen assailants in the surrounding buildings.

The men of Hyades kept a constant stream of fire against the invaders, but to little avail. The power armour of the Space Marines rendered their defensive fire virtually useless. One Space Marine stumbled, but the rest forced their way through the roof of the Administratum building where they had landed with a combination of krak grenades and melta-bombs. The Thunderhawk was already gone, dispatching more troops on another rooftop.

The same scene was being repeated throughout Lethe. To this point, the air defences of Lethe had only slowed the Dark Angels, but nothing Hyades had to offer appeared able to stop them.

As more Space Marines landed, the Planetary Defence Force took action, turning their Earthshaker cannons from their positions aiming at the jungle to target their own city. A terrible explosion shattered the night as the first shell smashed into one of the Administratum buildings, just as a Thunderhawk lowered its ramp to discharge more Dark Angels.

The destruction of the building sent rockcrete in all directions, catching the evasive Thunderhawk in a shower of debris. The squad on its roof fell down into the rubble of the former building. Despite the blast, the power armour of the Emperor's finest still allowed some of them to survive. The remaining Space Marines inside the Thunderhawk blew their way free of their wounded vessel and started to make their way through the rubble and smoke that was all that was left of the Administratum building.

Cadmus had been watching everything from his command centre, assessing the enemy's tactics and guiding the battle to the best of his ability. As he watched the Thunderhawk's crash, he activated his vox. 'Now,' was his only command.

At that command, four Hellhound tanks emerged from hangars beneath separate buildings and raced towards the scene of the collapse. The tanks would incinerate the remaining squads of Dark Angels trapped in the rubble. Lethe would send the Space Marines to their own hells in promethium fires.

Cadmus didn't wait to watch the drama unfold from his command bunker. He had every confidence in the crews of his Hellhounds. And besides, he had other matters to attend to.

'Commander, how goes the battle?' crackled his comm. The voice was hushed, barely a whisper.

Cadmus paused for a moment before answering. 'As I told you, I will be able to hold out against the Dark Angels for a short while. Everything will depend on the Space Wolves,' he said, keeping his own voice low.

'Exactly, don't be concerned. Wolves will be wolves,' came the reply.

'I hope so. Now, with your leave, I have a battle to survive,' responded Cadmus.

'Of course. Remember, with every moment, we come closer to winning the war,' said the voice.

Cadmus clicked off the comm. He checked back on the scene of the Thunderhawk crash and building collapse. He could barely make out suits of power armour glowing from the heat of the Inferno cannons within the smoke. Three Hellhounds sprayed white-hot death into the rubble. With his tactical experience, he spotted the wreckage of the fourth Hellhound. A Dark Angels Dreadnought was moving away from the destroyed vehicle: a walking mechanical monstrosity containing the half-alive remains of a mortally wounded member of the brethren. It turned and levelled a twin-linked lascannon at another Hellhound which erupted into a fireball.

'The Lion still has its pride,' he remarked. 'Varnus, launch the suicide freighters filled with promethium. I want to give those Thunderhawks and the Dark Angels fleet something to think about.'

Cadmus wiped his brow and smiled. The Dark Angels had arrived. Phase one was complete.

Everything depended on the Space Wolf fleet arriving to patrol on schedule. It was all about timing and sequence.

* * *

THE DARK ANGELS kill team had begun its tactical withdrawal over two and a half hours ago. Jeremiah had decided that it was time for the withdrawal to become a redeployment. They had made the most of their head start on their pursuers, but with the enhanced senses of the Space Wolves, he knew that they would be found by their scent. He had hoped to get back to the jungle before things escalated, regroup and make another attempt to enter the city. That was not to be, however, and now Jeremiah had decided upon a new course of action.

'Marius, Sebastian and Gilead,' said Jeremiah. 'You will seek our brethren and support them. Report to the Interrogator-Chaplain on our progress.'

'Will you seek out the heretic yourself, captain?' asked Sebastian.

Jeremiah drew his blade. The reddish light of the mining machinery reflected off the polished weapon. 'By the winged blades, our mission has not failed. Elijah, Nathaniel and I will find our target. Further, if he commands the defences of this city, then we will decapitate the defenders, completing our victory. You have one final task, before rejoining the Brethren, a dangerous task, but essential to capturing our target. Engage the Space Wolves. Draw them after you as you retreat and lead them as far away from the city centre as you can. We three will find our way to the target.'

The three Dark Angels nodded their assent. 'The honour of the Lion shall be ours,' they chanted in unison.

Jeremiah said, 'I expect our adversaries will be in the tunnels to the north. They will find you if you do not find them. Engage and disengage, making your way to the surface swiftly.'

'Brother Jeremiah, what route will you take back to penetrate their defences?' asked Gilead.

'Our target is intelligent and understands that he fights a war with us, not just a battle. Though not a coward, he will be relentless in finding a way to continue his quarrel with us, and he will have planned a way to escape from our Chapter's holy strength. The best method of passing out of this city unnoticed and undetected would be these tunnels. We will find his escape route and follow it back to his lair. I have one idea of where to go. We passed a corridor built up like the rest of the refinery, but it was devoid of servitors and had few lights. I suspect that may be the path. If that proves false, we will find another. Do not underestimate the skills of the Space Wolves, and remember, the hand of evil guides our enemies. Your faith in the Emperor will be your shield and the pride of the Lion your strength. Go,' said Jeremiah.

The appointed three disappeared into the tunnels, moving quickly and quietly, guns drawn. Jeremiah knew they would fulfil their duty. The Space Wolves would not stop his team.

IT HAD BEEN several hours by Ragnar's reckoning since the Dark Angels had escaped from the Imperial palace complex in the city centre. Along with Torin and Haegr, he crouched quietly in a tight maintenance shaft, hoping that his plan worked.

If Ragnar was right, the Dark Angels would make their move at any moment. He hoped that he had anticipated things correctly. If he was wrong, then he, Torin and Haegr had just abandoned the rest of the search team.

An eternity passed with each second. Then, Ragnar caught the scent of anointing oils and heard the scrape of power armour against rock coupled with the swish of robes. The Dark Angels had taken Ragnar's bait. He had known that with their fanaticism, the Dark Angels kill team would not give up while there was any hope of completing their mission. With the help of the tech-priest, Ragnar had moved the servitors out of this tunnel and ordered the lights to be shut down. Ragnar had wanted to make this passage conspicuous with its lack of activity. He hoped that the Dark Angels might decide it would make a good place to hide, set an ambush or try to make their way back to the palace complex. It had all worked. The hardest part, besides waiting, had been fitting Haegr into the maintenance shaft.

Hidden behind the doors, Ragnar, Torin and Haegr couldn't see the Dark Angels, but with their well-trained senses, they could hear and smell them. Ragnar held himself in check, while his blood burned with anticipation of the fight to come.

'Here,' said the voice of one of the Dark Angels. He was undoubtedly the leader, as his tone wasn't muffled by his helm. 'We are blessed by the Emperor, my brethren. Nathaniel, remove the maintenance hatch.'

With a savage howl, Ragnar kicked the maintenance door from its hinges. The door struck the Dark Angel full in the chest, knocking him backwards and leaving him without his weapon drawn. From Ragnar's right, another Dark Angel whipped out a blade and drew his pistol with a speed worthy of a Blood Claw, although he paused before firing his bolt pistol, apparently rattled by Ragnar's howl. Torin engaged the quick one, because Ragnar had already chosen his target. There were only three of the enemy and the Wolfblade had the element of surprise in the darkened tunnel.

The helmetless Dark Angel had handsome, classical features, the sort sewn into tapestries to represent angels. Despite his youthful appearance, Ragnar could tell from his stance that he was a formidable fighter. Ragnar slashed at him. The Dark Angel just managed to parry the sudden attack. Ragnar's runed blade drove into the metal of the Dark Angel's sword. Ragnar heard the sounds of battle behind him as Torin pressed his foe. Something was missing.

'Let them know that mighty Haegr comes,' bellowed Haegr. Ragnar heard armour grate against metal. Haegr was having trouble getting through the maintenance hatch. 'Ragnar, Torin, leave some for me or I'll give you both a good thrashing.'

Ragnar kicked his foe as their blades locked. The Dark Angel fell backwards. Ragnar lunged forwards, nearly skewering his enemy with the blade gifted to him by House Belisarius.

The Dark Angel's eyes widened. 'You fight with a daemon weapon, wolf,' he spat, 'but it will avail you nothing against the Sons of the Lion. Just as Lion El'Jonson defeated Leman Russ, so I will defeat you.'

Ragnar looked at the Dark Angels. 'I am Ragnar of the Space Wolves, and I won't be defeated by a Dark Angel any more than Leman Russ was. If you wish to prove your strength against me, throw down your weapon, Dark Angel, and let us fight unarmed.'

Ragnar could hear Nathaniel extricating himself from the maintenance hatch, and was worried about an attack from behind.

With an echoing roar, Haegr burst free. The Dark Angel would have to get past the massive Space Wolf to reach Ragnar's back. From Torin's fight, Ragnar heard the distinctive clatter of bolter rounds ricocheting off ceramite.

'I, Jeremiah of the Dark Angels, accept your challenge, Ragnar of the Space Wolves.'

To Ragnar's surprise, the Dark Angel threw down his blade. Ragnar grinned and sheathed his own sword. The Dark Angel had undeniably realised that Ragnar had the better weapon, but if he thought he'd have a better chance in unarmed combat, Ragnar would prove him wrong.

'Brother Elijah, I'll help you with that one, once I've dispatched this giant,' said Nathaniel.

'Ho, the little Dark Angel thinks he can do something that no man can do. He thinks he can dispatch mighty Haegr of the Wolfblade!' Haegr laughed, swinging his mighty hammer. Nathaniel brought a chainsword up to defend himself, but against Haegr's onslaught, it was too little. Each blow echoed through the tunnels, booming like thunder. The Dark Angel was pushed back and smashed into a rock wall. Despite the pounding, he refused to fall. Haegr grabbed him and crushed him hard. The servos in the Dark Angel's power armour smoked as Haegr threatened to pop him like an overripe fruit.

Torin kept up his assault on his spirited foe, Elijah. The young Dark Angel lacked Torin's skills, but he made up for it with superhuman reflexes, arguably rivalling those of Ragnar. Still, little by little, Torin dissected the youth's defences, wearing him down with his finesse. Elijah caught Torin with his bolt pistol, but the shells bounced off the Wolfblade's chest plate. Torin realised that he had to end the fight quickly. The Dark Angel couldn't last, but he might get lucky.

Torin waited until Elijah managed to fire off another volley, then staggered, hoping that he had read his foe correctly. He had. Elijah rushed in with the sort of enthusiasm Torin would have expected from an untested Blood Claw. The feint worked. Torin thrust his blade up unexpectedly, catching it between his foe's helm and shoulder, right against the neck. Elijah's life was in Torin's hands, and they both knew it.

Ragnar grappled with Jeremiah. By Space Wolf standards, he was strong, but the Dark Angel's strength startled him. Jeremiah was a match for him.

Ragnar pushed and shoved, trying to gain an advantage, but every move he made, the Dark Angel countered.

Ragnar felt his anger grow. Jeremiah had insulted Leman Russ. While Ragnar may have lost the Spear of Russ, he would not fail his primarch in this challenge. He felt the rage of the wolf within him, giving him strength and enhancing his senses.

For a moment, Jeremiah appeared to have the advantage. As Ragnar struggled with the beast inside, Jeremiah hammered blows against him. Then with a howl, Ragnar found the strength he needed.

In a rage, he grabbed Jeremiah and hefted him off his feet, ramming him against the wall. The world went blood-red and Ragnar could no longer hear the battle around him. He smashed Jeremiah's head against the wall then smashed it again. Then, it seemed to shift to resemble the helm of the Thousand Sons, the traitor Chaos Space Marines who were the eternal enemies of the Space Wolves. He could no longer think about anything but the honour of the Space Wolves and Leman Russ.

'For Russ!' he screamed and smashed his head into Jeremiah's, drawing blood.

'Lad, that's enough. We want them alive for questioning,' Haegr said, grabbing Ragnar and pulling him off Jeremiah. Ragnar looked at Haegr, taking a moment to recognise his old friend. Finally, the anger subsided.

Jeremiah lay unconscious, his handsome face covered in blood. Nathaniel groaned on the ground. His power armour had not yielded to Haegr's strength, but his bones had not fared as well. Torin's blade remained at Elijah's throat, and the young Dark Angel had lost his weapons.

'You're the only one awake, so I guess it's up to you to surrender,' offered Torin.

'Dark Angels don't surrender to Space Wolves,' snarled Elijah.

Haegr smashed the young Dark Angel on the head, dropping him instantly.

'So that would make this case a special exception,' remarked Torin.

Ragnar retrieved his weapons and tried the comm. 'Markham, do you read me?'

The comm crackled with static before coming to life. 'We've suffered some casualties among the men, Wolfblade Ragnar, but we've got them on the run. They are making their way to the surface. I'm broadcasting the location to Commander Cadmus. I believe we have them. The rest of the Wolfblade are giving chase,' said Markham.

'Good work. You are a tribute to House Belisarius. Ragnar out.' He clicked off his comm.

Ragnar was impressed. The Dark Angels had split up to try and draw his men away. In some ways, the members of this kill team thought like Space Wolves.

'Are you all right, brother?' asked Torin.

Ragnar nodded. He had come close to losing control and letting the wolf come out. Within every Space Wolf lived a beast, a primal savage. They all had to work to control it, to constantly keep the beast in check. Now that the adrenaline had died, Ragnar was starting to feel aches and bruises. Jeremiah had given him a good bout.

'Let's take these prisoners back up to the surface and see how the defences are holding. We need to know why they are here. Perhaps they know something we don't,' said Ragnar.

'Perhaps they think they know something we don't,' offered Torin.

'I suspect that they all needed a good sound thrashing, and once they heard that Haegr was here, well, they knew they'd found the most solid thrashings in the galaxy. What say you to that?' Haegr kicked Nathaniel.

The Dark Angel groaned.

'I'd say he agrees,' said Ragnar.

An explosion rocked the mines. The scent of the anointing oils intensified heavily. More Dark Angels were coming, most likely from the surface. Some of them had penetrated the mine, and it was bad luck that they had entered near the Space Wolves' location.

'They better be careful. Too many more explosions like that and they'll puncture one of the pipes and set the promethium ablaze,' said Torin.

'This whole place, the refinery and the mines, could turn into an inferno!' said Haegr.

'I hope not,' said Torin. 'I believe that the machine-spirits would shut down parts of the pipes where any explosions took place. This whole set of tunnels is convoluted simply because they have an array of pipe systems in case a section malfunctions... Maybe if someone intentionally sabotaged the system.'

'What?' asked Ragnar. 'You mean that if one of us shot one of the pipes it wouldn't cause all of these tunnels to erupt?'

'Exactly,' said Torin. 'Ragnar, did you think... That's why you looked so nervous about the man with the flamer.' Torin chuckled. 'If the whole place was likely to erupt, Lethe would have been destroyed a long time ago. Even the servants of the Machine-God aren't flawless. You'd start a large fire, Ragnar in one section of tunnel, like this one, roughly like getting roasted by a heavy flamer point-blank or an Inferno cannon. Hardly healthy, but that's why we are Space Marines in power armour.'

'So, it's not much more than using a heavy flamer?' asked Ragnar.

'No,' said Torin. 'Believe me if it was, I'm sure one of the Dark Angels would have shot that promethium pipe during our hand-to-hand combat. I know I would have if I was sure that we'd die on an espionage mission rather than be captured by the enemy. However, I think, rather than debate the explosiveness of the tunnels, we need to consider getting out of here. I smell more Dark Angels.'

The tunnel where the Wolfblade stood connected the abandoned mines to the working refinery. The sound of bolter fire came from the direction of the refinery. Ragnar could smell Space Marines from both ends of the tunnel. It was hard to tell just how far away they were. 'Don't worry,' said Ragnar, 'Varnus told me that the maintenance shaft we hid in leads to an old command centre for the unused sections of the mines.'

'What?' asked Haegr. 'Tell me that I didn't hear that right?'

'He's right old friend. We may have to leave you behind. Too many pies, roast meat and barrels of ale.' Torin paused to sigh. 'I doubt you'll fit in the shaft, so you won't make the climb.'

'That's only because Haegr has so much power that he needs food worthy of his stature,' said Haegr.

They heard more bolter fire from the direction of the refinery, and the explosions of grenades. A flash of light came from that direction as well, along with a blast of heat.

'See, they detonated part of the promethium,' said Torin.

In a strangely serious tone, Haegr said, 'Don't worry, I'll fit in the maintenance shaft, even holding one or two of these Dark Angels. I'll bring up the rear.' Then he added, 'Besides, that way I can best protect you two in case the enemy comes down this tunnel and decides to check the maintenance shaft.'

'I'll go last. I'm going to discourage any pursuit,' said Ragnar.

'Fine, I'm not going to waste time debating.' Torin grabbed Elijah and pulled him into the maintenance shaft.

'Are you sure about bringing up the rear, Ragnar?' asked Haegr.

'I'm sure, but I may need your help with Jeremiah.'

The giant heaved Nathaniel and Jeremiah, laying one over each shoulder. The large Space Marines looked like children on Haegr's shoulders. 'Even if I have to go on my knees,' Haegr said ducking down and entering the shaft.

Ragnar was torn. He had decided to turn this tunnel into a flaming ruin. On one hand, maybe he should wait until the last moment to see if he could catch any Dark Angels in the blast. He still felt that it was dishonourable, even if it was no worse than using a heavy flamer. These were the hated Dark Angels, but they were Space Marines as well.

Once again, he had to make a choice: to remain loyal to House Belisarius and to his oath of duty, or to listen to his heart and trust in the Emperor.

He missed life on Fenris.

The Dark Angels, whatever their motives, were the enemy, and had to be treated as such. In their place, he doubted the Space Wolves would have behaved any differently.

Hearing enemy approaching, Ragnar clicked his belt and a grenade came free. With one hand, he set the charge and threw it towards the large refrigerated promethium pipe in the centre of the tunnel. Without waiting, Ragnar leapt as far as he could into the shaft. Behind him, the grenade went off.

The initial blast was a simple burst. Then, there was a rush of flame and a great roaring, as the promethium ignited and split the pipe, spilling its deadly contents into the tunnel. Ragnar reached a ladder at the end of the shaft and began climbing up it. Below him the shaft filled with light as the fireball flew into it.

'By the Fire Wolf itself,' said Haegr, reaching down and grabbing Ragnar's arm, 'you managed not to kill yourself, lad.'

'That should discourage them from entering the tunnel, and I suspect the lower part of the ladder melted,' said Ragnar.

'Do you think you got any of them?' asked Haegr.

'No, I was trying to stop them pursuing us,' said Ragnar.

They had climbed up the ladder into an empty corridor, fitting Varnus's description of the unused mine monitoring station. In Imperial

Gothic, a sign on a metal door at the hall's end declared it to be a security station. The three Space Wolves exchanged glances, gathered their prisoners, one each, and made their way forwards.

Haegr placed his Dark Angel on the ground, roared, and threw himself against the security door. The door groaned, but didn't budge.

'Haegr...' said Torin.

But there was no stopping the massive Space Wolf. He took his hammer and pounded the door, again and again. The booming strikes resounded in the hall. After several blows, Haegr threw down his hammer and charged the door once more. This time the enormous girth of the Space Wolf was too much for the door and it collapsed beneath Haegr, falling into the room.

'There,' declared Haegr. 'Now Torin, what were you going to say?'

Torin clapped his large battle-brother on the shoulder. 'I was going to say something unimportant about knowing the House Belisarius security override codes.'

Ragnar laughed and then his battle-brothers joined him. 'It was much more impressive Haegr's way.'

'Indeed,' said Torin, 'and after that clamour, we know that our enemies are truly unconscious, but, perhaps I can use the security codes on these vid-screens.'

Haegr and Ragnar carried their unconscious prisoners into the room, laying them apart and keeping a watchful eye on them, while Torin worked on the command centre's controls.

The security station had several vid-screens, but based on the signs and indicators, Ragnar could tell that it was more for monitoring the unused sections of the mines than for city security. Still, Torin stood in front of one of the vid-screens and gave the codes, performing the required ritual to activate the machine-spirits within the security monitors.

Amazingly, half of the screens flickered to life. At first, they showed only darkened images of the mines. Then, with a few gestures, Torin moved dials and changed indicators and views of the city filled the screens.

'Torin, you did it,' said Ragnar. 'Are you sure you aren't part Iron Priest?'

Torin didn't answer, pointing to the screens instead.

The activated vid-screens showed the ongoing battle. On one large screen, a dramatic encounter drew the attention of the Space Wolves. A Dark Angels Dreadnought strode through the streets of Lethe. Three Imperial Guard Sentinels closed on it, each one carrying deadly saws and blades, designed for cutting through the jungles of Hyades, but now put to deadly use on the battlefield. A twin-linked lascannon from the Dreadnought made short work of one Sentinel, while the others covered the Dark Angels war machine in promethium fire. The Dreadnought disappeared in a cloud of smoke for only a moment, before striding out to smash one of the Sentinels with its massive power fist, shattering it as if it was a child's toy.

Other screens showed the defence guns firing at Thunderhawk gunships and drop-pods. Ragnar also saw the people of Hyades fighting back as best they could. The entire populace used makeshift weapons, along with flamers, grenades and lasguns to defend themselves. Ragnar was impressed with the raw courage, and he saw that the Dark Angels were not unscathed.

'People fight hardest protecting their homes. It's true even here,' said Ragnar.

'One of the smartest things you've ever said,' said Torin. 'We need to find out why the Dark Angels attacked, and that means waking these men up.'

'They won't tell us willingly. Maybe they think we're Chaos-tainted,' said Ragnar.

'What is this bunker?' he asked Torin. 'It seems more to be than an old mine security room.'

'It appears to be a secondary command post. Commander Cadmus probably has a couple of backups hidden throughout Lethe.'

Ragnar found a communications station. Messages flashed across the screen. One in particular caught his attention. It read 'Dark Angels escaping, Wolfblade in pursuit on the street. Quadrant three, sector five north, target on Markham'.

'Can we see quadrant three, sector five?' asked Ragnar.

'Give me a moment.' Torin fiddled with the dials and levers. 'Yes, this screen,' he said.

A message flashed across the screen: 'Bombardment imminent'.

Cadmus was going to kill both sets of Space Marines.

SEVEN
Betrayal

THE DARK ANGELS had surprised Lieutenant Markham and the Space Wolves with their sudden attack and withdrawal. Markham's team had given pursuit, only to be ambushed a second time. They suffered three casualties, but the lieutenant didn't have time to tend to them, as the enemy was close. He and his men had followed the Dark Angels through an access hatch back into the streets of Lethe.

The city of Lethe was in a state of pure carnage. Down the street, a squad of men fired their lasguns at an unseen foe in the ruins of a habitation complex. The night breezes had a caustic tinge and particles of ash floated in the air. Explosions punctuated the night, bright flashes of light followed by booming sounds as if a hundred storms were competing to make the loudest thunder.

In the light from burning buildings, Markham saw three Dark Angels crossing the street, seeking cover provided by the sparking rubble of what might have been a manufactorum due to its many wires and bits of twisted machinery. The Wolfblades accompanying him howled. 'We'll take care of this,' one of them ordered. 'Head to the wall.'

Just as the Space Wolves charged, Markham's vox buzzed. 'This is Commander Cadmus. Belay that order. Stay with the Space Wolves and keep your vox ready for further orders.'

'Yes, sir,' replied Markham, leading his men after the Space Wolves.

The lieutenant was a hard man, a veteran of countless wars. In his time, he had seen massive green-skinned orks tear the guts out of living men with their teeth. He had seen violent act upon violent act, and he had committed more than his fair share of them too, but he knew that he and the PDF would be no match for the Dark Angels and little help to the Space Wolves in a fight. Nevertheless, he would perform his duty.

The Space Wolves engaged the Dark Angels in the middle of a cratered street, 'Wait for a clear shot,' Markham ordered his men as he watched the genetically altered warriors attack each other with chainswords and bolt pistols.

'Lieutenant, I thank you for your fine service,' said Cadmus over the vox.

Markham felt his heart leap into his throat. Both groups of Space Marines fought hard, exchanging bolter fire and blows that would have left squads of guardsmen dead. 'Disengage,' Markham yelled to the Space Wolves and the men around him.

If the Wolfblade heard him, they paid him no heed. They were lost in battle. Markham heard an eerie whistling noise. He dived towards a shallow crater in the street, even as his brain told him that he, the Space Wolves, the Dark Angels, and his men were all about to die.

RAGNAR, TORIN AND Haegr watched the vid-screen in the old command post, while the message 'Bombardment imminent' scrolled across the screen. The Dark Angels still lay unmoving on the ground. Ragnar kept a close eye on them; they were Space Marines and would recover soon. On the grainy vid-screen, Space Wolves were fighting Dark Angels in the city streets, guard units close behind them.

'It's the rest of the Wolfblade,' said Haegr as a Space Wolf knocked a Dark Angel to the ground. 'And isn't that Markham?'

Ragnar felt his blood quicken. The Space Wolves had the Dark Angels outnumbered, but the outcome was by no means certain. He tried to raise the other members of the Wolfblade on the comm, but all he received was interference.

'Torin, do you think the PDF will fire on them?' asked Ragnar.

'Doubtful, it probably means that they expect the Dark Angels to bombard that area. Keep trying to establish contact with them. We need to let them know they are in danger,' he answered.

Markham's men still had not engaged or retreated for cover. Perhaps the message was wrong, because surely someone would have informed the PDF. Then, Lieutenant Markham looked skywards, shouted, and dived towards a crater. For the briefest moment, Ragnar saw the blurred outline of a massive shell hurtle towards the battle scene, then there was a blinding white flash.

Bodies of Space Wolves, Dark Angels and PDF troopers flew into the air.

'They've used Earthshakers,' Torin gasped.

The Earthshaker was a ground-based artillery piece, and the Wolfblade knew that Cadmus had several of them in the city. Unlike the encounter at the kill zone, Hyades's Planetary Defence Force wasn't taking any chance with killing Space Marines.

The scrolling message changed from 'Bombardment successful' to 'Targets destroyed'.

'No...' gasped Jeremiah, sitting up from where he lay on the floor. He lunged towards the monitor and fell, obviously still groggy from the fight. His companions remained motionless.

Ragnar didn't even care that the Dark Angel had been faking his unconsciousness, as he, Torin, Haegr and Jeremiah all watched their companions die. They were stunned and shocked. Of the nine Wolfblade who had come to Hyades, only the three of them and perhaps Magni survived.

Ragnar decided to try Magni. The younger Space Wolf was supposed to be with Lady Gabriella, guarding her, and he was due for some luck with the comms.

Torin and Haegr turned their attention to their prisoners. Both of them looked more than ready for another fight.

'Magni,' shouted Ragnar into his comm unit.

Surprisingly, he received an answer. 'Ragnar? No need to shout! I can still hear. My ears weren't damaged. I'm still holding out with Lady Gabriella and Governor Pelias. The house guard is here as well. We're secure in a bunker beneath the Imperial palace,' answered Magni. 'Do they need me out on the streets to help fight off the Dark Angels?'

'Which house guard? The ones we brought from Terra or the ones here on Hyades?'

'Terra, why? What's wrong, Ragnar?' asked Magni.

'I'm not sure.' Ragnar looked around at the consoles, hoping he could figure out the situation. 'We may have just lost every member of the Wolfblade except for Torin, Haegr, you and me. Stay with Gabriella, and trust no one. I'll report back when I know more, Ragnar out.'

Ragnar's comm buzzed immediately.

'Ragnar, this is Commander Cadmus, I'm surprised that you answered. Was your mission a success? I'm afraid that you lost several of your men, according to my information.'

'You bastard! You ordered those strikes against the Wolfblade! I knew that I couldn't trust you,' growled Ragnar. 'I'm sure that Markham didn't survive that close to four Earthshaker blasts, and he was one of your own men.'

'I'm impressed that you found a way to stay aware of the situation,' said Cadmus. 'Unfortunately, you survived, Ragnar. I'm afraid that although I need Space Marines, they don't have to be alive. Thanks to this little communication, I've located your position. Don't worry, Space Wolf, I won't underestimate you again. Oh, and you do have my admiration. You and the Wolfblade are worthy of your reputation. This is your last communication, so give my regards to Leman Russ when you see him.'

The power went off through the room. All of the monitors died at once. Ragnar suspected that the commander had cut the power to the entire building. As if to demonstrate Cadmus's authority, Ragnar's comm went dead with a burst of static as well.

Haegr and Ragnar activated the torches at their belts in unison.

Torin stood over Jeremiah with his thin blade at the Dark Angel's throat. He hadn't given Jeremiah an opportunity to take advantage of the darkness. Without glancing over at Ragnar, he clicked his comm. 'My comm is dead too, brother.'

'They have even jammed the communicator of mighty Haegr. They will not escape Haegr's vengeance,' growled the largest Space Wolf.

'We should kill our prisoners,' pronounced Torin in a flat tone.

Jeremiah looked over at Ragnar. Dark Angel or not, Jeremiah was an honourable opponent, and had fought well. He had also lost his men in that salvo.

'What is going on? Why are you here? Who is Cadmus? Is he the reason that you are here?' asked Ragnar, going from question to question without pausing to let the Dark Angel answer.

'He will kill us all if you let him. I need a weapon,' answered Jeremiah. 'Can my brethren, Nathaniel or Elijah, be revived?'

'I don't know,' said Haegr, 'both received a mighty thrashing at my hands.'

'We should kill them,' said Torin. 'Their Chapter is destroying the holdings of House Belisarius, and I don't think we can break them, brother.'

'Ragnar, I pledge to you by my faith in Lion El'Jonson and the Emperor, that my men and I will remain your prisoners, unless the time comes when our brethren free us or you release us. Give us weapons. We are Space Marines, just as you are, and we share a common enemy, this Commander Cadmus,' said Jeremiah.

Something about the sincerity with which Jeremiah made his pledge made Ragnar believe him. Furthermore, he knew the Dark Angel was an enemy of Cadmus, and Cadmus had proven his treason by threatening the Space Wolves. He decided they had to trust the Dark Angels. 'Torin, give the Dark Angel a weapon. We can trust him.'

'Lad, have you gone mad?' asked Haegr. 'These are Dark Angels. We *can't* trust them.'

'Haegr, Torin, old friends, we *need* to trust them. They know something about Cadmus. You both heard him threaten us and we all know that he ordered the Earthshakers to bombard the other members of the Wolfblade,' said Ragnar. 'They came here to remove Cadmus. We share a common enemy.'

'You have good instincts, Ragnar of the Space Wolves,' said Jeremiah. 'I will handle my men.'

Torin reluctantly handed Jeremiah his sword. 'I try to keep good weapons, even if they are slightly damaged.'

Jeremiah nodded, and raised his sword skywards. 'In the name of the Lion, I swear upon my soul that the lives of my brethren: Gilead, Sebastian and Marius, will be avenged.' He then sheathed his blade and wiped the caked blood from his face.

Ragnar found a medi-kit under a console and gave it to Jeremiah who went over to Elijah first.

'Hurry, we don't have much time,' said Ragnar. 'Cadmus killed our electricity and he knows where we are. If he thinks we are still a threat to him, then he'll send troops to kill us.'

Jeremiah nodded and injected Elijah with a stimulant. 'We won't surrender,' gasped Elijah as he woke. The young Dark Angel swung his fist wildly in the air.

'Stop,' commanded Jeremiah. 'We did surrender, Brother Elijah; we are prisoners of the Wolfblade, and we will fight alongside them and not attempt to escape. They know we have a common enemy. Say nothing more. Our mission has not failed.'

Elijah nodded and moved slowly. Distrust filled his eyes. 'I will obey,' he said, reluctantly.

Jeremiah helped Nathaniel up and woke him using the same litanies that he had used on Elijah. 'Brother, we triumphed?' asked Nathaniel before his eyes focused on the Space Wolves.

'No, but we've come to an understanding. How bad are your wounds?' Jeremiah asked.

'I can fight.' Nathaniel stood, determined not to fall.

Seeing the Dark Angels this way reminded Ragnar of life with the Space Wolves. The Dark Angels made him think of a Claw of young

Space Wolves, a group bound together in fellowship, even friendship in some cases. Although Torin and Haegr were truly Ragnar's battle-brothers, the feeling was different. These Dark Angels were men who had become accustomed to working together in a battle zone. They had a bond stronger than words, a constant sense of shared purpose.

'We need to find a way out, besides the main doors to this section of the building or the mines below,' said Torin.

Ragnar knew he was right. The seldom-used corridor they had used to enter this monitor room was just a maintenance corridor and access route to the mines and refinery below. Ragnar could see that the large sliding double doors were made of plasteel and marked with the double-headed Imperial eagle. Cadmus's forces would come through those doors and there were probably more Dark Angels in the tunnels below.

'The walls are reinforced,' said Haegr, 'but we can burn through with melta-bombs.'

'Good thing that our prisoners brought some with them.' Torin produced a pair of melta-bombs, confiscated from the Dark Angels and set them against what Ragnar hoped was the outer wall.

'What are you doing?' Jeremiah asked Torin. 'What's behind that wall?'

'We aren't sure,' answered Ragnar, 'but if the Emperor smiles on us, it will be the outside world and even if he doesn't, it'll be a new exit that Cadmus's men won't expect to be there.'

'Why don't we run out of the main entrance?' asked Jeremiah. 'Surely the enemy isn't waiting for us.'

'Cadmus had men throughout the city. If they aren't there now, it won't be long,' said Torin.

'I can smell the stench of something foul behind those doors,' said Haegr. 'Someone's there.'

A gentle tapping started at the plasteel doors, and they could hear muffled voices. Someone was behind them, probably trying to get inside. It was time to go.

Ragnar and the others pulled back and put their heads down. The melta-bombs flashed and the wall crackled as they detonated. The rock-crete vaporised under the tremendous power of the blast. The hole they left was a decent sized door. Ragnar couldn't help but wonder if Haegr would fit through it, but he didn't have much time to worry about it.

The main doors flew open and gunfire blasted through the room, destroying consoles and vid-screens and pelting the power armour of the Space Marines. Giant hulking shapes shambled in. For a moment, Ragnar thought someone had cloned Haegr and ripped off his power armour.

'Ogryns,' said Jeremiah.

The ogryns were huge mutants, one of the few altered humans allowed in Imperial forces. Imposing figures, they dwarfed the Space Marines, standing a full head higher than even Haegr. Ragnar had heard stories of ogryns strong enough to lift tanks.

The massive creatures were pure muscle and stupid as rocks, with no mind except for killing. Unfortunately, that meant that their brains took longer to realise when they were wounded or even dead. Ragnar had once seen an ogryn fighting with a large hole in his chest, until a medic had pointed the wound out to him and he fell over.

The ogryns wore a mishmash of armour and were armed with ripper guns. The solid weapons had such a kick that only the large mutants could keep them steady, but they unleashed a massive barrage of fire, so much so, that each ogryn wore belts of ammo around their arms and chests. Moreover, each gun was at least as deadly as a club in hand-to-hand combat.

'We never received word of ogryns,' said Torin.

'They must be part of Cadmus's special forces, the ones he brought with him,' said Ragnar.

'Raaarhh!' Haegr charged, as quickly as Ragnar had ever seen him move. He crashed solidly into the first ogryn that entered the room. The monstrous creature didn't move its feet but swung its arms back into its fellows, spraying the foot of one with its ripper gun.

'Go, Torin, get the others out,' yelled Ragnar. 'I'll cover for Haegr.'

'Elijah, Nathaniel, go with Torin. Remember what I told you and stay true to our pledge. Do not betray him. I'll follow in a moment,' said Jeremiah.

'Jeremiah, we must first deal with these abominations. We cannot allow these mutants to live,' Elijah responded.

'You will follow my orders, Elijah. Now go!' Jeremiah's order was reluctantly obeyed.

Ragnar exchanged glances with Jeremiah. The Dark Angel looked like he had something to prove. Ragnar grinned. So did he.

'Armour man, get off,' shouted the ogryn as Haegr literally hammered him, striking him with blow after blow. The size of Haegr and the size of the ogryns was buying everyone else precious time. The door was completely blocked.

'Haegr, move!' Ragnar said.

'Ha! You've gone mad, little brother,' said Haegr, turning his head. 'I'm winning.'

It appeared that Haegr was right for the moment. Then an ogryn with a metal plate for a forehead brought the stock of his ripper gun around, striking Haegr on his backswing, hard enough to crack the ceramite of his power armour. The Space Wolf fell backwards into the ruins of the command consoles.

Jeremiah took advantage of the moment to put a bolter round into the ogryn's skull, directly under the metal plate. The Dark Angel put a second bolter round into one of the beast's large yellow teeth, shattering the tooth and spraying blood and bone into the air. Ragnar was impressed with Jeremiah's precision, but he wasn't about to be outdone by a Dark Angel.

He charged into the mass of ogryns, leaping over fallen Haegr. His runeblade took the knee off one ogryn, although it felt to Ragnar as if he had sliced through a tree trunk. Instinctively, he fired off several shots from his bolter pistol into another, blowing off most of its arm in the process. Behind the ogryns, Ragnar could see troopers from the Planetary Defence Force.

An ogryn kicked Ragnar with its large steel-shod boot, knocking him back from the fray. He rolled with the blow, and between his reflexes and his armour, managed to ignore most of the impact. He brought his sword up to defend himself, only to find that Jeremiah's precision bolter fire had eliminated his enemy.

This seemed a perfect time to escape before the sheer weight of numbers took them down.

'Let's go,' said Ragnar.

For once, Haegr didn't argue. Instead, he thrust himself through the hole in the wall. Thankfully, he fit.

'Wolf, hand me a melta-bomb,' said Jeremiah.

Ragnar hesitated for only a fraction of a second before tossing a melta-bomb to Jeremiah.

The Dark Angel leapt onto a ruined console and attached the bomb to the ceiling. Ragnar covered him, firing bolter shots one-handed into the oncoming ogryns. Almost without thinking, Ragnar stopped firing the moment Jeremiah finished setting the charge. The Dark Angel dived through the hole with Ragnar immediately behind him, as if the two of them had practised the manoeuvre a hundred times before.

The melta-bomb detonated with a deafening noise. The ogryns howled in agony, then fell silent. A low rumble indicated that the ceiling in the room had given way, crushing everything beneath it.

The others had moved a few dozen metres down an unmarked rockcrete passage.

'Where are we?' asked Ragnar.

'I don't know,' said Torin and Elijah simultaneously.

'We need to find Cadmus,' said Jeremiah.

'No,' said Ragnar, 'first we find Lady Gabriella and Magni. Then, we'll both go after Commander Cadmus.'

'I have men to avenge,' said Jeremiah.

'And I have an oath to keep and my last battle-brother to keep alive against a world full of potential enemies and the invasion of you Dark Angels. If you want to give me the truth about what's going on maybe you can convince me, otherwise, we make sure Lady Gabriella of House Belisarius is safe, first and foremost. Do we still have an understanding?' asked Ragnar.

Jeremiah stared directly at Ragnar. 'I gave you my word. I do not break oaths.'

'Good, then you understand,' said Ragnar.

'Let's keep moving,' suggested Torin. 'She'll be at the palace. We just need to get out of here.'

'Ah, what a great day for battle,' said Haegr.

The six Space Marines made their way down to the end of the passage where a reinforced door was marked 'Lethe defence forces only'. The security lock on the door looked intact and everything about the door gave the impression that short of a lascannon, nothing was going to get through it.

Nathaniel was having trouble keeping up with the rest, wheezing and limping. Haegr's bone-crushing grip had hurt him badly. As if sensing what the others were thinking, Nathaniel spoke, 'My faith in the Emperor will sustain me.'

A squad of the Planetary Defence Force appeared at the other end of the passage, while the Space Marines were inspecting the door. Now they were trapped at the end of the passage.

'They've found us,' snarled Torin.

The defence forces fired their lasguns down the passage at the Space Marines. Although none of the shots pierced their power armour, Ragnar knew that they could not remain in their position long.

Slowly, the door grated open.

'It's open, let's move,' said Jeremiah.

Torin and Nathaniel fired their bolters down the passage to deter the oncoming troopers, while Jeremiah, Elijah, Ragnar and Haegr went through the door, quickly checking for enemies in the room beyond.

They stood in the hangar of a large vehicle pool. The outer doors stood open, giving them a view of the city. Ragnar could only see smoke and rubble, punctuated by flashes from lascannons and exploding munitions. A few servitors tended to wires and consoles on the edges of the room. The large hangar was mostly deserted with the exception of a single Chimera.

'We may have found a way to get to Gabriella,' said Haegr.

'But who opened the door?' asked Ragnar.

'This must be a trap,' said Jeremiah.

'No, it's not. We have a friend on the inside,' said Torin as he and Nathaniel stepped inside the room between bolter shots.

Torin hit a control, sealing the door once again, now ironically, holding the Lethe defence forces on the far side. He put a bolter round into the control in the hope of shorting it. 'I contacted Tech-Priest Varnus after I activated the vid-screens and told him to do his best to monitor us. I suspect we would have had more help if the power had stayed on, but there's power here, probably from an independent back-up generator.'

Ragnar was pleased that Tech-Priest Varnus was still on their side. Just as he had helped the Space Wolves ambush the Dark Angels, he was helping them now. Faith in the Emperor was rewarded in the strangest ways.

'It's not a trap. Into the Chimera, we're heading to the palace,' announced Ragnar.

'I'll drive,' said Torin.

Torin opened the front hatch and got in. The rear hatch opened to reveal a small cramped space, complete with gun ports for the exterior lasguns. Elijah was the first in the rear, Ragnar second, and then Jeremiah.

Haegr paused. 'You want me to get in there?'

'Yes,' said Ragnar, gesturing Haegr over to the bench. The massive Space Wolf managed to climb in, but Ragnar could tell that the space made for Imperial Guardsmen was tightly cramped for the large Space Wolf in power armour. Torin started the engine. Nathaniel made it to the ramp, but barely, shooting off covering fire as the Planetary Defence Forces entered the hangar.

Ragnar heard the Planetary Defence Force outside even over the roar of the Chimera's tracks. The men hadn't taken long to breach the security door. One of them must have had the proper security codes and Torin's bolter shot probably hadn't done much to the doors controls on the opposite side. The men showed no hesitation in firing, but their guns couldn't penetrate the armour of the Chimera. Elijah returned fire with the Chimera's built-in lasguns.

Ragnar gestured for him to stop. 'These men are following orders, trying to defend their home. They aren't enemies of the Imperium. They don't know what is happening.'

Jeremiah nodded in reluctant agreement, but Ragnar knew what he was thinking. The men of Hyades would fight against the Dark Angels' own battle-brothers.

The Chimera roared out into the city, which had become a battlezone. Rubble and debris were strewn everywhere. Ragnar could hear the big guns of Lethe booming and smell the familiar scent of burning promethium. From the hatches, he saw the blackened bones of Lethe's defenders. Broken tanks lay in the streets, and although the Chimera was an all-terrain vehicle, it shook violently as it ran over the craters and through the rubble left in the streets. A few civilians staggered through the smoke, some screaming for help, while others did their best to run to cover. Ragnar estimated that they were about halfway between the outer walls of the city and the central complex with the Imperial palace.

'We won't make it to the palace,' said Nathaniel. 'Our brethren will take out any transport they see, just in case.'

'In case what?' asked Ragnar.

Jeremiah placed a hand on Nathaniel's shoulder. 'Ragnar, we have our own Chapter's secrets and honour to keep. I'm sure you respect that.'

Ragnar was getting tired of these conversations. 'I just hope that whatever your Chapter is doing it's worth destroying an Imperial planet for.'

GABRIELLA PACED ABOUT within the governor's bunker below the palace. It had been hours since the Dark Angels had first entered the Imperial palace complex. The governor had requested she come to the bunker with him for her own safety. Gabriella had brought a few of her House Belisarius guard and Magni of the Wolfblade with her. She had ordered the rest to join in defending Lethe from the Dark Angels. Since Magni had given her the news about the possible deaths of five of her Wolfblade, she was worried and the communication systems from inside the bunker were only receiving interference.

The interior of the main room in the bunker was lavishly decorated with portraits of ancient leaders of Hyades, thick carpets and hand-carved wood furniture. It seemed more like a formal stateroom than a bunker. Commander Cadmus had informed her that this was the safest place on Hyades, with reinforced plasteel and rockcrete walls behind the inlaid wood panelling.

Gabriella looked at Magni. 'This is terribly wrong. Space Marines shouldn't be attacking us.'

'I'll protect you, m'lady,' Magni said. 'I'm sure that the defence forces will hold out against the Dark Angels.'

Gabriella looked around the room. Even within the bunker, they could feel explosions rocking the city. Suddenly, she shook her head. A glow came from her forehead, shining through her black scarf.

'Lady Gabriella, what sorcery is this?' asked Magni. 'Are you all right?'

Gabriella moaned, collapsing to her knees. 'There's a disturbance in the warp, I can feel it. Something's coming.'

'Excuse me, everyone,' said Commander Cadmus, entering the room with an entourage of heavily armed men in carapace armour. These soldiers appeared to Magni to be the elite of Lethe's defences, armed and equipped like Imperial Guard stormtroopers. 'Thank you, governor, for staying put and keeping Lady Gabriella with you as I requested. I'm afraid that we've had to make some changes due to the current invasion.'

'Changes? What sort of changes?' asked Governor Pelias.

'Changes in leadership, sir,' Cadmus said, drawing his plasma pistol nearly as fast as Magni's eyes could track him. A blue-green fireball engulfed the governor's head, killing him instantly. His second shot took Magni in the knee, burning straight through the Space Wolf's power armour and dissolving the knee, severing his left leg.

Cadmus's elite troops opened fire on the House Belisarius guard. Taken completely by surprise, Gabriella's defenders stood no chance and the fight was over in seconds. Cadmus and his men stood in the centre of the room; only Magni and Gabriella remained alive.

Magni writhed in pain and shock from the betrayal. Cadmus walked close to the fallen Space Wolf, careful to stay just out of arm's reach. 'I have a message for you to relay to your fellow Wolfblade. Tell them that I have Gabriella, and that the only way they'll see her again is for them to kill every Dark Angel on Hyades. Am I clear?'

Magni shook his head.

'I'll take that as a yes. This woman is now my prisoner.'

The commander aimed his pistol at Gabriella while one of his men took her and pinned her arms behind her. Still weakened by her vision, she was unable to resist. A set of binders locked her wrists together. Cadmus roughly pulled her to her feet by her left arm. 'Come.'

Gabriella tried to shake him off, but her captor held her with an iron grip. Magni was dimly aware that he was hurting her.

Cadmus's men had fanned out, securing all entrances and exits. In a strange moment of compassion, one threw a rug over the headless governor's body. There would be no statue in the courtyard for Pelias.

Despite the pain, Magni was a Space Wolf, and he would fight to the end. Slowly, carefully, he slipped his bolt pistol out of its holster. While Cadmus was half-leading and half-dragging Gabriella out of the room, Magni took aim at the commander's back.

Cadmus spun without warning, placing a perfect shot with his plasma pistol. The Space Wolf's hand was consumed instantly in blue-green fire. Magni screamed involuntarily. He had never felt pain so intense.

'I can't believe how hard you Space Wolves fight. It's quite remarkable. You should know when you are outmatched and defeated, and just die. Do you understand? Now, Fenrisian, I hope there's enough left of you to deliver my message. Gabriella is depending on it.'

The shock of his action roused Gabriella. She had no doubt that if she tried to struggle, he'd gladly shoot her, but she was determined to make her feelings known. 'Let me go. You're committing treason, commander,' said Gabriella. 'Have you gone mad?'

'Hardly; this is simply the act of a rational mind in an irrational situation, my dear Navigator,' said Cadmus. 'Now, let me take you away from the screams of this young Space Wolf. It's not proper for a member of a noble house to be surrounded by such violence. You are my prisoner, and I hold all the cards. The Dark Angels aren't going to spare you either. Every breath you take is at my whim. Please don't displease me. You are only alive because it amuses me to torture Ragnar. To think I apologised to him.'

'You are a walking dead man. I felt a disturbance in the warp and that can only mean one thing, the Space Wolves are here,' said Gabriella.

'You did? How amusing. You are quite a potent Navigator then. I'm sure if your father were alive, he'd be pleased,' answered Cadmus.

'I recognised the warp signs. The Space Wolves' patrol of the sector must have just arrived. Within hours, you won't have to worry about Dark Angels. The Great Wolf has an alliance with Belisarius. The Space Wolves will be here in untold numbers.'

Cadmus stopped. When he looked at her, all she could see was a malicious gleam in his eyes. When he spoke, he did so in a very soft voice.

'My dear Lady Gabriella, not only did I know that the Space Wolves were coming, that's exactly what I'm counting on. Everything depends on the Space Wolves getting here, everything. It's good to know that I won't be disappointed.'

Gabriella's blood turned cold.

EIGHT
Arrival of the Space Wolves

WOLF LORD BEREK Thunderfist strode through the corridors of the *Fist of Russ*. He hated long patrols, too much time onboard ship made him uneasy. He stroked his beard as he walked, unconsciously flexing his power gauntlet. His mind wandered back to the battle in which he had lost his natural arm and smiled slightly. In that battle, he had squared off with Kharn the Betrayer, the legendary berserker of Khorne, a Chaos Space Marine whose name brought fear to even his own side. Now that was a battle, Berek thought to himself.

Berek entered the bridge, two of his Wolf Guard flanking either side of the entrance. Berek took inventory of the bridge, ensuring all was how it should be. The warriors of Fenris who worked here were proud men, selected for lifelong service to the Space Wolves. They dressed as warriors, complete with weapons and whatever honours they had earned during their service, such as bits of fur or runes. Symbols of Fenris adorned the room, from shields mounted on rune-covered pillars, to the wolf pelts used as carpets. Indeed, many of the control gauges rested in the jaws of sculpted wolves and the consoles were made to appear as worked stone or even ice. Banners hung from the vaulted ceiling, and the command chair was set as a throne. The impression of the bridge was more one of a lord's great hall, than the nexus of machine-spirits.

371

Berek held the crew of the *Fist of Russ* in high regard, and he clapped many of them on the shoulder or nodded to them as he passed. The men who served aboard this ship were here by choice, free men devoted to the Chapter, unlike other ships of the Imperium who enlisted the use of thralls and convicted criminals or mindless servitors to crew their vessels.

The *Fist of Russ* had finished its patrol of the Euphrates system, a star and its worlds considered insignificant by most within the Imperium. However, it was a place that fell under the watchful and protective eye of the Sons of Russ. For that reason alone, it was given the same consideration as any other system under the protection of the Space Wolves. Everything was in order, so they had executed a warp jump and proceeded to Hyades, the next stop on their patrol route to fulfil the Space Wolves' ancient pact with House Belisarius. As the stop was a recent addition to the patrol, Berek wondered if House Belisarius and the Wolfblade even knew they were coming.

As Berek thought about House Belisarius, he couldn't help but recall the young Blood Claw, Ragnar, now part of the Wolfblade. That reckless and honourable youth had left an impression on the Wolf Lord during his time with his company. Ragnar had served well, and then, he had lost the sacred spear on the planet Garm. The Blood Claw had halted a Chaos invasion by throwing the holy spear into a Chaos portal, collapsing it, and saving him and his great company. In Berek's mind, it was a deed worthy of song, even if one of the Space Wolves' greatest relics had been lost and a Chaos invasion had been stopped.

Had Ragnar been rewarded for his heroic action? No. In fact, Ragnar was immersed in the political infighting between the Chapter's Wolf Lords. In an effort to discredit Berek, his rivals lobbied the Great Wolf to exile Ragnar. So it was that the young Space Wolf had been exiled to Holy Terra to serve in the Wolfblade, a cadre of loyal Space Wolves serving House Belisarius. One day, Berek hoped that he would once again see Ragnar walking the halls of the Fang.

A warning alarm sounded, interrupting the Wolf Lord's reverie. 'Jump to normal space will commence in one minute,' the herald announced ship-wide. Berek, having been brought back to the here and now, gave one last look around the bridge. His crew was prepared for the jump back to normal space, attending their stations, saying the proper blessings, and performing the proper rituals. His Wolf Guard departed the bridge to secure themselves in their acceleration couches.

A warning alarm preceded the next countdown announcement, 'Jump to normal space will commence in thirty seconds.'

Even though Berek had made more warp jumps than he could remember, he still had moments of uneasiness. The warp was not devoid of entities, indeed it was a place where unspeakable horrors dwelled, horrors that one had to pass through when travelling amongst the stars in service of the Emperor. Deep in the Wolf Lord's heart, he was still a superstitious warrior from Fenris with a healthy distrust of magic, or anything that smelled like it.

'Jump to normal space will commence in fifteen seconds.'

Slowly, the bridge seemed to stretch and lengthen. Light danced across the ship's interior, emanating from no apparent source. A low rhythmic hum grew in Berek's ear. The process had already begun. Even now, the ship was trying to escape the warp.

'Jump to normal space will commence in ten seconds.'

The hum transformed into murmuring, sickly, twisted voices speaking in an unintelligible tongue. Every surface within the ship began to glow. Bulkheads screamed as if they were buckling under a terrible strain.

'Jump to normal space will commence in five seconds.'

Suddenly sound, light and motion blended together in a collage of horrors.

'Jump.'

In that instant, there was everything and nothing.

The jump to normal space was complete. Berek gave quick, silent prayers to the Emperor, Leman Russ and the old gods of Fenris.

The Wolf Lord checked the bridge and his crew. Everyone was removing their restraints and moving back to their positions. Berek took his time, making sure each member of the crew had survived the passage unscathed. The dangers of warp travel could never be underestimated. Having confirmed that all was in order, he slapped the restraining harness release.

As he stood, he turned to his men. 'Begin system scan. Comms, announce our presence and extend my compliments to Governor Pelias. Let's see if they have some hospitality to offer.'

'Wolf Lord!' said Hroth. 'Scans show a battle-barge in low orbit over the planet. Civilian ships are scattered throughout the system, fleeing the planet. There's an orbital defence platform in a decaying orbit, and I think she's scrap. I'm also reading weapons fire on the surface. It appears that the capital city of Lethe is under attack.'

Hroth was a warrior upon whom Berek had bestowed the title of ship's guide. Though not a Space Marine, Hroth had proven to Berek his ability to quickly assess tactical situations. Had he remained on Fenris, his tribe may well have slaughtered krakens due to his skill in suggesting ship movements.

'I'm unable to contact Lethe, Lord Berek. Their comms appear to be jammed,' the herald added.

A slight grin emerged on Berek's face. 'It would appear that our routine patrol has proven to be most timely.'

Berek did not believe in random chance. If he and the *Fist of Russ* were here at this place and time, it was destiny, providence. Berek was here to bring this conflict to an end, and that was exactly what he would do.

He crossed the bridge to the tactical console. 'Let's find out what we're up against.'

The tactical display sprang to life, showing a hologram of Hyades and all orbiting vessels. The unknown battle-barge was indeed in a low orbit over Hyades. Thunderhawks flew back and forth from the battle-barge to the planet's surface.

Berek was confused. These were ships of the Adeptus Astartes. What were they doing here and why by the frozen wastes of Fenris were they attacking a planet under the protection of the Space Wolves?

'We are receiving a transmission on gold priority Imperium frequency 7590.4.' Confusion was apparent in the herald's voice.

Berek waved his hand, indicating that the herald should put the transmission through to the speakers. The Wolf Lord's curiosity had turned to frustration. Berek had had many dealings with other factions within the Imperium. None of them had yet proven worthy of his trust, but he had never witnessed anything like this blatant violation of Imperial law.

'Unidentified vessel, this is the *Vinco Redemptor* of the Dark Angels. You are hereby ordered to leave Hyades's orbital space. This planet is under Imperial quarantine. Do not approach or attempt to enter orbit.'

Berek clenched his power gauntlet into a fist tight enough to make its servos whine in protest. He had dealt with the Dark Angels before. They were worthy of only one thing: their untrustworthy reputation. Although no Terran official would label them traitors to the Imperium, Berek had always known that one day the true nature of that self-serving Chapter would be revealed.

'This is the *Fist of Russ*, flagship of Berek Thunderfist, Wolf Lord of the Space Wolves. You have moved against an Imperial world under the protection of the great Wolf Logan Grimnar and the Space Wolves. What do you mean by "quarantine"?'

'*Fist of Russ*, this is the *Vinco Redemptor* of the Dark Angels. This planet is under Imperial quarantine. Do not approach,' the metallic-sounding transmission from the battle-barge replied.

'Who gave the order to quarantine Hyades?' asked Berek.

'The quarantine order comes from Interrogator-Chaplain Vargas. Do not approach any closer,' came the response.

'Why is Hyades under quarantine? If I were to be made aware of the circumstances perhaps I could aid my brother Astartes.' Berek's patience was wearing dangerously thin.

The Space Wolf crew remained silent waiting for the answer to the offer of assistance. Moments passed and then the answer finally came.

'Wolf Lord, their weapons are tracking us,' Hroth said.

Although the Chapters had a strong rivalry, both the Space Wolves and the Dark Angels had a glorious history of service to the Emperor. The Imperium would not take kindly to a conflict between two of their own Chapters, and although both organisations were formidable, neither could hold out against the fury of the Imperium. The endless numbers of Imperial Guard, coupled with dozens of Chapters of Space Marines, could spell the end for the Dark Angels or the Space Wolves. Berek had made every effort to avoid an engagement with the Dark Angels, but enough was enough. Berek smashed his fist onto the comms activation rune.

'Withdraw your forces immediately or you will face the fury of the Sons of Russ! So you understand, that means we will remove your forces for you.' Berek waited for a reply, certain that the Dark Angels would back down.

'Their weapons are still tracking us, Lord Berek.'

'My lord, shall we move her back?' asked the helmsman.

'No, we won't back down,' said Berek. 'We're in the right and they know it. They wouldn't dare fire on us, warning shots or not.'

A barrage of shots came from the *Vinco Redemptor* towards the *Fist of Russ*, missing high. The Space Wolf ship continued to approach Hyades, undeterred.

'Get away from our planet... Now!' barked Berek. 'I don't care for your Chapter's tactics and I can fire off warning shots myself.'

'We will fire another barrage. This will be your last warning,' came the response.

Berek looked over at the ship's guide. 'Hroth, fire a volley at them. Make sure you come close. I want them to understand that Space Marines or no Space Marines, we will defend our own.'

'Ready, fire,' ordered Hroth, but just then, another barrage erupted from the *Vinco Redemptor*. The laser batteries struck the *Fist of Russ*. Just as the Space Wolf vessel fired her guns, a Dark Angels torpedo salvo was detected.

The explosion shook the vessel. 'We've been hit, Wolf Lord,' cried Hroth.

Berek clenched his fist. The Wolf Lord knew this was an accident. The Dark Angels were fanatics, but they wouldn't have the guts to fire on the Space Wolves first.

'You have attacked us, you barbaric idiots! Now, feel the wrath of the Dark Angels.' The *Vinco Redemptor* began rising from low orbit. 'You will suffer from our next volley.'

'My lord, the battle-barge is departing orbit, moving to engage, weapon batteries are charging,' Hroth announced.

Berek hated the Dark Angels. The Space Wolves were in the right and he was tired of being threatened. They had shot his ship and tried to make it look as if he shot them first. That was the conniving under-handed backstabbing way of the Dark Angels. If they wanted a fight, then so be it. He'd find a way to explain once he'd exposed whatever convoluted rationale the Dark Angels had for attacking a Space Wolf planet. 'I warned them,' he said under his breath.

The Wolf Lord triggered the comms activation rune on his console. 'Wolf brothers, Russ be praised, for he has brought us here to Hyades in their time of need.' Berek could feel the electricity building aboard ship. His Space Wolves had hungered for conflict for far too long. Soon, there would be a feeding frenzy.

'Prepare for battle, my brothers! We launch as soon as we are in range.' Berek deactivated the comm unit. 'Helmsman, bring us within lance battery range. Herald, keep trying to reach the Hyades command centre. We'll need to coordinate our efforts with them.' The crew rushed to execute Berek's commands. The Wolf Lord could see the pride in each of them.

The *Fist of Russ* was smaller than the Dark Angels battle-barge. Berek knew that in a close range ship-to-ship engagement, the Dark Angels had the advantage. Their bombardment cannons would rip the Space Wolves to shreds. The *Fist of Russ*, however, was not without teeth. Her lance batteries had much greater range than the bombardment cannons. Using the longer range, Berek would bring the *Fist of Russ* close enough to launch his Thunderhawks and drop-pods, and carefully deploy his smaller ships. Using their speed and manoeuvrability, he could avoid a direct exchange of fire. The Space Wolves would win this battle on the surface of Hyades.

The *Fist of Russ* moved into position, entering Hyades space above the opposite hemisphere to the Dark Angels ship. Berek moved his ship into a low orbit to deploy the Thunderhawks. Drop-pods would be an entirely different matter to launch. Unlike Thunderhawks, which could manoeuvre themselves into position once they were free of the launch bays, drop-pods operated exactly as they were named. Berek would need to risk a quick pass of the *Vinco Redemptor*, bringing the *Fist of Russ* within range of the bombardment cannons.

Many songs would be written this day. Berek longed to join his brothers on the surface, but he knew that his place was on board the *Fist of Russ*. This was one case where rank did not have its privileges.

Mikal, Captain of the Wolf Guard, Berek's personal bodyguard and most trusted warrior, confidently took the bridge. He was shorter than Berek by half a helm, but much broader across the shoulders. A full beard covered his face.

Berek greeted his friend. 'The fortune of Russ does not smile on us this day, my old friend. I have a grave mission for you.' His concern was etched across his face.

'You know you have but to ask, my lord, and it is my honour to attend to it.' Mikal's words brought the faintest of smiles to Berek's face.

Berek clasped his hand. 'Mikal, I need you to lead the ground forces on Hyades. I need you to discover why the Dark Angels have chosen to fire upon us.'

'Then it's true – the Dark Angels have attacked us?' Mikal replied.

Berek tapped a rune on the display console. An expanded map of Hyades appeared, the capital city highlighted on its surface.

'Take your Thunderhawk and establish contact with the governor here in Lethe. Find out what's going on. Coordinate with his Planetary Defence Forces, establishing a command post for our forces. If attacked, by all means defend yourselves, but I must have answers, Mikal.'

'As you wish, Wolf Lord! When we see each other again we will tap a keg of the Fang's finest, and I will tell you of our heroic deeds,' said Mikal slapping Berek on the shoulder as he left.

'Good hunting, my friend.'

Mikal had served with Berek for a long time and was Berek's most trusted Wolf Guard and his most trusted friend. They had saved each other's lives more times than either of them could remember. They had fought side-by-side against some of the most horrific creatures mankind had ever encountered and celebrated victories over insurmountable odds. There was no one Berek would rather have leading this assault, no one more qualified.

But before Mikal could lead the assault, Berek had to get him to Lethe and to do that, he had to get the *Fist of Russ* past the Dark Angels battle-barge. Berek looked at the power gauntlet that replaced his natural hand and grinned. It should be one hell of a battle.

The *Fist of Russ* lunged forwards, engines at full burn. As soon as they made range, laser batteries lanced out, striking the *Vinco Redemptor*.

Blue energy sparked as the defensive shields absorbed the initial barrage. A volley of torpedoes surged from their tubes, rocketing towards their target. Space Wolf Thunderhawks launched from the *Fist of Russ* and fanned out behind the torpedoes' makeshift skirmish line, using the salvo to shield their approach.

The *Vinco Redemptor* came about, going head to head with the attacking ship. Weapons batteries swung into action, unleashing their firepower at the incoming torpedoes. One torpedo after another collided with the protective umbrella opened by the weapon turrets. Using the wall of exploding torpedoes for cover, the first flight of Thunderhawks dived on the battle-barge. Their speed, size and manoeuvrability made them virtually impossible for the turrets to track at such close range. The Thunderhawks strafed the battle-barge in unison, targeting the *Redemptor's* bombardment cannons. Missiles and battle cannon fire rained down, pounding the hull of the Dark Angels ship. Explosions erupted across the battle-barge.

While the first flight attacked, the second flight of Thunderhawks dived hard, entering the atmosphere at such an angle that friction fire blazed across the leading edges of their noses and wings. If the crews had not been Space Marines, their bodies would have been turned to bloody pulp by the forces involved. Once deep into the atmosphere, the Thunderhawks levelled off, on course for Lethe.

The first flight had strafed up the central axis of the barge until they reached the command centre superstructure. At that point, they split up. Circling around the superstructure, they regrouped and strafed down the central axis once again. A Thunderhawk disintegrated from the turrets' defensive fire. Realising the Dark Angels turret crews had analysed their flight path, the Thunderhawks broke off, peeling off the central axis in opposite directions, diving down below the firing plane of the weapons turrets and accelerating towards the planet. Another Thunderhawk erupted in flame before the rest escaped into the atmospheric shield of Hyades.

Meanwhile, the *Fist of Russ* closed on the *Vinco Redemptor*. Both vessels exchanged torpedo fire. Weapon battery rounds streaked across the void between the two vessels. Ripples of blue energy ran across both hulls as shields absorbed the weapons fire that splashed into them. As the defensive shields overloaded from the strain, secondary explosions blossomed on the hulls of both vessels.

The ships raced towards each other. It was time for battle to be joined in earnest. In their zeal, both vessels accelerated, closing the void between them faster than either anticipated. Simultaneously, the command on both ships realised the potential danger of collision. The

Vinco Redemptor cut to starboard and the *Fist of Russ* did the same. Port Dark Angels weapons and port Space Wolf weapons erupted in violent broadsides. The ships tore into each other.

Finally, the *Vinco Redemptor's* bombardment cannons pivoted to port. The strafing run of the Space Wolf Thunderhawks had concentrated its fire on the bombardment cannons. Now, Berek would find out if their gambit had paid off.

Two of the four cannons were unable to bring themselves to bear upon the smaller cruiser. The Space Wolf vessel shuddered from the salvo of the remaining two as wide holes appeared in the cruiser's hull.

The *Fist of Russ* was severely damaged, as was the *Vinco Redemptor*, but the vessels had finished their pass. As the starships widened the gap between them, each looked to distance itself from the other to repair and regroup. The *Fist of Russ* had succeeded. Space Wolf drop-pods accelerated down towards Lethe. Berek's radical strategy had worked; the battle would indeed be decided on the ground.

MIKAL'S THUNDERHAWK RACED across the sky, flanked on both sides by several others. The Wolf Guard captain sat at the tactical station in the control den of the aircraft, just behind the pilots' chairs. He analysed the current deployment of the Dark Angels and sent attack plans to his battle-brothers. The other Thunderhawks peeled off, vectoring towards their assigned deployment coordinates. Mikal continued directly towards Lethe.

The ordered city blocks and streets of the city were gone, buried in rubble and debris and obscured by smoke. Planetary Defence Forces scrambled to establish a perimeter, but the Dark Angels drop-pods made it impossible. Space Marines did not fight by their opponents' rules. Drop-pod tactics were specifically random. They fell behind enemy lines, causing havoc.

The Planetary Defence Forces were faring better than Mikal had expected. They appeared to have highly effective defence strategies against the Space Marine invasion, and several buildings in the capital had become redoubts for the defending troops. The defences of Lethe were set up so each group acted under its own command and control. The Dark Angels wanted to decapitate the Hyades defence forces, but they couldn't find a head.

LIEUTENANT PAULINUS AND his platoon paused as he checked his map, barely able to keep up with the events that were unfolding. He kept asking himself if it was true: were the Dark Angels attacking the city? He could not believe it. They moved through the streets with orders to reinforce the southern city entrance, reporting any activity along the way.

His hands shook as he held the map. His nervousness was impossible to hide. He'd been with the Planetary Defence Force for just under a year, and most of that time he had been stationed in observation outposts, monitoring orbital traffic. He had requested a transfer to Lethe in hopes of gaining some recognition that might help his post-military career. Now, he wished he was still tracking transports instead of down here in the streets of Lethe, acting as bait.

They had been moving through the streets for a while and had not come across any Dark Angels, just explosions from unseen artillery, and rubble. He could hear fighting, but the platoon couldn't find the sources. The streets were a maze and every new street looked like the last. All Paulinus knew was that they were in the workers' section of the city.

Paulinus was from a rather prominent family on Hyades, and normally lived a lifestyle befitting his family's wealth and prestige. The seedier section of the city was a place that he had seldom ventured into before. Carnal pleasure rooms and gambling dens lined the streets, marking this area of town as the sort of place where human filth could acquire contraband and explore their secret vices. Paulinus was disturbed that it seemed relatively unscathed.

The men carefully stepped out into an intersection where three streets converged. Every street still looked like the last. Lieutenant Paulinus thought they were lost. He tried to think back to his younger days when he and his friends would drive down into these areas of the city. They had been callow youths looking for some cheap thrills. He had tried to distance himself from those days, but now, he needed his memories. He looked for familiar signs, for anything that would give him a clue to where they were. He saw nothing.

They approached a building that less than a day ago had been a gambling den; now it was simply another abandoned building. Paulinus raised his hand as a signal to his men to stop. He pulled out a map as he tried once again to determine where they were. He could call in, but he didn't want the humiliation. If his men found out, then they might lose morale.

Using the map, he managed to orientate himself using the street layout and nearby buildings as his guide. If they headed north, they should be able to find their way back to their checkpoint. The lieutenant gestured, instructing his men to move out.

None of them saw the Dark Angels until they opened up with their bolters. A red spray of blood splashed across Paulinus's face and drenched his map as his sergeant was ripped in half by bolter fire. The lieutenant watched in horror as men all around him twisted and fell before the Dark Angels' attack.

Lieutenant Paulinus ran to find cover from the hailstorm of rounds. He couldn't focus on his men, they were dying and he needed to live. After all, he had to give orders and he just didn't want to die, not here, not like this. Paulinus looked back at the gambling den, the source of the shooting, only to see another man die on the ground behind him with his chest ripped open by a bolter round.

Five Dark Angels strode from the gambling den, mowing down troopers as they came. Their dark green and black armour added to their aura of menace. Paulinus's remaining men made a vain attempt to return fire, but their intense fear made their shots worthless. All of the men, including Paulinus, were shaking with shock. The Dark Angels holstered their bolters, drew their close combat weapons and charged.

It was clear to all of them how this engagement would end. The Space Marines would slaughter them.

The street was instantly bathed in light and a searing wind struck everyone in the street as the gambling den imploded. A cloud of dust and debris obscured everything. The defence forces clutched at their breather masks as the dust and rockcrete particles clogged their lungs and scratched their eyes. The Dark Angels continued to close.

Lieutenant Paulinus raised his sabre, making a feeble attempt to defend himself. The Dark Angel advancing on him easily countered his weak thrust. The lieutenant's arm felt numb as the Dark Angel knocked his sword away.

Paulinus screamed, 'I don't want to die!'

Then, the Space Marine's arm exploded. The Dark Angel's chainsword clattered to the ground. The explosive whirring of an assault cannon drowned out Paulinus's screams.

Five more figures emerged from the building just abandoned by the Dark Angels. They were Space Marines, but their armour was different, making them appear larger. They did not wear the dark green colour of the Dark Angels, but the icy bluish-grey of the Space Wolves.

Paulinus didn't know what to think or hope. The newcomers moved surprisingly quickly, unleashing a volley of rounds into the Dark Angels. Taken by surprise, the Dark Angels tried to change tactics and engage the new threat, but the twin advantages of surprise and firepower made this a futile gesture. A few rounds from storm bolters and the spray of the assault cannon reduced the Dark Angels to piles of broken armour. Paulinus could not believe his eyes. He couldn't believe how quickly the new Space Marines had killed his attackers.

The Space Wolves wore armour adorned with the totems of wolf pelts, tails, and teeth strung on leather necklaces. The ground vibrated with each of their footfalls as they moved protectively around the defence forces.

One of the Space Wolves approached Paulinus, 'Lieutenant, we are here to assist in the defence of Hyades. Berek Thunderfist sends his greetings and respects. We are his Wolf Guard.'

'Lieu-Lieu-Lieutenant Paulinus, Hyades defence forces, I th-th-thank you for your assistance,' Paulinus stuttered.

FIERY CONTRAILS STREAKED across the sky as drop-pod after drop-pod plummeted towards Lethe. Thunderhawks touched down, pouring Space Wolves onto the streets. Dreadnoughts lumbered through the carnage laying waste to all who opposed them. Throughout the city, Space Wolves engaged the Dark Angels.

MIKAL'S THUNDERHAWK CIRCLED the city while the Space Wolves reconnoitred the battle zone. Mikal knew that the best plans only lasted up to contact with the enemy. His fellow Wolf Guard were on the ground with orders to protect the citizens of Lethe and to obtain any information as to the cause of this so-called quarantine. He needed to contact the governor, but so far radio contact had been unsuccessful.

'Sigurd, bring us about. Set course for the governor's palace. Put us down on the parade ground,' said Mikal, addressing the pilot.

After a Space Wolf was initiated and the canis helix implanted, he truly become one of the Sons of Russ. However, it took time for all the physical changes to manifest within the Space Marine. These new Space Marines were designated Blood Claws. During this time of service, they learned and grew.

Once they learned to control the wolf within and proved themselves in battle, they were promoted to the status of Grey Hunters. During this period, some Space Wolves showed an aptitude for specific skills. The Grey Hunters then trained to pilot aircraft, crew tanks and handle other attack craft.

Sigurd was one such Grey Hunter and Mikal had grown to trust Sigurd's instincts and respect his skills.

The Thunderhawk banked hard, changing course as instructed, flying low over the city. Wing-mounted weapons turrets spun rapidly, firing short controlled bursts. Small-arms fire from below bounced harmlessly off its fuselage.

Alarm sirens blared in the cockpit as anti-air defence missiles leapt into the sky, vectoring towards the Thunderhawk. Sigurd's hands darted across the panels, tapping activation runes for defensive system counter measures. Then, pulling the control arm back hard and turning the control wheel, the Thunderhawk executed evasive manoeuvres. Sigurd evaded three of the pursuing missiles. Unfortunately, the last one was proving to be persistent.

'This one's like a pack of Fenrisian wolves on the hunt,' Sigurd continued, executing evasive manoeuvres. 'Brace for impact, brothers.'

The missile struck the starboard wing, sheering off two-thirds of it. The severed section of wing struck the vertical stabiliser as it passed over the main fuselage. Sigurd struggled with the controls as the heavily armoured craft plunged towards Lethe. The force of the dive pushed the Space Wolf passengers against their restraints.

Sigurd desperately attempted to regain control over his wounded craft. Fire alarms activated as the fuel escaping from the severed wing ignited. Sigurd and his flight crew could have ejected to safety, but there were three packs of Grey Hunters and an ancient one in the transport hold. He had to bring this craft down safely, his crew would not abandon their passengers.

Mikal heard Sigurd curse under his breath, 'By Russ, Mikal will owe us a barrel of ale when this is all over, and not that swill he usually gets! I want the good stuff.' Sigurd's co-pilot laughed, as did Mikal.

The Thunderhawk shook and shuddered, as if trying to tear itself apart. Sigurd levelled the aircraft out as it raced on its crash course; he had done everything he could. The Thunderhawk was too badly damaged. They would crash, hard and fast. There was only one last tactic he could try.

Something caught Mikal's ear. Among all the clutter of noises, he heard singing. He swung his seat around and looked into the cockpit to see Sigurd and his crew belting out an old Fenrisian song about heroic deeds, courage and friendship. He simply grinned and joined them. Soon every passenger on board did the same.

They were still singing when the nose of the Thunderhawk ploughed into the ground. Mikal heard the impact and the sound of metal shearing away before the force of the crash rendered him unconscious.

MIKAL AWOKE, STILL strapped into his seat. The walls and ceiling of the Thunderhawk were misshapen. He saw several of his battle-brothers slumped in their restraints. His head was spinning, and he could feel where the straps had held him in place. He wasn't sure exactly what had happened after the initial impact.

Slapping the quick release, he unbuckled his restraints and attempted to stand. He rose to his feet, reeled and stumbled forwards. He had survived the crash with only minor bumps and scratches, the worst of which was on his forehead. Touching his fingers to his injury, he felt blood, but he was alive.

The emergency security door completely blocked the cockpit. The door was designed to protect the crew from fire or debris. It must have activated on impact. Mikal tried to force the door open, but it wouldn't budge. He looked for something to use to pry the door open, but saw nothing. Suddenly, the shrieking sound of metal on metal pierced his ears. The sound was so intense Mikal had to cover his ears. Turning towards the source of the noise, he saw a claw protrude through the bulkhead of the Thunderhawk, and then the bulkhead wall simply ripped open. Standing outside the newly formed exit was the massive form of Dreadnought Gymir.

Mikal shook his head to help clear his senses. The once proud ship lay atop a pile of rockcrete and glass rubble, twisted and broken, like an animal with a snapped neck. Mikal could see plumes of smoke rising in the early light of dawn, and rubble in all directions.

'Mikal, it is good to see that you are alive,' said Gymir the Dreadnought. Mikal thought that the electronically generated voice sounded relieved.

'Yes, ancient one, I am alive,' Mikal said as he clambered out of the makeshift opening.

On its descent, Mikal could see that the Thunderhawk had struck the top of a building, knocking apart the upper floors before crashing into the street, creating a trench as it gouged itself to a halt. The nose of the ship was completely buried in rubble and debris. Several Grey Hunters had set up a perimeter around the crash site, while others searched the wreckage for fallen battle-brothers. Mikal searched for Sigurd, but his comrade wasn't among the living. He glanced at the cockpit canopy where a large plasteel support beam jutted through the framework. Mikal bent his knee and mourned the loss of his old friend.

NINE
Dilemma of Belisarius

SMOKE HUNG HEAVILY in the air rank with the stench of burning flesh, machine fuel and the residue of promethium. Buildings that had stood for decades were nothing more than burned-out shells. Craters riddled the ground from repeated artillery bombardments. Pieces of bodies lay scattered throughout the ruins, all that was left of victims who were unable to get to the bunkers in time to avoid the shelling. Water from ruptured underground lines flowed freely through the streets, winding its way through the rubble and debris, filling craters and turning the newly exposed dirt to mud.

Impact tremors created ripple effects on the surface of the standing water, first one, followed by another, then another, the intensity increasing with each one. A large beetle, disturbed by the vibrations, scurried out of one piece of debris in a mad dash for the protection of another.

A mechanical footpad crushed the beetle and the rubble beneath it. The Dreadnought Gymir the Ice-Fisted surveyed the landscape. He'd seen bombed out streets before, having served the Imperium for centuries. He had been recruited from some forgotten battlefield on Fenris, and served as a Space Marine for hundreds of years until he was so badly injured that even the Wolf Priests were unable to mend his wounds. However, they were not willing to risk the loss of Gymir's decades of experience and knowledge, so the honour of eternal service was bestowed upon him with the privilege of entombment within one of the ancient Dreadnought sarcophagi. From within his metal shell, Gymir was a living keeper of the Space Wolf lineage. He spent his time resting deep within the Fang until called upon to serve once more.

Gymir slowly traversed the rubble. His visual sensors, much more efficient than genetically enhanced eyes, swept the debris field as he advanced. The holy assault cannon that formed his arm tracked first left and then right. His power claw opened and closed instinctively, in anticipation of impending conflict.

His heavy footfalls sent vibrations through the ground. Dreadnoughts were not known for their ability to sneak up on the enemy. Gymir did not hide his presence. His visual sensors allowed him to separate organic heat signatures from artificial ones and identify them. He sensed a potential threat hiding behind the rubble twenty metres straight ahead. Locking his assault cannon on the possible threat, he continued forwards, stopping fifteen metres from the target.

The signal was too small to be a Space Marine. Dark Angels were treacherous, but not cowardly. His quarry would not be able to hide from him for long.

'Stand and be recognised,' Gymir's mechanical voice commanded.

A solitary figure slowly rose from behind the debris, his empty hands raised above his head. Gymir recognised the uniform of a Planetary Defence Force officer, although the cloth was tattered, torn and blood-soaked from the soldier's numerous injuries. The man's face was badly burnt, and his left cheek was swollen enough for his eye to be forced shut. Blood trickled from both of his ears.

'Don't fire. I'm not armed,' the officer stated.

From this closer vantage point, Gymir detected eight other heat signatures, hidden throughout the debris. Gymir advanced towards the officer. 'Identify yourself,' he said, his deep mechanical voice leaving no doubts as to his intentions. The officer limped slightly as he stepped further from cover, moving slowly so as not to appear threatening.

'My name is Lieutenant Paulinus of the Hyades defence forces.'

THE CHIMERA CRASHED through the palace gate. Electrical sparks bounced off the hull of the transport as wires were severed and torn from wall conduits. The bent and twisted gate gave way to the war transport, wrapping itself around the nose of the Chimera until it was dragged under the tank's persistent treads. Leaving its metal victim behind, the Chimera careened across the circular entrance road, tearing across the flower garden in the centre. A wave of dirt and vegetation flowed out of the garden splashing onto the pavement. The vehicle erupted from the opposite edge of the garden, losing speed before finally coming to rest on the front steps of the palace entrance.

The rumble of the drive system of the transport roared and then suddenly went silent, as if accepting that it had travelled as far as it could. Pressure seals gave way, sending jets of trapped dust and dirt from the hatch's seam as the internal atmosphere equalised pressure with the exterior environment. Hydraulic cylinders hissed as the rear hatch began to lower. The sound of metal against metal screeched in defiance, as if announcing that a long awaited dignitary had finally arrived. Slowly Ragnar and Jeremiah stepped from the vehicle, taking up positions on either side of the rear door, covering the deployment of the rest of the passengers. Haegr, Nathaniel and Elijah followed closely by Torin fanned out as they leapt from the Chimera.

The palace grounds appeared abandoned but untouched thus far by the conflict that surrounded them. The city outside the old walls was a different story entirely. Columns of smoke rose into the sky in the city surrounding the palace compound. The air was filled with the sounds and the scents of combat. The streets were devoid of activity, and paper and other rubbish rolled across the ground, pushed along by the warm breezes. Grave concern crossed their faces as the sights and sounds reinforced their determination to bring this conflict to a quick end.

The Space Marines bounded up the steps towards the main palace doors. Torin and Nathaniel took the rear, watching for signs of trouble. As they entered the palace foyer, they discovered that the palace had been evacuated. Tables and chairs were overturned and papers lay strewn about the floor. The main power was out. Emergency lights dimly lit the rooms and corridors.

Ragnar directed the others swiftly through the palace. Gabriella should be in the command centre in the lower levels. When they had left the palace Magni had been with her and he could only hope that in the confusion that was still the case. So far however, attempts to contact him had been unsuccessful. Ragnar hoped it was just Cadmus's electronic jamming or promethium interference.

When the Wolfblade had first arrived, Ragnar had reconnoitred as much of the palace as he could, attempting to commit as much of its configuration to memory as he was able. He felt more comfortable and in control when he knew his surroundings. The hallways seemed longer and more maze-like than he remembered, but he knew it was just a trick of his mind.

His concern for Gabriella was distorting his perception. He needed to regain his focus, control his emotions. Ragnar cursed under his breath – he should never have left Gabriella's side.

The mixed squad of Space Marines had almost reached the command centre elevator when Ragnar scented blood. As he rounded the last corner before the elevators, Ragnar found the source of the scent. Bodies of the House Belisarius Guard were sprawled out on either side of the elevator doors. The stench of blood and burnt flesh hung heavily in the air. Ragnar summoned the elevator as the rest of the group examined the bodies.

'They were caught by surprise,' said Torin.

'How can you tell?' Elijah asked.

The elevator doors opened, and the group entered the lift. 'They never drew their weapons,' Ragnar answered.

Torin and Haegr nodded. 'If it was their trusted commander, why would they?' Torin replied.

Elijah, Nathaniel and Jeremiah exchanged quick glances. Jeremiah subtly shook his head, not wanting to be noticed. He could not tell the Space Wolves their secret. Until this night, Jeremiah's perception of the Space Wolves was that they were barbaric, more interested in their next tankard than concepts like duty and honour. Ragnar and the others were proving that his beliefs may not have been wholly accurate.

THE ELEVATOR CAME to a stop as the door slid open. Ragnar's senses were instantly assaulted by the overwhelming array of olfactory stimulus present in the command centre. The six Space Marines entered the room. Static danced across every display console, bodies of the House Belisarius Guard were everywhere, and another corpse lay in the midst of them. Ragnar did not need the scent to know that it was Governor Pelias.

Ragnar continued to scan the room. His relief grew when he did not see Gabriella's body amongst the carnage. That relief fled from him as his eyes crossed to the body at the far side of the room.

'Magni!' Haegr shouted as he ran across the room.

Their young colleague was slumped against a wall. A trail of smeared blood stretched across the floor from where he had dragged himself. Haegr fell to one knee, sliding to Magni's side. Magni was clutching the burnt, curled remnants of his right hand to his chest. The plasma fire had cauterised the wound, slowing his blood loss. The stump that was now his left leg was an entirely different matter. Plasma had burned completely through his leg melting away power armour, flesh and bone. Severed arteries, strips of muscle and tendons hung from where the knee and lower half of Magni's leg were once attached. Blood had pooled around him where he rested.

'Magni, come on lad! Say something,' Haegr pleaded.

Magni's voice was weak and raspy. 'By Russ, please don't let the last thing I hear be your whining, Haegr.'

Magni slowly raised his head. His skin was ash-grey and dark circles surrounded his eyes, giving him a deathly appearance. 'Cadmus is a traitor. He took Gabriella. I failed the Wolfblade! I failed her!'

'Try not to talk about it, lad. Save your strength,' Torin said.

Torin looked at Ragnar, and his eyes spoke for him. Ragnar knew that Magni would not survive. Torin turned to the other bodies, unwilling to watch as his fellow Wolfblade passed on. Ragnar saw anger and rage in Torin's normally calm eyes.

Ragnar felt the same way. To die in the service of Russ and the Emperor was how every Space Wolf expected to meet his end: on his feet facing the enemy. To be betrayed in this way was a death almost beyond a Space Wolf's comprehension.

Ragnar knelt next to the young Blood Claw. He saw that Magni was in great pain. Ragnar wished he could ease the lad's suffering.

Magni slowly raised his eyes to meet Ragnar's. 'Ragnar, Cadmus had a message for the Wolfblade.' He paused, labouring to get his breath. 'He took Gabriella, and he will kill her... kill her if we... don't...' Magni took another deep painful breath.

'Take your time, Magni. What does he want from us?' Ragnar wanted him to stop and save his breath and to rest, but they had to have every detail, everything that Magni knew.

Magni fought to carry on speaking. 'I'm sorry... Ragnar... the Dark Angels... He said he'll kill her if we don't... eliminate... every Dark Angel on Hyades... must kill... them all.' Relief crossed Magni's face as he finished.

Ragnar leaned in closer. 'Where was he taking her, Magni?'

Magni shook his head slowly. 'I... don't know... but... he knew... Space Wolves... were coming... counting... on it, killed everyone... evil.'

Ragnar wiped blood from Magni's face. The youngest Wolfblade struggled to stay conscious. He looked up at Ragnar, fighting to keep his eyes focused.

His body was failing. Space Marine bodies were designed to withstand almost any injury, to survive poisons and toxins, and they were immune to virtually any disease. Their respiratory systems allowed them to survive without oxygen for extended periods of time. Special organs were implanted to change the composition of their blood. This normally enabled their blood to coagulate almost instantly. Even with all these genetic manipulations Space Marines were not indestructible. Sometimes, in cases like Magni's, without immediate medical treatment, the enhancements weren't enough.

'Ragnar… you did… the right thing! I just… wanted you to know that…' Magni's body slumped to the floor as his life drained away.

Ragnar reached out and brushed Magni's hair off his face. Slowly sorrow grew to anger in the hearts of the Space Wolves. Their battle-brother was gone.

Ragnar rose and turned from Magni's body, reaching out and placing his hand on Haegr's shoulder.

'Cadmus has Gabriella. We must find her and bring her to safety.' Grim determination filled Ragnar's voice.

Haegr crossed the room towards Jeremiah. 'Sounds simple enough, we just have to eliminate all the Dark Angels,' he said, raising his bolt-gun at the Dark Angels captain. 'And we might as well start right here.'

GYMIR THE ICE-FISTED, ancient warrior of Fenris, stood in the centre of the street, his hulking mechanical form towering over the officer of the Hyades defence forces. The officer's platoon had scattered amongst the ruins, in an attempt to hide from the Dreadnought. On his command, Lieutenant Markham's troops emerged from their hiding places. Gymir's targeting system locked on each one in turn. Should the need arise, they would be quickly cut down.

'Mikal, I've encountered and secured planetary forces,' Gymir's voice came over the comm system.

Mikal and his Grey Hunters quickened their pace through the city streets. Reaching Gymir's position in under sixty seconds, they surrounded Lieutenant Markham's forces. Mikal approached the lieutenant. He needed to coordinate with the defence forces, but this officer was not what he'd expected. There were many unanswered questions here on Hyades.

'Lieutenant Markham, My name is Mikal, Wolf Guard to Berek Thunderfist.' Mikal extended his hand, engulfing Markham's.

'We were attempting to coordinate defensive efforts with the commander of the planetary forces. We were en route to the palace when our Thunderhawk was shot down.'

Mikal caught the scent of fear coming from Markham. Normally this reaction was not unexpected when dealing with forces from the Imperial ranks. However, Markham's reaction was different. Markham's demeanour changed when he mentioned the planetary commander.

The lieutenant met Mikal's gaze. 'Commander Cadmus is a traitor,' he said, rage and betrayal dripping from his words.

'The commander of the planetary defences a traitor? Explain yourself, lieutenant,' Mikal said.

'Cadmus intentionally fired an artillery barrage on our position. He was trying to kill the Space Marines. He would have killed us all were it not for them,' Markham explained.

'The Space Marines saved you?' asked Mikal.

'Yes, sir. Just before the barrage hit, some of the Space Marines managed to throw several of my men to cover. The others attempted to shield them from the blasts with their own bodies,' Markham answered.

'Please, lieutenant, start from the beginning.' Mikal gestured for Markham to follow him out of earshot of the defence forces.

The lieutenant walked beside Mikal. 'The Dark Angels dispatched a kill team to infiltrate the palace prior to the invasion.'

'Have we established what the kill team's objective was?' Mikal asked.

'We all assumed that Lady Gabriella was their target.' Markham was growing more comfortable as he answered Mikal's questions.

'Lady Gabriella is on Hyades?' Mikal was familiar with House Belisarius, Lady Gabriella and the ancient pact between Belisarius and the Space Wolves.

'Yes! She arrived only a few days ago with a contingent of Wolfblade from Holy Terra.'

'Please go on.' The lieutenant continued to relay his tale of treachery to Mikal as they moved through the streets towards an abandoned Administratum building. As it was still relatively intact, Mikal decided that this would be the best location to establish a command post.

He dispatched two battle packs of Grey Hunters to locate and establish communications with their Wolf Brothers. When completed he would be able to create a command and control centre from which he could direct his forces in the defence of Hyades. Once the Space Wolf forces were organised he would ask for Lieutenant Markham's assistance in identifying and locating the loyal planetary troops, giving him overall command of all the Hyades defence forces.

Across the city Space Wolves and Hyades defensive forces linked up to establish a definitive perimeter. The tide was turning.

RAGNAR LEAPT TO his feet, grabbed Haegr's boltgun, and forced it up. Craters created by boltgun rounds trailed across the ceiling. Jeremiah, Elijah and Nathaniel drew their weapons. Torin growled and drew his sidearm. Dark Angel squared off against Space Wolf. Ragnar stood between the two groups, arms raised, trying to exert his will on a situation that was fast spiralling out of control.

Eyes darted from friend to foe, each one trying to ascertain the next move. Fingers tensed on triggers. The standoff between the Wolfblade.

and the Dark Angels seemed to last forever. Ragnar looked from Jeremiah to Haegr. Everything would be decided by the actions taken in the next few seconds.

'Haegr, Torin, drop your weapons,' Ragnar ordered.

'Magni is dead because of their treachery, Ragnar,' Haegr roared. Ragnar could hear the beast in his giant friend. The wolf was dangerously close the surface.

'Cadmus is the enemy here, Haegr. It was his treachery that killed Magni.' Ragnar fought his own rage at Magni's death but it was not Jeremiah and his team who had killed their battle-brother.

Torin was the most controlled Space Wolf that Ragnar had ever known, never allowing even the slightest hint of the beast within. The brother he had always relied on to be the voice of reason and calm held his bolter on Elijah and Nathaniel. He could see the rage in his eyes, almost as a reflection of the madness that was all around them. He could not believe that after everything this was where they had ended up: at each other's throats. He gestured for Torin to lower his weapon. Torin looked blankly at him, as if he didn't know who he was. Then Ragnar could see rationality returning to his eyes. Slowly, Torin lowered his boltgun and Ragnar knew that his friend was back.

'Ragnar speaks truthfully, Haegr. I mourn Magni's passing as well. Cadmus will pay for his treachery. This, I swear by all the frozen hells of Fenris.' Torin walked over to Haegr and placed a hand on top of Haegr's weapon. 'We don't do what Cadmus demands.'

Haegr turned in disgust from his brothers. 'The decision rests with you Ragnar, just be certain it's the right one.'

In a very short time, Ragnar had learned that Jeremiah was a man of his word and held honour above all else, in direct contradiction to what he thought he knew about the Dark Angels. Treachery and deceit were the ways of the Dark Angels, or at least that was what most Space Wolves believed. Jeremiah's actions thus far indicated otherwise, but he had not been completely forthcoming with Ragnar on the subject of Cadmus. He had told Ragnar that he was unable to discuss the details of his mission because of loyalty to his brethren. That was something that Ragnar himself would do if the roles were reversed.

Things were different now. It was no longer the Wolfblade versus a Dark Angels kill team. From the Chimera, they had seen the assault landing of the Space Wolves. Recognising the symbol emblazoned on the side of the landing craft, Ragnar knew that the great company of Berek Thunderfist was planet-side. Here on Hyades, two of the Adeptus Astartes' greatest Chapters were at war.

Ragnar raised his hand, pointing a finger towards Jeremiah. 'It's time for answers, Dark Angel. If we are to survive this, you must tell us the truth.'

'I've told you all I can, Ragnar.'

'No! You've told me all you've chosen to,' Ragnar corrected the Dark Angel.

Jeremiah knew Ragnar was right. There was more to Cadmus than he was saying, but his hands were tied. He could not divulge the commander's true nature.

Two Chapters of Space Marines waging war meant nothing compared to what would happen if the terrible secrets of the Dark Angels were revealed. Ragnar had proven himself to be a man of conviction and courage, a far cry from the barbarian that he expected a Space Wolf to be.

Jeremiah weighed the situation up in his mind.

He could not reveal to Ragnar the whole truth. Perhaps however, he did not need to. He might be able to tell some of what he and the Dark Angels knew without betraying his Chapter.

'You are correct; I have chosen to withhold some of our information in regards to Cadmus.'

'Jeremiah, do not betray the honour of our Chapter!' Nathaniel protested.

Jeremiah held up his hand to silence Nathaniel. 'The history of distrust between our Chapters is long. In a very short time, I've discovered that the mutual distrust we share for each other may be unwarranted.' Jeremiah stepped towards Ragnar. 'I will tell you what I can and nothing more.'

'Well, get on with it, then,' Haegr shouted at Jeremiah.

'Haegr,' Torin warned, realising that Haegr wasn't helping the situation.

'All this cloak-and-dagger makes my head hurt.' Haegr walked towards the elevator shaft. 'I don't know why Ragnar was so excited about getting back into the galaxy anyway! Doesn't seem any different than Holy Terra! Everyone has a secret.'

Torin followed Haegr to the elevator. 'Ragnar, I'll take Nathaniel and Elijah and maybe we'll reconnoitre the rest of the palace.' Ragnar nodded in agreement.

'Nathaniel, you and Elijah should go with Haegr and Torin.' Jeremiah's words were more a request than an order. Nathaniel looked concerned as his gaze passed from Jeremiah to Ragnar and back. Jeremiah crossed the floor to stand next to his oldest warrior.

'Do you trust me?' he asked.

'I always have,' responded Nathaniel.

'Then trust me now, brother,' said Jeremiah.

Nathaniel nodded and walked towards the Wolfblade.

'Come on, little one, let's help these Space Wolves. At least that way we can all keep an eye on each other.' Elijah looked annoyed as he stepped into line with the others.

As the four of them reached the elevator doors, Torin gave Ragnar a last look. Ragnar nodded. Torin returned the affirmation and entered the elevator.

'We'll meet up in thirty minutes or less, Torin,' Ragnar said as the elevator doors slid closed.

Jeremiah turned his back to Ragnar. Dropping his gaze to the floor, he began, 'Cadmus and the Dark Angels have a history. My team was dispatched here to confirm our suspicions, capture him and if possible deliver him to my superiors for questioning.'

Ragnar judged Jeremiah not only by his words, but if the Dark Angel wasn't telling the truth, his scent gave no indication of it. His body language was another matter: he was holding something back.

'What do the Dark Angels need with the commander of a Planetary Defence Force?'

'We believe that he has been conspiring with the dark powers of Chaos,' Jeremiah explained.

'Chaos?'

Ragnar's mind travelled back to the Chaos temple and the sacrificial altar that the Wolfblade had discovered. He had distrusted Cadmus from the start. Now all the pieces of the puzzle started to fit together. When he and the Wolfblade had made the discovery of the Chaos temple and entered the kill zone, the Planetary Defence Forces had instantly engaged them. The attack was not an accident as Cadmus had claimed, but must have been an attempt to destroy the Wolfblade as he had suspected.

Jeremiah turned to face Ragnar. 'I believe that Cadmus lured my team here intentionally, and allowed us to gain entry to the city wall and reach the palace unhindered.'

This caused Ragnar a momentary pause. 'Why would he lure you to Hyades when he knew that there were Wolfblade here, and that the Space Wolves would be conducting a patrol of the system?'

'I believe he has orchestrated this conflict from the beginning, using the Space Wolves and Dark Angels' ancient distrust to spark this conflict,' Jeremiah continued. 'Perhaps he intended to create a full-scale war between our Chapters.'

Ragnar pondered Jeremiah's words, trying to fathom what Cadmus could possibly gain by setting such events into motion. What could be gained by a conflict between two of the Emperor's greatest servants? Ragnar had learned enough about the forces of Chaos to know that if what Jeremiah was saying were true then there had to be a reason. Ironically, the forces of Chaos did nothing random. There was always a plan, always a reason. The same had to be true here. If Cadmus had set these events into motion, there had to be something to benefit him. The difficulty would be determining what that was.

'If what you are saying is true then we must no longer allow ourselves to be manipulated,' Ragnar said.

'Yes, but blood has been spilled on both sides. How can you and I bring this to an end?' Jeremiah's question was valid. How would they achieve this?

'Your team and the Wolfblade have managed to set aside our differences and forge an alliance, fragile as it is. If we can do it, then so can our Chapters. We must find and defeat the true enemy. We must succeed, Jeremiah. We must.'

Ragnar headed for the elevator. They had to move and move quickly. Each moment that the battle raged would make ending it even harder. Reaching the control panel to summon the elevator, Ragnar realised that Jeremiah had not followed. He turned to face his new Dark Angel ally.

'Ragnar, there is one more thing I must ask of you. Cadmus is an enemy of the Dark Angels and I must complete my mission,' Jeremiah said with guarded confidence.

'Cadmus killed Magni and abducted Gabriella, his life ends at the point of my blade.'

'I understand how you feel, Ragnar, but you must understand that I am a Son of the Lion, and Cadmus is mine.' Jeremiah's voice was unwavering and firm. He could see the anger cross Ragnar's face. His eyes were filled with rage.

He made one last attempt to gain the Space Wolf's understanding.

'You just told me that we must get our brothers to set aside their ancient distrust and bring this conflict to an end. We're not even out of this room and already we're back to this.' Jeremiah continued. 'I, like you, have made an oath to serve, an oath of loyalty! I cannot – will not – set that aside. I pledge to you that I will stand by your side and do anything we need to bring this conflict to an end, but I personally must deal with Cadmus.'

Ragnar considered what the Dark Angel had just said. Evaluating the events of the last few days, he put himself into Jeremiah's position. Again, he asked himself what he would do if things were reversed. He would not allow anything to deter him from his goal. Jeremiah was not what he would have expected from a Dark Angel. In fact, he was surprised at how alike they actually were, and if this was about redemption… He wondered what he would do to make up for the Spear of Russ.

Ragnar extended his hand to Jeremiah. Jeremiah accepted his gesture of friendship and trust.

'I know that there is more between the Dark Angels and Cadmus than you have told me,' said Ragnar. 'I also know that you've risked much in sharing with me what you already have. I understand what it means to risk something for the greater good, and that I cannot ignore. Cadmus will be yours to deal with as you see fit. You have my word as a Space Wolf.'

TEN
A Thousand Pains

CADMUS STOOD AMONG servitors wired into the monitor systems, in one of Lethe's command bunkers. These former criminals served out their sentences for cowardice, heresy and their other crimes by helping to power the many surveillance systems of Lethe's defences. They were more machines than men and as such, they were beneath Cadmus's notice. As far as he was concerned, he was alone, surveying the carnage throughout the city. Watching the battle unfold gave Cadmus a sense of power. He had orchestrated everything that had happened.

The door behind Cadmus opened, and Lieutenant Carson of the Hyades Planetary Defence Force hurried inside. Carson was a young man who had risen quickly through the ranks, a tall charismatic man who had earned his rank. Carson's bravery and calm command were legend among the rank and file, but Cadmus could tell that his officer's vaunted courage was wavering as the Space Marines assault continued.

'We don't have much time, commander. The Dark Angels have breached many of our defences, and the Space Wolves...' the lieutenant swallowed. 'Sir, why are we attacking the Space Wolves?'

Cadmus fixed the lieutenant with his gaze. Faint beads of perspiration showed on the man's forehead. Cadmus sighed. It wouldn't do to have the other men see Carson afraid. It was a pity. Carson had been the type of tool that Cadmus would have forged into a legend on other worlds in times long gone.

'Come with me, Carson.' Cadmus led the lieutenant out of the monitor chamber. None of the servitors even registered the fact the two men had departed.

'Sir, where are we going?' asked Carson.

Cadmus raised his hand in answer and led the young officer down the hall to a large plasteel door.

'This is the most secure chamber in the city. I even had the servitors eliminated after its completion to maintain the security. Once we are inside, I'll explain the plan.'

Cadmus pressed the correct runes to activate the security door. With a rumble, the massive door slowly opened.

The lieutenant strained his eyes to see inside, but the room was pitch black.

'Go in,' ordered Cadmus. The commander followed the lieutenant inside. The door slid closed quickly, surprising the lieutenant as it slammed shut. The room was cold as well as dark. Carson felt as if they had entered a tomb. The two men stood in near darkness.

'Lieutenant, you were born and raised here on Hyades, were you not?' asked Cadmus.

'Yes, sir.'

'Did you know that the people of Hyades, particularly Lethe, are some of the most defence-minded that I've ever met? Your people adamantly refuse to give in to the wilderness and you refuse to adapt to the world. Instead, you try and force the world to adapt to you, an admirable quality. Unfortunately, you don't seem to realise that your world only exists at the whim of the Emperor, or should I say, the Imperial bureaucrats.'

'What?'

Cadmus smiled. 'Surely, you know that the Emperor is dead in that Golden Throne of his. He's been dead for ten thousand years. The Imperium is a lie, and the greatest liars are those devout Dark Angels come to butcher you. So, lieutenant, I'm going to give you a bit of honesty.'

'Sir?' The lieutenant took a step backwards. 'I don't understand,' he said.

'Lieutenant, I don't care about you or anyone else on this planet. I only care about my brothers and myself. To secure my safety and defeat my enemies, I'm afraid that I've had to make a deal and I'm going to sacrifice Lethe to my new allies,' Cadmus said.

The commander swept his arm out in front of him. As he did, an arcane circle sparked to life in the centre of the room. A bloody red light emanated from its twisting runes. Smoke swirled within the circle, and the lieutenant thought he could see something translucent moving inside it. Whatever it was, it was fascinating, and merely gazing on it made the lieutenant's blood freeze with terror.

'The power of the Lord of Change flows there,' whispered Cadmus. 'I can tell you are intrigued. The flames mesmerise even the strongest willed men. It's even more impressive when fully activated.'

'Why would you...? What does this...?' The lieutenant struggled with his words and emotions.

'Blood sacrifice activates it,' said Cadmus in a tone as cold as ice. His sword flashed through the air, slicing neatly through the lieutenant's throat. Cadmus carefully caught the soldier's body with his free hand, pushing it into the circle. The smoke turned a deep red, and a hissing sound filled the room.

Cadmus paused for a moment and wiped his sword clean as he watched the lieutenant's blood pulsing into the circle.

'The time is now,' said Cadmus, addressing the circle of power. 'I have done everything you requested. The bodies of Space Wolves and Dark Angels litter Hyades. I even have the Wolfblade here as you wanted.'

A moment of silence followed. Then a commanding voice boomed from beyond space and time.

'You have done well, Fallen. As promised, your enemies will be destroyed. Vengeance shall belong to both of us, for though you hate the Dark Angels, there is nothing that can compare to the hatred for the Space Wolves that belongs to the Thousand Sons! As for me, soon I shall personally end the life of one who has ever proven himself to be a thorn in the side of my master.'

'Surely you speak of the Wolf Lord Berek?' asked Cadmus.

'No, I speak of the whelp, Ragnar!' The portal crackled. Blue bolts of lightning cascaded from the centre, and a large form took shape.

Cadmus took a step back and gripped the hilt of his blade. Though he wouldn't admit it, seeing the image of the huge armoured shape manifest before him put him on his guard. The Chaos Space Marine wasn't truly in the room, he reminded himself, just appeared to speak to him via dark sorcery. Still, Cadmus couldn't escape a feeling of dread in his gut.

'My apologies, Lord Madox,' offered Cadmus.

The huge Chaos Space Marine sorcerer wore blue armour traced with gold covered with ever-changing sigils of Tzeentch. It was an artefact, a relic of Chaos in its own right, exposed to the power of Tzeentch and the daemons of the warp for untold millennia. Madox's eyeplates burned with a bright yellow-white light, and Cadmus could feel the hatred within this master of the Thousand Sons.

'The Space Wolves destroyed our planet. They betrayed us. Our master, Magnus the Red, attempted to save the Emperor, but he was ignored. Only Horus believed us, and even he did not fully accept the truth! We could have saved the Imperium then, but we will destroy it now! I have walked the surface of Fenris. I have beheld the return of my primarch from the warp. Only one thing has stopped me from being the greatest of the Thousand Sons, that insignificant wolf pup, Ragnar.'

Madox threw his head back, raised his arms, and laughed.

Cadmus was sweating. He had seen hundreds of battles and faced terrifying enemies. He had even barely escaped the Dark Angels on two occasions, but the presence of the Chaos sorcerer chilled his soul.

Madox's voice took on a maniacal tone, and the lightning from the portal struck in tune with his laughter. 'My lord Tzeentch truly is the master of Chaos, the Master of Change, the Master of Magic, and the Almighty God of Fire! Truly, he tests my resilience. Were my adversary a Wolf Lord, or a hero of the Imperium, then my defeats would find excuse, but to face an ignorant warrior has driven me to aspire to greater heights! Thank you, Tzeentch, for Ragnar, for he and he alone has shown me the way to destroy his entire cursed Chapter.'

Laughter responded in a blasphemous cacophony from the portal.

Madox looked directly at Cadmus. 'Now, Fallen, as you said, it is time.'

The Chaos sorcerer raised his arm and fire raced from his fingertips into the ceiling of the bunker, burning purple, blue, indigo, yellow, green and deep red all at once.

'Let the fire in the blood of this world bring Tzeentch's blessing.'

Cadmus heard shrieking. The sound was soft at first, but soon it echoed from all around him.

'The deaths of the Space Marines must provide fruit. I need more than just their lives; I need their very essence. The children of Tzeentch shall come and they shall reap the souls of their enemies.'

'Lord Madox, what more do you need?' asked Cadmus. 'Have I not given you everything you requested? I have made a war.'

Madox fell quiet, and the shrieking fell to an almost imperceptible scream. 'I wanted more than a war. I wanted bodies. Now, I want gene-seed.'

The gene-seed was the part of every Space Marine that made them what they were. Each gene-seed contained a piece of the DNA of the primarch, the Chapter's founder. When a warrior was chosen to become a Space Marine, the Apothecaries implanted the gene-seed within their body. Other organs would be implanted alongside the gene-seed, which controlled and regulated not only the genetic changes but also the body's acceptance of them.

The gene-seed was the essence of a Space Marine; it was what separated them from ordinary men, far more than their signature power armour or even their faith in the Emperor.

Cadmus suddenly realised that he was just a tool for the Thousand Sons. Everything he had done meant nothing to them. He was merely a pawn in their games. His anger brought courage. He wasn't going to let anyone, not even an ancient evil ten thousand years old, play games with him.

'My lord, I expect you to honour the terms of our agreement,' said Cadmus, 'and if you don't...'

Madox tilted his head and stared directly at the commander, and the protest died in Cadmus's throat. The Fallen felt as if Madox looked into the depths of his soul, as if he knew everything about him. 'I know that you don't wish to finish your threat. Emotion makes you weak. Cadmus, you are not worthy of honour. In that way, you are the same as your former Chapter. I will, however, send allies to you in your time of need,' Madox laughed. 'Now, we have gathered all of our pieces and set the Wolf and the Lion against each other. We must reap our bloody harvest, so we may plant the seeds of destruction for my Lord Tzeentch.'

With a burst of multi-coloured flame, the image of Madox was gone.

Cadmus found himself sweating and trembling. His heart raced in his chest, and he felt the blood burn on his cheeks. The ritual had exhausted him physically and emotionally.

'By Luther's blade,' cursed Cadmus. He walked over to the wall in the darkened room and activated the light. Carefully worked lenses shone into the room from sculpted gargoyles and daemons. Everything about the room had been made in secret to allow this summoning circle to work, just as the sorcerer had requested.

Cadmus glared at the quiet summoning circle. 'Don't trifle with me. I'm not one of your blind cultist pawns,' he muttered to the floor, but he knew that he was the only one listening. He would survive, and one day, there would be a reckoning for all of his enemies.

The commander took a moment to regain his composure. It wouldn't do for the men to see his anger, and he couldn't afford to have his thoughts clouded. He checked his uniform for blood and carefully removed a few incriminating droplets. There was no sign of the lieutenant's body or even his blood in the room. The spell had completely consumed the corpse. Cadmus shuddered.

He activated the door, and then cut the lights. He was worried, even though he knew that everything had gone according to his plan. It was all about time and sequence, one event following another. He had set this in motion and he would see it to the end. He had contacted the Thousand Sons, hadn't he? He was the master manipulator, he reminded himself, but try as he might, he could not dispel his doubts.

Cadmus followed the security corridor past the monitor chamber and the hall to the city complex. The plasteel door at this end of the hall was a duplicate of the other. Two of his loyal men saluted as they maintained their posts. The guards were his people, subservient to his every command.

'Open the door,' he snapped. The guard nearest the control activated it as soon as he dropped the salute. The door slowly slid open and lights activated as Cadmus stepped inside.

The largely empty chamber was nondescript, a storeroom that could easily have been on a thousand planets or even starships throughout the Imperium. The room had one occupant who lay on the ground in the middle of the chamber.

Gabriella lay shackled and bound. She glared up at her captor with hate in her eyes. She looked tired from struggling. It was a pity that she was so dedicated to her house. Despite her lack of classic beauty, Cadmus admired her spirit.

Gabriella had tried in vain to free herself from her bonds, and although she realised that she was probably wasting her strength, she wasn't going to accept any part of this power-hungry officer's plan. 'I felt the presence of Chaos. Tell me, Cadmus, are the dark forces part of your plan as well? Because if they are, you are a bigger fool than I thought.'

Cadmus knelt down over the Navigator and slapped her hard across the face. The small release of anger felt good. 'I promise you, Lady Gabriella, if I die, you'll die as well. Fortunately, I expect that your Space Wolves will show their typical lack of control and spend their energy rending the Dark Angels. While that happens, my men will kill them both. Soon, we will be in a city of the dead, and my allies will put an end to all of this.'

Gabriella smiled; she didn't believe a word of what he said.

ON THE STREETS of Lethe, battle raged between the Dark Angels and the Space Wolves. Both sides fought fiercely against their fellow Space Marines, while the men of Lethe did their best to defend their ruined city. Two ancient champions of the Chapters met on the cratered streets.

The Dark Angels Dreadnought, Arion the Unchallenged, levelled his twin-linked lascannons at his Space Wolf counterpart, Gymir the

Ice-Fisted. The blasts scored a hit, but the Space Wolf war machine took the shots on his arm instead of the sarcophagus on his chest. The glancing strike set a massive Fenrisian wolf pelt ablaze, but failed to disrupt the mind of the entombed Space Marine housed within the venerable Dreadnought's body. The combatants on both sides paused in awe and reverence at the duel unfolding before their eyes.

The Space Wolf Dreadnought kicked aside the remains of a dead Dark Angel as if it were a child's toy and charged, conjuring images in the minds of soldiers on all sides of a sprinting soldier rather than a lumbering mechanical walker. The Dark Angels Dreadnought met the challenge full on, swinging his power fist. Metal clanged on metal like the sounds of a giant forge.

Lieutenant Markham staggered away from the battling Dreadnoughts. He prayed that with the aid of the Space Wolves, House Belisarius would emerge triumphant. Wolf Guard Mikal had contacted the other Imperial Guard units. Markham had been lucky to encounter the Wolf Guard. Word of Cadmus's treason was spreading, but despite that many men would stay loyal to him and assume the rumours were just a Dark Angels trick. Still, the Space Wolves were coordinating the battle. The Dark Angels had adjusted to the challenge and the battle for Lethe was in full swing.

A Leman Russ tank, reinforced with siege armour, drove down a side street. It paused to fire its massive battle cannon at a target that Markham couldn't see. Although the Leman Russ was the main battle tank of the Imperial Guard on countless worlds, the Planetary Defence Force kept few of them on Hyades. The vehicle's size made it difficult to manoeuvre in city streets and in the jungle, yet each one of the tanks received more attention from the tech-priests than the Hellhounds or Chimeras. That was because of the pride that House Belisarius took in the vehicle named for the primarch of their allies, the Space Wolves.

Markham could see the ruins of the city's outer defence wall down the main plaza. Bombardment from the assault had turned it into a mountain of rubble. It was badly breached. Dark shapes crawled through the rubble. If they were some of the defence forces, maybe he could rally them. Commander Cadmus had betrayed him, the Wolfblade and House Belisarius. Markham did not give his loyalty lightly, and something churned in his stomach as the impact of the betrayal struck him. He knew that he was still reeling from the near miss of the Earthshaker cannon earlier, but he felt as if the betrayal was what truly kept his head spinning.

Cadmus had made a mistake. Markham was originally from Catachan, a real death world, not some planet where the people hid behind walls and feared the mines more than they feared the plants. He'd find a way to survive and do his duty. He knew that he'd gained some respect from Wolf Guard Mikal when he had demanded a weapon so that he could rejoin the fighting. Markham wasn't going to let a few scrapes, bruises or even a concussion slow him down.

He squinted to see more clearly. The dark shapes that he had spotted moved strangely, and he was sure that there were many more of them than before. Lethe burned from the ongoing war, and with his addled brains, Markham wasn't sure exactly what he was seeing. He wiped his eyes.

The shapes weren't human, they were reptos. Dozens of the creatures were gathering around the breach, all the while the humans on the planet were busy blowing each other to bits. The reptos appeared to be gathering, waiting.

Markham had a vox that he had scavenged from a dead soldier so he could to stay in touch with the Space Wolves. 'Wolf Guard Mikal,' he voxxed. 'I believe we have a problem. The wall has been breached and the reptos have come to scavenge.'

'Lieutenant, what are reptos?' came the reply. Markham heard storm bolter shots echo through the vox.

'The reptos are native creatures from the jungle surrounding Lethe. They've been attacking the mines and anything outside the walls. They are mammalian reptiles,' responded Markham.

Static answered him. Communications were jammed again.

Markham crouched down behind a bit of rubble and took a better look. The reptos shook and convulsed. He was confused. He'd never seen this behaviour. The creatures then poured into the streets, heading to the bodies of Dark Angels. Strangely, they ignored the bodies of the defence forces.

The creatures fell upon their targets, ripping and tearing. Through extreme effort, they found cracks and weak spots in the power armour, and ripped into the dead flesh underneath. Markham shook his head. He hated watching the reptos scavenge and devour any humans, even if the Dark Angels had attacked Hyades.

The reptos were tearing large bloody objects free from the Space Marine bodies. Markham wasn't sure what they were collecting. At first, he thought it might be hearts, but the organs were too large. The reptos gathered in clusters, hissing and snapping at the body parts, as if they were celebrating. Then, they retreated.

All of the reptos moved back to form a semi circle around a single large member of their species. The large one wore different scaled pelts and held a long staff. The sight fascinated and enthralled Markham. He forgot the sounds of battle behind him, completely oblivious to everything but the scene he was witnessing.

The repto with the staff suddenly ignited, bursting into flame. At first, Markham thought that someone, an infiltrating soldier perhaps, had taken a hand flamer to the beast, but the creature didn't burn with the purifying white fire of promethium. Instead, the flame burned with an unearthly rainbow of colours. As the fire consumed the repto, something even more unexpected took place. Markham cleared his eyes. With the haze of battle he wasn't sure at first that what he saw was real.

Tendrils burst from the body of the flaming creature. Then something covered in mouths and eyes floated out of the fire. The creature was bright blue with streaks of red and pink. It floated above the ground and a nimbus of rainbow fire curled around it. Markham's mind laboured to accept the sight before him. He was a survivor, a man born on a deathworld. He had endured challenges and pain. He had encountered the deadliest predators on planets across the galaxy.

Somehow, he knew that what he saw was not from this galaxy. He felt terror in every fibre of his being.

The reptos gave a shrill greeting sound as one, and handed over their trophies. The abomination took each of them with its tendrils, tenderly grasping them. Then it pulled itself back into the flame and vanished. The reptos spread out, hunting for more trophies, save for one, who picked up the staff from the charred hand of its former owner.

Markham fell on his knees and sobbed a prayer of thanks to the Emperor. The unnameable horror that he had seen was gone. He would not have felt so relieved if he had known that similar scenes were taking place across the city. The harvest had begun.

IN THE PALACE complex, Haegr, Torin, Elijah and Nathaniel searched for Cadmus. Ragnar and Jeremiah were searching together elsewhere, and the other Space Marines assumed that they might be negotiating more details of their alliance without the complications of everyone else's thoughts. The four focused on their search, each one hoping that they would discover the commander first. So far, they had found nothing but bodies, and the lasgun wounds on the bodies coupled with still-secure doors indicated that their killers hadn't been other Dark Angels. The dead men appeared to have been killed by members of the Planetary Defence Force.

Torin looked over at Haegr after sniffing the air. 'So, lad, your nose can tell us everything else. Where is he? I can't find him.'

Haegr shook his head. 'I'm not sure. There are too many scents.'

'Are you really trying to sniff him out?' asked Elijah. The Dark Angel sounded incredulous. 'I thought that was Space Wolf talk for tracking or something.'

'Young one,' said Nathaniel, 'the Space Wolves are known for their senses.'

'Unfortunately, some of us spend our time trying to track nothing but food,' said Torin.

'What's wrong with that?' questioned Haegr. 'Without my ability to find sustenance, we could die out here if things stay bad. Torin, I think you've gone too long without a good thrashing.'

Haegr had to admit to himself that hearing the banter made him more relaxed. He kept finding scene after scene of death, and he didn't know where Cadmus was. Torin placed his hand on Haegr's shoulder and leaned over to whisper to him in that conspiratorial manner that came so easily to him.

'Brother, are you tracking Cadmus?' he whispered.

'I'm trying,' said Haegr.

'Focus on Gabriella's scent instead. You know it better,' recommended Torin.

Haegr gave his friend a look. He wasn't sure if Torin was implying something or not. Haegr knew that he had a strange feeling for Gabriella, but he told himself it was a sense of protectiveness.

From one of the palace windows, Haegr could see drop-pods descending amidst the fire and smoke of the combat. The Space Wolves had arrived! Just catching sight of the wolf symbol made his blood race, although he felt a sense of disquiet as well. He should be in one of those drop-pods with his battle-brothers. Then, he realised that the symbol belonged to Wolf Lord Berek Thunderfist.

'Impressive, isn't it?' asked Torin. The other Space Marines were gathered around, momentarily distracted by the scene of drop-pod after drop-pod coming down.

'Look,' said Elijah, pointing out of the window. More Dark Angels drop-pods were descending. The Dark Angels were still coming. The battle was escalating.

They were running out of time.

GABRIELLA STRUGGLED AGAINST her bonds as the commander pulled her through dark passage after dark passage. She had lost all sense of time and place. Guards walked behind them, hard-looking men with scars and oddly mixed armour and unique weapons. There were at least six with them, but she couldn't tell if there were more. These were Cadmus's hand-picked troops: men who had followed him to this planet.

She knew that the Wolfblade would come for her. The Space Wolves would not relent until they found her. Cadmus would die for his treason.

Yet she could feel other forces at work. In her mind's eye, colours swirled, vibrant and bright. She could feel the power of Chaos coursing through these dark passages. She saw images of Madox and the Thousand Sons, just as she had felt them before when Cadmus had contacted them in his ritual. They were coming, and they had something with them, something that they had brought from the warp.

Then, she saw an image that she knew from ancient tapestries and paintings. She saw the Spear of Russ, the artefact that Ragnar had lost. It was in the possession of the Thousand Sons, they must have recovered it from the warp. She knew the story about Ragnar and how the Thousand Sons had nearly opened a gateway between the warp and the physical world, attempting to summon their primarch, Magnus the Red.

Would they succeed this time?

ELEVEN
Dark Angels and Wolfblade Unite

A WAR RAGED in the city of Lethe between the Space Wolves and the Dark Angels. The ten thousand year-old distrust of these two founding members of the Adeptus Astartes was being exploited by the powers of Chaos.

Ragnar and Jeremiah were in unexplored territory. The mixed band of Space Marines was setting out to find Cadmus and bring him to justice, rescue Gabriella, and work out a way to bring this conflict to an end without sacrificing the honour of either of the proud Space Marine Chapters.

Torin, Haegr, Nathaniel and Elijah had just completed their search of the palace. There were no additional signs of Cadmus anywhere to be found. During their search of one of the communication temples they did, however, come across Tech-Priest Varnus. Varnus was monitoring several communication channels while directing his servitors to areas and equipment that needed to come to the assistance of the Adeptus Mechanicus. The tech-priest accompanied them, walking between Haegr and Torin, his scarlet robes lightly dusting the floor. With the exception of a few minor scraps and some fresh oil stains on his robe, he looked exactly the same as he had when the Wolfblade had first met him.

As the group approached the entrance to the command centre the heavy metal doors slid open as Ragnar and Jeremiah entered the corridor.

'Ragnar, Jeremiah, allow me to introduce Tech-Priest–' Torin began.

'Varnus, it is good to see that you are alive.' Ragnar's surprise and relief were apparent. 'We are in your debt. Had you not opened the blast door, Cadmus's treacherous attempt to destroy us would have succeeded.'

'Indeed, your plight seemed rather perilous. I'm sorry I could not have been of assistance sooner. It had only recently become apparent to me that the governor's forces had been compromised.' There were no emotional inflections in the tech-priest's voice and his mechanically assisted breathing remained eerily rhythmic.

'Compromised is an understatement. Cadmus is undoubtedly in the service of Chaos.'

'Haegr will wipe his Chaos taint from existence,' Haegr promised.

'Yes, Haegr, we will, but first things first,' Ragnar responded.

'What could be more important than cutting out his treacherous heart?' Haegr's words revealed his simplistic perception of the universe.

'I believe that Ragnar is talking about our newly landed brethren who are fighting and dying on the streets of Lethe,' Torin said.

'Perhaps I can be of assistance,' Varnus interrupted. 'Shortly after the Dark Angels began their assault, the Space Wolf patrol fleet commanded by Wolf Lord Berek Thunderfist arrived.' Varnus paused as if checking his facts.

'Yes they were the forces of Thunderfist. After several attempts by him to determine why they had quarantined Hyades, he was forced to engage the Dark Angels, and through a daring ship-to-ship engagement was able to deploy his forces. It was here that I discovered the treachery of Commander Cadmus. His troop deployments were not consistent with defending the city. He had removed his most experienced forces from the city, leaving his less experienced troops defending the brunt of the attack. That, combined with several communications between Cadmus and his stormtroopers that I was able to monitor, forced me to take action. I only regret that my actions did not come soon enough.'

'Have you made contact with the Space Wolf landing forces yet?' Ragnar asked.

'No, but I believe that their commander has been successful at contacting some of the loyal Hyades ground forces,' Varnus answered.

'Once the Space Wolves were on the ground they established communication with the loyal factions of the Planetary Defence Forces. It was through this alliance that they were able to establish a defensive perimeter within the city, right around the palace compound. With the defensive lines firmly established, the allied forces have begun to push back the Dark Angels,' Varnus concluded.

Ragnar and the rest of the Wolfblade were relieved to hear that the tide of battle appeared to be swinging in their direction. Ragnar, however, knew that what was good news for him and his Wolfblade brothers was worrying to his new-found allies. The alliance forged with the Dark Angels kill team was tenuous at best, and if they were going to bring this conflict to an end it would be this relationship that would be the catalyst.

'This madness has to end,' said Ragnar. 'Cadmus has been pulling the strings from the beginning. Everything that's happened has been according to his design.'

'That is true, Ragnar, everything except one element: our alliance! Cadmus could never comprehend that the Lion and the Wolf would be capable of setting aside ten thousand years of distrust. It is this alliance that gives us the advantage,' Jeremiah said.

Ragnar was relieved that Jeremiah's thoughts were the same as his. However, the Wolfblade's first duty was to House Belisarius. The information provided by Varnus left them free to pursue the traitor and rescue Lady Gabriella.

'Varnus, can you establish communications with the Spaces Space Marine forces here on Hyades, and inform them of Cadmus's treachery? Ragnar asked.

'Yes, I believe that I can,' Varnus replied.

Ragnar hoped that Varnus would be able to use his skills as a techpriest to establish communication channels with the Space Wolves and the Dark Angels. This could be a useful resource when the time was right.

'Our priority is to locate Cadmus,' Torin exclaimed.

'Yes, but he could be anywhere. In fact, I would be surprised if he was still on the planet at all,' Haegr said.

'No, he's still here. He wants to ensure that his plan works,' Nathaniel added.

'How can you be certain?' Ragnar asked.

The Dark Angels remained silent, exchanging glances between themselves until Jeremiah finally spoke.

'Shortly after our first encounter with you on the palace grounds we were contacted by Interrogator-Chaplain Vargas, who had arrived on board the battle-barge that orbits Hyades. While we were reporting our need for additional time to locate and secure our target, the transmission was interrupted by Cadmus, who we now know to be our quarry. Chaplain Vargas had just agreed to give us the time we needed. However, once the transmission was compromised Cadmus provoked the chaplain into this full-fledged assault. We've been unable to reach the battle-barge since,' Jeremiah concluded.

'Cadmus has gone to great lengths to ensure that these events unfold exactly the way he intends. I find it difficult to believe that he would simply slip away,' Nathaniel added.

'He wouldn't,' Torin agreed.

'Yes. He must still be here on Hyades, but where?' Ragnar asked.

'He would need a place where he could plan events without detection, and free from interruption. That means it would not be within the palace compound,' Varnus concluded.

'How can you be so certain?' Haegr asked.

'The compound is heavily monitored by security surveillance skulls.' Ragnar remembered the command centre's monitors, almost every corridor and room under constant scrutiny.

'Yes,' Varnus confirmed.

'Then he would need to establish his base in a secluded location away from the palace compound,' Jeremiah added.

'The temple,' Haegr said, almost shouting.

The silence of the group was deafening as each member of the Wolf-blade reached the same conclusion. Haegr was right – the temple would be the best place to begin their search for the treacherous Cadmus. It was secluded, and out of the way.

'Temple?' Jeremiah asked.

'Upon our arrival on Hyades we conducted a search of the jungle around the city. While there, we came upon an ancient temple. It appeared to be abandoned,' Ragnar explained.

'We just need to find a way to get there without attracting the attention of our brother Space Marines,' Torin explained.

'I think I can help with that,' Elijah said as he walked past the group. Jeremiah looked to Nathaniel who simply shrugged and entered the command centre as well, followed closely by the rest of them.

When they entered the command centre Elijah had pulled several tubes from a plasteel box that rested between the wall and one of the monitoring consoles.

'I saw these when we were in here earlier, I think that they can help.'

Elijah read the label on each tube in turn. 'This one,' he said, pulling the parchment from the tube and unrolling it across the table.

'It's a city map,' Elijah said.

The others watched as Elijah began to trace a path from the jungle to the city walls and on to the palace.

'What are you doing?' Torin asked.

'This is the path we used to gain access to the city,' Jeremiah explained.

'Our insertion went exceptionally well. In fact, I thought at the time that it went too well.' As he continued, Jeremiah pointed out the key locations along the line on the map. 'We teleported in here and made our way through the jungle to the wall here.'

'That's great, but there's a war going on out there.' Haegr's words rang true. There were forces throughout the city: forces that they would have to avoid.

'This is correct. We will need to move undetected if possible. Any contact with either side would spell disaster for our mission,' Nathaniel said.

Varnus looked at the map and then spoke. 'The Dark Angels dropped into the city here, here and here. At first they moved unobstructed towards the palace. Fortunately, the governor's guard report directly to the governor who dispatched them right away, slowing down their advance.'

'I'm impressed. Defence forces going head-to-head against Astartes,' Torin commented.

'That was not their mission. Their numbers were too small to mount an actual defence. Their orders were to harass them, slow them down. With the use of mines and explosives charges they were able to topple several buildings in an attempt to slow their advance on the palace. This gave the governor some time to locate and deploy those forces still loyal to him.'

The Astartes warriors watched and listened as the tech-priest pointed out the most current troop and Space Marine deployments that he had, committing almost every detail to memory.

'These locations are somewhat out of date but they should give you enough information to move through the city, decreasing your chances of encountering any of the forces engaged on Lethe,' Varnus concluded.

'Again, Varnus, we are in your debt.' Ragnar placed a hand on the tech-priest's shoulder.

'Once you've departed I will attempt to contact both Adeptus Astartes forces and explain the situation to them. May the Emperor and the Machine-God protect all of us.' Varnus bowed and left the command centre.

'Let's get to it then,' Ragnar commanded. 'Torin, go to the Chimera and bring it to the parade grounds, where we first discovered the Dark Angels.'

'I'll go with Torin and Jeremiah, just in case,' Nathaniel said.

'Good idea,' Jeremiah agreed.

'The rest of us will proceed to the armoury to re-supply.'

'The palace armoury? We need bolter rounds not lasgun power cells,' said Elijah.

'Haegr, would you be so kind as to lead us to the armoury where the Wolfblade supplies were housed upon our arrival?'

'It would be my pleasure, Ragnar. Right this way. Fortunately we have to go right past the kitchen. One can not be expected to wage war on an empty stomach.'

Ragnar and the others prepared, re-equipping and re-arming for the journey ahead. Upon their arrival several stowage crates had been offloaded. The Wolfblade were always on the move, supporting and protecting House Belisarius's interests. Since supplies for a contingent of Space Marines were hard to come by on most worlds, the Wolfblade always brought their own. Once the team was ready they left to rendezvous with Torin and Nathaniel.

HAEGR AND ELIJAH were the last to enter the Chimera transport. Elijah moved past the rest towards the front while Haegr took the seats next to the deployment hatch. Chimeras were not designed for Space Marines, especially ones his size.

'I do not know how you expect a man to go to war when all he's had to eat are food packs,' Haegr grumbled.

Torin looked back from the driver's seat. 'What's got Haegr's blood up?'

'We stopped by the kitchen on our way here, and all he could find to eat were food packs,' Elijah said with a grin as he took the tactical seat.

Suspicion and distrust ran through Torin's mind as Elijah sat down, visions of ambush or the Chimera pulling right into a Dark Angels command post flashing in his head. Torin attempted to run a mental checklist of the troop concentrations that Varnus had depicted on the map. He hoped his memory would not fail him.

'I thought I might be able to help with the navigation through the city. I'd hate to round a corner and find we'd entered a Space Wolf command centre,' Elijah said.

'Well said, my friend, we'll keep each other honest,' Torin said with a grin.

'I would hate to have our new alliance severed because I failed in my duties,' Elijah replied with a smile.

Ragnar exchanged a quick glance with Jeremiah. Both had witnessed the exchange. Perhaps there was a chance that they would succeed. With some minor exceptions they were at least setting aside the distrust that stood between their two Chapters. If they could do it then maybe there would be a chance to bring this conflict under control once

Gabriella was rescued and Cadmus was dealt with. As the Chimera rolled out Ragnar smiled a slight smile of relief. Haegr simply grunted in disgust.

THE TEAM STOOD at the entrance to the maintenance tunnel where the Dark Angels had first gained entry into Lethe. Sounds of conflict were all around them; explosions and weapons fire from different directions. During their journey several quick direction changes had been needed, but Torin and Elijah worked very well together. Ragnar was relieved that something finally seemed to be going well for them.

Elijah was the first to enter the maintenance tunnel, followed closely by Nathaniel, and then the rest of the group. Haegr was the last one in. Emergency lighting panels illuminated the dull grey rockcrete walls. Elijah moved quietly, until finally reaching the exit door. It still wore the scars from the kill team's creative lock picking techniques.

Elijah slowly opened the door and stepped into the waiting jungle, scanning the immediate surroundings. He moved slowly forwards, trying to get a clear scan. The auspex display screen distorted and blinked out for a split second and then reset and blinked out again. It was still useless.

Nathaniel stood about three metres behind Elijah, visually scanning the surrounding area.

'How does it look, Eli?' Nathaniel asked.

'Hold your position, Nathaniel, the auspex isn't functioning,' Elijah replied.

The rest of the team cautiously stepped into the jungle, fanning out along the wall. There was no kill zone. The jungle grew right up to the walls. Vines and other forms of foliage had even begun to grow up along the wall, covering it with a thick layer of greens and browns. As Ragnar and the other Space Wolves moved into position they exchanged quick glances.

'It must be the heat or the promethium still causing interference,' Elijah said, preoccupied.

Jeremiah and Nathaniel noticed a change in their Space Wolf companions. They were almost frozen in place, eyes locked on the jungle. It was as if they saw something that was not there. 'Put that contraption away Elijah,' Nathaniel ordered.

'Seems to be clea...' A red cloud rose just above Elijah's left shoulder, drizzling red mist on his armour's shoulder pad and the side of his face. The shot spun him around, causing him to lose his footing and fall.

One of their own was down, and the ragtag Adeptus Astartes group reacted instantly. Nathaniel ducked his head and ran towards his fallen comrade while the rest laid down a pattern of suppression fire at their unseen attackers. Ragnar and Jeremiah each broke to opposite flanks while Haegr and Torin stood the middle ground.

Nathaniel moved through the tangle of vines and branches that clogged the jungle floor finally reaching Elijah. He found him lying prone, face down in the dirt. Grabbing his right arm, he spun the younger Space Marine over onto his back. The round had managed to penetrate the armour at the lower rear section of the shoulder pad, grazing the upper arm. The wound was minor and Elijah was already climbing to his feet.

Branches erupted all around them as the enemy began to fire once again. Firing short controlled bursts they retreated back through the jungle to rejoin their companions.

Once the six Space Marines were together again, Ragnar activated his internal comm system.

'If we stand here we're just waiting to get shot,' Ragnar declared.

'Then what would you suggest?' Nathaniel asked.

'The best defence is always a good offence. We charge,' Ragnar answered.

'Agreed,' Jeremiah confirmed.

Ragnar slung his boltgun, drew his bolt pistol and sword, thumbed the activation rune as he'd done hundreds of times before, and dived through the dense foliage separating them from their unseen enemies. A bestial howl rose as he charged, the Wolfblade offering their own howl to the battle cry.

The six warriors crashed through the jungle on a head-on collision course. Firing blindly into the barrier of trees and brush in front of them, their swords arched through the air cleanly slicing branches away as they cut a path through the harsh foliage. Ragnar emerged from the jungle onto a path and the scent of Chaos poured into his nostrils. At least they were not facing their fellow Space Marines.

A ragged, feral-looking guardsman leapt from the jungle slashing wildly at Ragnar, striking the armour of his chest plate, which stopped the attack cold. The clumsy attack reminded the Space Wolf to stay focused and to keep his mind on the events of the here and now. A simple flick of his wrist and a downwards strike imbedded Ragnar's sword deep in the enemy's neck, severing the head from his body.

Members of Cadmus's elite unit of stormtroopers poured from the cover of the jungle onto the Space Marines. The remnants of their once-proud uniforms hanging from their bent and twisted bodies were the only indication of who these inhuman beasts had once been. Tooth and claw, talon and horn replaced the once cherished weapons of humanity.

Some still carried these weapons but they were now merged with their wielder in an unholy union of flesh and metal. These creatures were greater in number, fierce, and showed no hint of fear, but they were incredibly outmatched. Undeterred, the stormtroopers swarmed over the combined members of the Wolfblade and the Dark Angels.

Haegr's weapon howled from his roundhouse swings, sending the mutated attackers sailing back into the jungle when his hammer struck home. Jeremiah made quick work of the filth surrounding him, his efficiency wasting neither time nor energy. Torin's speed and finesse with a blade allowed him to dance around his opponents, throwing them off-balance. Nathaniel and Elijah fought back-to-back encircled by attackers, using their decades of service together to combine their fighting prowess to overwhelm and confuse. Ragnar, meanwhile, used sheer ferocity to wade into the filth of Chaos.

In a matter of minutes, the Chaos-tainted troopers lay dead on the jungle floor. Ragnar knelt down next to one of the fallen warriors, wondering if this poor soul realised that his misplaced loyalty to Cadmus had led him to this end.

The acrid scent of Chaos nauseated him; the air was heavy with it. When they had first explored the jungle, a few days ago, birds and other indigenous life had been extremely active, now there was nothing. Even the buzz beetles that had constantly harassed them were no longer anywhere to be found.

The Space Marine squad followed Ragnar through the tainted jungle, ignoring the footpath. They simply made their way through the foliage, cutting and slicing through the vines and bushes. Ragnar stopped occasionally to confirm they were heading towards the temple, moving on quickly when he was reassured, for time was of the essence and caution was a luxury that they could no longer afford.

As Ragnar moved through the trees he came across a huge number of tracks, cutting a swathe through the jungle, moving directly towards Lethe. He held up his fist, signalling for the rest to stop.

'What do you have, Ragnar?' Torin asked.

'Fresh repto tracks, hundreds of them, moving towards the city,' Ragnar answered.

'Why should we be so concerned about a bunch of reptiles?' asked Haegr.

'These new forces pose a threat to both the Lion and the Wolf. A new faction is approaching the city,' Jeremiah replied.

'Exactly! The forces in Lethe must be made aware of this new development. We must contact Varnus,' Ragnar said.

* * *

SERVITORS SHUFFLED AROUND the command centre, having moved the bodies of Magni and the governor, ready to conduct the necessary repair rituals. Varnus hunched over the comms pulpit. He did not like the new information he had just received. The reptos had been causing work delays for a while on Hyades, and it would appear that they were moving in force on the city. Their objective was still unclear to him, but Ragnar was right, the Space Marines needed to know about the new threat.

The heavy steel doors of the command centre opened with a clang and five Astartes warriors entered, their ancient armour glittering with a blue-yellow glow. Spikes like thorns on a vine ran up the sides of both legs. Horns erupted from the sides of their helmets, curving up and rising high above the green glowing eye-lenses. These were not Astartes. These were Thousand Sons Space Marines.

Three Traitor Space Marines moved to the body of the fallen Space Wolf while the other two remained at the entrance. It was then that Varnus noticed a sixth figure, standing in the shadows just beyond the entrance, revealing only a vague silhouette. Terror rose up within the tech-priest as he faced these ancient enemies of mankind.

'Foolish son of Mars, your time is at an end,' announced the figure at the rear of the group.

Those words were the last that Varnus would ever hear as the melta gun superheated his body from the inside out.

RAGNAR AND THE other Space Marines broke into the clearing that surrounded the entrance to the temple. The surrounding area was exactly as he remembered, the tiered pyramid, faces leering out from the stones. When they had first found the structure he had wanted to enter and investigate it. Things might be different now had he followed his instincts then, but at the time they'd had other issues to contend with. He would see to it that he corrected that mistake. Signalling the others, he headed in.

The entrance of the structure was primitive in design, crudely hewed blocks of stone with mud used for mortar. The jungle did not intrude here as it did at the city; it was as if it had simply accepted the structure. The interior floor was hard-packed dirt. They moved through the temple, the blue-green phosphorescent glow from the foliage dimly lighting the winding corridor. Deeper and deeper into the pyramid they descended. The dim light cast shadows across the stones, exaggerating the evil faces with even more vile expressions. Ragnar took point, followed by Jeremiah and the others. Besides the sounds of the Space Marines walking through the corridors, there was only the sound of the wind that whispered softly.

Ragnar wondered how long the temple had stood here. Had the reptos built this place, or their ancient ancestors? And for how long had they worshipped the gods of Chaos?

As the Space Marines descended into the temple, the light started to change. Eventually, the rough, primitive, construction transformed into a smooth rockcrete corridor, and the natural phosphorescent light was replaced with glow-globes. The hard-packed dirt floor was replaced with the standard textured plasteel plating. The sudden change in the corridor caused the Space Marines to stop and evaluate their situation.

Torin approached Ragnar, followed closely by Jeremiah. As the three huddled in intense conversation, Haegr, Elijah and Nathaniel took a rear guard position.

'I sense that we're close,' said Ragnar.

'Yes, little brother, I sense it too, but let's not rush in,' Torin replied.

'How can you be sure? This doesn't confirm that Cadmus is here, only that at one point he could have been,' Jeremiah explained.

'You should learn to trust your instincts, Jeremiah,' Torin said.

Concluding their conversation, Ragnar turned and moved down the corridor. Jeremiah signalled Elijah to join him. Ragnar and Elijah moved down opposite sides of the corridor, the rest following behind them. The complex seemed more command centre than bunker. Until this point, the corridor had slowly descended while gently winding. Now it made a ninety-degree turn to the right. Slowly, Ragnar and Elijah approached the corner. Ragnar tested the air, but it was too thick with the ripe stench of Chaos for him to get any kind of a scent trail.

Elijah crouched on the left side of the corridor when Ragnar signalled that there were sentries of some kind around the corner. Acknowledging the information, Elijah reached for his trusted auspex. Then, remembering the attack in the jungle, he decided that his own eyes would be his most useful tools. Leaning out, he saw that the corridor extended for another five metres, ending in a set of double doors. Two stormtroopers of Cadmus's elite guard stood on either side of them.

Ragnar looked first at Torin and then to Jeremiah. Both realised exactly what he was thinking. Jeremiah momentarily considered protesting, but then he recalled a ferocious Space Wolf crashing through an Administratum building, tackling him to the ground. It was that ferocity that had halted their incursion. He and Torin nodded their agreement. Ragnar signalled for the charge, grinning as he activated his sword.

Ragnar and Elijah erupted into the corridor, Ragnar's howl filling the air. Both guards were dead before they were able to turn to face their attackers. Without slowing, they crashed into the double doors. Unable to withstand the combined impact of two Space Marines, the doors gave way.

Six of the Emperor's finest warriors poured into the room. Cadmus stood in front of a door on the opposite side of the room, clutching Gabriella by her hair. 'Well, the Wolf and the Lion have joined forces, how unexpected.' The renegade commander growled in disgust, surprised and frustrated.

'It's over, Cadmus. Let her go,' Ragnar shouted.

'I've heard how persistent you can be, mongrel son of a rabid dog, but you have no idea who I am or what I've seen. It's over when I decide it is,' Cadmus said, yanking harder on Gabriella's hair.

Jeremiah slowly manoeuvred himself along the wall, trying to get himself closer to Cadmus, closer to the Fallen. This was his chance, but he would have to move quickly.

Cadmus pointed his pistol at Jeremiah. 'Stop right there, young lion.'

'It's over Cadmus! It's time for you to—' Jeremiah was interrupted as the walls on either side of the commander began to distort. Gabriella started to convulse violently. Blood flowed from her ears and nose, her muffled screams reflecting her pain and terror. Whatever was going on was tearing into her mind.

'Meet my new battle-brothers, young lion,' said Cadmus. 'Now if you will excuse me, it's time for me to depart. I'm sure the Interrogator-Chaplain will forgive your failure.' The commander released Gabriella and stepped through the door. Suddenly, six Thousand Sons stepped out of the distortion into the room. Unlike the Space Wolves, their armour was not adorned with personal trophies or remembrances from previous battles, the eye of Tzeentch emblazoned across their chest was the only indication of their allegiance. The Chaos Space Marines stood like a wall between the Space Marines and their quarry.

Ragnar knew instantly that the real masterminds had finally revealed themselves. With a savage howl, he threw himself at the Thousand Sons.

TWELVE
The Real Enemy

CADMUS WAS FURIOUS. The Wolfblade were an enigma. His plan had been perfect; he never made mistakes. When the Space Wolves arrived on their patrol to discover the Dark Angels invasion force, war broke out. The Dark Angels kill team should have joined them in the fight, leaving Ragnar and the other Wolfblade to rescue Gabriella and meet their doom. They should not be working together: the Space Wolves hated the Dark Angels. Apparently, Ragnar was as troublesome as Madox said. He would think on this later, but for now he needed to make his escape.

He reached the back wall, and sliding his hand down along its surface, activated a hidden panel that slid up, revealing a keyed access pad. He entered a pass code.

The panel buzzed its rejection. Cadmus quickly re-entered the code, only for it to be rejected again. He entered the code a third time, this time taking even more care to ensure that he was entering it correctly. Again, the panel buzzed its refusal.

'Running to hide again, Fallen?' The voice seemed to emanate from the walls themselves. Cadmus spun around to see a figure in the corner of the room.

It was Madox, his blue and gold armour shimmering slightly with mystical energies. Spiral horns curved up from his helmet and green light emanated from his eyes. In his right hand he clutched a staff tipped with a glowing orb.

Madox stepped lightly from the shadows.

'I sent the assistance you requested from me, Cadmus, and now you leave my warriors as you left your own battle-brothers all those centuries ago.'

'You don't expect me to believe that you're concerned about a few of your followers do you, Madox?' Cadmus asked, while turning back to the access panel.

'No, you are right. I've been waiting here for you Cadmus,' Madox said.

Again Cadmus tried the access panel, and again it failed to respond. He smashed his fist into the wall in anger.

'The panel no longer works, Cadmus, I've had it disabled,' Madox said.

'I've kept my part of the bargain! I lured the Dark Angels to Hyades! I've orchestrated a war between them and the Space Wolves, and I've even brought the Wolfblade here, as you wanted. Why are you blocking my escape?'

Madox's maniacal chuckle filled the chamber. 'Because Ragnar still lives and as far as you're concerned, I have no further need of you.'

'But we had a bargain! I set all this in motion. You seem to forget, Madox, that without me none of this would have been possible,' Cadmus said, his voice quaking with anger.

'Are you really so naïve that you actually think this all came about because of you? You really believe that all of this was part of your design?' Madox asked.

Cadmus filled with rage. Had he really been a pawn to Chaos? Was he really that easy to manipulate and deceive? He searched his memory for any sign, any clue that he had not been in control of any of it. Drawing his plasma pistol, he stepped towards Madox.

'So, you see the truth of it,' Madox gloated.

'I'm going to kill you,' said Cadmus. Raising his plasma pistol, he pulled the trigger.

'You are truly naïve,' Madox's laughter filled the room as he vanished.

CADMUS'S DEPARTURE LEFT Ragnar and the others squared off with the Thousand Sons. Gabriella lay unconscious on the floor at the back of the room. Crates, boxes and furniture lay strewn around. The Thousand Sons were not noted for their outstanding prowess in hand-to-hand combat, approaching a battle slowly and purposefully, laying down a hail of bolter fire, giving their sorcerers time to win the day. Ragnar guessed the Thousand Sons were merely a delaying tactic to buy the commander time to escape. With a battle howl, Ragnar and the rest of the team leapt at the Chaos Space Marines.

Fire sparked off combat weapons as the two sides clashed. Deflecting an attack with his sword, Ragnar crashed into one of the Thousand Sons, driving his shoulder deep into his opponent's abdomen. He had faced this menace before and although not known for their hand-to-hand fighting skill they were stalwart warriors, able to withstand a tremendous amount of damage. As the Thousand Son stepped forwards, Ragnar leapt, stepping on one of the plasteel crates elevating himself above the Chaos Space Marine. Wedging the point of his sword where his opponent's helmet and neck armour met, he drove it straight down. The Thousand Son buckled and collapsed to the floor and the energy holding him together was released.

Haegr swung his hammer in an uppercut stroke bringing his target off his feet, and dumping him on the ground with a thundering crash. Raising his weapon over his head, he delivered a crushing blow. The helmet of the Thousand Son exploded into hundreds of pieces. The ancient dust that was once the physical form of the Space Marine poured out onto the rockcrete floor.

Jeremiah bolted for the door that Cadmus had left through moments ago. A Thousand Sons Chaos Space Marine stepped in his path. His chainsword ripped across his chest plate, the force of the attack sending Jeremiah stumbling backwards.

Although quickly regaining his footing, his opponent pressed his advantage, forcing the Dark Angel to retreat, deflecting blow after blow from the Chaos chainsword. The Thousand Son brought his bolt pistol around. Seeing this, Jeremiah deflected the weapon, but this left him exposed, a mistake that was soon exploited as the chainsword crashed down into his shoulder, driving him to his knees.

The Chaos Space Marine knew he had the advantage and intended to bring the fight to a quick end. As the killing blow came down, Jeremiah reached up, grabbing his opponent's hand, while jabbing his own pistol into his enemy's midsection, firing several rounds. The hollow, lifeless armour fell to the floor.

Torin found himself backed against the wall as one of the Chaos Space Marines closed on him. Ragnar had warned him that the Thousand Sons were slow, but he didn't think the assessment was entirely accurate. He ducked his head as a chainsword dug into the rockcrete wall. It was the mistake he had been waiting for. Swinging his sword up and around, he sliced clean through his opponent's armour, sending the chainsword and arm greave clanging to the floor. Using the momentum of his attack, Torin tucked into a shoulder roll which brought him up beside and just behind his opponent.

Spinning his sword in his hand, inverting his grip and placing his other hand over the pommel, he spun around, sinking his sword into the joint at the waist of the Chaos Space Marine's armour. He continued his spin and the sword ripped through the entire side, cleaving the Thousand Son in two.

Nathaniel eliminated his adversary quickly and turned to assist Elijah. As he ran to the aid of his young battle-brother, a Chaos Space Marine helmet bounced across the floor past him. The Traitor that was facing Elijah slumped to its knees and then collapsed to the floor.

Within a few moments, the empty armour of six Thousand Sons Space Marines lay inactive and crumpled on the floor of Cadmus's command centre.

Haegr stood at the side of the room, picking up a chest plate, bewildered by the fact that it was empty. Torin, Jeremiah and the other Dark Angels checked the room ensuring that they were safe.

Ragnar leapt to Gabriella's side, removing her gag and bonds. 'Gabriella, are you all right?' he asked.

The Navigator was barely conscious and felt so fragile, nothing like the person he knew. Her face was bruised and swollen. Red stripes of dried blood curved down the side of her face from the corner of her right eye. Fresh blood pooled in her ears.

Slowly, she opened her eyes, but it took her some time to focus properly. 'Ragnar, is Magni alive?' Gabriella asked.

'Do not worry about that now, my lady. We must get you to safety,' said Ragnar, his voice reflecting his concern.

Gabriella started to wipe the blood away from her face, and Ragnar could tell that her faculties were returning. In her eyes he saw the grim determination and confidence that she had always possessed. She looked at Ragnar. 'You must stop Cadmus,' she demanded.

'Once you are safely away from here, my lady. We must get you out,' Ragnar argued.

Gabriella grasped the edge of Ragnar's armour and pulled herself up to a sitting position. 'I will be fine. Cadmus must be stopped,' she said again, only this time Ragnar knew it was not the request of a delirious woman, but the request of a member of House Belisarius. Gently placing her against the wall, he stood. He was a warrior of the Astartes, a Son of Russ, and he knew what had to be done.

'Torin, see to her wounds. Haegr, cover the door,' Ragnar commanded.

Jeremiah and Nathaniel crossed the room to join Ragnar. Together, the three Space Marines went through the door Cadmus had left by.

As they entered the room beyond they found Cadmus, weapon in hand, staring blankly at a blazing blue-green fire in the corner. He seemed oblivious to the Space Marines' presence. Ragnar took in the Chaos markings that adorned the floor and walls of the room as well as various racks of arcane-looking weapons.

When he saw Jeremiah, Cadmus broke out in laughter.

There was really nothing more for Ragnar to do except honour his oath to Jeremiah. Gabriella was safe with the Wolfblade; his duty was to bring this conflict between the Space Wolves and Dark Angels to an end. 'It's over Jeremiah,' he said. 'I honour my oath to you. Cadmus is yours.'

'Ragnar, I have a message for you from an old acquaintance of yours,' Cadmus said.

'Silence, heretic,' Nathaniel shouted, striking the commander across the face.

Cadmus was defeated, his plan thwarted. What message could he possible have, Ragnar asked himself? He knew better than to listen to the final pleas of a condemned traitor. However, he was still unaware of what Cadmus's true objectives were.

'What could you possibly have to say that I would want to hear, Cadmus?' Ragnar asked.

'I know why you were sent to Terra, and I know of your failure. I know you were sent to the Wolfblade in disgrace for losing the Spear of Russ,' Cadmus said, speaking quietly and with precision.

Jeremiah and Nathaniel exchanged quick glances, unsure of what to make of this information. Jeremiah began to grow concerned. He knew what Cadmus was trying to do. He was trying to divide them, trying to use this information to create a rift between the allies.

'You speak in vague generalities hoping to sound as if you know more than you really do. You speak as someone who is about to be brought to justice and scrambles to find a way out,' Ragnar said.

'That may be, Wolfblade, but I digress; as I said, I have a message for you from and old friend. Madox sends his greetings,' Cadmus said.

Ragnar failed to hide his surprise. He had spoken of the Spear many times while on Hyades. Cadmus's surveillance equipment could have provided him with that information about the Spear of Russ, but how would he know its true name? Logic and reason told him that this was another of Cadmus's attempts to manipulate the situation in his favour, to fracture the fragile alliance between the Space Wolves and the Dark Angels. He needed to proceed carefully.

'How do you know that name?' Ragnar growled.

'As I said, boy, I have much information, but all of it comes at a price.' Confidence grew in Cadmus's voice.

'Ragnar, don't listen to him,' said Jeremiah. 'He is a heretic, a pawn of the Dark Ones.'

'Don't interfere, Dark Angel! Or perhaps you'd like me to discuss other issues. Issues of a more personal nature, perhaps,' Cadmus threatened.

'As I said, Cadmus, how do you know that name?' Ragnar asked again.

'A price, Ragnar. You should know that all information has its cost,' Cadmus said, almost gloating.

'Name it, then,' Ragnar demanded.

'A trifle really, not much at all. I just want my life,' said Cadmus, all the fear gone from his voice.

'Tell me what I want to know and your life will be yours,' Ragnar said.

'Ragnar, you swore an oath! Is this how a Son of Russ keeps his word?' Jeremiah asked, stunned.

Ragnar saw the betrayal Jeremiah felt in his eyes and understood his anger. He had given his oath that Cadmus would be his to deal with as he saw fit, but this was a new development. He had to know how Madox fit in to this. Ragnar remembered his first encounter with the Chaos sorcerer. He had never known true evil until that day and never truly understood the scope of the danger that Chaos represented to the Imperium.

The learning machine had taught him of the nature of Chaos and shown him many battles between the forces of the Imperium and Chaos. However, being told what evil is and experiencing it first hand were entirely different. Madox hated everything about the Space Wolves and the Imperium. If he was involved, then everything that had transpired on Hyades had little or nothing to do with House Belisarius, Hyades or its promethium mines. Was that information more important than his oath or his honour?

'If Madox is here then it is imperative that we have all the information, Jeremiah.'

'Ragnar, we had an agreement! I trusted you,' said Jeremiah.

'Then continue to trust me, Jeremiah,' said Ragnar. 'You do not know what Madox is capable of. We must have answers.'

He looked to Jeremiah and then to Nathaniel, trying to determine their course of action. He did not want a conflict with them, since they had earned his respect several times over, but he would have the answers, above all else he would have them.

'Get on with it, Cadmus! What does Madox have to do with what's going on here?' Ragnar demanded.

'He wants you dead, wolf, and once you are dead he intends to destroy the rest of Russ's sons,' Cadmus explained.

'How does he intend to do that and what does Hyades have to do with all this?' Ragnar asked, a growl rising in his voice.

'Hyades is merely a battlefield. He wanted to spark conflict between the Lion and the Wolf. This would give him access to one of the two components he would need, the sacred gene-seed,' Cadmus continued.

'Gene-seed!' The three Space Marines were horrified. The future of every Chapter of Space Marines rested in the gene-seed. The most sacred of all things: without it each Chapter would eventually diminish and become extinct.

'I see that got your attention.' Cadmus's voice lowered to a sinister growl.

'You mentioned two components. What's the second?' Ragnar demanded.

Madox hesitated. 'Some kind of ancient relic, a weapon or a device. It was imperative that he have both of these components for the ritual. That much I am sure of,' Cadmus answered.

Ragnar's mind raced back to the day when he had lost the sacred spear. He saw himself wielding the most cherished of his Chapter's relics. In painstakingly vivid recollection, he witnessed himself throwing the spear into the portal, striking the giant, one-eyed primarch of the Thousand Sons. Ragnar had forced the evil primarch back into the warp, saving his battle-brothers, but forever losing the spear! Could Madox have found it? If so, then his failure was even greater than he had thought.

'What artefact is it, and does he have it?' Ragnar asked.

'I'm not sure if he actually has possession of the bauble. If not, I am fairly certain that he knows where to find it,' Cadmus answered with a devious smile, enjoying the effect his words were having on Ragnar.

'So you started this conflict to give Madox access to the gene-seed for use with this unknown artefact for some sort of ritual. To what end?' Ragnar asked.

'A ritual that he is confident will bring about the destruction of the Sons of Russ,' Cadmus explained.

'But why involve the Wolfblade?' Jeremiah asked.

Cadmus pointed at Ragnar. 'Oh, it's not the Wolfblade he's after, It's Ragnar,' Cadmus replied. 'I told you all I am prepared to. Now it's time for me to leave.'

'Very well, Cadmus, you've kept your word and I in turn will keep mine,' Ragnar said.

Ragnar crossed the room as if clearing the way for Cadmus's departure. Nathaniel and Jeremiah closed ranks, blocking his exit. Jeremiah looked anxiously towards Ragnar, longing to trust his oath. Cadmus stopped, looking puzzled, wondering why he was not being allowed to leave. He looked over his shoulder in Ragnar's direction. 'I've told you all I know. Anything else you will have to find out yourself. You gave me your word that I would be able to leave.'

'Ragnar, I cannot allow him to leave! He has unfinished business with the Dark Angels,' Jeremiah said, controlling his tone, but not his intentions.

'Jeremiah, I gave him my word,' said Ragnar stopping in front of one of the weapons racks on the opposite wall.

'You are not bound to keep your word when it is given to a traitor such as this,' Nathaniel said, compelled to voice his opinion.

'If that were the case then you would be no different than those you call enemies,' Cadmus said.

'Loyal servants of the Emperor cannot choose. They must honour their oaths and follow their masters regardless of the path. I know this better than anyone, and so do you, Son of the Lion,' Cadmus said, sorrow and regret apparent in his words.

'Cadmus is correct, Jeremiah. I have given him my oath. I cannot break my word, just as I am bound to honour my oath to you,' Ragnar said.

'They are in conflict Ragnar,' said Jeremiah.

'Yes, Wolfblade, they would appear to be in conflict,' Cadmus said, spitting the words out like poison.

'Actually, they are not in conflict at all. Jeremiah, I swore to you that Cadmus would be yours to deal with once we had rescued Gabriella,' Ragnar said calmly.

'Yes, and you gave me your word that if I helped you, I'd be free to go,' said Cadmus, the words almost dancing from his lips. He was growing impatient.

'That's not entirely correct,' Ragnar said, pulling a chainsword from the wall. 'I promised you that your life would be yours, and it is.' Ragnar tossed the chainsword to the ground at Cadmus's feet. 'I suggest that you defend it.' Ragnar crossed back across the room past Cadmus, and stopped next to Jeremiah, placing a hand on his shoulder.

'He is yours to do with as you see fit. I'm sure that you will do the right thing,' Ragnar said, before turning and leaving the room.

Jeremiah turned his full attention to Cadmus, who was kneeling to retrieve the sword. For a moment there was fear in his eyes: the fear that someone feels when justice is finally served on them after a lifetime of betrayal. This caused a smile to cross Jeremiah's face. His original mission was to deliver the Fallen to the Interrogator-Chaplain, but Jeremiah knew that path was no longer possible. Cadmus had lured his battle-brothers, Dark Angel and Space Wolf alike, to their deaths, sacrificing his men to further his own means. Redemption was not possible for the likes of Cadmus. Right or wrong, this was the path that Jeremiah was on.

Drawing his sword, Jeremiah swore to himself that he would see Cadmus dead whatever the consequences.

'So, this is how I will meet my end, killed by the Emperor's lapdogs, on this backwater world, left to rot in this forgotten dungeon.' Scorn dripped from Cadmus's voice as he prepared himself for combat.

'Too good an end for the likes of you,' Nathaniel declared, drawing his sword.

'No, Nathaniel. Leave the room,' ordered Jeremiah. 'Trust me in this. If I fall, keep him from running like the coward that he is.'

Nathaniel wanted to protest but he knew better. He would honour Jeremiah's last order regardless of the price. He nodded, then left the room. He had served with Jeremiah for many years and had unwavering confidence in his skills.

'So, Jeremiah, you intend this to be a single combat: you and I to the death?' Cadmus inquired.

'Absolutely, you and I, single combat, to the death,' Jeremiah answered.

'You know you don't stand a chance. I walked the stars when the Lion himself commanded the legion. I was there when Caliban cracked. Even without my armour you are no match for me.' Cadmus said, gloating.

'You will not leave here victorious, Cadmus, but should I fall this day you will be able to leave here unhindered. My brethren will honour my word in this,' Jeremiah commanded.

Jeremiah knew what he had to do, but Cadmus was right about one thing: he had centuries more experience. Jeremiah would not falter, he couldn't; this evil must be stopped. His faith and determination were all he had. He knew that would be enough.

Jeremiah and Cadmus circled each other in the centre of the chamber. The Dark Angel's heart filled with rage. All he had witnessed on Hyades, all the atrocities were the work of one man, but more than that it was the work of one of the Fallen. The Dark Angels had been paying for the betrayal of the Fallen since the Horus Heresy, and even though Jeremiah was responsible for bringing several members of the Fallen before the Interrogator-Chaplains, he had never witnessed the corruption of one of the Fallen so closely before.

'You can't beat me, young lion. You haven't got the skills or the experience,' Cadmus said.

'Your arrogance astounds me, Cadmus. You have turned your back on everything you once stood for, on everything you once held dear. Your fate was sealed the moment you stepped foot on Hyades. Neither my skills nor experience will have much effect on the outcome. Your own actions have determined your fate. I am just an instrument of redemption,' Jeremiah said, speaking from his heart.

Cadmus and Jeremiah slowly circled each other around the centre of the chamber. Both warriors were looking for an opening, a sign of weakness that they could exploit. Suddenly, Cadmus swung his sword in an arcing downwards stroke. Jeremiah parried, and then countered. A quick exchange of attacks and parries were exchanged, each combatant measuring the other's skills.

'You speak of betrayal? You speak of things you know nothing about. Should I tell you of betrayal, should I speak to you of turning your back on your brothers,' Cadmus said, goading his opponent.

Jeremiah knew that Cadmus was trying unbalance him and force him to make a mistake. He knew that he must not listen, must not allow himself the luxury of an emotional response. He would not allow himself to be distracted by mere words.

Jeremiah lunged, striking low, trying to catch Cadmus off-guard. Cadmus easily parried the attack, and then turned his parry into an offensive strike at Jeremiah's midsection. He was barely able to parry the attack without putting himself off balance, a fact that Cadmus quickly exploited, as an armoured gauntlet struck Jeremiah squarely in the mouth, knocking him to the ground. Cadmus did not press his advantage, stopping his attack instead to allow Jeremiah to rise to his feet.

Blood trickled from Jeremiah's nose, which he quickly wiped away. 'Keep your lies to yourself Fallen. We are well aware of your treachery. We all bear the burden of your actions. We are the unforgiven, Cadmus, unforgiven for your cowardly actions and for the actions of the rest of the Fallen. It is a burden we will continue to bear until you and all those like you are redeemed.'

Cadmus leapt towards Jeremiah. Their swords clashed and locked at the hilt. The Fallen leaned in, bringing himself face to face with Jeremiah. 'You spit out words like the programmed fool you are, regurgitating the propaganda that the real betrayers of Caliban concocted. We did not betray the Imperium. We did not allow the Emperor to perish,' Cadmus said, his voice full of rage.

Jeremiah had heard all he could take. 'You may not have thought you were a traitor then, Cadmus, but the seeds of treachery can take a long time to take root. You've given in to Chaos. You've abandoned everything, just as your newfound allies have abandoned you. We hunt the Fallen in an attempt to allow them a chance for redemption. You are no longer a Dark Angel. You're not even one of the Fallen any more. You are nothing more than a pawn that Chaos used to lure a disgraced Space Wolf into a trap. You are pathetic. You are beyond redemption and I will hear no more of your lies!'

Jeremiah pushed Cadmus away, allowing his rage to control his actions. He brought his sword around as he spun, an easy parry for the older warrior. However, Jeremiah attacked anew, with blinding speed and fury. Not allowing Cadmus a moment's respite, each attack came quicker and stronger than the last. The Fallen was giving ground, backing up, unable to ward off the flurry of attacks being thrown out by the young Son of the Lion.

Cadmus's footing finally gave way and he fell to one knee, barely able to parry the latest blow, which knocked him off-balance. Jeremiah spun around, thrusting the sword through the abdomen of the Fallen Dark Angel. Blood erupted from Cadmus's mouth.

Jeremiah bent down to stare into the eyes of his adversary, mimicking the Fallen's last offensive move.

'Your time is at an end, betrayer. Confess your sins and be redeemed,' he spat.

'I will confess nothing,' Cadmus said, coughing up blood.

'The betrayal was not mine but that was your beloved primar-' The Fallen's final words would never be heard as Jeremiah's sword tore up through his chest plate, ending Cadmus's life.

THIRTEEN
An Uneasy Peace

THE TWO GROUPS OF Space Marines stood at opposite sides of Cadmus's secret bunker. Both had private reports to make to their superiors and had respectfully stepped away from each other. Since both teams had comms in their helmets that they could use to subvocalise, the physical separation was more a matter of propriety than practicality. Gabriella sat on the floor near the Space Wolves, rubbing her wrists where her bonds had cut her flesh. Her ordeal had obviously exhausted her, and she seemed focused on recovering her strength.

'Interrogator-Chaplain Vargas, this is Captain Jeremiah of Kill Team Lion's Pride. The threat was eliminated. Our mission has been accomplished,' Jeremiah said, hoping that the signal would reach the Dark Angels battle-barge far above the planet. The static seemed to have died down on the comms.

Nathaniel and Elijah flanked Jeremiah, waiting for the response and watching their Space Wolf counterparts. The mission was over. All that remained for them to do was to protect their secret.

With one eye on the Dark Angels, Ragnar also made contact with his superior. 'Wolf Lord Berek Thunderfist, this is Ragnar of the Wolfblade. The Dark Angels have completed their mission here and will be leaving soon. There is no reason to continue your attack.'

Torin and Haegr stood quietly, weapons at the ready. The tension hung thick in the air. Both sets of Space Marines hoped that the fighting would end.

Jeremiah moved further away, hoping that he would be far enough from the Space Wolves to avoid being overheard. He didn't want to reveal his Chapter's secrets to their most intense rivals, no matter how honourable they were individually.

'Captain Jeremiah, is the heretic dead?' asked Interrogator-Chaplain Vargas, his voice ringing cold and metallic.

'Yes, my lord.'

'Do you have possession of his remains?' asked Vargas.

'We do, yes.'

'Activate your beacon. A retrieval team will come for you,' ordered Vargas.

'Interrogator-chaplain, may I boldly suggest that we break off the conflict with the Space Wolves?' asked Jeremiah.

'You overextend yourself, captain,' replied Vargas.

The conversation between the Wolfblade and the Wolf lord fared no better.

'Young Ragnar, it is good to hear you.' The booming voice of Berek Thunderfist came over the comm. 'Aye, the battle is nearly over, and we will have these traitors and hang their suits of green armour in the Fang as trophies. Bring about the guns again! Blow them into space, lads!'

Ragnar cringed. He had heard that tone in the Wolf Lord's voice before when he had stood shoulder to shoulder with Berek in battle against Chaos Space Marines. He knew what kind of warrior the Wolf Lord was: he lived for battle, and would never stand down.

'Lord Berek, the commander of the PDF forces was a traitor. Chaos has infested this planet. The Dark Angels only attacked to eliminate that threat. We need to stop the fighting. There's no reason for either side to continue this battle.'

'Ragnar, you know that I wish you were still one of my lads instead of a member of the Wolfblade, but I hope your time on Terra hasn't made you soft,' replied Berek. 'The Dark Angels are still firing, and I'll suffer in the frozen hells of Fenris before I drop my shields or let up, so you had better get them to stop first.'

'I understand,' said Ragnar turning off his comm. He looked over to the Dark Angels, to see if the sensitive part of their conversation was over. Jeremiah nodded and waved Ragnar over, even as Jeremiah continued his conversation.

'Interrogator-chaplain, please hear me out,' said Jeremiah, looking at Ragnar. He knew that Ragnar could not stop the Space Wolves, and in truth, Jeremiah knew that the Wolves were merely defending their territory, no matter how things had escalated. He hoped that the next words he spoke would be inspired by the Lion himself.

'We are in possession of the target, his comm, and his bunker. We have all of his information secure but only because a group of Space Wolves have agreed to a truce with us. If we do not cease hostilities and agree to open negotiations, we will come into conflict with them,' Jeremiah said. Then he looked at Ragnar and added, 'The target put up a hard fight, and we will not be able to hold against the Space Wolves. When we fall, they will have possession of all our target's secrets,' he stated aloud for the benefit of the Space Wolves.

Static crackled over the comm. The Dark Angels and Space Wolves fell silent, waiting for the Interrogator-Chaplain's response. Ragnar could feel the apprehension as everyone waited for the reply. The only sound came from one of the infernal beetles, floating in the air, oblivious to the moment.

Elijah grabbed the insect in mid-flight and crushed it in his gauntlet. Despite themselves, the six Space Marines grinned.

'It is my decision, Captain Jeremiah of Kill Team Lion's Pride, that we open negotiations. Such an action will be to our advantage. Maintain your truce. Recover what you need. The Lion watches over you.' The metallic voice of Interrogator-Chaplain Vargas made the last blessing sound far more like a threat.

Torin sub-vocalised over his comm to Ragnar. 'Are you sure about leaving this bunker in possession of the Dark Angels?'

Ragnar nodded ever so slightly. He knew Torin would see the answer. They had Gabriella. She was more important than whatever secrets Cadmus held. Besides, Ragnar was sure that Jeremiah would not end his quest against Chaos. To Ragnar's surprise, he trusted the Dark Angels to ceaselessly battle their mutual enemies. Jeremiah wouldn't give up, any more than Ragnar would.

'Our duty is to protect Lady Gabriella. Jeremiah, I trust you and your battle-brothers will take care of this bunker and of Cadmus,' said Ragnar.

Jeremiah looked Ragnar in the eye. So much had happened between them in such a short time. 'You have my respect, Ragnar of the Wolfblade. You and your brothers are men of honour,' he said.

Ragnar nodded. Saying nothing, he, Torin and Haegr turned and left. Ragnar offered Gabriella his arm for support, but she shook her head.

'I can walk, Ragnar,' she said, favouring him with a weak smile.

'My lady, this bunker is out in the jungle, and you might do well to conserve your strength until we've returned to the city,' he offered.

'Very well, you may assist me,' she said, regaining the tone of authority.

The Space Wolves paused to wordlessly exchange salutes with the Dark Angels, although Gabriella did not acknowledge their recent allies. Jeremiah and his men said nothing, and began their search of the bunker for any information left by Cadmus.

'Come! There are lizard-ape creatures that mighty Haegr wishes to add to his legend,' Haegr said, raising his hammer. 'Follow me,' he bellowed and led the way out of Cadmus's secret base.

INSIDE LETHE, THE battle continued. About halfway between the city centre and the outer walls, Mikal and the Wolf Guard had encountered a squad of Dark Angels. The Dark Angels' weapons were covered in blood and gore, evidence of the many men they had slaughtered since the assault had begun.

Mikal roared as he and the other Wolf Guard fired into the Dark Angels. Seven of their enemy fell as bolter rounds smashed into their ranks. They weren't dead yet, as Space Marines could survive extreme amounts of damage, but they were out of the action. The three remaining Dark Angels reached the ranks of the Wolf Guard, swinging their chainswords and firing their bolt pistols. Mikal licked his fangs. Like most Space Wolves, he preferred dealing with his enemy in hand-to-hand combat.

Chainsword struck ceramite as a Dark Angel thrust at Mikal. The Wolf Guard swung his power fist into the helm of his attacker, disregarding the chainsword strike, trusting that his armour would hold. It did, and the power fist made short work of his opponent's helm.

A shrill cry cut through the air, followed by hissing from all directions. Mikal caught movement in his peripheral vision. New attackers swarmed the Space Marines. Large reptilian humanoids leapt from buildings and rushed into the warriors from all sides.

These new foes stood as tall as the Space Marines. Grey-green scales covered their bodies along with tufts of green, brown and red fur. Their large eyes were yellow with diamond-shaped black pupils. Long fangs and sharp teeth filled their jaws, although they moved more like primates than lizards. Many of them had strange warpaint in red and purple streaked across their bodies. Fearlessly, they launched themselves at the Space Marines.

The attack startled the Wolf Guard, but it did not deter them. No matter the foe, they would fight for their Chapter and the Emperor. If these creatures did not already know enough to fear the Space Wolves, then by the end of the day they would.

Serrated jaws clamped on Mikal's arms, although they had less of an impact than the chainsword had moments before. Mikal threw the creature aside, and blew the guts out of another with his storm bolter. In their power armour, the Space Wolves were nearly impervious to the creatures' blows, but the sheer weight of the attackers' numbers threatened to drag Mikal and the Wolf Guard down.

Mikal redoubled his efforts, giving the wulfen its head and letting the anger and fury within his breast guide him. He was a berserker, slashing and smashing his foes. Mikal tore through tails and teeth, heads and hearts, pushing himself to the limits to overcome his enemies.

The Wolf Guard were hard-pressed. Mikal saw his men pulled down under the horde of aliens to his left and right. They still moved in their armour and he had every hope that they still lived, but the tide of beasts was too much. They could not hold.

The ground shook violently. Mikal didn't notice at first, thinking that it was more explosions. Then screeching started from the horde of creatures. Several hissed and turned to face something down the street. A large shadow blocked out the sun and one of the beasts fighting Mikal unlocked its jaws and leapt away.

A giant metal claw flung the bodies of three lizard creatures skyward against the smoke- and flame-filled heavens. Mikal felt his blood boil with pride. The shadow belonged to a massive venerable Dreadnought. Towering over the enemy, Gymir the Ice-Fisted reached down to slay them in massive swathes. The mighty Dreadnought had come to the aid of his fellow Space Wolves.

'Die, xenos scum! Face the fury of Fenris,' Gymir boomed through his array of speakers.

Gymir continued to wield his power claw like a scythe, moving it back and forth, and cutting down the creatures in a gory harvest. Bones snapped as the Dreadnought unleashed his might against the beasts. The mere presence of the ancient machine shook the aliens, who stared and hissed at the machine in fear, frustration and rage. Ultimately, fear won out over the other emotions, and the surviving lizards broke off their attack and scattered in all directions. Gymir stood, surrounded by mounds of bodies, looking for more of the creatures to fight. Finding none, he turned with a whirr to face Mikal.

'Are you well, my brothers?' asked Gymir.

'Aye,' answered Mikal.

As the Wolf Guard clambered to their feet and re-formed, Mikal noticed something unusual. The bodies of the Dark Angels lay shredded. Mikal walked over and knelt down beside the body of one of the fallen Space Marines.

During the attack, some of the creatures had opened up the Space Marine's power armour and dug their claws into his flesh. Mikal felt a chill run through him. Chunks had been dug out of the Dark Angel. Organs had been removed, including the Space Marine's gene-seed. He checked the other bodies; all of them showed the same signs. The beasts had been collecting the gene-seed of the Emperor's finest.

Mikal looked over at the Wolf Guard and then up to Gymir. 'The creatures stole the Dark Angels' gene-seed,' he roared.

Mikal's comm crackled to life. 'Wolf Guard Mikal, this is Lieutenant Markham. We have reptos entering the city in untold numbers.'

ABOVE THE PLANET, the *Fist of Russ* hung in space and for the moment her guns lay silent. The Dark Angels' fleet backed away from the Space Wolves' ships while Thunderhawks from the planet below docked with their parent vessels.

From his bridge, sitting in his stone command chair, Wolf Lord Berek Thunderfist could not believe his eyes. The battle runes indicated the Dark Angels' retreat, as did the holographic projections of the battle. The Dark Angels were breaking off their attack. The ship's herald called to him, 'M'lord, we are receiving hails from the Dark Angels' battle-barge.'

Berek waited for a moment. He couldn't believe that Ragnar had negotiated something like this. He knew that the young lad had courage to spare and a zeal for battle, but Ragnar wasn't a diplomat unless his time with the Wolfblade had changed him quite a bit.

The Wolf Lord's men held their posts, waiting for orders. They would follow Berek into the Eye of Terror itself if he so commanded. The Wolf Lord stood up. 'Herald, accept the transmission from the Dark Angels.'

The herald touched a rune and two of the carved wolfs' heads opened their jaws to reveal hidden speakers.

A cold metallic voice came over the speaker. 'Space Wolf commander, this is Interrogator-Chaplain Vargas of the *Vinco Redemptor*. We are withdrawing our forces from your planet. We trust that you have the strength to keep Chaos in check, now that you are here in numbers. We have stopped our assaults on your vessels, but be assured, we will defend ourselves if you do not break off your attack immediately.'

Berek cleared his throat and took the comms console. The ship's herald stepped back. 'This is Wolf Lord Berek Thunderfist, Interrogator-Chaplain. I'm sure you realise that I'm familiar with your Chapter's history of treachery and duplicity.'

'Just as we are familiar with your reputation as ignorant barbarians,' replied Vargas.

'Good,' said Berek baring his fangs. 'Since we understand one another, you are retreating, and you are asking us not to fire upon you. I can understand that, since we've nearly crippled your precious battle-barge and bled you white on the surface. We will stand down. After all, I don't want to leave the Imperium without one of its Chapters of Space Marines, even the Dark Angels, but my men might like to hear you announcing your retreat.'

'I will not rise to your bait, Space Wolf. We will only fire if fired upon. We have accomplished our purpose. The rest of the mess is yours, Wolf Lord. I also do not wish to leave mankind without several of its defenders, even when they've let their territory be infiltrated by Chaos.'

'Good, so you are retreating,' said Berek.

'We will withdraw once we have retrieved all of our men from the surface,' answered Interrogator-Chaplain Vargas.

The battle in space was over.

THE MEMBERS OF the Wolfblade made their way through Hyades's jungles back towards the city. Ragnar supported Gabriella, while he, Torin and Haegr kept up as fast a pace as they could. Choker vines lashed out at them, and they splattered through swarms of buzzing beetles.

One of the trees tried to trip up Haegr with its roots. The giant Space Wolf swung his hammer around and smashed through the living wood. The entire tree shuddered. 'And don't try that again,' Haegr warned it.

When Torin, Haegr and Ragnar burst from the jungle into the kill zone, several columns of smoke and clouds of dust greeted them. Mounds of broken rockcrete marred the once invincible walls of Lethe. One of the gates hung open. Thunderous explosions echoed from the city. The battle hadn't ended yet.

'We've made it to the city. Now we just need to get through the fighting to the palace and find a shuttle,' said Gabriella. She still looked tired, but she had regained her air of command.

Ragnar's comm crackled to life. 'This is Wolf Lord Berek Thunderfist. Ragnar, lad, if you're out there, answer.'

'This is Ragnar. Have the Dark Angels retreated?' Ragnar was curious since the explosions hadn't stopped.

'They are retreating. I'm impressed, young one. Only one thing prevents us from removing the Dark Angels. The Hyades defence forces keep firing on them. The governor doesn't answer his comm, and well, I know about the commander. Where is Lady Gabriella? Aren't you her bodyguard? I need someone to order the planetary defenders to stand down against the Dark Angels,' the Wolf Lord chuckled. 'Mikal went out onto the battlefield, but I'm having trouble raising him. Do you have Lady Gabriella?'

'Yes, Wolf Lord. She is here with us,' Ragnar replied.

'Wolf Lord Berek Thunderfist is on the comm. He asks you to order the Hyades Planetary Defence Force to stand down against the Dark Angels,' said Ragnar.

Gabriella leaned over to speak into the comm system. 'This is Lady Gabriella of House Belisarius, Wolf Lord Berek Thunderfist. I will immediately give the order to cease hostilities against the Dark Angels.'

'Good to hear your voice, my lady,' said the Wolf Lord. 'We're still ready to defend House Belisarius. I understand that you have a xenos problem on the ground, but I think it's time to start by removing the Dark Angels.'

'House Belisarius will not keep them here. I'm giving the orders now.'

'Aye. Berek Thunderfist, out,' responded the Wolf Lord.

Gabriella adjusted the comm codes. 'Hyades Planetary Defence Forces, this is Lady Gabriella of House Belisarius. You are ordered to cease hostilities against the invading Dark Angels. They have agreed to withdraw. The Space Wolves will help restore order. Governor Pelias and Commander Cadmus have fallen, and as of this moment, you will take all orders from Wolf Lord Berek Thunderfist or myself. Again, cease all attacks on the Dark Angels immediately.'

'Now, we just need to listen,' said Torin. 'If the guns stop, you did it m'lady. If not, then we're in for a long bout of fighting.'

Without saying anything, the four stood in the kill zone and listened. The regular blasts of the guns slowed, and then stopped. The only sounds Ragnar could hear were servos in the Space Marines' armour and the ever-present buzz of beetles.

'They stopped,' said Ragnar.

'Pity,' said Haegr, 'I would have preferred to thrash the lot of them.'

'Now, we just have to survive the reptos,' said Ragnar, 'and with Berek's company here, we will.'

'Lady Gabriella,' offered Torin, 'let's get you to the House Belisarius shuttle, assuming it's in one piece, and safely off this planet.'

'Finally, Torin has a good idea,' said Haegr.

The four of them clambered over the remnants of a wall and entered the city.

THE WOLFBLADE'S TREK to the city centre revealed the full extent of the devastation. Buildings lay shattered and broken. Craters pockmarked the roads, and the landscape more resembled a volcanic badland than a city. Despite the devastation to the landscape, the real horror came from the number of bodies lying strewn everywhere.

Bodies lay scattered, rotting in the ruins. Some of the corpses wore the colours of the Planetary Defence Force, but far more were civilians. The stench of death and decay burned Ragnar's nostrils. The dead had looks of pain and horror on their faces. Ragnar had a new respect for the terror that Space Marines could inspire in their foes. Lethe had suffered horribly, there was nothing but ruins and flames in all directions. Torin kept pausing and checking his auspex to make certain that they were heading in the proper direction.

'By the Emperor,' said Gabriella, as she stared at the limp body of a child at the edge of a crater, 'what evil guided Cadmus?'

'The worst kind of evil, Gabriella,' said Ragnar, 'Chaos... and not only Chaos, but the work of our worst enemies, the Thousand Sons.'

The mere thought of the Thousand Sons made Ragnar's anger rise within him. Throughout his entire career as a Space Wolf, they had proven to be the most relentless of foes. The legends all spoke of the Thousand Sons as the greatest enemies of the Space Wolves, and Ragnar would vouch for every one of those stories. The passionate rivalry between the Space Wolves and the Dark Angels was a mere shadow of the shared hate between the Space Wolves and the Thousand Sons.

For Ragnar, battling the Thousand Sons was personal. He had served with Berek when he had last fought the Thousand Sons and defeated them using the Spear of Russ. How ironic that he had come face to face with more of that traitor Chapter while Berek's great company fought the Dark Angels both in orbit and on the surface of Hyades.

Still, it was a day of victory. The Dark Angels were leaving, and although they had encountered Chaos Space Marines, the members of the Wolfblade had defeated them. Cadmus lay dead, his body in possession of the Dark Angels.

The ground shook. Then, it shook again and again... and again. The sound of the explosions kept growing in volume, one after another, after another. A column of white flame burst from the street in front of the Space Wolves. It became a wall of white fire, extending in both directions and rising to nearly thirty metres. The scent of burning promethium was unmistakable.

'Take cover,' yelled Torin.

The next blast threw all of them off their feet, even Haegr. The ground was scalding hot. The explosions weren't like any they had experienced so far in the battle.

Ragnar took cover with the others behind a large still-standing wall with an overhang from what had once been the second floor of a building. Now, it was shelter against a burning rain. He tried to comprehend what was happening. The aerial bombardment had stopped some time ago, what could be causing these explosions?

The smell of promethium was so strong that he wondered if the refineries were blowing up. He could even taste the fuel on his tongue.

The explosions continued in all directions and smoke billowed upwards from cracks in the streets. The blasts were coming from below.

'What is happening?' asked Haegr.

'I'm not sure,' said Gabriella.

'With the smell of promethium everywhere...' started Ragnar.

'The only thing that I can think of is that something in the refineries, the tunnels or the mines has gone terribly wrong,' finished Torin.

Gabriella looked at the members of her Wolfblade, and then settled her gaze on Ragnar. 'We've got to get to the shuttle now,' she said.

'I know. If the promethium has ignited,' said Ragnar, 'we'll cook if we stay here.'

'I see something ahead,' said Haegr. 'Follow me.'

'Be careful,' said Torin.

Ragnar saw Haegr's target. A Chimera sat quietly in the street with its ramp down. The bodies of the men who had once occupied the vehicle lay scattered around the ramp. Bolter holes in the bodies and the distinctive cuts of chainswords indicated that these men had encountered the Dark Angels and things had not gone well.

Torin went to the main hatch, which appeared to have been forced open. He reached down into the driver's compartment and pulled out a charred corpse. 'They killed the drivers too,' he said, scooping out another blackened body and throwing it down to the pavement with a wet thunk. The stench was awful. 'I'll make this thing work. I'm driving. With your permission, m'lady, I believe that this vehicle will allow us to reach the shuttle much more safely,' he said.

'Take us there, Torin. Let's go inside, away from this burning debris,' said Gabriella. Wisps of ash and promethium gently fell from the sky, contrasting with the continuing eruptions.

'You want me to get in one of these, again?' asked Haegr.

'Yes,' said Ragnar. He wanted no delays.

Torin shook his head and climbed into the front of the vehicle. Haegr swore upon the private parts of Fenrisian wolves, but he crouched and angled his way inside.

Static crackled over Ragnar's comm, and he cursed under his breath. He banged his fist against the driver's compartment. 'Torin, I can't get a signal again.'

'I suspect we have interference,' replied Torin.

Ragnar wasn't in the mood for Torin's ability to state the obvious, although he knew his battle-brother faced the task of driving the Chimera through the exploding hell that Lethe had become. He had to think for a moment.

'Torin, what about the Chimera's comm system? Could I access that? Shouldn't it have more signal?' asked Ragnar.

'Try it yourself. There's a comm station right next to your seat,' said Torin.

Ragnar activated the comms on the tank as it rumbled through the debris towards the palace. Gabriella had strapped herself in, but Haegr was fighting with his seat. 'Just how do ogryns ever fit in these things?' he asked.

'Ogryns are smaller than mighty Haegr, I suspect,' said Ragnar, finding the heart to joke. Inside, he prayed to the Emperor to let the comm work. All he received was static.

'By Morkai's Axe,' said Ragnar, 'I can't contact Berek.' He shook the comm, frustrated with the constant signal interference adding to everything else falling apart around them.

A crackle came over the system. Ragnar had a signal. It was weak, but it was a signal nonetheless.

'This is Ragnar to Wolf Lord Berek. Can you hear me?' asked Ragnar.

'This is the *Fist of Russ*, Ragnar, ship's herald here. The Wolf Lord is busy,' came the reply.

The Chimera struck something in one of the roads, bounced, and then got very hot. Haegr cursed again as his head hit the roof of the cramped transport chamber. 'We had better get there soon,' he growled.

'I need to talk to the Wolf Lord. All this isn't just the work of the traitor Cadmus,' said Ragnar.

'This is Berek,' said the voice of the Wolf Lord over the comm. 'Wolfblade Ragnar, the events on the planet below are the work of Chaos. Since you have Lady Gabriella with you, leave the surface of Hyades as soon as you can,'

'Someone ignited the promethium mines,' said Ragnar. 'Everything's exploding.'

'Heh, lad,' said Berek. 'You should see the view from space.'

'What do you mean, my lord?' asked Ragnar.

'The pattern of the burning forms an oval. In fact, it looks like a flaming eye glaring up from the planet, and it's visible from space. I can see it from the observation decks. From your signal, you should be near the centre–'

The comm died. 'In the name of Russ,' said Ragnar. He dropped the comm quietly, taking in the impact of what he had heard.

Gabriella screamed. Light glowed from beneath her headband and she shook violently.

She gurgled something incoherent. Tears streamed down her cheeks and she banged her head against the Chimera's restraints. Ragnar saw her muscles tense. A vein bulged in her neck.

'Gabriella. What's wrong?' asked Ragnar.

'How can we help her?' asked Haegr as Ragnar pulled a med-kit from its storage bin in the back of the Chimera.

Gabriella started hyperventilating.

Ragnar grabbed her hands.

'Hold on, come back to us, your Wolfblade. We're in the Chimera on Lethe.'

Gabriella's breathing slowed and her eyes met Ragnar's. 'Ragnar, something terrible is happening. There are... many disturbances in the warp.'

'Hold on,' shouted Torin from the driver's seat in the front. 'We're heading through a wall of fire.'

Everything became extremely hot and there was a loud bang. The Chimera lurched to the right, sending Haegr flying across into Ragnar. Neither Space Wolf was wearing safety restraints, but fortunately neither of them landed on Gabriella. Torin swore something from the driver's seat in front as he fought for control of the tank.

Another loud bang sent the Chimera lurching back to the left. The two Space Wolves tumbled to the other side of the tank. Gabriella's restraints kept her secure.

'In Russ's name!' said Haegr as Ragnar smashed into him.

Ragnar thought the Chimera had become airborne for a moment, and then a third loud bang reverberated through the vehicle, followed by a metallic grinding. He knew that at the least, the tank had broken multiple tracks. Ragnar smelled oil and the terrible grinding sound continued from the right side of the transport vehicle. With a loud boom, the Chimera shook and jolted from side to side, before coming to a rest with a resounding thud. At least they had stayed upright. Ragnar and Haegr both climbed to their feet.

'Everyone alive back there? Sorry about that – driving conditions are rather poor at the moment,' snarled Torin.

Ragnar ignored Torin for the moment. 'Gabriella, are you all right?' he asked. He looked at her bloodshot eyes and immediately realised it wasn't one of the brightest questions that he had ever asked.

Gabriella managed a smile, as she seemed to notice what a stupid question it was.

'Mighty Haegr is getting out,' announced Haegr. He pushed open the rear access ramp. Stepping outside, he drew his hammer.

Ragnar took a moment to examine Gabriella for additional injuries. Once he was confident that she was relatively unharmed, he joined Haegr.

Reptos swarmed all around them, leaping and running as explosions went off in all directions. There were hundreds of them, milling around in a frenzied mass. One of the creatures paused to stare at the Space Wolves. As if given a silent signal, the others stopped as well, and then the mass of creatures turned their heads as one to glare at the Space Wolves.

Showing their fangs and hissing, they advanced on the Space Wolves, their previous panic apparently forgotten.

'Hah,' said Haegr, clapping Ragnar's shoulder and raising his hammer. 'Lad, the two of us have them outnumbered.'

FOURTEEN
The True Enemy

Surrounded by reptos, Ragnar and Haegr took the only course of action that made any sense at all: they charged.

Ragnar remembered when his squad of Blood Claws had dropped in the wrong location on Garm and had been overrun by hundreds of Garmites. Only the actions of his old friend Sven and their fallen sergeant Hakon had saved him that day. Then, he had fought like a man possessed; now it was time to do so again. He just wished he had a heavy weapon to provide some covering fire.

Haegr swung his thunder hammer around, scattering reptos with the force of the blow. The huge warrior seemed almost inhuman, as if he were a miniature Dreadnought rather than a man. Bodies of reptos flew into the air and the hammer boomed like its namesake. A spray of flesh, scales, bone and blood erupted with each swing and Haegr laughed.

Where Haegr used large strokes to scatter the enemy before him, Ragnar leapt into a knot of the creatures. His blade sliced through bodies, sending blood running into the streets. One clamped its jaws on his sword arm, so he took his bolt pistol and put a shot into its skull. He flung the corpse off his arm into the midsection of two others and finished them both with shots. Without hesitating, Ragnar spun around, swinging his sword in a deadly arc that took down two more that were attacking him from behind.

He slammed a repto with the front of his bolt pistol and then fired. The round ripped through the first creature and blew a hole out of the back of the second. Claws raked at his armour, trying to find a weakness. Ragnar felt the scrapes and scratches and the impact of the blows threatened to unbalance him. If he fell, they would win by sheer weight of numbers, but he wouldn't let that happen.

He looked to Haegr. In one hand the giant still held his hammer, but with the other, he swung a repto by its tail. He slammed the creature back and forth into its brothers as if it were a reptilian blackjack. The repto screamed and its brethren hesitated, uncertain how to react to Haegr's improvised weapon. Taking advantage of the moment, Ragnar sprang into the air, flipping over some would-be attackers and crossing to Haegr.

Haegr smashed the street with his lizard flail again and again. The creature was just a sack of skin now, barely holding its remains inside.

Torin dived out of the driver's hatch of the Chimera, firing shots from his bolter as he moved. With a blade in one hand, he expertly decapitated the closest repto, as he maintained his firing. Another repto sprang high into the air at Torin, but the Space Wolf's reflexes allowed him to sidestep the creature's pounce and bring his blade around in a downwards stroke that severed the beast's spinal cord.

All three Space Wolves moved towards each other, forming a circle of blades and bolter fire. The frenzied mass of reptos lost member after member, but it seemed they would never stop coming. Then, the knot of alien beasts was gone. The Space Wolves had broken the horde. The survivors turned tail and disappeared into the smoke of the burning city.

Gabriella walked down the ramp of the Chimera. She had a slight limp, but still managed to hold herself tall. She cradled a lasgun in her arms, and she had a med-kit slung over her shoulder. 'I shot a few on the other side of the Chimera,' she said, looking at the ruined tracks of the vehicle. 'How far are we from the shuttle hangar in the main city complex?'

Torin took an auspex from his belt, while Ragnar and Haegr instinctively checked the area for more signs of immediate danger. 'We're less than five hundred metres from the city centre. Despite the interference, I can still pick up on the signals from the palace. It's this way, follow me,' said Torin. 'We'll have to walk the rest of the way.'

BEREK WAS STANDING on the bridge of the *Fist of Russ*, glaring down at the surface of Hyades, with Morgrim, his skald, standing beside him. The face of the Wolf Lord was contorted with rage at the sight of an eye burning on the planet below.

'Curse the Dark Angels for their arrogance,' he snarled. 'Bring us around. What damage have we suffered?'

An Iron Priest, one of the Space Wolves' own Techspace Marines, stood on the bridge, alongside the many Fenrisian warriors assigned as crew. A huge servo-arm shifted on his back and he held a massive thunder hammer with many wolf tails hanging from it, a sign of worth over his many years of service. 'My lord, the battle has drained many of the ship's spirits. The strength of the generators is spent. The proper rites and rituals are replenishing their energy, but for now, providing shields and engines is the extent of their ability. To restore them would take time.'

'Restore the spirits as quickly as you can. I trust in the rites and rituals of my Iron Priest,' Berek said, flexing his power fist for emphasis.

'My lord, I am picking up some strange signals,' said Hroth. 'I'm detecting ships at the edge of Hyades's space.'

'More Dark Angels?' asked Berek. 'Do they ever stand ready to interfere in our business?'

'No, my lord, these are not Imperial vessels...' Hroth's expression hardened. 'Wolf Lord, a Chaos fleet approaches!'

The guide touched the activation runes of the holographic projector. The Dark Angels ships moving to the edge of the display appeared green, while the Hyades defence patrol and the Space Wolf vessels showed blue. Flickering red shapes indicated the incoming enemy ships.

'Give me a tactical report,' growled the Wolf Lord.

'The fleet appears to be composed of a number of cruisers, escort ships and one larger vessel, a Styx-class heavy cruiser,' replied Hroth.

'Let's hope we didn't cripple that Dark Angels' battle-barge too badly, lads,' snarled Berek. 'We'll need her guns. Herald, open a channel to the Dark Angels. Iron Priest, how long until the generator spirits have their strength renewed? Has Mikal reported on withdrawing from Hyades? I want my Thunderhawks back and my men ready to board the enemy vessels.'

Berek considered the tactical possibilities. Most Imperial strategists would say that the Chaos fleet should split, sending half their force to one side of the Imperial vessels and half to the other and trap them in the middle. It would be a good strategy, considering the range and armaments of the Chaos ships, and it might work.

These Chaos ships must have known about the battle between the Space Wolves and the Dark Angels to be ready to take advantage of them so quickly. Analysing the tactics of his enemies, he determined that they would soon close for the attack, bringing their guns to bear and attempting to board his ships. After all, they had a battered Space Wolf fleet in their sights.

'A large number of Chaos fighters have launched and are forming up ahead of the main cruisers,' announced Hroth. 'I believe that they are meant to screen the cruisers from our guns and shoot down any Thunderhawks we launch, milord.'

'I suspect you are correct, Hroth. Alert the fleet to be ready for the enemy to close directly with us,' said the Wolf Lord. 'Iron Priest, see if the spirits can find us a bit more essence. I will need all our weapons for this battle.'

'Of course, milord. I will oversee the libations and rituals on the generators myself.' The Iron Priest strode off the bridge past the banners and carved wolf heads.

'Half of the Thunderhawks have returned to the ship,' announced the ship's herald.

'Where's my channel to the Dark Angels?' demanded Berek.

'I have them now, Lord Berek,' responded the herald.

The *Vinco Redemptor* had moved down towards Hyades, nearly touching the atmosphere. On the holographic display, several Thunderhawks were docking with the Dark Angels' battle-barge. The Dark Angels were pulling all of their troops back.

'Interrogator-Chaplain Vargas, this is Wolf Lord Berek Thunderfist. I hope that you and your men are ready to defend the Imperium from an actual enemy,' said Berek.

'Wolf Lord Berek Thunderfist, this is Interrogator-Chaplain Vargas. We have agreed to withdraw and withdraw we shall. The enemy has numbers and both of our fleets are weary. We are currently receiving the last of our vessels. Hyades is lost to us. We shall return with the wrath of the Lion at the appropriate time.' Interrogator-Chaplain Vargas's voice was metallic and inhuman, which Berek felt matched Vargas's heart.

'Get out of the system, and don't worry, we won't need you watching our backs. You've done enough damage. This isn't over,' snarled Berek.

The last green blips representing Thunderhawk gunships disappeared as they touched the holographic image of the *Vinco Redemptor*. The Dark Angels' withdrawal was complete.

'It is over. May the Emperor watch over you if you decide to throw away your lives defending this corrupt planet,' said the Dark Angel commander.

'We understand about defending a man's home world,' retorted Berek.

He cut the channel on the Interrogator-Chaplain, hoping to annoy the Dark Angels by having the last word. The Dark Angels' lack of compassion and lack of apparent desire to defend the Imperium annoyed him deeply. Berek hoped that Vargas would catch the reference to losing a home world and take it as he meant it, as a reminder that the Dark Angels had failed to defend their own world during the Horus Heresy.

'All the ships fire with full guns,' commanded Berek. 'Let's blow through the Chaos fighter screens quickly and cripple those Chaos cruisers before the Styx joins the fray.'

Even as Berek gave the order, he could see the cloud of red blips on the holographic display descending on the blue ones.

THROUGH THE HAZE of promethium smoke, Ragnar could see the palace. The structure was burning, like everything else, although the banner of House Belisarius still waved. Five ogryns stood in front of the palace, the same ones that the Wolfblade had fought earlier. They looked relatively untouched from the day's events. Ragnar couldn't believe that the monstrous mutants were still on guard. The abhumans hadn't appeared to notice the Space Wolves' approach due to the smoke all around them.

Haegr readied his thunder hammer. Torin calmly unsheathed his sword and raised his bolt pistol. Ragnar stepped in front of Gabriella. He didn't want to take a chance on the ogryns' ripper guns shredding her. He would protect her with his armoured body if need be.

As the Space Marines approached, the ogryns finally spotted them. The huge mutants leered down at the Space Wolves and readied their guns more as clubs than shooting weapons. The largest of them roared and flexed his huge arms. If he meant to intimidate the Space Wolves, then he failed.

'Wait,' said Torin, 'they aren't firing,'

'So?' Ragnar and Haegr responded as one.

'Don't you see? They are obeying orders. In their simple way, they are doing what they were ordered to do, guard the palace,' said Torin.

'And we need to enter the palace, Torin, so we need to kill them,' said Ragnar.

'Wait,' said Gabriella, 'if they are so devoutly following orders, maybe they would follow new orders.'

'My thoughts exactly,' said Torin.

Gabriella stepped in front of Ragnar and addressed the ogryns. 'I am Lady Gabriella of House Belisarius. Commander Cadmus is dead. I am in charge. Go fight the reptos. Kill them all.'

Ragnar exchanged looks with Torin. Gabriella folded her arms across her chest. The ogryns tilted their heads from side to side as if they were trying to understand.

'Yes, lady,' said the lead ogryn. 'Bring you dead ape-lizards.'

Gabriella pointed back the way the Space Wolves had come. 'That way,' she prompted.

The ogryns nodded, and then the five abhumans charged off into the smoke and flame with their ripper guns at the ready, never glancing back. Ragnar watched them disappear in the promethium haze.

Gabriella touched her temple and winced. Ragnar could see her forehead wrinkle around her headband. Her third eye was active. There was psychic activity somewhere, disturbances in the warp. It was straining Gabriella. Ragnar wondered how much of a curse these psyker gifts were. For a moment, he gave a fleeting thought back to Lars, a fey touched youth who had been part of his first pack. The youth had always suffered from haunted visions before giving his life for the Imperium. Ragnar thought Gabriella was stronger than Lars had been, despite the fact that she was no Space Wolf. Still, whatever was happening was taking a greater and greater toll on her.

'What is it?' asked Torin.

'An ancient evil approaches. We need to get off the planet and join up with the Space Wolf fleet. Then we can worry about defeating the enemy,' said Gabriella.

ON THE BRIDGE of the *Fist of Russ*, Berek cursed. 'By the blood of Russ! Those cowards,' shouted the Wolf Lord. The Dark Angels vessels were fleeing the engagement. They had accomplished their task, ruined Hyades's defences, damaged the Space Wolf fleet, and now they were leaving. Berek had hoped that his final taunt about defending a home world would have changed their minds, but it wasn't so.

The Chaos fleet was closing in on the Space Wolves and its fighter screen had already arrived. Guns blazed across the battle-barge as it shot down dozens of small enemy craft. A Chaos fighter crashed against the hull of the *Fist of Russ*. Two Chaos cruisers closed the kilometres quickly, readying their broadside guns. The screen of Chaos escorts was scattered space dust, but they had fulfilled their mission. Nothing would stop the enemy cruisers from bringing their big guns to bear.

Berek turned to his skald. 'Horgrim, make sure that a Thunderhawk is ready for me. If Mikal's back from the surface, get my Wolf Guard, if not, I want Krom's Grey Hunters. I'm going to give these Chaos bastards a taste of the Thunderfist.'

'Yes, Wolf Lord.' Horgrim knew that Berek wanted this task completed immediately, otherwise he wouldn't have given it to his most trusted advisor.

Berek knew if he could fire the Nova cannon without completely draining the ship, the *Fist of Russ* had a chance. If they could take out one cruiser with a single shot, and that's all that they'd have, then they could board the other while the Iron Priests strengthened the ship's spirits. He wouldn't concern himself about the other vessels. The powerful engines of the Chaos cruisers had put them further forwards than the rest of their fleet. If the Space Wolves could deal with this threat, then they would have time to figure out the rest.

'The Iron Priest reports that we have enough power for the Nova cannon, my lord,' shouted the ship's guide with unabashed enthusiasm.

'Excellent,' said Berek, smiling. 'We'll only have time for one shot with it before they close. Horgrim, have my Thunderhawk wait.'

The *Fist of Russ* shuddered as the spirits of the Nova cannon drew all available power. Berek watched the lights dim across the bridge, growing dark in the wolfs' heads. He could see the glow from the engines of the escorts and Thunderhawk gunships streaking around his ship like the auroras of Fenris. Russ was with them. 'Fire!' he ordered.

The beam exploded out from the prow of the *Fist of Russ*. It felt as if the legendary Firewolf itself had opened its maw and unleashed the fury of every volcano on Fenris as one.

'Lord Berek, the spirits of the Nova cannon have drawn too much power in their zeal,' said the voice of the Iron Priest.

Warning runes glared red across the bridge. The hull of the *Fist of Russ* roared. Berek clenched his teeth and raised his power fist.

The beam struck home against the Chaos cruiser, spearing it through and erupting from the other side to continue tearing through space. The holographic display showed the blast continuing unabated, glancing another distant cruiser, but all eyes on the bridge focused on the main target. The enemy ship shivered, and was replaced for an instant by a new sun in the Hyades system. As the light faded, there was nothing left.

Cheers came from the officers and crew of the *Fist of Russ*. Several men pumped their fists and more than a few threw back their heads to howl.

Berek shouted, 'Let's go and show those treacherous spawn how warriors of Fenris fight! To the Thunderhawks!'

THE SURVIVING MEMBERS of the Wolfblade and Gabriella had arrived at the shuttle hangar in the heart of the Imperial palace. Once they had passed the ogryns, they had fought through minimal opposition, just a few Planetary Defence Forces holding to a misguided loyalty to the now-dead Cadmus.

Torin activated the locks to the hangar doors. The inside of the hangar was stacked with supplies and a few servitors went about their duties. The House Belisarius shuttle sat, remarkably unscathed, in the centre of the hangar. Her hatches were closed, indicating that the crew was on board and that they had taken the proper defensive stance. The lights on the shuttle activated as the Space Wolves and Gabriella entered. Russ be praised, thought Ragnar.

They had barely taken three steps when the speakers on the shuttle crackled to life. 'Lady Gabriella, Wolfblade, behind you!'

'What? Who would dare?' asked Haegr, apparently forgetful of the traitors, xenos and Chaos Space Marines on Hyades.

Clad in glittering blue and gold armour, nine Chaos Space Marines had entered the open hangar doors. Each one wore his own heraldry, but each of them had the symbol of Tzeentch emblazoned upon his power armour. The power of the Chaos god infected the warriors, causing their armour to glow with faint tongues of fire. Ragnar could feel the hate of ten thousand years burning in them. Every one was a potential match for a Wolfblade. One among them wore a glittering cape and had a tall spiked helm. A blue flame wrapped itself around his left gauntlet.

The Chaos Space Marine sorcerer gestured, raising the blue flame towards the ceiling. A voice came from the fire itself.

'We would dare.'

The silky mocking voice echoed in Ragnar's soul. He'd know that voice anywhere. It was Madox, the same Chaos Space Marine who had assaulted Fenris, the mastermind behind the theft of the Spear of Russ and the one who had nearly killed Ragnar's best friend, Sven.

'Madox,' shouted Ragnar.

'As always, Ragnar Blackmane, it is good to be recognised. Alas, I shall not have the luxury of killing you personally, but we must all make some sacrifices.'

The Chaos Space Marines aimed their bolters at the Space Wolves. Gabriella dived for cover behind some supply crates, holding onto her lasgun. Ragnar felt his blood run cold for an instant, but he was shocked out of any hesitation by his battle-brother, Haegr.

Haegr shouted, 'Hah! They didn't account for you and Ragnar, Torin. There are barely enough of them for me.' Then the giant bellowed and charged.

Torin readied his bolter and growled softly.

For once, Ragnar agreed with Haegr; all they could do was fight. 'For Fenris,' he yelled, and joined Haegr's charge.

FIFTEEN
Escape to Fenris

NINE CHAOS SPACE MARINES, including a sorcerer, confronted Ragnar, Torin and Haegr in the shuttle hangar. The crew of the shuttle had activated their ship's systems in preparation for launch, but the Space Wolves wouldn't be able to board unless they stopped the Chaos Space Marines first.

Haegr charged the enemy with a tremendous roar. Though hardened from thousands of years of combat, even the Chaos Space Marines appeared taken aback by the giant Space Wolf's charge. For a moment, they hesitated as Haegr closed with them.

Three of the Chaos warriors swung their bolters at Haegr. Ragnar heard shrieks come from the Chaos bolter rounds as they burned through the air, smashing into the Space Wolf. Ragnar heard the crack of power armour, yet Haegr had reached full speed and the force of the shots wouldn't slow him. Three more of the Thousand Sons commenced firing on Haegr.

Perhaps the real reason for their hesitation was that they hadn't decided how best to kill the giant Space Marine.

Looking at the Thousand Sons, Ragnar did not see them as much as feel the emotions they radiated. Their ornate gold and lapis lazuli armour evoked racial memories of the most ancient of humanity's gods with its ancient shapes and markings. Daemonic forms twisted and melted on the polished surfaces of the metal. Ragnar saw the hate burn inside them as they mercilessly fired at Haegr.

Ragnar knew this foe was a full-fledged sorcerer; not as powerful as Madox, but truly an enemy to be reckoned with. Ragnar and Torin didn't wait. The last two members of the Wolfblade drew their weapons and charged. Ragnar's runeblade glowed as he closed with the enemy. Torin thumbed the activation rune on his blade.

The sorcerer gestured at his attackers. Ragnar saw a flash, and a bolt of dark energy lifted him into the air and threw him backwards as if he was merely a child's toy. Instinctively, he twisted and came down in a crouch. Torin was not as agile as his battle-brother and landed hard on his shoulder.

The shuttle's engines roared as they started up. The defence forces of House Belisarius appeared as the shuttle's ramp lowered. The men held lasguns at the ready, but they didn't fire at the Chaos Space Marines. Haegr was almost in the midst of the enemy, and they wouldn't chance shooting one of their own. Gabriella saw the ramp open and made a dash towards the shuttle, from her cover behind a crate.

Haegr had reached the Chaos Space Marines. 'You face the mighty Haegr,' he shouted, swinging his hammer into the large helm of a Thousand Son. The hammer struck with a loud echoing boom, and the Chaos Space Marine crashed backwards. Flickering flames escaped from the hammer-sized hole in the Chaos Space Marine's armour. The creatures facing them were dead spirits haunting the shells of their ancient armour.

Ragnar howled and charged at the sorcerer. The Chaos Space Marines levelled their bolters at him. Their shots struck with deadly accuracy, but Ragnar broke off his straight-line charge to roll, and then leap, making himself a moving target. Ragnar was powerful, but his reflexes had always been his greatest physical asset.

Torin braced himself and opened fire with his bolter, drawing the enemy's attention. Shot after shot struck the enemy squad. Unfortunately, their arcane armour held, but Ragnar knew that Torin had bought him just enough of a respite. He would be in their ranks in a second.

The sorcerer intoned a phrase in a strange tongue and another bolt of dark magic raced from his hands. Ragnar dodged to his left, but the bolt followed him. The Space Wolf howled in pain as the arcane energy threw him back into a pile of crates, knocking him off his feet. Spots danced in front of his eyes and pain came from each place a bolter round had struck him. He clutched a refuelling line as he tried to pull himself to his feet.

Torin tried to duck the return fire from the Thousand Sons, but they had numbers. Possessing a skill that matched the Space Wolves, they blasted Torin. Haegr had three fighting him. Although they could not match the giant Space Wolf's strength or his skill with the hammer, they were still formidable adversaries. Haegr was breathing heavily and the hammer was swinging slowly and wildly. He was being pushed back, and the enemy were gaining the advantage.

Anger raged within Ragnar's heart. The wolf in his soul howled and he joined in chorus; his pack needed him. He threw himself at the sorcerer and the Thousand Sons. This time, Ragnar reached the sorcerer and thrust his blade through the Thousand Sons helm, breaking through ancient ceramite and arcane protections to jut out of the back of the Chaos Space Marine's helmet.

Ragnar roared and took his blade to the next Chaos Space Marine. The ancient warrior raised his bolter in an attempt to parry, but Ragnar sliced through the gun. Ghostly smoke came from the ruined bolter. On the down stroke, Ragnar brought up his other arm and levelled his foe with two point-blank bolt pistol shots.

Then, a mighty blow cracked Ragnar on the back of the head, dropping him to the ground.

The sorcerer's other guard stood over Ragnar and fired his bolter into the Space Wolf's back. Ragnar heard his armour's backpack crack and felt the shot through his spine. Ragnar's genetically altered hearts pounded as his enhanced physique raced to repair the damage.

Ragnar rolled from his stomach to his wounded back and kicked up into the Thousand Son. The Chaos Space Marine fell back, nearly losing his balance. Somehow, Ragnar got back to his feet and brought his sword up into his foe's abdomen.

Flames flared within the helm of the Thousand Son. Even as the Chaos Space Marine's essence was leaking out of his armour, he reached for Ragnar's throat, impaling himself further on the blade. 'Madox will be pleased with your death,' his foe grated.

'Go to hell,' said Ragnar, placing his bolt pistol squarely on his opponent's forehead and pulling the trigger.

The Chaos Space Marine fell limp on the end of Ragnar's blade.

Ragnar realised that he had killed three of their foe in the last few seconds. He took an instant to assess the battle. Haegr stood near him and had felled another in addition to his first kill. Haegr swayed and Ragnar wondered how much longer he could stand. Torin was on the ground, slightly closer to the shuttle, struggling to get to his feet. The odds were almost even, four Chaos Space Marines against three Space Wolves, and despite Ragnar's wounds, he knew that victory was in their grasp.

The body of the sorcerer rose from the hangar floor, pulled as if by invisible strings. Blue flames wreathed the sorcerer's gauntlets. The hair rose on Ragnar's neck and his eyes widened as the lifeless body raised its hands.

Reality shuddered. Fire burst forth from the armour and Ragnar brought his arm up to shield his face. He heard insane laughing echo from all sides and a sickly sweet scent filled his nostrils.

Something started to materialise in the middle of the chamber. A creature floated in the air, drifting on nonexistent winds. Its flesh was blue and pink with one colour replacing the other. Tendrils sprang from bubbling twisting flesh and flailed towards the Space Wolves.

A wave of horror and revulsion swept over Ragnar and he raised his sword defiantly. If this was the end, he would go out like a true Space Wolf. He threw his head back and howled for as long and loud as he could, until his cry drowned out the laughter of the daemon.

When he lowered his head, he heard an answering howl, one with a mechanical undertone. With a huge crash, the wall of the hangar bay cracked. Large rents appeared in the rockcrete. Suddenly, a large section fell inwards, crumbling to dust.

Gymir the Ice-Fisted, venerable Dreadnought of the Thunderfist great company, howled once again as he strode into the hangar. *Russ takes care of his own,* thought Ragnar, *and we take care of his enemies!*

The ground shook with each step of the towering Dreadnought. Behind the mighty one, Space Wolves, members of Berek's great company, rushed in. It was an entrance worthy of a song.

The sight of the ancient Dreadnought and the arrival of so many battle-brothers inspired Ragnar. Chanting a prayer to Russ, he charged into the daemon with renewed vigour. He slashed with his blade to his left and right, transforming himself into a whirlwind of mayhem and destruction. Tentacles flew through the air, spraying black ichor everywhere.

'Ragnar Blackmane,' shouted Mikal, as he and his fellow Space Wolves followed the Dreadnought into the hangar. Ragnar had saved Mikal and the Wolf Lord once on a space hulk, and Mikal had always sought an opportunity to repay him.

Ragnar forgot himself for a moment and glanced over at Mikal. With preternatural speed, a tentacle grasped his sword arm and another wrapped itself around his neck. One of the dismembered limbs snaked across the floor and wrapped itself around Ragnar's leg. He spat at the daemon as he tried to loosen its hold on his neck with his free hand.

'For Russ!' boomed Gymir. The great Dreadnought swung a massive power fist full into the central mass of the daemon. Energy cascaded from the power fist and the daemon's tendrils snapped away from Ragnar as the creature looked to its own defence.

One of the Chaos Space Marines knocked the thunder hammer from Haegr's grasp, while a second attempted to slice through his power armour with a chainsword. Sparks flew, but they had seized their advantage too late. Two Grey Hunters engaged the Thousand Sons, swinging axes and firing bolters into their foes at close range. The Chaos Space Marines turned their attention from Haegr to their new attackers.

Mikal and three other Space Wolves tackled the two Chaos Space Marines attacking Torin and with a howl, the four of them charged into the enemy. Mikal smashed one of the Chaos Space Marines with a power fist, tearing a gaping hole in his armour. A shrieking exhalation of smoke and fire came from the rent, leaving only empty armour.

The second Thousand Son brought his chainsword up to defend himself against the first Grey Hunter who reached him. With a skilful parry, the Chaos Space Marine not only blocked the Space Wolf's attack, but disarmed him as well. A bolter shot to the chest dropped the first Grey Hunter, even as the second sprang upon his foe.

This Space Wolf seemed fresher and more determined, toppling the Thousand Son. The two engaged in brutal combat, rolling on the hangar floor, each trying to gain the upper hand and make a lethal blow. In the end, the blade of the Grey Hunter claimed the Thousand Son, finding enough of a weakness in a joint to sever the helm.

The Grey Hunters attacking Haegr's foes seemed evenly matched by the Thousand Sons. The Chaos Space Marines were unrelenting in their attacks as if they could not feel pain or fatigue, while the Grey Hunters' blows became weaker after the initial charge. Haegr reclaimed his thunder hammer and rose again. He swung it into the back of one of the ancient warriors. With a loud boom, the Chaos Space Marine's backpack shattered in a burst of gold and lapis lazuli. The Chaos Space Marine fell, not to rise again.

Ragnar tried to regain his feet as he watched the final moments of the battle. A Grey Hunter took a double-bladed axe in one hand and slashed through the last standing member of the Thousand Sons. Gymir the Ice-Fisted had locked both power fists against the central mass of the daemon. The thing from the warp lashed tendril after tendril around the mechanical body of the entombed Space Marine, but the horror held no terror for one who had faced death. Strange warp fire leapt in an aura around the daemon, but Gymir held firm. Then the Dreadnought forced his arms apart, tearing the daemon into pieces. The lights in the hangar bay flickered and a terrible screaming began, but was cut short. Nothing was left of the daemon, and the Dreadnought stood triumphant.

The fight was over and the Space Wolves stayed on guard for a moment before allowing themselves a respite. Haegr leaned against his hammer, standing over his fallen enemies and recovering his strength. Lady Gabriella examined Torin's wounds, and House Belisarius's men formed a semi circle around her. The other Space Wolves moved together, gathering around waiting for orders. As for Ragnar, he could feel the world spinning as he walked over to the shuttle and Lady Gabriella.

Mikal's voice seemed distant, 'Blackmane! How many other members of the Wolfblade do you have?'

Ragnar was exhausted. 'As far as I know, we are the last three Wolfblade on the planet. I believe that the others are dead.'

'Lady Gabriella, I have orders from the Wolf Lord to return to the *Fist of Russ* immediately. Your shuttle looks large enough for us. Does its cargo bay have room enough for a Dreadnought?' asked Mikal.

Gabriella looked to the men of House Belisarius. They nodded affirmatively. The shuttle had extra cargo space to deliver supplies to Belisarius's custodial holdings. 'We're ready to take you to the Wolf Lord,' she said.

THE SHUTTLE STREAMED skyward, its wings touching the licking flames from the towering columns of fire bursting from beneath Lethe. Ragnar knew that he would not return for a long time, if ever. He glanced back towards the city from the viewport.

'By Russ,' he cursed. It was as Wolf Lord Berek had described it – the fiery explosions traced an eye of flame across the devastated city. Anger mixed with superstitious fear inside him. What type of ritual demanded a symbol so vast? Ragnar shook his head, tearing his eyes away from the foul symbol.

Ragnar's superhuman healing had allowed him to recover from most of his wounds from the battle. Haegr and Torin both sat quietly, Torin with his eyes closed. Ragnar had not realised just how many bolter shells his battle-brothers had taken. To his credit, Torin made no noise, instead he focused inwards, willing his wounds to close. Ragnar knew that his brothers would be ready for battle again soon.

He looked over at Mikal and the other Space Wolves. They all showed signs of the combat, but Ragnar could feel their desire to join their Wolf Lord in space. They had fought in countless battles and they would fight in countless more.

Compared to these warriors, Ragnar thought the Wolfblade looked out of place. Torin's well-manicured moustache and disparate awards seemed foppish. Haegr looked like a horribly out of shape rotund caricature of a Space Wolf. Yet, they were Ragnar's battle-brothers with a prowess that he would never have guessed at on a first glance. He wondered how he looked. Moreover, he wondered what Berek's men thought of him.

He had been a member of Berek Thunderfist's great company when he had lost the Spear of Russ. Had he brought shame on the company? How could he not have? Ragnar wondered if his former brothers cursed his name. These men would not give him any sign, and he knew that Mikal Stenmark had never cared for him.

Mikal looked over at Ragnar. 'We will arrive at the *Fist of Russ* and disembark to join the ship-to-ship fighting.' Ragnar's heart leapt, he would be fighting alongside the Space Wolves. Mikal continued, 'You and the Wolfblade will wait aboard this shuttle for further orders. I suspect you'll return to the *Wings of Belisarius*. Don't worry. We will deal with this Chaos incursion.' Ragnar's heart sank at first, and then anger and frustration rose in his chest.

Lady Gabriella entered from the cockpit and strapped herself into one of the seats. She was paler than usual, but she had recovered her grace and inner strength. She turned to Mikal. 'We have a problem. I have spoken to the Navigator on the *Fist of Russ*. Unusual turbulence in the warp has blinded the astropaths. We cannot send word of what has happened to Fenris.'

The shuttle made a hard turn into a cloud of silent explosions. They dived towards the *Fist of Russ*. Ragnar thought he could feel the ship turning as it approached the landing bay.

The Wolf Guard checked their weapons. They nodded to each other in acknowledgement and Ragnar could see the exchange of grins. They were ready for battle. Ragnar longed to be one of them.

The shuttle landed fast and hard in the hangar bay. The landing gear screeched against the deck of the *Fist of Russ*. Sparks shot across the viewports. Ragnar heard the cargo hold doors drop, and he felt Gymir the Ice-Fisted lumber out of the shuttle.

The other Space Wolves immediately released their restraints and followed suit. Mikal paused and gave Ragnar a last look. 'Rough battle down there, Blackmane. You have a gift for finding trouble. May the Emperor watch over you,' he said and without another word, Mikal left.

Ragnar wondered what his words meant, but he was tired of pondering such things.

'Lady Gabriella, the Wolf Lord wishes to speak to you,' said the pilot. Gabriella unstrapped herself and walked up to the front of the shuttle.

With his sharpened senses, Ragnar could hear Gabriella's half of the conversation.

'Yes, Wolf Lord. I would be honoured to deliver word of this incident to Fenris,' she said. 'Pilot, take us to our cruiser, the *Wings of Belisarius*. Wolf Lord Berek has entrusted us to deliver news of this battle to the Great Wolf. Let the *Wings of Belisarius* know that we must traverse the warp to Fenris.'

Within moments, the shuttle left the hangar of the *Fist of Russ*, bound for the *Wings of Belisarius*.

WITHIN MINUTES, THE shuttle docked with the *Wings of Belisarius*. The cruiser was warp-capable, and it had a fair complement of guns, although it was hardly a match for the powerful vessels of the Space Wolf fleet. Ragnar knew that they were being left out of the battle, sent to Fenris because Wolf Lord Berek Thunderfist felt that the Wolfblade couldn't help him defeat the Chaos fleet. What angered Ragnar most was that he knew that the Wolf Lord was right.

The members of the Wolfblade and the crew of the shuttle disembarked swiftly. The servitors in the hangar had already begun securing the shuttle for the larger ship's warp travel. There was no time to waste. Gabriella was already on the comm to the bridge.

'Captain, we are aboard and we will be strapped in as quickly as possible. Once we are secure, we shouldn't waste any time. We need to reach Fenris as quickly as we can,' she said.

'Haegr will once again return to Fenris. Let the gods themselves tremble in their halls,' bellowed Haegr.

A beetle flew out from under Ragnar's shoulder pad as the group left the hangar for one of the main corridors to the restraining couches. Ragnar crushed it against the wall. 'We're done with Hyades.'

'Brilliant holiday idea,' offered Haegr cheerfully, but Ragnar wasn't smiling.

Torin waved his hand over the activation runes for the door to one of the ship's transport chambers. He stepped back to let Gabriella enter the room first with enough of a flourish for Ragnar to be certain that he had fully recovered.

'Captain, we're ready,' announced Gabriella over her comm. She sat down and pulled the restraints. The others hurried to do the same.

'Activate restraints and harnesses. Prepare to enter the warp,' came the command from the ship's speakers.

Gabriella looked over at Ragnar. 'I'm sorry. You served with them before the Wolfblade,' she said.

'Sorry about what?' asked Ragnar as he finished adjusting his restraints.

'There are too many Chaos ships. They won't survive,' she stated flatly.

Ragnar set his jaw. 'They are Space Wolves.'

Before Gabriella could respond, reality folded in on itself and the colours of the room lengthened and shifted. Ragnar lost all sense of space and time. The *Wings of Belisarius* had entered the warp.

FROM THE OBSERVATION window on the bridge of the *Fist of Russ*, Wolf Lord Berek Thunderfist watched the attackers come for them. Waves of enemy attack craft swarmed out of the bays of the Styx cruiser. Like monstrous bats, they covered space, blocking the light of the sun and blotting out the stars. Berek knew that it was time to find his place in the sagas, but, by Russ, they would remember him and his men for this day!

The cloud of death descended towards the Space Wolves. Berek cursed under his breath. The men of his great company had outdone themselves. They had fought the Dark Angels to a standstill and yet they had found the heart to destroy far more of the Thousand Sons than any tactician would have deemed possible.

Berek remembered the run through the Chaos cruiser. Ah! Those were the experiences that made a man's blood burn with life. They had killed her mutant crew and detonated her power core. Two Chaos cruisers had fallen to the *Fist of Russ*. Now, the Styx cruiser came at them, and they limped through space, badly damaged. Berek knew that the hull of the Space Wolf vessel wouldn't hold for much longer. 'Come on you treacherous bastards! Come and destroy us if you can,' he said waving his power fist at the enemy.

'My lord, Lady Gabriella and the *Wings of Belisarius* have made it into the warp,' reported the ship's guide.

'All is not lost. She'll get word to Logan Grimnar,' the Wolf Lord said, and then continued to shout at the Styx. 'Burn in hell, you traitors!'

Then, as if it was intimidated by the cursing of the Wolf Lord, the wave of enemy bombers and fighters wavered and turned, breaking up and retreating towards the Styx.

'What in the name of the Gates of Morkai?' asked Berek.

The Dark Angels battle-barge suddenly filled the view screens on the *Fist of Russ*. The *Vinco Redemptor* opened up on the Styx with all of her guns, beams of energy illuminating the void with holy fury. A myriad of smaller Dark Angels vessels erupted from behind the mighty battle-barge, guns blazing.

The Dark Angels were back. Dark Angel escorts flew in behind the remaining Chaos ships sending ravening blasts of white-hot energy into the hulls of the enemy vessels. The *Vinco Redemptor* showed no mercy as it launched barrage after barrage into the Styx. Large sections of the Chaos cruiser glowed and exploded into molten fragments.

The Astartes were victorious. Berek raised his fist and his heart pumped wildly.

'Wolf Lord Berek, incoming transmission,' reported comms.

Interrogator-Chaplain Vargas appeared. 'Wolf Lord Berek Thunderfist, I offer my congratulations and praise for your efforts and for those of your men. Your distractions allowed us time to repair and flank the enemy. The Lion will be victorious this day. Praise to the Emperor!' His voice retained a metallic ring.

'Praise to the Emperor! You abandoned us! You fled and left us to do the fighting,' shouted Berek, as anger replaced the feeling of victory. 'You said that you were leaving!'

'We could not speak the truth over open channels, Wolf Lord. We are a proud Chapter just as you are. We always intended to flank them. I will grant you this: we never expected to discover that you destroyed so many. Our praise to you, Wolf Lord. Now, let both our Chapters fight as brothers against this foe and let Chaos be destroyed.'

Berek nodded. 'Let Chaos be destroyed.'

The transmission ended. Berek didn't trust the Dark Angels, but thanks to them, they would win the day.

'Engines, get us full power,' ordered the Wolf Lord. Berek turned on the ship's full comms. 'The Dark Angels have decided to join the fray. Let's remind them who won this battle. For Fenris! For Russ! For the Emperor!'

Berek could hear the cheering of his men fill the *Fist of Russ*.

SIXTEEN
Return to Fenris

THE *Wings of Belisarius* had traversed the warp to Fenris, making the journey in good time. Upon entering orbit, Gabriella and the surviving members of the Wolfblade had boarded the same shuttle that had taken them to Hyades. Now, they rode the vehicle to Fenris. The foursome sat quietly, Gabriella beside Ragnar, who stared out of a viewport, with Haegr and Torin seated further down on the same side at another viewport. The Space Wolves all longed to see their homeworld.

Ragnar gazed out at the planet below. He was almost home. He could see the raging seas and the mountainous icebergs surging with the waves, great white shapes rocking back and forth. Storm clouds crackled with lightning, voicing their power with peals of thunder, and a wall of weather threatened to shroud the surface of the planet. Fenris was a harsh world, a cold and bitter place where only the strong survived, but most of all it was home.

He struggled to avoid shaking from the emotions he felt. He knew that he had thought a great deal of home, brooded on it in fact, but he hadn't expected to feel this strong a reaction. He shook his head, and then grinned with exultation. Finally, he was returning to the Fang.

'Aye, I know how you feel, lad,' said Haegr. 'Nothing stirs a warrior's heart like a return home. Now, poor Torin who was completely corrupted by civilisation, he's in for a bit of misery.'

Torin looked over. 'I harbour strong feelings for Fenris as well. It's the home world of our Chapter. Beyond that, I can't feel too sentimental over endless winters, krakens, and a harsh life filled with nothing but battle and cold. Still, I understand why my brother Ragnar loves Fenris so much, and well, as for you, I expect you'll be the cause of decades of starvation once you find the Fang's pantries.'

'Hah, it'll just make the rest of the Wolves tougher, weed out the frail and weak,' responded Haegr.

Ragnar could almost taste the Fenrisian ale and hear the stories of the grizzled veterans concerning battles against the ork, the eldar and Chaos. He had stories that he wanted to tell too, stories about fighting cultists, Imperial assassins, Dark Angels and Thousand Sons. He couldn't wait to see his old friends, especially Sven and the old Wolf Priest, Ranek. Sven had been with Ragnar since his choosing and was a member of Ragnar's first claw, a bonded group of Blood Claws. Ranek had chosen Ragnar as a warrior, and although he trained hundreds of Space Wolves, Ranek had the ability to make him feel as though he were the only Space Wolf that Ranek had ever recruited.

The Fang came into view. It was the eternal fortress of the Space Wolves, the greatest mountain on all of Fenris, a spike of rock and ice so high that it pierced the sky. It dwarfed the other mountains surrounding it, and its peak even rose above the oncoming storm clouds. The warriors of Fenris viewed the Fang with superstitious awe as the home of gods. In some ways, they were right; compared to ordinary men, the Space Wolves might as well be gods. Unlike other Chapters though, the Space Wolves had never forgotten that they had once also been men.

Ragnar felt a chill race along his spine and spread outwards to cross his body. The Fang still inspired awe in his heart, and he knew that no matter what the future held, how many battles he fought or where he travelled, the Fang would always affect him this way. For him, it represented the heart of the Space Wolves and their desire to fight for their ideals against all mankind's enemies.

Excitement mixed with dread in his gut. He was still an exile. This was a temporary visit. Seeing his friends would be bittersweet indeed, because he would have to leave again. Ragnar wanted to watch the Fang for the entire descent, but he thought that seemed like the action of a young Blood Claw and Ragnar knew that he should wait like the others.

Ragnar looked over at Gabriella, who turned her head to look away. Had she been looking at him? Ragnar realised that Gabriella had seemed quiet and reserved since her rescue, especially around him.

'Gabriella, is something bothering you?' Ragnar whispered, although he knew that Haegr and Torin could both hear.

Gabriella met Ragnar's eyes. 'Yes, I had a vision on Hyades.'

'What was it?' he asked.

'I'm not exactly sure. It was many things, colours, shapes and images. It's hard to know what was real and what was delusion,' she whispered, 'but I think I saw a great spear, perhaps the Spear of Russ.'

'What?' asked Ragnar. His hearts nearly burst from his body. 'Tell me. I have to know'

'I don't know much, Ragnar. I think that I saw the Thousand Sons with the Spear of Russ, but there were so many other images that I can't be certain. It happened when I was in the bunker in the Chaos temple. I don't know whether it was a real vision, it may just have been a hallucination. Perhaps it was a scene from the past, but I felt like the Thousand Sons had retrieved the spear from the warp. As I said, I'm not sure, but I know how you feel about it. I just thought I should mention it. I'll speak to the Great Wolf and the Rune Priests and see if they think it's real.' Gabriella turned away.

'I have to find it. We have to have the chance to bring it back. That's my chance,' said Ragnar.

The shuttle suddenly angled, making its final descent into the hangar of the Fang. The shadow of the mountain fell over the craft, darkening the viewports.

'Ho! Enough talk,' said Haegr. The shuttle decelerated and Ragnar saw the mighty sculpted wolves that stood guard over the hangar. A large emblem of the Great Wolf marked the side of the hangar. This was Logan Grimnar's territory. The shuttle soared into the hangar and then he heard the crunch of landing gear on ice.

'We've landed. We are home, brothers,' said Haegr.

As the four walked out onto the icy surface of Fenris, Torin took Ragnar's arm and pulled him aside. 'Brother, listen to me and listen well. Both Haegr and I overhead what Gabriella said to you, our ears are too sharp for small quarters. Let Gabriella speak to Logan Grimnar. Don't speak of the Spear of Russ yourself. Trust the Great Wolf.'

Ragnar swallowed. His friend was probably right. Torin understood politics. If there was any justice in the galaxy, Ragnar would get his chance, and if any leader was just, it was Logan Grimnar.

Ragnar felt chills as he walked out of the hangar into the halls of the Fang with his Wolfblade brothers, following Gabriella. The imposing majesty and strength in the rock gave this hallowed ground an indescribable feeling. Other Space Wolves walked all around, along with the human warriors who dedicated their lives to serving the Chapter. It had been a long time since he had seen so many of his fellows. The Fang was where his life as a Space Wolf had started and it was his home.

Ranek, the ancient Wolf Priest, stood in the centre of the great passage, awaiting them. 'Wolfblade Ragnar, let me see you,' he said.

Ragnar immediately came to attention.

Clad in black power armour, the Wolf Priest wore a cape made from the pelt of a massive Fenrisian wolf. Like all Space Wolves, he wore teeth and wolf tails along with runes and wolf skulls as per his station. He was a large man, grey and dominating, old and strong like the mountain of the Fang itself. His fangs protruded like tusks and his beard was so grey and fine that it evoked comparisons to the colour of snow at twilight.

Ranek's glacial blue and piercing eyes studied Ragnar, assessing him. He felt as if the Wolf Priest knew everything that had transpired in his life since he had joined the Wolfblade.

'Lady Gabriella, may I have a moment with this member of your Wolfblade?' asked Ranek.

'As you wish, Wolf Priest Ranek,' she answered. Ragnar thought that he saw a hint of a smile in her eyes. Gabriella, Haegr and Torin continued into the Fang, leaving Ragnar behind.

The old Wolf Priest sized up Ragnar, pacing around him with a stern eye. Ragnar stood to attention, feeling as nervous as he ever did under the watchful eye of the Wolf Priest. How long ago it seemed that Ranek had taken him to be reborn as a Space Wolf. Indeed, to Ragnar, it seemed long ago that Ranek had seen him, before the judgement that led to his exile. 'You look good, laddie. Your time in the Wolfblade has helped you. Do you still feel like just a bodyguard?'

'No, I... I've learnt quite a bit,' Ragnar said, momentarily surprised at Ranek's observations, but then, he realised that he had changed and Wolf Priests were known for their abilities to look into the hearts of men.

Ranek raised a bushy eyebrow. 'I see judgement and wisdom in your eyes to go with that fire in your heart. You'll need it.'

'Need it? For what?' asked Ragnar.

'To defend the Imperium and Fenris, as you were chosen to do. Join your battle-brothers. I want to hear your report on Hyades as well. We'll speak more later.' Ranek clapped Ragnar's shoulder, held his eyes for a moment, and then strode off towards a group of bellowing Blood Claws.

Ragnar hurried to rejoin the Wolfblade. Torin was grinning and Haegr looked slightly annoyed as they paced respectfully behind Gabriella.

'He was not,' said Haegr.

'Aye, that he was,' retorted Torin.

'What are you talking about?' asked Ragnar.

'We saw some new Blood Claws,' answered Torin, 'and one of them was larger than Haegr, except perhaps in the belly,' Torin chuckled.

'There is no Space Wolf larger than mighty Haegr. Don't you agree, Ragnar?' asked Haegr.

Ragnar laughed. The banter and kinship of his battle-brothers gave him relief. 'Well, not that I've seen.'

'See, Torin? That settles the matter,' said Haegr. 'Later, I'll give you a good thrashing. Maybe it'll put some sense back into your head.'

As they approached the Hall of the Great Wolf, the members of the Wolfblade fell into silence.

Lady Gabriella led her champions into the hall of Logan Grimnar. Great stone-carved wolfs' heads looked down upon them. Ice coating parts of the walls of the cavernous hall made it seem like a deep cave, yet the banners and heraldry proclaimed that this was the hall of the greatest of lords. Advisors and warriors of the Chapter stood silently around the chamber, almost forming an honour guard, yet at the same time appearing as impassive as statues, as if they were part of the mountain itself.

The Great Wolf sat on the wolf throne, two Fenrisian wolves sitting quietly on either side. Even these massive beasts were humbled by the presence of their master. Logan Grimnar was the heart of the Fang, impassive and old beyond reckoning, yet as strong as the world. He rested a gauntleted hand on a double-headed frostaxe. He had a hardened face, craggy like the rocks and worn, yet strong, stronger than that of any man Ragnar had ever met. His beard framed his face like the ice on the sides of the Fang.

Ragnar took a deep breath and made sure to keep his eyes on the Great Wolf. He would not show fear or cowardice in front of his Chapter Master.

Gabriella knelt before the master of the Wolf Lords, as did the members of the Wolfblade in a proper show of respect.

'Lady Gabriella of House Belisarius, what tidings do you bring?' asked Logan Grimnar.

Gabriella rose to speak, and Ragnar, Torin and Haegr followed suit. Gabriella seemed like a thin dark shadow in the massive hall of the Wolf Lord.

'I bring ill tidings, Great Wolf. The capital of the planet Hyades was overrun by Chaos, and there was conflict as well with the Dark Angels. Our House was betrayed from within and the forces of the Thousand

Sons are responsible for the deaths of many of my people including many noble Space Wolves.'

He replied, 'Tell me everything.'

Ragnar listened as Gabriella recounted the events on Hyades. He noticed that she emphasised the heroics of the Wolfblade, although she told the truth. One did not lie to the Great Wolf.

Gabriella finished with her revelation, 'There is more as well. I had a vision on Hyades. I believe that in my vision, I saw the Spear of Russ in the possession of the Thousand Sons.'

Although Ragnar did not hear a noise, he felt a collective gasp come from the assembled advisors. Such news could cause even the unwavering to waver.

'I believe that it may be possible that the Thousand Sons will once again attempt to draw Magnus the Red from the warp back into Imperial space,' she concluded.

Logan Grimnar remained impassive. Silence filled the chamber. The quiet lasted an eternity for Ragnar. It took every ounce of his self-control not to shout an oath to Leman Russ and the Emperor before the Great Wolf himself, that he would find and return the Spear of Russ. Still, he kept his tongue, but at that moment, he looked into the eyes of the mighty Wolf Lord and made the oath in his heart.

Ragnar thought that Logan Grimnar nodded, ever so slightly.

The doors to the great hall opened and a messenger came in, running swiftly. He went over to Logan Grimnar and whispered something to the Great Wolf. Ragnar had a sudden feeling of déjà vu. At his last meeting with Logan Grimnar, a messenger had also interrupted to bring word of the death of Gabriella's father, the Great Wolf's old friend, Skander.

'Good news coupled with more grim tidings,' announced the Great Wolf. 'Berek Thunderfist and his fleet have returned battle-worn from Hyades, but the astropaths have reported attacks on many worlds. The Thousand Sons have launched an offensive, unforeseen in recent centuries against planets protected by our Chapter. Our enemies have declared war, and boldly, but we will rise to the challenge. There will be a council of war. Lady Gabriella, you and the Wolfblade may go. I will call upon you later.'

Gabriella knelt before the Chapter Master of the Space Wolves and departed with the Wolfblade following behind.

FOR THE NEXT several hours, Ragnar volunteered to spend his time guarding Lady Gabriella's chambers. He wanted the time to brood and think. Gabriella had wanted to sleep. Haegr had needed food, Torin looked as if he wished to explore so Ragnar decided to volunteer for the first shift of guard duty.

Ragnar wanted to recover the Spear of Russ. He knew that it should satisfy him if the Chapter found it, but he wanted to have a chance to restore his honour and he felt that it was his responsibility. He had lost it. He had been exiled and he wanted the chance to set things right.

After a several hours, Torin came up to him. 'Still on guard, brother?' he asked

'Aye,' said Ragnar, 'she still rests.'

'Well, Haegr will be eating a few more krakens before we see him again,' Torin said, shaking his head. 'I hope that the Chapter's stores will recover.'

Ragnar just looked at him.

'Brother,' said Torin, 'you have a great deal on your mind, but you can't change any of it. You look tense. I knew there was a problem when you didn't argue with Haegr or myself about guard duty and volunteered. Let me relieve you. Besides, someone important is in the observation chamber near the hangars, wanting to speak with you.'

'Who?' asked Ragnar.

'I think it best that you find out yourself. You'll know soon enough,' said Torin.

'Thank you, Torin. I'm on my way,' Ragnar said, slapping his fellow Space Wolf's shoulder. He walked quickly, and then broke into a jog as he headed to the observation chamber.

Someone wanted to speak to him. Ragnar wondered who it could be. Ranek, perhaps, wanting to give him advice?

Ragnar opened the stone doors, marked with Logan Grimnar's dancing wolf crest. The chamber looked out over the hangars, and from its vantage point, an observer could watch the Thunderhawks and shuttles arriving and departing. The panoramic view of Fenris seen through floor to ceiling panels was impressive. He could see the lesser mountains under the shadow of the Fang with their icecaps and forests, and the dark shadows of deep valleys. Far off, he could even make out the stormy oceans and a few of the distant islands as well as the mighty icebergs that floated on the cold seas.

Ragnar saw a Space Wolf standing by the viewing window. 'I've come as quickly as I could,' he blurted out, before he even took a good look at whoever was waiting for him.

'Well, not bad for someone as slow as you.' Ragnar instantly recognised the voice of Sven, his long-time friend. He smiled at the sound of the voice. Sven had been with Ragnar since the beginning. They had been chosen at the same time from the battlefields of Fenris. It had been so many years ago that Ragnar had lost count. They had survived initiation together, both confronting their personal struggles with the wulfen. They had seen many battles and were made members of the same claw. Sven had been with him when the Spear was lost, fighting alongside him against the Thousand Sons and the Sorcerer, Madox. Sven had lost a hand that day and more. The hellblade that had wounded him had cut deep.

Sven's hair was now silvery grey and his face far more lined than it should be. He reached out to Ragnar. Sven was more than a friend. He was a battle-brother, and closer to Ragnar than anyone else in the galaxy.

'Ragnar,' Sven said, grabbing him in a bear hug. 'It's good to see you. I had hoped to make planetfall on Hyades and find you.'

'Sven!' Ragnar returned the bear hug.

The two men broke their embrace and smiled at one another, but Ragnar knew that Sven could tell that something was wrong.

'Don't look so excited to see me,' said Sven.

Ragnar shook his head. 'I'm sorry, it's just…'

Sven held up his hand. 'I know, my brother. The Thousand Sons are back, and last time, you jammed the Spear of Russ into the eye of their primarch and got made into a Wolfblade. You know how I feel, especially about Madox. When I see him again, I'm going to take my blade and thrust it straight up his…'

'I remember,' said Ragnar, grinning. 'It is good to see you, Sven.' He gave Sven a hearty clasp.

'I can't believe that you have been living the soft life on Blessed Terra,' said Sven.

'You'd be surprised at life on Terra. Besides, what happened after we left Hyades?' asked Ragnar.

It was Sven's turn to grow quiet. 'The Dark Angels showed up and helped us finish the battle. We drove the Chaos fleet back, but we had to abandon Hyades. We had too much damage to stay there, and the Dark Angels left little in the way of facilities in the system to repair our ships. I think the future of Hyades is no longer ours to determine.'

The two friends exchanged a meaningful look. Word of what had happened on Hyades would reach the Imperium… and the Inquisition.

'While you were on guard duty, we finished a major briefing. The Thousand Sons have attacked across the sector. Some of the Wolf Lords got hit hard. Even as we speak, battle rages on,' said Sven. 'I suspect that you would have been invited if you weren't assigned to guard Lady Gabriella.'

'I see that the two of you are once again attempting to chart the future of the galaxy. Sven, you are needed with your company. Go,' said a deep voice.

Ragnar and Sven both jumped, startled, and reached for their weapons, before they realised that it was Ranek. Despite their senses, neither Ragnar nor Sven had noticed the Wolf Priest enter the chamber. Ragnar wondered how long he had been there.

'Of course,' Sven said removing his hand from his bolter. 'Good to see you again, Ragnar. Hope Terra hasn't made you too soft.' Sven clapped Ragnar's shoulder and left the chamber.

Ragnar came to attention, as he always did under Ranek's eye.

The Wolf Priest waited until the door closed before he spoke. 'The Thousand Sons have attacked us on all sides. Even now, we are looking for help wherever we can find it. The Wolfblade will be needed. The alliance between the Space Wolves and House Belisarius works both ways.'

'Laddie, you look as if you lost Hyades to the Thousand Sons. I have some terrible news for you. We lost a city on Hyades, not the planet, and it wasn't just you, but our entire Chapter, and we may be on the verge of losing much more. Ready yourself for your duties in the fight, wherever they may take you.'

'Yes, of course,' Ragnar said, taking a deep breath. Whatever he did, he would help his Chapter.

A gleam shone in the old man's eyes. 'Besides, I hear that there's a wolf around who stuck the primarch of the Thousand Sons in the eye.'

Ragnar grinned and to his surprise, Ranek grinned back. 'Go back to your duties,' said the Wolf Priest.

Ragnar nodded and left, heading back to Torin. When he arrived, the older Wolfblade stood at Gabriella's door, straightening his moustache. Ragnar had a strange feeling his friend knew everything that had transpired.

'So, everything went well, I take it?' asked Torin.

'Indeed,' said Ragnar. 'Thank you. I'll take over guard duty again.'

'No need,' said Torin. 'Get yourself some food. I'll call if I need you.'

Ragnar decided to take his friend's advice and get something to eat. As he walked through the halls, the impact of the Fang and of Fenris struck him again. He was glad to be home. He made his way through the ice and rock-hewn corridors to the great hall, where he had enjoyed several feasts as a Blood Claw.

When Ragnar entered the great hall, he was astounded to see Berek Thunderfist's company. They were his friends and battle-brothers, and he had fought alongside them against the Thousand Sons. Many of them had fresh scars. Others wore gleaming cybernetics, a sure sign of their newness. A few also carried Dark Angels helms, obvious trophies. Ragnar felt strange to see so many who knew him so well. They knew of the Spear of Russ, and they had been on Hyades.

Ragnar saw Haegr, sitting alone at the other end of the hall. He paused, wondering if the others would recognise him. He wondered if they hated him as a disgrace to the company, if any of them would even acknowledge him. He was who he was, and he couldn't change the past.

He decided to make his way towards his giant battle-brother and the debris that Haegr had left on the table. As he walked, he thought about Magni and the young Wolfblade's last words.

Halfway across the room, he was noticed. Several Space Wolves stood up as he went towards Haegr. Ragnar felt the eyes and the stares. He remained focused on Haegr, who seemed to be the only person in the room oblivious to his presence. Haegr was too busy devouring a huge joint of meat and drinking a keg of Fenrisian ale, apparently at the same time.

'Ragnar,' shouted a Grey Hunter. Ragnar stopped and turned.

'To our battle-brother Ragnar! May he have another chance to drive a spear into the eye of Magnus the Red.'

'To your health, little brother.'

'It hasn't been the same without you.'

Suddenly, the voices came from all sides and so did the cheers. Then, a number of Space Wolves were all around him, attempting to commiserate for his assignment to the Wolfblade, asking about his part in the battle on Hyades, wishing him well, and hoping that he'd get a chance to get back at the Thousand Sons. It all seemed overwhelming and wonderful all at once. His battle-brothers knew the truth.

Ragnar was home. Someone thrust a drink into his hand and he gulped it down. It was the best-tasting ale he had ever had. 'To Berek's great company!' he shouted.

Cheers of agreement followed. 'When are you rejoining us?' yelled a Space Wolf. 'You should be there when we drive the Thousand Sons into the warp.'

'Ho!' roared Haegr, before belching loudly.

Haegr pushed his way through the crowd. 'Hands off, he's a Wolfblade now.' Ragnar could tell by the way that Haegr was swaying that the giant had drunk too much, even for him.

Haegr clapped Ragnar's shoulder.

'I am a Wolfblade,' announced Ragnar, 'but I will always be the battle-brother of any member of Berek Thunderfist's great company.'

There was a loud cheering and then, much drinking.

SEVENTEEN
Councils of War

LOGAN GRIMNAR STOOD at the window looking out over the mountains of Asaheim. His grey hair flowed like a mane, blending with the wolf pelt cloak he wore, making it hard to tell one from the other. This was the tallest tower in the Fang, and he often found himself here at times like this. Looking out over the mountain ranges of Asaheim brought him focus. He was the Chapter Master of the Space Wolves. He'd been the Great Wolf for several centuries, so long in fact that he was sometimes referred to as the Old Wolf. He sometimes found that title humorous for it was only at times like this that he actually felt old.

The Thousand Sons, the Space Wolves' ancient hated nemesis, were once again wreaking destruction and mayhem within Space Wolf-controlled space, on a scale that had not been seen since their assault on the Fang, many years ago. The actions on Hyades were just one of a series of events that were unfolding; several worlds were under siege.

Logan knew the Thousand Sons all too well. They did not just initiate random assaults, mindless violence, or kill for the sake of killing. He wondered if the Sons of Magnus might be hiding their true intentions within several attacks. Perhaps a mastermind among them had devised a terrifying scheme. Maybe they were hoping to spread the Space Wolves so thin that their true objective would go unnoticed until it was too late. Dealing with the Thousand Sons was always problematic.

Logan pondered the challenges that lay before his Chapter and his battle-brothers. Upon hearing of the attacks he had instructed the Rune Priests to consult the runes in an attempt to unravel the mystery of Thousand Sons' true intentions. He had called on his available Wolf Lords to seek the advice of their veteran leadership. He had even woken one of the mighty Dreadnoughts to hear the wisdom of the ancient one. This information was imperative to allow him and his Wolf Lords to develop a cohesive plan of action and bring the incursion of the Thousand Sons to an abrupt halt.

The door to the Great Wolf's chamber slid open and Rune Priest Aldrek entered the room, accompanied by Ranek and two other Rune Priests. Grimnar stood gazing out of the window with his back to them, apparently oblivious to their presence. The four priests stood perfectly silent, waiting for the Great Wolf to acknowledge them before daring to speak. Several minutes passed before Aldrek took a breath as he prepared to interrupt the Great Wolf's concentration.

'Yes, Aldrek, I know you are here. You've consulted the runes, I take it?' Grimnar asked.

'We have, Great Wolf,' Aldrek said.

'What do they tell you?' Logan took a deep breath and slowly turned to face the priests.

'The news is grave, Great Wolf, far worse than we first thought. The runes suggest that the Thousand Sons have recovered the Spear of Russ, and the signs indicate that they will attempt far more than they did in the past.' Dread filled Aldrek's voice as he continued.

Aldrek left unspoken the fact that when the Thousand Sons had last possessed the Spear of Russ they had attempted to summon their primarch, Magnus the Red from the warp. All of the Space Wolves had heard the tale of that battle.

'The runes show that the ritual they are attempting could bring about the destruction of Fenris and the entire Space Wolf Chapter!'

WITHIN HOURS, THE leadership of the Space Wolves had gathered in the Great Hall of the Fang at the command of the Great Wolf. Five Wolf Lords, each a leader of one of the Chapter's great companies, sat at an oval table, carved from rare woods. A large circular stone tablet hung at one end, the grand annulus with the symbols of each great company. Dominating them all was the rampant wolf, symbol of Logan Grimnar. The Great Wolf sat on a throne of stone, directly below his crest. Behind each of the Wolf Lords stood a small retinue of Wolf Guard, handpicked warriors from their companies, chosen to serve as the Wolf Lord's personal guard.

Other advisors and personages, such as Lady Gabriella of House Belisarius, held seats or stood behind the Wolf Guards. They included many Wolf Priests, Iron Priests and Rune Priests, the spiritual, technological and psychic advisors to their leaders.

Like the grand annulus, the table within the great hall depicted the symbols of each great company, each one having an assigned position. Several of those positions were empty, representing the severity of the situation facing the Space Wolves. It was not uncommon for a number of the great companies to be away from the Fang, on various missions, conducting Chapter business, however this time their absence indicated another threat within Fenrisian-protected space.

Logan Grimnar listened intently to Wolf Lord Berek's report on the events that had taken place on Hyades. Slowly stroking his beard, the Old Wolf had deep concentration etched on his face as he contemplated the course before the Space Wolves.

Logan rose to his feet and walked around the table, arms crossed. All eyes followed the Great Wolf as he paced across the room.

'The Thousand Sons manipulated us into fighting the Dark Angels and vice versa. This is not an isolated incident. On Gere, a Chaos uprising has destroyed valuable factories. Across the worlds we protect, numerous threats have arisen. Each one seems random, with no connection to the others, but we all suspect that this isn't coincidence. We are at a dangerous crossroads, my Wolf Lords.' The Great Wolf walked back to his seat. 'We have other indicators as well. Rune Lord Aldrek will explain further.'

Aldrek bowed to the Great Wolf and stepped forwards.

'Wolf Lords, at the behest of Lord Grimnar, I have gathered many Rune Priests and consulted the runes, interpreting the portents. The signs are disturbing. Dark castings indicate a terrible threat and show signs that the Chapter may be in even more danger than we imagined. We believe that the Thousand Sons may be seeking a powerful artefact, but we cannot be certain what and why. What we do know is that the runes indicate a threat to the Chapter as strongly as they ever have,' Aldrek finished.

'Iron Priest Rorik,' commanded the Great Wolf.

Holding a massive thunder hammer as the sign of his station, a large Iron Priest strode before the assembled lords. 'Wolf Lords, at the behest of Lord Grimnar, I have analysed the worlds attacked so far, along with others of my order and many of them held valuable resources. The Chaos Space Marines have attacked our production abilities, and although they have done nothing that we cannot rebuild, they have weakened our ability to maintain our production. We are not well-positioned for a protracted conflict.'

'Finally, Wolf Priest Ranek,' said the Great Wolf.

'I bring grim tidings indeed. In the battles that have unfolded in this conflict, we have harvested few gene-seed from our fallen battle-brothers. Although the number of gene-seed lost is small, every one is a precious gift from our primarch, Leman Russ and a terrible loss. Without them, we cannot recruit battle-brothers to replace those lost in battle.' Ranek stepped back.

Logan Grimnar stood once again, and this time he raised the double-bladed Axe of Morkai. 'The attacks have begun, and I believe that these random events are a prelude to the true ambitions of the Thousand Sons. I need every one of you, and every one of your men, to meet this threat. What you have not been told is this, and this information will not leave this hall without my leave: we have reason to believe that the Thousand Sons may have recovered the Spear of Russ from the warp. Each of you knows what the Thousand Sons attempted the last time they possessed the relic. You will find out the truth and discover the enemy's plans and intentions, as well as defending your assigned regions of space.'

Skalds entered the great hall, placing a scrolled parchment on the table in front of each of the Wolf Lords.

'The scrolls you've just been given detail the assignments for each of your great companies,' said the Great Wolf. 'We cannot let our personal ambitions cloud our judgement. We each must do what must be done. Now go and prepare your Wolves, for once again the Sons of Russ must cleanse the galaxy of the wretched Thousand Sons, just as Russ the Wolf Father did when he led our brothers to Prospero to destroy Magnus himself.'

A howl of agreement rose within the hall, as Wolf Lords and their Wolf Guards raised their weapons in salute to the Great Wolf. The howl continued even as they began to leave the great hall.

As Gabriella rose from her seat, Rune Lord Aldrek approached her. 'Lady Gabriella, might we have a few more minutes of your time?' Aldrek asked, gesturing towards the Great Wolf.

'Of course, Lord Aldrek,' Gabriella said, moving down the table to stand near the Great Wolf.

As Aldrek took his place beside the Logan Grimnar, Grimnar leaned forwards and rested his arms on the table. 'Lady Gabriella, our situation is dire, and our forces are spread thin.'

'Great Wolf, how may House Belisarius be of assistance?' Gabriella asked, her concern genuine. She had lived on Fenris and she valued the ancient alliance with the Space Wolves and the services of the Wolf-blade.

'It pleases this old warrior to hear the sincerity in your words, Lady Gabriella, again proving the wisdom of our ancestors in the forging of this alliance. I will need all the Space Wolves that we have to investigate and battle this threat. Although their numbers are few, the members of the Wolfblade have shown their abilities on Terra and on Hyades. I require their aid in unravelling this threat.'

'Great Wolf, House Belisarius and the Wolfblade are at your service.'

RAGNAR AWOKE WITH a start, and for an instant he did not recognise the group bunks in the guest chambers of the Fang. Then the blur that was the night before coalesced in his mind with images of toasts, song and heroic stories of battle. He felt as if he was sitting in the learning machine again as the images of last night's events poured through his mind. There were also the strangest images of Haegr entering some kind of bizarre eating contest. It had been a long time since Ragnar had consumed that much Fenrisian ale. A Space Marine's physiology was designed to resist almost any kind of toxin or poison, however, ale from Fenris was a different story entirely.

Standing up he looked around for Haegr and Torin, but they were nowhere to be found. He walked across the room, until his legs became a little wobbly, forcing him to take a seat. In all his recollections of Fenris, his reminiscences of the Fang, he hadn't remembered the ale being so potent. Placing his elbows on his knees, he rested his forehead in his hands.

He leaned back in the chair and started to laugh. He was so happy to be back in the Fang, even though he knew it would not last. Soon he and his battle-brothers would be at war again, but right at this moment he was pleased to be home.

The door to the sleeping quarters opened and Haegr entered the room. 'Have you been drinking all night, Ragnar? Why are you laughing?' Haegr looked puzzled.

Ragnar was amazed at the resilience of his fellow Space Wolf. He knew that Haegr had consumed much more ale than he had, but here he was this morning completely free of the effects. Ragnar stood up, not about to allow Haegr to see him in his true condition.

'Good day, Haegr,' Ragnar greeted his friend.

'Ragnar, the Great Wolf summoned all of his Wolf Lords into the great hall. They've been in there for hours,' Haegr informed Ragnar. 'They should have just finished. I thought you'd like to see if we can find out what's happening.'

'Give me a moment,' Ragnar said. He dressed quickly, and found that the ritual of putting on his power armour helped to clear his head.

Ragnar and Haegr entered the corridor, heading towards the great hall. Ragnar hoped that there would be a need for the Wolfblade. With so many systems under siege, Ragnar felt that every Space Wolf would be needed.

As they rounded the corner of one of the stone corridors, they saw Torin striding in their direction. As Torin approached, Ragnar wondered if his rebirth as a Space Wolf had an unseen flaw, because here was another of his battle-brothers who seemed to have no ill-effects from the night before.

'Greetings, Torin,' Haegr said. 'Ragnar and I are going to the great hall to find out what's happened, unless you already know?'

'I'll join you and make sure you don't get into too many fights. Meanwhile, I have special instructions for Ragnar. Our brother here needs to see Wolf Priest Ranek in his chambers. The old priest asked to speak to you once the meeting ended.'

'Very well, I'll catch up with you later,' Ragnar said, quickening his pace and heading down the corridor to the Wolf Priest's chambers.

As soon as Ragnar was out of earshot, Haegr turned to Torin. 'What's the story, Torin?'

'I'm not sure, old friend, but whatever it is I fear that things will never be the same,' Torin replied.

ONCE HE GOT out of sight of the other members of the Wolfblade, Ragnar stepped up his pace. Although he tried not to seem like he was an overly enthusiastic Blood Claw running through the Fang, he was failing miserably in his attempt. He couldn't help but move quickly, as his mind was running through the possibilities of why his old mentor might have summoned him.

Things were very confusing for Ragnar. Since his interrogation of Cadmus on Hyades, where Cadmus had mentioned the use of an ancient artefact by Madox, he had thought that it might be the Spear of Russ. Then with Gabriella's visions, he felt that his hopes might be affirmed. His excitement was matched only by his dread. If Madox was using the Spear of Russ again, that meant he would be responsible for more than the loss of the holy artefact, he would have given the Thousand Sons a deadly weapon.

These scenarios dominated Ragnar's thoughts as he moved through the corridors of the Fang. He wanted to have the opportunity to redeem himself by recovering the Spear.

If the Thousand Sons had the spear then maybe he had made a mistake using the weapon against Magnus. He had always told himself that he had made the decision in the moment and if called upon to make that decision again he would do so. Now, doubt crept into his mind, and doubt was the most deadly enemy of the warrior.

Ragnar chided himself silently. This was idle speculation, and he knew that his thoughts were getting away from him. Besides, the most important thing was the defence of the Chapter and the Imperium. That was his first duty, and he would live with his decision as long as he continued to serve the Emperor. There was a reason that the Wolf Priest wished to see him, and he would find out in a moment.

Ragnar weaved and sidestepped his way through the busy traffic of the Fang as skalds and servitors went to perform their required duties in this time of war. Finally, he entered the corridor leading to Ranek's chamber. He slowed his pace. Now that he was almost at the meeting, he hesitated, not really sure if he wanted to hear what Ranek had to say.

Rage filled Ragnar's heart, rage at his constant feelings of doubt. He was a Son of Russ and he would face his destiny, whatever it might be. Pausing for a moment, he cleared his mind, forcing himself to accept his actions for what they were. He would do whatever was required of him, but this self-doubt and desire for redemption needed to be set aside. His honour was not more important than his duty.

Large wolf skulls hung on the door to Ranek's chamber. Ragnar knocked and waited, calming himself and focusing. He was ready to meet with Ranek.

The Wolf Priest pulled open the door. 'Ragnar, thank you for coming so quickly,' Ranek said, stepping aside to allow Ragnar to enter. His quarters were sparse, exactly what one would expect for the living area of a Wolf Priest of Russ.

'It is my pleasure, Wolf Priest. How may I be of service?'

'It is actually I who may be of service to you.' Ranek walked across the room and sat down, gesturing for Ragnar to sit in the chair opposite him. Ragnar hesitated for a moment, and then sat.

'I'm not sure what you mean, Lord Ranek,' Ragnar said, confused.

'When you left here, Ragnar, you left under a cloud of political turmoil, with the Chapter split by your decision in regards to the Spear of Russ,' Ranek began. 'It was a decision that I and many others agreed with, a decision based on the choice of evils. Had you chosen otherwise then I believe that you and your brothers would be dead and the Imperium would have been plunged into war once again as the Thousand Sons invaded.' Ranek paused for a moment.

'Since your return from Hyades, Rune Lord Aldrek and his priests have deciphered their runes, and the Wolf Lords have studied the tactics and strategies of the Chaos Space Marines. They suspect that the Thousand Sons have a terrible plan for all of us.'

'Ranek, I understand the severity of the situation, and I would ask for your forgiveness for the bluntness of this question–'

Ranek anticipated Ragnar's question, interrupting him with the answer. 'Yes, Ragnar, the runes imply that the Thousand Sons have found the Spear of Russ. With the sacred artefact, combined with the holy gene-seed harvested on Hyades, we suspect that they plan on conducting a massive ritual that might somehow bring about the destruction of the Sons of Russ.'

Excitement and dread filled Ragnar's heart. In that moment he discovered clarity, clarity of mind that he had never known. He knew what must be done. The events that were unfolding were events that were directly tied to his actions, not just the loss of the Spear, but his actions prior to that as well. He had thwarted the Chaos Sorcerer Madox on two separate occasions. Madox's plot was as much about Ragnar as it was about the Space Wolves. His hatred of Ragnar was at the heart of his plan. That was why Cadmus lured the Wolfblade to Hyades. Ragnar knew that it fell to him to bring this situation to an end, regardless of the cost. Ragnar would stop Madox, redemption or not. It was his destiny.

'Lord Ranek, you know my heart better than anyone. You know that I will do whatever is asked of me. Madox is at the heart of this plan, and the Spear of Russ may be in their hands because of my actions. It falls to me to bring this situation to an end,' Ragnar said, meeting Ranek's gaze, without flinching.

'The Great Wolf made that decision earlier today Ragnar, and he asked Lady Gabriella for the services of Wolfblade. But, know this, what I have told you about the Spear of Russ is known only to a few and with the leave of the Great Wolf. Do not speak of it, save to Lady Gabriella, a Wolf Lord, myself or the Great Wolf himself. He bade me to tell you. He felt you deserved to know,' Ranek said beginning to smile. 'You've grown, Ragnar. I asked you here with the intention of guiding you through the turmoil that I had assumed these events would have thrown you into. However, it would appear that you are no longer the impetuous young warrior that I once knew.'

Ranek rose from his seat, extending his hand to Ragnar, who grasped his forearm in a warrior's handshake. Ranek's pride showed even on his hard face.

'Now, Son of Russ, go and fulfil your destiny.'

Ragnar left Ranek's chamber for the guest quarters he and the Wolfblade had been assigned. There was no longer any doubt in his heart, no question of where he belonged. Everything he had accomplished, every decision, his every failure had led him to this moment. For the first time in a long time, Ragnar's destiny was clear and he would face that destiny as a Space Wolf.

EPILOGUE

THE WAR FOR Corinthus V was nearly over. One more victory and the Space Wolves would break the power of the Night Lords. Yet the war had gone on for one day more than the Space Wolves had expected. With victory in their grasp in a battle on the streets of Saint Harman, Tor, a member of the Wolf Guard, had led his fellow Space Marines into an ambush meant to draw out the Wolf Lord and decapitate the great company. The strength and skill of the Space Wolves had allowed them to emerge defeated but unbowed. Based on information gathered by Space Wolf scouts, Ragnar Blackmane was ready to turn the tables on the forces of Chaos. This time, the main attack by the Space Wolves would provide a diversion, while Tor would get the chance to redeem himself in an assault against a Chaos sorcerer, possibly the leader of these renegades.

Wolf Lord Ragnar Blackmane paced back and forth in front of his men, as they readied themselves for an offensive into Saint Harman. The members of his force waited just outside the Administratum sector, the city's heart, the same sector of the city where the Wolf Lord had been ambushed only the day before.

Ragnar wanted to give the order to attack. He was ready to seize victory over the traitors and the souls who slavishly followed them, but he knew that timing would be critical. He had to wait until he received the signal that Tor was in place.

* * *

WITHIN THE FETID and rusted sewer tunnels beneath Saint Harman, over a kilometre away from the Wolf Lord, Tor led a group of Grey Hunters as they followed two Space Wolf scouts. A powerful sorcerer among the Chaos Space Marines had planned a ritual to open a portal into the warp. According to the scouts, the blasphemous servants of Chaos had chosen the Cathedral of Saint Harman, the city's namesake, as the site of their unholy ceremony.

Tor clenched and unclenched his fist. His Wolf Lord had chosen him from his Wolf Guard to lead this strike, while the rest of the Space Wolves provided a distraction. The day before, Tor had led his pack into an ambush and drawn another pack with him. He had nearly lost his life and had cost his Chapter a few of their great warriors, but Ragnar had chosen him, regardless. For that, Tor was thankful.

He felt responsible for what had happened, and he longed for a chance to restore his honour and make amends. Ragnar had taken him aside before dawn and explained the plan. Tor and a hand-picked group of Grey Hunters would interrupt the Chaos ritual and slay the sorcerer responsible. To provide cover, the Space Wolves would conduct a massive assault, hopefully drawing away as many of the enemy as possible. Tor was surprised that after his failure the Wolf Lord would select him, but one look in Ragnar's eyes and Tor knew that the Wolf Lord understood exactly how he felt. Tor would not fail.

The older scout, Hoskuld, raised his hand for Tor and his men to halt. The squad hesitated in the acrid dimly-lit sewers. Tor could hear the water dripping from leaking pipes and even in the dim light, he could see the colours of contaminants swirling in the water where he and his men stood.

Hoskuld indicated a set of metal rungs leading to a large grate to the street above. 'The alley next to the cathedral,' he whispered. With that, the scouts turned their backs on Tor and his men and jogged off into the deepening shadows of the sewers. Tor knew that they would find their own positions to support the assault.

It was time. Tor activated his comm and signalled to Ragnar, before deactivating it again. The attack would begin, and the rest would be up to him and his pack.

RAGNAR'S COMM BUZZED, and then went silent. Just as he had previously instructed, Tor had simply signalled, and then cut his comm. There was no need to risk the enemy intercepting their messages. The time to launch the attack had come.

Ragnar activated his comm, speaking to all of his Wolf Guard, save Tor, who were scattered throughout the force. 'Move out! The time has come!'

A soft chorus of howls began from one end of the Space Wolf force, and then raced to the other as each pack joined in. Ragnar enjoyed the sound and he could feel the excitement in his veins. There would be nothing subtle about this attack. The Wolf Lord wanted the Night Lords to know he was coming, and he counted on the fact that in their arrogance, the Chaos Space Marines would see the howls as the foolish bravado of a mob of barbarians, rather than realise this entire attack was a distraction.

Packs of Grey Hunters, Blood Claws and a team of Long Fangs made their way into the rockcrete and plasteel canyons of Saint Harman fanning out into different streets. Each group moved carefully, checking for booby traps and ambushes.

A pack of ten Blood Claws escorted the Wolf Lord. Ragnar's push through the street came with its own mobile cover. A tank, the Predator Annihilator *Wolf's Rage*, led the way, with a modified bulldozer blade fused to its front hull, allowing it to push through the debris-filled street. The tank's lascannons gave the *Wolf's Rage* the firepower to deal with almost any enemy. The vehicle was at a disadvantage in the narrow city streets, but Ragnar had chosen the vehicle and its crew because he knew that the threat they posed would draw attention.

The Night Lords didn't disappoint Ragnar. The front blade of the Predator struck a large chunk of rock, and then a melta-bomb detonated, incinerating the blade and sending a spray of hot metal across the front of the tank. Ragnar and the Blood Claws threw themselves to the ground, instinctively going for cover. Their instincts proved correct as bolter fire rained down from the windows of two buildings on each side of the street ahead of them.

'Everyone, follow me,' Ragnar ordered the Blood Claws on his comm. He got off the pavement and immediately broke into a full run, racing past the damaged tank into the building on his left. The only way to eliminate the enemy would be to carve them out of their holes. Skulls of long-dead scribes and bureaucrats stared blankly from the rockcrete facing of the building. Ragnar joked to himself that they had retained their personalities in death.

Bolter rounds ricocheted off Ragnar's power armour, pelting him like hail. He took a grenade from his belt and threw it on the run at the main doors to the building. They were large and darkened with a yellow Imperial eagle emblazoned upon them, which made a perfect target. The krak grenade blew the doors to pieces.

Within seconds, Ragnar and the Blood Claws entered the smoke left behind by the doors and found cover in the building. Now, Ragnar had to lead his men up and find the foe. He hit his comm. 'This is the Wolf Lord. My pack has engaged the enemy.'

TOR AND HIS men had waited for over half an hour in the sewer tunnel since giving the signal. He looked over at Jarl, one of the most experienced Grey Hunters, a warrior best known for his service against orks. Jarl wore a strand of ork fangs as a trophy, in addition to a necklace with a single wolf tooth. He rested a large axe on one shoulder and held his bolter one-handed. 'We're ready, sir, if the time is right,' Jarl said.

Tor realised that he had been looking to Jarl for consent to start the assault, but that wasn't Jarl's decision to make, it was his. Tor knew this was another reason why Ragnar had chosen him. Tor could make sound decisions and he needed to do so again before he let yesterday's events creep into his brain and make him doubt himself. 'The time is right. Let's move, quickly and quietly. We make sure the ritual is starting before we reveal ourselves.'

Tor grabbed the rungs and climbed up to the metal grate. He carefully opened the grate and stepped into an alley between two buildings. The alley was dark, the only light coming from the street visible at one end of the alley. Tor could hear the distant echoes of bolter shots and explosions. He raised his bolter and stealthily moved towards the street.

When he reached the end of the alley, he peered out. His augmented eyes adjusted to the low light just as the eyes of a nocturnal predator would, but he didn't need any enhanced vision to see. The alley opened to a street that ran into a main square in front of the cathedral. The giant religious edifice rose triumphantly above all of the surrounding buildings. Though he was about one hundred metres from the cathedral, the signs of heresy were unmistakable.

A large fountain in front of the cathedral was lit up, shining lights on a statue of Saint Harman, who appeared as an elderly monk, having devoted every waking breath to his devotion to the Emperor. Someone had chipped the face off the statue, leaving it to appear as an empty robe, and instead of clean water, the fountain was filled with blood. Just looking at the building, Tor felt something was very wrong, as if the beast within him could sense the unnatural events that the scouts had assured him were happening there.

A faint greenish light appeared for a moment from the cathedral's front windows. There could be no question in Tor's mind. It was time to set matters right and defeat the enemy.

'Let's move around the perimeter of the square, keep to as much cover as possible and make your way to the left side of the cathedral. We may be able to find an entrance besides the front,' he said.

Like true wolves of Fenris, the Grey Hunters stalked through the shadows and made their way along the edge of the square. If they were detected, the enemy gave no sign. Twice more, the greenish glow came from the cathedral.

The pack reached the outer wall of the cathedral and made its way around the side of the building. A modest door rested in an alcove on the side of the titanic structure, and a carved image of Saint Harman stood untouched over the door. 'The Emperor protects,' said Tor.

As Tor paused to reflect on the Emperor, he caught a faint scent from behind the door, the smell of sulphur and oils. It instantly made him think of the Chaos Space Marines from the previous day. Waving his men away, he readied his bolter.

He gave the door a hard kick, smashing it inwards and then whirled away.

A Night Lord blasted gouts of flame out of the door. In his ornate armour, the light of the flame reflected and burned all the brighter. The Traitor Space Marine advanced without a word, his flamer held ready to incinerate his target.

Tor had avoided the worst of the blast. He threw himself into the passage with no cover, trusting that his power armour and natural speed would provide enough protection. He activated his power sword, sending energy cascading from the hilt, without losing a step of his charge. Before the Night Lord could raise his weapon to fire again, the power sword sliced through the barrel. Tor jammed the blade into his foe, piercing his power armour and leaving him thrashing on the end of the sword. With a solid jerk, he pulled the weapon free and led his men up a staircase, and he hoped, into the main sanctuary.

RAGNAR LED THE Blood Claws up a battered flight of stairs as they raced to the upper floors of the building used by the Night Lords to fire down on the street. Ragnar took the stairs three at a time. He looked forward to running a few traitors through with his runeblade. A door at the top of the stairs marked this as the fifth floor of the building dedicated to the memory of the scribe Leonardus.

The door fell forwards and the servants of Chaos threw grenades down at the Space Wolves. Ragnar could see two of his foes, both Night Lords. They were tall warriors, even for Space Marines, made taller still by large horns jutting from their helms. 'Grenade!' shouted Ragnar as he continued forwards. The sudden attack had momentarily surprised Ragnar and all he could do was keep charging.

The first Night Lord drew a chainsword and interposed himself on the stairs in front of Ragnar. He showed no fear and no hesitation. With his off-hand, he ripped a large pouch off his belt and threw it at the Wolf Lord. This time Ragnar was ready, lashing out at the makeshift missile with his runeblade, and slashing open the pouch to reveal the bloodied helm of a Space Wolf.

'Look upon your fate, dog of the Emperor,' the Night Lord snarled then thrust at Ragnar with his whirring chainsword. Ragnar regained his wits and parried the blade with his own.

Behind him, the other Night Lord readied his bolter, looking for a clean shot at Ragnar.

These were worthy foes, thought Ragnar. In a moment, they had seized the initiative and blocked the stairs, enabling them to fight the Space Wolves one at a time, while the rest of their squad made ready for battle or made their escape. He decided that he had had enough of the Night Lords.

With a sweep of his blade and a howl, the Wolf Lord slashed through the chainsword, rendering it useless, and then raised his bolter to the helm of the Night Lord and squeezed the trigger. Round after round impacted the head of the Chaos Space Marine, blowing large holes in his skull.

Ragnar wasted no time, tossing the body of the first Night Lord aside. The second one mercilessly opened up on the Space Wolf with a torrent of bolter rounds. Ragnar growled and threw himself into the enemy. He took the large man off his feet, and then sat up to give himself enough room to plunge the runeblade into the Chaos Space Marine's gut.

The Night Lord glared at Ragnar even as he lay dying. Ragnar could feel the anger and disgust this traitor held in his heart for the Imperium, a hatred so great that he had sold his soul to Chaos. The Night Lord writhed, but reached for the grenades on his belt. Ragnar saw the move and pinned his foe's wrist to the ground with the barrel of his bolter and then pulled the trigger, blowing his foe's hand off.

With his final chance to kill the Wolf Lord gone, the light in the Night Lord's eyeplates dimmed, and his ghost left him, taking his hatred with it.

The Blood Claws rushed up around Ragnar and into a long corridor. Ragnar's men seemed relatively unscathed from the grenade attack. 'Find any more of them that you can, each of these foes costs the enemy dearly.'

Soon, the Night Lords would try something desperate. Ragnar could hear distant artillery echo from outside. He hadn't ordered artillery bombardment. If anything, Ragnar was hoping to keep the city as intact as possible. If the forces of Chaos had any artillery, then it would be precious indeed.

A Night Lord dropped out of an air vent at the end of the hall and began firing. The Blood Claws saw him and howled. Then they charged like starving wolves having sighted their prey. By the time Ragnar stood, the axes and blades of the Blood Claws had struck the Night Lord in dozens of places. He fell and the Blood Claws continued to reduce him to nearly unrecognisable gore.

Then, a blast shook the building. The Night Lords were willing to fire on their own men in order to kill their enemies. Ragnar looked down at the tall Night Lord he had dismembered and killed. In the remaining hand, the warrior clutched a comm. The attempt to reach the grenade had been a distraction. He might have signalled the enemy to strike the building with their ordinance.

'We need to get out, now!' shouted Ragnar. He hoped that Tor would be successful and soon.

Tor raced up a flight of stairs in the darkened stone Cathedral of Saint Harman, hoping that he had chosen wisely and found a way to the ritual site. Nine Grey Hunters followed their Wolf Guard, ready to complete their mission. The sight before them made all of them take pause.

The entire inner sanctuary of the cathedral had been gutted. Pews were thrown asunder, blood had been poured on the sacred stones of the floor, statues had been toppled and praises to the Gods of Chaos had been written on the walls, proclaiming their power. A billowing emerald bonfire roared between collapsed pews, and robed heretics stood with their arms spread at the edges of the flames, chanting in a strange undulating tongue.

A figure in a horned helm and long blood-red robes led them. Pale veined long-fingered hands extended from his sleeves, and as he gestured, the chanters changed their words and pitch, as if he was some sinister maestro conducting a choir of blasphemy. The flames also reacted to his every gesture, and Tor knew that this man was the sorcerer.

Then, there were the Chaos Space Marines.

Eight Night Lords held positions around the room, standing in four pairs with rubble nearby providing easy cover. Each one of the ancient Chaos Space Marines had his own distinctive armour, but all of them shared the same look. Spikes and blades designed to inspire fear doubled as practical weapons, while belts of ammunition were strung over their chests. The Night Lords were hard fighters and each individual was prepared to hold out against terrible odds. They showed no hesitation when the Space Wolves arrived, although Tor was certain that they must have surprised their enemy. They raised their bolters at the Space Wolves in well-drilled unison.

Tor knew what he needed to do. The Night Lords would be content to engage the Space Wolves in a firefight until the ritual brought something unholy from the warp to finish them off. Tor wasn't about to wait for that to happen. It was time to charge.

Bolter rounds crashed into the Grey Hunters as they charged. The Night Lords mercilessly fired shots as fast as their bolters allowed. Tor felt the rounds battering his power armour, but he clenched his teeth and focused on the sorcerer – his objective.

A Night Lord leapt over a crumbling statue and launched himself at Tor, realising that the Wolf Guard intended to kill the sorcerer. Circular chainblades spun on the Chaos Space Marine's armour, and he leapt at Tor, thrusting the blades forwards to slash through the Space Wolf's armour and then his flesh and bone. He moved with a speed that rivalled Tor's own.

Tor paused to bring up his power sword to defend himself, but even as he began, he knew that he would be too slow. Fortunately for him, Space Wolves ran in packs. Although Jarl was a step behind Tor, the Grey Hunter had been watching for an attack. He threw his body up as a shield and the Night Lord crashed into Jarl instead of Tor. Sparks flew as the Night Lord's chainblades ripped into Jarl's power armour. The decorated veteran with his ork trophies roared rather than screamed from the pain as he wrestled with the foe.

Tor turned back to the sorcerer. He would not let Jarl's effort go for naught. The mage gestured at Tor, breaking the ritual as he did so. Immediately, the emerald flame flickered and died. The monks screamed as one, while bolts of power flashed from the sorcerer's fingertips at Tor.

Ozone and brimstone mixed in the air as the bolts crashed into Tor. He felt all of his hearts seize up at once, and suddenly he couldn't breathe. He kept moving as if he were an automaton. The sorcerer clenched his fists and as he did, Tor's chest tightened. The Space Wolf's eyesight dimmed and his ears rang. He thought to himself that no matter what, even if it meant death, he would reach the sorcerer and complete his mission. He would justify Ragnar's faith in him. He had been given a chance to redeem himself and nothing, not even the dark magics of Chaos would prevent him from succeeding.

The Chaos sorcerer gazed at the Wolf Guard, and although his eyesight blurred, the Space Wolf glared back. The Space Marine's reaction surprised the sorcerer, and Tor watched the malicious confidence leave the robed figure. As it did, Tor almost felt his strength return. He closed the gap between them.

One of the monks tried to intervene, much as Jarl had gone to Tor's aid, but even half-blind and in agony, Tor still possessed enough strength to lash out with his power sword and cut down his blocker.

The energy flickered on the Chaos sorcerer's fingers. Tor couldn't tell if his foe said anything – the rushing in his ears was too great – but there was no longer any distance to cross. The sorcerer broke the spell and attempted to draw a blade to defend himself.

Breath flowed back into Tor's lungs and his hearts pounded. His sight instantly improved and the rushing in his ears faded. Instead of pausing to cherish the return of his senses and breathe, Tor brought his power sword up into the body of the sorcerer. Mystic robes, flesh and bone couldn't stop the stroke as Tor cut the sorcerer in half. The monks screamed again as one and then fell, like marionettes suddenly without strings.

The Night Lords redoubled their attacks against the Space Wolves. They had failed to protect the sorcerer and the Chaos Space Marines knew that only death would satisfy their Dark Gods. Tor felt power fill his body. He had completed the mission for the Wolf Lord. He activated his comm quickly. 'Wolf Lord, the deed is done,' he said and without waiting for a response, leapt to the aid of his fellow Space Wolves.

RAGNAR AND THE Blood Claws had escaped the building where the ambushers had lain in wait for them, but only moments before artillery fire rained down upon it. The bolter fire had stopped on the street and, cautiously, the Wolf Lord led his men forwards.

The Wolf Lord's comm crackled to life, 'Wolf Lord, the deed is done,' said Tor, triumph filling his voice.

'Well done,' said Ragnar, although he heard the sounds of battle on the other end of the comm. Still, he knew the battle would be over soon. Without the sorcerer, the Night Lords wouldn't have access to their daemonic allies and their material resources were too little for them to continue to hold out. Ragnar knew the enemy would have to retreat with whatever forces they had left.

Ranulf came running through a cross street with a pack of men. 'Hail, Wolf Lord! The foe appears to be in full retreat.'

'Good, that's how it was supposed to happen. Well done. Give me a moment, Ranulf.'

Ragnar opened a comm channel to Hoskuld, the old Space Wolf scout. 'Tor succeeded. Go ahead and help him.'

'Aye, Wolf Lord, we're there to back him up,' said Hoskuld.

Ranulf looked over at his Wolf Lord. Quietly, he asked, 'Why didn't you just have the scouts try to kill the sorcerer?'

Ragnar placed his hand on Ranulf's wide shoulder, 'Because, I'll need Tor's spirit on the next planet. He deserved a chance to take responsibility. It'll make him a better warrior.'

After a moment, Ragnar added, 'It worked for me.'

WOLF'S HONOUR

PROLOGUE
Heart of the Wolf

THE FOUR THUNDERHAWKS swept in at full power with the sun of Hydra Hydalis at their backs, plunging like a sheaf of iron-tipped spears at the dark leviathan drifting before them. If someone – or some*thing* – on the space hulk was watching for signs of attack, Ragnar Blackmane wanted to mask their approach until the last possible moment, concealing their emissions amid the raging solar winds given off by the system's three suns.

It hung in the void like the pitted shard of a broken world. Ridges of stone, plains of ice and towers of trapped metal stretched for more than ten kilometres, dwarfing all but the largest of Imperial battleships. *And not the biggest of its kind by any stretch*, Ragnar thought grimly, studying its ominous bulk through the viewports of the lead Thunderhawk's command deck.

Space hulks were the flotsam and jetsam of the warp, or so the theory went, drifting in and out of the immaterium as though carried on an invisible tide. Many were nothing more than hunks of lifeless rock, perhaps torn from worlds by the teeth of warp storms in ages past. Others, however, were studded with the hulls of entombed starships, some of them tens of thousands of years old and not all of them human in design. Such discoveries were legendary; often they contained treasure troves of lost technology and xenos lore.

Sometimes they also carried horrors hidden deep within their decks: foul alien raiders, hordes of twisted mutants, or worse.

When the space hulk first arrived at the edge of the system almost eight standard months ago the handful of decrepit ships that comprised the Hydalis system defence squadron drew close enough to perform a series of long-range auguries. Not long afterwards, the alarm had gone out via astropath, and three months later Fenris sent its answer.

Now all that stood between the oncoming hulk and the forty-five billion Imperial citizens of Hydra Cordalis was Ragnar Blackmane and his small company of Wolves.

The harsh light of Hydalis's primary gave the notional prow of the hulk a bleached out, blue-grey cast. Tendrils of steam wreathed the rocky surface as pockets of trapped ice boiled away beneath the suns' harsh glare. Here and there, the light flared painfully bright along a spar of metal or a shard of jagged hull plating. Abyssal shadows pooled in the depths of ancient impact craters. They seemed to shift with the changing position of the Thunderhawk, like the multiple eyes of some vast predator. The thought left a cold feeling in the Wolf Lord's gut. Ragnar was first and foremost a son of Fenris, and his people had a healthy dread for the horrors of the deep.

Baring his fangs in a silent snarl, Ragnar surveyed the red-lit interior of the command deck. It was a cramped space at the best of times, the pilot and co-pilot side-by-side at the forward end of the compartment. A master tech-priest and the senior augur operator situated directly behind them. The two bondsmen were fitted in bulky, armoured flight suits that made them look slope-shouldered and apelike, but Ragnar's power armoured bulk loomed head and shoulders above them all. With the Wolf Lord standing at the back of the compartment the atmosphere was nearly claustrophobic, but the crew did their level best to go about their work as though Ragnar wasn't there.

The Wolf Lord turned his gaze to the augur operator at his right. 'Any change?' he asked.

'None, lord,' the crewman replied, never taking his eyes from the wavering lines on the augur screens before him. The operator reached up with a gloved hand and made a minute adjustment to a set of brass fronted dials. 'No engine heat or augur signals. It's drifting at a constant rate, heading for the centre of the system.'

'Any power emissions at all?' Ragnar inquired.

The crewman shook his head. 'None so far,' he said. 'We'll know more as we get closer.'

Ragnar nodded thoughtfully, and then addressed the pilot. 'Where is the hull that the defence ships spotted on their augurs?'

The pilot glanced over his shoulder at the Wolf Lord; like Ragnar, the Space Wolf wasn't wearing a helmet. Bright blue eyes glittered beneath a pair of shaggy red eyebrows, and a web of fine scars indented the pale skin of his right cheek. 'We'll find it on the dorsal side of the hulk, lord,' the pilot said in a rumbling voice, 'roughly amidships, so they said. We'll be there in another few minutes.' Then he turned back and keyed the vox-bead behind his ear. 'Jotun flight: approach pattern Epsilon,' the pilot growled, 'and Snorri, keep your fat arse tucked into formation this time. If you get shot down again you're walking back to Fenris!'

Ragnar couldn't hear Snorri's reply, but the flight leader let out a booming laugh and pushed the throttles forward. The three other Thunderhawks in the flight shook out into a rough arrowhead formation, and their thrusters flared blue-white as they began the final phase of their approach.

The Wolf Lord shifted his weight and reached for a nearby stanchion as the assault craft pulled into a climb that carried them over the hulk's bulbous prow at a distance of less than a hundred metres. Jumbled plains of rock and twisted metal flashed by underneath the Thunderhawk's nose. Ragnar caught fleeting glimpses of broken hulls jutting from the surface: here the curved bow of an Imperial merchant ship, there the saw-toothed profile of an ork raider. Once he thought he caught the dull sheen of yellowed bone encased in a steaming sheet of ice.

Then he saw it, like a dark cathedral rising from a broken field of stone. 'There, off to starboard,' Ragnar said, pointing just to the right of their current course. 'That's it!'

'Where?' the pilot said, peering into the darkness. Then he straightened in his seat. 'Ah, yes. I see it now.'

The ancient warship rose from the centre of the hulk as though it had taken shape around her. Plains of broken stone stretched away on all sides, rising almost to the level of her dorsal turret deck. Her buttressed command bridge stood straight and tall, still remarkably intact after more than four thousand years. The prow of the Imperial battleship was almost completely buried, but Ragnar saw that instead of the customary eagle's head at its crown there rose the figure of an armoured warrior, sword and shield held ready.

The tech-priest shifted in his seat and pulled a thick, leather-covered tome from a satchel tucked underneath his console. The priest flipped through the yellowed pages, comparing the winged statue on the warship with the images pictured in the book. Suddenly he sat upright. 'Here it is,' he said, his voice tinged with awe. 'She's the *Dominus Bellum*.

One of Vandire's ships, according to the text. Disappeared right after the battle of Ophelia VII.'

Ragnar studied the derelict carefully. The condition of the ancient battleship was crucial to his plans. As soon as he'd received the report from the Hydalis defence squadron he knew that his lone strike cruiser, the *Stormwolf*, had no chance of destroying the hulk on its own. If the *Dominus Bellum's* reactors were still intact, however, it was possible they could destroy the drifting hulk from within.

'Any power readings?' the Wolf Lord asked.

The augur operator studied his screens and shook his head. 'No lord. It's... wait!' He began tuning a set of dials, and the lines on one of the screens suddenly spiked. 'I'm picking up energy spikes along the dorsal hull and z-band augur signals!'

'Morkai's teeth!' the pilot cursed, grabbing for his mic. 'Jotun flight! Evasive action!'

Just as he spoke, Ragnar saw pinpricks of fire flash and stutter along the length of the battleship's upper deck, and suddenly the Thunder-hawk was engulfed in nets of tracer fire and blasts of explosive shells. Hammer blows rang against the Thunderhawk's armoured hull, and the Wolf Lord was thrown forward as the assault ship dived even closer to the hulk's treacherous hull. The other Thunderhawks of Jotun flight followed suit, smoke streaming from minor hits along their fuselages and wings.

Ragnar tightened his grip on the stanchion as the Thunderhawk plunged through the chaotic storm of fire. The battleship's defensive turrets blazed away at the oncoming assault ships, filling the void with a wall of energy bolts, shells and streams of high-velocity slugs. Shrap-nel from near misses raked at the Thunderhawk's flanks, and a blow like a Titan's fist smote the craft on the starboard side. Lurid red icons flashed urgently on the tech-priest's console, and the young crewman began flipping switches hurriedly as he whispered a prayer of salvation to the Omnissiah.

The Wolf Lord growled under his breath. The plan had been to try and find an intact hangar deck to land on, but that was out of the ques-tion now. Ragnar realised that any hope of a rapid and orderly sweep of the derelict had just been thrown out of the airlock. He reached for-ward with his free hand and gripped the pilot's shoulder. 'Full assault profile!' he yelled. 'Get us on board any way you can.'

Nodding his head, the pilot keyed his vox-bead to relay orders to the flight. Another blow shook the assault ship, and Ragnar's keen nose caught the smell of burning circuitry. Quick as he could, the Wolf Lord turned and stepped through the rear hatchway, heading down the ladder beyond to the assault bay where his Wolf Guard and the company's priests waited.

Ragnar dropped down to the metal clad deck with a clang. The cavernous assault bay, large enough for thirty fully-armed Space Marines, was crowded with ten warriors in massive Tactical Dreadnought armour. Though slow and ponderous, the ancient suits of Terminator armour were ideal for the close confines of a space hulk's passageways, and Ragnar had brought every one of the ancient suits he could muster. Power fists flexed and armoured heads swivelled to regard the Wolf Lord, and a chorus of rough howls greeted Ragnar from the Wolf Guard's vox-units. Jurgen, the company's Iron Priest, waited at the far end of the bay, flanked by four powerful thrall servitors. Jurgen was locked into his assault cradle like the other Wolves, his helmeted head bowed as he read a litany of protection from a small, metal clad book in his gauntleted hands.

Next to Ragnar, an adamantine helmet worked in the shape of a massive wolf skull turned slightly to regard him. Pale golden lenses the colour of lupine eyes studied him from the depths of the helm's black oculars. The vox-unit on the Wolf Priest's Terminator suit crackled. 'I take it the hulk is hostile,' he said laconically.

Ragnar chuckled, stepping to his assault cradle and reaching for his waiting helmet. Normally he hated wearing the thing, preferring to feel the thunder of battle and the hot touch of blood on his skin. That sort of thing required air, however, and there was no way to know if they'd find any inside the battleship's hull. 'Frankly, it never occurred to me that it might be otherwise,' he replied. 'I didn't expect this hot a reception, though.'

He pulled the helmet on and locked it into the adamantine gorget. There was a moment of darkness, and then, immediately, the helm's optical systems flickered into life. Icons and readouts shone in dull colours at the corners of his vision, showing the status of his suit and those of his pack. With a murmured command, he tapped into the Thunderhawk's command channel and received status icons from the rest of the company as he locked himself into the assault cradle. The Wolf Lord noted grimly that three icons in Hogun's Blood Claw pack were flashing amber. *Jotun Four's been hit hard,* Ragnar thought grimly. *Three men out of action and we haven't even reached the target yet. An ill omen.*

A massive impact struck the rear quarter of the assault ship, hard enough to throw Ragnar against the cradle's restraints. His stomach lurched for half an instant as the whole ship seemed to slew sideways. The battle lanterns flickered. In the darkness, one of the Wolf Guard threw back his head and howled like a fiend. Fist and sword clashed against armour, and rough voices barked out battle chants as old as Fenris itself. Ragnar bared his teeth in the close confines of his helmet and felt his blood burn.

Then there was a thunderous roar, and the Thunderhawk shook from stem to stern. A bright red icon flashed a warning but Ragnar already knew what was coming. 'Here we go!' he bellowed, and the assault craft touched down on the battleship's hull with a bone-crushing impact and a scream of tortured metal.

Ragnar rebounded from the cradle restraints and smashed a fist against the quick release. With a murmured benediction, he queried the Thunderhawk's machine-spirit and gauged the position of his forces. Jotun flight had broken formation at the flight leader's order and their high-speed approaches had scattered them in a wide arc across the battleship's dorsal hull. Jotun Four was closest to Ragnar's Thunderhawk, landing parallel to the Wolf Lord's assault ship almost 750 metres away. Jotun Two had landed in the shadow of one of the battleship's massive dorsal lance turrets, well over a kilometre distant. There was no way to tell by the readout if the assault ship would be able to take off once more. Jotun Three was nowhere to be seen, the Thunderhawk's icon conspicuously absent from the readout.

Ragnar bit back a sulphurous curse. He gestured to Jurgen. 'Ventral breach,' he ordered, and the Iron Priest leapt into action. Slipping out of his assault cradle, Jurgen moved nimbly among the hulking Terminators and knelt before a hatch on the deck in the centre of the bay. The Iron Priest's voice rolled sonorously from the vox-unit of his ornately worked power armour, asking forgiveness from the ancient spirits of the *Dominus Bellum*, and then pronouncing the Benediction of the Fiery Breach as he flipped open an access panel beside the hatch. Jurgen lifted a heavy lever, and the shaped melta charges attached to the ventral breaching unit detonated with a leaden *thump*. There was a shrieking of incandescent gases as the focused plasma charge drove like a molten spear tip through more than half a dozen metres of heavy armour and pierced the battleship's hull.

Moving with the speed and ease of veteran warriors, the Wolf Guard quickly formed up around the ventral hatch, ready to jump off. Ragnar keyed open the command channel on his vox-unit. For the moment, he could tap into the vox-network of Jotun Flight's transports and communicate with his scattered forces. He knew from experience that would change once he was inside the hull of the huge warship. 'Strike Team Surtur, status report,' he called.

The company's Wolf Scouts and Leif's Grey Hunter pack aboard Jotun Two checked in first. 'We're going in now,' the Wolf Guard pack leader reported. 'I mark your position at twelve hundred metres. Hogun's pack is closer. Do you want me and Petur to link up with the Blood Claws first?'

'You look to your own pack, Leif,' Hogun cut in. The Blood Claw pack leader's voice was rough-edged with fury. 'The Blood Claws hunt alone!'

The vehemence in Hogun's voice surprised Ragnar. The Wolf Guard had proven to be a cold, clear-eyed warrior, which was why he'd been given command of the hot-headed Blood Claws in the first place. 'What's the status of your pack, Hogun?' Ragnar snapped.

'Three brothers are badly wounded. They have slipped into the Red Dream,' Hogun snarled. Space Marines, with their enhanced physiology and redundant vital organs, were extraordinarily difficult to kill. Space Marines in the field who had been incapacitated by their wounds often went into a life-sustaining form of suspended animation until they could receive proper treatment. 'A burst of shells tore through the assault bay,' the pack leader continued. 'The rest of us got away with minor wounds.'

'Does anyone know what happened to Jotun Three?' Ragnar asked.

'They were hit hard, just short of the target,' Leif reported. 'I can't be certain, but I think they overshot and landed on the starboard side of the ship.'

'Have they contacted you?'

'No, lord. It's possible their vox system was knocked out. As I said, they were hit hard.'

That left a pack of Grey Hunters and the company's Long Fangs unaccounted for and possibly dead. Ragnar drew his bolt pistol and considered his options. 'All right,' he said. 'I and my pack will activate our beacons now. Leif, you and Hogun home in on our signal. Petur, take your scouts and see if you can locate Jotun Three. We'll hold here until everyone has linked up. Then we'll head aft to the reactor vault. Now go, and Russ be with you.'

'For Russ and the Allfather!' Leif answered, and the channel went silent.

Satisfied, Ragnar activated his power armour's recovery beacon and instructed his Wolf Guard to do the same. Then he gave Jurgen a curt nod, and the Iron Priest turned a heavy dial on the control panel beside the hatch. With a sharp hiss and a column of scalding steam, the breaching hatch slid open. Ragnar stepped to the edge and peered down into a circular shaft of semi-molten metal that dropped away into darkness. Baring his fangs in the close confines of his helmet, the Wolf Lord leapt into the shaft.

The drop was longer than he expected. Ragnar fell through the breaching shaft and into a cavernous space beneath, hitting the canted deck twenty metres below with an echoing boom. He landed in a crouch, servos whining, and then leapt to his feet and dashed forward, pistol at the ready. His chainsword flashed from its scabbard, its diamond-hard teeth whirring to deadly life with a faint, ominous moan.

He found himself in a long, high-ceilinged passageway crowded with debris. Armoured viewports let in the faint gleam of starlight, giving the silent corridor a ghostly cast. Fallen support beams and smashed masonry from toppled statues and broken containers were strewn everywhere. The dust of ages swirled in faint eddies around Ragnar's feet. His armour registered heat and atmosphere, heavy with nitrogen and laced with an acrid stink that set the Wolf Lord's teeth on edge.

The Wolf Priest landed next, power crackling menacingly from his crozius arcanum, and then came the Wolf Guard Terminators in rapid succession. The Terminators faced outwards in a circular perimeter to allow Jurgen and his thralls to lower down their cargo: an armoured case containing a plasma breaching charge. The Iron Priest reckoned that they would need a minimum of three charges to pierce the battle-ship's reactor cores and destroy the hulk. Ragnar had brought four, just to be safe. Leif's pack had one, Hogun's pack another, and Einar, the Grey Hunter pack leader on Jotun Three, had the spare. With Einar missing, however, they'd lost their safety margin, which Ragnar didn't like at all.

Powerful searchlights cut through the darkness as the Wolf Guard activated their suit lights. 'Ho, lord!' one of the warriors called out. 'Have a look at this.'

Ragnar followed the beam of the warrior's searchlight and saw a curious pile of weapons lying in the dust. Frowning, the Wolf Lord walked over and inspected them. They were crude swords and axes shaped from bulkhead plating, the hide grips tattered and grey. A massive, ungainly firearm, clearly built for something much larger than a man lay nearby. A long, twisted belt of corroded shells lay pooled beneath the weapon.

'Greenskins,' Ragnar growled. 'There were orks on this ship at some point, but what happened to them?'

'The previous owners must have seen them off,' the Wolf Priest replied. '*Someone* turned those turrets on us.'

'Not so,' Jurgen said, lowering the breaching charge carefully to the deck. With a hiss of pneumatics, the Iron Priest's powerful servo-arm retracted against his backpack. 'It could have been an automated response triggered by the ship's machine-spirit,' he said, and shrugged. 'At least now we know the battleship's reactors are still active.'

Ragnar nudged the pile of crude weapons with the toe of his boot. 'Then what happened to the greenskins?' he mused, 'and why were their bodies removed, but their weapons left behind?'

A sense of foreboding crept upon the Wolf Lord, prickling the hairs on the back of his neck. Something was very wrong. He turned and peered warily down the rubble strewn passageway leading aft. Ragnar could feel a chill creeping over him, like a rime of frost spreading inexorably across the surface of his brain. He suddenly regretted not having the services of a Rune Priest at his disposal.

Ragnar keyed his vox-unit. 'All packs report in,' he ordered.

A hissing screech of static answered. Words came and went in the torrent of noise. It might have been Hogun, but Ragnar couldn't be sure. 'Damned armoured bulkheads,' he muttered.

'Hist!' The Wolf Priest said. 'Did you hear that?'

Ragnar cocked his head and listened, straining his enhanced senses to the utmost. There! He heard it, a whispery sound, like wind over broken stones or the hiss of a distant tide.

Or like the dry clatter of claws, hundreds and hundreds of them, scrabbling along the deck of an ancient battleship.

They swept up the passageway in a seething wave of chitin, their armoured shells shining dully in the searchlights. The xenos swarm flowed over obstacles and along the pitted walls like a swarm of spiders, their four arms and powerful legs scrabbling for purchase on the slick metal bulkheads. They were almost as large as Space Marines, with broad, taloned hands that looked capable of rending adamantium plate, and armoured carapaces that shone a mottled green beneath the Wolf Guard's suit lights. Their heads were bulbous and vaguely humanoid, each with a leering, fanged mouth and black eyes as cold as the Abyss itself.

The people of Hydra Hydalis were in far greater danger than anyone imagined.

'Genestealers!' Ragnar snarled, raising his bolt pistol and firing into the oncoming mass. Carapaces burst, and torn limbs spun through the air as the mass-reactive shells found their marks. Keening, inhuman shrieks echoed along the passageway, and were lost in the rattling thunder of storm bolters as the Wolves of Fenris answered their foes.

The front ranks of the xenos horde writhed and rippled as streams of explosive shells tore through them, blasting frenzied monsters apart. One of the Wolf Guard stepped forward with a roar and levelled a heavy flamer at the oncoming horde. Scores of shrieking creatures vanished in a seething blast of promethium, but the rest came on, trampling their burning kin beneath the weight of hundreds of clawed feet.

Shouts and gunfire echoed from the forward end of the passageway as well. The xenos monsters had them surrounded. Ragnar caught a glimpse of the Wolf Priest on the other side of the perimeter, directing fire from half the Wolf Guard into the new wave of attackers. A second Terminator opened fire with his heavy flamer, sweeping the forward passage in an arc of all-consuming flame.

A genestealer leapt at Ragnar from high on the starboard wall of the passageway, reaching for the Wolf Lord with its taloned hands. Ragnar pivoted on his left foot and shot the creature point-blank, hurling its shattered body into the oncoming mob. More alien monsters were leaping at him, dropping from the walls or bounding ahead of the oncoming horde. Ragnar's frost blade howled as he decapitated one attacker in mid-leap, and then spun and severed the limbs of another. A fourth monster reared before him like a cobra. Howling his battle lust, Ragnar shot the creature in the face. Then the air filled with mindless, screeching cries as the tide of horrors swept over the Space Wolves.

Claws slashed and rang against Ragnar's armour. Rending talons jabbed like knives, striking hip, shoulder, neck and face. The Wolf Lord's heart hammered in his chest, and his blood seethed with righteous rage. He swept his ancient sword in devastating arcs, splitting torsos, severing limbs and slicing throats. The stink of xenos fluids filled the air, and every blow the monsters landed on Ragnar only enflamed him further. The battle madness was upon him, and he embraced it gladly.

Ragnar's vision narrowed. A howling filled his ears, rising and falling in volume like a spirit of the damned. The sounds of battle blurred, as though echoing from far away. Even the blurring speed of the aliens seemed to slow. A talon found a chink in his armour and bit deep. The Wolf Lord decapitated the monster with a backhanded slash, and then coolly shot three more monsters point-blank. A warning icon at the corner of his eye told Ragnar his pistol was empty. He smashed the butt of the pistol into the skull of another leaping xenos and dashed its body to the deck.

All around him, the Wolf Guard lashed out at the frenzied creatures with fist and blade, their Terminator suits splashed with alien blood. Ragnar glimpsed Jurgen the Iron Priest hurling knots of broken creatures through the air with sweeps of his powerful servo-arm. The Wolf

Priest stood at the other side of the circle, laying about with his fiery crozius arcanum and bellowing a fell battle chant in the tongue of Fenris.

A monster leapt at Ragnar from the left. Without thinking, the Wolf Lord stunned the creature with a blow from his pistol and then split it from shoulder to hip with his blood-stained blade. Another, seeing its opportunity, dashed in from the opposite side, talons slashing for Ragnar's throat. Yet before it could reach the Wolf Lord, the monster was torn apart in a stream of storm bolter shells from a nearby Wolf Guard.

Ragnar spun around, seeking more foes to slay, but everywhere he looked he found only the heaped bodies of the fallen. Terminators moved among the enemy dead, smoke rising from the barrels of their storm bolters as they finished off the wounded. Three of the Iron Priest's thralls were dead, their flesh-and-metal bodies ripped apart by alien claws. Jurgen knelt beside the fourth, attempting to repair a damaged leg joint. The Wolf Priest stood off to one side, bloody and indomitable, his Terminator armour limned in lurid red light from still burning pools of promethium.

The Wolf Lord breathed deeply, trying to master the fire burning in his blood. His hands worked of their own accord, dropping the bolt pistol's empty magazine and slapping in another. The howling continued to echo in his ears, a savage, bestial sound, devoid of reason or sanity.

With a chill, Ragnar realised that it was coming over the command channel. It sounded like Hogun's voice.

'Hogun?' Ragnar called over the vox. 'Hogun, answer me!' Abruptly, the howling ceased, but Hogun made no reply. Cursing silently, the Wolf Lord switched channels. 'Leif? Do you read?' Immediately Ragnar heard a response, but it was too garbled by static to make out.

Suddenly the Wolf Priest whirled, raising his storm bolter. 'More scrabbling sounds,' he warned, 'coming from further aft.'

Now that they had been discovered, the genestealers were swarming from their hiding places and seeking out the intruders. It was likely that all of the packs were under attack, and the Blood Claws sounded like they were in dire trouble. If Ragnar didn't act quickly the whole company might be overrun, and the fate of the system would be sealed. 'Follow me!' he ordered, heading down the forward end of the passage in the direction of Hogun's pack. 'Heavy flamers cover the rear. I don't want any of those xenos beasts overtaking us.'

The Wolf Guard fell into formation without a word, surrounding Jurgen and his demolition charge as they moved down the passageway at a rumbling trot. The Wolf Priest loped silently beside Ragnar, peering warily into the gloom. No doubt he'd heard the howls over the vox-net as well, and could guess what they portended.

It had been a long time since Ragnar had heard such a cry from a brother Wolf. Every Space Wolf had to contend with the beast within. The gifts Russ gave to his sons were double-edged, like everything else about Fenris. The strength and ferocity of the wolf could not be tamed, but constantly tugged at its chains, testing the will of its master, and made no distinction between friend or foe. To the wolf, there was only the hunt and the joy of the kill.

Ragnar had travelled almost seven hundred metres down the passageway when he came upon the first xenos bodies. The dead monsters had been burst by bolt pistol shells or split by axe and sword, and the further he went the more numerous they became.

The field of slaughter stretched for almost a hundred metres down the passageway, with dead aliens piled in drifts almost as high as Ragnar's chest. Hogun's Blood Claws had waged an epic fight, driven slowly but steadily backwards by the sheer weight of their foes. Ragnar fought back a wave of dread, expecting to find the torn corpses of the pack somewhere ahead.

Instead, a trio of gore-splashed warriors leapt from behind a pile of alien corpses, levelling their bolt pistols at Ragnar's head. One of the Blood Claws had lost his helmet in the battle, and his eyes were wild with battle lust. Recognising their lord, the Blood Claws lowered their weapons at once and stepped aside. 'Hail, Ragnar Wolf Lord,' the bare-headed warrior cried breathlessly.

'Hail, Bregi,' Ragnar replied, stepping past the warriors. He found himself at a corridor junction, occupied by eight restless Blood Claws. Their armour was battered and rent, spattered with gore from head to toe. They raised their stained weapons in salute, and Ragnar saluted in return. 'What happened here?' he asked.

Bregi stepped forward, head held high. 'We were on our way to meet you, lord,' he said, 'and the cursed xenos were waiting for us. They were hiding in the debris and hanging in the shadows along the walls. Hogun tried to lead us out of the ambush, but there were just too many of them.' The Blood Claw glanced down the passageway, his expression grim. 'They forced us all the way back here, and then they hit us from the junction, too. They broke through our cordon, and then it was every warrior for himself.' The young warrior faced Ragnar. 'I lost count of all the monsters I slew, but for every one I struck down it seemed ten more were waiting to take its place. Then Hogun… he began to howl,' Bregi said, and a haunted look came over him. 'He hurled himself at his foes, slaying half-a-dozen monsters with every sweep of his axe. It was… terrible to behold.'

Ragnar nodded grimly. 'I know of what you speak. What happened then?'

'Hogun fought like a wild beast,' Bregi continued. 'The xenos filth couldn't stand against him. He killed everything he could reach, and then, when there weren't any monsters left to kill, he took to hacking up the corpses. We... we tried to stop him, tried to calm him down, but when Erdwulf and Halvdan laid hands on him he turned and split Erdwulf's skull.' The Blood Claw's gaze fell upon the bodies of his three packmates. 'Halvdan and Svipdaeg fought him, thinking Hogun possessed, and perhaps he was. Hogun lost his helmet in the fight, and I saw the look on his face.' Bregi looked up at Ragnar. 'He was wolf-bitten, lord. I saw it in his eyes. He's been lost to the Wulfen.'

'Where is he now?' Ragnar asked.

'He killed Halvdan and Svipdaeg and then ran off down that junction, howling like one of the damned,' Bregli replied. 'He took the demolition charge with him. It was still strapped to his back.'

Ragnar bit back a curse. 'You're pack leader now, Bregi,' he said. 'The Old Wolf will hear of your pack's courage when we return to the Fang. Now see to your men.'

Bregi nodded gravely and turned to his waiting pack.

A terrible howl echoed from the junction corridor. It was a fearsome, hungry sound, fraught with madness and pain.

Memories rose unbidden in his mind, down the long span of years: of the fighting on Charys and the ill-fated journey of the *Fist of Russ*; of Gabriella and his old companions, Torin and Haegr. He saw in his mind's eye the storm wracked plain, and heard the mournful howls of the Wulfen. They had all experienced the curse of the Wulfen-kind on that dark campaign, each in their own way. For a time, they had all known what it meant to be lost.

The Wolf Priest stepped close, his gaze penetrating and inscrutable. 'What now, Wolf Lord?' he asked quietly.

In truth, there was only one thing he could do. 'Tend to the fallen,' Ragnar said. 'I'm going after Hogun.'

ONE
Sealed in Blood

'TWELVE SECONDS TO insertion!' Mikal Sternmark shouted over the vox, his voice rising over the shrieking wind and the thunder of the guns. 'We're entering the flak barrier now.'

As if on cue, a heavy shell exploded close to Berek Thunderfist's drop-pod, peppering its armoured hide with shrapnel, and shaking the Wolf Lord in his restraints like a rat in a terrier's jaws. More shells exploded in rapid succession, like staccato drumbeats against the drop-pod's skin, as the assault force streaked at near-supersonic speed through the capital city's air defence zone.

The Imperial Guard commanders on the ground had assured him that most of the city's anti-aircraft guns had been knocked out of action in the last few weeks. Another blast rang like a hammer blow against the pod's flank, hard enough to rattle Berek's teeth. If this was their idea of light AA fire, by Russ he didn't want to know what a full barrage felt like.

'Hang on, lads,' he said with a fierce laugh, 'here's where the ride gets rough!'

The Chaos uprising was in its fourth month on the planet Charys, an agri-world ominously close to Fenris. Servants of the Ruinous Powers had arisen on dozens of worlds spread across the Space Wolf domains, overthrowing local governments, staging suicide attacks and disrupting vital military and industrial networks. Many of the uprisings had been brutally dealt with by the Space Wolves and local Imperial Guard units, but the speed and ferocity of the campaign had left the Chapter scattered and their resources stretched thin. Elements of the Space Wolves' twelve great companies were in action on more than two dozen worlds, and several important sectors were teetering on the brink of anarchy.

The attacks were anything but random. The Old Wolf Logan Grimnar, Master of the Chapter, had seen that at once. It had begun with a Chaos uprising among the primitive xenos tribes on Hyades, triggering near-simultaneous attacks across vast stretches of space. A complex and devious plan had been set in motion, one that had clearly been in the works for a great many years. The enemy's ultimate objective remained a mystery, but one thing was clear: if the Chaos forces were not stopped soon, the damage inflicted to many of the local sectors could take decades, if not centuries to repair.

Berek and the Old Wolf had studied the pattern of the uprisings for months, looking for the lynchpin of the Chaos campaign. Every indicator pointed to Charys, which was why he'd brought his entire great company to the agri-world and assumed command of the planetary defences. Within hours of his arrival he'd laid plans for a counter-offensive aimed at driving a spear into the uprising's heart. He and his Space Wolves were the tip of that spear, plunging on trails of fire from the company's battle-barge high overhead.

Battle reports from the planet's surface indicated that two local Guard regiments and the vast majority of the local Planetary Defence Force had forsaken their holy oaths and sworn fealty to the Ruinous Powers. Opposing them were seven loyal Guard regiments shipped in from neighbouring worlds, each of them locked in bitter urban combat to recapture the world's major population centres. Interrogations of captured officers and militiamen pointed to the former governor, Lord Volkus Bredwyr, and his family as the leaders of the revolt. Evidently, Lord Bredwyr and his household had nurtured an obscene cult within the bounds of the governor's palace, from where they continued to issue orders to their followers all over the world.

Berek swore that all that was going to change in the next few minutes.

The capital city of Charys was heavily defended, occupied by one of the rebels' traitor regiments and units of heavily armed planetary militia. Weeks of artillery and aerial bombardment had levelled the city walls and reduced entire districts to smoking rubble, but rebel forces had placed strongpoints at every intersection and turned the narrow streets into mined kill zones. Loyal Guard regiments operating from the nearby star port had only managed to seize a narrow foothold on the eastern fringe of the city, almost a dozen kilometres from the fortress of the governor's palace. The air over the massive, walled compound shimmered with the dark haze of an Imperator-class void shield, proof against the heaviest shells the Guard could throw at it.

As the drop-pods streaked down through clouds of anti-aircraft fire a holo-slate built into the drop-cradle above Berek's head projected a detailed display of the battle unfolding below. Mere minutes before the *Holmgang* launched her drop-pods, the Guard regiments at the edge of the city had begun a fierce offensive, driving hard for the city centre.

Heavy tanks and armoured personnel carriers were assaulting rebel strongpoints, advancing under a steady rain of heavy artillery shells. Dark masses of infantry advanced doggedly in their wake, dashing from one shell hole to the next in the face of intense enemy fire. Lascannon bolts and rocket trails leapt from the rebel positions, and streams of tracer fire raked through the struggling infantry formations. Casualties mounted as the Imperial forces charged across the killing ground. Tanks and armoured personnel carriers exploded in balls of fire, incinerating the hapless squads inside.

The traitors were throwing everything they had at the oncoming troops, and the augurs of the Space Marine vessels overhead took careful note of their positions.

An amber warning icon flashed along the margin of the holo-display as the *Holmgang* and her attendant strike cruisers opened fire. Salvoes of bombardment rounds, each one massing as much as a Leman Russ tank, impacted in a curtain of fire four seconds later, stretching in an arc five kilometres wide in front of the Imperial advance. Rebel strongpoints disintegrated. Entire city blocks vanished in boiling clouds of flame and pulverised ferrocrete. In a single instant of righteous fury, the traitors' defensive line was shattered. Even the Imperial advance faltered for a moment, stunned by the sheer ferocity of the attack. As the Guard units watched in awe, the bombardment shifted, marching inexorably towards the city centre, and the regiments surged forward once more, forcing their way past the shattered rebel positions.

The warning icon flashed an insistent red as the drop-pods neared the terminal phase of their approach, and the second phase of the Space Wolf bombardment began.

'Here it comes,' Berek said, settling deep into his restraints as the icons of five Nova-class escorts in high orbit flashed crimson and unleashed their lance batteries on the shields of the governor's palace. Ravening beams of energy stabbed downwards amid the plummeting drop-pods. One passed so close to Berek's pod that the ionisation caused the onboard lights to flicker, and sent waves of static coruscating across the holomap. The superheated air outside the pod howled like the Stormwolf of legend, and Berek Thunderfist howled along with it.

Five lance beams played across the palace's shields for almost a full second, setting off a ripple of concussive blasts that hammered at the falling drop-pods and rattled the Wolf Lord's bones. The blasts were so intense that Berek didn't even realise the pod's retro thrusters had kicked in until he saw the landing countdown flash on the holo-display. Three seconds later the drop-pod slammed to earth and explosive bolts fired, lowering Berek's assault ramp to the ground. The Wolf Lord hit his quick release and, with a roar, charged into the mouth of hell.

The company's dropsite was a kilometre square parade ground that stretched before the gates of the governor's palace. A hot wind roared across the scorched plain, buffeting the Wolf Lord's bare face and tangling his braided blond hair. Columns of smoke and fire coiled into the sky from the palace grounds and the buildings surrounding the square.

Corpses and parts of corpses littered the parade ground, many burned beyond recognition. Men staggered across the scorched ferrocrete, their eyes glassy with shock and their uniforms blackened by heat. Berek glanced quickly around and saw more than a dozen armoured vehicles arrayed around the square. Some were on fire or had been overturned by the bombardment, but most still appeared functional. The company had dropped right into the middle of a mechanised battalion that had been using the square as a staging area.

Fifty metres away, the rear assault ramp of a Chimera armoured transport dropped, and a squad of stunned rebel Guardsmen scrambled out. Berek turned and raked them with a long burst from his storm bolter. Explosive rounds stitched across the chests of the surprised traitors and flashed along the rear deck of the APC. Before the torn bodies had even hit the ground, the Wolf Lord activated his beacon and keyed the command channel on his vox-unit. 'Blood and thunder!' he roared, sounding the war cry of his company. 'Wolf Guard, to me! All packs, form up and clear the square!'

Even as he spoke, the staccato *thump thump thump* of storm bolters and the more measured fire of boltguns echoed across the square as the Space Wolves leapt into action. Off to Berek's right there was a draconian hiss as a cyclone missile launcher fired, sending an armour piercing rocket into the side of another Chimera. The APC exploded in a huge fireball, and the battle began in earnest.

The four Terminators accompanying Berek in his drop-pod took up positions around their lord, snapping off shots from their storm bolters. One of the Wolf Guard levelled his assault cannon at a charging squad of rebels and tore them to pieces with a two-second burst.

Streaks of fire criss-crossed overhead as Deathwind launchers on several of the Space Marine drop-pods went into action. Explosions ripped across the square amid the growing crackle of lasgun fire.

A rocket hissed across the battlefield and struck one of the Wolf Guard standing beside Berek. The krak missile struck the Space Marine full in the chest, knocking him back a step, but the anti-tank round could not penetrate the adamantine breastplate of the ancient Terminator suit. The Wolf Lord caught sight of the rocket team, killed them with a quick burst, and then turned his attention to the disposition of his troops.

Anti-aircraft fire and cyclonic winds had scattered the company's six drop-pods all across the parade field. From where he stood, Berek could see the tops of four other pods, one to the north-west, one to the north and two to the east. 'Aldrek! Where are you?' he called. The Rune Priest had been in the drop-pod containing the rest of Berek's Wolf Guard.

Aldrek responded at once. 'I mark you three hundred metres to my east,' he said over the vox. 'We are on our way.'

A loud boom echoed from the edge of the square, and the drop-pod to the east exploded. The voice of Thorvald, one of Berek's Grey Hunter pack leaders, rang out over the command net. 'Battle tank at the eastern edge of the square! I'm taking casualties.'

'We see him, brother,' a gruff voice answered. It was Gunnar, one of the Long Fang pack leaders. 'We're some way off to the west, but we're manoeuvring to line up a shot. Stand by.'

The Wolf Lord nodded in satisfaction. The volume of lasgun fire was increasing, stitching threads of blazing light across the square from every direction, but the company had sorted itself out and was responding decisively to the threat. Berek was just about to order his Wolf Guard forward when the air shook with a roar of dual petrochem engines and a Chimera APC came charging out of the smoke directly at the command squad. The forty-tonne armoured vehicle sideswiped the drop-pod behind the Wolves, toppling it onto its side, and bore down on the Space Marines like an enraged rhinodon. Multi-laser bolts spat from its squat turret, flashing among the Terminators as they scattered to either side of the onrushing war machine. One bolt detonated against the pauldron of Berek's Terminator armour, making his ears ring and leaving a scorch mark on the curved ceramite. The Wolf Lord bared his fangs as he turned to face the APC, his power fist crackling. 'Blood and thunder!' he cried, and met its charge head-on.

Berek gauged the vehicle's approach with an experienced eye. More laser bolts snapped harmlessly overhead as the Chimera drew too close for the gunner to target him. The Wolf Lord raised his storm bolter and rattled off a long burst at the driver's vision block. The explosive rounds smashed into the armourplas, and the driver panicked, slewing the vehicle slightly to Berek's right. At that moment, he stepped forward and smashed his power fist into the APC's right quarter. There was a thunderous detonation. Armour crumpled, partially converted to plasma by the power fist's energy field. The forward axle snapped, hurling a spinning tyre past Berek's head, and the APC flipped heavily onto its left side. Moments later, the rear assault hatch was shoved open, and the bloody survivors of the infantry squad staggered out of the smoking wreck into the Wolf Guard's merciless fire.

'Well struck!' Aldrek cried, raising his gory rune axe in salute as he and four more Terminators jogged heavily out of the swirling smoke. 'Gunnar knocked out the battle tank with his lascannons, and he reports that the traitors are falling back to the east. What now?'

Berek pointed north. 'Forward, to the palace gates,' he cried. 'We have to get inside before the rebels recover from our bombardment and launch a counter-attack. If the traitors bring up more heavy armour we'll be overrun before our Guard allies can reach us.' Without waiting for a reply, the Wolf Lord set off at a ponderous run, heading north.

Lasgun fire flickered over Berek's head as he drew closer to the palace walls, growing in volume with each passing minute. Streams of tracer shells stitched their way through the smoke as rebel gunners opened fire with heavy stubbers mounted on the square towers of the palace gatehouse. Missiles hissed through the air and exploded above the battlefield, showering the Wolf Lord and his companions with clouds of red-hot shrapnel.

Berek reached the bulk of his company a minute later, just a few hundred metres short of the palace gates. Two of his three Grey Hunter packs had taken cover behind the burning wrecks of a pair of Chimeras, while his two Long Fang packs fired at the palace defences from the rims of a pair of shell craters nearby. As he watched, two lascannon gunners from Thorbjørn's Long Fang pack targeted the battlements of the leftmost gate tower. The red beams vaporised a corner of the structure in a cloud of pulverised ferrocrete, spilling burning bodies onto the square sixty metres below.

At the Wolf Lord's approach, one of the Grey Hunter pack leaders rose from cover and dashed over to Berek. 'Well met, lord,' the pack leader said. 'It appears we have a problem.'

Berek scowled at the helmeted pack leader. 'What kind of problem, Einar?' he asked. A few metres away, one of the Terminators fired a

Cyclone missile at the rightmost gate tower, blasting away a section of its battlements.

'It's the damned gate,' Einar said, nodding his head towards the palace. 'It's a great deal stronger than we'd been led to believe. Gunnar and Thorbjørn's lascannons can't scratch it.'

A line of stubber shells marched across the ferrocrete a few metres away and up the leg and chest of one of the Wolf Guard. The Terminator was knocked back a step by the heavy impacts, but the slugs shattered harmlessly against the heavy armour. The Wolf Guard made a rude gesture with his power fist in the direction of the palace wall, and fired a burst from his storm bolter in reply.

Berek studied the distant gates with his enhanced vision, nodding thoughtfully. 'The former governor had ample time to prepare for this day,' he growled. 'How many melta bombs do you have?'

Einar glanced back over his shoulder at his assembled pack. A lasgun bolt, possibly from a long-las sniper rifle, struck the side of his helmet with an angry *crack*. The Space Wolf appeared not to notice. 'We've got four, and Ingvar's pack has two left.'

'Hand them over,' Berek ordered, and the pack leader began gathering up the heavy plasma charges.

Mikal Sternmark stepped up alongside his lord. 'Going for a walk, are we?' he asked, surveying the killing ground between them and the palace gates.

'The Grey Hunters and Long Fangs will provide cover fire while we take down the gates,' Berek said, gesturing for Einar to hand the charges over to the Wolf Guard. 'Once we're inside, don't waste time clearing the walls or the palace grounds. Aldrek has cast the runes, and believes we'll find Bredwyr in his audience chamber. If we only kill one man inside that palace, it must be him. This uprising has gone on long enough.'

The Wolf Guard answered with growls of assent. 'Lead on, lord,' Mikal said sardonically. 'First man out always draws the most fire.'

Berek threw back his head and laughed. 'Last man to the gate can clean the scorch marks off my armour,' he answered. 'Blood and thunder!'

'Blood and thunder!' the Wolf Guard howled in reply, and they charged for the gates as one.

The Space Wolves were rushing into a storm of enemy fire within moments. Intersecting lines of lasgun fire wove a burning web around the Terminators. Tracer fire arced through their ranks, and explosive shells dug craters the size of feasting plates out of the scorched ferrocrete. Bolters roared as Berek's Grey Hunter packs opened fire at the rebel positions along the walls, stitching chains of red and yellow flashes along the battlements. Lascannon beams and missile trails lanced towards the gatehouse, punching molten craters in the ornately carved stone façade, and spilling curtains of shattered masonry onto the pavement below.

Lasgun bolts and autogun shells rang off the Wolf Lord's armour. A burst of rounds from a heavy stubber struck his left leg, and a bloom of fiery pain caused Berek to stumble. Mikal drew close and reached for Berek's arm, but the Wolf Lord waved him towards the looming gates instead.

An autocannon let off a loud, rattling burst at a Terminator to Berek's right. Red and yellow detonations hammered across the Space Wolf's chest. The Wolf Guard staggered out of the cloud of dust and smoke, his storm bolter still firing despite the three bloody craters punched into his breastplate. After two halting steps, the warrior fell to his knees and pitched over onto his face.

Moments later, the Space Wolves were flattening their bodies against the scarred surface of the palace gates, underneath the arc of the remaining guns along the walls. Many of the Wolf Guard were splashed with blood from numerous minor wounds, but they immediately went to work setting the demolition charges. 'No need to blow the whole gate down,' Berek said through gritted teeth as he probed the wound in his leg. He could feel the shell in his leg, lodged close to the bone. 'Just make us a hole big enough to charge through.'

The breaching charges were ready in seconds. Berek took half of the Terminators to the right of the gate, while Aldrek and the other half went to the left. 'Clear!' The Wolf Lord called out, and when he heard an answer from Aldrek he keyed the detonator.

There was a bone rattling *whump* and a rush of superheated air, and the stink of vaporised metal made Berek grimace. 'Go!' he roared, and the Wolf Guard rushed to the breach.

The melta charges had blown a roughly circular hole three metres across in the thick metal gate, just large enough for one Terminator to pass at a time. Beyond lay a long, rectangular courtyard, bordered by statues of forgotten saints, which the rebels had transformed into a charnel house. Priests and adepts from the local Ecclesiarchy had been brought here and slain, and then hung by chains from the worn, grey statues. A thick cloud of noxious smoke hung over the scene, reeking with strange compounds that seared Berek's nostrils and made his flesh crawl.

An improvised rebel strongpoint made from steel supports, flak-board and bags of ferrocrete stood about twenty metres from the gate.

Lascannons and heavy stubbers had been sited there to cover the entrance to the compound, but now the sloped face of the strongpoint was ablaze, its surface ignited by molten shrapnel from the melta bombs. Berek dashed forwards, firing bursts from his storm bolter into the roiling fire and smoke. Other Wolf Guard snapped off short bursts with their storm bolters as well, unleashing a hail of deadly fire into the position.

Berek reached the sloped front embrasure of the strongpoint and leapt through the flames, landing next to a heavy stubber and its dead crew. Lasgun fire struck him along the right side, and the Wolf Lord grabbed the stubber by the barrel and hurled it at the squad of traitors who'd shot at him. The rebels scattered out of the way of the spinning weapon, leaving them easy targets for Berek's storm bolter.

A rasping cry from Berek's left brought the Wolf Lord around just as a traitor wearing the tattered uniform of a Guard officer lunged out of the smoke and swung a crackling power sword at his head. Berek deflected the sword with the back of his power fist and shot the rebel point-blank.

The hissing crackle of power weapons hummed amid the smoke and the screams of the dying. Dark shapes flitted through the roiling haze. Aldrek appeared from the smoke like a giant of old, his black beard glistening with spilled blood, and his heavy axe streaming gore. The traitors' false courage broke before the onslaught and they fled in every direction, calling vainly to their newfound gods for deliverance. Those that fled in the direction of the palace were cut down as they ran, reaped like wheat by the blazing guns of the advancing Wolves.

Berek and his men reached the far end of the courtyard in moments. The Wolf Lord climbed the shallow steps of the palace entrance and without breaking stride he smashed his power fist into the ornate wood and metal doors. There was a clap of righteous thunder and the portal exploded inward. Shouts and screams of pain greeted Berek as the Wolf Lord crossed the smoking threshold.

The nave outside the governor's audience chamber was once majestic. Soaring arches decorated with winged saints rose high overhead, their carved hands outstretched towards an octagonal ceiling of coloured armourplas that filled the chamber with shafts of jewel coloured light. Square columns carved with the likenesses of Imperial heroes stood at attention down the length of the chamber, their stern features judging the worth of every soul that strode along the marble floors.

The great space was crowded with a mob of twisted degenerates, gibbering and shouting imprecations to the false gods of the warp. Foul sigils covered the walls and pillars, and many of the carved heroes had been smeared with layers of blood and filth. Naked, rotting corpses lay in heaps at the feet of the columns, their torn faces twisted into masks of horror and despair.

Hundreds of mutants and Chaos worshippers recoiled in shock and anger from the Wolf Lord's sudden arrival. They brandished stained cleavers and chainblades, laspistols and looted autoguns, and the air of the defiled nave shook with their bestial cries. More streamed in from side corridors to the left and right, adding to the mass. It was a sight to shake the heart of even a stalwart hero, but Berek looked upon the shrieking masses and was unmoved. He was one of the Emperor's chosen, a Space Wolf, and he knew no fear.

Berek clenched his crackling power fist and raised it high. His furious voice smote the unbelievers into silence. 'Oathbreakers!' he roared. 'I am Berek Thunderfist! Look upon me and despair! The Allfather knows your crimes and has set his Wolves among you.'

An answering roar echoed Berek from the far end of the nave. An impossibly-muscled, four-armed mutant reared head and shoulders above the rest of the mob and made to answer the Wolf Lord. Berek shot the monster between its three eyes, and with a bloodthirsty howl he leapt among his foes.

The Wolf Lord swept his storm bolter in an arc before him, cutting a vengeful swathe through the packed throng. At such close range the heavy shells tore through two or even three bodies before their explosive tips travelled far enough to detonate. When he'd emptied the weapon's twin magazines he swung it like a club, crushing skulls and smashing ribs. His power fist rose and fell, hurling broken bodies in all directions. Clubs, chainswords and cleavers rained against his ancient armour, but none could find purchase. He was a storm of righteous fury, the embodiment of the Emperor's wrath, and nothing could stand against him.

Aldrek and the remaining Wolf Guard stormed into the nave behind Berek, adding their strength to the battle. Two Terminators stepped to either side of the broken doorway. One launched a pair of Cyclone missiles down the length of the nave, showering the rear ranks of the mob with red-hot shrapnel. The other levelled his whirring assault cannon and unleashed a stream of deadly shells over the heads of his brother Wolves.

Within seconds, the battle had transformed into a slaughter. Even the mutants' fanatical devotion to their new gods was not enough to sustain them in the face of the Space Wolves' fury. They tried to flee, but their large numbers worked against them as they tried to fight their way to the nave's narrow side-passages. They clawed and trampled their kin in their desire to escape, while the Wolves continued their remorseless advance, blood streaming from fist and blade.

By the time Berek reached the far end of the nave there were hundreds of dead rebels heaped in his wake. Aldrek and the Wolf Guard gathered around him, weapons ready. The Wolf Lord eyed the Rune Priest as he reloaded his storm bolter. 'What now, priest?' he asked.

Aldrek took a step towards the audience chamber doors, his hand tightening on the haft of his rune axe. 'I smell the stink of sorcery,' he said. 'Bredwyr must lie within.' He turned back to the Wolves, his face lined with terrible strain. 'There are terrible forces at work in the chamber beyond,' he warned. 'The fabric of reality is... unsettled.'

Berek frowned. 'Unsettled? Speak plainly, Aldrek.'

'This is as plain as I can make it,' the Rune Priest replied, his expression vague and haunted. 'Reality is... shifting, like sand. Forces are mingling, compelled to weave together...' Aldrek shook his head fiercely, trying to drive the image from his mind. 'I cannot explain it. I've never known the like.'

Berek raised his storm bolter. 'Then let us see for ourselves,' he said, and put his power fist to the door.

The portals swung open silently. A wavering nimbus of light washed over the wary Space Wolves, and unseen energies clawed invisibly at their minds.

The Wolf Lord strode forward into the dimly lit chamber. His boots crunched on brittle bones. The entire chamber was littered with human skeletons and cast-off husks of withered skin. The air was hazy with foul incense, streaming from tall, wrought iron braziers placed apparently at random along the room. Sheets of bloody skin had been tacked to the tall pillars by the hundreds, each one carved with intricate patterns of blasphemous runes. It was these runes that filled the room with its tenebrous light.

Berek strode through the detritus of scores of sacrificial victims. His brain felt as though it was on fire. The Wolf Lord passed unheeding through the blasphemous tableau, his gaze fixed dreadfully on the abomination that reared behind the governor's broken throne.

The wall behind the throne was fifteen metres tall and ten metres wide, and in the days of the palace's construction it would have been carved with the likeness of the holy Emperor. Now, the wall was covered in glistening flesh and pulsating organs, stitched together by some form of silver wire that shone like liquid in the sorcerous light. Veins and arteries throbbed, and hearts clenched and unclenched, driving blood through the vile mass. Berek glimpsed naked brains trapped in webworks of palpitating muscle, and eyes rolling in gelid masses of fat. Intestines writhed like snakes across the surface of the towering mass, bound in place by silver wire. Vast and unnatural energies radiated from the thing, like heat from a forge. The abomination was alive, somehow, and on some deep, primal level Berek also knew that it was not some maddened act of depravity. It had been built to serve a very particular purpose.

'Blessed Allfather,' Aldrek gasped, his face turning pale. 'We've found Bredwyr and his entire household.'

Gritting his teeth, Berek raised his storm bolter. 'Then let's finish what he came here to do.'

The Space Wolves fired as one, pouring streams of explosive shells into the horrid mass of flesh. Berek watched with revulsion as the construct writhed beneath the storm of fire. A pink haze of vaporised blood and flesh filled the air around the abomination, but, almost as quickly as they were made, the shell holes sealed shut again.

A wave of unholy power radiated from the construct and swept over the Space Wolves. Vertigo washed over Berek, overwhelming his enhanced senses. It felt as though the room was expanding in every direction, stretching away into the vastness of space. Reeling, the Wolf Lord turned to Aldrek. 'Priest!' he cried. 'Your axe!'

Aldrek had been driven to one knee by the force of the construct's power. His eyes had rolled back in their sockets, and tendrils of smoke curled from the silver and brass connections wired to his skull. And yet, the heroic priest heard Berek's call and nodded. He tried to speak, but only a guttural growl escaped his bloody lips. With a mighty effort, Aldrek rose to his feet, raising his rune axe high, and a black blade carved with blasphemous, glowing runes burst from the Rune Priest's chest.

A towering figure clad in ornate blue and gold armour had appeared behind Aldrek, as though coalescing out of the shadows. The Chaos sorcerer pulled his hellblade from Aldrek's body, and the Rune Priest staggered, blood pouring from his open mouth. With a strangled roar, Aldrek spun about, swinging furiously with his axe, but as he did so two more armoured giants materialised like ghosts to either side of him and drove their swords into the Rune Priest's chest.

More figures were taking shape from the darkness: dreadful warriors clad in baroque versions of power armour eerily similar to those the Space Wolves wore. Berek recognised their blue and gold heraldry at once, and fought back a surge of righteous revulsion and dread. Every son of Russ knew the colours of the Chaos Space Marines known as the Thousand Sons. Twisted nightmares of muscle and flesh emerged alongside the Traitor Space Marines, and reached for the Space Marines with glistening, ropy tentacles and fanged mouths.

The ambush had caught the Wolf Guard unawares, but their surprise lasted only an instant. 'For Russ and the Allfather!' Mikal Sternmark cried as the sorcerers and daemons rushed in from all sides, and the air rang with the thunder of bolters and the clash of blades.

Aldrek had fallen to his knees, blood flowing from his wounds. As the sorcerers closed in again, he slashed at one with his rune axe, but the Chaos warrior parried the blow with his hellsword and knocked the axe from Aldrek's bloodless fingers. The Rune Priest howled defiantly at his foes, but the sorcerers laid their hands upon him, and they vanished as swiftly as they appeared, taking Aldrek with them.

Berek Thunderfist let out a furious bellow. 'Stand fast, sons of Fenris!' he cried, blasting a pair of daemons into gobbets of protoplasm. 'Our brothers are coming,' he said, knowing that Einar and the rest of the Grey Hunters could not be far behind them.

'Indeed,' said a silken voice behind the Wolf Lord. 'As a matter of fact, my plan depends upon it.'

Quicker than the eye could follow, Berek spun on his heel, his power fist reaching for the source of the voice, but the gauntlet closed on empty air.

A fearsome impact struck Berek in the chest. Terrible pain, cold and black as the abyss, spread beneath his ribs.

The Chaos sorcerer stood just out of reach. His ornate power armour was wrought with blasphemous sigils of power, and decorated with the writhing skulls of serpentine gargoyles. Terrible, inhuman intelligence burned from the eye slits of the baroque, horned helmet.

With a single, fluid motion, Madox drew the Spear of Russ from Berek's chest. The Wolf Lord felt his strength leave him all at once. His legs failed him, and the Space Wolf fell to his knees.

Madox raised the tip of Russ's spear to Berek's face, showing him the blood dripping from the point of the sacred relic. 'The fate of your Chapter is sealed, Berek Thunderfist,' the Chaos champion said, as darkness filled the corners of the Wolf Lord's vision. 'When you go to stand before your false emperor, tell him that you are the one to blame.' As the sorcerer spoke, his armoured form blurred before the Wolf Lord's eyes, fading from view as if he were a ghost.

The last thing Berek heard was the sound of triumphant laughter, as cold and cruel as Old Night itself.

A MOANING WIND keened ceaselessly in the crimson temple that Madox had built. Ruddy light seeped from the very stones, and the unnatural wind plucked at the corners of the bloody scraps of skin nailed to the temple columns. The runes inscribed on their surface were black as the void, drawing in the energy that surrounded them.

The blood of the Wolf Lord ran in thin rivulets down the haft of Russ's Spear and across the sorcerer's knuckles. As Madox watched, the insubstantial figures of Berek's Wolf Guard withdrew from sight, dragging the body of their lord through the piled bones and skin that littered the chamber in the physical realm.

Where the governor's throne had stood in the audience chamber, Madox had placed his temple's altar, a single block of black stone carved with runes of power. Offerings covered its surface, gleaming like rubies in the hellish light.

A trio of sorcerers approached Madox, dragging the body of the Rune Priest. The Space Marine still clung to life, despite his terrible wounds. The Chaos sorcerer smiled. 'Hold him up,' Madox commanded.

With inhuman strength the Traitor Space Marines lifted Aldrek nearly to his feet. Madox placed a taloned gauntlet over the rent in the Space Wolf's breastplate and thrust it within. The Rune Priest stiffened. Pure agony focused Aldrek's gaze on the sorcerer.

Flesh ripped, and Madox tore his hand free. The Rune Priest slumped, eyes glazing in death as the sorcerer showed Aldrek what he held in his hand. 'Now the circle is complete,' he said, and laid the progenoid glands on the altar beside nearly a dozen more.

Aldrek's body fell to the bleeding stones with a lifeless clatter as the sorcerers raised their hands and began to chant. Madox felt the power of the great ritual begin to take shape, and turned to face his master.

Madox held up the Spear of Russ to the blazing eye that hovered in the air before him. 'The end of the Space Wolves is at hand,' he said, showing the Wolf Lord's blood to his dreadful master.

TWO
Alarums and Excursions

THE NARROW BLADE scored a thin cut across Ragnar's powerfully muscled chest as he pivoted to avoid the killing thrust. Baring his teeth in a feral snarl, he brought his iron sword around in a blurring arc and chopped down hard on Torin's exposed neck.

It was a blow that would have hacked a normal man's head clean off. Instead, Torin pivoted on the ball of his right foot, nearly too fast for the eye to follow, and Ragnar's heavy blade rang against the Space Wolf's reinforced collar-bone. The dulled sword split the skin in a pressure cut a quarter of a metre long across Torin's chest, drawing a hiss of pain from the older warrior, and filling the air of the practice arena with the coppery scent of blood. At virtually the same instant, Torin's sword swept down and struck lightly at Ragnar's left thigh before the Space Wolf's lunge carried him past his opponent, opening the distance across the sandy training ground.

Dried blood crackled faintly along Ragnar's brow. The enhanced clotting factor in his blood had already stopped the bleeding from the scalp wound Torin had given him seconds before. Both warriors were bare-chested, clad only in loose fitting breeches, torn and stained from dozens of blows. Most Space Marine Chapters preferred to practice their close-combat skills with automated sparring drones or combat servitors, but the Space Wolves kept to the old ways of their home world: man to man and iron against iron.

Both Wolves were covered in angry red weals and shallow cuts. They grimaced at the pain from torn muscles and wrenched ligaments. The wounds sharpened their wits and tested their wills in a way no mindless combat servitor could.

Torin continued to give ground, gliding effortlessly across the black volcanic sand. His iron sword was a little longer and thinner than the heavy broadsword in Ragnar's hand, lending the warrior a slight advantage in speed and reach. The weapon suited him. Torin was tall and lean, almost lithe compared to Ragnar's broad-chested bulk. His blade flickered back and forth through the air, more often than not avoiding directly blocking the younger Space Wolf's more massive blade and leaving Ragnar swinging at empty air. The older warrior's blows were fluid and precise, striking sharply along leg or arm and withdrawing again, as though intended to goad Ragnar into anger rather than strike a killing blow.

If that was Torin's plan, Ragnar had to admit it was working.

The young Space Wolf lowered his head and charged at Torin with a furious bellow. Gauging the distance carefully, he aimed a fierce blow at the older Space Wolf's temple, and then checked the feint at the last moment and reversed the angle of the blow, slashing hard at Torin's thigh. Quick as he was, Torin was still faster. Instead of trying to parry Ragnar's blade or turn aside, he leapt forward and past Ragnar's right side. The sleek blade scored another shallow cut on the inside of Ragnar's right arm.

Snarling furiously, Ragnar spun and lunged for Torin's retreating back, jabbing the blunt tip against his opponent's shoulder blade hard enough to draw a painful grunt from the older Space Marine, but not enough to translate into a killing blow. Torin threw himself forward into a shoulder roll across the black sand, coming up facing Ragnar a few metres away with his sword at the ready. The older Space Wolf's lean face quirked into a faintly mocking grin. 'Good, but not good enough,' he said.

'I came down here to fight, not dance,' Ragnar growled. 'If you'd sit still for half a second you'd be dead.'

Torin's mocking grin deepened. 'A compelling reason not to sit still, don't you think?' he replied.

'Morkai's frozen bollocks,' boomed a thunderous voice from the edge of the arena, 'will you two quit yapping and get on with it?' A massive figure rose ponderously from a stone bench near the arena entrance, ~andishing a gnawed leg bone in his knobby fist like a greasy, gristly
Rich, honey coloured ale sloshed from an enormous drinking ~hed in Haegr's left hand and splashed over his thick fingers.

'If I were in there I would have killed the both of you and be halfway back to the mead hall!' The huge warrior's bushy red whiskers and bristly eyebrows lent Haegr the appearance of an enraged walrus.

Torin laughed. His voice was light, but his dark eyes never left Ragnar's face. 'Iron sword against ice mammoth haunch? I think I'd like to see you try.'

'Bah!' Haegr exclaimed, pausing to lick the spilled ale from his scarred knuckles. 'The mighty Haegr doesn't play at fighting, Torin. What he fights, he kills. You should know that by now. And if I killed the two of you, who would be left to guard the lady Gabriella besides me?'

The older Space Wolf rolled his eyes in mock disdain. 'Who can argue with wisdom like that?'

Ragnar nearly had him. Just as Torin spoke, he lunged forward, his blade slashing in a blurring figure of eight. For a fraction of a second, Torin appeared to be caught off-guard. He blocked one cut with a ringing blow that sent sparks flying from his sword and barely ducked aside a brutal cut from the opposite angle. Again, his swift blade flicked out, biting painfully at Ragnar's groin, but this time the young Space Wolf kept right on coming, hammering at Torin's head, neck and shoulders. The older Space Wolf back-pedalled furiously, his face growing taut with strain. He was forced to block one blow, and then another. Then a third stroke snapped the thinner blade with a discordant clang. Ragnar's sword continued along its arc and cracked hard against Torin's left cheekbone, knocking the Space Wolf onto his back.

Ragnar leapt forward, stomping down hard on the inside of Torin's right thigh to pin him in place, and then pressing the blunt tip of his blade into the hollow of his opponent's throat. 'This dance is over,' he growled, his hand tightening on the grip of his sword. 'Next time you fight me, try something other than a toy sword.'

Blood flowed in thick streams down Torin's ragged cheek and into his thin moustache. He regarded Ragnar coldly. 'The fight ended five seconds before my sword broke,' he said. 'I killed you, but you were too thick-headed to realise it.'

Ragnar let out a bark of laughter. 'What? That bee sting?'

Torin pushed Ragnar's blade aside and climbed slowly to his feet. He pointed at the spot where his last blow had fallen. 'Femoral artery,' he said. He then pointed to the cut along the inside of Ragnar's sword arm. 'Brachial artery.' Torin jabbed at a fading red mark on Ragnar's abdomen. 'Main pulmonary artery. Even with the clotting factor, I'd have bled you white about two minutes ago.' He turned away and limped over to the broken half of his blade, sticking up from the sands a few metres away. 'You should have paid more attention, my friend. Half a dozen minor blows are just as deadly as one big one.' Torin bent and picked up the battered shard of iron. He frowned, turning it over in his hands. 'I had to have this specially made, you know.'

Torin's cold dissection of the battle drained all the heat out of Ragnar's blood, leaving the younger Space Wolf vaguely shamed. 'You're right, of course,' he said heavily, tossing his notched sword onto the sand.

'Forgive me, brother,' Ragnar said, holding out his hand. 'Give me the pieces of the blade and I'll beg a boon from one of the Iron Priests to have it remade.'

The older Space Wolf shook his head, waving Ragnar's hand away with the broken shard of iron. 'There is nothing to forgive, my friend,' he said. 'The fault is as much mine as yours. I prodded you on purpose, trying to draw out some of the melancholy that's gripped you these last few months.'

'Much as it pains me to say it, Torin's right,' Haegr said, worrying at a piece of gristle with his fangs. 'Here we are back on Fenris, the land of heroes, and all you've done since we got here is mope.'

Scowling, Ragnar turned away, heading for the bench where the rest of his clothes were laid. 'The Chapter is at war,' he said darkly, reaching for his wool and leather tunic. 'We should be out there, fighting alongside our brothers.' Ragnar thought of Sven, his old pack mate, fighting with Berek Thunderfist's great company on Charys. No doubt they were celebrating their victory in the governor's palace even now, while he haunted the stone halls of the Fang like some *nithling*.

'Our place is at Gabriella's side,' Torin said evenly. 'We have a sacred duty to House Belisarius, Ragnar, now more than ever, after the losses we suffered at Hyades.'

'I hear you, Torin,' Ragnar replied, sitting on the bench and reaching for his dragon skin boots. They were members of the Wolfblade, bodyguards assigned to the Navigator House of Belisarius by the Great Wolf, in keeping with an ancient pact that was as old as the Imperium. There were never more than two dozen Wolfblade at any given time, and most of those were stationed on Holy Terra, guarding high-ranking members of the Belisarius line and training their House troops.

Ragnar, Torin, Haegr and six of their brothers had left Terra more than six months ago to accompany Lady Gabriella, one of House Belis-
is's highest ranking Navigators, on an inspection of the House's
ns on Hyades, a jungle world valued for its promethium mines.
however, they had been caught up in the machinations of

a Chaos tainted warlord named Cadmus, who had sworn himself to the service of Tzeentch and to the Space Wolves' ancient foes the Thousand Sons. Cadmus's schemes orchestrated a violent battle between Berek Thunderfist's great company, which was patrolling in the region, and a contingent of Dark Angels. The Dark Angels were one of the most secretive of Space Marine Chapters, and nursed a bitter rivalry with the Space Wolves that stretched back thousands of years. The fight that ensued – and Cadmus's own treachery – claimed the lives of their fellow bodyguards, leaving only Torin, Haegr and himself to keep Gabriella safe. Though Cadmus had ultimately been defeated and the Thousand Sons driven off, Hyades was the first spark in the conflagration sweeping across the Space Wolf domains.

Ragnar rose from the bench and reached for his sword belt. The ancient frost blade, a relic borne by the Wolfblade for thousands of years and given to Ragnar by Gabriella was settled comfortably on his hip. 'It's just… if Gabriella isn't safe in the *Fang* of all places, she isn't safe anywhere. The Old Wolf needs every stout sword-arm he can muster and we're being wasted here.'

Torin gave Ragnar a probing look as he settled a heavy bearskin cloak around his shoulders. The months on Fenris had changed Torin somewhat. On Terra the Space Wolf had adopted many of the fashionable airs of the local aristocracy. When Ragnar had first met him, his hair was cut short and his moustache trimmed pencil-thin, in the Terran fashion. Now, his hair was growing out again, and bore none of the scent of perfumed pomade he'd favoured among the Imperial elite. His ability to read people, however, was just as sharp as ever. 'This isn't about doing your duty as a Space Wolf. This is about the Spear of Russ.'

The observation stung Ragnar. Though assignment to the Wolfblade was ostensibly a posting of great honour, most Space Wolves saw it as a form of exile, far from the glory of the battlefield. Ragnar could not see it any other way. He had been sent to Terra by Logan Grimnar after he had lost one of the Chapter's most sacred relics: the Spear of Russ. Once wielded in battle by the primarch, in the glory days of the Great Crusade, it had been kept for millennia at a sacred shrine on the planet Garm, waiting for the day Russ would return for the Last Battle. But an arch-heretic named Sergius had stolen the spear during a bloody uprising on Garm, and Ragnar, then a Blood Claw in Berek Thunderfist's great company, had been among the warriors sent to crush the revolt. After numerous battles, Ragnar came face-to-face with his old nemesis Madox, who had manipulated Sergius into taking the spear in an effort to summon Magnus the Red, his Legion's infernal primarch, into the physical realm.

Lee Lightner

The foul sorcerer nearly succeeded, but just as Magnus began to cross the threshold from the depths of the warp, Ragnar seized the spear from Sergius and hurled the legendary weapon at the fearsome primarch. The spear struck Magnus like a thunderbolt and the daemon prince was hurled back into the raging maelstrom of the warp. Garm had been saved, but the Spear of Russ had been lost, possibly forever.

He'd had no choice. Ragnar knew this. Even the Old Wolf had once told him that he would have done the very same thing had he been in Ragnar's place. That didn't change the fact that he'd betrayed a sacred oath that the Chapter had sworn to their primarch nearly ten millennia ago. To the people of Fenris there were few things more terrible than an oathbreaker, and the realisation haunted him.

The young Space Wolf shook his head, dragging blunt fingers through his tangled mane of black hair and probing at the cut on his scalp. Unlike Torin or Haegr his square chin was clean-shaven, in the custom of the Blood Claws. A Space Wolf grew his beard only after being accepted into the Grey Hunters or the Wolf Scouts, and those avenues had been closed to him when he'd been sent away to Terra.

'The spear is gone, Torin,' Ragnar said at last. 'I know this. It's just... I haven't been sleeping lately. That's all.'

'Ha! Clearly you haven't been drinking enough,' Haegr interjected, raising his massive ale horn. 'A cask of ale and a good brawl is what you need, Ragnar my lad! Why don't we go to the mead hall and see what we can find, eh?'

Ragnar stole a glance at Torin. The older Space Wolf seemed unconvinced by Ragnar's clumsy evasion. 'I've had enough of waiting, brothers,' he said gravely. 'I'm going to speak to the Old Wolf and demand he send me to the battle line.'

'*Demand?*' Haegr repeated, his expression incredulous. The massive Space Wolf threw back his head and roared with laughter. 'Did you hear that, Torin? The cub thinks to command Logan Grimnar!' Haegr's huge face split in a ferocious grin. 'The Old Wolf will hit you so hard Russ himself will feel it!'

Ragnar felt a flush of anger rise to his cheeks. Before he could reply, however, the vox-bead behind his right ear hummed, and Gabriella's calm, quiet voice filled his head. 'Ragnar, I would have you attend upon ⸱ please.'

⸱ young Space Wolf paused, mastering his temper. He reached ⸱ ⸱e vox-bead. 'As you wish, my lady,' he answered grimly. *Per-* ⸱ *t time.* 'Where will I find you?'

'In the Great Wolf's council chamber,' Gabriella replied. 'A ship has arrived from Charys bearing grave news, and there is much to be discussed.'

A cold sense of foreboding prickled the hairs on the back of Ragnar's neck. 'I'll be there at once,' he replied.

Torin watched the change in Ragnar's expression. 'What's happened, brother?' he asked.

The young Space Wolf could only shake his head. 'I don't know,' he replied, 'but I fear it's something terrible.'

WHITE SUNLIGHT FLOODED the Great Wolf's council chamber. The armoured shutters had been drawn back from the tall windows that dominated the east side of the large room, providing a panoramic view of the cloud-wrapped Asaheim range and the distant, iron-grey sea. Fenris was swinging close to the Wolf's Eye once more, ending the harsh winter and heralding the even harsher Time of Fire. The rising temperatures had banished the heavy overcast and the clinging mist that enfolded the Fang for much of the year, and for a short time Ragnar knew that the seas would be mild and relatively free from storms. The kraken would rise from the deeps, and the people of Fenris would take to the sea in their long ships to hunt and to fight. *The Iron Season*, Ragnar recalled, *a time of feasting and of battle, of betrothals and births: a time for offering sacrifices to the gods who watch from the clouds.*

Logan Grimnar was standing before one of those tall windows as Ragnar entered the room, his wide hands clasped behind his back as he brooded upon the unsuspecting world below. The Great Wolf was in his armour, his shoulders wrapped in a cloak of sea-dragon scales. Runic charms and wolves' teeth were woven into the thick braids of his iron-grey hair, and parchment ribbons from hundreds of major campaigns fluttered like raven's feathers from his scarred grey and yellow pauldrons. Old and fierce, as indomitable as the Fang itself, some said that Logan Grimnar was the greatest living warrior in the Imperium, and Ragnar could not help but feel awed by his presence. Nearly a dozen other Space Wolves stood around the council table, mighty priests or members of Logan's Wolf Guard, each one a towering figure in his own right.

At once, Ragnar caught a familiar scent among the fearsome Wolves and searched among the crowded warriors for its source. Lady Gabriella, Master Navigator of House Belisarius, sat in a high-backed wooden chair at the far side of the table, studying the assembly over slim, steepled fingers. She wore the dark dress uniform of her House, ornamented with epaulettes and polished gold buttons fashioned with the wolf-and-eye symbol of Belisarius. Medals and ceremonial braid covered the front of her jacket, proclaiming her personal achievements and the great deeds of her household, and a small pistol and a gracefully curved sabre hung from a belt around her narrow waist. Her long, black hair had been bound up in glossy braids that hung about her narrow shoulders and framed her severe, angular face. A scarf of black silk covered the Navigator's high forehead, concealing the pineal eye that was the source of her psychic talents.

Gabriella turned her head slightly as Ragnar's gaze fell upon her and nodded a curt greeting. Then she rested her hands in her lap and turned her attention back to the Great Wolf.

Ragnar stepped forward and knelt before Grimnar. 'Lady Gabriella said a ship has come from Charys bearing news,' he said without preamble. 'What has happened? Why didn't the astropaths–'

'According to the Lady Gabriella, you encountered the Chaos sorcerer Madox on Hyades,' the Great Wolf said, cutting Ragnar off. 'What did he say to you?'

The question took the young Space Wolf aback. 'We did not meet face to face,' he replied. 'He only revealed himself through one of his minions, just as we were about to leave the planet.'

'And?' Logan growled.

'He said his men were going to kill us,' Ragnar said with a shrug.

Grimnar turned, fixing the young Space Wolf with an icy gaze. 'What of the Spear of Russ? Did he say anything about it?'

Ragnar frowned. 'No, lord, he didn't. The traitor Cadmus, however, claimed that Madox was seeking a relic that was a crucial component of a ritual he sought to perform, a ritual that also depended upon Space Marine gene-seed.' A chill raced down Ragnar's spine. 'This was all in my earlier report. What is all this about?'

'Madox has been sighted on Charys, lad,' spoke a voice beside the council table. Ragnar turned to meet the gaze of Ranek, the great Wolf Priest. 'He has the Spear of Russ with him.'

Ragnar leapt to his feet, startled by the news. 'The Spear!' he said, forgetting himself. *Russ be praised,* he thought, *perhaps all is not lost.*

'This is hardly a cause for celebration, lad!' Ranek snapped. 'Now the full scope of the Chaos incursion becomes clear.'

'How so?' Ragnar asked.

Ranek reached down and touched a rune at the edge of the council table. A hololith mounted in the tabletop glowed to life, creating a detailed star map of the sector. Fenris lay near the centre of the map. Systems currently under attack or in revolt shone brighter than the rest. Minor attacks or incursions were coloured yellow, while major attacks were red. Ragnar was shocked to see that more than thirty systems were affected.

'We have been studying the pattern of the Chaos incursion since it began,' the Wolf Priest said, 'trying to ascertain their ultimate objective. Many of the initial uprisings made sense from a military standpoint: forge worlds, industrialised hive-worlds and trade centres, attacks designed to sow confusion and cripple our ability to respond. But many others confounded us.' He pointed to a pulsing red system. 'Ceta Pavonis, an airless rock occupied by gangs of pirates and slavers. Or here: Grendel IV, an old world all but abandoned three centuries ago when the last of its radium mines played out. Even Charys is nothing more than a minor agri-world, with little strategic value other than its proximity to Fenris. Yet, in each of these places there are major uprisings and reported sightings of Chaos Space Marines.'

Ragnar considered this. 'Diversions,' he concluded, 'meant to draw our attention from the true objective. What else could they be?'

Ranek gave the young Space Wolf an appraising look. 'What, indeed? We wondered much the same thing.' The Wolf Priest shrugged. 'If they were meant as diversions, then our foes chose poorly. There are far more important systems that require our protection. But we know that our enemies are not fools, however much we would like to believe otherwise. There was a plan at work here, but we could not see it at first.' Ranek gestured at the collection of Rune Priests standing quietly around the table. 'The runes were consulted, and they suggested we seek a new point of view on the problem.'

The young Space Wolf turned, pensive. 'Well, I'm not sure how much help I will be, but if you think I can be of use–'

A melodious laugh rose from the far side of the table, and in moments the assembled Space Wolves joined in, breaking the tension in the room. Gabriella covered her mouth with one pale hand, her human eyes twinkling with mirth. 'Ranek was referring to me,' she said, not unkindly. 'He and the Great Wolf thought I might see a pattern where a warrior might not.'

Ragnar fought to control the flush rising to his cheeks. 'Ah, of course,' he said quickly, 'and were you successful?'

Gabriella's angular features turned sober once more. 'Unfortunately, yes,' she said. She turned to Ranek. 'If you will permit me...'

'Of course, lady,' the Wolf Priest said, stepping away from the table.

Gabriella rose from her chair and stepped over to the hololith controls. 'The problem was that everyone was viewing the incursion as a military campaign, not unlike a Black Crusade,' she said. 'As Ranek said, nearly all of the minor targets had military value, but if we just focus on the areas with a major Chaos presence, we are left with this.' She touched a rune and the yellow indicators faded from view, leaving thirteen systems scattered in a roughly spherical arrangement around Fenris.

Ragnar studied each of the systems in turn. 'None of these are major military or industrial targets,' he said, a puzzled look on their face.

'Indeed,' she said, 'but, being a Navigator, another prospect suggested itself to me: what if the systems weren't important because of what they were, but rather, *where* they were?'

Gabriella touched another rune. The hololith drew blinking red lines connecting each of the systems together. Ragnar watched them converge, and his eyes went wide. 'It's a symbol of some kind.'

'Not a symbol *per se*,' Gabriella replied. 'It's a sorcerous sigil, and Charys lies at its centre.' She glanced up at Ragnar. 'Do you remember what the city of Lethe looked like when we left for the *Fist of Russ*?'

Ragnar nodded. 'Fire from the burning promethium lines stretched all across the city. It looked like... well, I remember thinking it looked like a ritual symbol of some kind.'

She nodded. 'That was the ritual symbol establishing Hyades as an anchor point for this larger sigil,' she said, pointing to the blasphemous sign hanging before them. 'Madox has laid the foundation for a sorcerous ritual of enormous proportions. If what you learned from Cadmus is correct, he now has all the elements he needs for the ritual to begin.'

The scope of the sorcerer's plans staggered Ragnar. He looked to the Great Wolf. 'A ship arrived from Charys, bearing news. What has Berek found?'

The Old Wolf's expression turned grim. 'Berek has been gravely wounded,' he said, 'and the Rune Priest Aldrek is believed to be dead.' Logan turned away from the window and stepped heavily to the table. 'When Gabriella revealed the importance of Charys I sent Berek's great company there to bring an end to this monstrous scheme. It appears that Madox was waiting for him. Berek and his men were lured into a trap.' The Old Wolf leaned forward, resting his scarred knuckles on the table's glass surface. His lined face was grim. 'Mikal Sternmark commands the great company for the moment, and he and the Guard regiments continue to fight against the rebels, but warp storms are growing in the region. Soon the system will be isolated altogether, and the Chaos uprisings have scattered our forces across the sector.' The Old Wolf banged his fist on the tabletop. 'Madox and his one-eyed master must have been planning this for decades. They've outmanoeuvred us, and their teeth are at our throats.'

A low growl began to build in Ragnar's throat. Suddenly he was very aware of the blood rushing through his veins and the pounding of his hearts. Every Space Wolf in the room sensed the change. Hands clenched and heads lowered as they caught the scent of the Wulfen.

'Master yourself, young one,' Ranek said in a low, commanding voice. 'Save the wolf's rage for our foes.'

Ragnar struggled to control his rising fury. 'What of your company, Great Wolf?' he said in a choked voice. 'Surely they can turn the tide at Charys.'

'My company is scattered across our domains, bolstering the efforts of the other Wolf Lords who are hard-pressed,' Grimnar replied. 'Berek's company was our reserve force.'

'Send the Wolfblade to Charys, then,' Ragnar snarled, unable to contain himself.

The Old Wolf's fists clenched. 'What, the three of you?' he thundered. 'Do you imagine you'll turn the tide all by yourselves?'

'I'll die in the attempt, if I must!' Ragnar shot back. 'I'd rather lie on a field at Charys than live another day here.'

'Arrogant pup!' Grimnar roared. He straightened to his full height, his fierce presence seeming to fill the entire chamber. He crossed the space between him and Ragnar with a single step, and lashed out with his open hand, cuffing Ragnar on the side of the head. 'I couldn't have said it better myself!'

The Wolves roared with laughter. After a moment, Ragnar joined in as well. Gabriella studied the giants' bloody-minded mirth with an expression of startled bemusement.

'You will have your wish, young Space Wolf,' Grimnar said, clapping Ragnar on the shoulder. 'We are sending every warrior we have left to add their swords to the fight, and Lady Gabriella has pledged her skills to guide our reinforcements safely to Charys,' the Old Wolf said, nodding respectfully to the Navigator. 'Report to Sternmark when you arrive. I'm sure he'll be glad for every stout arm he can get.'

In a flash, Ragnar's anger turned to a fierce, bloodthirsty joy. Death might wait for him on Charys, but so be it, he would face it as a Space Wolf, fighting alongside his battle-brothers. 'The Spear of Russ will be ours once again, lord. On my life and on my honour, I swear it!'

'I hear you, Ragnar Blackmane,' the Old Wolf answered solemnly, 'and Russ hears your oath as well. Spill the blood of our foes and return to us what was lost, and try to set a good example for the lads when you're getting yourself hacked to pieces, eh?'

THREE
Darkness and Ice

THE RUMBLE OF the Thunderhawk's engines drummed soundlessly across Ragnar's aching bones, rising inexorably to a punishing crescendo as the heavily laden transport clawed its way into the night sky. He dimly heard the approaching roar of the engines, the sound attenuated into a brassy rattle by the thin atmosphere, and the thick blanket of clouds below the rocky ledge began to glow a faint blue. The climbing spacecraft burst through the cloud layer like a spear, riding a column of cyan light into the purple vault of stars where the *Fist of Russ* awaited. Ragnar tracked its course through frozen, half-closed lids until it was nothing more than another fiercely burning speck in the firmament above the great mountain.

Within moments, the last notes of thunder faded, leaving Ragnar to his silent vigil. He had lost track of the hours since he'd climbed above the clouds and settled himself high atop the Fang. Clad only in his woollen clothes and wolfskin cloak, he had knelt in the snow and drawn forth his ancient frost blade. Resting the tip against the frozen ground and placing his hands upon its hilt, he had prayed to the Allfather and to blessed Russ, the First Wolf, until ice crystals clogged this throat and rattled in his lungs. All through the night he waited, his face upturned to the endless expanse of space, hoping for a brush with something he could not rightly name.

For a time after his brief audience with the Great Wolf, Ragnar's spirits had been lifted. The chains of duty had been loosened at last, and fields of war beckoned. More importantly, the Spear of Russ had been spotted on Charys, and for the first time, Ragnar felt that he might have a chance to redeem himself and restore the honour of his Chapter.

However, as the day wore on, and he began preparing his wargear for the journey, his thoughts turned dark once more. The news of Berek's fate at the hands of Madox was a terrible blow, and the picture that the Old Wolf had painted of the overall situation was woefully grim. Restoring those worlds already lost to Chaos would take centuries to complete, if it could be done at all. He'd heard of worlds scoured down to the bedrock by virus bombs and cyclonic torpedoes, once they'd been deemed too tainted to reclaim. Again and again, his mind turned back to that moment in the temple on Garm when he had held the Spear of Russ in his hand. *I threw it away,* he thought, *and everything that came after is because of me.*

He could not help but think of what the Old Wolf had said in the council chamber. *Madox and his one-eyed master must have been planning this for decades.* Could it be true? If so, hadn't he been nothing more than a pawn, pushed and pulled across a vast, invisible board that only the Chaos sorcerer could see? The idea left him sick at heart. It was one thing to strive mightily and fail – at least that was a noble failure, pure in spirit and done with honour – but to dance to the bidding of evil powers… that could not be borne.

So, he had climbed to the highest slope of Fenris he could reach, far beyond the grasp of mortal men, to stare up into the heavens and seek… something, a brush with holiness perhaps, such as he'd felt in the sacred shrine on Garm. He remembered the peace he'd felt then, the sense of rightness that banished pain and weariness and doubt.

Not this time, however. Poised between heaven and earth, fire and ice, Ragnar Blackmane was left with nothing but silence and doubt.

Ice crackled faintly as the Space Wolf slowly bowed his head. His breath no longer left faint wisps of mist in the thin air, having slowed and cooled almost to the point of hibernation. He could hear the sluggish flow of blood through his veins, and the slow, alternating beats of his hearts.

It was several long moments before the buzzing sound of voices registered in his numbed brain. They were approaching from the thick cloud layer, several dozen metres below. Haegr appeared first, broaching the pearly mist like a grey flanked whale. His beady eyes spotted Ragnar at once. 'Ha!' he exclaimed, his booming voice strangely distorted by the altitude. 'I told you we would find him here! That's three kegs of Ironhead Ale you owe me, Torin the Doubter.'

The barrel-chested Space Wolf plodded resolutely up the icy slope towards Ragnar, the heavy armour he wore lending weight and power to his steps. Ice glittered along the shoulders of Haegr's bearskin cloak and dragged down the bristles of his walrus-like moustache, and his cheeks were vivid red. Despite the climb, the huge warrior still carried his massive ale horn in his right hand. Behind him, lighter of step but no less burdened by the savage conditions, came Torin, helmet-less, but wearing an arctic hood that shielded his lean face from the worst of the cold. 'It was two kegs of ale, not three,' the older Wolfblade replied, 'but you won them fairly for a change. How did you think to look here?'

'Mighty Haegr's muscles aren't just in his arms,' he declared, tapping an armoured finger against his skull. 'You saw the look in his eyes when he left the arming chamber this afternoon. When he's in one of his black moods just think of the worst, most inhospitable place a Wolf can get to under his own power, and that's where you'll find him.' The burly Space Wolf climbed onto Ragnar's ledge, and peered sternly at him. 'Been up here all night, by the looks of him. His skin's blacker than an inquisitor's heart.'

Torin slipped past Haegr and knelt beside Ragnar. The older warrior studied him so intently that for a moment Ragnar wondered if Torin thought he might be dead. He took in a deeper breath and spoke, the words coming out in a raspy cough. 'Needed time to think,' he said gruffly. He tried to give Torin a hard look, but his frozen eyes refused to obey.

The older Wolfblade glanced back over his shoulder at the vast sea of cloud below. 'If you'd waited here a few hours longer you'd be watching our Thunderhawk take off and be thinking about how you were going to walk to Charys,' he said. 'Gabriella is taking her breakfast, and wants to be aboard the *Fist of Russ* before daybreak. We tried to call you, but you switched off your vox-bead, or it's frozen solid; I can't tell which at this point.'

Ragnar forced his eyes to close and concentrated on his breathing for a moment. His pulse began to quicken, slowly increasing his body's core temperature. Trickles of water ran from his eyes like faux tears, and froze upon his cheeks. The young Space Wolf clenched his fists around the hilt of the sword and felt ice crackle across his knuckles. When he opened his eyes again he saw that the skin of his hands was blue-black. He would be scraping the dead skin cells away for quite a while. Gritting his teeth, Ragnar climbed to his feet. Fierce pains stabbed through his joints, but he suppressed them with an effort of will. 'I would have come down by dawn,' he grumbled, shaking still more ice from his shoulders.

'Perhaps a note to that effect next time would be helpful,' Torin observed.

Now Ragnar did manage a forbidding glare. 'If I'd done that you would have come looking for me straightaway. I told you, I wanted to be alone.'

'What a bloody stupid thing to say!' Haegr barked. 'A Wolf's nothing without his pack, Ragnar. Even you're bright enough to know that.' He brandished his horn before the young Space Wolf. 'Why, you missed a true hero's feast in the hall last night! There was mead enough to float a long ship, and the eating-board groaned with all the food piled upon it!'

'Which Haegr tried to eat all by himself,' Torin said wryly.

The huge Space Wolf puffed out his barrel chest. 'Don't blame me for your faint heart,' Haegr replied, eyes wide with outrage. 'You could have taken your share at any time.'

'Except that I like my fingers where they are,' Torin remarked wryly. 'I've heard of battle madness before, but feast madness? Were you bitten by a goat at a young age, Haegr? I think you tried to eat the board itself between courses.'

'Don't be stupid,' Haegr shot back. 'I just needed a splinter to get a piece of venison caught between my teeth.'

'That wasn't venison, that was Rolfi, one of the new Blood Claws,' the older Wolfblade replied. He glanced at Ragnar. 'For a while, the cubs just sat and stared at everything that was going down Haegr's throat, but finally Rolfi had enough. He reached for a piece of venison and this great fool tried to take a bite out of him. Started quite a fight. The Claws pulled Haegr down eventually, like a pack of wolves nipping at a bear.'

'And you sat by and did nothing!' Haegr growled, full of dudgeon.

'Not so. I saw my chance and had a fine dinner amid the debris,' Torin answered mildly, and then regarded the young Space Wolf again. 'Did you find what you came here for?' he asked.

Ragnar raised the gleaming frost blade to the starry sky, inspecting the weapon carefully in the faint light. 'No, I didn't,' he said after a moment, and then slid the blade back into its scabbard. 'Perhaps the answer lies elsewhere.'

'On Charys, you mean?' Torin asked.

'Perhaps,' Ragnar said darkly.

Haegr shook his head in exasperation, staring out across the cloudscape. 'You're a good lad, Ragnar, but you think too damned much,' he observed. 'Still, you can pick some fine spots to brood.' The huge warrior spread his arms and sighed. 'By Russ, it feels like we barely got here before we're leaving again,' he said, a touch wistfully, and then chuckled. 'See, now you've got me doing it. I'll be moping about for years when we finally get back to Terra.'

'You're getting ahead of yourself,' Ragnar said. 'We have to win on Charys first.'

'Ha!' Haegr replied, his expression brightening at once. He clapped his hand on Ragnar's shoulder hard enough to stagger the young Space Wolf. 'That's a good one, lad! Haven't you ever heard the old saying? The wolf wins every fight he's in!'

'Every fight but his last,' Ragnar added, his expression grim.

The burly Space Wolf threw back his head and laughed. 'Then Mighty Haegr will live forever!' he roared, raising his ale horn to his lips. He paused, and then lowered the horn and peered into its depths. 'Morkai's black breath,' he cursed, 'my mead's frozen. Let's get below quick. There may be just enough time to thaw it out and get a quick bite to eat before we lift off.'

RAGNAR WATCHED THROUGH the shuttle's viewports as they began their approach to the *Fist of Russ*. The huge warship appeared out of the darkness like a battered fortress, her vast grey flanks bearing deep scars from enemy lances and cratered by salvoes of macro-cannon shells. Her imposing, armoured prow was scorched and pitted by weapon blasts, and her superstructure was a blackened, twisted ruin along nearly half of its length. Smaller repair tenders hovered around the enormous warship, using huge servo-arms and plasma blast torches to replace ruined sections of hull plating. Ragnar's keen eyes picked out swarms of repair servitors climbing like ants over the warship's massive dorsal lance turrets, working furiously to make sure they would be ready for action.

She had once been a Mars-class battle cruiser that had served with distinction alongside the capital ships of Battlefleet Obscuras, nearly fourteen centuries before. In those days she had been called the *Resolute*, but that name fell into infamy when the Arch-Hierophant Vortigern began the Alphalus Insurrection late in the 39th millennium. The petty officers and crew of the *Resolute* had sided with Vortigern and mutinied, murdering the ship's officers and turning the battle cruiser over to the Arch-Hierophant's forces.

For three hundred long years she served as Vortigern's flagship, until Berek Thunderfist's predecessor, the Wolf Lord Hrothgar Ironblade, captured her during the Battle of Sestus Proxima. Hrothgar claimed the ship for his own shortly thereafter, as his previous flagship had been lost, and *Resolute* returned to Imperial service as the *Fist of Russ*. She had fought many great battles since and earned a place of honour in the Chapter's battlefleet, and it grieved Ragnar to see her in such woeful shape. At Hyades the *Fist of Russ* had faced off against the heavy bombardment cannons of the *Vinco Redemptor*, a battle-barge of the Dark Angels Space Marine Chapter, and then later fought a small armada of Chaos warships summoned to assist Cadmus in the uprising on the planet's surface.

Though she'd survived, and even triumphed, in both battles, the *Fist of Russ* had paid dearly for her victories. Ragnar could see that the warship needed months, perhaps years, to repair all the damage she'd received, but that was a luxury the Space Wolves currently didn't have. All the Chapter's other great ships were already in action, along with their smaller escorts, so the *Fist of Russ* was needed at the battle line once more. Crews from Fenris would continue to make repairs up until the very last minute, returning to their tenders only when the battle cruiser was about to enter the warp.

Ragnar knew that there had been reports of Chaos warships lurking at the edges of the Charys system. He offered a prayer to the Allfather that the repairs would be enough.

'You seem troubled.'

Ragnar turned away from the shuttle's porthole. Unlike the Thunderhawk transports that had ferried the new Blood Claw packs to the *Fist of Russ* during the night, Gabriella was coming aboard the warship on an elegantly appointed personal shuttle from her family's cruiser, the *Wings of Belisarius*. The young Navigator sat at ease in a curved, high-backed acceleration couch in the shuttle's spacious passenger compartment, her face half-hidden in shadow.

The young Space Wolf cast a glance towards the pilot compartment, where Torin was guiding the shuttle to the warship's starboard hangar deck. Haegr, true to his word, had dashed off as soon as they'd come down from the mountaintop and appeared at the shuttle, just moments before launch, with a huge haunch of meat clutched in one armoured fist. He'd eaten the whole thing, bones and all, before the shuttle had even left the lower atmosphere, and now he sat in the back of the shuttle compartment snoring like an idling Land Raider.

Ragnar considered how to respond. 'The ship has no business heading back to the battle line,' he said after a moment. 'Are you certain you will not reconsider this?'

A faint smile touched the corners of Gabriella's thin lips. 'After everything that you and your Chapter have done for my House?' she replied.

'This is the very least I can do. But you're being evasive. It's not the ship that's bothering you.'

Ragnar folded his arms tightly across his chest. 'Are you peering into my thoughts?' he asked gruffly. The Navigator Houses of the Imperium were some of the most powerful psykers humanity had ever known, and their psychic abilities allowed them to guide ships of all sizes safely through the maelstrom of the warp. Their powers made travel through the Imperium possible for its warships and merchant fleets, and it was the source of their families' enormous wealth and power.

Gabriella let out a small sigh of exasperation. 'Don't be foolish,' she chided. 'When it comes to your emotions you're about as subtle as Haegr,' the Navigator said. 'You've been in a dark mood for the last few weeks,' she continued. 'What is it?'

She spoke calmly and carefully, as she always did, but Ragnar felt a flush of irritation at her persistent questioning. He started to snap at her, lips pulling back from his curved fangs, but caught himself at the last possible moment. *What is wrong with me,* Ragnar thought? He had sworn an oath to serve and protect House Belisarius. For all intents and purposes Gabriella was no different in authority than Berek Thunderfist or even Logan Grimnar. The young Space Wolf tried to mask his consternation, but gave up with an explosive sigh. 'Honestly, lady, I do not know,' he replied. 'I've been troubled since our escape from Hyades, but my mood has only darkened since arriving on Fenris.'

'I would have thought that returning to your home would please you,' she said.

'Please me?' Ragnar said. 'How could it? My Chapter is at war, and the more I consider it, the more I believe that I am partly to blame.'

'How? By casting the spear into the warp? Ragnar, if Madox had wanted that done, do you honestly think he would have needed your help to do it?'

Ragnar shifted uncomfortably in his seat. 'Well, no, I suppose not, but it troubles me all the same.'

Gabriella sighed and folded her pale hands in her lap. 'Ragnar, I understand what it's like to feel obligated to the people around you, but what's done is done. Be ashamed if you must, but don't wallow in regret. It won't change a thing.'

The young Space Wolf dropped his gaze to the tips of his armoured boots. 'I see your point,' he said reluctantly, 'but lately, I just can't get the thought out of my head. I haven't been sleeping well for days. Lately I've been having strange dreams. I think the spear figures into them, but I can't quite remember what they were about when I awake.'

He glanced up worriedly. 'I think Madox may be in my dreams as well. Could he have put some kind of curse on me?'

Gabriella raised an eyebrow. 'A curse? Unlikely,' she said. 'It sounds more like guilt to me.' She gestured gracefully at the massive warship looming large in the shuttle's forward viewscreen. 'Ranek said there was a young Space Wolf Priest leading the Blood Claws we're taking to Charys, perhaps he could help you.'

At the rear of the shuttle, Haegr let out a snort and straightened in his chair. 'A Wolf Priest?' he said fuzzily, wiping drool from his chin. 'I know him, a young lad named Sigurd.'

Ragnar glanced back at the burly Space Wolf. 'How do you know him?'

'He was at the mead hall when those cubs of his stole my rightful share of the feast,' he said indignantly. 'Tried to lecture *me* about discipline and respect! I've got scars older than that pup,' Haegr grumbled. 'He's got a stick shoved so far up his arse I could use him for a hand puppet on feast days,' he said, and then frowned. 'Are we there yet? Mighty Haegr could use a bite to eat to keep at peak fighting condition.'

The rumble of thrusters ebbed as the Belisarius shuttle began its descent into the battle cruiser's hangar deck. Ragnar found he had one more reason to be concerned about the voyage to Charys.

FOUR
Devils in the Darkness

A LOW GROAN of tortured metal echoed hollowly down the length of the broad passageway, and Ragnar thought he felt the heavy deck beneath him tremble as the *Fist of Russ* was buffeted by energies beyond mortal ken.

They were three weeks out from Fenris, and more than four days past their scheduled return to real space at the edge of the Charys system. They had encountered the first warp storm more than a week ago, and the intensity of the ethereal winds had only grown more intense since then. At first, the storms were almost imperceptible to Ragnar and the rest of the Space Wolves, but over time the first creaks and groans began to reverberate through the hull. Now, the terrible sounds were nearly constant, rising and falling in volume as the unseen gale wracked the warship's Geller field. There were already scores of hull breaches in still-damaged parts of the ship. The crew, overwhelmed by the simple day-to-day tasks of keeping the *Fist of Russ* operational, were forced to seal off entire sections of the warship rather than spend precious resources on temporary repairs.

The mood of the crew was tense. Unlike most Space Marine Chapters, which made extensive use of servitors to man secondary crew stations throughout their ships, the Space Wolves preferred human bondsmen to operate their starships. Many of these were former Space Marine aspirants that had fallen short of the enormous demands of training, but were still deemed worthy to serve the Chapter in another capacity. Others were chosen from among the peoples of Fenris specifically because of their skills as ship-handlers. They were among the finest shipmen in any Imperial fleet, but when Ragnar passed them in the corridors of the embattled ship he could smell the acrid scent of fear on their skin. If they didn't find a way through the storms soon, the *Fist of Russ* might not reach Charys at all.

For their part, the Wolves had grown more restless with every day spent in the confines of the great ship. Despite the battle cruiser's vast size, the individual rooms and passageways took on an increasingly claustrophobic feel, as though the warp storms had a physical weight that pressed in on the ship from every side. The Wolf Priest, Sigurd, kept the Blood Claw packs busy practising boarding drills and mock combats along the length and breadth of the battle cruiser, driving the young Wolves hard, but keeping their minds busy in the process. Ragnar could not help but approve of the Wolf Priest's diligence and dedication, but Sigurd didn't seem to know when to stop. Day-long battle drills would be followed by unannounced inspections or surprise attacks during sleeping hours. Packs were assigned complicated navigation problems to solve within the labyrinthine corridors of the warship, and were not allowed to eat or rest until they were completed. Tempers were growing frayed with each passing day, but the Wolf Priest would not relent. Even Ragnar was growing increasingly irritated about it, and he wasn't even taking part in the training regimen. Torin had approached Sigurd early on in the voyage, offering the services of the Wolfblade, but the older Space Wolf had been coldly rebuffed.

The Wolfblade spent their hours tending their wargear and practising their close combat techniques when the Blood Claws weren't using the training arena. Even Haegr had been persuaded to join, more from boredom and lack of food than anything else.

Sleep continued to elude Ragnar. It had been many weeks since he'd last managed a full rest cycle, and what little sleep he did manage was fraught with strange, fragmentary dreams. Although a Space Marine could function without proper sleep for months at a time if necessary, Ragnar could feel the strain beginning to affect his ability to think and react. He had contemplated approaching the ship's Apothecary for help, or even entering the Red Dream for the duration of the voyage, but the thought of what strange dreams he might encounter in such a state gave him pause.

From time to time, he considered Gabriella's advice about consulting the Wolf Priest for help. As the keepers of the Space Wolves' sacred lore, the Wolf Priests were considered the spiritual heart of the Chapter, and sources of great insight and wisdom. Sigurd, however, was rarely available to anyone outside the Blood Claws, driving himself as hard as, or harder than, his charges, and the one request that Ragnar had left at Sigurd's quarters had gone unanswered. These days, when sleep eluded him, he went to the battle cruiser's bridge and stood watch over the armoured capsule where Gabriella fought to guide the *Fist of Russ* through the warp.

Ragnar intended to return there after the evening meal, for he could already tell that he was too agitated to get any sleep. He had spent the entire day sparring with Torin and Haegr while the Blood Claws practiced boarding drills near the bow of the ship, and his body ached in a score of places where his comrades had landed telling blows. He'd kept fighting long past the point of exhaustion, but while his body felt almost leaden with fatigue his mind was tense and agitated. Strangely, even Torin and Haegr seemed to echo the young Space Wolf's mental state. They'd fought just as fiercely as him in the arena, hacking and slashing at one another with silent, murderous intent. Torin brought none of his cunning to bear, reverting back to simple, brutal blows, and even Haegr had little or nothing to say. They padded along silently in Ragnar's wake as they made their way to the ship's mead hall, drawing worried stares from every bondsman that passed by.

The raucous sounds of feasting rolled down the passageway as they approached the mead hall. Ragnar paused, biting back a surge of irritation. The whole reason he'd chosen this time to visit the hall was because normally the Blood Claws were elsewhere. Since the voyage began the Wolfblade had kept their distance from the young Wolves, and the sentiment had been returned in kind. Ragnar had little doubt that Sigurd had painted the Wolfblade as a pack of outcasts and exiles, as many other Space Wolves were wont to do.

'Are you going to stand there all day?' Haegr growled. 'Can't you hear that? The pups are eating our supper!'

Torin sighed, a little exasperated. 'There will be more in an hour or so, you great fool.'

'Then they can wait their turn,' the huge Space Wolf rumbled. 'Pups ought to learn their place, if you ask me. Here we are, three mighty heroes – well, one mighty hero and two fair to middling ones – who deserve their due, and those un-blooded younglings think to snatch the meat and ale from our very mouths. Well, I won't have it!' Puffing out his chest, Haegr pushed past Ragnar and rolled like thunder into the mead hall.

Torin cursed under his breath. 'I must be going mad,' he said. 'Haegr almost made sense there for a minute.' He glanced at Ragnar. 'He's sure to start a fight, you know. On the other hand, I'm almost as hungry as he is. What about you?'

Ragnar almost turned on his heel and headed back to his cell. In the mead hall beyond, the clamour of young voices and the racket of plates fell into a sudden and tense silence. All at once, a surge of irritation washed over Ragnar, raising the hackles on the back of his neck. 'Come on,' he growled, and strode swiftly into the hall.

The hall was full of Blood Claws. At first glance, Ragnar reckoned that all three of the young packs were taking their meal at the same time, something that hadn't happened since leaving Fenris. Shaggy heads hung low over gnawed haunches of meat, and dark eyes surveyed Haegr and his brethren with open hostility. Low growls rumbled across the hall and the air was thick with the scent of challenge, setting Ragnar's teeth on edge.

In older times the warship's mead hall was the officer's wardroom. Now three massive red oak tables were arranged in a rough Y-shape in a room capable of holding easily three times that number. Haegr stood between the two lower tables, his wide hands planted on his hips as he glared back at the Blood Claws. Heads turned to the high table, where the strongest pack typically sat, and the lesser packs would take their cues from them. The pack leader at the high table was a broad shoul-dered, blond-haired warrior with a hatchet face and hooded eyes. He picked a grox's thigh bone from the debris on the table and cracked it between his powerful jaws, his gaze never leaving Haegr as he sucked out the sweet marrow.

'What in Morkai's name do you want?' he asked with a raspy sneer.

Haegr glanced back at Ragnar and Torin, and gave them a wide grin. 'Now there's a stupid question if ever I heard one,' he replied, his rum-bling voice low with menace. 'This is the mead hall, isn't it? We're here to eat and drink our fill, as Wolves ought,' he said, turning back to the pack leader. 'Only you dogs happen to be in our seats.'

More growls rose around the Wolfblade. Ragnar caught Torin, giving him a sidelong glance. He knew that he should say something, a quick word of greeting or an offer to toast the coming battle, but he felt his body responding to the challenge, almost of its own accord. If the cub thought he was the toughest Wolf in the hall, Ragnar was eager to prove him wrong. In fact, he *hungered* for it.

A lean, red-haired warrior to the pack leader's right gave Haegr a wolfish grin. 'I think the walrus is ready for another beating,' he said.

The blond warrior's sneer widened. 'You want to eat? Here,' he said, and tossed the cracked bone at Haegr's feet. 'When you're done you can beg for more. I expect we can find a few more scraps for a bunch of outcasts like you.'

Laughter filled the mead hall. A bone arced from the table to the right and bounced off Haegr's shoulder. A crust of bread flew past, and then a fish head.

Haegr straightened to his full height, his chest swelling like a thundercloud, but by the time he'd opened his mouth to bellow his rage, Ragnar had swept past him in a dozen long strides and reached the high table opposite the pack leader. The blond warrior leapt to his feet, his eyes alight with the promise of battle, and Ragnar slapped him with his open hand hard enough to knock the warrior off his feet.

The pack leader crashed back into his chair and bounced back with a furious snarl, his face twisted with fury. He snatched a carving knife from the table and made to lunge at Ragnar, but the Blood Claw might as well have been standing still. Ragnar chopped his hand down on the pack leader's wrist, breaking it with a brittle crunch of bone, and then backhanded the Blood Claw off his feet.

There was a shout from the pack leader's right and the warrior's red-bearded lieutenant lunged from his chair. The rest of the pack at the high table followed suit, shaking the air with howls of rage, and the mead hall erupted into a wild, wheeling brawl.

The Blood Claws came at Ragnar from every direction, swinging fists, steins or whatever else came to hand. A hurled plate buzzed past his head and a drinking cup shattered against his chest, spraying Ragnar with mead. The young Space Wolf took a step back from the table as the first of the Blood Claws reached him, spoiling the pup's aim as he threw a wild punch at the side of Ragnar's head. Ragnar smashed him to the deck with a bone-cracking punch to the jaw. Another warrior rushed in from Ragnar's right, bent low and aiming to tackle him. The young Space Wolf laid the pup out with an elbow to the back of his head, and then two more warriors crashed into him from the left, driving him off his feet.

The three Space Wolves crashed to the deck with a thunderous clatter of ceramite. Fists rained down on Ragnar, hammering his chest, shoulders and face. One fist raked across his right cheek, opening a ragged cut all the way back to his ear. Snarling, Ragnar grabbed a handful of one Blood Claw's hair and smashed his forehead into the pup's face. The warrior rolled away, momentarily stunned, but the second Blood Claw drove his fist into the side of Ragnar's head. A flurry of bright spots burst across Ragnar's vision, but he shook off the blow with a savage growl and planted his foot against the Blood Claw's chest. Another punch glanced across Ragnar's forehead, and then the young Space

Wolf kicked with all his strength and sent the Blood Claw flying backwards. The warrior hit the heavy oak table and flipped over it, scattering plates and bits of food in all directions.

A heavy chair spun through the air to Ragnar's right and smashed a Blood Claw off his feet. The three packs were fighting the Wolfblade, and battering one another with wild abandon. Ragnar glanced over his shoulder and saw Haegr lift two Blood Claws by the scruff of their necks and knock their heads together. Two other warriors had their arms wrapped around the burly Wolfblade's legs and hips, trying to pull Haegr down, but they might as well have been trying to pull down the Fang itself. Farther off to Ragnar's left, Torin was weaving through the melee like a ghost, felling men with swift, precise blows and picking choice morsels of food off the battered tables as he went.

Ragnar heard the whirring approach of the flung beer mug half a second before it struck. He ducked, letting it pass harmlessly overhead, and glanced back at the high table to see from whence it came. Instead, he saw the red haired Blood Claw just a few steps away, swinging a massive chair in an underhanded blow that was aimed squarely at his face.

Ragnar got his arms crossed in front of his head a split second before the blow struck home. Old oak splintered, driving his heavy vambraces into his face, and the force of the blow sent the young Space Wolf sprawling. He landed in a tangle of splintered debris, blinking blood from his eyes, and his attacker was upon him in an instant, swinging a thick chair leg like an improvised mace.

A heavy blow struck Ragnar high in the chest, and then another landed on his chin. Pain burst across the young Space Wolf's face, and for a split second Ragnar's vision went black. He kicked out blindly and connected with the warrior's side. Then he drew back his boot and drove it against the Blood Claw's left knee. The warrior's leg gave out, dropping him into a painful kneeling position, but before he could react, Ragnar sent the warrior sprawling with a vicious kick to the side of his head.

Ragnar clambered to his feet, shaking his head to try and clear his vision. His keen senses detected someone rushing at him from the left, and he spun to meet the threat. A hand lashed out at him, angling in towards the side of Ragnar's neck, and he barely managed to block it by grabbing his attacker's wrist. With a cold shock, Ragnar felt the prick of a knife-point dig into the side of his throat.

The Blood Claw pack leader let out a wordless snarl and pressed his attack, swinging at Ragnar's head with his free hand. Ragnar let the blow strike home, scarcely feeling the pain. A sudden wave of murderous fury washed over him, and he closed his right hand around the pack leader's throat.

'*Stand fast in the name of Russ and the Allfather!*' shouted a furious voice from the far end of the hall. 'What is the meaning of this?'

Ragnar squeezed the pack leader's throat hard enough to feel the reinforced cartilage creak beneath his fingers. He watched the veins throbbing furiously in the pack leader's face and felt his pulse beneath his palm. At that moment, he wanted nothing more than to tear the fool's throat open.

Dimly, he heard Torin answer. 'Your pups required a lesson in manners, Sigurd,' the older Wolfblade said coldly.

The other voice replied with an iron note of command. 'I think it's the three of you who forget yourselves,' it said. 'Unhand that warrior, Wolfblade, or suffer my wrath!'

Ragnar whirled, dragging the choking pack leader with him. A young Space Wolf, not much older than Ragnar, stood at the far end of the room. He was a handsome youth, with a pale, square-chinned face and sharp, flinty grey eyes. His hair was white-blond, pulled back in a heavy braid that curved around the heavy wolfskin mantle on his shoulders and hung down across his breastplate. No scars marred his close-cropped beard, and his armour, while ancient, showed no sign of recent battle. A massive cross of gold inlaid adamantium, blazoned with a snarling wolf's head, hung from a heavy chain around the Wolf Priest's neck. The crozius arcanum, sacred badge of the priesthood, crackled menacingly in the priest's fist.

The look of fury in the Wolf Priest's eyes took Ragnar aback, extinguishing his rage almost at once. The priests of the Chapter existed apart from the great companies, and in effect were living embodiments of the Chapter's history and traditions. They demanded deference and respect by virtue of their position alone. Even the Great Wolf treated them with the utmost respect. It was what they were trained to do from their first days at the Fang. Without hesitation, Ragnar let the pack leader go, but it was harder to let go of the insult he and his brothers had been dealt. Leaving the pack leader gasping for breath, Ragnar strode towards the young priest. 'Blame the Claw,' he growled. 'He thought fit to challenge his betters.'

'Betters?' the Wolf Priest snapped. Young as he was, he had the look of a prince, and a manner that came from one born to authority. 'Harald has no betters here save for me. This is a hall for warriors, not exiles like you.'

Ragnar's fists clenched. Haegr let out a threatening hiss, and even Torin stiffened at the insult. It was all Ragnar could do not to strike the high-handed priest. 'It is an honour to serve in the Wolfblade, as anyone versed in the Chapter's lore would know,' the young Space Wolf replied with care, 'and we were treated as such in the halls of the Fang.'

The young Space Wolf Priest was unmoved. 'I do not speak of the Wolfblade,' he replied coldly. 'I speak of the three men I see here before me, exiles and outcasts, one and all,' he said. Sigurd took a step closer to Ragnar. 'I know your crimes,' he said. 'I know how you lost the Spear of Russ, the self-same weapon used to strike down your former lord!' His grey-eyed gaze transfixed the young Space Wolf. 'Do you deny it?'

Ragnar trembled with the effort to hold his rage in check. He could not guess what would happen if he gave in to his fury at that moment, and he didn't want the blood of a priest on his hands. 'You know I cannot,' he replied.

'That is so,' Sigurd answered with a grim smile. 'You do not belong here. None of you do. If you would eat, take your meals in your quarters until we reach Charys. You do not belong in the company of true warriors,' the Wolf Priest declared. 'Now get out of my sight.'

For a moment, silence reigned in the hall. No one moved. Sigurd glared implacably at the Wolfblade, merciless and indomitable in his anger. Finally it was Torin who relented. 'Let us go, brothers,' he said coldly. 'Sigurd is right. This is no place for the likes of us.'

The three Wolves filed silently from the hall, each one struggling to contain his rage. Ragnar turned at the doorway, and glared a challenge at the red-faced Harald and his brethren. When he met the pack leader's eyes he saw equal measures of anger and doubt. The young Space Wolf bared his teeth in a snarl. *Try me again and you'll get more of the same, and worse besides*, his look said to the Blood Claws. Then he closed the doors to the hall and stalked alone into the labyrinthine passageways of the warship.

RAGNAR DREAMT OF wolves that walked like men.

The thick, hot air echoed with the snarling of beasts and the sounds of battle. Ragnar could smell spilt blood and the stench of death all around him, and bodies littered the stones at his feet. He saw men and women in bloodstained robes, their bodies torn by tooth and claw, and their lifeless faces frozen in masks of terror.

The wolves wore armour like his own, but they had the faces of savage beasts. They struggled all around him, grappling and tearing at shadowy figures that writhed and lashed at the wolves like snakes. For every one the wolves tore apart it seemed two more rose to take its place. Howls of anger and despair smote Ragnar's ears.

He was standing in a vast chamber, like a ruined temple. Another armoured figure stood at the far end of the room, his face hidden behind a horned helmet. Ragnar didn't need to see the tall spear clutched in the man's armoured fist to know who the figure was. 'Madox!' he snarled, and threw himself at his bitter foe.

His veins turned molten with rage. A guttural growl rose in his throat as he slashed left and right with his keening blade. The ancient sword carved a deadly path through the shadow creatures, but Madox made no move to resist as Ragnar drew closer with each long stride. Ragnar could feel the power swelling in his limbs, his bloodlust quickening his steps until he was little more than a blur.

Voices were calling out to him, shouting warnings he could not understand. None of it mattered; the spear was almost within reach. A howl of triumph rose to his lips as he reached for the sacred weapon, and then his legs seemed to buckle beneath him.

Ragnar collapsed to the stone, his muscles writhing like snakes beneath his skin. The frost blade fell from his hands as his fingers contorted into claws. The only thing that remained constant was his anger, burning as bright as a hunter's moon.

Ragnar fell onto his belly, writhing. He threw back his head and howled in rage, feeling the bones of his face distend, centimetre by centimetre, into a blunt, toothy snout. Snarling, lashing at the air with his talons, he thrashed onto his side and snapped madly at the silent figure of the sorcerer just out of arm's reach.

As he did so, his gaze lit on a pale figure a metre to his right. She lay on the stones beside him, her alabaster face spotted with blood. As she spoke, vital fluids gushed from the terrible bite marks in her throat.

'*The beast waits within us all,*' Gabriella said to him, and then he watched the life go out of her eyes.

HE AWOKE WITH a shout of dismay, lashing about wildly in the darkness with his fists. One hand rang off a thick metal pipe and the violent motion thrust him backwards, causing him to crack his head against a heavy steam fitting. Ragnar collapsed back into a heap, blinking stupidly into the blackness. He had no idea where he was, or how he'd got there.

Asleep, he thought, struggling to make sense of the situation. *I must have fallen asleep.* Within moments his keen eyes adjusted to the gloom, and a second or two later he realised he was in some kind of narrow tunnel, deep within the bowels of the old battle cruiser.

Still blinking, Ragnar rubbed a hand over his face and tried to recall how long he'd been wandering through the ship, a great many hours;

that much was certain. The rage he'd felt after the encounter with Sigurd refused to go away, no matter how hard he tried to master it. He'd stalked along the passageways, swearing every vile oath he could imagine to have his vengeance upon Harald and that upstart priest.

The last thing he clearly remembered was deciding to head for the part of the ship where the Blood Claws were stationed, and to lie in wait for Harald's return.

Something like horror washed over the young Space Wolf. Slowly, dreading what he might find, he raised his hands to his face. They were covered in a thick layer of grease and grime, but he smelled no fresh blood on them.

'Blessed Russ,' he sighed. 'What's the matter with me?'

Then a dolorous howl echoed down the conduit, sending Ragnar reaching for his weapons. It was a few moments before he realised that the sound wasn't coming from a living throat, it was the ship's battle klaxon, summoning the crew to their stations.

That was when he realised that the battle cruiser's litany of creaks and moans had fallen silent, and her deck no longer trembled with strain. The *Fist of Russ* had dropped out of the warp at last.

They had arrived at the Charys system, and they were under attack.

FIVE
The Fist of Russ

THE OLD DECKPLATES rang with the tramp of booted feet as the bonds-men crew of the *Fist of Russ* readied the battered ship for combat. The grey uniformed crew raced nimbly past Ragnar as they ran to their sta-tions, but the Space Wolf could not help but see the strain on their faces or smell the fear on their skin. The battle cruiser was in no shape for a fight.

It took Ragnar almost half an hour to find his way to the command deck, high upon the citadel-like superstructure near the aft end of the ship. Blood racing at the prospect of battle and his head still reeling from his strange dream, Ragnar charged past the two bondsmen stand-ing guard at the armoured hatch. The command deck was dimly lit, and despite the high, cathedral-like ceiling the air felt heavy with ten-sion. Officers and midshipmen stood at their stations, consulting brass etched logic engines, and conferring in low voices. Ragnar saw the hunched figure of the Officer of the Deck at the far end of the space as he gripped the edges of the command pulpit and bellowed orders to the bondsmen and servitors of the ship's bridge, half a deck below. The young Space Wolf saw the green and grey orb of Charys filling three-quarters of the high, arched viewports along the bow end of the bridge. They were approaching the world from its night side, and his keen eyes picked out the scattered embers of farming settlements and trade cities burning sullenly across the planet's surface.

A handful of dark, angular shapes hung like cinders above the burning world, limned with pulsing green light from their plasma drives. Raiders, he thought grimly: traitor warships whose crews had sworn themselves to the Ruinous Powers. Some had once been vessels of the Imperial Navy, while others had been built at corrupted forge worlds at the edge of the Eye of Terror. Individually, they were less than a third the size of the *Fist of Russ*, but they were swift, agile craft, and in large numbers they were a threat to the largest battleship.

'What's happening?' he demanded, approaching a small group of senior officers who were standing around the rim of a large hololith table and speaking to Sigurd the Wolf Priest. Among the officers, Ragnar recognised Wulfgar, the ship's master and, half-hidden by the shifting patterns of the holo map, he caught sight of Gabriella. The Navigator's face was paler and more strained than Ragnar had ever seen it, and he could see that she was clenching her fists at her side to keep them from trembling. As near as he could tell, Gabriella remained standing by sheer willpower.

The Wolf Priest whirled around at the sound of Ragnar's approach. Sigurd fixed the young Space Wolf with a baleful glare. 'Return to your quarters, exile,' he snapped. 'The ship is at battle stations. This is no place for the likes of you.'

Ragnar felt a rush of anger so intense that it was all he could do not to throw himself at the arrogant young priest. Several of the ship's officers drew away from Sigurd, their expressions wary. The Wolf Priest's eyes narrowed, his hackles rising in the face of the sudden threat. His gauntleted hand tightened around the haft of his crozius.

Save your fury for the real foe, Ragnar told himself, forcing his body to relax and his fists to unclench. Like it or not, as the highest ranking Space Wolf aboard, Sigurd was the acting captain of the ship, and his word was law. He was bound to heed the counsel of Wulfgar and his officers, but little else. Ragnar wasn't about to bare his throat so easily, however. 'My place is with her,' he said, inclining his head towards Gabriella. 'Where she goes, I go, especially during times of battle.'

Sigurd's aristocratic face twisted into a grimace. He glanced back at Gabriella, and then looked to Wulfgar and the rest of the ship's senior officers as though gauging the strength of his authority. Finally he acquiesced with a curt wave of his hand. 'Very well,' he growled, 'but for the lady's sake alone.'

With an effort, Ragnar nodded curtly to the Wolf Priest and worked his way around the perimeter of the broad table to reach Gabriella's side. As he did so, the young Space Wolf quickly took in the situation unfolding in the air above the hololith. The *Fist of Russ* was less than an hour from entering orbit around Charys, but no less than nine enemy raiders stood in their way. Flickering runes and directional icons on the hololith showed that the raiders were breaking orbit at high speed and heading their way.

Ragnar saw no signs of Imperial ships anywhere in the vicinity. *Where is Berek's fleet?* The Wolf Lord had brought a battle-barge, two strike cruisers and half a dozen escorts to Charys. What could have happened to them?

Wulfgar and two other officers resumed a tense but quiet exchange with Sigurd as Ragnar stood beside Gabriella. The Navigator managed a weary smile. 'You look terrible,' she said.

The comment took him aback. 'I might have said the same about you, lady,' he said quietly, his brows drawing together in a worried frown. 'You suffered much to get us here, it seems. How long have we been in real space?'

Gabriella took a deep breath. Her lips pressed together in a tight line, and Ragnar could sense her disquiet. 'Less than an hour. I brought us in as close to Charys as possible,' she said after a moment. 'It was… difficult. I can't quite explain how.'

'Warp storms?' Ragnar ventured.

'No, nothing like that,' she said, her expression troubled. 'The currents around Charys are fierce, though, like… a vortex, of sorts.'

'A vortex?' the young Space Wolf asked. 'You mean, like a whirlpool?' He knew them well from the craggy coastlines of Fenris, and understood the danger they posed.

'Perhaps,' she said tentatively. She pressed a trembling hand to her forehead. 'I've never encountered anything like it. It took everything I had to guide the ship past the tidal forces. A lesser Navigator wouldn't have stood a chance.'

Ragnar chuckled quietly. 'My lady has spent too much time in Haegr's company, methinks.'

Gabriella smiled up at Ragnar. 'Save the wry humour for Torin,' she said. 'But what troubles you, my Wolf? There is a fey look in your eyes that I've never seen before.'

Ragnar paused, recalling the wolf dream. What could he tell her? What would she believe? He didn't understand it himself. Before he could answer, however, Sigurd's angry voice brought Ragnar's head around.

'Flee? You expect me to turn tail and run from the enemy?' the Wolf Priest snarled. Sigurd loomed angrily over Wulfgar and his officers. 'Where is your honour, Shipmaster Wulfgar?'

Wulfgar's men bristled at the insult. Though not Space Wolves, they were men of Fenris still, and such talk did not go lightly with them. But Wulfgar, the veteran shipmaster, was unmoved. 'There were no reports of an enemy fleet at Charys,' he said. 'The ship is not battleworthy. Most of our repairs are temporary, lord. A single, well-placed hit could cripple us, leaving us almost helpless.' The old bondsman leaned forward, his expression intent. 'We must disengage now, while we still can. The charts show an asteroid field nearby. We can hide there and try to come up with another approach to the planet.'

'And spend days skulking like a whipped dog while the Thunderfist's company is ground to pieces on the planet's surface? No. I swore an oath to Logan Grimnar that I would deliver our reinforcements to Charys without delay, and I will do so if I have to fight my way through hell itself!' The Wolf Priest glanced coldly at Ragnar. 'I'd sooner die than be called an oathbreaker.'

Once again, Ragnar fought to contain a flash of murderous rage. This was not the time or the place to issue a challenge, but for a brief, dizzying moment he found that he did not care.

His hand drifted to the hilt of the frost blade at his hip, but Gabriella gripped his fingers instead. The slight pressure was enough to shock him back to his senses. Ragnar took a deep breath. 'The Wolf Priest's words are ill-chosen,' he said to Wulfgar, 'but nevertheless, he is correct. Our reinforcements are desperately needed on Charys, and even a single day could make the difference between victory and defeat.'

Sigurd gave Ragnar a brief, appraising look, as though surprised at the young Space Wolf's backhanded show of support. Wulfgar listened, and his wrinkled face creased in a deep frown. 'If we must fight our way through then so be it,' he said heavily. 'Load your warriors aboard their Thunderhawks, lord. If our engines fail you may have to launch quickly and fly the rest of the way in.'

The Wolf Priest nodded solemnly. 'Russ is with us, Shipmaster Wulfgar,' he said solemnly. 'Let us bare our blades and begin the battle song!'

'I hear you, Wolf Priest,' Wulfgar answered, and seemed to draw strength from Sigurd's iron conviction. He turned to the officer of the deck. 'Ahead two-thirds!' he ordered. 'Bring us two points to starboard and charge the dorsal mounts! Gun crews fire as you bear!'

THOUSANDS OF KILOMETRES distant, the black-hulled raiders shook off the grip of Charys's gravity with a flare of plasma drives, and swung their rakish bows towards the oncoming Imperial ship. Their hulls were matte black, like dark iron, etched with foul runes that had been sanctified in blood and blessed by the dread hand of Chaos. Gargoyle figures of verdigrised brass crouched atop squat turrets or leered from the armoured mantlets of their towering superstructures, their mouths gaping hungrily. Their viewports gleamed balefully with pale, eldritch light. They leapt from their parking orbits like a pack of jackals and scattered into a loose arc in the path of the oncoming battle cruiser, scanning the void with uncanny augurs and looking for signs of weakness. Gun turrets squealed ponderously on their corroded mounts, training upon the *Fist of Russ* as the range between the two sides decreased.

In response, the distant Imperial ship swung to starboard, showing the raiders her battle scarred flank and her broadside of heavy guns. Along the battle cruiser's dorsal hull, two massive turrets slewed to port, bringing their energy projectors to bear on the incoming enemy craft. Arcs of cyan light crackled and seethed within the huge accumulation chambers of the lance batteries, gathering intensity with each passing moment until the blunt projectors were shrouded in a haze of voltaic wrath. Though the *Fist of Russ* stood alone against the raiders, and her hull was battered and broken, the reach of her guns was longer than most other ships in the Imperial fleet.

The lance batteries fired half a second apart. Twin beams of irresistible force crossed the black gulf in the blink of an eye, converging on the foremost raider in the pack. The first energy lance crashed against the raider's void shield, blazing white at the point of impact and shooting arcs of cyan and magenta lightning across its curved surface. For perhaps a millisecond the powerful shield held, but then the semi-invisible shield flickered and flared as it struggled to dissipate the lance's tremendous power. It failed in a spherical flash of light, like a bursting bubble, and then the second lance beam struck home. It tore the raider open from stem to stern, ripping open its flank like a fiery talon until it penetrated the small ship's reactor decks. The Chaos ship disappeared in an incandescent ball of plasma and radioactive vapour, wreathing its fellows in streamers of purple and magenta fire. The *Fist of Russ* had claimed first blood.

Thrusters flaring, the rest of the pack raced on, plunging through the expanding cloud of debris. Though their main guns were still out of range, the raiders were far from toothless. Three of the Chaos ships surged ahead of the rest, ordering themselves into a rough line abreast. Blackened, pitted blast doors drew back from launch tubes recessed into the ships' angled bows, and a pair of powerful anti-ship torpedoes, each more than forty metres long, streaked towards the battle cruiser on boiling plumes of fiery gas.

* * *

'TORPEDOES INCOMING!' SHOUTED one of the tactical officers from his station on the command deck. Ragnar caught sight of the tense expression on the man's face as he glanced towards Shipmaster Wulfgar.

'Lance batteries switch to antimissile targeting,' the ship's master declared. 'Portside batteries lock on to those torpedo ships and fire at will!' Wulfgar turned to a trio of officers clustered around a set of consoles to his left. 'Ordnance officer! What is the status of our close-in turrets?'

'Defensive guns at sixty per cent to port,' the senior ordnance officer replied.

'Very well,' Wulfgar said gravely. 'At this range they're not likely to miss. Damage control parties stand by!'

THE SIX TORPEDOES fanned out in a broad arc, blanketing the area around the *Fist of Russ*. The weapons were powerful but unguided, their trajectories planned by the infernal logic engines aboard their parent craft. Swift as thunderbolts, they streaked towards the battle cruiser's kilometre-long flank. Though her thrusters were roaring at near full power, for all intents and purposes the Imperial ship might as well have been standing still.

Twin cyan beams lashed through the darkness at the oncoming torpedoes, detonating four of them in globes of nuclear fire. The final pair of deadly missiles slipped past the raking beams and plunged towards the *Fist of Russ*.

At fifty kilometres the battle cruiser's defensive turrets clattered into action, hurling a torrent of energy bolts and explosive shells into the path of the oncoming weapons. A close burst from one shell punctured the fuel tank of one of the enemy missiles and the resulting explosion blew it apart. The second torpedo flew on unscathed, flying by unholy luck through a gap in the ship's flak coverage. It struck the *Fist of Russ* just forward of the portside hangar deck, its nuclear warhead detonating like the hammer of an evil god.

THE ANCIENT WARSHIP shuddered beneath the blow, and a roar like thunder reverberated through the battle cruiser's hull. Men were thrown across the command deck by the impact. Gauges burst and sparks erupted from power conduits on the port bulkhead. On instinct, Ragnar gripped the hololith table to steady himself and wrapped a protective hand around Gabriella's waist. On the bridge deck below, wounded men cried in pain, and a tech-priest cried out a prayer to the Omnissiah.

'Damage control report!' Wulfgar roared from the command pulpit.

'Hull breach from decks thirty-five to thirty-eight at frame 412,' the damage control officer reported. Blood flowed freely from a cut on the bondsman's scalp, and he wiped it away with a savage swipe of his hand. 'Fire on the flight deck!'

'All available crew to the flight deck and commence firefighting procedures,' Wulfgar ordered. The master of the ship turned and addressed Wulfgar. 'I advise you make for the starboard hangars at once, lord.'

Ragnar shot Gabriella a worried glance. The *Fist of Russ* was hit hard, and the battle had only just begun. The Navigator caught his eye and gave a stern shake of her head. The young Space Wolf nodded and raised his head to Wulfgar. 'We stand with you, Shipmaster Wulfgar,' he said. 'Fight on, in Russ's name!'

The ship's master turned back to his task. Ragnar caught Sigurd glancing his way, and was surprised at the Wolf Priest's approving nod.

Off to the right, one of the ship's gunnery officers looked up from his data screen. 'Enemy ships in range of our broadsides!' he said with a vengeful snarl. 'All gun decks report weapons lock!'

'Then give the bastards a taste of hell,' Wulfgar replied.

THE FLANK OF the battle cruiser was limned in red from the molten wound of the torpedo hit. Jets of burning atmosphere vented from the hangar decks aft of the impact site, casting a flickering glow over the dozens of huge gun turrets that swung into action. Macro-cannon barrels elevated into position, aimed by complex gunnery rituals performed by machine-spirits on the battle cruiser's bridge. The enormous weapons fired in sequence, hurling shells the size of land raiders at the oncoming Chaos ships.

Salvoes of explosive shells bracketed the three oncoming torpedo ships, hammering relentlessly against their void shields in staccato bursts of fire. Without warning, the shielding on one of the raiders faltered, and a cluster of shells erupted on the warship's rune covered bow and superstructure. One shell tore through the iron decks and found the raider's forward magazine. The resultant explosion ripped the traitor vessel in half.

Half a second later, another raider succumbed, its hull pierced in a dozen places and its superstructure ablaze. The last remaining torpedo ship continued on, its shield overloaded, but otherwise unharmed... until a cyan bolt from the battle cruiser's lance batteries tore the raider apart.

Nearly half of the raiders were gone, but the rest plunged ahead. They were less than fifteen seconds from entering gun range.

* * *

'Two of the raiders are angling aft!' the senior auspex officer declared. 'They're going after our engines!'

'Hard to port!' Wulfgar ordered. 'Show them our bow!' The ship's master chuckled bleakly. 'Maybe if we're lucky one of the blasphemers will try to ram us!' He turned to the gunnery officers. 'Port and starboard broadsides, stand by for salvo fire!'

With a tortured groan of metal, the command deck angled beneath Ragnar's feet as the huge ship swung onto its new course. He could see streaks of red and yellow through the tall viewports as the first enemy shells began hurtling past the struggling warship. Once again, he looked to Gabriella, but her eyes were closed, as though deep in thought or prayer. He thought to ask her once more if she wished to head for the hangar bay, but after a moment's thought he chose to hold his tongue.

The battle would be decided in the next few seconds. If the battle cruiser was doomed they would never reach the hangar deck in time.

Slowly, streaming a trail of frozen oxygen and melted debris, the *Fist of Russ* turned to face her attackers. Wulfgar had timed his move carefully, bringing the warship's heavily armoured prow into position just as the enemy ships hove into range. Macro-cannons and magna bolt projectors spat torrents of fire at the oncoming Imperial ship, bracketing her void shields with an unrelenting storm of explosions. The first layer of shielding failed. Then, seconds later, the inner shield gave way as well. Fierce blasts pummelled the battle cruiser's bow and superstructure, leaving scorch marks against fifteen-metre thick adamantium plate.

Moments later the raiders were plunging past the warship like burning meteors, their weapon batteries still blazing away at their foe. The *Fist of Russ* answered, her broadsides roaring to port and starboard at the swift moving Chaos ships. The nearest raider to port flared cyan under the lash of one of the battle cruiser's lance batteries, before a salvo of macro-cannon shells blew it apart.

Scores of explosions ravaged the Imperial ship's flanks. Many were turned aside by the vessel's armour plate, but here and there the enemy shells struck home. One of the battle cruiser's huge lance turrets blew apart, its massive power capacitors detonated by an enemy shell. Hundreds died on the Imperial ship's gun decks as armour piercing shells opened airtight compartments to space.

A raider on the starboard side of the ship was struck by a salvo of heavy shells that collapsed its shields and tore into its thruster banks.

The small ship spiralled out of control, trailing a blazing wake of plasma and molten debris until its reactors overloaded moments later in a spectacular burst of light.

Then the surviving raiders were gone, hurtling aft of the *Fist of Russ* and opening the range while the battle cruiser's beleaguered crew struggled to keep the ancient vessel alive.

FLAMES BILLOWED FROM the bridge, sending clouds of dark smoke roiling over the command deck. Men screamed in terror and pain as the emergency lighting flared to life. Officers picked themselves up off the deck and staggered back to their stations. Ragnar held on to Gabriella and peered warily through the smoky gloom, wishing to the Allfather for a foe he could come to grips with.

The senior damage control officer sang out through the smoke. 'Hull breaches on multiple decks! Dorsal lance battery out of action! Starboard gun decks report heavy casualties. Shields at fifty per cent. Our reactors are stable, but power output is limited.'

'Very well,' Wulfgar replied as he staggered back up to the pulpit. 'Helm! Can we still manoeuvre?'

'Aye, sir,' the chief helmsman replied. 'She's sluggish, but she's still answering the helm.'

'Bring us two points to port,' the ship's master ordered. 'Let's clear our wake and see where those raiders went.'

All starships were blind directly aft, where the roiling wake from their thrusters made sensor returns impossible. Slowly, ponderously, the battle cruiser swung around, streaming twisting ribbons of fire.

The seconds stretched upon the command deck as the ship's augurs searched for the Chaos raiders. Fire-fighting crews were hard at work on the bridge deck, and already the choking smoke was dissipating. Ragnar breathed slowly and evenly, allowing his enhanced respiratory system to filter out the worst of the fumes. He bent low over Gabriella. 'Are you all right, lady?' he asked. 'Shall I call for a medicae?'

'No, no,' the Navigator protested waving a soot stained hand. Her eyes were bleary from the smoke, but her expression was determined. 'The God-Emperor knows they've more serious problems to worry about.'

'Fire-fighting teams on the flight deck say they have evacuated the hangar and vented it to space,' the damage control officer reported. 'The fire is out.'

'Very well,' Wulfgar replied. 'Where are the enemy ships?'

The chief auspex officer looked up from his screen. 'No contacts aft,' he replied, his voice tinged with relief. 'The remaining enemy ships have shut down their augurs and gone silent. They've disengaged!'

A ragged cheer went up from the command crew. 'Belay that foolishness!' Wulfgar bellowed. 'We're far from safe harbour yet. Gun crews and augur teams will remain at their stations. All other crew will report to local damage control stations and lend assistance.'

The ship's officers scrambled to obey. Wulfgar stepped wearily down from the command pulpit and approached Sigurd and Ragnar. Neither of the Space Wolves had moved from their places. Barely four minutes had elapsed since the battle had begun.

Wulfgar bowed his head to the Wolf Priest. 'We've fought our way clear for the moment,' he said grimly, 'but I fear the *Fist of Russ* is crippled, lord. A Thunderhawk can reach Charys orbit in less than three hours. I suggest you and your warriors depart for the planet at once. The enemy could return with reinforcements at any time.'

Sigurd nodded gravely. The young Space Wolf Priest looked around the damaged command deck, apparently stunned by the devastation his orders had wrought. He slowly raised his crozius over Wulfgar's head. 'Praise Russ and the Allfather,' he intoned in a powerful voice. 'You and your crew are to be commended, Shipmaster Wulfgar. It was wrong of me to suggest that a man like you was without honour. The courage of you and your men shames me.' The priest placed his hand on Wulfgar's head and pronounced the Benediction of Iron, an honour normally reserved for members of the Chapter. When Sigurd was finished, Wulfgar looked up at the Wolf Priest in speechless awe, nodded respectfully to Ragnar and returned quickly to his station.

Ragnar watched as Sigurd looked around the damaged command deck one last time, clearly shaken by the fierce battle. When the Wolf Priest's gaze fell upon him and Gabriella, however, his expression hardened once more. 'We will leave for Charys at once,' he snapped at Ragnar. When he turned to Gabriella, his voice was far more moderate. 'Will you accompany us aboard one of our Thunderhawks, lady? It is no longer safe for you to remain aboard, I fear, and it will be some time before the *Fist of Russ* has need of your talents.'

'Your concern is noted, holy one,' Gabriella replied smoothly, 'but I and my Wolves will follow in my personal shuttle.'

'As you wish,' Sigurd replied with a curt bow. To Ragnar, he said, 'Report to headquarters as soon as you've made planetfall.' Then he strode swiftly from the command deck.

Ragnar watched the young priest depart, admiration mixing with outrage. Later, he vowed, Sigurd would answer for his insults to Ragnar's honour. For now, they had a war to fight.

SIX
Unto the Breach

By ACCIDENT OR a pernicious twist of fate, the enemy rocket attack began just as the landing craft from the *Fist of Russ* began their final approach. Two kilometres north across the cratered and smouldering expanse of the Charys star port, the barrage siren began to wail from the central bunker complex, the notes barely perceptible above the rising shriek of the Thunderhawks' turbines. Seconds later a salvo of rockets roared in from the rebel artillery positions to the east, just as the first assault transport raised its armoured prow and flared in for a vertical landing. The unguided warheads fell at random across the ten-kilometre square star port, detonating amid empty revetments, burned-out warehouses and blackened administration buildings. One came down on the other side of a storage shed less than two hundred metres from where Mikal Sternmark and the assembled honour guard were waiting at the edge of the landing field. The blast hurled chunks of burning flakboard and pulverised ferrocrete into the air with a thunderous explosion. Neither the Space Marines nor the armoured platoon of Imperial Guardsmen seemed to notice.

Roiling clouds of dirt and grit sped in a widening circle as the descending craft touched down in a rough diamond formation at the centre of the landing field, less than a hundred yards away. The hot wind tangled Sternmark's dark hair and pulled at the tattered ends of the black wolf pelt across his shoulders. Needles of pain stabbed along the length of the ugly, ragged wound that marked the left side of Stern-mark's head, but the Wolf Guard grimaced stoically into the hot, stinging wind and tightened his grip on the haft of the power axe in his left hand. He'd had little occasion to carry it recently, and he drew comfort from its familiar weight.

He'd carried an entire world on his shoulders for the last three weeks, and now he could gladly set that burden aside. It was one thing to lead men into battle and come to grips with the enemy face to face, Mikal had done that for more years than he could count, and he was good at it. Directing a planetary campaign from a dimly lit bunker, with thousands of troops and tens of millions of civilians to contend with was something else again. Once upon a time, he'd dreamt of rising to the lofty rank of Wolf Lord and holding the fate of star systems in his hands. Charys had shown him the folly of his ambitions. He was a warrior, and a leader of warriors, and he longed to return to the front lines where he belonged.

The ferrocrete landing pad trembled as the transports touched down. Mikal saw with some bemusement that one of the craft wasn't a Thunderhawk at all, but a richly appointed shuttlecraft with the insignia of House Belisarius emblazoned on its flank. Must be some kind of advance party, he thought, and waited patiently as the transports' assault ramps lowered with a clang and the first troops clattered out into the late afternoon sun.

Dust swirled around the legs of the Space Wolves as they loped onto the ferrocrete and formed up in ranks. Here and there the billows of dust seemed to mask larger, more hulking shapes that stalked menacingly at the corners of Mikal's vision. He shook his head sharply to try and clear it, which only set his wound throbbing again. The hellblade that had struck him during the frenzied retreat from the governor's audience chamber had not been poisoned as far as the company's Wolf Priest could determine, but the injury wasn't healing as it should.

Within moments, three large packs of Space Wolves were standing in ranks before their transports, heads held high and weapons ready at their sides. Blood Claws, Mikal noted with a slight frown. His expression of unease deepened when he saw that none of the warriors bore the heraldry of the Great Wolf on their shoulders.

Movement at the end of the line caught his eye. Mikal saw a Wolf Priest step forward and raise his crozius in salute to the waiting honour guard. The heavy mantle of wolfskin and the bulk of the priest's polished armour made the wearer seem almost childlike in comparison, like a son trying on his father's wargear. After a moment, he recognised the young, aristocratic face. *Sigurd, son of a rich jarl in the Dragon Isles, young and unblooded. Blessed Russ, what is he doing here?*

Off to the west, a heavy drumbeat shook the ground as the Earth-shaker batteries of the Imperial Guard fired a counter-battery salvo against the rebel rocket launchers. Nearly a third of the Blood Claws flinched at the sound, weapons jerking in their hands. Sternmark's unease transformed to irritation.

He strode towards the Wolf Priest, lips curling back from his teeth. Silent as a shadow, Morgrim Silvertongue followed in Sternmark's wake, watching the scene unfold with a storyteller's eye. *Marking my every mistake, noting every telling failure,* the Wolf Guard thought sourly. *Every king and hero wanted a fine skald at his side, but pity the warrior whose deeds were not worthy.*

Sigurd watched Mikal approach and smiled, making the sign of the wolf. 'The blessings of Russ and the Allfather be upon you, Mikal Sternmark,' he intoned. 'All of Fenris knows of your deeds on Charys, and we have come to add our swords to your own–'

'Where is he?' Sternmark growled.

The Wolf Priest's smile faded. 'I don't... I don't understand,' he stammered.

'Where is the Great Wolf?' Mikal said, still advancing on the young priest. With his terrible wound and his battered Terminator armour, the Wolf Guard was a vision of war incarnate, looming over Sigurd and the front rank of the startled Blood Claws. 'When will he and his company make their landing? Has he been delayed by the space battle?'

Sigurd lowered his crozius, an apprehensive look on his face. 'He... he's not here, lord,' he answered.

'Berek is lord here, not I!' Mikal shouted, suddenly struck with anger. 'I am his lieutenant and champion, and control of this war zone must pass to Grimnar as soon as he arrives.' He took another step forward, teeth bared, his face mere centimetres from Sigurd's. 'Can you tell me when he and his company will make planetfall or not?'

The Wolf Priest blanched at Sternmark's palpable fury, but gamely held his ground. 'He won't,' Sigurd said flatly. 'He can't. The Great Wolf's company is scattered across the war zone, supporting the actions of the other Wolf Lords.'

His answer stopped the Wolf Guard in his tracks. The shock left him painfully aware of the spectacle he'd made of himself. Sternmark fancied he could feel the skald's dark eyes burning accusingly into the back of his neck.

'I don't understand,' he said, not quite able to keep the stricken tone from his voice. 'Did he not read my report? Berek has fallen. Madox is here, with the Spear of Russ. This is where the war will be decided.'

Sigurd nodded, more composed now, but still unable to conceal the look of resentment in his eyes. 'Even so,' he replied, 'the Great Wolf cannot come. We have been sent in his place to aid you in whatever way we can.'

Once again, a tide of anger and despair threatened to overwhelm Sternmark. He shot a look at the waiting Blood Claws and choked back the words that first rose to his lips. *How am I to save our Chapter with three packs of initiates and a boy-priest? Why has the Old Wolf forsaken me?*

Instead, he drew a deep breath and struggled to push his feelings aside. As he did so, he caught sight of another small group approaching the ranks of newly arrived troops. Though distant, he recognised their scents at once.

Ragnar Blackmane, and the Navigator, Gabriella, with Torin the Wayfarer and Haegr the Mountain in tow. What in Morkai's name are they doing here? The answer suggested itself almost at once. *It's the Spear. Grimnar's sent them to reclaim it somehow. Either the Old Wolf is truly desperate, or he knows something I don't.*

Sternmark chose to believe the latter. He'd banked a great deal on the report he'd sent to Fenris, believing that once Grimnar understood how dire things were on Charys, the Old Wolf would gather his warriors and take charge of the campaign. Mikal had clung to that hope for days, knowing he was not up to the task that had been thrust upon him. Now he would have to see things through to the bitter end.

With as much dignity as he could muster, Sternmark turned to the assembled Blood Claws. 'Praise Russ!' he declared. 'Look upon blood-stained Charys, and know that your deeds here will be remembered in the sagas of our Chapter. Glory awaits you, in the Allfather's name!'

The Blood Claws didn't respond for a moment, still stunned by the Wolf Guard's earlier outburst. Then Sigurd raised his crozius and added his voice to Sternmark's. 'For Russ and the Allfather!' he cried. 'Glory awaits!'

Harald, leader of the first Blood Claw pack, took up the cry. 'Russ and the Allfather!' he roared, raising his axe. Within moments the rest of the Space Wolves had joined in, banging their weapons against their breastplates and howling at the smoke stained sky.

Mikal Sternmark listened to the shouts of his young brethren and fought to master his emotions. Ghostly images played at the corners of his vision: huge, leaping shapes that were neither beasts nor men, and strange, distorted sounds whispered in his ears. *The wound,* he thought despairingly. *That damned hellblade has laid a curse on me.*

He looked to Silvertongue, and caught the skald staring at him with those unreadable eyes of his. Mikal could guess how his own saga would end. Not all the tales ended gloriously. Some ended in tears, or infamy. The thought shamed him, but he resigned himself to it.

Off in the distance, the barrage siren wailed.

THE COMMAND BUNKER was red-lit and stank of unwashed bodies and bile. From what Ragnar could determine, the Guard commander in chief had chosen the star port bunker complex as her headquarters upon first arriving with her regiments on Charys, and what started out as a temporary post became permanent as the campaign wore on. Field cots and piles of empty ration tins in the corners of some of the low-ceilinged rooms suggested that Athelstane's general staff worked, slept and ate at their posts. Judging by the pasty faces and red-rimmed eyes he'd seen on his way inside, Ragnar thought that many of her staff hadn't felt the touch of sunlight in weeks.

That one observation told him all he needed to know about how desperate the situation on Charys truly was.

Athelstane's harried officers all but ignored the newcomers as they were escorted into a small auditorium that had been converted into an improvised situation and planning room. The hard pews had been cleared away, replaced with tables and portable work stations. Harried aides darted between the narrow aisles, carrying flimsy printouts to staff officers who were monitoring battle reports from half a world away. Tense conversations and muted orders rose above the dry clatter of logic engines and vox teletypes. Enginseer acolytes hovered in the corners of the room, muttering prayers and lighting votive candles to keep the data channels open.

Mikal Sternmark led Sigurd, Ragnar and Gabriella across the crowded room to a large, ornate hololith table that had been set up on the auditorium's former stage. There, he introduced them to Lady General Militant Esbet Athelstane. The commander of all Guard forces on Charys was a thin, raw-boned woman with a severe, patrician face and large, dark eyes. Her iron-grey hair was cropped as short as a rank and file sergeant's, and to Ragnar she smelled of leather, amasec and fine machine oil. Athelstane wore the Medallion Crimson among the many campaign ribbons and decorations on her officer's greatcoat, and from the faint sounds of servomotors and pistons, Ragnar reckoned that her right arm and both legs were expertly crafted augmetics.

Athelstane greeted them all with weary professional courtesy, and then introduced an older, balding man in a dark green suit, who reluctantly joined the gathering from a seat at the back corner of the stage.

He was taller than the general, with a hook nose and red-rimmed, grey eyes. There was a defeated air about the man; he limped haltingly on his left leg, and his angular shoulders were hunched. As he stepped into the dim light, Ragnar saw that the right side of the man's face and throat was covered in a glistening film of wound sealant, and both hands were wrapped in flexible bandages.

'This is Inquisitor Kadmus Volt, of the Ordo Malleus,' the general said. 'He and his team have been on Charys for the last three years, investigating reports of forbidden practices among the local farming cartels. Since the uprising began, he has advised us on the enemy's capabilities and possible intentions.' From the steely sound in Athelstane's voice it was clear that Volt had been of little use in that regard.

Inquisitor Volt bowed cordially to Gabriella. 'May I ask what brings so esteemed a member of the Navis Nobilite to such a dangerous place as Charys?' he asked.

Gabriella acknowledged Volt with a cool nod and a narrow gaze. The Navigator Houses had a long, antagonistic relationship with the Inquisition. 'House Belisarius and the Wolves of Fenris have been allies for centuries,' she replied coolly. 'Honour requires that we aid our esteemed friends in whatever manner we are able.'

'Without Lady Gabriella's assistance our reinforcements would never have reached Charys at all,' Ragnar said. 'Turbulence in the warp has all but isolated the system.'

'So we surmised,' Athelstane said with a nod. 'Whatever the enemy is attempting at Charys has taken a fearful toll on our astropaths. We have been awaiting your arrival with great anticipation.'

Both Athelstane and Sternmark looked to Sigurd, and the Wolf Priest picked up on the unspoken cue and began his report of the war council on Fenris. The commanders listened carefully as the Wolf Priest recounted the Great Wolf's deliberations and their subsequent journey to Charys. Ragnar took the opportunity to lead Gabriella to a nearby seat. The Navigator was still somewhat unsteady on her feet, and though she took pains to conceal it, Ragnar could tell that she was deeply unsettled. Gabriella accepted the seat with an absent nod, one hand clinging to his forearm for support.

As strained as her manner was aboard the *Fist of Russ*, it had only grown worse once their shuttle had landed. There was something strange at work on Charys. Ragnar felt it, too, a strange sense of dislocation, as though the world around him had no more substance than a hologram. Shadowy shapes flitted at the corners of his vision, and faint sounds whispered in his ears. The agitation he felt on Fenris seemed magnified tenfold. It was all he could do not to rise and pace across the crowded stage like a caged animal. From time to time, his gaze wandered to Mikal Sternmark's grim face, and he wondered if the legendary champion felt the same as he did.

'Thanks to the Lady Navigator's skill, we emerged very close to Charys, whereupon we came under attack from a force of enemy raiders that had been at anchor in high orbit,' Sigurd continued. 'We had thought to find Berek's fleet waiting there.'

'The enemy has a sizeable naval presence in the system,' Athelstane replied. 'We believe that there was a large armada of raiders hiding within the outer asteroid fields for some time. Since the uprising began, they have been joined by a growing number of escorts and cruisers. Berek's fleet commanded the approaches to Charys for almost a week, and we were able to defeat a number of enemy ground offensives with their support. As the enemy was able to commit more and more ships against Berek's force, casualties began to mount, and it became clear that if they left the system to make repairs, they might not be able to return.' The general glanced briefly at Inquisitor Volt. 'It was decided that the fleet would withdraw to the edge of the system and make what repairs they could. They've remained there ever since, as our force of last resort. Much of the enemy fleet has been drawn off to hunt for them, although groups of raiders have appeared from time to time to bombard our positions from orbit.'

Gabriella straightened in her seat and drew a deep breath. 'How has the enemy managed to communicate with their fleet across the system?'

The general shrugged. 'We don't know. Sorcery, perhaps? That's not my area of expertise.' Once again, she gave the inquisitor a sidelong look. 'Maybe they aren't talking with one another. Their orbital attacks don't seem to coincide with their ground operations as far as we can tell, not that they aren't damaging enough all by themselves.'

'Well,' Sigurd interjected, clearly a little agitated by Gabriella's interruption, 'you've heard our tale. Now, what would you have of us?'

Athelstane rested her hands on the hololith table's smoked glass top and glanced at Sternmark. 'That's an interesting question,' she said slowly. 'We had been led to believe that Fenris would be sending a great deal more troops and heavy weapons to support us. We'd hoped for a spear that we could thrust into the enemy's heart. Instead, it appears that the Great Wolf has gifted us with a handful of brand new knives.'

The bald statement took all of the Space Wolves aback. It wasn't a disparagement, but a cold assessment of the facts. Ragnar saw the Wolf Priest stiffen nevertheless. This is the second time he and his men have been dismissed as irrelevant, the young Space Wolf thought, a hard thing to take, for the son of a powerful jarl.

When Sigurd didn't reply at once, Ragnar ventured, 'Even a knife can be lethal when used properly,' he said. 'Tell us, how goes the war on the ground?'

'Badly,' Athelstane replied. 'At first we believed the uprising was the work of a small cabal of government officials and officers in the local PDF regiments, but now it's clear that outside forces planned and organised this campaign for many years. More than two-thirds of the Planetary Defence Forces mutinied over the course of a single night. What heavy weapons and vehicles they didn't take they managed to destroy. Bureaucrats in key positions sabotaged the planetary logistical network and crucial emergency response plans. By the time my regiments and I arrived, Charys was almost completely in enemy hands.' She reached down and keyed a control panel recessed into the edge of the table. A holo-map of the planet instantly appeared in the air above the table, showing nearly sixty small cities and townships scattered across the world's vast plains. More than half of the settlements had a skull superimposed over them. They existed in name only, having been abandoned or wiped out by the rebels. The rest showed a red aquila, indicating that they were battlegrounds where neither side could claim total control.

'We managed to establish footholds at a number of points around the planet, but we weren't able to achieve significant gains because we had been misled as to the size of the rebel force and the lack of support we would find on the ground.' The general turned a brass knob and the view switched to an operational map of the capital city. Nearly eighty-five per cent of the districts were red, with only a narrow band of Imperial blue around the outlying sectors to the east that stretched back to the star port outside the city. 'When Berek Thunderfist and your brethren arrived, we attempted a lightning thrust aimed at decapitating the rebel leadership and retaking the capital.' She pressed a stud and a trio of broad, blue arrows leapt from the eastern districts and drove deep into the heart of the city. 'The orbital bombardment and follow-on attacks inflicted very heavy rebel casualties and allowed us to push all the way to the governor's palace.'

Athelstane's expression darkened. 'Unfortunately, the Wolf Lord's attack met with disaster. Sternmark and his warriors managed to break out of the enemy ambush and withdraw from the palace with Berek's body, and then linked up with our lead armoured elements.'

Ragnar glanced over at Mikal. The look in the warrior's eyes was one he knew all too well. He curses himself for retreating, the young Space Wolf thought, and no wonder, but what other option did he have?

'Where is Berek now?' Sigurd asked. 'Does he still live?'

'We think he lingers in the Red Dream,' Sternmark said dully. 'Our instruments detect faint life, but his body will not respond to our priest's unguents and balms. We had hoped that Grimnar would at least send Ranek or one of the senior Wolf Priests to tend to Berek...' The Wolf Guard left the rest unsaid, but the implication was clear.

'What of the palace?' Ragnar interjected.

'Before we could mount another attempt to retake the palace the rebel forces launched a massive counter-offensive,' Athelstane replied. 'This time the rebels were supported by Traitor Space Marines and packs of daemons. The enemy struck out of thin air, exploiting weak spots in our lines with diabolical skill.' She sighed bitterly, clearly haunted by her failures stemming from that fateful day. 'Fighting raged around the city centre for almost forty-eight hours, but in the end we were forced to withdraw.'

Gabriella leaned forward in her chair. 'How are the Chaos Space Marines managing these feats of teleportation?'

Inquisitor Volt folded his arms and scowled at the holo-map, as though the secret was somehow hidden there. 'We don't know,' he admitted. 'It's not technological. They appear and disappear like ghosts, coming and going apparently at will, and not just here in the city, but across the entire *planet* as well.' He shook his head in exasperation. 'We've laid wards to protect the star port perimeter from attack. They seem to have worked so far, but the cost of maintaining them is enormous. If I knew *how* the enemy was accomplishing this, I could perhaps devise a better way of countering it, but I can't find a reference to anything like this in my records. The scale is unprecedented.'

Gabriella considered this. 'It is interesting that you mention the notion of scale, inquisitor. I have been studying the efforts of the enemy sorcerers at the subsector level. Perhaps if we were to compare notes, I might be able to give you more insight into the situation.'

Volt stared dumbstruck at the Navigator for a moment. 'That is... unexpected,' he finally managed. 'Of course, I would be happy to hear your thoughts on the matter.'

Gabriella nodded at Volt, and then gestured to Athelstane. 'Please forgive the interruption, general. Pray continue.'

The general keyed another stud, and the blue arrows shrank back from the palace. 'For a time we were able to stabilise our lines with help from the ships in orbit, but once they withdrew the tide turned against us. The enemy has pushed us back bit by bit. The Traitor Space Marines crack open our lines with precision assaults, and their ground troops pour right through. Berek's company has been divided up among war zones all over the world in an attempt to stem the tide, but all we've done is slow their advance. At this point, we've been driven back to the edge of the city, and there are indications that the enemy is preparing another major offensive.' The holo-map shifted again, returning more or less to the thin blue line at the city's eastern edge. 'Their objective is the star port. If it falls, we lose our one and only air base and supply point. Our regiments will then be isolated and eventually over-whelmed.'

For a moment, Sigurd and Ragnar considered the map in stunned silence. Ragnar glanced up at the general. 'What about the Imperial Navy and the Guard?'

'When I left Corianus with my staff, the lord governor subsector had sent out the call for more regiments,' she said. 'At best, the first units won't get here for another five months, even assuming the Navy can get ships through the local warp turbulence.' She eyed the map grimly. 'We'll be lucky if we can hold out another five days.'

Ragnar walked over to the map table, studying the riot of symbols that depicted the locations of Imperial and enemy units across the city. 'You forget, general, that one ship has already made it through,' he pointed out, 'and, although they are untested in battle, you have almost fifty Space Wolves to add their strength to the fight. Do not be so quick to dismiss us.' He looked pointedly at Sternmark, but the Wolf Guard would not meet Ragnar's eyes.

Athelstane sighed. 'Your courage does you credit,' she said heavily. 'I've had the honour of fighting alongside the Space Wolves several times in my career, and I know very well what you're capable of, but you must understand, even with twice your numbers I doubt we could defeat the forces arrayed against us.'

Ragnar set his jaw and looked the general in the eye. 'You said you wanted a spear to thrust at the heart of the enemy,' he said. He indi-cated the enemy positions on the map with a sweep of his hand. 'Suppose the Great Wolf had arrived with his company, where would you have employed them?'

The general regarded him appraisingly for a moment. 'For starters, I wouldn't have committed them to the city at all.'

She adjusted a set of dials and the map's viewpoint pulled back until it showed the countryside within sixty kilometres of the city. 'There is a large PDF base approximately twenty kilometres west of the capital. Before the uprising it was the supreme headquarters for the Charys defence forces.' The map shifted, focusing in on a large, fortified mili-tary base some five kilometres across. 'We've suspected for some time that the traitor regiments were still using it as their command centre.

Naturally, we've bombarded it at every available opportunity, but the base's bunker complex was built to shrug off that kind of attack.'

With another turn of the dial the map zoomed in on the rebel base. Ragnar observed tall, thick perimeter walls sited with dozens of gun emplacements that commanded a flat, featureless killing ground for kilometres in every direction. He saw tank parks and reinforced barracks large enough to hold four or more armoured regiments, defended by Hydra anti-aircraft positions. The central bunker complex alone was over two kilometres across, and Ragnar suspected that it extended even farther underground.

'Once Berek's company arrived we inserted three packs of his scouts into the area around the base to see what we could learn,' she continued. 'Our suppositions proved correct. The rebels were indeed still using it as their headquarters, and recently they have observed the arrival of numerous high-ranking officers and their aides. They are still there, which is why we believe they've been gathered to plan a major series of offensives.'

'And you wanted the Old Wolf's company to destroy this base?' Ragnar asked.

'Not just destroy it,' Athelstane replied. 'We planned a lightning assault to capture the rebel high command and deliver them here for interrogation. Inquisitor Volt assured me he had the means to make the traitors tell us everything they knew.'

Ragnar nodded appreciatively. 'How many enemy troops?'

'A reinforced armoured regiment: at least fifteen hundred troops with heavy weapons and almost forty battle tanks.' She spread her hands. 'We reckoned even Grimnar's great company would have a tough time taking the base.'

The young Space Wolf nodded thoughtfully. 'It's good for you then that we're here instead of the Old Wolf,' he said with a feral grin. 'We'll go in at first light.'

SEVEN
Hit and Run

THE BATTLE CRUISER'S brass and steel teleportation chamber rang like a swordmaster's forge as the Space Wolves made ready for battle. The Wolves of Harald's Blood Claw pack congregated in a tight group, checking their weapons and adjusting the heavy load of extra equipment they would be carrying with them on the raid. Most had their helmets off and were talking with one another in low, sullen voices. Ragnar had insisted that the warship's ancient teleporters were vital to the success of the raid, but the Space Wolves hated the thought of placing themselves at the mercy of such an arcane, unreliable device. A few metres away, Sigurd the Wolf Priest stood alone, both hands clasped on his crozius and his head bowed in prayer. Iron Priests and acolytes in full ceremonial vestments moved slowly around the perimeter of the room, checking and anointing the vast network of power couplings and matrix field collectors.

Ragnar stepped through the armoured hatch into the chamber just a few minutes before jump-off. They had returned to the *Fist of Russ*, in high orbit over Charys only a few hours ago, and he'd spent most of the intervening time meditating in his old quarters. A grim sense of foreboding dogged his steps. Although the sense of dislocation had ebbed since leaving the planet's surface, he could not ease the tautness of his nerves or banish the wisps of shadow that flitted at the corners of his eyes.

He could not afford to be distracted once the raid began. Even a moment's hesitation could mean disaster.

The assembled warriors paid Ragnar no heed as he strode across the chamber. He took careful note of Sigurd and the Blood Claws, and then caught sight of Torin on the opposite side of the room. The older Wolf-blade was finishing an inspection of his chainsword as Ragnar approached.

'Where's Haegr?' Ragnar asked with a frown.

Torin slid his chainsword into its scabbard and grinned ruefully. 'Where else?'

'Morkai's black breath!' Ragnar cursed. 'If that overfed walrus is late–'

'Peace, brother,' Torin chuckled, raising a gauntleted hand. 'Haegr can be a fool sometimes, but I've never known him to shirk his duty. He'll be here when the time comes, probably clumping along with an ale bucket on his foot, but he'll be here nonetheless.' The older Space Wolf studied Ragnar carefully. 'What's troubling you? I've never known you to get a case of nerves before a battle, even one as risky as this.'

Ragnar shrugged. 'It's nothing,' he began, but stopped trying to pretend when he saw Torin's disbelieving glare. 'Nothing I can explain, at least,' he said grudgingly. 'I don't know, Torin. Truth be told, I haven't felt right since we returned to Fenris. My temper is on a hair trigger, and I feel like I could crawl right out of my skin.' He shook his head savagely. 'Even my eyes are playing tricks on me.'

Torin's eyes narrowed thoughtfully. 'You, too?'

Ragnar froze. 'You mean you feel the same way?'

The older Space Wolf lowered his voice to a conspiratorial whisper. 'Since we arrived on Charys I've been seeing things, like shadows or wisps of smoke, flitting at the edge of my sight.'

'Yes! Exactly!' Ragnar whispered excitedly. He leaned close to Torin. 'Anything else? Did everything planetside feel... I don't know... *unsettled*, somehow?'

'Like nothing was solid or real?' Torin breathed a sigh of relief. 'Thank Russ. I was starting to think I was losing my mind. But wait, you said you were feeling like this back on Fenris?'

Ragnar frowned. 'Well, not exactly. I didn't start seeing things until later, once we'd set off for Charys. On Fenris it was mostly just strange dreams.'

'Dreams about what?'

'Monsters,' Ragnar answered. 'Monsters in the shape of men.'

Torin frowned. 'Monsters... or Wulfen?'

Ragnar felt his hackles rise. 'Does it matter?' he asked.

'Of course it does,' Torin answered. 'Have you talked to the Wolf Priest about it?'

'Even if I'd thought of it, there was no time to talk to Ranek,' the young Space Wolf replied.

'What about Sigurd?'

Ragnar snorted. 'Don't be stupid. We're just a bunch of *nithlings* as far as he's concerned. The only things I plan on sharing with him are my fists.'

The older Wolfblade shook his head. 'Don't be so quick to judge him, Ragnar. Yes, he's a bit of an idiot, but we all were at that age. He still thinks he's the son of a jarl, not a young priest who's just earned his crozius. He's unsure of his authority and overwhelmed by the role he's been thrust into. Basically, he's terrified of failure.' Torin looked pointedly at Ragnar. 'Sound like anyone you know?'

'I'm not sure what you mean,' the young Space Wolf growled.

'Fine, consider this instead: Sigurd wouldn't have been raised up unless Ranek and the other priests saw some potential in him. Talk to him about the dreams. Give him the benefit of the doubt, and perhaps he'll learn to do the same for the rest of us.'

Ragnar thought it over. Finally, he shrugged. 'All right,' he said, 'as soon as we get back, provided we don't get blown to pieces in the meantime.'

Torin grinned and clapped Ragnar on the shoulder. 'That's the cheery soul I used to know. Trust me on this, brother. I know what I'm talking about.'

The young Space Wolf turned and surveyed the chamber once more. 'Is that so? Then where is Haegr? We jump off in thirty seconds–'

A booming laugh rolled down the passageway outside the chamber. Haegr's bristly, grinning face appeared in the hatchway, his massive drinking horn clutched in one great fist. 'Mighty Haegr is here!' he roared, sloshing a bit of frothy ale onto the deck. 'Draw your swords and beat your shields, sons of Fenris! Battle and red glory await!'

For a moment, it looked as though Haegr wouldn't be able to force his bulk through the narrow hatchway. Iron Priests and acolytes hurried over to help, but the huge Space Wolf paid them no heed. First one foot, then the hand bearing the ale horn, then a hip the size of a boar's flank and a torso half again as large as a mead cask, and with a grunt and a creak of metal, Haegr squeezed sideways into the room. Still grinning, he took a long draught from his ale horn and licked the froth from his whiskers. 'Next time I see the Old Wolf,' he said to Ragnar, 'remind me to tell him we need bigger ships.'

* * *

FAR BELOW, ON the surface of the embattled world, the first stages of Ragnar's plan were swinging into motion.

At Gorgon-4, an Imperial Guard firebase five kilometres east of the star port, a vox teletype began to clatter in the company commander's blockhouse. The sound jolted the vox operator awake, dragging him from a pleasant dream about a girl he used to know back home. Rubbing his bleary eyes, the young Guardsman read off the script as it printed and confirmed by the message header that it had been sent to the proper unit. Then he tore the flimsy copy from the machine and dashed out into the trenches to find the artillery officer.

The vox operator found the battery commander sipping lukewarm recaff from a tin cup as he watched the sun start to rise through the smoke-stained horizon to the east. The officer, a veteran of many campaigns, took the proffered script without a word and read the orders between sips. His dark eyes widened a bit as he saw the time stamp on the page, and he turned to rouse the gun crews with a stream of leathery curses.

Within minutes, the long barrels of Gorgon-4's Earthshaker batteries rose into the sky. Six hundred kilo shells had already been fed into the guns' open breeches, and bare-chested Guardsmen were still blinking sleep out of their eyes as they wrestled propellant bags from their armoured caissons.

Still watching the glow on the eastern horizon, the battery commander slowly raised his right hand. All along the line, the gunnery crews scrambled clear of the gun carriages. Each gunnery sergeant in the battery checked his gun, checked his elevation, checked his crew and then shot his right hand into the air.

The battery commander smiled in satisfaction. At that exact moment, the first rays of the sun broke through the haze.

'Fire!' he cried, dropping his arm, and the eight heavy guns roared. Thunder shook the earth to the north and south as five other firebases added their guns to the barrage.

FIVE KILOMETRES WEST, the vox-units crackled in the cockpits of Mjolnir Flight. 'Mjolnir Lead, this is Echo five-seven. Green light – repeat, green light. Good luck and good hunting.'

Ten pilots and their crews straightened in their jump seats and put away their pre-flight checklists. They had been wakened in the dead of night, briefed and taken out to their birds an hour before dawn. Now wide awake, they reached for the throttles and brought idling turbojets to a full-throated roar.

One by one, eight Valkyrie gunships and two Thunderhawk assault transports rose heavily from their revetments and headed off to the west. They would be over their target in just twelve minutes.

BACK ABOARD THE *Fist of Russ*, the Iron Priests and their acolytes filed one by one from the teleportation chamber. An unearthly hum began to fill the air, sinking deep into Ragnar's bones.

'Form up!' Ragnar ordered, drawing his bolt pistol and sword. The Blood Claws fell silent at once, separating into three teams as Ragnar had planned. Three of the Claws trotted over to join Ragnar, Torin and Haegr. Raising his crozius, Sigurd moved quickly to the head of another team of five Claws. Harald stood ready with the remaining six members of the pack. There were no dark looks, no challenges or recriminations. Whatever Sigurd or the Blood Claws thought of Ragnar and his companions, none of it mattered now. They went to war as battle-brothers, as their forebears had done since the dawn of the Imperium.

Sigurd the Wolf Priest turned to his brethren and began the Benediction of Iron. One of the Blood Claws clashed his axe against his breastplate and started his battle-chant, singing of salt waves and splintered shields in a low, rumbling voice.

Haegr threw back his head and drained his ale horn in a single draught. Foam dripping from his whiskers, he gave his companions an enormous grin. 'By Russ, these are the moments that make a man's blood sing!' he roared, laughing like a drunken god. 'Try to keep up with mighty Haegr if you can, little brothers, lest he claim all the glory for himself!'

Chainblades growled to life. Power weapons crackled and moaned. Bolt pistols rattled as shells were driven home, and then the teleporter activated with a searing flash of light.

THERE WAS A moment of terrible, blind dislocation, and in the space of a single heartbeat the Space Wolves found themselves near the southern edge of the sprawling rebel base, caught up in a storm of fire, thunder and steel.

Ragnar staggered and dropped into a crouch as the earth shook beneath the Imperial barrage. Heavy shells howled overhead, falling across the rebel base with thunderous detonations and tall pillars of dirt and smoke. They were well within the base's defensive walls, perhaps two hundred metres from the broad ferrocrete bunkers of the tank park. The mangled wreckage of a staff car blazed brightly nearby, its passengers scattered in smoking pieces for a dozen metres around the impact site. No one else could be seen. The base's garrison had run for the shelters the moment the barrage began.

Red-hot shrapnel rang off Ragnar's armour. He ducked his head and shouted at the top of his lungs. 'Go for objective one!' he shouted into the cataclysmic storm. 'Go!'

Without hesitation, the three teams of Space Wolves separated, charging off into the howling storm of shells. They had to deal with the anti-aircraft batteries first. Their air support would be over the base in less than ten minutes.

It was General Athelstane's comment about bombarding the PDF base that had given Ragnar the idea. Despite his protestations, he knew full well that the Blood Claws stood no chance facing the base's garrison in a conventional fight. Dealing with them one element at a time, however, was another matter. One pack, he reckoned, would be enough for what they had to do. Any more and they risked taking unnecessary casualties from their own artillery fire. As it was, there was a good chance that some of them would be caught by an unlucky blast, but that was a risk Ragnar was willing to take.

There were three large Hydra anti-aircraft batteries situated around the base, consisting of four quadruple cannon mounts and a high-power auspex unit. Ragnar chose the battery furthest from the insertion point as his team's objective. The Space Wolves dashed through the pall of smoke and dirt, navigating more by memory than sight. Concussions smote at them with invisible fists, and steel fragments whizzed past their heads. Ragnar heard Torin grunt in surprise and pain, but a quick glance showed that the older Wolfblade was still running alongside him. Bright blood leaked from a shrapnel wound in his arm.

They covered the distance to the battery in just over three minutes. The gun mounts were in concrete revetments arrayed in a diamond around the central auspex unit and barrage shelter. Ragnar signalled to his men, and the warriors peeled away and headed for the guns, leaving him to take care of the battery's crew.

He vaulted a slit trench connecting two of the batteries and ran to the low ferrocrete bunker in the centre. Pulling a grenade from his belt, he put his armoured boot to the bunker's steel hatch. The door crumpled and fell inward on the third kick.

Bolts of blue light snapped out of the interior of the bunker, detonating against his breastplate. One shot sizzled past his head, close enough to leave an angry welt on his cheek. Ragnar fired a pair of wild shots from his bolt pistol and ducked to the left of the door as he chucked the grenade inside. A chorus of shouts was silenced by a sharp *bang* as the grenade exploded. Moving quickly, the young Space Wolf dashed into the smoke filled bunker and made certain the occupants were dead before heading back outside.

By the time he was finished the four gun mounts were wrecked. Ragnar waved to his men and keyed his vox. 'Objective one-one clear,' he shouted.

'Objective one-two clear,' came Sigurd's reply.

'Objective one-three clear,' Harald answered a moment later.

Ragnar nodded in approval. So far, so good. 'Go for objective two!' he called.

The Space Wolves converged on the centre of the base from three different directions, heading for the garrison's cluster of barrage shelters. Two and a half more minutes elapsed. According to the plan, the Imperial barrage was about to lift.

Ragnar and his men reached the first of the barrage shelters. Each one was a low, ferrocrete bunker capable of holding a hundred men, with a reinforced steel door and a set of narrow vision slits running along their flanks.

A hundred traitors versus five Space Wolves, Ragnar thought, taking cover to the right of the door. Those were odds he could deal with.

He motioned to a pair of Blood Claws. The Wolves ran to the door, one of them detaching a heavy melta charge from his backpack. Working quickly, they attached the charge's magnetic clamps to the door and keyed the timer.

The bunkers' ferrocrete construction made them strong enough to shrug off a direct hit from an Earthshaker round. It also made them strong enough to channel the blast of a melta charge instead of bursting apart and dissipating it. Ragnar had seen what melta charges did to the crews of enemy tanks. He expected a similar result here.

With a hollow *thump* the charge detonated, vaporising the steel door and hurling it inwards as a plume of incandescent plasma. The concussion wave struck the far end of the bunker and rebounded through the open door with a thunderclap of superheated air. Grinning fiercely, Ragnar signalled his warriors, and they swept inside, hunting for survivors.

They didn't find many.

RAGNAR'S MEN CLEARED fifteen bunkers in just under four minutes. By the time the last Imperial shells landed across the enemy base its garrison had been almost completely destroyed.

The three teams linked up again on the west side of the central bunker complex. A quick head count showed that three Wolves were missing. Two had been unlucky running through the barrage, and one

Blood Claw had got over-eager assaulting the bunkers and had stepped in front of a rebounding concussion wave. He lay inside a bunker awaiting extraction, deep in the Red Dream.

A chorus of petrochem engines growled off to the west, on the other side of the bunker complex. The tanks would be rolling out of their shelters soon. The faint roar of jet engines off to the east told Ragnar that the traitors were about to be in for a brutal surprise.

'Here's where the fighting begins in earnest,' Ragnar told the assembled Space Marines. 'We don't know how many troops are inside the central complex, but Russ knows they'll put up a stiff fight. Expect anything,' he said. 'You've all got maps of the complex loaded into your memory cores. If you get separated, fight your way to the vault or head back outside for extraction. Kill everything that gets in your way.'

The Blood Claws growled in assent. Ragnar glanced at Torin and Haegr and nodded. 'All right, let's go.'

They ran to the western side of the bunker, emerging like vengeful spirits out of the smoke and haze. Autogun fire and bolts of energy snapped out at them from the bunker's firing slits, but the enemy was too startled to draw beads on the fast-moving Wolves. Two Blood Claws ran ahead and started fixing their last demolition charge to the western bunker doors. They keyed the timer just as Ragnar and the rest of the force arrived.

The concussive blast buffeted Ragnar and his companions from ten metres away, checking his headlong charge for half a step. Then, with a howl, he plunged into the searing heat and smoke beyond the gaping doorway. The young Space Wolf found himself in a short narrow corridor, emerging after a few moments into a large, square room that reeked of hot metal and burned flesh. A squad of rebel stormtroopers had been formed up inside the room. At least three of them had been caught by the force of the blast and torn apart, while the rest were hurled like rag dolls against the stone walls. Ragnar burst upon them just as they were staggering to their feet. Their sergeant let out a yell and shot the young Space Wolf full in the chest with his hellpistol. The crimson bolt cracked harmlessly against the ancient ceramite breastplate. Ragnar hacked off the sergeant's left arm and head with a backhanded swipe of his frost blade, and then shot two more troopers as they tried to flee from the room.

Another sharp concussion rang from the bunker walls as Haegr stepped to Ragnar's left and smashed two more rebels to bits with a swing from his thunder hammer. The last surviving stormtrooper threw down his hellgun and raised his hands in surrender. Torin stepped into the room and shot the man in passing. They were going to have enough trouble with prisoners as it was.

Two corridors led out of the entry room, heading left and right. Ragnar recalled the maps he'd studied of the bunker layout, looked to Sigurd and pointed left. The Wolf Priest, his pale face speckled with fresh blood, nodded and led his and Harald's teams down the corridor. There were two staircases in the complex that led down to the lower level where the vault was located. They would work their way across the bunker to the stairs on the west side, while Ragnar and his companions fought their way to the closer staircase. That way they could ensure that none of the rebel commanders got past them if they decided to flee.

Shots and lasgun bolts whipped through the entry room from the right-hand corridor as rebels opened fire on Sigurd's team. Ragnar pulled another grenade from his belt and hurled it down the passageway. A second before it detonated, he nodded to Haegr, and the burly Wolf charged into the wake of the blast. Screams and brutal thunderclaps echoed down the corridor, punctuated by the Space Wolf's booming laugh.

Ragnar readied his bolt pistol and dashed off after Haegr, running past broken bodies and shattered weapons that littered the passageway floor. The massive Space Wolf was ploughing ahead like a stampeding mastodon, crushing any resistance in his path. Ragnar and his men charged, more than once, into a bloodstained room, and found themselves fighting stunned guardsmen, who Haegr had simply overrun and left behind.

They caught up to Haegr several long minutes later, at a four-way junction deep within the complex. The huge Wolf had his back against the wall near the corner of the junction, wrapped in swirling tendrils of smoke. The smell of ozone and shattered stone filled the air.

Haegr looked over at his battle-brothers as they approached. Ragnar saw that the right side of Haegr's face was red and blistered, and half of his unruly whiskers had been burned away. 'Mighty Haegr is unusually nimble for one of his heroic girth,' he grumbled, 'but these tight corridors make it hard to dodge plasma fire.'

'Like shooting fish in a barrel,' Torin said tightly. He glanced at Haegr. 'Sorry. More like spearing whales.'

'Must I do the foe's work and thrash you myself?' Haegr said. 'That would be tragic, would it not?'

'Where is the plasma gunner?' Ragnar said.

Haegr jerked his head to the left. 'Around the corner, about twenty metres,' he replied, 'and he's not alone. Looks like another squad of stormtroopers is covering the staircase.'

The young Space Wolf nodded. 'Did you try any grenades?'

Haegr blinked at him. 'Grenades. Yes. A good idea,' he agreed.

Torin rolled his eyes. 'What did you do? Eat yours?'

The burly Wolf glowered at Torin. 'The mighty Haegr prefers to look the foe in the eye before ending his life, not cowering behind a cloud of shrapnel.'

'Meaning your thick fingers can't work the grenade dispenser,' Torin said drily.

Haegr shifted uncomfortably. 'Yes, well, possibly that, too,' he growled.

Ragnar couldn't help but chuckle. 'Now I know why the pair of you were sent to Terra,' he declared, shaking his head. He sheathed his sword and drew a grenade from Haegr's belt. Thumbing the fuse, he tossed it around the corner. Immediately, a hail of fire chewed along the length of the stone wall and ricocheted across the junction. Seconds later the grenade went off, and Ragnar spun around the corner, firing as he ran.

The young Space Wolf saw at once that Haegr had neglected to mention the barricade a few metres down the corridor.

A barrier of layered flakboard had been erected across the width of the passageway, and his grenade had left a scorch mark at its feet. The stormtroopers taking cover behind it were just popping back up from behind cover as Ragnar started his charge. Scarlet bolts of hellgun fire burst across his breastplate and pauldrons, leaving scorch marks across the ceramite plate. He saw the rebel plasma gunner pop up and level his weapon. Ragnar brought his pistol around and shot the man in the head.

Another bolt detonated against his thigh, and Ragnar felt a jolt of pain as the shot burned through his armour. He stumbled, and then redoubled his pace, charging headlong at the enemy barrier while he dragged his frost blade from its scabbard.

Two more shots struck his midsection as he leapt over the barrier. Ragnar's frost blade flashed and two stormtroopers toppled in a welter of blood. He landed on a third rebel, driving the soldier to the floor before shooting him in the neck. Ragnar spun to the right, slashing downward with his sword and slicing another screaming trooper in half.

The remaining storm-troopers fell back, snapping off shots from their hellguns as they went. Drunk with battle lust, Ragnar stalked after them. He shot the closest man in the head. Then the crowd before him parted, and he was facing a sergeant with a glowing power sword in his hand, and a trooper with a hissing flamer levelled at Ragnar's chest.

There were two loud booms behind Ragnar, and a pair of heavy rounds hissed past the young Space Wolf's head. The first shot struck the man with the flamer in the shoulder, and the second tore through the trooper's throat. The stormtrooper spun to the right, his finger tightening on the trigger, spraying his comrades with a stream of liquid fire.

Ragnar dodged to the right, away from the flames, and the stormtrooper sergeant rushed forward, slashing at the young Space Wolf's chest. Ragnar caught the glowing sword on the diamond-hard teeth of his frostblade and ripped open the rebel's chest with a back-handed blow. The survivors fled down the hall, firing wildly as they went, abandoning their post at the head of the staircase to Ragnar's right.

The young Space Wolf looked back the way he'd come and saw the rest of his team rushing up to join him. Haegr was out front, smoke curling from the barrel of his bolt pistol. Ragnar scowled at the burly warrior. 'You could have warned me about the barricade,' he growled.

'Barricade? You mean this pitiful thing?' Haegr drew back a foot and kicked the layered flakboards apart. 'I thought it was just a pile of rubbish.'

Shaking his head, Ragnar gave the wound in his leg a cursory check. Finding nothing serious, he bent and picked the flamer and plasma gun off the bodies of the dead stormtroopers. 'Take these,' he said, passing them over to two of the Blood Claws. 'Flamer up front. Let's go.'

The Blood Claw with the flamer nodded curtly and stepped to the head of the staircase. The iron rungs receded into darkness.

A breath of cold air rose up from the depths, smelling of old stone and lingering rot. Ragnar bared his teeth and slapped the lead Blood Claw on the shoulder. Slowly, cautiously, they began their descent.

EIGHT
Descent into Darkness

THE IRON STAIRS rang as the Space Wolves made their way into the command bunker's lower level. With a draconic hiss the flamer spat a stream of burning promethium down the length of the dark staircase. Ruddy orange light pushed back the cave-like shadows for a moment, revealing a steep descent to a ferrocrete landing and a switchback leading farther down. Teeth bared, the lead Blood Claw clambered slowly down the stairs with Ragnar and the rest of the team close behind.

Bolt pistol trained over the Blood Claw's right shoulder, Ragnar strained his senses to the utmost, listening for tell-tale signs of ambush. In the distance, he thought he could hear the crash and echo of gunfire, but the stone walls of the bunker made it hard to gauge where the sound was coming from.

Once again, a cold wave of vertigo swept through him, and the young Space Wolf fought to control his balance on the narrow stairs. Shadow shapes flitted at the corners of his vision, further disorientating him. Ragnar growled softly and forced himself to concentrate on the feel of the weapons in his hands and the presence of the Blood Claw in front of him as they made their way down the stairs.

Ragnar signalled for the lead Wolf to halt at the bottom of the first staircase. They listened in the gloom. Faint sounds reached Ragnar's ears. Was it whispering, or the faint scrabble of claws on metal? Whatever it was, the sound was coming from around the corner of the staircase. Ragnar signalled to the Blood Claw, who nodded and swiftly thrust the flamer around the bend. An all-too-human scream of horror was quickly swallowed in the flamer's hissing roar.

The Blood Claw held down the trigger for a full second before drawing back out of the way. Ragnar swept past, bolt pistol levelled, and pumped shells at the burning, flailing forms writhing on the staircase. He advanced into an inferno, killing men with shots to the head and chest or ending their agonies with a sweep of his blade. Power packs and ammunition cooked off all around him, filling the narrow space with thunderous detonations and deadly ricochets. Behind him, the rest of the team swept down in Ragnar's wake, eager to come to grips with the foe.

There was a small landing at the base of the stairs, piled with smouldering corpses. In the dim firelight, Ragnar's keen senses picked out an open doorway to the left of the landing. As he approached, he heard the distinct double *click* of a pair of grenades being primed, and the twin silver canisters were lobbed through the doorway at his feet. A lesser man might have panicked. Ragnar simply knocked them back the way they'd come with a sweep of his armoured boot. They detonated less than a second later, close enough to pepper him with bits of searing shrapnel, but the effect on the rebels in the chamber beyond was far worse.

Ragnar charged through the doorway into the reeling squad of rebel troopers, knocking two men off their feet with bolt pistol shots before slashing into the rest with his frost blade. The room was nearly pitch-dark. Ragnar's keen senses caught the ultrasonic whine of thermal-vision goggles and marked the locations of the rebel Guardsmen in the stroboscopic flashes of their weapons. Light burst from a lasgun to his right, sending a beam point-blank into Ragnar's breastplate. The flash revealed a snarling Guardsman little more than a metre away, his sunken cheeks crudely carved with blasphemous sigils. Ragnar spun on his heel and lashed out with his sword, eviscerating the soldier with a sweeping cut.

A shotgun went off, spraying his right shoulder and the side of his face with lead pellets. Ragnar howled in fury and fired a round in the direction of the flash, hearing the meaty sound of the shell striking home in the rebel's chest. As Ragnar drove deeper into the room a chainsword slashed in from the left, glancing off his left pauldron and tearing open his chin. Without hesitation, the young Space Wolf tore upwards with his keening frost blade, severing the rebel's arm near the elbow.

There was another flash, this time behind Ragnar, as Haegr fired at another target. The young Space Wolf glimpsed the rebel who'd struck him, reeling away, blood jetting from his shorn arm. Another traitor cowered on the floor near the far wall, his blood spattered hands pressed to his face. Ragnar shot them both for good measure.

Thunder and man-made lightning burst again and again in the confined space. Guardsmen thrashed and spun, hammered to the ground by bolt pistol shells. Within moments, the survivors broke and ran, loosing ragged volleys of lasgun fire as they fled down an adjoining passageway to the north.

Ragnar heard Haegr and Torin step to the mouth of the passageway and fire on the retreating troops. The young Space Wolf stood near the centre of the dark room and tried to get his bearings. He swayed unsteadily on his feet. Strange smells assaulted his senses over the reek of propellant and the stink of ruptured organs. The hairs on the back of his neck prickled. Somewhere, impossibly far away, he thought he heard a howl.

The rest of the team spread out into the room. In the darkness, Haegr chuckled cruelly. 'The fools should have stayed put,' he said. 'I've never met a man who could outrun a bolt pistol shell!'

'There's a room at the far end of the passageway,' Torin cut in. 'I can see some sort of faint, purple glow.'

Sorcery, Ragnar thought. That had to be the source of his hallucinations. Madox and the Thousand Sons served the dreaded Changer of Ways, a vile god of madness and illusion. Now, it appeared that the rebels were turning to their unholy patrons for help against the implacable Wolves.

Ragnar peered around the dark room, struggling to focus. Time was running out. Beyond the danger of whatever sorceries the rebels were trying to invoke, the extraction flight would be over the base, circling and strafing any traitor vehicles that emerged from their shelters. They couldn't remain for long. If they weren't back on the surface within a few minutes, there wouldn't be anyone waiting to take them back to base. He didn't want to try his odds fighting his way back on foot with half a dozen enemy prisoners in tow.

The young Space Wolf tried to summon the maps of the bunker complex to the forefront of his mind. He knew that the vault adjoined the main war room on this level, but how many passageways connected to it? The spilled blood in the room made it difficult to think. Ragnar started to pace, fighting the urge to charge off into the gloom in search of something to kill. Sounds echoed in the darkness. A howl seemed to echo from another passageway to the south.

'Did you hear that?' he hissed.

To Ragnar's surprise, Torin answered at once. 'I did. It could be Sigurd or the other team. If they're pinned down, we're the only ones in position to reach the vault.'

Ragnar stifled a curse. Torin was right. He was letting his imagination get the better of him, and time was wasting. He worked his way past the fallen bodies of the rebel soldiers and reached the mouth of the north passageway, where he too could see a dim, purple glow pulsing slowly at the far end. As he passed Torin, he whispered, 'Is there anything else you feel? Do you see shadows?'

'Yes,' Torin whispered back, 'perhaps worse than before, but let's worry about that later. For now, let's just get down this corridor.'

Ragnar nodded to himself. He shouldered his way alongside Haegr and checked the ammo load for his pistol. Satisfied, he focused on the light in the distance and set off at a loping run with the rest of the team behind him.

They passed through half a dozen small rooms along the way, cluttered with debris and devoid of life. As they drew closer to the pulsing, ethereal light, Ragnar could feel the invisible tides of sorcery washing over him in waves of oily filth. A strange, acrid stench burned in his nostrils and set his teeth on edge. Buzzing, atonal notes echoed in his ears, growing louder with each step he took.

Distracted as he was, Ragnar didn't notice the flakboard barrier until he was within three metres of the end of the passageway. The enemy had laid boards over the doorway to well above human height, their grey sides reflecting the shifting purple light from the ceiling of the room beyond.

Ragnar slowed his pace at once. 'Barrier ahead,' he said gruffly, his voice sounding tinny and distorted over the infernal buzzing in his ears. 'We'll get the plasma gun–'

Haegr laughed. The sound was deep and guttural, like the growl of a bear. 'A barrier for you perhaps,' he growled, 'but not for mighty Haegr!'

The huge Space Wolf charged right at the slabs of flakboard, his thunder hammer ready in his hand. With a bloodthirsty shout, he crashed against the barrier. The flakboard exploded inward in a shower of debris, falling apart so easily that Haegr stumbled forward with an awkward shout into a hail of gunfire and a chorus of excited cries.

'Morkai's black breath!' Ragnar shouted angrily, and then chased off after Haegr. Shouts and war cries echoed after him as Torin and the Blood Claws took up the chase.

Sharp blasts of thunder rang from the walls of the chamber as Ragnar charged through the doorway and found himself in the bunker's expansive war room. Situation tables and logic engines had been overturned or moved to create defensive positions across the wide, rectangular room, and more than a score of huge, burly figures stood or crouched behind their barricades and unleashed a storm of fire upon Haegr and Ragnar both. Beyond them, at the opposite side of the war room, Ragnar saw a pair of gleaming steel doors: the entrance to the bunker's emergency vault.

Stubber shells whipped through the air around Ragnar or rang off his ceramite armour. One gouged a fiery path across the side of his head before ricocheting off his thickened skull. Tracer fire criss-crossed around him in a deadly web of shells. A few metres away, Haegr had crashed against the face of an upended hololith table and was smashing at the traitors on the other side with his crackling, blood smeared hammer. Bullets sparked and howled off the curved surfaces of his armour, though Ragnar saw where almost half a dozen rounds had left red-rimmed holes in the burly warrior's arms, waist and legs. The hits didn't seem to slow Haegr in the least.

A heavy blow struck Ragnar in the left arm, and fiery pain blossomed just above his elbow. Snarling, the young Space Wolf turned and blasted away at the rebels taking cover behind the barricades to his left. A huge figure reared up behind a broken logic engine. Ragnar caught sight of a twisted, misshapen hunk of gleaming muscles and a scarred lump that might once have been a human head. The mutant turned its beady red eyes on Ragnar and levelled a short-barrel heavy stubber at him. Roaring, the young Space Wolf charged at the mutant, blazing away with his bolt pistol. Shell after shell rocked the monster, blowing gory holes through its massive arms and torso, but the mutant refused to die.

Its heavy stubber hammered at Ragnar, spitting a stream of tracer rounds at the onrushing Space Wolf. Hammer blows struck Ragnar in the chest and abdomen, but the blessed armour plate held against the heavy stubber rounds. Howling like a beast, Ragnar leapt onto the toppled logic engine and buried his blade in the monster's cartilaginous skull. Sickly grey and yellow matter spewed from the frost blade's whirring teeth, but the mutant refused to die. It howled and thrashed, throwing down its smoking gun and reaching for Ragnar's blade. Horrified, Ragnar shot the monster twice in the face and dashed its blasphemous corpse to the floor.

Howling, gibbering figures rushed at the young Space Wolf from every direction. A Guardsman with a skinned face swung a chainsword at Ragnar's left leg. Ragnar parried the stroke with his frost blade and kicked the onrushing rebel in the head, bursting it like a melon. Another mutant, this one wearing the tattered uniform of a PDF staff officer, wrapped a long, barbed tentacle around Ragnar's left ankle and with surprising strength hauled the Space Wolf off his feet. He landed heavily, smashing his head and shoulders against the metal and glass case of the logic engine before rolling, senseless, to the floor.

For less than half a second he was too stunned to move. Sounds rolled like surf in his ears: shouts, gunshots, screams and thudding blows. A blade of some kind smashed into Ragnar's back again and again, grinding off the armour. Figures crowded above him; a gun went off, the round burying itself in his backpack. Then a tentacle squirmed wetly around his throat and began to squeeze.

Ragnar roared like a wounded beast and lashed out with his whirring blade, shearing through ankles in an arc around his head. Mutants shrieked and toppled like felled trees, bleeding their lives out onto the floor. Ragnar used the impetus of the swing to flip onto his back, his bolt pistol hammering at the foes still looming above him. Three mutants reeled backwards with smoking holes in the backs of their heads. The tentacle around Ragnar's throat came away with a spasmodic jerk.

An upended table nearby exploded in a blue ball of plasma, scattering flaming debris across the room. Two mutants staggered away from the explosion, blinded and firing wildly into the melee. Battle chants and bloodthirsty cries rang from the stone walls as the Blood Claws in Ragnar's team charged into the fray. Ragnar caught sight of Haegr carving a gory path through a knot of struggling mutants, bursting them apart with earth shaking blows from his hammer. A shadow passed across the young Space Wolf's vision, but this time it was Torin, leaping nimbly over a barricade of smashed logic engines and opening the throats of the mutants hiding behind them.

For a moment, the room seemed to spin. Ragnar felt as though he was falling, but then he heard a guttural voice snarl into his ear. *'Watch your head!'*

Something in the tone of the voice galvanised him. Ragnar rolled to the left, just as a roaring chainblade smashed into the ferrocrete where his head had just been.

Heart racing, Ragnar threw a blind swing behind him as he lurched to his feet. His frost blade swept through empty air, and then he heard the chainblade's throaty rasp, and a terrible blow struck him in the back of his left thigh.

The pain was immense. For a brief, agonising instant, Ragnar could feel the teeth of the chainblade tearing through his flesh. He staggered, but his sacred armour sensed the impact and locked his left knee-joint to keep him upright. Snarling in agony, the young Space Wolf spun on his immobilised leg, barely warding off a second blow aimed at his neck.

He found himself staring at an enormous, hyper-muscled mutant, wielding a two-handed chainsword in its clawed fists. Ragnar recognised the weapon at once: it was an eviscerator, a ponderous but devastating weapon favoured by would-be martyrs in the Guard's Ecclesiarchal auxiliaries. The young Space Wolf realised that the leering mutant was wearing the tattered remains of a priest's homespun robes. An Imperial aquila, once the priest's most prized possession, hung upside-down on a necklace of body parts strung around the mutant's bull-like neck.

The mutant gibbered a stream of blasphemies and pressed its attack. The eviscerator was a clumsy weapon in human hands, but the muscle bound traitor wielded it like a willow-switch. Ragnar blocked one powerful blow after another, knowing that if his defence failed, even for a moment, the mutant would hack him in two.

A blurring stroke leapt at Ragnar's face. The young Space Wolf blocked the eviscerator in a shower of sparks, and shot the mutant in the left knee. The monster staggered, bellowing through a mouth full of pointed teeth, but it pressed its attack without pause.

The mutant charged forwards, slashing across Ragnar's left pauldron and leaving a deep gash in the ceramite. A lightning-fast return strike nearly took off half the young Space Wolf's face. Ragnar shot the mutant twice more, once in the belly and once in the groin, and this time, when the mutant lurched beneath the impacts, the young Space Wolf lashed out with his frost blade and severed the traitor's left hand at the wrist. Hot blood spurted onto Ragnar's face as the mutant howled in agony, and the young Space Wolf rushed in to finish off the traitor, but the former priest dropped its weapon and seized Ragnar's sword wrist in a vice-like grip.

Ragnar felt servos whine under intolerable pressure as the mutant closed its fist. The cuff of his gauntlet began to deform under the pressure. Bones grated in his wrist. Ragnar put the bolt pistol to the mutant's head and pulled the trigger, but the weapon was empty.

The mutant looked into Ragnar's eyes and hissed cruelly. Ragnar felt a wave of panic as the bones in his wrist and arm began to splinter. It was as though a wild beast came howling up from deep in his breast. With a savage growl, Ragnar leapt forward and buried his teeth in the mutant's over-muscled neck.

He bit deep, feeling flesh and cable-like muscle tear within his powerful jaws. Blood, hot and bitter, filled his mouth. The mutant shrieked, pummelling Ragnar with the stump of its left arm, but the young Space

Wolf wrenched his head left and right, widening the wound and digging for the pulsing arteries buried within the neck.

Ragnar could feel the heat of the mutant's heart-blood. He hungered for it, longing to feel it spilling in a flood over his gaping jaws. It was the purest, most vivid thing he'd felt in his entire life. For a fleeting instant, Ragnar was gone. What remained behind was something raw and elemental: a wolf in name and deed.

He tore out the mutant's throat, and then he started to feed.

NINE
Wolf-bitten

A POWERFUL BLOW smote Ragnar on the side of the head. The force of it knocked the young Space Wolf onto his side, but he was back upright in moments, showing his red slicked fangs and crouching protectively over his kill. Sigurd's pale face appeared before him, blood spattered and severe.

'*By the holy name of Russ the Primarch I take your soul into my hands, Ragnar Blackmane!*' The priest's voice trembled, but the words were powerful, infused with the strength of centuries of faith. Ragnar blinked, drawing back from the image of a wolf's skull amulet that Sigurd brandished before his eyes.

'*The wolf cannot have you! Your heart is not yours to give, but belongs to the Allfather, now and forever more! Remember your oaths, son of Fenris! Remember who you are!*'

The words were like the tolling of a bell inside his head, cold and bright and irresistible. He fell heavily onto the floor, shaking his head dazedly.

After a moment, Ragnar's vision cleared. Sigurd the Wolf Priest loomed above him, his wide eyes fearful, but his expression hardened into a mask of determination. His Iron Wolf amulet was clenched in one gauntleted hand.

Ragnar could feel blood trickling over his lips and staining his breastplate. A shudder passed through him. The young Space Marine rose to his knees with an effort, and as he did so he noticed the bloody figure sprawled beside him. Ragnar looked down at the mangled corpse of the former priest and felt a wave of horror and revulsion crash down upon him. Blessed Russ, he thought despairingly, I'm wolf-bitten.

'Forgive me,' he said hoarsely, unable to tear his eyes away from the gaping wound in the mutant's throat.

'Forgiveness is earned in battle,' Sigurd said coldly. 'Stand and fight like a man, Ragnar, not an animal.' The Wolf Priest brandished his crozius before the young Space Wolf. 'Just as Russ overcame the wolf inside him out of love for the Allfather, so too must you rise above the beast within. Now get up. The foe awaits.'

Nodding, Ragnar lurched to his feet. The battle in the war room was over. Sigurd and the remaining Blood Claws had arrived and overwhelmed the remaining traitors as Ragnar struggled with the huge mutant. Smoke and the stench of burned flesh hung in the air, and the bodies of the traitor Guardsmen lay in bloody heaps behind their makeshift barricades. Harald and his pack-mates stood among the carnage, clutching their weapons and watching the exchange between Ragnar and Sigurd with wary, fearful eyes. It was all Ragnar could do not to hang his head in shame.

A heavy blow to the shoulder nearly knocked the young Space Wolf off his feet. Haegr loomed over Ragnar, chuckling deep in his throat. 'You call that a bite? Mighty Haegr would have taken that monster's head off with a single snap of his jaws!'

The huge Space Wolf's laugh was infectious. Soon, every warrior in the room was laughing along with him, but for Sigurd and Ragnar.

'You want something to chew on, come over here and try your teeth on this,' Torin said, pressing his fingertips to the cold steel doors of the vault. 'Our time is almost up, and the Allfather alone knows what they're up to inside.'

Ragnar rubbed his chin with the back of his hand and turned to Sigurd. 'Have you got any charges left?'

'Two,' the Wolf Priest said, and nodded to Harald. The Blood Claw pack leader waved a pair of his men forward, and they began setting the charges against the door.

Harald turned to Sigurd. His eyes passed over Ragnar, as though afraid to see what lurked within the young Space Wolf's gaze. 'We're sure to kill everyone inside when these go off,' he said.

'No,' Ragnar replied, shaking his head as he reloaded his pistol. 'These doors are doubly reinforced, designed to protect the general staff in the event of a major attack. More likely the shockwave will rebound back on us, so I suggest standing well off to either side of the door.'

The battered and bloodied Space Wolves quickly took up positions around the vault. Ragnar could still feel the sickly wash of unclean energies rippling from within. He nodded to the Blood Claw waiting at the threshold. The warrior keyed the fuse and leapt clear.

Sure enough, a tremendous concussion shook the entire room, throwing the armoured warriors back against the stone walls and sending clouds of broken debris flying through the air. When the smoke cleared, Ragnar leapt forward, weapons ready, and found a hole melted through the thick steel doors just wide enough for a Space Marine to fit through. He threw himself into the gap while the metal edges were still red-hot, with Torin, Haegr and Sigurd just a few steps behind him.

The vault was a small redoubt, with a narrow, thick-walled passageway beyond the molten doors that opened into an octagonal chamber barely ten metres across. Two bodies, charred almost beyond recognition, were sprawled on the stone floor at the far end of the passageway. Beyond them lay a scene of bloody pandemonium.

There were perhaps twenty officers and staff aides crammed into the chamber, shouting and babbling desperate pleas to their newfound gods. Their ornate uniforms were torn and stained where they had dug into their flesh with ceremonial knives, and their faces were painted in fresh blood. More blood had been spilled on the floor. A young orderly, little more than fifteen, had been dragged to his knees and slit from ear to ear, and the red flood that had poured from his narrow throat had been used to paint a blasphemous circle in the centre of the room. It was towards this terrible sigil that the rebels directed their pleas, their gore-stained hands outstretched in abject worship. As Ragnar charged into their midst he saw a ghostly figure take shape within the sigil. It was a towering form clad in ancient, baroque armour of blue and gold, its edges inlaid with blasphemous sigils, and its curved plates decorated with charms and fetishes of bone and withered skin. Flickering purple flames glinted hungrily in the oculars of the Chaos champion's horned helmet, fixing Ragnar with a glare of eternal malice. In one hand, the sorcerer held a sword made from tooth, horn and soulless, black iron. Flames leapt hungrily in the palm of his other hand, hissing and spitting in the dank air.

For a fleeting moment Ragnar's heart leapt with bloodthirsty joy at the thought that he'd come face-to-face with Madox himself. Yet there was no glint of recognition in the sorcerer's strange eyes as he raised his blazing hand and called out a horrific string of syllables in a raw, hateful voice.

A howling torrent of pink and purple fire burst from the sorcerer's hand, aimed right at Ragnar's chest. The bolt struck one of the rebel officers a glancing blow as it passed, and the traitor dissolved right before the young Space Wolf's eyes. Cursing fearfully, Ragnar threw himself to the side and the sorcerous flame struck his right pauldron a glancing blow. He heard the ceramite hiss and scream beneath the blast, scattering molten droplets upon the floor. The bolt continued on, missing Haegr by a hair's breadth and crashing into the onrushing form of Sigurd.

The sorcerous flames washed over the Wolf Priest in a chorus of thin, unearthly howls and a crackle of brittle thunder. Two Blood Claws to either side of the priest were thrown to the floor by the blast, but Sigurd was unmoved. The flames curled away from the rosarius that the Wolf Priest held before him, and he called out in a powerful voice, 'Traitor! Servant of false gods! I abjure you, warrior of the Thousand Sons! Look upon the sons of the Wolf and despair!'

The Thousand Sons Chaos Space Marine laughed at the Wolf Priest and uttered a stream of vile curses that caused the rebel Guardsmen to fall thrashing to the floor. Baring his teeth, Ragnar gathered his courage and charged at the unholy warrior, snapping off shots with his bolt pistol as he went.

Explosive rounds detonated harmlessly against the champion's breastplate and helm, leaving scarcely a mark on the ensorcelled armour. Undaunted, Ragnar stepped close and unleashed a storm of deadly blows with his master crafted frost blade, fully intending to chop the Chaos Space Marine to pieces.

Not a single blow found its mark. Whether by sorcery or pure, deadly skill, the champion blocked or evaded Ragnar's every move. The huge figure moved like quicksilver, seeming to anticipate the young Space Wolf's attacks, and countering them with disdainful ease. At one point Ragnar sensed he'd found an opening in the sorcerer's guard and nearly found himself impaled on the champion's unnatural blade.

A shadow flowed into Ragnar's field of vision to his left. Torin was there, catching the sorcerer's blade against his chainsword. Sensing an opportunity, Ragnar lunged forward with a slashing cut to the champion's shoulder, but the Chaos Space Marine fell back, dodging the blow.

Shouts and battle cries echoed in the confined space as the rebel troops reared up from the stone floor like beasts, and threw themselves at the Space Wolves. Dimly, Ragnar heard Sigurd repudiating the traitor Guardsmen in a loud, sonorous voice over the roar of chainblades and the bark of laspistols. Then a mountainous form loomed to the young Space Wolf's right and unleashed an earth shaking blow upon the Chaos champion. Haegr laughed as the sorcerer leapt backwards out of the path of the falling hammer. 'That's it, traitor! Dance like a maid!' he roared. 'You can't match blows with mighty Haegr!'

The sorcerer's hateful gaze never wavered, however, as he fell back, step by step, across the chamber. Ragnar counted the steps and gauged their distance to the far wall. He'll have his back up against the bricks in a few more metres, he thought, pressing his attack, and the bastard's too good not to know it, too. He's trading space for time.

A flash of understanding nearly stopped Ragnar in his tracks. 'Ambush!' he cried out, just as the air seemed to thicken and tear like rotted parchment, and a host of gibbering horrors appeared in the Space Wolves' midst.

Something heavy and rank landed wetly behind Ragnar and uttered a piping, lunatic cry. Fearful of turning his back on the deadly Chaos Space Marine, the young Space Wolf pivoted on his back foot and thrust out his pistol at a writhing column of pink and purple flesh. The daemon's four thorny tentacles wrapped around Ragnar's arm and chest, and the column of muscle contracted, hauling the young Space Wolf towards the creature's serrated beak.

Ragnar cried out as the black beak gaped mere centimetres from his skull. Then he felt the lash of another set of tentacles around his neck and waist, and he was jerked to a painful halt. Yet another daemon had trapped him in its talons, and now the two unholy creatures gibbered and squawked at one another as they vied for his flesh.

An entire pack of tentacled horrors filled the octagonal space, snapping and lashing out at everything that moved. As Ragnar struggled, he saw a pair of rebel Guardsmen torn to pieces in a messy spray of blood and entrails. Sigurd reeled within the grasp of a trio of snapping monsters, thick purple ichor smoking from the crackling edges of his crozius. The Blood Claws were beset on every side, but Harald stood in their midst, holding the burning husk of a daemon in his power fist and shouting a rallying cry to his men.

Growling angrily, Ragnar squeezed the trigger and the bolt pistol bucked in his hand, blowing a smoking hole in the daemon standing before him. Shrieking, the monster recoiled, drawing its tentacles still tighter. The daemon behind Ragnar pulled back just as fiercely, and the young Space Wolf felt the bones in his neck creak from the strain. With a savage curse, he lashed out with his free hand, and the frost blade slashed through two of the tentacles that bound him. Ichor gushed over Ragnar's armour as the daemon in front of him unwrapped its remaining tentacles and tried to slither away. Immediately, the young Space Wolf was hauled backwards towards his second assailant, but Ragnar levelled his bolt pistol and fired twice more at the wounded daemon, blasting its head apart in a shower of dissolving flesh. Then he spun in mid-air, levelling his frost blade and impaling the daemon that had been so hungry to draw him into its embrace. The rune-marked chainsword tore through the daemon's abominable form, causing it to discorporate into a cloud of foul, clinging mist.

Ragnar twisted as he fell, landing hard on his back and skidding across the stone floor. His bolt pistol came up, seeking targets. The entire chamber was filled with a riot of struggling, slashing bodies, and the crash of battle roared surf-like in his ears. The light inside the chamber seemed to pulse and shift. Shadows flitted at the corners of the young Space Wolf's eyes, but he muttered a prayer to Russ under his breath and focused on the battle at hand.

He caught sight of a Blood Claw grappling with a snapping, strangling daemon a few metres away and put a bolt-round through the monster's nominal head. Another warrior went down beneath the thrashing tentacles of a pair of purple horrors. Ragnar pumped shell after shell into the daemons' muscular bodies until the Space Wolf managed to tear his sword-arm free and hack one of the monsters in half.

A severed head bounced across the floor. The face was masked with blood, but Ragnar knew from the scent that it was one of Harald's battle-brothers. Some distance away, the young Space Wolf saw Haegr pull a lashing, snapping daemon from his chest with one broad hand and smash it against the wall beside him. Another monster darted in, bloodstained beak clashing hungrily, but the Wolfblade crushed it with a downward sweep of his massive hammer.

Another daemon erupted in a gout of purple ichor. Harald raised his dripping power fist in triumph, his fangs glinting in the faint light. Then Ragnar saw the monster rising like a snake behind the pack leader, its tentacles rearing back to strike.

Ragnar drew a bead on the daemon, and a dark shadow fell over him. He heard the rasp of ancient armour and the hungry sweep of the Chaos champion's blade as it drew back for the killing blow.

In a split-second, the young Space Wolf made his choice. Commending his soul to the Allfather, he fired an explosive round past the pack leader's head and into the daemon's gaping beak.

Shadows danced above his head. Metal crashed against metal, and Ragnar heard a rumbling, liquid growl.

Blood pounding in his temples, Ragnar faced his attacker, only to find the sorcerer grappling with a huge Space Wolf in scarred, gun-metal-grey armour. The warrior fought the champion bare-handed, one powerful hand gripping the sorcerer's sword wrist, while the other closed inexorably around the Chaos Space Marine's throat.

There was wiry grey fur matted along the back of the Space Wolf's hands. Ragnar caught a glimpse of curved, black talons, and then he noticed the shaggy mane and the strange shape of the warrior's head.

The Space Wolf sensed Ragnar's eyes upon him. He glanced back at Ragnar, furred snout wrinkling as his lips pulled back in a bestial snarl.

Cursing wildly, Ragnar hurled himself to the right, rolling away from the struggling figures. In moments, he clambered unsteadily to his feet and whirled around, weapons raised, but the struggling warriors were gone. They had simply vanished, as though they'd never existed.

Bolt pistols hammered, the shots echoing from the walls. Chainswords sang their harsh battle song, tearing through unnatural flesh, and then, abruptly, the only sound was the panting of exhausted men and the pained breaths of the wounded.

The stone floor seemed to sway beneath Ragnar's feet. Numb with shock, he surveyed the blood spattered chamber. Harald and half a dozen Blood Claws were still on their feet, their eyes wide and their armour splashed with gore. Three others knelt or lay among the bodies on the floor, wounded grievously but still alive. Two battle-brothers would not rise again, their bodies ripped apart by tentacles and snapping, serrated beaks.

Haegr knelt by Torin's prone form a few metres to Ragnar's left. The older Wolfblade was struggling to rise with Haegr's help, despite a deep wound in his hip.

A feeling of dread settled in Ragnar's stomach as he began to inspect the dead. Every one of the rebel officers had been torn apart by daemons or melted by sorcerous flames.

Of Sigurd, there was no sign. The young Space Wolf Priest was gone.

THEY RODE BACK aboard the Thunderhawks in silence, each warrior lost in his own grim thoughts. Harald had suggested looting the war room of every bit of useful information they could find, and they dragged away makeshift boxes full of maps, data-slates and memory cores. As they loaded up their wounded and dead, however, the Wolves could not help but feel that they had failed.

Ragnar reported to Mikal Sternmark while the raiding party was still in the air, apprising him of what had happened. The loss of Sigurd was an exceptionally hard blow to Sternmark, recalling as it did the ambush at the governor's palace a few weeks earlier. Ragnar accepted full responsibility for what had happened in the bunker, lauding the courage of Harald and his pack as well as his fellow Wolfblades, but he wasn't sure Sternmark paid attention to any of it.

The return flight took them low over the southern outskirts of the city, and it was obvious to everyone on board that the forces of the enemy were on the move. Plumes of blue-black petrochem exhaust hung in a poisonous haze over the cratered transit ways leading into the capital, as regiments of infantry and armour moved towards the tenuous Imperial lines. White flashes stuttered and strobed beyond the hills west of the city as rebel gun batteries pounded the eastern rim of the capital. More than once the Thunderhawks and their Valkyrie escorts had to dive behind broken ridges or weathered hilltops to evade rebel anti-aircraft rockets or gun positions, and it was more than an hour after dust-off before the assault ships reached friendly lines and could land at Charys star port.

They disembarked in the middle of another rocket attack, carrying their seriously wounded brothers to the port's medicae facilities through a storm of fire and shrapnel. Torin wanted no part of the packed and chaotic field hospital, with its exhausted chirurgeons and outdated equipment. He insisted his wound was minor and would heal quicker on its own. 'I'd rather lie down in the dark somewhere like a wounded hound than risk getting my limbs cut off by some drunken bone-cutter,' he declared, and his protests grew so vehement that even Haegr shrugged his broad shoulders and relented. Of course, they hadn't the faintest idea what to do with the older Wolfblade, so finally Ragnar and Haegr turned around and carried him back to the Thunderhawk.

Once they'd settled Torin back in the same suspensor-web he'd lain in on the flight out of the PDF base, Ragnar left Haegr to watch over their battle-brother and headed to the command bunker to report to Athelstane and Sternmark. On the way there he thought to check with Gabriella and ensure that she was safe, but the memory of what he'd done back at the rebel base was still painfully fresh in his mind. I'm as much a danger to her as the enemy is, he thought in despair, wondering what was going to happen to him now.

Every Space Wolf struggled with the wolf inside him. The gifts of the Canis Helix made them into peerless warriors, but such savagery was two-edged. The wolf within was always testing its limits, seeking escape in the fire of battle to rend and tear until its appetite was sated. Once the wolf had got its teeth in a man, there was no turning back, so far as Ragnar knew. Little by little his mind slipped away and his body succumbed to the influence of the helix's bestial influence. Sometimes there were Wolf Lords who took one of the Wulfen into battle with them, but most often the wolf-bitten were given into the care of the Wolf Priests and taken from the Fang, never to fight for the Chapter again.

Now he understood from whence his dreams had come, and why he had been feeling so strange of late, but the realisation gave him little comfort. He would probably be dismissed from the Wolfblade, he reasoned, and without a Wolf Lord willing to speak for him, this campaign would doubtless be his last.

Ragnar gritted his teeth and pushed such thoughts from his mind. For now, there was a battle to be fought and won.

The young Space Wolf found an open crate of field rations in the command bunker, and forced himself to eat. It had only been a few days since he'd last had a meal, but focusing on his body's mundane needs kept more troubling thoughts at bay. The ration paste also helped kill the taste of blood that still lingered in his mouth.

'WE SHOULD HAVE expected this all along, after the ambush at the governor's palace,' Sternmark said bitterly. 'What I want to know is how they knew when we were going to strike?'

The Wolf Guard was pacing along the back wall of the bunker's war room, gauntleted hands clasped tightly behind his back. Sternmark's face was fierce and brooding, his dark eyes darting from Ragnar to Athelstane and back again. The Guard general sat in a nearby camp chair, fixing the situation holo with a dark stare. From the beleaguered look on her face Ragnar suspected that she hadn't slept in days.

Ragnar stood at parade-rest at the foot of the table opposite the general. He raised his scarred chin and addressed them both. 'I don't believe it was an ambush at all,' he said. 'If the rebels wanted to lay a trap for us at the base they could have done it easily enough without putting their generals in the crossfire.'

'At this point I'm starting to have my doubts that they were generals at all,' Athelstane said with a frown. She gestured at the holo with a gloved hand. 'Their planned counter-offensive hasn't skipped a beat. Reconnaissance imagery shows that the traitors have moved another forty thousand men into the city since daybreak, and they'll be in a position to hit us by tomorrow. The Emperor alone knows how we're going to stop them.'

Ragnar shook his head. 'You didn't see the looks on their faces when we broke into the vault. Those men were high-ranking officers, all right, and they were desperate to escape,' he said. 'They had painted some kind of symbol on the floor. It looked like they were calling for help, honestly.'

'Yet the Chaos champion and his daemons killed those same men during the fight,' Sternmark pointed out. 'If the champion killed the army commanders, who then is leading the counter-offensive?'

The young Space Wolf shrugged. 'The Thousand Sons themselves, I would think,' he replied. 'We know this world is the lynchpin to their entire campaign. I can't imagine that they would trust a cabal of Guard officers to defend it.' He glanced uncomfortably at Athelstane. 'No offence, ma'am.'

Athelstane brushed the remark aside with an impatient wave of her hand. 'If the Thousand Sons are commanding the planet's defence, where are they? They must have a base somewhere on the planet, correct?'

'Not necessarily, I'm afraid.'

Heads turned at the sound of Gabriella's voice. The Navigator and Inquisitor Volt stood at the edge of the former stage, their arms piled with dusty books. She looked to the Inquisitor, who nodded and addressed the general. His face was pale and grim.

'We think we know where the Thousand Sons are striking from,' he said. 'If we are right, we are all in far greater danger than we imagined.'

TEN
Tripwire

'It was Lady Gabriella who provided the key,' Volt said quickly. The inquisitor shuffled up onto the stage and spread his weathered books on the situation table. The holo image above the table warped into a storm of rainbow hued static as Volt covered many of the hololith's projector eyes.

'What's all this about?' Athelstane asked, unable to conceal a note of irritation in her voice.

The inquisitor didn't seem to hear the general at all. 'As focused as I was on events here on Charys, I failed to pay close attention to reports from the other affected worlds across the subsector,' Volt said, fumbling with his trembling, bandaged hands at the iron lock and hinge securing one of the tomes. The book's cover was smoke stained and charred along the edges, and one corner of its heavy, cream-coloured pages was spotted with red.

'A… a campaign of this size, with so much preparation, it should have been obvious that there were deeper patterns in play,' Volt said, almost to himself, as he rifled through the thick pages. 'The diversionary attacks, yes, and the choice of targets… Ah! Here,' he said, gripping the bottom of the open book with both hands and turning it around so that Athelstane and Sternmark could see. 'This is what I'm talking about.'

The general and the huge Space Wolf leaned over the table. Volt had opened the book to a page covered in hand lettered High Gothic script. Spread across the pages was a vast, intricate circle, inscribed with dense patterns of blasphemous runes. Athelstane caught just a glimpse and turned away, making the sign of the aquila and muttering a prayer under her breath. Sternmark raised his eyes and studied the inquisitor carefully.

'This is not the symbol I saw in the governor's palace,' he said.

'No, not at the palace!' Volt snapped, his grey eyes blazing. He turned and beckoned to Ragnar. 'You were at Hyades, were you not? Tell me what you see.'

Frowning bemusedly, Ragnar stepped over to the table. The lines etched in red across the page burned into his mind, calling up a memory of the tense shuttle flight off the beleaguered Imperial world. He glanced from Volt to Gabriella. 'It's the symbol we saw burning over the capital city,' he said.

'Aha!' Volt said, pleased to hear the young Space Wolf's confirmation. 'This is what is known as a cornerstone, an anchoring sigil designed to shape the boundaries of a much larger occult symbol,' he said. 'In my time, I've seen them spread across the hab blocks of a small hive city, even once across the breadth of an entire island.' He traced a finger across the surface of the page. 'Only once in history has anyone attempted such a feat on an *interstellar* scale.'

Volt turned his attention to the remaining books on the table, searching through them impatiently. Gabriella stepped forward quietly and handed over a battered tome from the top of her stack. The inquisitor looked up with a grunt of surprise and took the volume with a mutter of thanks. 'It happened around thirteen hundred years ago,' he said, flipping quickly through the ancient pages. 'A traitor named Arsenius Talvaren tried to open a permanent gateway to the Eye of Terror, centred on Holy Terra itself.'

Athelstane, Sternmark and Ragnar shared incredulous looks. The general shook her head. 'Obviously, he failed,' she said.

'Obviously, yes,' Volt replied. 'The attempt was doomed almost from the very start, but the madman's underlying theory was *entirely sound*, from an arcane standpoint.' He paused at a particular page, reading closely, and then nodded to himself. Volt looked up from the book. 'Lord Sternmark, come here and take a look at this for a moment,' he said. 'Tell me if this is more familiar to you.'

The powerful champion moved slowly around the perimeter of the table, a look of dread settling like a mask over his features. He looked down at the book, and grimaced at once. 'It is similar,' he admitted, 'very similar.'

'So you're telling me that the traitors are trying to pry open the Eye of Terror?' Athelstane asked, her stoic expression tinged with concern.

Volt snapped the tome shut. 'No, not this time,' he said. 'Talvaren, the mad genius, overreached himself. He could not master the forces necessary for such a feat, and even if the Inquisition hadn't stopped him on Luna, the demands of the ritual would have destroyed him.' The inquisitor glanced at Sternmark and the general. 'Here on Charys we're dealing with forces that are altogether more powerful and sophisticated.'

'Then what, pray tell, are they attempting?' Athelstane asked, her patience clearly nearing its limit.

'A bilocation,' Volt said gravely. 'A... link, if you will, between Charys and a daemon world within the Eye.'

The lady commander rubbed her brow with an augmented hand. 'I thought you just told me that wasn't possible,' she growled.

Lady Gabriella cleared her throat diplomatically. 'A co-location is not the same as a conduit,' she said, setting her books on the table. 'Because the Eye of Terror is a location where the warp spills into physical space, the notion of distance and time within the region is fluid,' she said. 'This is the same reason why we use the warp to travel between the stars.'

'Yes, yes, I know all that,' the general said with an impatient nod.

'Well, think of the warp as a fast-flowing river,' the Navigator continued. 'A person could either walk along the bank to get from one town to another downstream, or he could leap into the water and be rushed there at a much faster rate. Now, what Talvaren tried to do was create a tributary of that river, allowing the water to flow from the Eye of Terror directly to sacred Terra, a tremendous feat that had little chance of success.'

Gabriella reached into her belt and removed her vox-unit. 'We think Madox is trying to strain the fabric of reality around Charys and create a shadow of the world inside the Eye of Terror.' She extended her hand slowly, edging the rounded vox-unit into the projector field of the hololith. As the object occluded the edge of the projection field it created an oval shaped dark patch in the shimmering, distorted map.

Sternmark glowered at the shadow before him. 'The Eye of Terror is hundreds of parsecs away,' he protested. The Eye was a vast stellar region within the Segmentum Obscuras, where the Chaotic energies of the warp bled into the physical universe. It was a realm of horror and madness, an eternal battlefield where the worshippers of Chaos warred for the favour of their uncaring gods. After the Horus Heresy, the Traitor Legions of the Warmaster Horus fled into the Eye, where they continued to plague the Imperium with deadly raids and ruinous Black Crusades.

'Remember that within the warp there is no notion of space or distance,' the Navigator said. 'A location can be fixed by will and ritual alone, and Inquisitor Volt suspects that a series of daemon worlds within the Eye are maintaining cornerstone sigils to stabilise the shadow world as well. The sigil within the governor's palace provides the glue that conjoins the two worlds.' She turned to Ragnar. 'It's this ritual that is causing the strange turbulence in the warp I spoke of.'

Ragnar nodded thoughtfully. *It also explains the sense of dislocation Torin and I felt, and perhaps even the hallucinations.* 'Then the Thousand Sons are simply stepping between worlds when they attack us.'

Gabriella nodded. 'Yes, exactly.'

'But to what end?' Athelstane demanded. 'I'm going to assume that what you just told me is possible, but even so, surely pulling it off would have to consume enormous resources.'

'Yes, indeed,' Volt nodded. 'We can't even speculate on what the traitors had to do in order to create the cornerstones within the Eye, but it's obvious that they devoted many years and a huge investment of effort to arranging the rituals across this subsector.'

'Then what do they stand to gain from all this?' the general asked.

'Several things,' Volt replied. 'First, it gives them a secure base of operations from which to pursue their efforts on Charys. They can strike us anywhere, at any time, and retreat to safety without fear of pursuit. It also allows them to tap into the limitless power of the Eye to fuel their sorcery.'

'But what's their objective?' Athelstane snapped. 'That's the one piece of information I need, inquisitor. If I know what they're after, I can try to counter it.'

Ragnar remembered the war council back on Fenris. 'The runes say that the Thousand Sons have a plan to bring about the downfall of our entire Chapter,' he said. 'That's why Madox is here.' *And the spear as well,* he thought.

Inquisitor Volt looked sidelong at Ragnar. 'As to what their ultimate goal is, neither I nor Lady Gabriella can say,' he continued, 'but we do know that the heart of the enemy's power lies not on Charys, but upon its shadow twin within the Eye.'

'Then that is where we must strike,' Ragnar said at once.

Athelstane interrupted with a harsh bark of laughter. The bitter amusement died at once as she saw the look on the young Space Wolf's face. 'You're serious,' she said incredulously. 'But... that's not possible.'

Volt glanced at Gabriella. 'We think it is,' the inquisitor said, gesturing to her. 'Please explain.'

Gabriella nodded. 'The *Fist of Russ* made orbit not too long ago,' she began. 'Shipmaster Wulfgar reports that she has sustained severe damage, but her warp drive is intact. We could place a strike team onboard and use the ship to enter the warp.' The Navigator took a deep breath. 'Providing we activated the drive close to the planet, the ship would cross the barrier into the immaterium at the point where the shadow world is anchored.'

The general interjected with a peremptory sweep of her hand. 'Now, forgive the interruption, my lady, but I know enough about warp travel to know that the ship is surrounded by a force field that keeps it isolated from the immaterium–'

'The Geller field, yes,' Gabriella said. 'It projects a pocket of reality around a ship travelling through the warp that keeps the forces of Chaos at bay. Naturally, we would have to deactivate it before making the attempt.'

Athelstane was struck speechless. Finally she stammered, 'That would be suicide.'

'Normally, yes,' Gabriella agreed, 'but not in this case. Just as the co-location causes some of the warp to spill over into the physical realm, the reverse would apply to the shadow world. There should be a pocket of stable reality around the planet strong enough to keep the ship from being destroyed outright.'

'*Should,*' Athelstane echoed. 'All of this is theory. You haven't one shred of proof that any of this is true.'

Volt raised his chin. 'It fits the evidence at hand,' he replied archly.

'I can only take your word for that,' Athelstane replied. 'My experience doesn't help much in matters like these, but I *do* know what will happen if you've guessed wrong and you head off into the warp without a Geller field. You, the ship, and everyone on board will be destroyed.'

Mikal Sternmark folded his arms and glowered thoughtfully at the books scattered across the situation table. 'I'll gather the Wolf Guard,' he said, 'plus a pack of Grey Hunters and Einar's Long Fangs. We could–'

'No lord, you can't,' Athelstane declared. 'I won't let you do this.'

Sternmark slowly turned to the general. 'You forget yourself, lady commander,' he said coldly. 'You have no authority over the Sons of Russ.'

Athelstane rose to her feet and stared up at the towering Space Wolf. 'Perhaps not,' she said, 'but you swore an oath to protect the people of this world, and without you Charys is most assuredly lost. Every squad you pull out of the battle line makes our defence that much more precarious. Are you willing to risk losing an entire world for the sake of a suicidal gamble like this?'

'What other choice do we have?' Sternmark shot back. 'Volt is right. The Thousand Sons can strike our lines at will, and there are no reinforcements coming. At best, we're just delaying the inevitable. Better to strike a blow against the enemy than sit in our holes and let them come for us!'

'And what if they're wrong?' Athelstane said. 'If that ship hits its warp drive and there's no stable pocket of reality on the other side, you'll have thrown away not just your life, but *millions* of others as well. Make no mistake, without you and your men we won't last twenty-four hours once the rebel counter-offensive begins.'

'Send the Wolfblade,' Ragnar interjected. The words burst from his lips before he fully knew what he was saying. 'Us and Harald's pack as well.'

Sternmark shot Ragnar a disdainful look. 'What, thirteen of you against Madox and the Thousand Sons?'

Inquisitor Volt spoke up. 'Actually, I was thinking along much the same lines,' he ventured. 'It is unlikely that the enemy is expecting this kind of attack, and a small force would have a better chance of avoiding detection.' He spread his bandaged hands. 'Of course, given the situation, I would assume command of the expedition. My skills will be able to further protect the strike team and lead it to its target.'

The Wolf Guard regarded Volt balefully for a moment, and then relented with a curt nod. 'There's still the matter of the warp turbulence,' he said. 'How do you plan on getting past that?'

Volt turned to Gabriella. She raised her head and said calmly, 'The mission will have need of an expert Navigator. Otherwise the ship could be hurled deep into the Eye and meet with disaster.'

The Wolf Guard's eyes went wide. 'No,' he said, 'I can't allow this.' He glanced at Ragnar and Volt for support. 'Lady, surely you can see that this mission is a forlorn hope at best. Even if everything goes as planned and the mission is a success, the survivors will face the full wrath of the Thousand Sons. With an attacking force this small, no one is going to survive.'

Gabriella only nodded. 'I understand, lord, and I appreciate your concern, but just as the lady commander has no authority over you or your men, neither do you hold any sway over me.' She met the Wolf Guard's eyes and gave him a faint smile. 'Rest assured, the Navis Nobilite are no strangers to sacrifice in the name of the holy Emperor.'

Sternmark thought it over. 'The Old Wolf will have my hide for a rug when he hears about this,' he growled, but he threw up his hands in surrender. 'All right. Make your preparations to depart,' he said. 'Ragnar, I'll leave it to you to give Harald the good news.'

Ragnar bowed his head to Sternmark, and with a worried glance at Gabriella he took his leave. The Navigator sketched a bow to Athelstane and the Wolf Guard. 'I'll contact the *Fist of Russ* and inform Shipmaster Wulfgar of our plans,' she said, and departed as well.

Sternmark watched them go while Inquisitor Volt gathered up his scattered tomes. Finally he sighed. 'I hope you know what you're doing,' he growled.

'As do I,' Volt answered. He straightened and fixed the Wolf Guard with a commanding stare. 'It's time we contacted the *Holmgang*.'

THE BLOOD CLAWS weren't at the staging area near the star port's command complex, and none of the headquarters staff seemed to know where they'd gone. Ragnar wasn't all that surprised, but the discovery irritated him nonetheless. As more enemy rockets plunged like arrows across the cratered expanse of the star port, Ragnar was reduced to tracing his route back to the Thunderhawk they'd flown in, and then tracking Harald's pack by scent.

He finally found them in an isolated supply bunker not far from the Thunderhawks' armoured revetments. Ragnar followed the trail down a shallow ferrocrete ramp that led to an open doorway in the bunker's flank. Two Blood Claws posted as sentries rose silently to either side of the interior doorway as the young Space Wolf stepped inside.

The bunker had been emptied out long ago, and the pack sat on the bare floors in the gloom, tending weapons and making field repairs to their armour. The three men that they'd taken to the field medicae unit had either been released or they'd decided to release themselves. They rested against one of the ferrocrete walls, letting their enhanced constitution and their armour's medical systems tend to their injuries.

Harald was sitting with a pair of packmates, cleaning and checking their weapons when Ragnar appeared. The pack leader glanced up and his face darkened into an angry scowl. 'What in Morkai's name do you want?' he snarled.

Ragnar strode purposefully into the bunker. The two Blood Claws to either side of him closed in quickly, intending to bar his way, but he stopped them in their tracks with a steely glare. 'I bring tidings from Mikal Sternmark,' he declared. 'We're going back into action.'

He sketched out the planned expedition quickly and concisely, entertaining no questions from Harald or his packmates. As he spoke, the

Blood Claws shared disbelieving looks that only turned grimmer as the inquisitor's plan took shape.

When he was done, Ragnar turned back to Harald and planted his hands upon his hips. 'If you have something to say, pack leader, now is the time,' he said. He could see the challenge building behind Harald's eyes, and part of him hoped that the Blood Claw would try to do something about it.

'Who is commanding this expedition?' Harald asked. 'The last time you led us, we lost our Wolf Priest and a third of our pack. Surely Sternmark isn't about to place us in your hands again.'

The rest of the Blood Claws were silent, glaring angrily at Ragnar. The young Space Wolf bared his teeth. 'There's an inquisitor on the planet, a man named Volt. He'll be leading the force.'

Harald snorted in disgust. 'First an exile, then an inquisitor. By Morkai, we're an ill-fated bunch,' he told his men. They growled their agreement. The pack leader sneered at Ragnar. 'Next thing you know, that damned three-eyed maid of his will try her hand at us.'

'Get up,' Ragnar said coldly.

The pack leader smiled. 'Well, well,' he said. 'Struck close to home, did I?'

'I said *on your feet.*' Ragnar took a step forward. 'Take your beating like a man, not grinning up from the floor like a dog.'

Harald leapt off the floor with a snarl, blue fire crackling between his fingers as he activated his power fist. Startled shouts filled the bunker as the rest of the pack threw their bodies between the two men and tried to push them apart.

'Enough!' yelled Harald's second, the red-haired warrior called Rolfi. He grabbed Harald by the front of his armour and shook him. 'No challenges during war time! That's the Old Wolf's law!'

Harald pushed himself away with a snarl, but anger still smouldered in the pack leader's eyes. 'When we return to Fenris, then,' he declared, pointing at Ragnar with his crackling fist. 'You're going to answer for Sigurd, exile. That I swear.'

Ragnar shook off the men gripping his arms like a bear shakes off a pack of hounds. 'Let Sigurd speak for himself,' he shot back. 'I for one choose to believe he still lives.' He glared savagely at the assembled Wolves. 'Muster for battle at Thunderhawk Two in an hour,' he said. 'We're going to go and get him.'

Ragnar turned and headed for the doorway. He paused at the threshold, and looked back over his shoulder at Harald. The pack leader was still surrounded by his men, gazing angrily at the young Space Wolf's back.

One fight at a time, Ragnar thought, and stepped out into the sunlight.

THE GUARD'S POWERFUL VOX transmitters were only a short walk from the bunker's situation room. Inquisitor Volt led the way, with Sternmark pacing only a few steps behind him. The stormtroopers stationed at the door shouldered their hellguns and admitted them without a word.

Inside, Volt surveyed the crowded room. Half the space was given over to humming vox consoles, where soldiers hunched over flickering cathode screens and read off messages from sheets of flimsy parchment passed from the war room across the hall. The rest of the dimly lit room contained rack upon rack of transmitters, receivers and power supplies. The stink of ozone hung heavy in the cramped space. Nodding in satisfaction, he dismissed the on-duty vox operators and tech-priests with a murmured command. When the door had shut on the last of the men, the inquisitor walked over to the central console and began adjusting the frequency controls on the system's orbital relay.

Sternmark put his back to the door and folded his arms. For once he was glad not to have the watchful eyes of the skald boring into his back. A sense of despair gripped him. He could not shake the feeling that the situation was spiralling out of control and nothing he did could alter its course. 'You don't have to do this,' he said grimly.

'It is now or never,' Volt replied, fine-tuning the frequency. 'You said it yourself. There is virtually no chance that any of us will return from this mission. I must set things in motion before we depart–'

'That's not what I meant,' Sternmark said. 'It's too premature to call for Exterminatus.'

Volt turned to face the dour Space Wolf. 'Do you think I'm doing this lightly? I've been an inquisitor for a hundred and fifty years, and do you know how many worlds I have condemned? *None.* Not a single one.' The inquisitor took a step towards Sternmark, his bandaged hands trembling. 'There was always another way to deal with the traitors and save the innocent, *always*. We... we always found a way.' He took a deep, shuddering breath. 'But not this time. The enemy was too well prepared. We worked for years, slowly penetrating the governor's household and the PDF hierarchy, but they were aware of us the entire time. When the traitors finally revealed themselves my... friends... were the first to die.' Volt's face grew haunted, his gaze turning inwards as he relived that bloody night in the capital. He shook his head. 'Now... there's nothing left. If we don't succeed on the shadow world, then it's only a matter of time before your positions are overrun.' Volt regained his focus with a start, like a man waking from a nightmare. 'We have to be prepared for that eventuality.'

Sternmark tried to formulate a reply, but the inquisitor turned his back on the Wolf Guard and keyed the transmitter. '*Holmgang*, this is Citadel,' Volt said, using the code name for the planetary headquarters. 'My authorisation is five-alpha-five-sigma-nine-epsilon. Please respond.'

For several long moments nothing emerged from the vox-unit except for the ghostly hiss of static. Then, faintly, a voice replied. 'Citadel, this is *Holmgang*. Countersign is gamma-alpha-seven-four-omicron-beta. What is your message?'

The battle-barge and her surviving escorts had been hiding out in the asteroid belt for weeks, powered down and maintaining vox silence to avoid detection. Volt had insisted that the ships be held in reserve once it had become clear that losses were mounting against the Chaos fleet. The barge's powerful barrage cannons and cyclonic torpedoes were a force of last resort in the event that the Imperial defenders on Charys were overwhelmed.

Volt took a deep breath and invoked the wrath of the Holy Inquisition. 'Implement Tripwire,' he said. 'Acknowledge.'

Silence hung heavy in the air as the signals crossed the void. Finally, the voice replied, 'Tripwire acknowledged. *Holmgang* out.'

The inquisitor slowly reached up and switched off the transmitter. 'Mark the hour,' he said to Sternmark. 'From this day forward the all-clear code must be sent at exactly the same time.' He turned back to Sternmark, and his expression was bleak. 'If you or Athelstane fail to send the code, the ship's master will assume that the headquarters has been overrun, and by order of the Inquisition, Charys will die.'

ELEVEN
Into the Storm

THE SHELLS FELL from orbit with a rumbling, clattering roar, passing high overhead and falling beyond the horizon to the west. White and yellow flashes lit the undersides of the thick clouds of billowing smoke above the capital, and a roll of man-made thunder sent a shiver through the ground beneath the Space Wolves' feet.

An early dusk was coming on as the strike team finally began to board their ships and rendezvous with the *Fist of Russ*. Their departure had been delayed more than four hours by rocket attacks and a surprise air raid by a squadron of rebel Valkyries late in the afternoon. Fires were still burning out of control at the fuel depot on the other side of the star port, and several of the Guard's aircraft had been damaged or destroyed. Rocket attacks had continued over the course of the afternoon as well, making repair work hazardous. It was clear to Ragnar and the rest of the Wolves that these were the opening stages of the coming enemy offensive.

The delays were further compounded by Shipmaster Wulfgar, who, upon receiving his orders from Sternmark, insisted on evacuating the cruiser of all non-essential personnel and transferring the ship's supply stores down to the planet. The off-loading took more than three hours, during which time the battle cruiser's surviving weapon batteries bombarded rebel positions in and around the capital. Wulfgar wanted to do as much as he could for the embattled defenders while he had the chance, and no one, not even Sternmark, sought to gainsay him. No one said it aloud, but everyone knew that once the *Fist of Russ* broke orbit and entered the warp, there was little chance the crippled warship would ever return.

A grim mood hung like a storm cloud over the Wolves of Harald's pack as they queued up to board Thunderhawk Two. Thunderhawk One, where Torin had chosen to rest and recuperate from his wound, had been hit during the air raid and badly damaged by enemy bombs. Though the injured Wolfblade had managed to put out the fire raging in the assault ship's fuselage, the damage was so extensive that the Thunderhawk had been put out of action. Smoke stains still smudged the older Wolfblade's lean face, giving him a dark, glowering mien as he limped around the exterior of the Belisarius shuttle on a pre-flight inspection.

There was a scent in the air, something thin and acrid that cut through the smell of burning petrochem and flakboard and set Ragnar's hair on end. He could see by the hunched shoulders and hooded eyes of the rest of the Wolves that they felt it, too, all but Haegr, who seemed serenely oblivious of everything but the grox thighbone he had between his teeth. Something's got under our skin, he thought, watching the Blood Claws climb aboard their waiting assault ship a few dozen metres away. *Something's burning in the blood.* The thought perplexed him, but he found himself strangely assured that he wasn't the only one in an ill humour. *It's not just me, not just the wolf inside. Surely the curse can't be clawing inside each of us.*

Gabriella seemed troubled as well, in her own way. She arrived at the shuttle silent and withdrawn, clad in partial carapace armour drawn from the Guard's meagre stores. She walked with great care across the tarmac and up the ramp into the shuttlecraft, as though burdened by the unfamiliar weight of breastplate and greaves. Ragnar had stood at the bottom of the ramp, immobile as a statue, and she passed him without a word or a sideways glance. He'd long since gone over every argument he could think of to dissuade her from joining the expedition, and not one of them seemed sufficient. It was her right, indeed, her duty, to place her life in harm's way for the good of the Imperium, and yet he could not help but feel as though he and his brothers had failed her somehow. It should never have come to this, Ragnar thought darkly.

Inquisitor Volt arrived, a short while later, disembarking from the armoured squad bay of a scarred Chimera APC. He emerged alone from the idling transport, carrying nothing more than a battered leather book case in one hand and a scabbarded sword in the other.

Polished armour gleamed from beneath the folds of his dark, red robes, and the unmistakeable bulge of a bolt pistol rested upon his hip. Ragnar saw at once that the war gear had been made with Volt in mind, but the inquisitor bore it awkwardly. He reminded Ragnar of an aged veteran, long past his prime, who'd put on his old gear for the first time in a great many years. Another salvo of heavy shells rattled overhead as Volt strode across the tarmac, and he turned to mark their passing as they fell upon the far-off capital. Ragnar watched the man stare contemplatively at the distant horizon for several long minutes. Then the inquisitor raised his hand, as though in farewell. With that, he straightened and resumed his course in a swirl of crimson robes and nodded wordlessly to Ragnar as he joined Gabriella inside her shuttle.

Torin completed his check of the shuttle's thrusters, and limped over to Ragnar. His armour had been patched where the sorcerer's hellblade had torn through his hip, but the pale line of the chemical weld showed how large the wound had actually been. His voice was a husky growl, no doubt from the clouds of toxic smoke he'd inhaled fighting the fire. 'She took some fragments during that air raid, but she'll fly,' he said, 'providing Haegr hasn't managed to put on any more weight since we've been here.'

Haegr cracked open the end of the bone with his granite-like molars. 'If I have, I can work it off in a few moments by giving you a good thrashing,' he said idly.

Torin gave his battle-brother a wolfish stare, and for a moment it looked as though he welcomed the chance for a fight. The sight startled Ragnar. 'Head inside and start up the engines,' he said quickly. 'I want to launch as soon as Harald's men have boarded.'

The older Wolfblade nodded, almost sullenly, and then nodded at something past Ragnar's shoulder. 'Sternmark's coming,' he rasped, and headed up the shuttle ramp.

Bemused and deeply unsettled, Ragnar turned to see half a dozen Wolf Guard striding purposefully through the smoke towards the strike team. Sternmark led them, his helmet tucked beneath his arm and his long, black hair unbound. He seemed a different man, Ragnar thought at once. Gone were the troubled expression and the hunched, almost defeated look that he'd had inside the command bunker. Out in the open air, with guns pounding and enemy shells flying overhead, the Wolf Guard held his head high and there was a fell look in his dark eyes. He strode through the fury of war like a hero of legend, the true son of a hard and warlike people. Some of Harald's pack caught sight of Sternmark and called out his name, raising their chainblades in salute. Ragnar did so as well, drawing his frost blade free and lifting it to the sky. Even Haegr tossed his splintered bone hurriedly aside and gripped the haft of his thunder hammer.

'Mikal Sternmark, lord and captain, hail!' Ragnar called in a deep, powerful voice.

Sternmark nodded gravely to the warriors and returned their salute with a raised fist. 'There is no lord here but Berek,' he said, 'I am only his sworn man, acting in his name.' He stopped before Ragnar and called out to the nearby Blood Claws. 'Harald! Come here!' At once, the pack leader broke into a run, covering the few dozen metres between them in moments. He arrived with a clatter of armour and the faint whine of servomotors, bowing his head respectfully to the Wolf Guard. Ragnar lowered his sword, suddenly very conscious of the silent figure of Morgrim Silvertongue, the company skald, watching the proceedings from the rear of the group.

'I am heading for the front line soon,' Sternmark said without preamble. 'The enemy offensive has begun, and every warrior will be needed to hold the traitors at bay.' He paused, a frown momentarily creasing his brow as he struggled for the proper words to say.

After a moment, he continued, 'The survival of Charys depends upon you. If the Rune Priests speak true, the fate of the entire Chapter rests upon your shoulders as well. Whatever evil our foes are working you must somehow destroy it, no matter the cost.'

Harald's expression turned sombre. This was the first time he'd heard of the priests' dire predictions regarding the future of the Chapter. 'No matter the cost,' he echoed. 'You have my oath upon it.'

'And mine,' Ragnar said.

Sternmark nodded. 'I am no priest, so I have no benedictions to offer you. Nor am I a lord, to gift you with gold rings or titles. I can only give you this,' he said, offering his hand, 'and wish you good hunting.'

They clasped forearms in silence, warrior to warrior, as more rockets howled overhead. Ragnar was last, and Sternmark gripped his arm a moment longer. 'Fight well,' he said quietly. 'If we do not meet again, know that you are redeemed in the eyes of Berek's company.'

Ragnar understood what Sternmark intended. He sends me off to die with honour, he thought, and was moved. Yet he shook his head. 'No,' he answered, 'not yet, not until the Spear of Russ is returned to Garm. That is my oath to the Great Wolf.'

The Wolf Guard smiled grimly and nodded. 'So be it,' he said. 'Russ will know your deeds, even unto the depths of the warp.' Sternmark took a step back and saluted the two Wolves one last time. 'Until we meet again, brothers, in this life or the next,' he said. As he started to turn away, the Wolf Guard caught Haegr's eye. 'And if you get to the Halls of Russ before me, save me a sip of ale and a crust of bread, will you?'

Haegr watched the Wolf Guard and his retinue stride off, his brow furrowed in consternation. 'Now what do you suppose he meant by that?' he mused aloud.

NOT FAR FROM the star port's command bunker, the warriors of Berek's company had taken their fallen lord and laid him in state like a king of old, clad in gleaming armour and stretched upon a table of stone. His blond hair was unbound, and but for the deathly pallor of his face, Berek Thunderfist might have been sleeping, lost in red dreams of glory. His scarred power fist was laid across his chest, and his helm, which the Wolf Lord almost never wore, had been dug out of his arming chest and set by his side.

Twin braziers burned low inside the abandoned bunker, one at each end of the long table. When it became clear that the Wolf Priest's salves and incense did nothing to rouse their stricken lord, Sternmark had the censers removed and the braziers put in their place. He'd lit the wood fires himself, as his people had done on Fenris for thousands of years. The orange fire threw martial shadows against the thick walls. In the weeks since Berek had fallen, his warriors had heaped their war trophies around their lord's feet. Swords and axes, pistols and rifles, skulls of mutant and human alike filled the space around Berek nearly to ceiling height, and more were arriving every day.

A single Wolf Guard stood vigil over the fallen lord. It was all the company could spare in these desperate times. Old Thorin Shieldsplitter filled the doorway with his fearsome bulk, barring the way with his two-handed power axe. He had been the company champion before Mikal, and now he bowed his head and stepped aside as Sternmark approached to pay homage to his lord.

He entered the bunker alone, hard footsteps echoing strangely in the crowded space. The faint crackling of the fire and the smell of wood smoke reminded Sternmark of home, and for the first time in months he found himself thinking of Fenris, so many light-years away.

Sternmark approached the bier carefully, set his own helmet upon the floor, and slowly drew Redclaw. The ancient, rune-etched blade gleamed in the firelight as he rested its tip on the floor and sank to one knee. For a long time he stared at the blinking status runes flickering from an exposed access panel on Berek's armour. The Wolf Lord still clung to life, so faintly that the armour's powerful systems could only barely detect it. On Fenris, perhaps, something could possibly have been done, but here, on Charys, all they could do was wait, and they were nearly out of time.

The Wolf Guard cast his eyes downward, to the blinking red telltale of the melta charges set beneath the bier. If the star port perimeter was ever breached and the Imperial defenders overrun, then Thorin's last duty was to hit the detonator and ensure that their lord would never become a trophy for the enemy.

A sense of inevitability hung over Sternmark. It was like riding a long-ship into the teeth of a storm and perching atop a towering wave, waiting for the moment when the prow would start to dip and the ter-rifying plunge would begin. *Death comes for us all, sooner or later*, but it was not death that the warrior feared. A part of him welcomed the com-ing foe and the brutal simplicity of battle. When the swords sang and blood flowed, a man's decisions meant life or death for him alone, not uncounted thousands half a world away.

What Sternmark feared was the stain of failure, and the realisation that he was not worthy of the challenge laid before him.

'Why?' he said softly, his hands tightening on the hilt of his blade. 'Why me?'

'If not you, Mikal Sternmark, then who?'

Sternmark leapt to his feet. For the briefest instant he thought it was Berek's voice that he heard, but then he recognised the smooth, prac-ticed tones of Morgrim the skald. Sternmark felt his cheeks burn with the shame of his confession. He whirled, teeth bared, and saw Morgrim standing silently just within the bunker's entrance. His expression was unreadable as ever, but his eyes were sharp and clear.

Watching me. Marking my every mistake.

White hot rage boiled in Sternmark's breast. The weight of the sword felt good in his hands, and then he saw that the two of them were alone. I could kill him now, he thought wildly. My shame will die with him.

He took a single step forward... and then realised what he was doing. 'Blessed Russ!' he cried, wrestling with his revulsion and rage. He glared at Morgrim, furious at himself and the skald besides. 'No wonder you skalds are called stormcrows,' he growled, 'always sticking your beaks where they don't belong!' With a conscious effort Sternmark slammed Redclaw back into its scabbard. 'What will you say of this moment, I wonder?'

Morgrim cocked his head curiously. 'I will tell of a hero and a dutiful warrior who spent his hour before battle paying homage to his lord,' he said. 'What did you imagine I would say?'

'Don't lie to me!' Sternmark roared, once again feeling the rage claw through him. A vision danced before his eyes of the skald thrashing on the bunker floor, his eyes wide and his hands pressed to the shredded ruin of his throat. The Wolf Guard shook his head savagely, trying to drive the image from his mind. Blessed Russ, he thought, what is wrong with me?

'Do you think I haven't seen you these past few weeks?' Sternmark shouted. 'Dogging my steps and noting every false move I've made? Do you think me blind to the way you judge every decision I make?'

The skald's eyes narrowed. 'It's not my place to judge you,' he said carefully. 'My duty is to bear witness, and remember the deeds of our company.' He spread his hands. 'Do you think I do this out of spite, or for an evening's entertainment? No. I remember all the deeds of our brothers so that when times are desperate and our leaders are in need of advice, I will be able to help.'

'And now you've got a fine tale of a man's failure!' Sternmark shouted. 'If you manage to survive my blunders here on Charys you'll have a cautionary tale for the next lord who comes along.'

'What blunders are those?' Morgrim asked, and the sincere interest in his voice gave Sternmark pause.

The Wolf Guard groped for the right words. 'This... this looming *defeat*,' he said, clenching his fists. 'Nothing I've done here has stemmed the tide one whit, and you well know it. We're about to be overrun. Berek's great company is about to die, and *the blame is mine.*'

Morgrim did not answer at once, instead tugging thoughtfully at his beard. Finally, he said, 'Do you imagine Berek could have done any better?'

'Of course!' Sternmark snapped. 'How many battles has he won? How many times has he led us against impossible odds and stood triumphant?'

'Five hundred and thirty-seven.'

Sternmark frowned. 'What?'

'You asked how many battles Berek's won, and I told you, five hundred and thirty-seven. That's major battles, of course. We don't concern ourselves with skirmishes or raids unless they lead to something noteworthy.'

'Are you *mocking* me, stormcrow?' the Wolf Guard asked, incredulous.

'By the Allfather, I'm not!' Morgrim said with a laugh. 'Think on this: in five hundred and thirty-seven battles, do you not imagine that Berek had occasion to feel the exact same way you do now?'

Sternmark glowered at the skald. 'Why don't you tell me?'

'Morkai's black breath! Of course he did,' Morgrim replied. 'Paxos VI; Manes Primus; the whole of the damned Lucern Suppression,' he said, ticking them off with his fingers. 'And those are just the most recent ones. That's the burden of command, Mikal Sternmark: holding the lives of your brothers in your hands and knowing that no matter what you do, they could still die. Sometimes the enemy is stronger, or more clever, or just luckier. You can only do the best that you can, and the rest is up to fate.' The skald walked past Sternmark and stood next to the bier. 'Berek is a fine lord and a mighty warrior,' he said, 'but he still walked into an ambush in the governor's palace.' He shrugged. 'Perhaps he would have done things differently, perhaps not. Every light fails in time,' the skald said. 'Battles are lost. Heroes die.'

Sternmark looked down upon his stricken lord. 'I failed him, Morgrim.'

'No,' the skald replied, 'you never shirked from your duty. What man can do more?'

The Wolf Guard considered this, and found he only had one answer. He bent and picked up his helmet, turning its battered shape over in his hands. 'When the time comes we can fight and die like Wolves,' he said softly.

'And so we shall, brother. So we shall.'

THE FIST OF *Russ* limped away from Charys at half power, trailing a glittering stream of leaking air and coolant in her wake. Her augurs swept the void, searching for signs of danger, while the skeleton crew aboard prayed to the Divine Emperor that they would find none. Her shields were weak, only half her guns worked, and all but one of her port thrusters were out. The crippled battle cruiser wouldn't last long against a determined group of raiders, but the young Navigator on board told them not to worry. The voyage, she assured them, would be a short one.

Smoke still stained the bulkheads on the warship's command deck, and the air still smelled of burned wiring and scorched flesh. Techpriests walked in solemn circles across the deck, swinging censers and intoning damage control catechisms. Shipmaster Wulfgar was alone on the deck, save for a handful of his senior officers. Their faces were grim as they went about their tasks, calling out orders with an almost funereal solemnity. Every one of them had volunteered for the mission. Sailors down to their bones, they had refused to give up the ship.

Shipmaster Wulfgar stood at the command pulpit, his hands gripping the lectern before him as he looked out over the bridge, below. He had been reading passages aloud from the *Lexicanum Imperialis* as the ship sailed on through the endless night, but he had fallen silent as Gabriella had climbed quietly inside the Navigator's vault. Torin and Haegr took positions at either side of the vault's adamantium hatch, as though their presence could somehow shield the Navigator from harm.

Ragnar understood how they felt. The young Space Wolf caught Volt's watchful eye, and the inquisitor gave him a nod. Ragnar took a deep breath and moved quickly to Wulfgar's side.

The ship's master turned slightly at Ragnar's approach. Despite the added height of the pulpit, the bondsman was still a few centimetres shorter than the towering Space Wolf. Ragnar saw a pair of faded picts laid across the illuminated pages of the *Lexicanum*: a young boy in a bondsman's black tunic, grinning up at the imager, and a woman, tall and severe, wearing the armoured coveralls of an engineer. Wulfgar's right hand settled protectively over them as the young Space Wolf approached.

'The engine decks report ready,' Wulfgar said. 'We are merely awaiting word from the Navigator to commence jump. The Geller field has been shut down.'

Ragnar nodded slowly. 'I understand your concerns, Shipmaster Wulfgar,' he said, 'but I trust the Lady Gabriella with my life. If she and Inquisitor Volt say that there is a world on the other side, then there is.'

Wulfgar began to speak, but thought better of it and simply nodded instead.

'She also says that there is little chance we'll find any hostile forces above the planet's surface,' Ragnar continued, 'so our arrival should go unchallenged.' He looked Wulfgar in the eye. 'So you should have no problem completing the jump cycle and returning back to real space as soon as the strike team is deployed.'

The master of the ship turned fully about to face the young Space Wolf. 'That would be your death warrant,' he said. 'It takes many hours to recharge a warp drive under optimal conditions. You'd be dead before we could return to get you, providing we could even find our way back to the proper time and place.'

Ragnar nodded. 'But the ship – and her Navigator, our solemn charge – would be able to escape.'

Wulfgar studied Ragnar for a long moment. 'You've talked this over with the inquisitor?'

'I have. We are all agreed.'

The ship's master sighed, and then nodded solemnly. 'So be it. May the Allfather protect you all.'

Ragnar nodded solemnly, secretly relieved that he'd at least found a way to place Gabriella out of harm's way. The Thunderhawk carrying the strike team could deploy within minutes of reaching the shadow world. Gabriella wouldn't even need to leave the safety of her heavily armoured vault.

A red telltale began flashing on a screen set into the lectern. Wulfgar knew its meaning with a glance. 'Signal from the Navigator,' he said, turning back to the pulpit. He drew a deep breath and cried out across the bridge. 'All hands, stand by to jump!' As an afterthought, he glanced over his shoulder at Ragnar. 'You'd best find something to hang on to. Russ alone knows what will happen when we engage the drive.'

Ragnar looked dubious. 'And holding on to a stanchion is going to help?'

The ship's master shrugged. A faint grin touched one corner of his mouth. 'It can't hurt.'

Ragnar thought it over and shrugged. It was bad enough that they were going to leap headlong into the warp without protective shielding; there was no sense tempting fate any further. He stepped over to one side and closed his hands around the railing overlooking the ship's bridge.

Moments later the jump siren began its shrill cry. 'Stand by!' Wulfgar shouted. 'Stand by... *jump!*'

Without warning, a howling wind tore across the command deck, cutting deep into Ragnar's bones. The massive battle cruiser pitched and yawed like a longship in the teeth of a gale, her massive superstructure groaning against the strain. Lights and strange, reflected shapes flowed like oil through the cathedral-like viewports of the bridge. The air curdled. Men screamed in terror, or ecstasy. Ragnar felt the unbridled desecration of Chaos crash over him like a wave and called out to the Allfather for deliverance.

As if in answer, the howling, groaning storm simply ceased. Ragnar staggered, clutching desperately at the rail as his body tried to compensate for the sudden shift in motion. A sense of unreality passed through him. For a moment he feared that his hand might pass through the metal rail as though it were made of smoke. Just like Charys, he thought.

The air tasted strange on Ragnar's tongue. He looked around and saw men sprawled upon the deck. Two of the tech-priests were in convulsions, sparks flying from their augmented eyes and foam speckling their lips. Even Torin and Haegr were on their hands and knees, shaking their heads drunkenly from the shock of the brief transit. Inquisitor Volt was climbing slowly to his feet, his mouth working in a silent prayer.

Red light flooded through the viewports, thick as congealed blood. Ragnar brought his head around and forced his eyes to focus on the realm beyond the stricken ship. He saw the dark curve of a world, like a sphere of ebon glass. Skeins of purple lightning ravelled across its surface, silhouetting vast, arrowhead shapes drifting like leviathans high above the shadow world.

The sky was full of Chaos ships.

TWELVE
No Matter the Cost

THE LAST SALVO of the rebel barrage landed right on target, bursting along the entire length of the Imperial barricades blocking the Angelus Causeway. Huge siege mortar rounds and Earthshaker cannon shells blew gouts of pulverised ferrocrete and structural steel dozens of metres into the air and turned human bodies into clouds of blood and vaporised flesh. Ten metres to Mikal Sternmark's right, a bunker made of salvaged masonry and quick-setting ceramite compound took a direct hit and vanished in a cloud of grey smoke and razor-edged shrapnel. Guardsmen manning firing positions to either side of the bunker were tossed into the air like broken dolls, their armour melted and their clothes alight.

Nearly three weeks of constant shelling had turned the once-prosperous commercial district that lined the causeway into a nightmare landscape of gutted buildings and smoking, debris-lined craters. The causeway itself passed through the centre of the Imperial lines. Fed by four major transit lines, the broad, six-lane road was made to ferry the produce of Charys's sprawling agri-complexes into the arms of the mercantile syndicates at the nearby star port. Columns of local granite had been raised along the entire length of the causeway, topped by severe-looking angels bearing the scales of commerce or the upraised sword of war. Nearly all of the angels had been destroyed during the long weeks of combat: all save one, who seemed to tower defiantly over the right end of the Imperials' defensive line, his sword raised to strike down the Emperor's foes.

The defenders had built their barricade from the carcasses of the bombed-out buildings that lined the causeway. Heavy slabs of ferrocrete had been dragged into place by cargo walkers brought up from the star port, and engineering teams had gone to work constructing firing steps and gun pits out of masonry and layers of flakboard. The line of fortifications stretched for a full kilometre, from one side of the causeway to the other. An entire regiment, the Hyrkoon Grenadiers, one of Athelstane's veteran units, had been ordered to hold the causeway at all costs. A full platoon of Leman Russ battle tanks had been assigned to support the defenders, their squat, blocky turrets rising threateningly from ferrocrete revetments built just behind the barricade. From their firing steps, the defenders could see for almost two kilometres down the wide, flat causeway. It was an ideal killing ground, one that any sane commander would dread having to cross, but it also stretched from the city like an out-thrust spear, reaching right for the heart of the Imperial forces on Charys. If the enemy forced open the causeway they could reach the star port in little over an hour.

Sternmark had no doubt that the causeway would be the traitors' main objective. He and his Wolf Guard had joined the surviving members of Einar's pack just as the first enemy shells had begun to fall. Now, amid the deafening thunder of the rebel bombardment, his enhanced senses detected a different timbre to the impacts landing on the far side of the barricade. Sternmark placed a boot on the firing step and raised his head above the lip of the stone embrasure. A thick wall of grey vapour was swelling silently across the concertina wire and tank traps laid before the barricade, fuelled by the bursts of dozens of rebel smoke rounds. At the same time, the roll of artillery blasts dwindled, and beyond the wall of smoke Sternmark heard the distant growl of petrochem engines and the war-shouts of the rebel host.

A grim smile touched the corners of the Wolf Guard's soot stained face. He keyed his vox-unit. 'Here they come!' he called out, both for the benefit of his battle-brothers and for the platoons of Guardsmen huddled against the fortifications to Sternmark's left and right. 'Stand ready!'

Shouted orders echoed thinly along the barricade as sergeants broke the spell of the enemy barrage with a shower of fiery curses and got the men onto their feet. The long, grey line seemed to swarm with darkly coloured beetles as the grenadiers scrambled onto the parapet and readied their weapons. The cries of wounded men rang shrilly through the air, mingled with angry shouts and the piping notes of officers' whistles. Not far from Sternmark one of the Leman Russ battle tanks started its engine with a throaty roar, its turret tracking slowly from left to right as its gunner sought targets beyond the curtain of smoke.

Frantic activity swirled about Sternmark's towering figure. A priest staggered from a makeshift shelter no bigger than a penitent's cell, furiously chanting the Litanies of Extermination. A young grenadier, barely old enough to serve, clambered over the debris behind the barricade and picked through the body parts of his dead comrades in search of spare power packs for his squad mates. A trio of soldiers grappled with a tripod-mounted autocannon, struggling to lift it back into position after it had been dislodged by a shell impact. More grenadiers raced past the towering Space Wolf from shelters further to the rear, and climbed awkwardly onto the firing step. Rifles were checked. Some men laid grenades on the chipped stone parapet where they would be close to hand. Bayonets were pulled from their sheaths and locked in place. A tall, cadaverous-looking sergeant strode quickly along the line, eyeing the grenadiers' preparations with a practised eye.

Volleys of crackling red las-bolts began lashing their way through the smoke, detonating against the stone barricades or buzzing angrily overhead. Bursts of shells kicked up puffs of dust or ricocheted crazily off the edges of the parapet. The roar of the engines was closer now, as well as the demented howls of the rebel infantry.

Sternmark closed his hand around Redclaw's hilt and drew the great blade from its scabbard. Sunlight played along the mirror finish of its edge and the runes carved along its length. He held the sword up and rested his forehead against the flat of the blade. Then he closed his eyes and offered up prayers to Russ and the Allfather. When he was done he thumbed the sword's activation rune and felt the familiar hum of its power field sweep reassuringly up his arm. A sense of calm settled like a mantle onto the Wolf Guard's shoulders. For the first time in almost a month, the anger and frustration that had gripped him at the command bunker receded from his mind. On the verge of battle, he felt whole once more.

Looking left and right, he could just see Haakon and Snurri. His battle-brothers were a hundred metres to either side, and the Wolf Guard and Einar's pack was stretched thin along the entire length of the barricade, ready to lend their strength to any breach in the line. Sternmark considered keying his vox and shouting words of encouragement to his brothers, but nothing came to mind. He had never been much good with words, and besides, what was there left to say? While he'd been driving himself mad with route maps and logistical tables they

had been out on the front lines, doing the work of warriors. They knew
what was at stake far better than he did.

Ahead, the smoke was thinning. Sternmark could see the dark shapes
of Chimera APCs heading down the causeway towards him, their mul-
tilasers and heavy bolters spitting fire. Platoons of infantrymen ran
along in their wake, snapping off wild shots with their lasguns as they
advanced.

Bolts of energy tore through the air around Sternmark, and the Imperial defenders opened fire, unleashing a storm of energy bolts and
deadly shells into the ranks of the oncoming enemy. A Chimera was
struck by a lascannon beam and lurched to a stop, smoke pouring from
its burst hatches. Men staggered and fell as lasgun beams or heavy stubber shells found their marks. The foe pressed on, drawing closer to the
barricades with each passing moment.

Sternmark raised his sword heavenward and began the battle chant
of his ancestors. Looking up at the iron-grey sky he thought of Ragnar,
and wondered if the young Space Wolf and his companions were still
alive.

THE FLEET OF Chaos ships turned upon the *Fist of Russ*, trailing glittering
arcs of grave-light from their thrusters as they broke orbit, and closed
on the Imperial battle cruiser like a swarm of hungry sea drakes. Bolts
of pulsing light stabbed from the weapon batteries studding the hulls
of the Chaos ships, but their aim was wide and the first salvoes streaked
harmlessly into the battle cruiser's wake.

'Helm, hard to port!' Shipmaster Wulfgar roared from the command
pulpit. His voice was calm and assured, but the bondsman's knuckles
were white as he gripped the edges of the lectern. 'Ahead full! All
batteries fire as you bear!' The master of the ship glanced at Ragnar, and
then turned and fixed his engineering officer with a commanding glare.
'Run the reactors at one hundred and twenty per cent.'

The engineering officer paled, but nodded nevertheless. 'Reactor at
one-twenty, aye,' he confirmed, 'but the containment wards won't hold
for long.'

'Very well,' Wulfgar replied, as the battle cruiser started her turn.
Deep, groaning sounds echoed aft from the engineering decks as the
warship increased power, her tortured superstructure suffering under
the strain. Thunder rang through the deckplates as the first of the
enemy salvos struck home against the warship's weakened shields.

Ragnar's mind raced as he studied the nearby plot table and studied
the flashing lines marking the courses and positions of the Chaos
ships. The *Fist of Russ* was turning its armoured prow to the oncoming

enemy ships, but within moments the battle cruiser would be surrounded and vulnerable. His worried glance fell on the still-sealed Navigator's vault. Then he addressed the ship's master. 'We can be at the hangar deck and launch our Thunderhawk in ten minutes,' he said. 'Alter your course and open the range, Shipmaster Wulfgar. We can slip past the Chaos ships in the confusion and make planetfall.'

Wulfgar glowered at the young Space Wolf. 'You wouldn't last ten seconds, lord,' he said with a snort. 'We've got to get you as close to the planet as we can before you launch, or they'll blow you apart.' Greenish light flickered through the high viewports as an enemy salvo flashed past the battle cruiser's bridge. Wulfgar turned back to the command lectern. 'Once we're through and you're on your way, we'll come hard about and jump again. With Loki's luck we'll still be in one piece when we come out on the other side.'

A series of deafening blasts battered the port bow of the stricken battle cruiser. Men were thrown to the deck by the impact. Only Ragnar's speed and strength kept him upright, although his grip creased the command deck's metal rail. A bloom of orange and red swelled in slow motion on the port side of the warship, just aft of the armoured prow. Ragnar saw molten hull plating streak like meteors down the length of the battle cruiser and tumble into the void.

'Shields have failed!' cried the ship's deck officer. 'Augurs report an enemy ship dead ahead, coming about on a collision course! We have to come about-'

'Steady as she goes!' Wulgar roared back as he pulled himself to his feet. The ship's master pressed a hand to a cut, smearing blood across his forehead. 'Dorsal lance battery, fire at will!'

Ragnar could see the Chaos ship now, a distant, arrowhead shape, glimmering with pale, unnatural light. It lay squarely in the battle cruiser's path, firing bolt after bolt at the Imperial ship's prow. The young Space Wolf shook his head. 'A single lance won't be enough, Shipmaster Wulfgar,' he said.

'So now you're a ship master, lord?' Wulfgar snapped, but he gave the young Space Wolf a fierce grin. 'They suspect what we're doing, and they're moving to stop us. If we alter our course even a single degree it will make the task of reaching orbit that much harder.' The bondsman shook his head. 'No. We'll plough right through that bastard if he doesn't bear away. You have my oath on it!'

A cyan flare from beyond the viewport showed that the battle cruiser's remaining lance battery had gone into action. The arcs of voltaic force leapt across hundreds of kilometres in the blink of an eye, and flared in a raging storm against the shields of the onrushing Chaos ship. The battery charged and fired again within seconds, and once more the powerful beam weapon battered against the still-glowing curve of the enemy cruiser's void shield, until it failed in a blaze of light.

More explosions battered the flanks of the Imperial ship. Sparks showered from a power conduit along the starboard bulkhead, and alarms began to wail across the command deck. Wulfgar quickly checked the readouts on the command lectern, and his expression turned grim. 'Engineering, increase reactor output to one hundred and thirty-five per cent. Helm, bring us to ramming speed.'

The *Fist of Russ* was almost completely surrounded and taking fire from all sides. Her surviving batteries answered, and the space around them was so dense with enormous ships that every shot found a target. Macro cannon shells smashed aside enemy shields and blasted deep craters in the flanks of the Chaos ships. One cruiser sheered abruptly to starboard, streaming molten debris from a blast that had smashed its command deck. Its sudden manoeuvre carried it directly into the path of another Chaos ship, and the two collided in a spectacular eruption of blazing plasma, and shorn hull plating. However, deprived of her shields, the damage to the ancient battle cruiser was mounting swiftly. Fiery explosions rippled along the length of her hull, and she bled ragged streamers of burning oxygen that tangled in her wake.

Then, like a wounded bear, the *Fist of Russ* surged forward, her surviving thrusters blazing. Caught unawares by the sudden change of speed, many of the enemy salvoes fell harmlessly behind her as she bore down on the lone enemy vessel in her path. The two ships closed the distance rapidly, still blasting away at one another with their remaining weapons. Lance fire had wrought terrible damage along the Chaos ship's bow, and the battle cruiser's armoured prow and superstructure had been repeatedly cratered by high-energy bolts.

The Chaos ship swelled in the battle cruiser's forward viewports. 'Sound collision!' Shipmaster Wulfgar cried. 'For Russ and the Allfather!'

Ragnar had just enough time to grip the command deck rail with both hands and check to make sure that Gabriella was still sealed in her vault, before the two ships collided.

Though the *Fist of Russ* was burned and broken, she was still a massive ship, weighing tens of millions of tonnes. The armoured prow of the battle cruiser struck the cruiser's bow and split it open like a rotten fruit. Crumpled hull-plates and shorn bracing beams burst outward from the impact, propelled by a cloud of superheated metal and escaping gas. The Imperial ship tore through the cruiser from stem to stern, plunging like an iron tipped spear thrust by a wrathful god.

The wounded battle cruiser suffered too. Ragnar was thrown hard against the deck rail and the air reverberated with the groan of tortured metal and the scream of tearing hull plates. Several of the bridge officers were thrown forward by the impact, hurled over the deck rail and onto the bridge crew below. Sparks exploded from a pair of overhead conduits, and then suddenly the lights went out. Ragnar heard screams of pain and terror, and the deck trembled with powerful explosions from deep below decks.

Then, with a flare of multicoloured light, the Chaos ship's reactor exploded, wreathing the forward end of the battle cruiser in fire. The *Fist of Russ* shuddered, and Ragnar felt an ominous tremor pass along the warship's battered keel. Then, all was silent, save for the faint cries of the wounded.

Red emergency lighting slowly illuminated the command deck. A faint haze of acrid smoke hung in the air. Ragnar surveyed the deck in the dim light and was amazed to find many of the crew still at their stations, working hard to keep the warship in the fight. Shipmaster Wulfgar still stood at the command pulpit, bent with pain, but quickly scanning the readouts on the lectern before him. 'Damage report,' he ordered in a raspy voice.

'We are on emergency reserve power,' the damage control officer replied. 'No one is responding on the engineering deck, but indications are that the reactors have failed. There are reports of multiple fires below decks, but most of our damage control stations are not responding.'

Wulfgar nodded. 'What about the hangar decks?'

The damage control officer checked his gauges. 'Both hangar decks report ready, though I don't know for how much longer.'

Ragnar listened to the exchange and felt a cold ball of dread settle in his stomach. 'What does this mean, Shipmaster Wulfgar?' he asked, even though he already suspected he knew the answer.

Wulfgar slowly straightened and addressed the young Space Wolf. His face was pale, and a trickle of blood leaked from the corner of his mouth. 'It means we've gone as far as we're able,' the bondsman said. 'Take your lady and make for the hangar deck as fast as you can. There's not much time.'

Ragnar felt a surge of desperation. He glanced back at the Navigator's vault and saw that the armoured containment system was already starting to cycle open. 'But the jump–'

The master of the ship shook his head. 'We can't make the jump now that the reactors have failed.' Wulfgar replied. 'Now go, lord! Get to the surface and do what you came to do. We'll cover you for as long as we can.'

Ragnar bared his teeth in a silent snarl. 'I'll take your engineering officer and we'll try to reach the reactors. We can make repairs–'

'No,' Inquisitor Volt said. His voice was sombre, but there was cold steel in his tone. 'Shipmaster Wulfgar is right. We must reach the shadow world and confront Madox, or all of this is for nothing.'

A growl of anger welled from Ragnar's throat, but he knew that Volt was correct. Hard discipline asserted itself, and the young Space Wolf nodded curtly. 'I understand,' he told the inquisitor, and then nodded his head respectfully to Shipmaster Wulfgar. 'We'll take our leave of you, master,' he said. 'Inform Harald to load his men and stand by for launch.'

'I will,' Wulfgar said. Then, the bondsman reached forward and extended his hand. 'It has been an honour to serve, lord.'

The young Space Wolf shook his head. 'No, Shipmaster Wulfgar, the honour has been ours.' He clasped the master's bloodstained wrist. 'I shall tell the Old Wolf of your deeds,' Ragnar said. 'You have my oath on it.'

The bondsman smiled, and then straightened his tunic and turned away. He studied the pages of the book propped on the lectern before him, and began to read aloud in a strong, clear voice. *'For if the Emperor is with me, who may stand against me...'*

Ragnar turned to Inquisitor Volt, and the old man nodded silently. Torin and Haegr were already escorting Gabriella to the lift at the rear of the command deck. His heart heavy, the young Space Wolf hurried to join them.

THE DECKS BENEATH the battle cruiser's bridge were a hellish realm of fire, smoke and twisted wreckage. Torin salvaged an emergency air supply from the body of a damage control technician and gave it to Gabriella, while Haegr and Ragnar took turns forcing their way past the worst of the debris. More explosions hammered at the hull of the dying battle cruiser, and with every passing minute Ragnar feared that they would not reach the hangar deck in time.

Yet luck was with them once they were within a few decks of the hangar bay. They made it past the worst of the fires and quickly regained their bearings. The many days Ragnar had spent wandering the lower decks of the huge ship paid off, and he was quickly able to lead the party down a series of maintenance accessways that brought them directly to the waiting Thunderhawk. Harald had the engines idling as the group burst onto the deck, and Volt gave the order to launch as soon as they were aboard.

Ragnar struggled to reach the Thunderhawk's command deck as the assault ship roared down the launch platform and into a storm of enemy fire. The Chaos fleet had come about and was blasting away at the *Fist of Russ*. Ragnar saw at once that the battle cruiser's main thrusters had been reduced to a twisted mass of metal, and her dorsal superstructure had been all but ripped apart. Fires glowed like sullen coals in the deep wounds along the warship's flank.

The horizon spun crazily as the pilot rolled the assault craft and pulled away beneath the Imperial ship. Ragnar gripped nearby stanchions for support and kept his eyes on the dying battle cruiser the entire time, bearing witness to its final moments.

She went down fighting, her guns still defiantly answering the enemy barrage. Ragnar saw an enemy cruiser burst apart under a punishing strike from the battle cruiser's lance battery. Then an enemy shell found one of the Imperial ship's magazines. The *Fist of Russ* disintegrated in a massive chain reaction, a fitting pyre for her heroic crew.

Ragnar took a deep breath and looked through the forward viewports at the ominous curve of the ebon world. 'How long until we make planetfall?' he asked.

'Forty-five minutes, lord, give or take,' the pilot replied, his voice subdued. 'I'll keep the wreckage between us and the enemy ships until we're well out of range.'

Ragnar nodded. With the *Fist of Russ* destroyed, there would be no escape from the shadow world for any of them. Wulfgar and his crew were only the first among them to die.

Setting his jaw, Ragnar forced such thoughts ruthlessly from his mind. They had a mission to perform. Beyond that, nothing else mattered.

He was just about to turn and head back into the troop compartment when a warning telltale began to blink on the augur officer's panel. The crewman leant forward, twisting a series of dials.

'Russ preserve us,' the bondsman said, reading the icons on the screen. 'I have multiple contacts launching from the enemy ships. They look like fighters!'

Ragnar swallowed a curse. 'Full power!' he snapped at the pilot. 'Get us on the deck as fast as you can!'

Thrusters flaring, the assault ship dropped like a thunderbolt towards the shadow world. Behind them, the first of the sleek attack ships was already passing through the battle cruiser's debris field and starting to dive.

The hunt was on.

THIRTEEN
World of Darkness

'I COUNT TWENTY – no, thirty – contacts, closing fast!' the Thunder-hawk's augur operator cried, his eyes glued to the phosphorescent display screen. The bondsman's gloved hands played with the augur unit's tuning knobs. 'At present speed they'll be in range in seven seconds,' he calculated.

'Very well,' the assault ship's pilot replied calmly. He reached up and keyed his vox-mic. 'Gunners, look alive! Contacts at six o'clock,' he said, alerting the four crewmen manning the weapon stations in the compartment beneath the command deck. As an assault ship meant to carry troops into hostile landing zones, the Thunderhawk traded speed and manoeuvrability for weapons and armour. Along with a massive forward firing battle cannon and a pair of lascannons, the Thunder-hawk also mounted four twin-linked heavy bolters on remote hardpoints. Two of these hardpoints were mounted beneath each wingtip, allowing them to fire both forward and aft. Ragnar felt the vibration of the hardpoint gimbals and the clatter of the autoloaders as the two mounts swung about and began tracking the incoming Chaos fighters.

Ragnar's grip tightened on the stanchions to either side of the command deck's hatch. He hadn't counted on the possibility that the cruisers circling above the shadow world could carry attack craft as well.

'How long until we make planetfall?' he asked, eyeing the lightning-streaked curve of the ebon planet.

'Twenty minutes, more or less,' the pilot answered tersely. 'Setting up the proper re-entry angle is going to be tricky at this speed.'

'We'll be lucky to last twenty seconds,' the young Space Wolf growled. His hearts were hammering in his chest, and he thought he could feel the blood hissing in his temples. It took every ounce of will not to lash out, to feel something break and bleed in his hands. He closed his eyes and forced the Wulfen from his thoughts. The red tide seemed to ebb somewhat, after a moment, leaving his mind a little clearer.

'Is there any sign of a city on the planet's surface?' Ragnar asked. 'If this planet is truly a mirror image of Charys, there must be a shadow version of the capital as well.'

The pilot shook his head. 'I don't see anything but lightning,' he replied, and then glanced back at the augur operator. 'Otto, switch to navigational surveyors and sweep the planet.'

'What about the enemy ships?' the operator asked, looking up from his screen with a panicked expression on his sallow face.

'Forget about them!' the pilot snapped. 'You heard the lord. Find me a city down there.'

Swearing under his breath, the augur operator jabbed at a set of runes on his control panel, and the display screen shifted to a new set of oscillating lines. Frowning, the bondsman adjusted a series of knobs, and studied the pulsing readouts. 'I'm picking up small collections of ground structures at wide intervals. They fit the profile for agri-combines,' he said. 'Hard surface reflections from transit lines, but nothing… wait!' he leaned forward, gently twisting a pair of brass dials. 'Looks like a hard set of returns bearing zero-one-five, right at the planetary terminus. There's your city.'

The pilot nodded and brought the assault ship into a shallow turn to starboard. 'Lining up on zero-one-five and starting our descent,' he said, reaching up and adjusting a set of controls on a panel over his head. The Space Wolf looked over his shoulder at Ragnar. 'Good news, lord. The city is right at the edge of our glide path. We can touch down near the outskirts without adding any more time to our descent.'

Ragnar nodded. 'And the bad news?'

As if on cue, streams of seething energy bolts filled the darkness around the Thunderhawk, and the assault ship rang with a series of heavy blows along its fuselage. Warning icons flashed amber on the tech-priest's control panel, and the crewman began to recite the Litany of Atmospheric Integrity as he frantically jabbed at damage control runes. At the tips of the assault ship's wings, the twin-linked heavy bolters went into action, barking out stuttering bursts that reverberated through the Thunderhawk's armoured frame as the high-speed dog-fight began.

The enemy fighters were sharp and angular, like shards of polished obsidian. Faint, greenish light glowed from their angled cockpit view-ports, giving the ships a sinister, insect-like appearance. They descended on the larger Thunderhawk in a swirling, chaotic swarm, blasting away at the Imperial ship from a dozen different angles. Energy bolts burst across the assault ship's wings, fuselage and tail, wreathing it in a web of small explosions that ate away at the Thunderhawk's dense armour plate. The assault ship side-slipped abruptly left, and then right, trying to spoil the attackers' aim, but it wasn't enough to fully evade the storm of enemy fire.

Red tracer rounds slashed through the enemy formation in response as the Thunderhawk's heavy bolters returned fire. A pair of Chaos fighters blew apart in clouds of glittering fragments and glowing plasma. The shattered fighter craft dissolved in the ebon world's upper atmosphere, consumed by arcs of sorcerous lightning, but there was still more than a score of attack ships dogging the battered Thunderhawk's tail.

A powerful impact struck the assault ship's port side, causing the craft to slew sideways for a dizzying instant before the pilot could regain control. 'Number one engine is hit!' the tech-priest cried out. 'Pressure indicators are spiking!'

'Hold it together for another few minutes,' the pilot shot back. Another blast hit the nose of the attack craft just beneath the cockpit, limning the pilot's helmeted head in lurid green light. 'I'm going to increase our angle of descent and see if I can get the bastards to back off. Hold on!'

The Thunderhawk steepened its dive, coming into the planet's turbulent atmosphere at a sharper angle and increasing the speed of its re-entry. At once, the leading edges of the hull began to glow red with friction build-up. The Imperial vessel trembled like a ship in a summer gale, but her reinforced superstructure held against the strain. Several of the enemy fighters sharpened their dives as well, but their hunger for destruction proved their undoing, as the heat and turbulence tore their hulls apart. The rest of the swarm fell back, unable to match the assault ship's dangerous descent.

'Well, that bought us a minute or two,' the pilot shouted over the thunder of re-entry. The heat inside the cockpit was intense, and the assault craft shuddered violently as it plunged towards the planet's surface. More and more warning icons flashed an insistent red on the tech-priest's display.

Ragnar held on for all he was worth. It was clear that the pilot was pushing the Thunderhawk to the edge of its performance envelope and possibly beyond. 'Will this get us on the ground any faster?' he shouted.

To the young Space Wolf's surprise, the pilot threw back his head and laughed. 'Oh, aye, lord! One way or another, it surely will.'

They were close enough to the planet's surface for Ragnar to make out dark oceans and broad continents studded with mountain ranges. There were no lights that he could see, but the shape of the land masses was a perfect reflection of Charys as near as he could tell. All this just to facilitate a single ritual, Ragnar thought with a terrible sense of awe. He truly grasped the sheer scope of Madox's plans, for the first time, and felt something akin to dismay. He thought of the handful of Space Wolves in the troop compartment behind him and wondered how they could possibly challenge something so vast. *Who are we to overcome an entire world?*

The answer was obvious. We are sons of the Allfather, Ragnar thought, just as Madox once was. Whatever the traitor can bring to bear against us, we are its equal.

The Thunderhawk flashed past a rocky coastline, plunging towards the dark surface of the world like a fiery comet. Vast plains stretched beneath the descending craft. Ragnar was amazed to see the outlines of enormous agri-combines, their subdivided crop zones radiating like the spokes of enormous wheels more than a thousand kilometres across. The young Space Wolf could just make out the towering granaries and equipment hives at the hub of each combine, where legions of farm servitors would shuttle back and forth like bees to tend their carefully monitored crops.

Within minutes, the fierce shuddering began to subside as the assault ship passed through the upper atmosphere and dived through a dark sky empty of clouds. A torrent of green bolts slashed downward from high and to starboard. The daemon ships were closing the range once more. Ragnar eyed the multitude of warning runes flashing on the tech-priest's screen to his left. 'How long?' he asked.

'Otto?' the pilot said.

'Surveyor shows the city dead ahead at five hundred kilometres,' the augur operator replied. Then, suddenly, he straightened in his seat. 'Wait – I'm getting something–'

Bursts of green energy bolts howled down around the Thunderhawk from high and to starboard. The pilot muttered a curse. 'Never mind, Otto. I see them.'

'No! There's something else!' the operator exclaimed. He fumbled for a set of dials and adjusted them carefully, his head cocked intently to one side. 'I... I'm getting a signal on the vox. It sounds like one of our recovery beacons.'

The pilot looked back over his shoulder at Ragnar. 'How is that possible?'

Bolts impacted across the assault ship's wings and fuselage in a string of sharp detonations. The Thunderhawk shuddered beneath the blows and seemed to plummet downward for a vertiginous instant before coming under control. Ragnar leaned close to the augur operator. 'Can you get an identity code from the beacon?'

Otto shook his head. 'I can barely hear it at all,' he said, pressing a hand to his headphones. 'There's a lot of atmospheric interference—'

Another thunderclap smote the aft section of the transport, throwing the crew against their restraints. An alarm buzzed shrilly on the tech-priest's panel, but Ragnar was oblivious to everything but the signal that the augur operator was receiving. 'Can you isolate its location?' he asked.

The bondsman shook his head. 'I can get a bearing and an approximate distance,' Otto replied, shouting over the explosions battering the Thunderhawk. 'It... it looks like three-five-five degrees at about eighty to a hundred kilometres. That's deep in a range of low mountains on the far side of an agri-combine right ahead.'

Before Ragnar could ask further, the sound of the assault ship's engines changed pitch and the Thunderhawk slewed violently to starboard. The tech-priest let out a sharp cry. 'Number one engine's failed!' he said.

There was another stomach clenching drop as the assault ship fell like a stone. Both pilot and co-pilot wrestled with the controls. 'Increase power to number two,' the pilot ordered, his voice tense with strain. 'Can you restart number one?'

'No chance,' the tech-priest shouted back, 'turbine's seized!'

Ragnar was thrown forward as the Thunderhawk's nose dipped into a steep dive. The pilot was trading altitude for speed, trying to keep his ship in the air for as long as possible. The young Space Wolf clung to the stanchions and watched the ground rushing towards them through the cockpit viewports. He could see the pale ribbon of a transit route crossing the plain below them, pointing to the outskirts of the agri-combine that Otto had mentioned.

The Thunderhawk began to shudder violently. 'Controls are getting sluggish,' the pilot grated. 'Where's my hydraulic pressure?'

A flurry of energy bolts surrounded the diving assault ship, and multiple hits slammed into the Thunderhawk's tail and wings. The wingtip heavy bolters returned fire with a roar, but then there was a loud explosion aft and the world seemed to spin out of control.

'Number two engine's hit!' the tech-priest cried, and then lapsed into a desperate prayer to the Omnissiah.

'Well, that's it then,' the pilot said, his voice surprisingly calm as the horizon spun beyond the cockpit viewports. 'Cut power to number three! Hurry!'

The co-pilot threw himself against his restraints, reaching desperately for the throttle levers. Ragnar saw that the Space Wolf wasn't going to make it.

Praying to Russ, the young Space Wolf pulled himself towards the pilots' controls. Fighting hard against the G-forces pinning the crew into their seats, he pushed his armour's systems to the limit and strained forward with his right arm. The tips of his fingers brushed the steel throttle lever and drew it back far enough to get a solid grip. Ragnar wrapped his fingers around the lever and pulled back with all his might, nearly tearing it from its housing.

The howling wail of the engine fell silent. All Ragnar heard was the whistling wind and the impassioned prayers of the tech-priest in the few seconds before the assault ship slammed into the ground.

ANOTHER WAVE OF flesh and steel bore down on the Imperial positions at the Angelus Causeway. Clawed feet scrabbling for purchase, a huge mutant heaved itself up the shifting mound of bodies at the foot of the barricade and reached for Mikal Sternmark. Beady red eyes glittered with hate from within thick, pasty folds of fat, and the entire lower half of the creature's doughy face was nothing but a massive set of powerful jaws and a lashing, serpentine tongue. One clawed hand gripped a shock maul, of the type that Arbites riot troopers often carried, and its bloodstained tip crackled with lethal energies. A pack of lesser mutants swarmed behind the massive creature, armed with a collection of laspistols, slug throwers and gory chain-blades. They howled encouragement to their leader and scrambled along in its wake, eager to sweep over the Imperial defences and slaughter the soldiers on the other side.

Sternmark met them with a bloodthirsty shout, smoke curling from bolter and blade. His bare face and ornate armour were covered in blood and grime, and his fangs shone red in the fading light of day. The traitors had hurled wave after wave of assaults against the barricade over the course of the day. Burning vehicles and the bodies of the dead stretched for almost a full kilometre down the causeway, but each attack had brought the rebels a few hundred metres closer to the Imperial positions. Four times the enemy troops had attempted to scale the barricade, and four times the Space Wolves had driven them back.

The Wolf Guard levelled his storm bolter at the oncoming creature and fired a burst into its chest. Mass-reactive rounds punched clean through the mutant and felled a pair of gibbering monsters behind it, but the lantern-jawed monster only roared in bloodlust and kept coming. It swung its shock maul at Sternmark's head, but Redclaw blurred through the air to meet it. There was a sharp *crack* of electrical discharge and a blue-white flash as the ancient power weapon cut the maul in two. Teeth bared, Sternmark brought the heavy blade down in a diagonal cut, slicing through the mutant's shoulder and deep into its chest. Ichor flowed thickly from the wound. The creature snarled and snapped at the Wolf Guard, still trying to climb onto the top of the barricade, but its strength failed it all at once and it collapsed onto its face just short of its goal. The mound of dead now rose half a metre higher than it had before.

More of the mutants climbed over the corpse of their fallen leader. Las-bolts detonated across Sternmark's chest and shoulders, and a slug left a crease along the side of the Wolf Guard's right cheek. Sternmark tore his sword free of the mutant's corpse and split one of his attackers from groin to chin. Another tried to scramble past him, dragging a grenade from its belt, and he shot it point-blank in the chest. An arm came up, levelling a laspistol at his face. With a backhanded swipe of his blade, he severed the limb, and smashed the screaming foe off the barricade with a blow from the butt of his storm bolter.

Sternmark whirled in place, seeking more enemies to slay, but after a few moments he realised that he was alone among the dead and dying. Looking out along the causeway, he saw figures in tattered Guard and PDF uniforms retreating back into the smoke, chased by las-bolts and bolter fire from the Imperial defenders. The last of the mutants who'd tried to challenge him had stumbled back down to the base of the mound and were running for their lives.

The Wolf Guard threw back his head and howled at the red-stained skies. All along the line, a ragged chorus of voices joined his, celebrating the glory of the kill. The enemy had been broken for a fifth time and hurled back in disarray. Watching their fleeing figures, Sternmark felt the blood burn in his veins, and his mouth gaped in a wolfish grin. The urge to give chase, to fall upon the terrified enemy and tear out their throats was almost too much to bear.

He took a step down onto the slippery mound of corpses, then another. Sternmark could almost feel the rushing wind of the chase against his skin.

There was a buzzing in his ears, like the whine of a biting fly. Sternmark frowned, pressing a hand to his ear. Belatedly, he realized that he'd dropped his empty storm bolter, and he was tottering uneasily atop the shifting mound of the dead.

The last of the retreating traitors disappeared into the smoke. Slowly the tide of bloodlust ebbed, flowing restlessly into the back of his mind, and the buzzing in his ears resolved into words. 'My lord! What are you doing?'

Sternmark turned, as though in a dream. One of Einar's pack members stood a few metres away atop the barricade, a bolter and a bloody chainsword hanging loose in his hands. The warrior's silver-blond hair was braided, as was his bloodstained beard. It took a moment for Sternmark to dredge the young warrior's name from the red surf pounding in his brain. 'Sven?' he asked. 'What are you doing here?'

The young Space Wolf shifted uncomfortably. 'I'm here to report, lord.' He raised his bolter. 'My pack fired off the last of our ammunition in the last wave, even the rounds we gathered from Einar and Karl.'

'Einar? Karl?' Sternmark glared at Sven, trying to make sense of what the Grey Hunter was saying. 'What's happened to them?'

The question took Sven aback. 'Karl was killed during the third attack,' he said. 'A mutant with a meltagun got too close to the barricade.'

'And Einar?'

'Deep in the Red Dream. An eviscerator took his right arm and most of his shoulder, but he bloody well killed the traitor that did it.' Sven eyed the Wolf Guard with concern. 'We reported this over the vox. Is your system malfunctioning?'

'You tend to your wargear, brother, and I'll attend to mine,' Sternmark snapped. 'Who is in charge of the pack now that Einar is down?'

Sven paused, unsettled by the vehemence of the Wolf Guard's rebuke. 'By rights, that would be Freyr–'

'But Freyr isn't here making the report, is he? You're acting pack leader now, Sven. Return to your brothers and prepare for the next attack. I'll speak to headquarters about resupply.'

'I…' Sven's eyes widened. 'Lord, are you certain you are well?'

'Well enough,' Sternmark growled. His eyes narrowed in challenge. 'Do you think I've chosen poorly, brother?'

'No, lord!' Sven took a step back, clearly uncertain how to proceed. After a moment, the young Grey Hunter bowed his head in submission and backed away, his expression troubled.

Sternmark turned away, searching for his storm bolter among the dead. He found the weapon atop a trio of fallen grenadiers and bent to retrieve it. It felt clumsy and awkward in his hands. He fumbled with the magazine release for nearly a full second before he managed to drop the empty clips. Only the iron conditioning of many decades of campaigning kept him from hurling the weapon away in frustration.

The temptation stunned the Wolf Guard. Sternmark shook his head fiercely, as though trying to break the grip of a terrible dream. Shadowy forms flitted at the corners of his vision. He whirled, trying to focus on them, but saw only the bodies of the dead, stretching as far as he could see along the length of the barricade. The battle tanks that had supported the defenders were blackened hulls, destroyed by rebel suicide attacks or artillery strikes over the course of the long day.

He realised, dimly, that he had no idea how many of the Guardsmen were still alive, or where their commander was. He'd last spoken to their commander… was it after the second attack, or the third? Sternmark couldn't be certain. The regiment could be on the verge of retreat, leaving him and his battle-brothers to hold the causeway alone.

Sternmark looked left and right, searching for the Wolf Guard who'd accompanied him to the barricade. Rage and shame boiled inside him, making it difficult to think. 'Cursed,' he growled bitterly. 'This damned world has cursed us all.'

Rebel artillery howled overhead, crashing behind the Imperial positions. A chorus of battle cries rose from the rebel lines as the traitors resumed their attack.

RAGNAR AWOKE TO the dull ache of broken bones. Lines of pain pulsed across his forehead and down his face, almost as far as his jaw, and he tasted the coppery tang of blood in his mouth.

Lightning flashed beyond his closed eyelids. Ragnar blinked, and then carefully opened his eyes. He was lying on his back, staring up at a dark sky devoid of stars. The air smelled dry and musty as a tomb, tinged with the acrid stink of burning synthetics.

Two shadowy figures loomed over the young Space Wolf. One knelt closer. Lightning flickered across the empty sky, revealing Torin's angular face. The Wolfblade peered with worry at Ragnar's face, and then broke into a wry grin. 'See? I told you he was still alive,' Torin said to the second figure. 'Lucky for us his face absorbed most of the impact.'

With a deep breath, Ragnar pushed up onto his elbows. The fractures across his face and skull caused him to grimace in pain, but he could tell that the bone was starting to knit together already. He glanced up at the second figure and realised it was Harald. The Blood Claw pack leader scowled disdainfully at Ragnar and turned away.

The Thunderhawk was a twisted pile of wreckage a few dozen metres away, half-buried in a furrow of scorched earth that stretched for nearly three-quarters of a kilometre behind the mangled wreck. Somehow, the pilot had managed to crash-land the assault ship along the grey ribbon of roadway that he'd spotted during their descent. Twisting columns of black smoke rose from the wreckage. The cockpit of the Thunderhawk was burst open, its viewports shattered and the metal bracings peeled apart. The assault ship's port wing had been torn away during the crash, and the starboard wing jutted crookedly from the wreckage. Three warriors from Harald's pack were attempting to disassemble the remaining wing's heavy bolter hardpoint under the watchful gaze of the Thunderhawk's tech-priest. Four other figures in heavy flight suits were unloading a number of small packs and other survival gear from an open hatch on the assault ship's fuselage.

Torin followed Ragnar's gaze. 'We had to tear open the cockpit with Harald's fist to get you out,' he said. 'The pilot and co-pilot died in the crash, and the augur operator was dead by the time we pulled him out.'

Ragnar nodded painfully, realising sadly that he'd never learned the heroic pilot's name. 'Any other casualties?' he asked.

'Not yet, thank Russ,' the Wolfblade said, glancing up at the empty sky. 'We heard the enemy fighters fly overhead a few times as we were trying to cut our way out of the ship, but they were gone by the time we made it outside.'

'Lady Gabriella?' Ragnar inquired.

Torin indicated a spot off behind Ragnar with a curt nod of his chin. 'Haegr is watching her,' he replied gravely. 'She's not doing too well.'

His pain forgotten, Ragnar clambered quickly to his feet. Gabriella was sitting just a few metres away, her legs drawn up and her head resting on her knees. Haegr loomed protectively over the Navigator, his thunder hammer held at the ready. Inquisitor Volt knelt beside Gabriella, speaking to her in low tones. The rest of Harald's Blood Claw pack formed a security perimeter some way off, diligently scanning the surrounding terrain for signs of danger.

Ragnar approached the Navigator carefully and sank down into a crouch next to Inquisitor Volt. The inquisitor paid the young Space Wolf no mind. His head was bowed and he was reading from a small book resting in his bandaged hands. With a start, Ragnar realised that Volt was *praying*, reciting a litany in High Gothic that he'd never heard before. He sensed it was being done for Gabriella's benefit, but he could not follow the specifics.

Leaning forward, Ragnar spoke softly to Gabriella. 'Lady? Are you well?'

At the sound of his voice, the Navigator raised her head. Gabriella's pale face was smudged with soot and grime, and her expression was one of pure anguish. Her scarf was gone and her black hair hung loosely about her face. In the centre of her forehead the Navigator's pineal eye burned like a tiny star, stunning Ragnar with its intensity.

'I can feel it,' she said in a stricken voice, 'lines of terrible power stretching into the physical realm, anchored by the suffering of millions. The fabric of space turned inside out, warped by the will of...' A look of horror passed across her face. 'I cannot say it! I dare not say it! Blessed Emperor preserve us!'

'The Emperor is with us,' Volt told her, his voice trembling with conviction. 'His sacred light shields us, and he has set his Wolves to watch over us. Be strong, Gabriella of Belisarius,' he said, and laid a hand gently on her arm. 'What can you tell us of the ritual our foe is planning?'

'Planning?' Gabriella said. 'No, not planning, *performing*. It has been going on for some time. I can hear their voices in my head, whispering terrible things. Whatever the ritual portends, it is nearing its culmination.'

Volt squeezed her arm compassionately and glanced at Ragnar. 'It is worse than I feared,' he said quietly, but it was unclear if he was speaking about the ritual or the effect it was having on Gabriella. 'There isn't much time left.'

Ragnar nodded gravely. 'Lady, we need to get moving,' he said, as gently as he could. 'Can you walk? One of us can carry you if need be–'

'I can walk,' Gabriella said forcefully, though the strain of what she was feeling was painfully apparent in her eyes. 'I can do whatever I must.'

'Then rest for a few moments more,' Ragnar replied, and turned to Volt. 'Do you have any idea where we are?'

Volt closed his book of devotions and nodded, surveying the dark plain that surrounded them. 'We're about a hundred kilometres due south of the capital,' he said, and then pointed to the roadway. 'This is one of the main transit routes linking the southern agri-combines. It leads right into the heart of the city.'

Ragnar scowled at the news. Time was of the essence. The Space Wolves could cover a hundred kilometres in less than seven hours at a forced march, but there was no way that Gabriella, Volt or the bondsmen would be able to manage such a pace. 'The roadway is too exposed,' he said to the inquisitor. 'The enemy fighters have gone for now, but I expect that something will arrive to search the wreckage before much longer.'

Volt nodded. 'I fear you're right.' He put away his book and then gestured to the north, where the grey stripe of the roadway bisected a dark green band that stretched across the horizon. 'We'll head for that agri-combine. It's much smaller than most, but the crops will give us some cover for at least twenty kilometres.'

Ragnar shook his head, bemused. 'What does a shadow world deep within the Eye of Terror need with crops and agri-combines?'

'It's the law of correspondence,' Volt said. 'The shadow world has to be an exact geographical copy of Charys for the co-location to work.'

'All right,' Ragnar said. 'What about the mountain range beyond the combine? If we follow it instead of the roadway, how close will it take us to the city?'

Volt pursed his lips thoughtfully. 'We could follow them to within ten kilometres of the city's south-west districts,' he said, 'but it would be rough going.'

Ragnar nodded. 'Then that's what we'll have to do.'

'What's this?'

Ragnar and Volt looked up at the sound of Harald's voice. The pack leader had arrived with his three Blood Claws and the surviving Thunderhawk crew in tow. Two of the warriors carried the heavy bolters stripped from the assault ship on improvised shoulder slings. The techpriest and the assault ship's gunners were carrying stubby lascarbines in their hands and had bulky survival packs on their shoulders.

Harald glared down at Ragnar. 'You're not in command here, exile,' the pack leader said. 'No one's taking orders from you.'

A shadow fell across Harald as Haegr leaned forward, his hands tightening around the haft of his hammer. 'Shall I thrash some sense into this pup, brother?' he asked.

Harald bristled at the threat. 'I'd like to see you try,' he said, baring his fangs.

'That's enough,' Volt snapped, rising to his feet between the two warriors. The Wolves stood head and shoulders above the old man, but the inquisitor's tone was hard and unyielding. 'Ragnar isn't in command of this expedition, but *I* am, and we're heading for the agri-combine. Harald, assemble your men. I want two of your Wolves on point and one covering each flank, understood?'

The pack leader stared down at Volt for a long moment, and Ragnar thought for an instant that Harald was going to challenge the inquisitor. Then, just as suddenly, he nodded an acknowledgement and began calling out orders to his men.

Volt began to gather up his gear without comment, as though nothing had happened. Haegr held out a hand to Gabriella and helped the Navigator to her feet. Torin appeared quietly out of the gloom. Only Ragnar noticed the older Wolfblade sliding his pistol back into its holster. The two warriors shared apprehensive looks.

'Not a good beginning,' Torin said softly, as the band prepared to move out. 'Harald's only barely holding it together.'

Ragnar glanced thoughtfully to the north. 'Aren't we all,' he replied.

FOURTEEN
The Lost

DISTANCES WERE DECEIVING on the vast, dark plains of the shadow world. When they'd set out from the crash site, Ragnar had reckoned they were only a few dozen kilometres from the edge of the agri-combine, but an hour later they still seemed no closer to their objective. The Space Wolves loped along at a tireless, ground-eating pace, their eyes restlessly scanning the horizon for signs of enemy activity. The bondsmen, accustomed as they were to the physical regimens of the Fang, kept up the pace without complaint. Inquisitor Volt and Lady Gabriella did the same, but Ragnar could tell that they were beginning to tire. Their scents were bitter, laced with crippling fatigue poisons. Gabriella in particular was suffering greatly after the difficulty of the warp transit, yet she held her head high and never slowed. Ragnar followed along in her wake, waiting for her to ask for help or to catch her up in case she should stumble.

He could hear the labouring beats of her heart, drumming a desperate counterpoint to the rhythmic cadence of her feet. When he breathed, he could taste the warmth of her skin and feel the heat of her blood on the tip of his tongue. Since he'd set foot on the shadow world his senses had become incredibly sharp. An almost electrical charge galvanised his blood and banished the weariness from his limbs. It felt as though he could run forever under this starless sky, pacing along in

Gabriella's wake and listening to the beat of her heart, waiting for her to stumble.

The surge of pure, soulless *hunger* that gripped him nearly took Ragnar's breath away. For a fleeting instant he could imagine her throat within his jaws and taste the hot rush of her blood. He staggered, bile rising in his throat, and fell out of step with his brothers.

The rest of the pack loped past Ragnar, all except for Torin, who slowed his pace and came up alongside the young Space Wolf. The older Wolfblade's expression was full of concern, but Ragnar waved him away with a savage sweep of his hand. 'Keep your distance brother,' he said hoarsely. 'I... am not myself.'

'I know, brother,' Torin replied quietly. 'I can smell it. Your scent is changing as the Wulfen grows in strength.'

'Russ preserve me,' Ragnar said, his hearts clenching in horror. He looked out across the featureless plain and for a fleeting instant he was tempted to run as fast and as far from his brethren as he could. 'I can't believe Harald or the others haven't noticed.'

'The reason is simple,' Torin replied, his voice grim. 'They can't tell the difference because it's happening to all of us.'

Ragnar scowled at Torin, thinking for a moment that he was being mocked, but then he saw the look in the older Wolfblade's eyes. Behind the concern there was a cold, desperate glint, hinting at the inner struggle going on inside the warrior. Ragnar suddenly noticed the tension gripping Torin's lean frame and caught the older Wolf's scent. There was a musky undercurrent that immediately set the young Space Wolf's teeth on edge. Instead of his battle-brother, Ragnar saw only another predator and a potential rival.

The sudden realisation struck Ragnar like a physical blow. He reeled away from Torin, his lips pulling back in a feral snarl.

Before he could react further, Torin's voice pulled Ragnar back from the brink. 'Peace, brother!' he said quickly, stepping forward and gripping Ragnar's wrist. 'Master yourself, or all of us are lost.'

Ragnar clenched his jaws and fought against the beast that threatened to suborn him. He focused on Torin's unwavering gaze and the steadying grip of his hand, and after a moment the fire in his blood subsided. When he could speak again he asked, 'How can this be, Torin? How is this possible?'

The older Wolfblade could only shake his head helplessly. 'I do not know,' he said. 'I've sensed the changes ever since we landed here. Even Haegr is being affected to some degree.' Torin grinned fleetingly. 'If we're not careful he might try to eat us all.'

The attempt at humour was lost on Ragnar. 'I've never heard of so many Wolves succumbing at once,' he said.

'Nor I,' Torin replied. 'At first I thought that the planet was affecting us – we are somewhere in the Eye of Terror, after all – but you were feeling the curse when we were still on Fenris.' The older warrior's shoulders slumped. 'I should have seen it then and brought it to Ranek's attention, but you can be so damned melancholy sometimes.' He sighed. 'Forgive me brother. I failed you.'

Ragnar shook his head ruefully. 'This is no fault of yours, Torin. You told me to speak to Sigurd aboard the *Fist of Russ*, but I was too stiff-necked to seek him out when I had the chance.' A thought occurred to the young Space Wolf. 'Could it be me?' he asked. 'Could I somehow be affecting the rest of you?'

Torin's brows knitted thoughtfully. 'Honestly, I don't know. I've never heard of such a thing, but who knows? Perhaps that's why the priests cull the Wulfen from the companies and isolate them.' After a few more moments' thought, he shook his head. 'No, if that was true then Haegr and I would have been affected ere now. Something else is causing this.'

Ragnar thought it over, and was forced to nod in agreement. 'That's a pity,' he said grimly. 'If I thought I could stop this by putting a bolt pistol to my head I would do it.'

'Don't be stupid,' Torin snapped.

'You wouldn't say that if you felt the same way I do,' Ragnar said. 'I'm becoming a danger to Gabriella, Torin. The thoughts that are going through my head...'

'I can guess,' the older Wolfblade replied. 'Don't worry, brother. I won't let you harm her. You have my oath upon it.' He sighed. 'Honestly, it's the younger ones I'm worried about. Harald and his packmates don't have the experience we have. They could succumb to the Wulfen and never know it until it was too late.'

Ragnar nodded gravely. 'I hear you, Torin. We can only pray to the Allfather that our oaths will sustain us long enough to deal with Madox and his infernal master. After that...' he shrugged.

'Aye,' Torin said. 'The rest is up to the Fates.'

The two Wolfblades had fallen several dozen metres behind the rest of the group. Ragnar nodded to Torin, and they began to pick up the pace. As they did so, Ragnar caught a hint of motion out of the corner of his eye. With a flash of irritation and a shake of his head he dismissed the phantom image, until he saw it again, streaking across the starless sky from the east.

'Hostile aircraft,' Ragnar bellowed. 'Take cover!'

The Chaos fighters howled across the plain less than fifty metres above the deck, opening fire the moment the Space Wolves began to scatter. Streams of green energy bolts raked along the dark ground and left melted craters in the surface of the roadway. The Space Marines reacted with blurring speed and years of experience and training, seeming to dance effortlessly among the streams of fire. One of the bondsmen wasn't so lucky, however. Two bolts took him high on the chest and shoulder, blowing the gunner apart.

Ragnar caught a glimpse of Haegr pushing Gabriella and Volt to the ground and placing his considerable bulk between them and the attacking ships. The two enemy fighters streaked overhead and split up, arrowing skyward on pillars of ghostly fire. An arc of red tracers fanned the air behind the southerly fighter as one of Harald's Blood Claws opened fire with his salvaged heavy bolter. The Chaos ship made a tight roll, avoiding the explosive shells, and disappeared into the darkness.

'Move, move!' Ragnar yelled, rising to his feet. The dark green border of the agri-combine appeared to be only a few hundred metres away. It wasn't much, but it was the only cover he could see for kilometres. 'Run for the fields! Go! Haegr, get Gabriella moving.'

The Blood Claws started moving at once, heavy bolters sweeping from horizon to horizon in smooth, controlled arcs. Haegr lifted Gabriella bodily to her feet, and then Volt as well, sending both running full-tilt down the roadway with the surviving bondsmen close behind. Torin fell into step beside Ragnar. 'Scout flight, you reckon?' he asked.

'Scouts or escorts,' Ragnar said, searching the sky. 'We'll know for sure in the next few minutes.'

The Chaos fighters made their second pass from the north-east, appearing without warning over the fields ahead. As bolts of energy tore through the pack of Wolves, Harald's gunners stopped in their tracks and filled the air with tracer fire. A burst of shells stitched a line of small explosions along the length of one of the attack craft. It roared overhead, trailing a ribbon of smoke and flame, and then went into an uncontrolled spin and crashed into the earth half a kilometre away.

Las-bolts chased vainly after the second fighter as the bondsmen vented their rage at the enemy ships. Ragnar gripped his bolt pistol and was tempted to loose a few pointless rounds, just for spite's sake. One of the Blood Claws was reeling, clutching at the melted stump of his left arm and cursing at the sky.

Ahead, Harald and his packmates had come to a halt before a knee-high barrier of pale metal that marked the outer boundary of the combine. Volt and Gabriella stood in their midst, staring motionless at the rustling fields beyond.

Ragnar charged past the smoking heavy bolters and made straight for Gabriella. He could almost feel the second fighter rolling in for a third pass, straight down the roadway behind them. 'What in the All-father's name are you waiting for?' he snarled. 'We've got to get under cover–'

Gabriella turned to him, and the look of horror on her face stopped Ragnar in his tracks.

A dry, whispering sound rose from the dark fields as the vast fields of the agri-combine rustled in the wind. Except, Ragnar suddenly realised, there was no breeze blowing against his face.

The tall, dark green stalks ordered in neat ranks beyond the barrier looked like gene-crafted corn at first glance. Long, drooping leaves, dozens of them on each stalk, trembled and whispered against one another, as though fearful of the Space Marines' presence.

Lightning split the sky to the east, painting the glossy leaves in pale, green light. Each leaf bore a human face, distorted into a mask of terror and pain. As Ragnar watched, the lips of each face moved in a silent scream or a plea for release.

'Blessed Russ!' Ragnar hissed. 'What in the Allfather's name is this?'

'A harvest of damnation,' Volt said gravely. 'These are the sacrifices that made this dark world possible. Field after field of them, stretching for thousands of kilometres all across the planet.'

'We have to burn them,' Harald said hoarsely. 'Our flamers–'

'Our flamers are not enough,' Ragnar said, 'and right now we need them.'

Then the heavy bolters began to roar again, and streaks of ghostly fire hissed past the stricken Blood Claws. Ragnar whirled and saw a stream of green bolts marching up the roadway towards him. 'Into the field!' he roared. 'Now!'

Raising his bolt pistol, Ragnar began walking towards the oncoming fighter, aiming and firing one shot after another as the Blood Claws began to scramble over the barrier. If the enemy fighter pilot wanted a target, he was going to give it one.

The attack ship was low and level, just a few dozen metres above the roadway. It plunged through a web of tracer fire, its cannons blazing. The two Space Wolf gunners blazed away at the Chaos ship just ahead of Ragnar. One of the Blood Claws was struck full in the chest by one of the energy bolts, blowing a hole the size of Ragnar's fist clean through the young warrior. The gunner staggered, and then sank to one knee, but the Blood Claw kept firing.

A volley of bolts filled the air around Ragnar. One glanced off his left pauldron and burned a molten furrow through the ceramite plate. The blow knocked the young Space Wolf back a step, but he continued to fire until his pistol's magazine was empty.

'Ragnar! Get back here!' Torin called from the combine's metal barrier.

The mortally wounded Blood Claw toppled forward, his hand still closed around the firing lever of his heavy bolter. Hits were beginning to register across the hull of the oncoming fighter however, as the surviving gunner found the range. Howling his defiance, the gunner stepped into the middle of the roadway, right into the attack ship's path.

Ragnar glanced back at the barrier. Torin was there, beckoning with his blade. 'Come on!' he shouted over the hammering blasts of the heavy bolter.

Explosive shells burst in staccato flashes across the nose and glowing viewports of the Chaos ship. Suddenly there was a larger blast farther aft, and the attack craft was haloed in a nimbus of burning gas and electrical discharges. The ship seemed to stagger in midair, and then plummeted like a thunderbolt towards Ragnar and the Blood Claw gunner.

Ragnar saw the danger at once, but the gunner continued to fire at the diving craft. 'Run!' the young Space Wolf yelled at the Blood Claw, but the gunner didn't seem to hear. He was still firing, the barrel of his heavy bolter glowing red with heat, when the fighter smashed into the roadway and crushed him beneath its skidding, tumbling bulk.

Cursing, Ragnar spun on his heel and raced for the combine's metal barrier as quickly as he could. He could hear the grinding, crashing screech of the attack ship disintegrating along the roadway behind him, growing closer with every passing second. At the last moment, Ragnar gathered his strength and leapt for the barrier. Something hard and unyielding smashed into his back the moment his feet left the ground, cracking his backpack and hurling him through the air. Tumbling, he struck the dark earth hard and rolled for several metres, flattening the morbid stalks, and digging furrows into the ground.

The attack ship spent the last of its energy against the combine's metal barrier, scattering steaming debris across the dreadful field. Twisted hunks of red-hot metal landed all around Ragnar, the pieces hissing against the dark ground. Within moments, Torin was at his side, all but dragging the young Space Wolf to his feet. 'I saw more thrusters burning off to the south,' Torin said. 'They're coming this way. Looks like those two were escorts after all.'

Ragnar climbed to his feet. His hands seemed to move of their own accord, dropping the empty bolt pistol magazine and slapping in a fresh one. 'Where's Gabriella?'

'Somewhere in this cursed field,' Torin replied, glancing warily to the south. 'She's with Haegr and Volt. The inquisitor told everyone to make for the buildings to the north.'

The young Space Wolf scowled at the news. 'We can't afford to get hemmed into a static defence,' he said. 'We've got to stay on the move or we'll be overwhelmed.'

'Tell that to Volt,' Torin said ruefully.

'First things first,' the young Space Wolf replied, breathing deeply of the dry, musty air. He tasted Gabriella's scent and felt his pulse quicken. 'Let's go find them.'

The two warriors dashed deeper into the sacrificial field, forcing their way down narrow rows carved between the dark green furrows. Slick, waxy leaves slithered against the plates of their armour and across their faces. When they brushed against his ears Ragnar thought he could hear the plaintive whispers of the souls trapped within.

He focused instead on the sounds of pounding feet echoing from the field in a wide arc ahead of him. It sounded like the Blood Claws had fanned out, or perhaps they had simply been separated by the field's endless, identical rows. Ragnar keyed his vox-bead and his ears were filled with a harsh, atonal sound, rising and falling like the howl of a demented wolf. He called to Haegr or Volt, but got no reply. He gave up after a few tries and concentrated instead on loping after the Navigator's scent.

Ragnar heard the approaching ships before he saw them, a rising crescendo of shrieking thrusters coming in low from the south. A dark shape roared overhead. Ragnar glanced up at a black, angular hull that glistened like polished iron and was studded with rows of curved spikes and jagged blades. Open portals gaped like mouths along the underside of the ship, and the young Space Wolf saw armoured, red-eyed figures crouching at their rims.

The assault ships thundered past Ragnar in a staggered line four abreast, riding boiling plumes of smoke and steam. More than a score of dark shapes leapt from the speeding craft, falling like stormhawks on shrieking pillars of superheated air. Ragnar saw at once that they were Chaos Space Marines, but their desecrated suits of power armour were fitted with bulbous, turbine-driven backpacks. They carried ornate bolt pistols and chainswords in their hands, and long trophy cords strung with human scalps hung heavily at their waists. The young Space Wolf recognised them with a surge of frozen dread: Chaos Raptors, the shock troops and flesh hunters of the Traitor Legions. They plunged like arrows into the field around the running Wolves, filling the air with their bloodcurdling shrieks.

Angry howls and the crack of bolt pistols echoed among the shifting stalks as the Raptors closed in from all sides. Ragnar howled a challenge of his own and drew his frost blade from its scabbard. Just as the rune-marked blade whirred into deadly life a dark shape burst into the narrow row ahead of the young Space Wolf. The Raptor spun on his heel, his trophy lines fanning out in a dreadful display as he brought his weapons to bear.

The Raptor's bolt pistol boomed and a mass-reactive shell flattened against Ragnar's breastplate. Snarling, the young Space Wolf broke into a full run, snapping shots at the foe as he came. The bolt pistol shells rang harmlessly off the Raptor's armour, and an answering shot ricocheted from the side of Ragnar's knee. With a fierce shout, Ragnar raised his sword and slashed at the Raptor's neck, but the Chaos warrior was a blur of motion, parrying the stroke with a sweep of its chainsword. Sparks flew from the clash of blades, but the attack was only a feint. Ragnar took another step forward, put his bolt pistol against the Raptor's left eye and pulled the trigger. The heavy shell burst the helmet apart, and Ragnar leapt over the foe's collapsing form.

Sounds of confused fighting echoed all around Ragnar as he tried to focus on Gabriella's scent. Las-bolts hissed through the air, and stray bolt-rounds carved paths through the dense rows of sacrificial stalks. Off to Ragnar's right, a man screamed in agony and a volley of wild las-bolts tore through the air. Bolter rounds rang off armour to the young Space Wolf's left, and then came the unmistakeable sound of a chain-blade rending flesh.

Gabriella's scent was growing stronger. She was close by, and Ragnar's pulse quickened when he realised that her trail led into the midst of a fierce battle that was raging just ahead. He was so intent on the sounds of battle that he didn't see the Raptor coming, until it leapt at him through a screen of rustling stalks to his right.

A chainsword roared through the air, slicing through the tall, green plants and scraping against Ragnar's right pauldron. The blade's whirring teeth sliced open the skin along his jaw, cutting the young Space Wolf to the bone. He whirled, bringing up his frost blade, but the Raptor blocked it with its snarling blade and raised his bolt pistol for a shot at Ragnar's unprotected neck. But before either Wolf or Raptor could react, a slim blade was buried deep in the attacker's neck. The Chaos warrior collapsed in a flood of steaming ichor as Torin pulled his sword free.

There was a sound like a thunderclap a few dozen metres ahead, and a bellow like that of an enraged bear. 'That would be Haegr,' Torin said with a grin. Ragnar nodded curtly and broke back into a run.

Within moments, they found themselves at the edge of a trampled clearing of sorts, where blades, bodies and tramping feet had flattened a rough circle within the blasphemous field. Gabriella, Volt, and Haegr stood back to back in the centre of the clearing, shooting and swinging at the pack of Raptors that encircled them. Bodies lay everywhere. Half a dozen armoured Chaos warriors were sprawled across the dark earth, close to the broken bodies of two of the Thunderhawk's gunners and Harald's one-armed Blood Claw. At the far end of the clearing the Thunderhawk's tech-priest was on his knees, choking for breath as he pressed red-stained hands to his torn throat. Haegr was trying to reach the mortally wounded bondsman, keeping the Raptors at bay with mighty sweeps of his thunder hammer.

Inquisitor Volt levelled his bolt pistol at one of the Raptors and fired. The shell took the armoured warrior square in the chest, and powerful blessings worked into the ammunition punched right through the armoured breastplate and consumed the man inside in a sheet of silvery flames. The inquisitor's armour burned bright with the glowing tracery of potent wards, and his unsheathed sword glimmered with pale blue lightning, similar to a Rune Priest's blade. A Raptor's gun barked, and a slug smashed into Volt's shoulder, knocking the old man off his feet. Three of the Chaos warriors rushed forward, leaping high on jets of shrieking air and plunging like falcons upon their prey.

To Ragnar's horror, Lady Gabriella rushed to protect the fallen inquisitor. She levelled a sleek-looking silver pistol at the lead Raptor and fired an indigo-coloured beam that burned a glowing hole clean through the armoured foe. The warrior collapsed with a screech, but before his companions could react, the Navigator slashed at them with a sweeping stroke of her sabre. The master crafted power blade glimmered like white-hot steel as it sliced through the legs of one Raptor and cut the thigh of the other. The wounded Raptor let out a sharp hiss and staggered backwards, shooting Gabriella twice in the chest. She pitched backwards and fell without a sound.

Ragnar charged into the clearing with a wild howl, sword ready and bolt pistol blazing. Two Raptors toppled, their throats blown apart by mass-reactive shells, and another had its chest split open by a stroke from the young Space Wolf's blade. Torin followed in Ragnar's wake, snapping off precise, deadly shots at the foemen near Gabriella's prone form.

Two Raptors spun around at the Wolves' sudden assault and slashed at Ragnar. The young Space Wolf took their raking blows against his battle worn armour, and struck off their heads with a single sweep of his sword. He stepped past their collapsing bodies and buried his sword into the side of another onrushing Chaos warrior. The Raptor's sword raked at the side of the young Space Wolf's face and cut deep into his neck before his lifeless form sank to the ground. Ragnar hurled the Raptor's body away, and with two more steps he reached the Navigator's side.

His enhanced senses told him at once that she was still alive; he could hear her heartbeat hammering in her chest. She sat up with a grimace, letting go of her sword and pressing her hand to the two slugs that had flattened themselves against her breastplate. 'I'm all right,' she said breathlessly. 'Help me up.'

Taking her at her word, Ragnar lifted Gabriella to her feet, while Torin helped Inquisitor Volt. Haegr whirled around, raising his stained hammer, and then his beady eyes widened as he recognised his brothers. 'Torin! Ragnar! Where the devil have you two been? I've been fighting the whole damned horde single-handed!'

'Never mind that now,' Ragnar snarled. 'How much farther to the buildings at the centre of the combine?'

Haegr straightened, peering over the tops of the sacrificial plants. 'Three hundred metres or so,' he said. A stray bolt-round whickered past the Wolf's shaggy head, causing him to duck down again.

'Let's go,' Ragnar said. 'I'm on point. Torin on the left, Haegr on the right. Lady Gabriella, Inquisitor Volt, you're in the middle. Now move!'

They set off once more down the narrow lanes between the sacrificial stalks, weapons held ready. The fighting seemed to be tapering off, and howls echoing back and forth from the fields ahead told Ragnar that at least some of Harald's pack still lived. As they ran across the remainder of the field, they stumbled over more trampled scenes of carnage, strewn with blood and scorched earth from the Raptor's jets.

Ragnar and his companions came upon Harald and his warriors all at once, nearly falling over them as they crouched behind a metal barrier at the north end of the field. The pack leader was studying the complex of darkened buildings ahead. Lightning flickered, banishing the shadows around the structures for a tantalising instant.

Harald shook his head. 'Gunther thought he saw movement behind one of those buildings, but with all the lightning it's hard to be sure.'

'Well, we can't stay out here,' Volt said hoarsely. 'We need to get somewhere defensible before those ships come back again.'

'No, we need to keep moving,' Ragnar said flatly. 'If we hole up in these buildings the enemy will surround us and wear us down. Time and numbers are on their side.'

'We agree on that much at least,' Harald growled.

The old inquisitor studied the buildings almost wistfully. Ragnar sensed that the man was exhausted, and Gabriella was not in much better shape, but Volt finally nodded. 'All right, we stay on the move,' he said, and then pointed at the buildings. 'We'll cross the compound and disappear into the field on the other side. That's the most direct route to the mountains north of us.'

Ragnar and Harald exchanged glances and rose to their feet as one. Weapons sweeping the open ground beyond the barrier, the Space Wolves emerged warily from the field. Lightning glittered across the surface of their ice-blue armour and on the whirring teeth of their chainblades.

The buildings were low, ferrocrete bunkers, most of them built to house the agri-servitors that tended the fields, plus a generator station and a logic hub. Four tall granaries towered from the centre of the compound, rising more than forty metres into the air. There were no lights, nor were there doors set in the buildings' doorframes or glass panels in the windows. Evidently, the structures alone were enough to make Madox's geomancy possible.

Ragnar surveyed the battered group that emerged from the depths of the sacrificial field. None of the Thunderhawk's gunners or its techpriest had survived, and three of Harald's pack were gone. Counting Volt, Gabriella and the Wolfblade, there were only twelve souls left against the might of an entire Traitor Legion.

It will be enough, Ragnar thought grimly. It will have to be enough.

They moved quickly and quietly down dark lanes between the empty structures. Ragnar felt his hackles rise as he watched the open doorways for signs of movement. The lightning played tricks on his eyes, hinting at movement down the dark side-streets.

Within a few minutes they had reached the foot of the towering granaries, and the lanes widened to a large ferrocrete plaza, where the agri-servitors could load and unload grain from the huge silos. Moving cautiously, the Wolves advanced across the open space.

Their boots echoed hollowly across the ferrocrete as they stepped into the midst of the towering granaries. Lightning flashed silently overhead. On impulse, Ragnar looked up at the arcs of unearthly light, and saw the silhouettes of horned helms and hulking shoulders ringing the tops of the four silos. 'Ambush!' he cried, raising his bolt pistol, but it was already too late.

The Raptors leapt from their perches atop the silos and dropped heavily among the surprised Wolves. Ragnar guessed that there were perhaps a score of them, attacking the group from all sides. They had been the true threat all along, he realised. The Raptors dropped into the field had been like hounds, driving the prey into the trap.

One of the attackers landed next to Gabriella, but was struck by Torin, Haegr and the Navigator almost simultaneously. Ragnar sighted on another Raptor a few metres away and shot the warrior through the neck. Then a pair of attackers rushed at him from the left, firing as they came. One shot smashed into his hip and another took him high in the shoulder, flattening against his armour, but nearly knocking him from his feet.

The sounds of fighting and the cries of wounded Wolves echoed from all sides. Ragnar howled a challenge at the oncoming Raptors and prepared to die like a son of Fenris.

He shot the first warrior between his red eyes, and then parried the sweeping stroke of the second foeman. The Raptor reversed its stroke in a blur of motion and slashed downwards at Ragnar's knee. The snarling chainsword found a gap in his armour and bit deep, grating across the bone. The young Space Wolf snarled and hacked downwards, slicing off the foeman's sword-hand at the wrist.

Then there was a flash of light, and a terrible, burning impact smashed into the side of Ragnar's head just above the temple. He heard a roaring sound in his ears, like a howling wind or the pounding of a stormy surf, and then he realised he was falling.

Ragnar landed face down on the ground, blood pouring from the wound in his head. Sounds of fighting raged above him. There was a crack of thunder and a shouted oath, and then the roaring filled his ears once again.

No, not roaring, howling, like a huge pack of Fenrisian wolves on the hunt.

The sound set Ragnar's blood hissing in his veins. He struggled to get his legs underneath him so that he could stand. He blinked, discovering that he could no longer see out of his left eye.

Something heavy fell on top of him. With a slurred curse, he shoved at the thing, grasping dimly that it was the riven corpse of a Raptor. Ragnar rolled awkwardly away from the thing and found himself lying on his back.

A dark silhouette loomed over him. Teeth bared, Ragnar tried to raise his sword, but the figure laid an armoured boot across his wrist and pinned it to the ground. The young Space Wolf raised his bolt pistol, only to find that his gun hand was empty.

The howling continued all around him. Lightning flashed, and in the flickering light Ragnar saw that the figure above him was cased in dark grey power armour similar to his own. Yellowed skulls and leather cords strung with long, curved fangs hung from the warrior's belt, as well as ancient tokens of iron etched with the runes of his people. A red wolf's head snarled fiercely upon the warrior's scarred right pauldron.

The warrior was huge, easily as large as Haegr. His broad shoulders were covered in a black wolf pelt, and his iron grey hair hung in two thick braids that draped heavily across his rune worked breastplate. His shaggy beard was still black as jet, however, and the eyes that shone beneath the warrior's craggy brow were yellow gold, like those of a wolf. In one hand he gripped a mighty, single-bearded axe, its curved blade marked with the scars of countless grim battles. Fell runes were carved into the dark metal, and it crackled with unseen and deadly energies.

When the figure spoke, his voice was cold and hard as the glaciers of Fenris, full of power and old beyond reckoning. To the young Space Wolf it sounded like the voice of a god.

'You must be Ragnar Blackmane,' the warrior said. 'We've been looking for you.'

FIFTEEN
The Company of Wolves

A BATTLE CANNON shell howled high overhead. The rebel tank gunner had been overeager and had fired too early, missing the fleeing Imperial troops by hundreds of metres. Grenadiers shouted and screamed at one another as they ran pell-mell down the debris choked causeway. Tracer fire from heavy stubbers and volleys of lasgun fire raked through the retreating soldiers. Men writhed, clutching at their wounds, or fell lifelessly to the ground.

Panicked grenadiers flowed in a dark tide around the impassive figures of Mikal Sternmark and his four Wolf Guard. The presence of the armoured giants was the only thing keeping the Imperial retreat from becoming a total rout. The Wolves moved at a stolid, measured pace, facing back the way they'd come and cutting down rebel squads that pressed too close.

'Haakon!' Sternmark called, levelling Redclaw at the rebel tank nosing its way among the squads of enemy troops a hundred metres behind them. The Terminator to Sternmark's right stopped in his tracks, raising the targeting module in his hand, finding the range to the target, and then loosing one of his few remaining Cyclone missiles. The antitank round streaked down the causeway with a hissing, spitting roar and detonated against the front of the battle tank's turret. Concussion and shrapnel scythed through the infantry surrounding the tank, and the Leman Russ lurched to a sudden halt. A good shot, but

Sternmark couldn't be certain whether it had knocked the tank out or not.

They had held the barricade beneath the towering angel for much of the day, throwing back no less than ten bloody assaults before they had been forced to withdraw under a storm of tank and artillery fire. By pure, evil chance a shell had struck the defiant angel at the start of the last barrage, blowing it apart and showering debris on the weary defenders below. Superstitious to a fault, the beleaguered grenadiers had taken it as an omen.

Surrounded by hundreds of their dead comrades and facing an apparently inexhaustible tide of enemy troops, the surviving regimental officers ordered a general retreat just as the rebels renewed their attack. Sternmark watched helplessly as the first squads began to stream away from the ruined barricade, but he knew from experience that there was no rallying the broken troops now that the withdrawal had begun. Instead, he formed the battered platoons around him into a rearguard, and sent Sven's pack racing down the causeway as fast as they could to form a second line of defence ahead of the retreating Guardsmen. He'd had no contact with the young Grey Hunter since. Sternmark could only pray to Russ that Sven had been successful. They were less than a kilometre from the edge of the city. If the rebel troops made it into the open terrain beyond the city there would be no stopping them from reaching the star port.

Sternmark caught sight of a rebel lascannon team struggling to haul their weapon into firing position, and cut them down with a burst from his storm bolter. The rebels responded with a hail of wild lasgun fire that burst across Sternmark's Terminator armour and pitted the ferrocrete roadway. The Wolf Guard ignored the flickering barrage, casting a quick glance over his shoulder to gauge the terrain along their path of retreat. Sternmark caught sight of a massive pile of rubble a hundred metres or so away. A building had collapsed onto the causeway, laying a natural barricade almost two-thirds of the way across the road. Armoured figures peered over the top of the debris pile, awaiting the approach of the rebel troops. They'd reached the second line of defence.

Mikal keyed his vox-unit. A shrill squeal of static filled his ears. The rebels had been trying to jam the Imperial vox-net since morning. 'We're holding here!' he called. 'Fall back and take position behind the debris pile!'

The Terminators raised their swords or power fists to show they'd received the order as they continued to fire at the advancing rebel troops. The first grenadiers were already swarming over the rubble or running around the far end of the pile. Sternmark fired another burst at the traitors and turned to run for the barrier. His mind worked furiously as he studied the terrain and tried to work out the best way to organise its defence. He could put his Wolves along the rubble pile to keep the infantry at bay and keep the grenadiers behind the barricade, out of the line of fire but ready to hit the flank of any attackers trying to force their way around the far end.

There was a loud boom and a battle cannon shell crashed against the debris pile, blowing a deep crater in the jumble of ferrocrete and steel. The Leman Russ was back in action, its treads clanking as it resumed its advance. Sternmark grimaced at the sting of shrapnel along the side of his face, and clambered up the jumbled slope of stone blocks and twisted girders. As he reached the summit, the Leman Russ fired again, blasting another crater in the barrier and showering him with a rain of dirt and stone.

Sternmark leapt over the summit and skidded down the other side until he was out of the line of fire. He found Sven and the two remaining members of his pack crouching behind the largest pieces of stonework they could find. The young Grey Hunter had acquired a Guard-issue meltagun at some point, and Sternmark was startled to see the two warriors beside Sven carrying hellguns instead of their blessed bolters.

'Where are your weapons?' the Wolf Guard snapped.

Sven shifted position to show his bolter stowed in its travel clip beside his suit's backpack. 'Ran out of ammunition hours ago,' he said.

'Why in Russ's name didn't you report it?'

The Grey Hunter looked bewildered. 'I did, lord,' Sven said, 'back at the barricade, just before the eighth bloody wave hit! Don't you remember?'

Sternmark shook his head angrily. The truth was that he couldn't recall. Everything seemed to be blurring together in his mind, dissolving into a jumble of half-formed images. The red tide in the back of his mind washed everything else away.

'Never mind!' the Wolf Guard snarled, turning away angrily to survey the state of the barrier's defences. He hoped to find at least a few hundred grenadiers and some heavy weapons dug into positions angling away from the barrier. With enough troops and a little luck, he thought, they could hold until nightfall, long enough to get some more ammunition sent up.

The only Guardsmen he saw, however, were the members of his rearguard, still retreating farther down the causeway. Sven and his two battle-brothers were alone on the barricade.

Shock and anger played across Sternmark's bloodstained face. 'Where are they?' he asked Sven. 'Where are the grenadiers? I ordered you to form a second line—'

Another explosion cut Sternmark off, raining more debris down on the beleaguered Wolves. 'We tried to form a line here,' Sven shouted back, 'but the regimental commander received orders from his superior to fall back to the star port.'

'The star port?' Mikal said incredulously. As he spoke, his four bodyguards appeared around the end of the barrier, still firing at the oncoming troops. Heavy stubber fire from the advancing tank rang off their armoured breastplates, scattering glowing red tracers in all directions. Sternmark waved his warriors back around the end of the barricade and out of the line of fire. Then he skidded to the bottom of the debris pile and keyed his vox-unit once more. 'Citadel, this is Asgard!' he shouted into the pickup. 'Citadel, this is Asgard! Do you read me?'

Sternmark strained to hear a response over the screech of the rebel jamming signals. Several seconds passed before he heard a faint reply.

'Asgard? Where have you been?' Athelstane asked angrily. 'We've been calling you for the past three hours.'

The Wolf Guard ignored the question. 'Why did you order the grenadiers back to the star port?' he shouted. 'We can't hold the causeway without them.'

'The causeway is already lost,' Athelstane shot back. 'The rebels broke through our lines four kilometres east of your position and have split our forces in two. If we don't pull back to the star port now our troops in the city will be surrounded and destroyed. That includes *you*, Asgard.' It was hard to tell over the jamming, but Sternmark thought the anger in Athelstane's voice had subsided a bit. 'There are reports that Chaos Space Marines have been sighted in the city, and we've lost contact with several of your packs scattered across the planet.'

Sternmark felt his blood run cold. 'Lost contact? What do you mean?'

'I mean they aren't answering our signals, much like you,' the general replied. 'You need to get back here right away, Asgard. Things are getting out of hand.'

Cursing bitterly, Sternmark switched off the vox-unit. The rumble of the rebel tank engine and the squeal of its treads were very loud now, sounding as though it was just a few dozen metres away on the other side of the barrier. He could hear the hoarse shouts of the traitor Guardsmen and the gibbering cries of the mutants in their midst as they raced for the barrier.

Mikal checked his storm bolter. He was down to his last magazine, and it was reading half-empty. His fellow Wolf Guard stood close by, ever courageous and resolute, but he knew that they must be nearly out of ammunition as well. Nevertheless, he was tempted to remain where he was, to make a stand at the barrier and fight to the last.

If the rest of the line had held, he wouldn't have hesitated, but what would it achieve now? Sacrifice was second nature to the Adeptus Astartes, but not without good reason. A final battle here would just be a waste of good men and precious wargear.

Still the red tide rose within him, demanding release. It promised nothing save spilled blood and dead foemen, and Sternmark longed to surrender to its embrace. I am no leader of men, he thought angrily. I'm a warrior, a wolf wrought of ceramite and steel.

Atop the barrier, Sven and his battle-brothers nodded to one another, and then went into action. The three Grey Hunters moved as one. The warriors with hellguns popped up and rapid fired into the approaching traitors, while Sven took careful aim with his meltagun. There was a draconic hiss of superheated air as the assault weapon fired, and a thunderous explosion sent the rebel tank's turret spinning into the air. Screams and shouts of alarm rang from the other side of the barrier as the Grey Hunters dropped back into cover and slid down the slope to the waiting Terminators.

'That took care of the tank!' Sven said with a feral grin. 'There must be a few hundred rebels left, though. What shall we do, lord?'

Sternmark gripped Redclaw's hilt and fought against the wolf inside him. 'We retreat,' he said grimly. 'We're falling back to the star port. The battle in the city is lost.'

RAGNAR BLINKED HOT blood from his eyes and bared his teeth at the bearded giant looming above him. A chorus of lusty howls filled his ears and set his mind to reeling. He could feel the curse of the Wulfen responding to the throaty cries. 'Who in the name of Russ are you?' he growled, letting the frost blade slide from his hand.

The giant narrowed his yellow eyes. 'Who am I?' he said, his voice rough edged with menace. 'I'm Torvald the Reaver, of Red Kraken Hold, and with this axe I've slain gods and men.' He raised the fearsome weapon in his hand and showed the gleaming edge to the young Space Wolf.

Ragnar could feel challenge in the giant's voice, like a blade against his skin. His blood seethed, and the Wulfen gripped him, body and soul. This time, he didn't try to stop it.

His empty sword hand closed around Torvald's ankle and pulled with all the wild strength of the Wulfen behind it. In the same motion, Ragnar rose up and drove his other hand against the side of the giant's hip. The speed and ferocity of Ragnar's attack took the giant by surprise. His heavy cloak flaring like dark wings, Torvald fell forward onto his knees. Swift as a shadow the young Space Wolf came up behind him, grabbing a handful of the giant's hair and pulling his scarred head back to reveal the corded muscles of the Reaver's throat.

Angry howls and bestial cries shook the air. Dark shapes rushed at Ragnar from all sides, and he glimpsed huge, swift forms in gunmetal grey armour with luminous, lantern yellow eyes. Lightning flickered across the empty sky, revealing shaggy heads and blunt, toothy snouts. Long, black talons glinted as the massive wolf-men lunged for Ragnar.

The world seemed to tilt beneath the young Space Wolf as the monsters closed in around him. These were the beasts that haunted his dreams and had fought the daemons in the command bunker at Charys! He let go of Torvald and staggered backwards, struggling to think. A low, animal growl rose in his throat, and the pack of wolf-men answered, snarling and snapping their fanged jaws.

'Be still!' shouted a clear, strong voice. 'In the name of Russ and the Allfather, be still!'

The wolf-men paused, hanging their heads and sniffing the air cautiously. The voice echoed strangely in Ragnar's head. He turned around, seeking its source, and his knees buckled beneath him.

A figure in familiar power armour was striding towards him through a press of hulking wolf-men, as a lord might move among his hounds. Lightning glimmered on the warrior's golden hair and the iron wolf amulet hanging from a heavy chain around his neck.

Sigurd the Wolf Priest approached Ragnar, his crozius arcanum held high. 'Remember your oaths, Ragnar Blackmane,' he said sternly. 'Master the wolf within you and stay your hand. We are all brothers here.'

The words seemed to echo strangely, as though from a great distance. Ragnar blinked his one good eye and looked for Gabriella, but all he found was darkness.

Fiery pain bloomed in Ragnar's head, dragging him roughly back to consciousness. He snarled, shaking his head, but an armoured hand closed fiercely around his jaw and held him fast.

Blinking furiously, Ragnar opened his crusted eyelids and saw Sigurd's pale face looming above him. He was lying on his back, surrounded by crouching figures. Faces swam into focus. Torin and Haegr watched the Wolf Priest work, their expressions guarded. Gabriella's face was bleak and etched with strain.

It was Haegr's hand that gripped him. Torin leaned close. 'Hold still a moment more,' he said to Ragnar. 'He's almost done.'

There was another bright flash of pain, but this time Ragnar was able to blunt it with the mental rotes he'd learned at the Fang. He felt a trickle of blood seep down the side of his head as Sigurd leaned back and inspected the blood-stained tip of a bolt pistol round. 'You must have a head made of solid ceramite,' the Wolf Priest growled. 'Still, you're lucky the shot hit at an angle, or it would have blown your brains out.'

Torin chuckled. 'No worries there, priest. That slug would have had to rattle around in Ragnar's head like a dice before it hit anything important.'

Sigurd offered no argument, tossing the bullet aside with a frown and digging a couple of metal jars from a pack at his belt. 'The shot hit you just above the left eye,' he said as he began applying the healing balms to Ragnar's wound. 'Are you having any trouble with your vision?'

Ragnar struggled to focus his thoughts. Visions of an axe-wielding giant and snarling wolf-men loomed like ghosts in his mind. 'I had some trouble before,' he said absently, 'but that might just have been the blood. I'm fine now.'

Sigurd nodded curtly, but his expression was dubious. He pressed a wound sealant to Ragnar's forehead, and rose to his feet. 'Watch him closely,' the Wolf Priest said to Haegr and Torin. 'I expect we'll be on the move very soon.'

Grimacing, Ragnar rose to his elbows as Sigurd turned on his heel and strode away, picking his way over the broken bodies of Chaos Raptors that littered the ground between the towering granaries. He saw Harald and his pack mates a few metres away, crouching beside Inquisitor Volt, checking their weapons and speaking to one another in low voices. Hulking forms stalked silently around the edges of the open space, sniffing warily at the empty sky. Ragnar caught the scent of the wolf-men and felt his hackles rise.

Ten metres away, Torvald stood with his axe raised to the sky. Lightning flickered upon his upturned face. The giant's eyes were open, but they glimmered green, like Gabriella's pineal eye, and Torvald's face was set in an expression of grim concentration.

Ragnar struggled to make sense of the scene. 'What in Morkai's name is going on here?' he muttered.

'We've fallen into the pages of a legend,' Torin said reverently, 'one that stretches back ten thousand years.'

The young Space Wolf scowled. 'What are you talking about?'

'Don't mind him,' Haegr said. 'I haven't understood a single thing he's said since the battle ended. If I didn't know any better I'd say he took the head wound instead of you.' The burly Wolfblade surveyed the scene of carnage and shrugged. 'The Raptors ambushed us. I'm sure you remember that part. But before mighty Haegr could put them to flight, Torvald and his... warriors... raced out of the shadows and tore our foes to pieces.'

'But who are they?' Ragnar asked, still haunted by the images in his mind's eye. 'They are clearly sons of Fenris, but the armour and insignia–'

'They haven't been seen since the Heresy,' Torin said, 'not since Leman Russ descended on Prospero to wreak his vengeance on the Thousand Sons.' He shook his head in wonder. 'They're part of the Lost Company, Ragnar, the Thirteenth.'

Haegr let out a snort. 'Listen to him. He thinks he's a skald, now.'

'Perhaps I was, once upon a time,' Torin said archly. 'There's more to life than just eating and fighting, you shag-eared lummox.'

'But what are they doing here?' Ragnar interjected. 'And how did Sigurd come to be with them?'

Torin shrugged. 'You'd have to ask them, brother. Sigurd wouldn't tell us a thing, and I gather Torvald is using his powers to hide us from our foes.'

'He's a priest, too?' Ragnar asked dumbly.

'Not just a priest, Ragnar. Torvald was one of the *first* Rune Priests,' Torin replied. 'He fought alongside Russ during the Great Crusade. Imagine that!'

'And you pitched him into the dirt as if he was a bare-chinned aspirant,' Haegr said, slapping Ragnar on the shoulder. 'That was well done, little brother! He's lucky he didn't try to shake his axe in my face. I might have bitten it off and spat it at his feet!'

The young Space Wolf paid Haegr no mind, staring instead at the huge wolf-men patrolling around them. 'They're all wolf-bitten,' he said, 'even Torvald. He has the mark of the Wulfen in his eyes.'

'According to the sagas, Magnus and the Thousand Sons escaped our wrath on Prospero by retreating through a portal into the warp, but Russ wasn't about to let them escape so easily. He ordered the Thirteenth to give chase, and they disappeared into the fading portal, never to be seen again.' Torin shook his head ruefully. 'It's a wonder any of them are alive at all.'

'Ten thousand years,' Ragnar echoed, trying to make sense of all he'd heard. 'What does Torvald want of us?'

'Not Torvald, he's here at the bidding of his lord, Bulveye. Sigurd said we're to head up into the mountains to meet with Bulveye and the rest of his warband. I expect we'll learn more when we get there,' Torin said.

Ragnar met Torin's eye. 'How do we know we can trust them?' he asked.

The question surprised Torin. 'They're our brothers, Ragnar!'

'Even so, they've spent ten millennia at the mercy of the warp,' the young Space Wolf countered. 'Who can guess what their motives are now?'

Torin shifted uncomfortably. 'We'll know soon enough. Torvald and his Wulfen mean to take us into the mountains, and I don't think we have much choice in the matter.' The older Wolfblade rose abruptly to his feet. 'Besides, we're not exactly unblemished ourselves.'

Ragnar watched, bemused as Torin stalked away. Haegr shook his head and rose to lumber after his long-time friend. The young Space Wolf turned to Gabriella, a questioning look on his face. 'What did Torin mean by that?'

The Navigator looked at Ragnar for a long moment, and then reached out and lightly touched his cheek. 'It's your eyes,' she said, a weary sadness in her voice, 'they're yellow-gold now, just like Torvald's.'

AT THE SAME moment, many leagues across the shadow world, a crescendo of pain and suffering rose within the walls of the crimson temple as the energies of the great ritual approached a critical mass. A thousand sorcerers and initiates knelt on the stone floor of the cavernous hall, their hands outstretched to the altar of black stone and the bloody scraps of flesh that lay upon it. Their lips were cracked and bleeding, their throats raw and their eyes seared shut by the awful energies emitted from the burning eye that hung like a blasphemous sun above the sacrificial stone.

Hellish light fell upon Madox. He could feel the terrible favour of his primarch resting like a fiery mantle upon his shoulders. The sorcerer lord stood before the great altar, leading the intricate ritual in a cold, implacable voice. In one hand he gripped the stolen Spear of Russ, and it was through this sacred icon that Madox channelled the force of his unholy spell. It was the fulcrum upon which the ritual would act. Without it, the great spell would have been for naught.

Madox felt the minds of the lesser sorcerers in the room, each one shaping a specific part of the malediction that he would channel into the spear. The elements were slipping inexorably into place, like the workings of a vast and terrible engine. He could sense the moment approaching and his voice swelled with triumph.

The Space Wolves had carried the seeds of their own destruction from the very beginning. Very soon those seeds would bear bitter fruit.

SIXTEEN
Red Tide Rising

Torvald the Reaver drove the Wolves hard, leading them out of the dismal fields of the agri-combine and towards the slate coloured mountains to the north at a dead run. Despite his age, the Rune Priest was fleet as a deer. Ragnar and the other warriors had to push themselves in order to keep up. During the first hour the dark green fields of the combine were just a faint line on the horizon, and the empty plains were giving way to low, rounded foothills of dark stone and lifeless earth.

Inquisitor Volt and Gabriella managed to keep the pace for the first half hour, but the exertions they'd endured after the crash of the Thunderhawk quickly took their toll. The older Volt faltered first, his pace slowing and his breath coming in ragged gasps. He stumbled, on the verge of collapse, but two of Harald's Blood Claws closed in on either side of the inquisitor and slipped their arms around his waist, carrying him along just as they would a crippled pack-mate. Gabriella lasted almost half an hour longer, but the sound of her pained breathing made it clear that she'd driven herself well beyond her physical limits. Before she could falter Haegr came up behind her and scooped the Navigator up in the crook of one arm, like a father might carry a child. Gabriella hung limp in the burly Wolfblade's embrace, too exhausted to manage much in the way of protest.

The Wulfen, no less than fifteen of them, Ragnar was shocked to discover, loped along easily beside the warriors. They moved with a swift, fluid gait, clawed hands swinging and shoulders hunched, their wolf-like heads held low as if to sniff for signs of danger. Their armour was dented and scarred from centuries of hard use, and Ragnar saw that many of their suits had been patched with scavenged parts. He couldn't be certain, but some of the replacements looked to have been taken from the suits of slain Chaos Space Marines. Their strength and speed were incredible, but there was little intelligence in their golden eyes save for the fierce cunning of a predator. When Ragnar met their flat stares he felt his hackles rise with an instinctive challenge, and more, a sense of mutual recognition.

Is this my future? Ragnar brooded over the notion as they raced across the twilit plain. He thought of Torvald. The Rune Priest was wolf-bitten, but for all that he seemed capable of holding the curse at bay. There must be a way, the young Space Wolf thought. He couldn't bear the notion that he was a prisoner to his fate.

There was only one person he could think of who could answer his questions. Gritting his teeth, Ragnar picked up his pace and sought out Sigurd the Wolf Priest.

Sigurd ran in the midst of Harald's Blood Claw pack, just a few metres behind Torvald. The younger warriors had gravitated around the priest since his unexpected return, like iron to a lodestone, and they glared belligerently at Ragnar as he worked his way into their midst.

The Wolf Priest noted his approach with a single, forbidding glance. 'What do you want, exile?' he said.

Ragnar gave the priest a sidelong glare. 'All of us are exiles now, priest,' he retorted. 'Our ship was destroyed, so there's no chance of ever returning home to our Chapter and kin.'

Sigurd said nothing at first, although the priest's stiff, silent demeanour told Ragnar that his point had hit home. Finally he said, 'We saw the battle unfold above the shadow world, but could only guess at the outcome.'

'The *Fist of Russ* is gone, and many brave men are feasting in the Halls of Russ now,' Ragnar said gravely. 'We detected a signal as we tried to make planetfall. Was that yours?'

'Yes,' Sigurd said. 'Bulveye was against it, but I thought it worth the risk. Lookouts spotted the aerial battle and the fires of your crash, and Torvald volunteered to search for survivors.' The priest spread his hands. 'The Wulfen caught your scent and led us to the agri-combine just in time.'

'It seems that the Wulfen saved you as well,' Ragnar said thoughtfully. Memories of the confused melee in the rebel command bunker flashed through his mind. 'The last I saw of you, you were surrounded by daemons.'

Sigurd gave Ragnar a hard look, but reluctantly nodded. 'It was a grim battle,' he agreed. 'They came upon me all at once, rising out of the aether like ghosts. This world we're on lies across Charys like a shadow, allowing them to step between the two at will.'

'I know,' the young Space Wolf replied. 'Inquisitor Volt and Lady Gabriella unravelled the mystery, which is what led us here in the first place.'

The Wolf Priest nodded in understanding. 'The daemons seemed to take particular interest in me for some reason. Perhaps a priest makes a better trophy than a mere warrior,' he said ruefully. 'I struck down several of the abominations, but to my shame the rest of them overwhelmed me. They pinned my arms and somehow dragged me back across the threshold into this nether realm.' Sigurd nodded to the towering form of the Rune Priest just ahead. 'But the foul creatures didn't realise they were being hunted. Torvald and the Wulfen ambushed the Chaos sorcerer and his daemons even as they ambushed us.'

Ragnar remembered the sight of the towering Wulfen grappling with the Chaos sorcerer in the vault beneath the rebel command bunker. 'So Torvald and his warriors can cross between the worlds as well?'

Sigurd frowned. 'Were that possible, I would have returned to the battle straight away,' he snapped. 'No, the crossing is affected by sorcery. Sometimes it's possible to be caught up in the spell and drawn across the threshold, but only for a moment.' He shrugged. 'The Wulfen pulled down the sorcerer and tore him apart, and Torvald turned his axe upon the daemons besetting me. When the battle was done I tended their wounds as best as I could, and they treated me as one of their own.'

'But how did they come to be here?' Ragnar asked. 'Torin says the Thirteenth Company was lost during the time of the Heresy.'

'Lost?' Sigurd seemed astonished by the notion. 'Bulveye's company was never lost, Ragnar. When a Wolf Lord is slain a new one is raised up to take his place. The same is true for the great companies, but a place for the Thirteenth remains at the table of the Great Wolf back on Fenris, as though they are expected to one day return. Think on that, Ragnar. The Thirteenth Company was sent into the Eye of Terror by Russ, and for ten thousand years they have continued their mission, regardless of the cost.'

The thought was a sobering one. Ragnar studied the grey, featureless mountains ahead and tried to imagine wandering them for ten thousand years, until Fenris was nothing but a distant memory. Unbidden, he felt the wolf within him stir. 'Their honour has cost them dearly,' he said.

'Honour always does,' the Wolf Priest replied.

For a while, they ran on in silence. The footfalls of the Wolves were like a heavy drumbeat across the sloping plain, beating out a war-song in time to the baleful lightning overhead. Ragnar considered his words carefully.

'How does a man come to be wolf-bitten, Sigurd?'

The Wolf Priest shot Ragnar a sharp look, but abruptly relented as he met the young Space Wolf's golden eyes. He considered the question for a moment before he replied. 'All of us have the wolf in our blood,' he said. 'It sharpens our senses and gives us the glad rage of the berserker in battle, but like any wild thing it tests its bonds constantly, waiting for the chance to break free.'

Sigurd stared thoughtfully at a pair of Wulfen loping silently along beside Harald's pack. 'It is a constant struggle between man and wolf,' he said, 'and not every soul is strong enough to keep the beast at bay.' The priest laid a hand on the Iron Wolf amulet at his breast. 'We bind the beast with sacred oaths to Russ and the Allfather, and we of the priesthood purify our battle-brothers with rituals and devotions to strengthen their resolve. For most, that is enough.'

'Yet not enough for Bulveye and his warriors.'

Ragnar expected a pious retort from the young priest, but when Sigurd spoke, his voice was surprisingly compassionate. 'It is not our place to judge these warriors,' he said with conviction. 'Even the ancient Dreadnoughts must sleep between times of war, lest they succumb to their feral natures. How hard must it be to keep one's soul intact after a thousand years of war, much less *ten*?' The Wolf Priest shook his head solemnly. 'It is a testament to their courage and honour that they have endured as long as they have.'

The young Space Wolf nodded thoughtfully. 'But… is there no way to restore them?'

Sigurd stiffened slightly. Ragnar was straying into the proscribed territory of the priesthood. 'The transformation is a gradual one,' he said guardedly, 'but once begun, the process is inexorable. As the wolf within gains power, it exerts physical changes on the body.' He gestured to the Wulfen nearby. 'Much depends on the will and the faith of the warrior. The degradation can be halted, sometimes indefinitely, but it cannot be undone.'

The priest's words sent a chill through Ragnar's veins. 'Gabriella says that my eyes have changed colour,' he said numbly. 'How much longer do I have?'

Sigurd frowned. 'Truly, I do not know,' he said reluctantly. 'Again, it depends upon the warrior. The process begins slowly, but accelerates as the wolf gains power.'

'How slowly?' Ragnar asked.

The Wolf Priest glowered at Ragnar. 'Are you trying to shame me with my lack of experience?' he snapped. 'I confess I do not know for certain. The curse usually strikes initiates hardest, because their minds are still adapting to the changes taking place within them. Once a warrior becomes a full-fledged battle-brother… the curse takes years for the transformation to take hold.'

'Years?' Ragnar exclaimed. 'But I felt nothing before I returned to Fenris, just two months ago!'

Sigurd stared sharply at the young Space Wolf. 'That's not possible,' he said. 'Even with an initiate, it takes at least a year for the first changes to make themselves known.'

'If I were wolf-bitten a year ago, Ranek would have known it,' Ragnar declared, 'and I would have never been sent to Terra to serve House Belisarius.'

The young priest thought it over, and his expression began to darken in consternation. 'It's true,' he said at last. 'Something else must be at work here, but I confess that I don't know what it could be.'

Ragnar nodded. 'Perhaps Bulveye or Torvald can tell us,' he said, daring to hope that things were not as hopeless as Sigurd suggested.

'Perhaps,' the priest allowed. 'We should reach the Wolf Lord's camp in a few more hours. I expect we'll learn a great deal then.'

They reached the first, wood-fringed foothills south of the grey mountains not long afterwards, and Torvald led the Wolves along the winding track of a dry streambed until they were hidden within the walls of a narrow, stony defile. Their pounding footfalls echoed crazily from the rocky walls as their course led north and east from one canyon to the next. The trail doubled back more than once, and without a pattern of stars to navigate by Ragnar soon lost track of where they were.

Within an hour Ragnar began to pick up the faint scents of other Wolves, and reckoned they were approaching the perimeter of the camp. His experienced eyes scanned the slopes of the rocky canyons through which they passed, but if there were sentries observing their approach he couldn't detect them. Then, abruptly, the canyon sloped steeply upward and the path narrowed to a cleft in the stone barely wide enough to admit the broad Space Marines.

Ragnar felt a prickling sensation race across his skin as he worked his way through the pass. Once through the cleft he quickly scanned the close-set walls of the defile that surrounded him and saw a pair of iron bars that had been driven into the stone on either side of the pass. Skulls and iron tokens carved with runes hung from each of the bars, and a wave of invisible power radiated from them.

'Those are way-posts, part of Torvald's system of wards,' Sigurd explained as he emerged from the cleft behind Ragnar. 'They confound attempts to locate Bulveye's camp using sorcery.' The Wolf Priest gazed upon the way-post with a mixture of awe and superstitious dread. 'Torvald and his kin have learned a great deal during their long campaign in the Eye.'

The path to Bulveye's camp had been carefully chosen, the approach forcing the Wolves to travel single-file and climb a steep, rocky approach into a high, sheer-sided canyon. At the southern end of the canyon, Ragnar saw the first of Bulveye's warriors: a pair of men crouching in the shadow of a boulder, covering the entrance to the canyon with a pair of plasma guns. Both warriors wore cloaks of tanned hide that had been covered in dirt and dust, and their motionless forms allowed them to blend in perfectly with their surroundings. Like Torvald, their long hair was thick and braided, and their beards hung halfway down their patched breastplates. They said nothing as the rescue party climbed past, studying them with cold, lupine eyes.

A little farther up the canyon a massive boulder had been rolled into a narrow place, creating a kind of dog-leg to prevent a clear line of fire into the area beyond. More warriors stood guard on the other side of the boulder, brandishing old, worn bolt pistols and ancient, rune carved blades. Their armour was decorated with intricate runes and carvings of battle scenes or voyages, and there were skulls or other battle trophies hanging from their broad belts. The warriors stared at Ragnar and the newcomers with frank but wary interest, stealing sidelong glances at one another and communicating in subtle gestures or nods.

More than a dozen metres further up the canyon they came upon a series of well-worn but serviceable wilderness shelters built alongside the rock walls. The camp looked as if it had been occupied for some time, and many of the shelters were marked with recent war trophies such as daemon talons and damaged pieces of blue and gold armour. More than a score of yellow-eyed warriors sat outside the shelters, cleaning their weapons or making repairs to their gear. On the surface, it looked no different from any other Space Wolf field camp that Ragnar had seen... except for the wary, challenging stares of the battle-brothers and the sense of history that stretched like an invisible tapestry across the camp and its inhabitants.

He'd felt such a thing once before, back when he was but a young lad plying the salt oceans of Fenris. His longship had been blown far off course during a storm, and they'd put in at a small island in search of fresh water. There they stumbled onto the camp of a small band of their clansmen who had been stranded there by a similar storm two years before. Ragnar still remembered the first time he'd set foot in their camp, and how the survivors had stared at him like a pack of wild dogs. They had lived in another world altogether since they had been lost, and their experiences had forged a bond that no one else could understand, much less share. It was a world in which he and his clansmen could not ever fully belong, and Ragnar felt the same sensation as he walked among the warriors of the Thirteenth Company.

They passed silently through the small camp and headed up to the far end of the canyon. Just off to the left, Ragnar was surprised to find a pack of huge, Fenrisian wolves stretched out in front of the entrance to a large cave. The wolves raised their shaggy heads as Torvald and the Wulfen approached, and the smallest of the pack rose onto its paws and loped into the darkness beyond the cave mouth. Torvald raised his axe, signalling for the party to halt, and went inside without a word. The Wulfen sank onto their haunches, some closing their eyes to rest while others dragged scraps of flesh from pouches at their belts and tore at them with their powerful jaws.

Harald's Blood Claws lowered Inquisitor Volt carefully to the ground. The old man spent several long minutes fishing a metal vial from his pack. He opened it with trembling hands and drank its contents in a single swallow. A little further away, Haegr set Gabriella on her feet. Though obviously tired, the Navigator was studying the Wulfen and the grim little camp with wide-eyed interest.

Ragnar slowly turned in place, surveying the canyon and its strange, forbidding inhabitants. He reminded himself that despite the differences between them, they were bound by the same oaths and the same world. The Thousand Sons were still their implacable foes, and Ragnar had no doubt that they would be able to count upon Bulveye and his warriors when the time came to strike at the heart of Madox's grand scheme. For the first time since crashing upon the shadow world, the young Space Wolf felt a spark of real hope.

Suddenly, a sharp cry echoed from the rocky walls. Ragnar whirled to see Gabriella stagger and fall to her knees, her hands pressed tightly to her face. Fierce green light from her pineal eye flared between her pale fingers.

'Lady!' Ragnar shouted, rushing to the Navigator's side.

The young Space Wolf had nearly reached Gabriella when a wave of sorcery buffeted him like an unseen wind. Its terrible energies sank through his armour and deep into his flesh, setting blood and bones afire. A cry of terrible agony tore its way past Ragnar's lips as he collapsed to his knees.

Dimly, he was aware that he was not alone. Harald and his Blood Claws had fallen too, and were writhing upon the ground. Even Haegr was down on one knee, his eyes screwed shut with pain.

Ragnar closed his eyes as another wave of agony wracked his body. His muscles roiled beneath his skin, and his flesh crawled. He tasted blood in his mouth, and then he was aware of nothing but a chorus of hungry, bestial howls filling the air and a red tide rising up to swallow his mind.

THE AIR ABOVE the rolling plain hissed with bolts of lascannon fire, and rumbled with the thunder of heavy guns. Pillars of black smoke rose into the sky from the burning hulks of tanks and armoured personnel carriers, painting the western horizon the colour of old blood.

Rebel troops had reached to within half a kilometre of the Charys star port before their offensive ground to a temporary halt. Outnumbered and outgunned, the Imperial defenders had managed to retreat in good order despite constant artillery barrages and furious assaults. The causeway linking the capital city to the star port was choked with bodies and wrecked vehicles, testament to the desperate rearguard action fought by the Twentieth Hebridean Foot and the Tairan Irregulars, two of Athelstane's veteran units. The tattered colours of the regiments fluttered in the rough wind blowing over the causeway, surrounded by the bodies of their fallen colour guard. Both units had died to a man, holding back the traitors' armoured assault long enough for the rest of the Imperial units to reach the port's fortified perimeter.

Now the frenzied rebel troops found themselves under the guns of the star port's defenders, forced to march across hundreds of metres of open ground covered by mines, anti-tank guns and artillery batteries. After two bloody assaults, the traitors were forced to pull back out of range until their heavy artillery could be brought forward to pound the Imperial positions.

Just over a kilometre from the beleaguered defenders, the first batteries of rebel guns were being rolled into position by the light of the dying sun. Bare-chested gun crews strained and cursed as they unlimbered heavy, stub-nosed siege mortars and tried to roll them into position along the reverse slope of a low, treeless hill. Other crews took pry-bars to squat, wooden crates containing the massive high-explosive shells. Within the hour they would be ready to fire the first salvoes.

The gun crews were exhausted, and they'd grown careless with the promise of impending victory. No sentries were posted to watch the surrounding terrain, so there was no one to take note of the eight armoured figures observing the battery from a copse of trees a hundred metres to the west.

Mikal Sternmark flexed his armoured fingers around the hilt of Red-claw and tasted the scents of the enemy troops. 'Ammunition?' he asked of his men.

Sven eyed his two packmates. 'Jurgen and Bors can shoot those bloody flashlights for another month before they run dry,' he said, scowling at the hellguns in the Wolves' hands. He checked the power meter on his meltagun. 'And I've got one shot left.'

Haakon cleared his throat. Several pieces of shrapnel had lodged in his neck over the course of the afternoon, leaving him hoarse. 'I'm out of rockets,' he grated. 'Bjørn, Nils and Karl are down to five rounds each.'

'Grenades?' the Wolf Guard asked.

Sven shook his head. 'Not since that fight back at the crossroads.'

Sternmark nodded, although he couldn't honestly say he remembered which fight Sven was talking about. The day had blurred into one long, deadly pursuit. They would retreat a few hundred metres, lay an ambush for their pursuers, and then strike, kill as many as they could and retreat to the next ambush point further down the road. The Wolves had left hundreds of dead traitors and wrecked vehicles in their wake, until finally they'd eluded their pursuers inside the drainage network at the edge of the city.

They could have slipped into the low hills south of the capital, lain low until nightfall, and then crept past the rebel positions under the cover of darkness and into safety behind the Imperial lines, but Sternmark would be damned before anyone said he slunk back to camp like a whipped dog.

The red tide was rising. He could feel it pressing against the backs of his eyes, and he welcomed it.

'We'll advance in standard skirmish formation,' he told his men, and then pointed with his bloodstained blade at a team of gunners who were fixing fuses to a trio of waiting shells. 'Sven, when we're in range, you put your last shot right there.'

Sven let out a low whistle. 'Pull the trigger and eat dirt. Aye, lord.'

The Wolf Guard ignored the Grey Hunter's impertinence. He was already moving, gliding swiftly from the shadows beneath the trees.

They raced across the low ground in moments, unnoticed by the labouring artillery crews. Sternmark measured the distance with a predator's eye, and then nodded to Sven and sank to one knee. Without hesitation, the Grey Hunter raised the meltagun to his shoulder and fired.

The three heavy shells detonated in a single, earth shaking blast that staggered the kneeling Wolves, and pitched Sven onto his back. For a single instant, the slope of the hill was painted in fiery orange. Then a shower of earth and smouldering pieces of flesh fell in a dark rain around the rebel battery.

Sternmark was on his feet before the flash had completely faded, charging among the stunned and wounded artillerymen. Redclaw flashed and hummed, splitting torsos and severing arms. A handful of gunners staggered to their feet and ran, screaming curses. Hellguns barked, and their smoking bodies tumbled to the ground. Within seconds, the slaughter was complete.

The Wolf Guard studied the guns. One of the mortars had flipped onto its side, but the rest seemed unscathed. 'Sven, you and your brothers right that mortar,' he said. 'Bjørn, Nils and Karl, fetch more shells.' He pointed to the summit of the hill. 'Haakon, you'll spot for targets.'

The Wolves leapt into action at once, realising Sternmark's plan. Haakon strode swiftly up the slope while the other three Terminators pulled apart more crates and hefted mortar shells like oversized bolt-gun rounds. Within moments, they were being fed into the breeches of the six waiting siege mortars.

'Targets?' Sternmark called.

Haakon peered over the slope. 'A motorised battalion between us and the star port,' he said, raising the targeting surveyor in his hand. 'Range six hundred and fifty to seven hundred metres.'

Sven and his packmates raced between the mortar tubes, dialling in the range. When they were ready he raised his hand to Sternmark. The Wolf Guard smiled coldly.

'Fire.'

The mortars went off in a staggered volley, spitting half-tonne shells high into the air. They screamed like the souls of the damned, and Sternmark threw back his head and howled along with them. By the time the first shells burst among the unsuspecting rebels Sternmark had crested the slope and was charging towards the foe.

Haakon had guided the shells right onto their target. The rebel unit had been assembling behind another line of low hills, their trucks and armoured cars massed in a disorderly knot behind the highest ridge line. Now the vehicles were smashed to pieces or tossed around like children's toys, spraying burning fuel across the blackened earth. Bodies and pieces of bodies lay everywhere, and wounded men tried to crawl or stagger away from the scene of carnage.

The Wolves raced among them, slashing and striking without mercy. Sternmark scythed his way through the screaming traitors, his teeth bared at the smell of hot blood. Las-bolts crackled through the smoky air. Once, an infantryman lurched upright, struggling to aim a melta-gun with a pair of charred hands, but Nils blew him apart with the last of his storm bolter shells.

Sternmark found the battalion commander trying to climb out from under a pile of bodies, and struck off his head with a casual swipe of his sword. Enemy return fire was intensifying as the survivors recovered from the shock of the barrage. He spied almost a platoon of soldiers retreating farther south, firing wildly at the warriors of Fenris.

Snarling, the Wolf Guard made to pursue the fleeing traitors, but Sven let out a yell. 'The way is clear, lord!' he said, waving his chain-blade from the summit of the next hill. 'We're fifteen hundred metres from the star port.'

Sternmark paused. For a moment he couldn't make sense of what Sven was saying. His bodyguard rushed up to surround him, firing well-aimed shots into the retreating traitors. Mikal tasted the blood of his foes upon his lips and eyed the fleeing rebels hungrily.

Somewhere, off in the distance, he felt a tremor, like the fall of a heavy shell or the first drumbeat of a coming storm. It tugged at him, making his veins tremble like plucked wires and catching the breath in his throat.

Mikal turned, seeking the source of the thunder. Haakon gripped his arm. 'What are your orders, lord?' he asked in his rough voice.

Sternmark struggled to focus on Haakon's face. He could sense the rebel troops escaping, drawing further away with every passing moment, and longed to run them down. 'We...' he began, struggling to pull the words from the red tide in his mind. *Chase them. Drag them to the earth and tear open their throats.*

Haakon frowned, worried. He, too, seemed to feel something strange in the air. 'The men are waiting, lord,' he said.

'The men...' Sternmark echoed. He breathed deeply, and then nodded towards the slope. 'Right. Let's go.'

The Wolves fell in behind their leader as he marched stolidly up the slope. At the summit he saw the broad expanse of the star port spread before him and the killing ground littered with the dead. Energy bolts and tracer fire sped back and forth across the corpse choked field as Imperial troops and rebel forces along the causeway traded volleys.

Sven eyed the field warily. 'A quick and easy run for once,' he said.

The Wolf Guard shook his head savagely. 'I've done enough running for one day,' he growled. 'From here, we walk.' And, raising his ancient blade to the sky, he started forward.

For ten minutes, the Space Wolves strode across the smoking plain, in full view of both sides. Redclaw caught the light of the setting sun and her blade shone like an evening star, drawing the eye of every soldier within sight. Almost at once, rebel gunners opened fire on the slowly marching warriors, but the las-bolts and stubber fire flew wide of their targets. Sternmark did not alter his pace in the slightest, his head straight and his stride measured. A chance shot cracked against his side, but his armour held and he missed not a single step.

By the time they reached the middle ground between the two sides, the Wolves could hear the cheering from the Imperial fortifications. Return fire stabbed out at the rebel troops, providing cover for the heroic Space Marines, and lone voices called out encouragement to Sternmark and his men. More shots flashed through the knot of bloodstained warriors. The rebels were firing grenades at long range, sending hot pieces of shrapnel ringing against the Wolves' flanks. A missile streaked from a rebel position to the south, but its aim was poor and the shot fell short.

Three hundred metres. Two hundred and fifty. A shot from a heavy stubber smashed into Sternmark's hip, shattering against the armour and sending splinters into his leg. Mortar rounds whistled overhead, smashing into the earth ahead of the Wolves like burning fists.

'Nice day for a walk!' Sven shouted into the din. A las-bolt cracked against his leg, and he brushed irritably at the scorch mark it left. 'Pity about the bugs, though!'

They were climbing the long slope up to the first of the Imperial entrenchments. Sternmark could see the grimy, cheering faces of the troops, calling out to him from their firing positions. They were less than a hundred metres away.

He faintly heard the clatter of treads far off to the west, and a lusty shout went up from the rebel positions. Then, too late, he heard the hollow boom of a battle cannon.

The world seemed to slow to a turgid crawl. Sternmark's senses grew supernaturally sharp. He could feel the rumble of displaced air as the heavy shell arced towards them. Pulverised rock and bits of dirt rang off his armour like tiny chimes as he turned, looking back towards impending doom.

The shell was a dark, thumb-shaped smudge in the air, spinning lazily as it fell. Next to him, Sternmark heard Sven draw in a sharp breath.

'Allfather protect us,' the Grey Hunter said, and the world vanished in an eruption of earth and flame.

SEVENTEEN
The Wolf King's Hall

SHOUTS AND BESTIAL snarls shook the air of the narrow canyon. Fists and blades clashed against ceramite plate as warriors clawed at their breasts in rage and pain. Ragnar howled in helpless fury, his fingers digging deep furrows in the lifeless earth. It felt as though his body was tearing itself apart from the inside out. His muscles writhed like maddened snakes, constricting around his reinforced bones and bending them with the strain. His eyes burned and his teeth ached to their roots, and it felt as though a swarm of stinging insects was crawling hungrily beneath his skin. Ragnar pitched forward and smashed his forehead against the lifeless ground again and again, trying to drive out the awful sensations with jolts of pure, honest pain.

The Wulfen snarled hungrily within him, setting its teeth deep in his bones. Ragnar tore clumsily at his armour, as though he could reach in and rip the beast from his body. The tips of his fingers ached fiercely, and mindless with rage, he tugged at the gauntlets with his teeth, trying to pull them free.

Voices were shouting all around him, but he could not make any sense of the words. Wolves snapped and snarled, clashing their fearsome jaws. The air was thick with the acid reek of anger and the sweet, heady smell of blood.

Something small crashed against him, and soft blows beat at his chest and face. A thin, piping sound reverberated in his ears. Shaking his head savagely, Ragnar gripped the flailing object and heard a gasp of fear. Breath ghosted against his face, and his eyes opened in surprise.

Gabriella's face was centimetres from his, her expression stern, but her eyes shining with fear. His hand was closed tight around her upper arm, hard enough to crack the carapace armour she wore.

She drew back her hand and slapped him hard across the face. The gauntlet came away slick with blood.

'Ragnar!' she cried, her voice sharp and faintly trembling. 'Listen to me! This is dark sorcery, and it feeds on conflict! The more you fight it, the stronger it grows! Don't struggle. Do you hear me? Let it wash over you like a wave, and then it can't affect you!'

The words echoed strangely in Ragnar's ears. He tried to grasp them, but they slipped from his mind like quicksilver. Every nerve was aflame, and he felt as though he was coming out of his skin.

Gabriella struck him again, and he tasted fresh blood on his lips. Ragnar bared his teeth at the blow, and his hands seemed to move of their own accord. He grabbed the Navigator by the hair and wrenched back her head, stretching the tendons of her pale neck.

'*Ragnar, no!*' Gabriella cried, her eyes widening in terror.

Fangs glistening, the young Space Wolf lunged for her throat.

A shadow fell over Ragnar at that moment, and an armoured fist closed around his neck like a vice. His lips scarcely brushed Gabriella's skin before he was hauled into the air and shaken like a newborn cub. A powerful voice, deep and sonorous, cut through the cacophony around the young Space Wolf and snapped his tormented mind into focus.

'Forget those soft words little brother, and fight the beast for all you are worth! You must struggle against the wolf in all its forms, as the primarch himself commands. That is the first oath of our brotherhood, and without it we are lost!'

Ragnar twisted his head to see who had seized him. He found himself staring down at a giant of a man, straight from the most ancient tapestries of the Great Wolf's Hall at the Fang. The warrior was tall and lean, cased in ornate armour wrought during the glory days of the Great Crusade. His pauldrons were edged in gold and finely carved with scenes of battle, and the pelt of the largest wolf Ragnar had ever seen was stretched across the man's broad shoulders. Trophies from a hundred campaigns decorated the warrior's breastplate or hung from his wide belt: fearsome skulls and cloven helms, medallions of gold and silver, polished scales and plaques of raw iron. In his left hand the warrior gripped the haft of a fearsome axe, wrought from a metal blacker than the night. Runes glittered like frost across its surface, and it exuded a cold nimbus of dread that chilled Ragnar's very soul. Unlike his kin, the warrior's head was bald, and his blond beard was close-shaven. Fierce blue eyes glittered like chips of polar ice beneath a grim, forbidding brow.

'Leman gave us the blessings of the wolf so that we would never be defeated by our foes,' he said, 'but his gifts come with a price. As we are born to battle, so are we called to prove our worth time and again, through strength, courage and guile. *War within. War without. War unending.* That is how we live, little brother. That is who we are.' The warrior shook Ragnar once more, as if to emphasise his point. 'I am Bulveye, axe man of the Russ and lord of this warband,' he said. 'Do you hear what I've said to you?'

Ragnar gritted his teeth and drew a deep breath as he summoned the catechisms of self-discipline he'd been taught as an aspirant. By force of will, he dampened the sensations wracking his body and struggled to clear his troubled thoughts. 'I... I hear you lord,' he said after a moment. 'I hear and obey.'

Bulveye nodded in approval and set Ragnar on his feet. The sheer force of his presence seemed to still the chaos sweeping through the camp. He paid no mind to Gabriella at all, turning his full attention to Haegr and Torin. 'What of you, brothers?' he asked, his eyes narrowing in appraisal.

Torin sank to one knee before the giant. His face was wracked with pain, and his eyes had turned yellow-gold, but a brief smile caused his moustache to twitch. 'I am no stranger to this fight, my lord,' he said breathlessly. 'The wolf may howl, but I am unmoved.'

'And you?' the warrior asked, turning to Haegr.

The burly Wolf puffed out his broad chest. 'The mighty Haegr fears no one!' he declared. 'Not even Haegr himself!'

Ragnar was cheered by his fellow Wolfblade's bravado, even as he saw signs of terrible strain around Haegr's eyes, but then he heard a bestial snarl off to his right, and saw that not everyone had been as fortunate as they.

Harald and his Blood Claws, all of them little more than aspirants, had suffered the worst under the sorcerous onslaught. Their faces were distended, already lengthening to form wolf-like snouts, and their skin was darkening with a fine pelt of fur. They crouched like beasts within a circle of the Thirteenth Company's Wulfen, snapping and snarling whenever the older beasts drew too close. Many of the warriors had tugged their gauntlets free and slashed at the air with thick, curved talons.

The sight stunned Ragnar, and a prayer to the Allfather came, unbidden to his lips. At that moment, the warrior that had been Harald glanced up and met Ragnar's eyes. The young Wulfen threw back his head and uttered a single howl of despair.

Bulveye looked upon the cursed warriors and shook his head sadly. 'Where are you, young priest?' he called.

Sigurd emerged from the pack of stricken Blood Claws. The Wolf Priest's face was ashen with grief. His eyes, once dark, were now a deep yellow-gold.

'Here I am, lord,' he said sombrely.

Bulveye nodded. 'Tend to your brothers, priest,' he said quietly. 'The first hours are always the hardest.'

Sigurd nodded, a bleak look upon his young face. Then he turned, spreading his hands, and began to chant a litany that Ragnar had heard only once in his time with the Chapter. It was the Litany of the Lost, a mournful observance for those who had been taken by the Wulfen.

Another, smaller figure elbowed his way through the snarling mob of wolf-men. Inquisitor Volt looked feverish with shock and fatigue, his eyes wide and his seamed face taut with strain. He caught sight of Ragnar and Lady Gabriella and rushed to their side. 'What has happened?' he demanded, falling to his knees beside the stunned Navigator.

Gabriella reached for the old inquisitor's arm like a drowning man clutches at a storm-tossed spar. Her pineal eye still burned brightly in her forehead, and her face was as white as chalk. 'A wave of psychic force,' she gasped. 'So much power, so much *hunger*, flowing like molten iron through the aether.'

'The ritual,' Volt said. He turned to stare at Harald and his monstrous packmates. 'Blessed Emperor,' he whispered, his voice filled with dread. 'They've completed the ritual. We're too late.'

The Navigator's gaze drifted back to Ragnar once again, and a look of horrified realisation drained the last of the colour from her face. 'You would have killed me,' she said, her voice leaden with anguish. 'Had it not been for Lord Bulveye, you would have torn out my throat!'

Ragnar stared speechlessly at the Navigator, struck dumb by the enormity of what he'd nearly done, but the Wolf Lord spoke.

'Allies we may be, Lady Belisarius, but we are not tame dogs to sniff at your heels,' Bulveye said sternly. 'Even a loyal wolf bites if provoked. You and your people would do well to remember that.' He fixed the inquisitor with his steely gaze. 'The lady I know by the heraldry she wears,' he said. 'Who are you?'

Volt rose to his full height and met the Wolf Lord's eyes. 'Inquisitor Cadmus Volt of the Ordo Malleus,' he said coolly.

Bulveye's craggy brows knitted in consternation. 'Inquisitor?' he asked. 'Is that anything like a remembrancer?'

The old man was taken aback by the Wolf Lord's reply. 'Certainly not,' he stammered.

'Good. Then I won't have to feed you to my wolves,' Bulveye replied gruffly. 'Now tell me of this ritual.'

The old inquisitor recovered his composure quickly and shook his head. 'First, tell me what this is,' he said, pointing to the Wulfen. 'At first, I thought your warriors had been twisted by exposure to the warp, but now I wonder if this is something deeper. The Inquisition has long suspected that there were flaws in the Space Wolf gene-seed. Is this true?'

The Wolf Lord's eyes narrowed coldly. 'I was wrong,' he said quietly. His hand drifted to the pistol at his hip. 'It appears I'll have to kill you after all.'

'It's the curse!' Ragnar snarled, overcome with horror and shame. 'I can feel it, like a hot coal buried in my brain. Madox has cast a spell to awaken the Wulfen in all of us.' He stared up at Bulveye. 'Even you, my lord! Surely you must feel it as well.'

The Wolf Lord set his jaw stubbornly, but there was a glimmer of doubt deep in his eyes. 'How do you know that thrice-cursed fiend, Madox?' he asked.

'There is a blood feud between us,' Ragnar answered. 'He has stolen the Spear of Russ, and I have sworn an oath to get it back.'

The news struck the Wolf Lord like a physical blow. 'Morkai's teeth!' he snarled, his eyes widening. He turned, seeking out the hulking form of the Rune Priest. 'Torvald! Did you hear–'

'No need to shout,' the Rune Priest said, making his way through the crowd of warriors towards Bulveye and Ragnar. 'The pup speaks the truth, lord. I've told you for some time that the air here stank of sorcery, and now I know why. I curse myself for a fool for not suspecting it sooner.' The bearded warrior gave Bulveye a meaningful look. 'And now these tidings of Madox and the spear. You see? The runes did not lie!'

'They may not have lied, but they tell their truths sideways,' Bulveye said. He raised his head to the empty sky, and for an instant Ragnar saw an enormous weariness etched into the lines of the Wolf Lord's face. Then it was gone, so quickly that the young Space Wolf could not be certain he'd seen it at all, and Bulveye surveyed his warband with a commanding gaze.

'Torvald, summon the pack leaders,' the Lord of the Thirteenth Company said. 'It's time we held a council of war.'

FOR A FLEETING instant, Mikal Sternmark was gripped by the jaws of a dragon. Fierce heat and a thunderous concussion buffeted him, and red-hot shrapnel raked at his face and neck. He staggered beneath the blow, but did not fall.

A shower of dirt and stone rained down all around him. Smoke curled from the surface of his Terminator armour, but he was still alive, and Redclaw still pointed defiantly at the sky.

It took several long seconds before Sternmark understood that he'd been spared. He looked around, dazed, and saw the stunned figures of his bodyguards, all of them battered and bloodied, but nevertheless alive. Among them, Sven and his battle-brothers were picking themselves up off the ground and looking off to the east in amazement. The battle cannon shell had landed just a few metres short of its intended target, gouging a deep, smouldering crater in the ground behind the Wolves.

Moments later the first cheer went up from the Imperial lines. A priest who'd been watching the scene from a nearby gun pit clambered atop the trench line and raised his arms to the sky. 'The Emperor protects!' he cried, and soon the Guardsmen took up the cry as well.

'The Emperor Protects! The Emperor Protects!' The shout echoed across the killing field, and men took heart again after the bitter retreat from the capital.

One by one, the Wolves turned and walked the last few metres into the Imperial fortifications. Sternmark waited until the last, his sword still gleaming in the sun's dying light. Then he turned his back on the traitors of Charys and joined his brothers in the trenches.

Sven and the others were waiting for him, surrounded by a ring of awestruck Guardsmen. The Wolves were joking with one another, the raw edge to their laughter betraying the tension of their brush with death. There was something almost feral in their wide eyes and rough-edged voices, raising the hackles on Sternmark's neck. His scalp prickled, and it felt like a swarm of hungry insects had crawled beneath his skin. 'Take half an hour to eat and replenish your ammo,' he snapped, 'then return to the line.'

The Wolves were startled by the harsh edge to their leader's voice, prompting a chorus of deep growls and a narrowing of eyes. For a fleeting instant, the air was charged with tension. Sternmark's hand tightened on the hilt of his blade, but then a powerful voice broke the deadly spell.

'That was boldly done, my lord,' Morgrim Silvertongue called as he moved through the throng of admiring troops. 'When you disappeared earlier in the day we feared you had been lost.'

Sternmark turned to the skald as though in a daze. The red tide was rising once more, threatening to overwhelm the last vestiges of reason he had left. His hands and fingertips ached, and abruptly he felt smothered inside the weight of his Terminator armour.

A sharp challenge rose to the Wolf Guard's lips, but it was Sven who spoke first. 'Another few moments and we might well have been, Silvertongue,' the Grey Hunter said grimly, and then pointed out across the killing ground. 'Look.'

Sternmark turned. Something was happening along the rebel lines. The very air seemed to thicken and deepen in hue, and purple lightning flickered above the traitors' heads. Cries of adulation and terror echoed across the killing ground as shifting, luminescent forms appeared among the rebel Guardsmen.

From the gun pit nearby the regimental priest made the sign of the aquila and began the Litany of Detestation in a harsh, trembling voice. Men clutched their weapons and pressed themselves fearfully against the packed-earth walls of the trench lines as hundreds of daemons howled a chorus of blasphemous curses at the Imperial defenders.

Still worse to Sternmark was the clashing, rhythmic sound of armour, rising and falling like a dirge beneath the cacophonous, otherworldly cries. He stepped to the trench parapet and studied the rebel positions carefully until he spied the first glimmer of blue and gold.

They towered over the cringing traitors in their baroque armour, their boltguns held at port-arms in perfect unison as they marched towards the battle line. Rebel soldiers flinched from the sound of their dreadful tread, parting like smoke before the Thousand Sons' inexorable advance. The heads of the towering warriors turned neither left nor right. No human curiosity shone from the glowing depths of their ornate helms. Their bodies had been consumed by sorcerous fires thousands of years ago. Nothing remained inside those armoured shells but spirits of pure, immortal hate and murderous skill. Fell sorcerers marched alongside the ghostly Chaos Space Marines, driving the warriors onward with fierce oaths and imprecations to their abominable god.

Sternmark counted almost two hundred of his Chapter's arch foes. In all his years of campaigning he'd never seen so many of the spectral troops assembled in one place. Even without the howling daemons and rebel battalions at their command, they could crush the star port defenders in an implacable, armoured fist.

Morgrim joined the Wolf Guard at the parapet. 'It seems you arrived not a moment too soon,' he said quietly.

'I wonder if the rabbit thinks the same thing as he sticks his head into the snare,' Sternmark hissed. He found himself thinking of his fallen lord Berek, and the melta charges laid beneath his bier. The cold demands of duty focused his mind somewhat, helping him ignore the awful sensations wracking his body. He bared his teeth, tasting the strange scents around him. 'How many of our brothers remain?' Sternmark asked.

The skald folded his arms thoughtfully. 'It's hard to say,' he answered. 'We've Gunnar and Thorbjørn's Long Fangs here at the star port, as well as half of Thorvald's Grey Hunters.' He paused, his lips pressing into a grim line. 'But we've lost contact with the rest.'

'Lost contact?' Sternmark gave the skald a hard look. 'What does that mean? Are we being jammed planet-wide?'

'There is some jamming, yes,' Silvertongue replied, 'but some packs have simply stopped responding to our calls. We aren't sure what's happened to them.'

'Not sure?' the Wolf Guard snarled. 'They're dead, Silvertongue. What other explanation could there be?' Sternmark brought his fist down on the ferrocrete parapet, sending up a spray of broken fragments. The rage was rising within him once more, and it was getting harder and harder to find a reason to fight it. He looked out across the killing field. 'What are they waiting for? Let's get to the bloody business of the day and be done with it!'

Silvertongue eyed the Wolf Guard warily. 'I expect they are still waiting for their heavy artillery,' he said. 'We have enough heavy weapons left to make a frontal assault very expensive, and before he left Inquisitor Volt instructed the priests to lay a series of wards that will keep the daemons at bay.' The skald peered closer. 'My lord? Your eyes... they've changed–'

The Wolf Guard seemed not to hear him. 'Wards?' he spat. 'Those won't last long with all those sorcerers out there.'

'Aye, that's true,' Silvertongue replied carefully, 'but we only need a few more hours.'

Sternmark glared at the skald. 'What in Morkai's name are you talking about?' he demanded.

Something in the Wolf Guard's face took Silvertongue aback. He recoiled slightly from Sternmark, as though suddenly confronted by a snarling Fenrisian wolf. 'I... I thought you'd been informed,' he said quickly. 'Lady Commander Athelstane has ordered every available ship made ready for launch. She believes that there are enough transports still able to fly to evacuate the entire star port in one go–'

'*Evacuate?*' Sternmark spat, the word bitter on his tongue. 'She would have us abandon our honour and slink away like whipped dogs?'

He staggered, overcome with fury. The red tide surged, angry and wild, and swallowed him up entirely.

Silvertongue shouted something, his voice urgent, but the Wolf Guard did not hear. He was gone, running like a shadow ahead of the crimson sunset towards the distant command bunker.

BULVEYE LED RAGNAR and his companions into the dimly lit cave, setting his wolves to guard its threshold once more with a quick gesture and a few whispered commands. Beyond the entrance, the cave narrowed quickly into a long tunnel that meandered for several dozen metres into the side of the mountain. To Ragnar's keen night vision the passageway seemed shrouded in twilight. Veins of dark ore ran in serpentine paths through the rough stone walls, and runes of warding were chiselled at every corner to foil the questing spirits of their foes.

Finally they came around another narrow turn, and Ragnar's eyes narrowed at a sudden blaze of firelight. The passageway emptied out into a large, high-ceilinged cavern almost twenty metres across, laid with furs and rough stone benches in the style of a lord's feasting hall. The warriors of the Thirteenth Company had felled some of the strange trees that dotted the foothills at the base of the mountain and had piled the logs in a crude pit at the centre of the cavern. The wood burned without sound or smoke, giving off a fey, otherworldly blue light.

At the far end of the cavern, ailing servos creaked and whined, and a pair of careworn servitors struggled upright at their master's arrival. Bulveye turned and addressed the newcomers sombrely. 'Enter my hall with the blessings of the Allfather,' he said, and beckoned to the servitors.

The Wolf Lord welcomed them according to the ancient tradition, with handclasps, bread and salt. The gesture was both strange and oddly reassuring. *Custom and tradition are all they have left*, Ragnar mused, as Bulveye bade them sit by the fire, and then strode off to a far corner of the cavern. He returned with guesting gifts: a gold ring for Gabriella and iron daggers for her Wolfblade. The weapons had been forged on Fenris, Ragnar noticed, and beautifully made.

Another piece of home, he thought, turning the blade over in his aching hands. He realised, for the first time that he would never see Fenris again, and a terrible melancholy stole over him.

A few moments later the first of the pack leaders filed into the cavern. They were silent, implacable figures, marked by ten millennia of warfare: the pauldrons of a World Eater champion sat on the shoulders of one warrior, while another wore the breastplate of a fallen lieutenant from Abaddon's infamous Black Legion. They wore cloaks of daemon hide or necklaces of hellhound teeth, and the twisted skulls of those they'd slain were spitted on iron trophy spikes jutting from their back-packs. The pack leaders took their places around the fire, each according to his position within the warband, and they spoke quietly amongst themselves as they waited for the council to begin.

Sigurd stole quietly into the hall shortly afterwards, his expression solemn. Rather than take a seat among the warriors he kept to the shadows at the back of the hall, arms folded, and deep in thought.

Ragnar stole a glance at Torin and Haegr. The two warriors were silent and withdrawn, their eyes hooded and shoulders hunched as they fought their silent struggles with the beasts beneath their skins. Beyond them, Inquisitor Volt and Gabriella sat on a bench to themselves. Volt was sitting ramrod-straight, his gaze moving constantly around the cavern, while the Navigator sat with her arms tightly folded across her chest, lost in some tormented reverie.

Torvald was the last to arrive, striding slowly past the fire and taking a seat at Bulveye's right. The Rune Priest surveyed the assembled warriors and nodded. Then he struck the cavern floor thrice with the butt of his axe. 'The blessings of the Allfather be upon you, brothers,' he said in the silence that followed. 'Our foes gather before us, calling us to battle. Ere the swords sing and the blood flows, hear what our lord has to say.'

Bulveye surveyed each of the warriors seated around the fire. 'It was Torvald's runes that led us to this place,' he said. 'He consulted the Fates, and when he took his hand from the leather bag, he was holding Tyr's Rune, the Rune of the Spear.'

One of the warriors let out a sullen growl. 'Yet when we got here, what did we find? A host of enemies and the shadow of an Imperial agri-world,' he said. 'If he was here we would have found him by now–'

'We have been here for some time, trying to puzzle out the riddles of this place,' Bulveye interjected sharply, throwing a warning look at the pack leader. 'Now our distant kin have arrived, with answers to some of the questions we seek.' The Wolf Lord nodded to Ragnar. 'Tell us how you and your brothers came to be here.'

The young Space Wolf eyed his companions and rose uneasily to his feet. As quickly and succinctly as he could, he related the events on Hyades and the Chaos uprising around Fenris, and then told the grim tale of the battle for Charys and their desperate foray to the shadow world. 'The heart of Madox's ritual lies here,' he said, 'within a great temple at the centre of the shadow city to the north.' He paused. 'Inquisitor Volt can tell us more about what our enemy intends.'

Ragnar gestured to the old inquisitor, who raised his head with a scowl and rose slowly to his feet. 'The enemy intends nothing less than the perversion of the Space Wolf gene-seed,' Inquisitor Volt declared. 'And in so doing, the Thousand Sons will inflict a wound upon the Imperium from which it may never heal.'

Bulveye glowered at Volt. 'How can you be so certain of this?'

'How? The evidence is sitting right here, before your very eyes!' Volt pointed to the Wolfblade. 'See how they have been changed already by Madox's spell?' He cast an accusatory stare at each of the warriors seated around the fire. 'You all feel it, don't you? Madox is reaching into the very core of your being, warping you from the inside out!'

'You speak of nothing that I and my brothers have not struggled with for ten millennia!' Bulveye growled. 'The warp twists everything it touches.'

'Do not dissemble, lord!' Volt snapped. 'We have no time for denials or deceptions! You saw what happened to Harald and his warriors. Has the curse Ragnar spoke of ever struck so quickly before? Somehow I doubt it.' The inquisitor turned to Sigurd. 'Come here, priest. It's your duty to safeguard the souls of your battle-brothers. Tell us then, are these transformations normal?'

The Wolf Priest stiffened at the mention of his name. Slowly, reluctantly, he stepped forward into the firelight. His eyes were yellow-gold, like two brass coins. 'No,' he said gravely, 'they are not.'

'There!' Volt snapped. 'You hear it from one of your own priests. Lady Gabriella felt the initial wave of sorcery as the ritual reached its culmination. That energy has crossed the aether into the physical realm, where it will wash over Charys and then down the sorcerous anchor lines until it charges the vast sigil that Madox painstakingly built.' The inquisitor began to pace, his hands clasped tightly behind his back. 'The Chaos uprising was both a cover and a lure to draw the Space Wolves within reach of the sigil,' he said. 'As the sigil becomes charged, every one of the great companies will be affected; even Fenris will be caught within the web of power.'

Sigurd scowled at the inquisitor, but he took a deep breath and spoke. 'The aspirants will succumb first,' he said, 'then the younger warriors. The senior pack members will hold out for some time, I expect, but slowly, they too will be overwhelmed. In the end, perhaps even the great Dreadnoughts beneath the Fang will awaken in the darkness and howl for innocent blood.'

Pandemonium broke out as pack leaders leapt to their feet, shouting angry oaths or denouncing Volt as a liar and a blasphemer. Bulveye sat in silence, brooding darkly over the news. Finally Torvald rose to his feet and raised his axe high. Lightning crackled from the blade and a sharp thunderclap deafened everyone in the cavern. '*Sit down!*' the

Rune Priest commanded, and the pack leaders reluctantly obeyed. Then Torvald addressed Volt directly. 'What you are talking about would require enormous amounts of psychic power,' he said.

'Naturally,' Volt replied. 'That is why Madox and his lord had to perform the ritual here, in the Eye of Terror. They can draw upon the warp to fuel their sorceries, and then channel those energies through the sigil around Charys. No one, not even Grimnar himself, could resist such a spell for long.'

'And then?' Torvald asked.

Volt's expression became a mask of dread. 'Then blood will flow across a dozen worlds,' he replied. 'The Wolves will turn upon the sheep they once swore to protect. I expect millions of Imperial citizens will die, and that would be just the beginning. The Inquisition would declare the Space Wolves *excommunicae traitoris*, and then there would be war.'

Ragnar felt his guts turn to ice. Volt was right; the Inquisition would spare no effort to hunt the Wulfen to destruction. Virus bombs would fall upon Fenris, and those that did not flee to the outer reaches of the galaxy, or into the Eye of Terror, would be slain. Of course, the Wulfen would not go meekly. By the time the war was over, entire sectors would lie in ruins. The Imperium would need thousands of years to rebuild, provided its foes did not decide to take advantage of humanity's weakened state and move against it.

'Now we know why the Chaos cultists were taking the progenoid glands from dead Space Marines on Hyades,' Ragnar mused. 'Madox needed Space Wolf gene-seed for his ritual.' He frowned as another thought struck him. 'But what of the Spear of Russ? What does he need with that?'

Volt shook his head. 'I've been wondering about that myself, and I can only speculate at this point,' he said. 'I believe that Madox required a relic of great significance to bind the ritual to your Chapter. The spear – tainted with the blood of Berek Thunderfist, a Wolf Lord – is the fulcrum for Madox's ritual.'

Once again, the cavern erupted in wild shouts as Bulveye's warriors reacted to the news, and this time it took the Wolf Lord himself to end the tumult and bring the council back to order. 'It is no surprise that Madox would have chosen the spear for his diabolical spell,' Bulveye told Volt. 'For we Wolf Lords swore our allegiance to Leman upon that self-same weapon and formed the great companies of our Legion. The most binding oaths of our brotherhood were wrought with it.'

The news stunned Ragnar. Did Logan Grimnar or the priests at the Fang realise the spear's importance, or had its true significance been lost over the course of thousands of years?

'But how did Leman lose his spear?' one of the pack leaders cried. 'It's inconceivable!'

'Morkai's black teeth!' Torvald swore, shaking his head. 'He was constantly losing the damned thing. You may not remember any more, but *I* do.' The Rune Priest pointed to Bulveye. 'Do you recall the time he drank all that stormwine on Sirenia and tried to throw the bloody spear at the moon? Took us four days to find it afterwards.' He chuckled ruefully and grinned at Ragnar. 'Truth be told, he hated that big boar-sticker, but the Allfather gave it to him as a gift, so he was stuck with it. He dragged it out for ceremonies, and then he'd stick it in a corner somewhere and forget about it. Drove his huscarls mad.'

'Never mind how he lost the spear,' Bulveye said, turning his attention to Volt. 'You said this sigil had to charge itself before it reached full power. Does that mean we can stop the ritual before it is too late?'

'Yes, I believe so,' the inquisitor replied. 'We must find a way to reach the temple at the centre of the city and wrest the spear away from Madox. Without that focus, the ritual energies will dissipate.'

Ragnar clenched his hands around Bulveye's iron dagger. He could feel his fingertips changing as thick talons began to take root. 'What about our brothers who have already succumbed?'

'If the ritual is disrupted before it causes too much corruption to the gene-seed, they may revert to normal,' Sigurd said, 'but every moment brings us closer to the point of no return.'

The young Space Wolf leapt to his feet. 'Then we must attack at once!'

Ragnar was greeted with loud roars of approval from the pack leaders, but Bulveye glowered at the warriors. '*Shut up*, for the Allfather's sake!' he bellowed. 'We've been watching the enemy come and go from that city for a long time. It's more than a day's march away, and the streets are guarded by an army of cultists and Thousand Sons.' The Wolf Lord paced in front of the fire. 'If we had the whole company here we could just charge right down their throats and *dare* the bastards to stand in our way, but there is only us.'

'What can we do, then?' Ragnar asked.

The Wolf Lord studied the faces of his pack leaders, and then stared thoughtfully into the cold flames. 'We must bring the enemy here,' he said.

EIGHTEEN
Wolf's Honour

THE FIRST HEAVY shells began to fall on the Imperial defences as Mikal Sternmark reached the command bunker complex. No barrage siren wailed this time as the earth shaking blasts pounded the fortifications to the east. The augur crews and communications staff were loading all the equipment they could carry on a trio of heavy cargo haulers as Sternmark came charging out of the twilight. Soldiers and technicians scattered out of the Space Wolf's path, intent on making good their escape from the impending rebel assault. The stink of defeat hung heavy in the air, stoking his rage even further.

No sentries remained to challenge Sternmark at the command bunker's entrance, but the narrow passageway beyond was filled with a procession of near-panicked Guardsmen carrying boxes of documents and crates of equipment. They recoiled before the grim, blood-spattered visage of the Space Wolf, flattening themselves against the ferrocrete walls as best they could to allow his armoured bulk to pass.

The burning beneath his skin had turned to a sharp, pulsing ache that reached down into his bones. Sternmark tasted blood on his lips, and a steady, agonising pressure was building behind his eyes. He lashed out like a maddened beast as he lurched down the corridors of the bunker, gouging craters in the reinforced ferrocrete with blows from his armoured fist.

709

A technician was hurrying out of the war room with a portable logic engine in his arms as Sternmark arrived. The man froze at the sight of the wild-eyed giant, and the Wolf Guard hurled him backwards into the chamber with a brutal shove. He hit the floor with a crash and a shout of pain, his arms still wrapped protectively around the precious machine.

Most of the equipment in the large chamber had already been removed, and a score of soldiers and staff officers were hard at work unhooking and packing up the rest. Heads turned at the sudden commotion, and the frenetic buzz of conversation in the room fell silent. Several of the Guardsmen took one look at Sternmark's horrific appearance and surreptitiously laid their hands on their lasguns.

Lady Commander Athelstane was standing on the stage at the far end of the room, surrounded by half a dozen of her senior officers. The men were carrying despatch cases bulging with maps and data-slates, and looked ready to depart at a moment's notice. They all turned at the Wolf Guard's sudden arrival, hands drifting to the butts of their laspistols.

Athelstane scowled at the blood-stained Wolf. 'Have a care with my equipment,' she said coldly. 'Those logic engines are difficult to come by.'

Sternmark bristled at the general's cynical tone. 'What is the meaning of this?' he demanded.

'I should think the meaning would be obvious!' Athelstane snapped. 'The enemy has driven us from the capital and is preparing for a final assault against the star port. Now, I must concern myself with preserving as much of my command as possible while there is still time. If you'd bothered to answer any of my vox transmissions you would have known about this hours ago.'

'You're fleeing from the enemy!' Sternmark roared. The savagery in his voice stole the colour from the Guardsmen's faces, but Athelstane was made of far sterner stuff.

'Have a care, sir,' she warned. 'I'm not in the mood for insults.'

Sternmark stalked towards the stage, his power blade gripped tightly in his hand. The pain in his head made it hard to think. It felt as though his very skull was being warped by the pressure. He lashed out with a clenched fist and smashed a table to pieces. Startled, the Guardsmen scattered out of his way and raised their weapons.

'Where is your honour?' Sternmark growled. The words were barely intelligible, as the Wolf Guard's lips stretched taut over prominent fangs. 'Our troops are dug-in. We have heavy weapons, and my men are well supplied–'

'How many of your men are left?' the general shot back. 'We haven't been able to contact anyone beyond the capital since mid-afternoon. My men are exhausted, and their vaunted heavy weapons are nearly out of ammunition. There's nothing more we can do here except die,' she said, 'and I won't waste the lives of good soldiers on a lost cause.'

Athelstane nodded curtly to her officers and checked her chronometer. 'It's almost time to check in with *Holmgang*,' she said. 'I was going to request that they return to Charys and cover our withdrawal, and then they can bombard the star port and the capital with everything they've got. We can at least make the enemy pay for massing so many of their troops in one place.'

She led her officers down off the stage and approached the Wolf Guard. 'Now that you're here, I could use your help convincing the *Holmgang* to support the withdrawal plan.' As the general drew closer, her eyes narrowed and she studied Sternmark's face closely. 'What's happened to you?' she said with a curious scowl. 'There's something wrong with your eyes–'

'*I cannot let you do this.*' The Wolf Guard's voice was little more than a deep, liquid growl. Redclaw fell with a discordant clang to the war room floor as a wave of agony swept over Sternmark. '*Better death than this.*'

His words gave way to a terrible howl. Sternmark pressed his hands to his face and felt the bones beneath his skin start to shift.

'Blessed Emperor!' Athelstane cried. 'He's suffering some kind of attack.' She turned to her men. 'Go and fetch a priest, quickly!'

'*It is too late for priests!*' the Wolf Guard snarled. Sternmark's head came up, his face distended into a toothy snout. Powerful jaws gaped at the stunned general and her staff. '*Cursed!*' he howled. '*I am cursed!*'

Guardsmen screamed at Sternmark's bestial transformation and brought up their guns. Bolts of energy detonated harmlessly against the Wolf Guard's Terminator armour.

Sternmark's body moved with pure, animal instinct, surging forward and smashing two of the Guardsmen across the room with blows from his powerful fists. Bones shattered. Men cried in mortal pain, and the scent of blood hung in the air.

Lady Commander Athelstane uttered a blistering curse and reached for the hellpistol at her hip. She fumbled open the holster flap and pulled the weapon free just as the Wulfen's teeth closed around her throat.

HALFWAY ACROSS THE Charys star system the *Holmgang* and her escorts drifted silently through the icy void. For weeks the battle-barge had played a deadly game of cat and mouse with Chaos ships in the asteroid field at the system's edge, but *Holmgang's* wily master reversed his course and slipped unnoticed through the enemy cordon. Since then the Space Wolf ships had been gliding on a parabolic course back towards the embattled agri-world, growing closer with every passing day.

The ship's master and his lieutenants gathered at *Holmgang's* signals room and eyed the minutes ticking away on the chronometer set above the vox station. Tripwire required at least three command officers present to confirm receipt of the scheduled signal. There could be no room for error with the fate of an Imperial world hanging in the balance.

The minutes ticked away. No one spoke. The silence in the signals room was broken only by the quiet hum of the vox-units and the ghostly whisper of static. At the appointed time the officers raised their heads to the crackling vox-speaker and listened.

They waited while the seconds passed, and their faces turned cold and grim. A full minute passed, and then another, until finally the ship's master could wait no more. With solemn ceremony he stretched out his hand and pressed a switch. The vox-unit fell silent.

Within the hour the orders were transmitted to the rest of the fleet. Thrusters glowed to angry life, and the Space Wolf ships put on speed. Belowdecks, Iron Priests garbed themselves in leaden robes and began the Rites of Atomic Redemption, unlocking the great seals that would waken the ship's cyclonic torpedoes. There was little time to waste.

The *Holmgang* would reach Charys in less than four hours.

BULVEYE'S PLAN WAS simple and direct. After issuing a few curt commands to Torvald, the Rune Priest left the cavern to set events in motion. Then there was nothing left to do but wait.

The Wolves passed the time in the same way as their ancestors of old, telling tales of the campaigns they had fought and the foes they had bested. Bulveye and his warriors spoke of the Great Crusade and the battles they had fought alongside Leman Russ. Their stories were told in the old tongue of Fenris, shaped in the chanting cadences of the ancient sagas. Ragnar learned of lost civilisations and long-dead races. Bulveye was a gifted storyteller, and painted vivid tales of fiery combat drops and titanic land battles, of desperate struggles and heroic stands fought for the sake of a young and hopeful Imperium.

They spoke of Russ himself, not the blessed Primarch Russ, but the black haired, flame eyed warrior who was more wolf than man. They spoke of his rough manner and intemperate heart, of his wild oaths and petty rivalries, of his melancholy nature and his merciless rage. 'He drove us all to distraction,' Bulveye said ruefully. 'I remember one time when he'd got Horus so worked up I thought they were going to come to blows. The Allfather got between them, and Leman punched him full in the jaw.'

Ragnar's eyes widened. 'What happened then?'

Bulveye laughed. 'The Allfather hit Leman so hard he was unconscious for a month. Spent the rest of the campaign flat on his back aboard the battle-barge.'

One of Bulveye's pack leaders, a warrior named Dagmar, shook his head and chuckled. 'That was the quietest month we ever had,' he said, and his companions laughed along with him.

'Leman didn't speak to the Allfather for almost a year, but eventually they came around,' the Wolf Lord said with a grin. 'That was how they were, like a jarl and his sons, always squabbling about one thing or another, but they never forgot the ties of blood and kin.' Bulveye paused, and his smile faded. 'Well, not until the end.'

Torin leaned forward, resting his elbows on his knees. His eyes shone yellow in the cold firelight, and there was a troubled look on his face. 'The legends say that Russ sent you into the warp to finish what was begun back on Prospero.'

'Is that so?' Bulveye replied conversationally, but there was a guarded look in his blue eyes. 'That sounds like an interesting story. You will have to tell it to me sometime.'

Silence fell around the fire. Ragnar glanced sidelong at the Wolf Lord. 'You came to this world because Torvald cast the runes and drew the spear,' he said. 'What were you expecting to find?'

The Wolf Lord considered the young Space Wolf for a long moment. 'You've already answered the question,' he said carefully. 'I came looking for the spear, and now you've helped me find it.'

'It wasn't just the spear, though, was it?' Ragnar said. 'You had no idea that Russ has been lost for ten thousand years, and that he'd left his spear behind on Garm. You expected him to be here.'

Bulveye gave Ragnar a wolfish smile. 'Leman is no more lost than we were,' he replied. 'I don't know where he's gone, but I do know this: he swore an oath to us a very long time ago, and one day he will keep it.'

'How can you be so sure?' Torin asked.

The Wolf Lord chuckled. 'Because, little brother, Leman of the Russ was a scoundrel and an axe-bitten fool at times, but he always kept his word, regardless of the cost.' Bulveye held out his right hand. 'When last we met, he clasped my wrist and swore that one day we would meet again.' The Wolf Lord lowered his arm and stared into the ghostly flames. For a fleeting instant Ragnar saw the terrible weariness once again in the warrior's blue eyes. 'In time, that day will come.'

A faint clatter of armour drew the attention of the assembled warriors. Torvald had returned to the cavern, and now strode quickly into the firelight. 'It's done,' he said curtly, returning to his bench.

Ragnar scowled at the cold, blue flames. 'How can you be sure the Thousand Sons will take the bait?'

'Because we've been a dagger in their side for ten millennia,' Torvald answered. 'Their sorcerers are always sniffing at our trail, waiting for the slightest mistake that will give our presence away. Now I've given them one. I allowed the wards concealing the camp to go out, for the briefest instant, before energising them again.'

'But how can you be certain they noticed the lapse?' Ragnar persisted.

The Rune Priest let out a snort. 'Who do you think we're fighting here, little brother? Of course they noticed!'

'And they will send every warrior and daemon they can muster,' Bulveye added.

'Then why are we still here?' the young Space Wolf asked in exasperation.

'Why, to fight them, of course,' Bulveye answered. 'If their warband arrives and finds the camp deserted, they'll suspect a trick and return to the city as quickly as they can.' The Wolf Lord raised his ebon axe and laid it across his knees. 'So, we'll let them spring their trap, and keep the devils busy while you fight your way into the temple and get back Russ's spear.'

The news stunned Ragnar. He glanced quickly at Haegr and Torin, noting their looks of shock. He'd expected that Bulveye and his more experienced warriors would claim the privilege of confronting Madox and reclaiming the artefact. 'This is a great honour, lord,' he managed to say.

'It's nothing of the kind,' Bulveye replied irritably. 'I'd like nothing better than to tear Madox apart with my bare hands, but if I'm not seen here with my troops the enemy might still see through our ploy.' He stared appraisingly at Ragnar and his companions. 'As far as we can tell, Madox doesn't know any of you are here. That's why you're staying in this cave until the attack is well begun.'

Ragnar's brain was whirling, trying to puzzle out the hidden elements of the Wolf Lord's deceptively simple plan. 'If we're still here when the attack begins, how in Morkai's name are we supposed to reach the city undetected?'

The Wolf Lord's eyes glittered with cold amusement. 'By the Allfather, you ask more questions than a Blood Claw!' he said. 'Suffice to say that we've got a few secrets that not even the Thousand Sons suspect.' He beckoned to Sigurd. 'Gather your charges, priest, and bring them here,' he commanded. 'We will not have much longer to wait.'

Sigurd nodded silently and left to find Harald and his packmates. After he had gone, the Wolf Lord turned back to his guests with a faint smile. 'Now, little brothers, speak to us of distant Fenris. Tell us tales of our home.'

Ragnar was taken aback by the sudden request. He'd never considered himself a storyteller, and as he felt the eyes of Bulveye and his pack leaders focus on him, his mind went utterly blank. An awkward silence hung in the air as the young Space Wolf groped for something worthwhile to say, but then Torin drew a deep breath and began to speak. At first his voice was rough and awkward, tainted by the beast inside him, but as he spoke of the tall cliffs and crashing salt waves of the islands, a change came over him. His tone grew stronger and more polished, falling into the smooth cadences of a skald, and the old warriors listened, rapt, as he told them of all that had transpired since the days of the Heresy.

Bulveye and the warriors were shocked to hear of all the changes that had befallen the Imperium in their absence. Their expressions turned grave as they heard how their glorious Legion had been reduced to a mere Chapter in the wake of Horus's rebellion, and they glanced thoughtfully at one another when they learned of Russ's departure. But the tales that gripped the warriors most of all had nothing to do with wars or strife. They wanted to hear of their homeworld, of the heaving seas and the tall mountains, of the Time of Ice and the Time of Fire. They asked how the fishing was off the Kraken Isles, of which clans had prospered and which had disappeared over the course of the centuries. They asked after villages and peoples that had vanished ages past, of legends that no one could now recall. Ragnar listened and watched the old Wolves, and saw the sense of loss etched on their faces.

Before long Sigurd returned, leading a shuffling pack of wary beasts that had once been men. Ragnar watched them gather around the priest a respectful distance from the fire, and heard the priest speaking to them in low, soothing tones. Inquisitor Volt and Gabriella had retreated from the circle, and sat cross-legged on a pile of rugs at the far end of the cavern. The Navigator's head was bowed and her eyes were tightly shut. For a moment, he considered going to her, but then he remembered the look of horror on her face when she'd glimpsed the Wulfen inside him. We are all of us forsaken, he realised bitterly. All of us have lost our way.

As Torin spun his tales, Haegr ran his wide hands over his whiskered face and glowered into the fire for some time. After a while he reached a decision and began rummaging quietly through the field bags attached to his waist. Slowly, carefully, he drew out a squat cylinder the size of a melta bomb and cradled it in his lap. Then he reached over his shoulder and drew forth his great ale horn.

Ragnar faintly heard the hiss of escaping air and thought nothing of it at first. Then he noticed a palpable change among the warriors sitting around the fire. The old Wolves were leaning forward, their expressions intent. Even Lord Bulveye had stopped listening to Torin and was watching Haegr's every move.

By this point Torin had noted the change as well, and his story came to a halt. Haegr, meanwhile, set the empty cylinder on the stone floor and started to raise the foaming horn to his lips.

'Is that ale?' asked Dagmar, licking his lips. His voice sounded almost reverent.

'Aye,' Haegr replied with a broad grin. 'Good, brown Iron Islands ale, tapped from the kegs in the Fang's deep cellars,' he said proudly. 'I've been saving this one for a special occasion, and this seems like the time! Bringing it all the way from Fenris was a saga all by itself, I can tell you.' He raised the horn to the warriors. 'Skoal!'

'We haven't had a drop of ale in six thousand years,' Bulveye mused, eyeing the ale horn appreciatively.

'Six thousand three hundred and twenty-two years, eighteen days, six hours and twenty-one minutes,' Dagmar said, 'give or take.'

Haegr froze, the rim of the horn touching his lips. His eyes flicked from one thirsty face to the next. 'Well, I suppose I could offer you a taste,' he said reluctantly, 'just a swallow, you understand–'

'That's fine!' Bulveye said, reaching eagerly for the horn. Prying it loose from Haegr's fingers, he raised it high. 'Drink deep, lads! The next taste we get will be in the Halls of Russ! *Skoal!*'

'*Skoal!*' the warriors cried, rising from their benches and crowding around their lord. Haegr watched the frenzy with a stricken grin frozen on his face.

Muffled thunder rolled down the winding tunnel, followed by the faint howl of wolves. Bulveye and the warriors froze, their celebrations forgotten. Then came another rumble, this one staccato and sharp edged, like the hammering of a heavy bolter.

'It has begun,' the Wolf Lord said.

NINETEEN
The Forlorn Hope

SVEN CROUCHED LOW and ran along the trench line, clambering over the twisted bodies of Guardsmen as bolter and missile fire crashed into the firing position he'd just left. Rebel artillery continued to fall, unleashing a storm of shrapnel and churning the earth behind the Imperial lines. The blasts strobed angrily in the darkness, painting the shattered fortifications in lurid colours and long, jagged shadows.

The Grey Hunter worked his way along the trench for a dozen metres, and then popped up and swept his bolter across the crowded killing ground.

The massed assaults by mobs of rebel troops had finally ground to a halt, and scattered platoons of infantry and bands of howling mutants crept their way forward metre by metre over the bodies of their fallen cohorts. Sven caught a small squad of traitors just as they rose from a smoking shell-hole and cut them down with a one-handed burst from his boltgun. Twelve rounds left, he thought, keeping the count in his head as he ducked to avoid the storm of return fire that clawed at the battered parapet.

Another salvo of shells crashed into Sven's section of the line, nearly pitching him forward onto his face and showering him with dirt and broken ferrocrete. The Space Wolf heard a fierce oath further down the corpse-filled trench, and saw a hulking, armoured figure on his knees, one hand pressed to the side of his neck. Teeth bared, the young Grey Hunter scrambled over to the wounded Space Wolf.

It was Gunnar, one of the company's Long Fang pack leaders. Bright red blood streamed between the old Wolf's fingers and spattered his dirt covered breastplate. Sven's eyes widened at the sight. 'How badly are you hurt, brother?' he asked, shouting over the roar of enemy shells.

Gunnar grimaced and spat a stream of blood onto the ground. 'I've had worse,' he grated, showing red-stained fangs. A krak missile slammed into the parapet directly over their heads, silhouetting their faces in yellow and orange. Both Wolves ducked as more fragments hissed over their heads. 'I don't think they like us very much,' Gunnar observed.

Sven couldn't help but grin. 'Must have been something I said,' he quipped. 'Where is the rest of your pack?'

'Thorin and Mikkal are fifteen metres back that way,' the pack leader said, jerking his head in the direction of the trench line to his left. 'I don't know where Ivo or Jan got off to, but they'd best hope the enemy finds them before I do!'

Sven shook his head. 'I've lost track of Jurgen and Bors as well,' he said. 'One minute they were with me, and the next...'

Gunnar nodded. 'I know,' he replied, tentatively pulling his hand from the wound in his neck. 'I thought Ivo and Jan might have heard the withdrawal order and pulled back. My vox isn't working.'

'Neither is mine,' Sven admitted. 'Not a single thing is going right, if you ask me.'

'Have you seen Sternmark?'

'He went charging off to the command bunker two hours ago and I haven't seen him since,' Sven answered.

The Long Fang growled deep in his throat, and then rose above the parapet and fired off a quick burst. Screams echoed up from the killing ground. 'Now would be a good time for Berek to get off his death bed and sort things out,' Gunnar said as he dropped back into cover.

'Not likely,' Sven muttered. He readied his bolter and waited for the storm of return fire to pass. Movement from further down the trench caught his eye. 'Someone's coming,' he said, pointing at the armoured figure swiftly working its way towards the two Wolves.

Gunnar peered warily at the approaching figure. 'That's Silvertongue,' he noted. 'Maybe now we'll get some damned answers.'

The skald looked in no better shape than they were. Streaks of blood and soot covered his long face, and shallow craters across his breastplate and pauldrons showed the impact of heavy calibre shells. 'Have either of you seen Sternmark?' he asked as he reached the two Wolves.

Sven and Gunnar shared a sidelong look. 'We were hoping you had,' the Long Fang admitted.

'Not since he headed off towards the command bunker,' the skald replied. 'His Wolf Guard is holding about a kilometre of the trench line back behind me, but I haven't been able to find anyone else besides you two.'

A rocket made a banshee wail right over the Wolves' heads, nearly close enough for Sven to reach out and touch it. 'There's something strange going on,' the Grey Hunter yelled. 'What's happened to the withdrawal? I thought we were pulling back to the ships?'

'Athelstane was supposed to give the order more than an hour ago,' Silvertongue replied. 'Some of the Guard units have already pulled back–'

'Pulled back?' Gunnar spat. 'They're retreating all along the line! If we don't do something soon this is going to turn into a rout!'

As ill fate would have it, screams and shouts of terror rang out along the Imperial line. In the fiery light of the rebel bombardment Sven caught glimpses of dreadful, sinuous forms rearing up from the trenches and scattering torn pieces of meat that moments before had been men.

'Morkai's teeth!' the Grey Hunter cried. 'The wards! The bloody wards have fallen!'

Battered, reeling figures were scrambling and crawling out of the trenches, firing wildly at the unholy monsters that had appeared in their midst. The Guardsmen had finally reached their breaking point, pushed past the point of endurance after a long day of blood, steel and flame.

Then, a dreadful, rolling drumbeat rattled from the depths of the killing ground. Fleeing soldiers staggered or spun about, torn by precise bursts of mass-reactive shells.

The three Wolves eyed one another grimly. They knew that sound and what it portended.

Sven popped up over the parapet and searched for targets. Down in the killing zone marched a thin line of figures cased in blue and gold.

The Thousand Sons strode like iron gods past the cowering rebel troops. Eldritch fires blazed from the oculars of their ornate helms and leaked from the joins in their ancient armour, and their rune-etched weapons spat streams of death at the fleeing Guardsmen.

Breathing an oath to the Allfather, Sven laid his sights on one of the advancing warriors and fired a quick burst. Detonations crackled along the foeman's breastplate and blew a fist-sized hole through its helmet. The Chaos Space Marine staggered, fires licking from the wound, but the warrior brought its weapon around and returned fire in the same motion.

A stream of cursed shells dug craters from the parapet, and burst along Sven's right pauldron. With a blistering curse, he ducked back into cover, absently smearing blood from a shrapnel wound across his cheek with the back of one hand.

Gunnar stole a look over the lip of the trench, and ducked back as another volley of shells tore into the parapet. 'We'll wait until they hit the trench line and give them a taste of our blades,' the Long Fang declared.

Morgrim Silvertongue shook his head. 'We three aren't going to stop this,' he said. 'The Guard regiments are in full retreat and our brothers have been isolated. We need to regain command and control or we're going to be cut off and slaughtered!'

'How?' Sven growled. 'The vox-units are being jammed.'

Silvertongue stared across the smoke wreathed star port and reached a decision. 'Head for the command bunker!' he declared. 'We can use the long-range vox system to rally as many troops as we can and form a rearguard.'

Sven eyed the distant bunker and nodded grimly. 'Let's go,' he growled. 'It's as good a place for a last stand as any.'

A SQUADRON OF Chaos raiders picked up the *Holmgang* on their scopes halfway to Charys, and swung about on an intercept course. Augur operators studied the unknown contacts, struggling to divine their identities as gun crews raced to their mounts and torpedo crews hauled at the loading chains of their rune-etched missiles. Commanders invoked the blasphemous names of their gods and ordered their ships to flank speed. Vast rewards had been offered to the first crew to find the hated Wolf ships and bring them to bay.

The Chaos ships fanned out in a broad arc across the *Holmgang's* path, casting a deadly net for the oncoming vessels. Converging at maximum speed, the two forces reached extreme weapons' range within moments. The augur operators muttered desperate incantations and brooded over the icons glimmering on their screens, but they were taken by surprise when the unidentified ships were obscured behind a cloud of flickering energy readings.

Upon command, the remaining Thunderhawks of *Holmgang's* battle group rammed their throttles forward and streaked from the sensor shadow of their parent ships. By the time the Chaos commanders realised what had happened the strike craft were already starting their attack runs.

Fifteen seconds later the Wolf ships passed through the expanding debris clouds of the Chaos raiders. Hours later the light from the violent explosions would reach the hunter-killer squadrons stalking through the asteroid fields, but by then it would already be too late.

The fate of Charys was sealed.

ANOTHER LOUD BLAST reverberated down the curving tunnel, stirring the air of the cavern and causing the flames to gutter and spark. The scent of smoke and burned flesh reached the Space Wolves, causing the Wulfen to lower their heads and growl deep in their throats. Sigurd moved among the former Blood Claws, murmuring prayers in a firm, quiet voice.

At a nod from Bulveye, the pack leaders raced from the cavern, teeth bared and weapons ready. The Wolf Lord passed the ale horn back to Haegr and took up his ebon axe. A strange, deadly calm settled like a cloak over the ancient warrior as the sounds of war echoed faintly in the valley beyond. When he turned to the Rune Priest his eyes shone like bale fires. 'Get them as close as you can,' Bulveye said, 'and stay with them until the last.'

'Until the battle's done, lord,' Torvald promised. 'In victory or in death. You have my oath upon it.'

Bulveye nodded and clasped the Rune Priest's arm in farewell. Then he turned to Ragnar. 'Your destiny awaits, little brother,' he said. 'There's no telling how many of the foe we've drawn from the city, but I don't need to cast any runes to know you've a grim battle ahead of you.' He held out his hand. 'Fight well, Ragnar Blackmane, and hold to your oaths. The honour of our brotherhood, nay, the survival of Fenris itself, rests in your hands.'

Ragnar gripped Bulveye's wrist. 'The spear will be ours again, lord,' he said fiercely, 'regardless of the cost.'

The Wolf Lord's eyes narrowed at Ragnar's grave oath. 'Even at the cost of all you hold dear?' he asked. 'Even unto your very soul?'

Bulveye's words chilled the young Space Wolf, but he answered without hesitation. 'Even so, lord.'

With a rattle and a wheeze of hydraulics, a servitor limped from the shadows, bearing a polished silver helmet fashioned in the shape of a snarling wolf's head. Bulveye took up the helm and studied its scarred face for a moment. 'Remember all that I told you,' he said to Ragnar. 'War within. War without.'

Then the Wolf Lord's face disappeared behind the snarling mask, and he was gone, striding swiftly from the cavern towards the sound of the guns.

'War unending,' Ragnar answered softly, and felt the Wulfen swell within his breast.

As soon as Bulveye was gone, the Rune Priest turned to the assembled Wolves. 'It is time,' he said, raising his axe. 'Gather round, brothers.'

Ragnar turned to Torin and Haegr. The older Wolfblade was already on his feet, weapons ready, while his burly companion stared disconsolately into the depths of his empty ale horn. Murmured verses echoed across the cavern as Sigurd summoned the Wulfen with the stern tones of the Benediction of Iron.

Inquisitor Volt touched Gabriella on the arm, and the Navigator's eyes blinked open. They spoke softly to one another, and then climbed slowly to their feet. Ragnar watched them approach, concern etched deeply upon his face. 'Are you well?' he asked as they approached.

Gabriella looked up at the young Space Wolf and summoned a resolute smile. 'Of course,' she said coolly. 'Don't concern yourself about me.'

The distant tone in the Navigator's voice struck Ragnar like a blow. A bewildered frown darkened the young Space Wolf's face, but before he could reply the old inquisitor spoke. 'I asked Lady Gabriella to try and contact Lady Commander Athelstane or Lord Sternmark and warn them of Madox's plan, but with no success. Though Charys and the shadow world are extensions of one another, the turbulence in the aether is too great for her mind to penetrate.'

'I need a physical link to them that I can focus upon,' Gabriella said. 'That would make all the difference.'

The young Space Wolf thought it over, but finally shook his head. 'I can't think of anything here that would help,' he growled, irritated at the idea of failing Gabriella yet again. 'I'm sorry.'

Volt sighed. 'No matter,' he said, although there was a look of concern in the old inquisitor's eyes. 'We will have to trust that they will endure until we can set things right.'

Ragnar nodded gravely. With a last glance at Gabriella, he turned to the Rune Priest. 'We stand ready, Torvald,' he said. 'Tell us what we must do.'

The old Rune Priest surveyed the assembled warriors and drew a deep breath. Pale blue arcs of power crackled along the length of his axe, and Torvald's bearded face split in a fearsome grin. 'Hearken to my voice, brothers,' he said in a booming voice. 'Hearken well, and follow me.'

Then the priest threw back his head and began to chant, the words ringing like hammer blows in the echoing space. Arcs of psychic power leapt from axe to priest and back again, growing more intense with each passing moment. Ragnar felt unseen energies crawl across his skin. The Wulfen snarled and snapped at the charged atmosphere, their yellow eyes narrowed in fear.

Lightning radiated outward from the Rune Priest, the arcs merging into a blue-white haze that surrounded the warriors in a nimbus of near-blinding light. Ragnar heard Gabriella let out a startled cry, and then the cavern floor seemed to tilt, propelling the young Space Wolf into the building storm.

RAGNAR FELT A dry, desert wind on his face and heard the cries of his companions echoing through the haze. He felt the first stirrings of panic as he tried to comprehend what has happening. His mind struggled to keep a mental image of the Wolf Lord's cavern, but his steps didn't match what he remembered. The faster he walked, the more the ground beneath him seemed to tilt, until it felt as though he were running downhill. Through it all, Torvald's voice rolled like thunder. Ragnar focused on the Rune Priest's chant and kept running, hoping that the old warrior's imposing form would take shape out of the whirling maelstrom at any moment.

Then, just as it seemed that the storm would go on forever, the white haze parted like mist and Ragnar found himself reeling like a drunkard down a rubble-choked street. The open sky stretched above him, dark and empty, hemmed by the jagged bones of burned-out buildings. His boot struck a large chunk of broken masonry and he went down on one knee, cursing fiercely under his breath. Wisps of grey smoke curled from the surface of his armour.

More cursing and startled shouts rang out behind the young Space Wolf. Ragnar heard Torvald let out a warning hiss. 'Quiet!' the Rune Priest warned. 'Not a sound.'

The young Space Wolf leapt to his feet, weapons ready, his eyes scanning his surroundings. Ruins stretched away from him as far as he could see. The road ahead of him was cratered by shell holes, but there were no vehicles or bodies that he could see. Off in the distance, Ragnar could see a broad, fortress-like structure brooding over the kilometres of devastation.

A column of shifting, pulsing energy rose from the dark palace, apparently woven like a burning thread into the night. Even from such a great distance the sight of it filled Ragnar with dread.

He knew where they were. Torvald had brought them to the very edge of the shadow city.

'How?' he gasped, turning to the Rune Priest. 'What manner of sorcery is this?'

Torvald was wreathed in vapour, like a blade drawn from the quenching barrel. His grin turned fierce, and tiny arcs of lightning flickered through his iron grey beard. 'We've learned a few of the enemy's secrets on our long hunt,' he replied. 'A keen mind and a bold heart can accomplish much, even in this terrible place. I can cross leagues in but a few steps, so long as I can see the destination in my mind.' The Rune Priest winked conspiratorially. 'Soon we'll be able to walk between the worlds as well as our enemies can.'

Inquisitor Volt stepped from the shadows across the street from Torvald. 'Pride goes before the fall, priest,' the old man warned. 'What you speak of dances upon the edge of damnation.'

Torvald gave the inquisitor a flinty stare. 'We've spent the last ten thousand years here, Volt. We've forgotten more about damnation than you will ever know.'

Dark shapes glided swiftly around the Rune Priest. The Wulfen recovered swiftly from the shock of the sudden transit, and whatever else had become of their minds, their training still held true. Sniffing the air, the former Blood Claws slipped silently into the shadows along both sides of the rubble-strewn lane, followed closely by Sigurd. Haegr and Torin paced into view behind Volt, warily eyeing the lightning-shot sky. Gabriella walked between them, her pineal eye blazing like a brand.

'We're at the south-east edge of the city,' Torvald continued. He pointed further east. 'A few hundred metres that way is the city's main transit route, but there's not much cover to shield our approach.'

Ragnar nodded, breathing in the crypt-like air and trying to clear his thoughts. He could still feel the curse clawing at his insides. Focus on the mission, he thought. 'What are we likely to encounter from here?'

The Rune Priest shrugged. 'I cannot say. This is as far as any of us has ever come.' His yellow eyes surveyed the ruined city blocks. 'The place is much changed since I was last here, and there are no signs of patrols. Bulveye's plan appears to have worked.'

'Or the Imperial troops on Charys have been driven from the capital,' Volt said, looking to the east. A look of horror leached the colour from the inquisitor's face. 'Blessed Emperor,' he said, fumbling for his chrono. 'What is the hour? Does anyone know? My timepiece isn't working.'

Torvald let out a grunt. 'Time is fickle in this place, inquisitor.'

'But not on Charys,' Volt whispered. 'If the Imperial forces have been forced back to the star port and Sternmark has been affected by Madox's ritual…' He gave Ragnar a stricken look. 'Before we left I ordered the *Holmgang* to destroy the planet if they didn't receive a signal from the planetary commanders at a set time each day. If Sternmark and his warriors have fallen under the sway of the curse, the surviving defenders will have been thrown into disarray–'

'Morkai's teeth!' Ragnar snarled. 'Have you gone mad, inquisitor?'

'Perhaps I have,' Volt said shakily. He ran a trembling hand across his face. 'We must be swift,' he said, thinking quickly. 'If we can disrupt the ritual in time, and Sternmark regains his senses, perhaps he can contact the battle-barge and stop the bombardment.'

'And if he can't?' Gabriella asked. 'What will happen here if Charys is destroyed?'

Volt turned to the Navigator. 'I don't know,' he said. 'Look around you. The shadow realm changes to reflect the reality of the physical world. If Charys burns...'

'Oh, damnation,' Torvald snarled. 'Not only have you put Charys in danger, but Bulveye and his warriors as well. You risk more than you know, Volt!' The Rune Priest took a step towards the inquisitor, his hand tightening on the haft of his axe.

'That's enough!' Ragnar snapped, stopping both men in their tracks. 'What's done is done. Our only chance to set this right is to get to Madox and recover the spear, and the sands are running from the glass as we speak.'

Torvald glared at Volt for another moment, and then relented with a curt nod. 'You're right, little brother,' he said. The priest pointed his axe in the direction of the palace. 'Lead on,' he said, 'but be careful. I've shielded us from sorcerous detection, but there may still be patrols guarding the streets.'

The young Space Wolf nodded, considering his options. 'Very well,' he said. 'Sigurd, take charge of the Wulfen and cover our flanks. Torin, Haegr, you're on point with me. Lady Gabriella, Inquisitor Volt, stay close to Torvald.' He locked eyes with each of the Wolves in turn. 'No shooting unless absolutely necessary. We can't risk being discovered before we get to the palace.'

Each of his companions nodded their understanding. Ragnar felt a welcome calm settle over him at the prospect of battle. 'All right,' he said, 'let's go.'

Torin and Haegr joined Ragnar without a word, and the Wolfblade set off at a swift, stealthy pace through the ruins. He breathed deeply, tasting the air for the scent of his enemies, and his eyes roamed the wasted landscape ahead for telltale signs of movement. The young Space Wolf bared his teeth in the darkness, glad to be back on the hunt once more.

They moved through the rubble wherever possible, avoiding the easier but more exposed roadways and charting a direct course for the distant palace. Ragnar caught multiple scents covering the broken stones, and thought he glimpsed distant movement in the direction of the palace, but the lightning made it difficult to discern truth from illusion.

It was Torin who saw them first. A warning hiss sent Ragnar scrambling for cover behind a toppled section of wall. His eyes darted warily left and right, but there was nothing to see.

Then he heard it, a thin, whistling sound, like wind over broken stones, approaching slowly from the north. Ragnar pressed closer against the stone and looked back along his line of march, hoping that everyone else had gone into cover as well.

Twin beams of lurid red light swept across the ruins from overhead, sweeping back and forth across the rubble. The whistling turned into a faint wail, and a strange, bat-winged figure glided swiftly overhead. Ragnar caught a glimpse of glistening, leathery wings and corroded metal ribbing, a long tail made of steel barbs and a pale, misshapen head. The creature's fleshy mouth was distended around the rusted grille of a vox-speaker, and the crimson beams shone from its augmetic eyes.

Still searching, the figure swooped off to the south, until the light from its eyes was lost in the distance. Ragnar waited a full five minutes before he rose slowly to his feet. 'What was that?' he mused softly.

'Some manner of daemon,' Torin muttered, still crouched low and scanning the dark sky. 'If we're spotted they'll draw every patrol in the city down on us.'

'Let them,' Haegr growled, gripping the haft of his thunder hammer. 'I haven't had a bite of food or a drop of ale in twenty-four hours. *Some-one* is going to get a good thrashing.'

Ragnar tried to gauge the distance left between them and the palace. As near as he could reckon, they still had five kilometres to go. 'We'll have to take that chance,' he declared. 'It's in the hands of the Fates now.'

They signalled to the rest of the warband and resumed their pace, dividing their attention between the path ahead and the skies above. As they drew closer to the centre of the city they saw more signs of movement along the shadowy streets. Ragnar's keen sight picked out the shapes of men, traitor Guardsmen like the foes they'd fought on Charys, lurking in the rubble at every intersection along the main routes leading to the palace. More of the flying daemons circled and swooped above the broken ground in between, painting the rocks with their bloody gaze. More than once, Ragnar was forced to call a halt and try to find a way through the net of flying sentries. Fortunately, their movements were predictable enough to create gaps that a small party could slip through if they were careful.

The trek into the city seemed to last for hours. Ragnar's earlier calm had melted away, leaving his body tense and his nerves raw. Each passing moment was like a weight piling onto his shoulders. Every flash of pale lightning caused his heart to skip a beat as he imagined the *Holmgang* unleashing her cyclonic torpedoes and setting the agri-world afire.

They were within a kilometre of the palace when they came upon a cross-street that intercepted their line of march. By this point they were close enough for the pillar of coruscating fire, towering over the ritual site, to cast strange shadows across the ruins, sending shivers along Ragnar's skin. He could see a pair of flying daemons searching a bombed-out district further off to the north, but sensed no other movement ahead. Signalling for his companions to halt, he crouched low and crept closer to the street.

Ragnar slipped silently through a defile of broken stone, and settled onto his haunches near the burned-out shell of a small building. Moving only his eyes, he scanned along the length of the street, first to the left, and then right... and froze.

Just twenty metres away, crouched against a low, broken wall, lurked nearly a score of traitor Guardsmen. Ragnar saw at once that they were not recent converts, like the rebels on Charys. Their armour was very old, and scribed with layers of blasphemous runes, and their bodies bore signs of terrible mutations. They clutched strange-looking autoguns tipped with serrated bayonets, and searched the darkness with cold, calculating stares. For the moment, their attention was directed to the north, towards the writhing column of Chaos energy.

The hackles on the young Space Wolf's neck rose. Faintly, he sensed movement behind him. Ragnar turned his head and saw several of the Wulfen moving across the rubble field towards him, and then Torvald, Gabriella and Volt. He bit back a curse. The rest of the warband had missed his signal in the darkness.

Moving as quickly as he dared, Ragnar slid backwards until his position was hidden by the same low wall that hid the daemon pack. Thinking quickly, he waved to his companions to head for the wrecked building. To his relief, the Wulfen changed course and slipped into cover behind the building's broken walls. Torvald and the others quickly followed suit, and Ragnar motioned for the Wolfblade to join them.

They made their way cautiously across the broken terrain and through a gaping window frame into the ground floor of the building. Part of the second storey's floor was still intact, as well as two of the structure's four walls. The warband crouched in deep shadow. Ragnar could hear the panting breath of the Wulfen, and saw the eerie glow of Gabriella's pineal eye. They watched Ragnar intently as he crouched down and described quietly what lay in their path.

'We can try to work our way further down the street, cross over, and then work our way back towards the palace,' Ragnar said, 'or we can wait and see if the patrol moves on.'

'Can't we just kill them?' Sigurd replied. The Wulfen shifted on their haunches and growled, as though in agreement.

'Not quietly,' the young Space Wolf said. 'We're still more than half a kilometre from the objective–'

'Then we'll cut our way through them and charge towards the palace,' Sigurd shot back. 'As you said before, we're wasting time.' The priest rose to his feet, and the Wulfen moved with him.

'Don't be a fool!' Ragnar hissed, bolting to his feet and stepping into Sigurd's path. Rage seethed within him as his body responded instinctively to the Wolf Priest's challenge. The Wulfen picked up on the change and bared their fangs. One of them, possibly Harald, took a step towards Ragnar and let out a warning snarl.

The bestial sound echoed like the roar of a chainblade in the confines of the ruined building. Sigurd hissed a warning at the Wulfen, but Ragnar waved him to sudden silence. Everyone froze as something sharp scraped along the ferrocrete above them.

Red light washed over the Wolves. Ragnar looked up and found himself staring into a pair of glowing augmetic eyes.

TWENTY
The Last Battle

It was no simple thing to turn a living world to ash.

Cyclonic torpedoes operated on the principle of igniting a planet's atmosphere and creating a self-sustaining firestorm that spread across entire continents. Kindling such a fire was no easy task, however; the warheads had to be seeded in a complex pattern and their detonations synchronised in such a way as to ensure a proper chain reaction.

The calculations began while the *Holmgang* was still an hour away from Charys. Like pieces of a puzzle, data about the agri-world's magnetic field, rotational speed and atmospheric density were computed, and orbital patterns for the bombardment took shape. This translated to manoeuvring orders for the fleet as the flagship choreographed insertion patterns for her attendant cruisers. Huge warships shifted positions with funereal grace, taking their places for the dreadful dance to come.

Holmgang's master and her command officers watched the green orb of Charys fill the grand viewports along the command deck and listened as the ordnance officers determined landmass ratios and population densities, turning over the last pieces of the puzzle and fitting them carefully into place.

The red-eyed daemon reared back like a striking cobra, its leathery wings spreading like a black hood around its misshapen skull. A squeal of static issued from the battered vox speaker that passed for the creature's mouth, and then it began a high, skirling wail that grew louder and more manic with each passing moment. More pairs of crimson eyes blazed to life in the shadows of the building's second storey. By ill luck, the Wolves had sought refuge right underneath the lair of an entire pack of the flying daemons.

Ragnar snarled a curse and brought up his bolt pistol, but the daemons were already in flight, leaping from their roost onto the surprised warriors. They moved with preternatural speed, diving low and lashing at their victims with their barbed steel tails. One of the creatures flashed past Ragnar, striking sparks across his breastplate and left arm with its raking tail. It spread its wings and raced skyward, but the young Space Wolf spun on his heel and shot the daemon in the back of the head. The smoking corpse struck one of the ragged walls and crumpled to the earth.

Unholy wails and the thunderous beating of wings shook the musty air as the daemons pressed their attacks. Haegr let out a wild yell and swept his hammer through the air at the darting figures, blood streaming from a ragged wound along the side of his face. Torin ducked low as a daemon swooped overhead, and sliced away one of its wings with a neat stroke of his sword. Other daemons crashed to earth in a tangle of wings and fur as the Wulfen grappled with their swift moving attackers and ripped them apart. The feral Wolves were every bit as swift as their monstrous foes, and their armour was proof against the creatures' barbed tails.

The surviving daemons fled skyward, circling above the ruined building and spreading the alarm far and wide. Bolt pistols barked, and within moments the last of the flying daemons crumpled and fell to the ground, but the damage had already been done. Ragnar could hear the sounds of armoured boots scrabbling across broken stone and heard the answering cries of other winged daemons approaching from every direction. There was only one thing left for the Wolves to do: fight their way to the palace, or die in the attempt.

Ragnar raised his keening blade. 'Follow me, brothers!' he cried. 'Our course is set, and the foe awaits. Let none stand against us. For Russ and the Allfather!'

Sigurd raised his crozius arcanum and began the Benediction of Iron. Torvald threw back his head and howled at the sky, and the Wulfen joined in, singing a hunting song older and more elemental than mankind.

Lightning raged overhead as the Wolves charged from the concealing shadows of the ruined building and crashed head-on into the oncoming platoon of traitor Guardsmen. Wild shots tore through the air, blasting craters from the rubble or ricocheting off ceramite plate. An indigo beam from Gabriella's pistol burned a hole through one onrushing Guardsman and toppled him to the ground. Inquisitor Volt cried an oath to the Emperor and shot another Guardsman full in the chest. The sanctified bolt pistol shell punched through the traitor's desecrated armour as though it were made of tissue, and the blessings carved onto the round's surface consumed the man in a sheet of silver fire.

Ragnar leapt a boulder-sized chunk of masonry and shot an oncoming Guardsman point-blank. The traitor staggered, and he finished the man off with a sweep of his blade. Another traitor lunged at him from the left, slashing at him with dagger-like claws, but he spun beneath the blow and sliced off the soldier's mutated arm at the elbow. Man-made lightning crackled as Torvald laid a traitor low with his rune axe, and Haegr smashed another apart with a furious blow from his thunder hammer.

'Forward!' Ragnar yelled, orientating himself on the distant palace. 'Don't stop for anything.'

Another Guardsman reared up in front of the young Space Wolf and they both fired point-blank. The traitor fell backwards, his head blown apart, even as the autogun shell ricocheted from Ragnar's ancient armour. He vaulted the Guardsman's bloody corpse and slid down a slope of shattered rubble, all but tumbling onto the debris choked street beyond.

A storm of shells criss-crossed over Ragnar's head or dug furrows from the roadway as more enemy patrols fired from either end of the street. Ragnar ducked low and crossed the street at a run, firing aimed shots at the mob of Guardsmen to his right. Torin and Haegr added their fire moments later as they emerged onto the street and followed the young Space Wolf's lead. Torvald, Gabriella and Volt followed, surrounded by Sigurd and the Wulfen. The inquisitor's armour and robes shone with burning silver runes, and the wards of protection seemed to confound the enemy's aim long enough for the group to reach cover on the far side of the street.

By that point Ragnar was already charging ahead through the lightning-shot darkness, stumbling, leaping and scrambling over piles of rubble and twisted metal while listening to the sounds of pursuit approaching from the east and west. Shrieks echoed overhead as more of the flying daemons joined the chase. One swept low, angling for Ragnar's back, but a shot from Torin's bolt pistol sent it tumbling to the ground. Shouts, curses and feral howls shook the night. Shots from the traitors' autoguns hissed through the air, but the broken terrain provided ample cover for the running warband. Ragnar couldn't afford a single backward glance. He could only trust that his companions were still behind him.

Ragnar cut the most direct course over the ruins that he could, navigating by the twisting column of Chaos energy rising from the palace roof. The traitors continued to pursue the racing warband, sometimes drawing close enough for a brief exchange of fire with the Wolves. Once Ragnar clearly heard a howl of pain, and he knew that one of the Wulfen had been hit. Steeling himself, the young Space Wolf pressed on.

After several long minutes, the broken walls and piles of debris abruptly ended at the edge of a vast, open square that stretched before the palace gates. The square was pocked with craters and scarred with blackened furrows that were the hallmarks of an orbital bombardment. Ragnar fetched up against the remnants of a shattered wall and cursed under his breath. He ought to have expected a parade ground or marshalling field in front of the palace. This one, near as he could tell, looked to be a kilometre across. Faint signs of movement at the far end revealed mobs of traitor Guardsmen rushing into the square from the west, drawn by the wailing daemons overhead.

Far across the plaza, the palace's tall gates stood open, but for how much longer, Ragnar wondered?

Torin and Haegr pulled up alongside Ragnar, their armoured forms coated in dust and splashes of ichor. Haegr was red-faced and breathing hard from the difficult run, but his expression was set in a determined scowl. Torin peered across the open square and shook his head. 'I don't like the look of that,' he declared. 'We'll be taking fire the whole way across.'

'Best get it over with, then,' Ragnar growled. He peered back over his shoulder, trying to ascertain where the rest of the warband was. He caught a glimpse of Sigurd and a few of the Wulfen, and then saw Torvald, Gabriella and Volt climbing over a pile of rubble just behind him. 'We'll stay close to the inquisitor and see how well those wards of his work. Let's go!'

Ragnar leapt from cover onto the edge of the square. Moments later Torin and Haegr followed, and then Sigurd, Torvald, Gabriella and Volt. The dark, swift forms of the Wulfen flowed like shadows out of the rubble to either side. They were close to the south-west corner of the square. Ragnar could see more movement farther north, where a side street emptied into the square, and saw more pursuing mobs approaching from the north and east.

He didn't see the traitors hidden in the rubble to the south until they rose from cover and opened fire.

A storm of shells tore through the surprised warband, ringing off the curved surfaces of ceramite plate, and buzzing through the air. Two shells flattened against Ragnar's armour; another clipped Haegr's right leg, nearly dropping the burly Wolfblade to his knees. One of the Wulfen dropped without a sound, shot through the head.

Gabriella spun, raking the ruins with bursts from her xenotech pistol. Then a shell struck her high in the chest, knocking the Navigator from her feet.

Ragnar roared in anger and opened fire on the ambushers, knocking one traitor backwards with a shell through his helmet. More enemy shells hissed past the young Space Wolf's head as he leapt for Gabriella. 'Head for the palace,' he cried. 'Go!'

Torvald took up the cry, leading Sigurd and the Wulfen towards the palace. Still firing, Ragnar knelt beside Gabriella. 'Are you hurt?' he asked.

'Fine... I'm fine,' the Navigator gasped. 'It flattened against my armour. Help me up.'

A shell ricocheted from Ragnar's left pauldron. Volt, Torin and Haegr stood their ground, trading shots with the ambushing Guardsmen. The young Space Wolf got his sword arm around Gabriella's shoulders and lifted her to her feet. 'Run!' he yelled, pushing her after Torvald. Holstering his pistol, Ragnar pulled a grenade from his belt, threw it towards the ambushers, and then loped along in Gabriella's wake.

Shells hissed through the air from three different directions as the Wolves raced across the square. Traitor Guardsmen were charging at the warband, forming an armoured barrier across the warriors' path. Torvald was hit again and again, skipping a single step when one of the shells found a weak spot in his armour, but the old warrior only redoubled his pace, his axe held high. The Rune Priest began a dreadful battle chant as he charged into the fire, a song of split helms and splintered shields, a merciless song of vengeance and red ruin.

If the traitors meant to bar the path to Madox, they would have to stand their ground before the Wolves of Fenris.

Torvald crashed into the enemy ranks like a battering ram, his axe reaping a terrible harvest among his foes. Armour plates split and smoking corpses were flung skyward with each upward sweep of the warrior-priest's blade. The traitors slashed and stabbed at him with chainswords or jagged talons, but none struck more than once.

The traitors reeled from the priest's terrible onslaught. Then the Wulfen struck. Having suffered a constant hail of shells since the battle began, the cursed warriors leapt at their foes with bloodthirsty howls and flashing, razor-edged claws. Sigurd charged alongside them, roaring out the Litany of Detestation and crushing skulls with his glowing crozius. The enemy line recoiled from the impact, its survivors pushed step by step back towards the waiting palace, and the mobs of Guardsmen along the flanks rushed forwards, trying to encircle the Wolves.

'Forward!' Ragnar shouted to his companions. 'Break through and keep going.' As he spoke, he snapped a pair of shots into the swirling melee and brought down another foe. Then he wove past the snarling Wulfen and crashed into the line alongside Torvald. His frost blade howled as the young Space Wolf hacked open a traitor's breastplate, and then severed another's claw arm.

An indigo beam flashed past Ragnar's shoulder and punched through two of the struggling foes. Then Volt appeared, brandishing a glowing silver falchion and shouting a prayer of detestation in a terrible voice. The traitors faltered before the furious inquisitor and his powerful wards. Many threw up their arms and staggered away, hissing curses at Volt and the Wolves.

Haegr rushed forward with a bear-like roar and smashed two Guardsmen aside with a sweep of his hammer. Ragnar saw the opening and shouted to Sigurd. 'Forward, priest!' He pointed to the palace gates, just a few hundred metres away. 'Keep moving!'

Sigurd blocked a traitor's sweeping blade, and then glanced quickly at Ragnar and nodded. The Wolf Priest shouted something at a trio of Wulfen close by, and the warriors surged forwards. In moments they had broken through the encirclement and were racing across the parade field, drawing fire from several of the traitors as they went. More of the Wulfen caught sight of their comrades and broke free as well, and within moments the warband was on the move again, firing at the mob of Guardsmen closing ranks in their wake.

Shells chased after Ragnar and his companions, but the shots were poorly aimed and flew wide of their mark. The war band was widely scattered in the wake of the melee, with Sigurd and a trio of Wulfen well ahead, followed by Torvald, Volt, Gabriella and the rest of Harald's pack. Ragnar, Torin and Haegr brought up the rear, firing shots at the pursuing traitors as they ran.

Ragnar saw that the palace gates were still open, and from what he could see there were no foes waiting on the pockmarked battlements. He turned his attention from the pursuing Guardsmen long enough to try and peer beyond the gateway into the courtyard beyond, but all he caught was a fleeting glimpse of flickering purple flame.

More traitor Guardsmen were racing onto the parade ground from the south and west, but they were too far away to reach the Wolves in time. Once past the gates it would be a short run into the palace, and the confined spaces would favour them rather than their foes.

The young Space Wolf turned to shout encouragement to Sigurd, and caught a flash of movement just beyond the palace gates. At first he thought it was a mob of traitors positioning themselves in front of the shifting flames, but then he realised that the flames were in motion, advancing implacably towards the gateway.

Ragnar's eyes widened in realisation. 'Sigurd!' he shouted, but his warning came a moment too late.

Sigurd half-turned, glancing over his shoulder at the young Space Wolf just as the Chaos Dreadnought lumbered through the gateway and opened fire, bathing the Wolf Priest and the trio of Wulfen in a blast of crackling plasma.

THE CRACKLE OF small-arms fire echoed through the darkness across the Charys star port, punctuated by confused shouts and the cries of dying men. Flames billowed skyward from warehouses or refuelling nodes hit by enemy fire, illuminating large sections of the landing field while leaving others plunged into abyssal shadow. Sven and his companions kept to the darkness as they raced back to the command bunker, their preternatural senses alert for signs of danger.

Strange, gibbering howls and blasphemous cries rose from all directions as packs of daemons stalked across the landing field after the fleeing Guardsmen. The regiments had all but ceased to exist. All that remained were isolated platoons fighting for their lives as they searched for some way to escape the slaughter unfolding around them.

Men screamed in the night, calling to the Emperor to deliver them. Sometimes, their plea was answered by a low, savage howl. The sound made Sven's blood run cold. He'd heard it often enough along the mountain slopes and ice fields of home as the Fenrisian wolves hunted their prey. After that there would be terrible, unnatural screams and savage cries as the daemons found themselves fighting a beast every bit as terrible as they were. Sven, Gunnar and Silvertongue shared uneasy looks at every wolf-like howl. *Our battle-brothers have gone mad,* the Grey Hunter thought dreadfully, feeling his skin crawl. His gaze turned to the north-east, where the company had laid Berek in state on a bier strung with melta charges. Sven pictured Thorin Shieldsplitter kneeling at Berek's feet, his hands trembling as he lifted the access panel to the first charge and awoke its detonation runes. *Not long now,* Sven thought bleakly.

As they ran the five kilometres to the centre of the landing field, Sven listened for the rising whine of engines, and scanned the dark skies for thruster flames. Nothing had taken off from the doomed star port as far as he could tell. He feared that when they reached the command bunker they would find a burning, cratered ruin, blown apart by a salvo of powerful Earthshaker artillery shells.

Instead, the three Wolves arrived to find the low, slope-sided bunkers largely unscathed. Three cargo haulers were parked outside the main entrance, their petrochem engines rumbling. The armoured doors to the bunker were open, but there was no one about.

They surveyed the scene for a moment from the deep shadows beyond the bunker floodlights. 'What do you make of this?' Sven asked, feeling his hackles rise.

Gunnar shook his head. 'No signs of a firefight. Maybe the Guardsmen lost their nerve and ran off?'

'Perhaps,' Silvertongue said, but the skald's voice sounded less than certain. 'Let's check out the back of those trucks.'

The warriors spread out and approached the cargo haulers at a crouching run, their bolters trained and ready. Sven reached the tailgate of the first truck and swung around, aiming into the bed. 'Logic engines, data-slates and a pair of generators,' he declared, lowering his weapon, 'but no soldiers.'

'Same here,' Silvertongue said from the back of the second truck. 'Gunnar? What have you got?'

'Crates and more crates,' the Long Fang said from the third cargo hauler. 'Looks like they were emptying out the bunker. Except…'

The skald looked back at the old Wolf. 'Except what?'

Gunnar nodded towards the bunker entrance, just a few metres away. 'I smell blood,' he replied, 'and it's fresh.'

Silvertongue looked over at Sven and indicated the bunker entrance. The Grey Hunter nodded and edged towards the open doorway, bolter at the ready.

When he was within three metres, he could smell the blood as well, along with the stink of scorched ferrocrete and overheated power cells. Sven crouched low and tried to peer into the tunnel beyond the threshold. Most of the lights in the passageway were out, but the Wolf's keen sight picked out a body slumped on the floor just beyond the doorway.

Another savage howl rose into the darkness off to the south. Sven took a deep breath and edged closer.

The body was clearly that of a Guardsman, collapsed against the right wall of the tunnel and sitting in a pool of blood. The soldier's left arm was flung out to the side. In the faint light Sven could see that it had been torn open from shoulder to elbow. More worrying, the soldier had been facing *into* the bunker when he'd been killed.

Moving carefully, Sven stepped around the body and entered the tunnel. The Guardsman's lasgun lay in his lap, covered in gore. A faintly blinking light on the weapon's power cell showed that it was completely empty. Scorch marks from wild lasgun fire marked the reinforced walls all the way down the narrow passageway.

Sven crouched low, aiming down the passageway. There was another faint scent in the tunnel, something savage and wild that set his nerves on edge. He was so intent on the strange smell that he didn't hear Gunnar and Silvertongue creep up to the bunker entrance behind him.

'What happened here?' the skald asked.

The Grey Hunter started, his finger tightening on the trigger of his boltgun. Heart racing, he half-turned to his battle-brothers. 'There's something in here,' he said quietly. 'I don't know what it is, but I can smell it.'

Gunnar looked down at the dead soldier. 'Looks like daemon's work,' he said grimly.

Silvertongue nodded thoughtfully. 'If so, they're between us and the vox-units,' he said. 'Sven, you've got point.'

The Grey Hunter nodded, checking his bolter. Six rounds left, he thought. If there's more than one of them in here, this is going to be a short fight.

Weapons ready, the Wolves made their way into the bunker. Outside, a chorus of hunting howls rose into the fire-lit sky.

THE CHAOS DREADNOUGHT's armoured hide bore the marks of ten thousand years of battle. Gruesome trophies from dozens of unholy campaigns hung from corroded spikes across its wide shoulders, and its scarred front hull was daubed with evil runes painted in the blood of the innocent. The war machine's sarcophagus was wrapped in black iron chains, and strange charms had been affixed to its metal surface. Wreathed in a nimbus of multicoloured fire, the oculars of the Dreadnought's pitted helm were as black as the depths of the abyss. Ragnar looked into those depths and knew that no living thing lay within that adamantine shell. The warrior within had been turned to dust by the sorceries of the Rubric of Ahriman, thousands of years past. All that remained was a hateful spirit that longed for nothing but slaughter.

In the middle ground between Ragnar and the Dreadnought, an armoured figure staggered amid three blackened and melted corpses. Smoke rose from Sigurd's armour, and the ceramite plates shimmered with heat, but the power of the iron wolf amulet had saved the priest from a gruesome death. The blast had left the Wolf Priest stunned, and for a moment he seemed unable to comprehend the peril looming before him.

With a groan of ancient servo-motors the war machine took a ponderous step forward. An inhuman growl issued from the Dreadnought's vox-unit as it reached for Sigurd with a huge, saw toothed power claw.

'For Russ and the Allfather!' Ragnar cried, charging between Sigurd and the war machine, and leaping at the Dreadnought's head. Purple and gold flames licked at him like deadly whips as he drew near, leaving long scorch marks across his shoulders and chest. His frost blade struck sparks as it rang from the war machine's heavy armour, but with all his strength he could not penetrate the thick adamantine plates.

Howling in fury, the Dreadnought turned at the waist and swiped its claw at the offending Wolf. Ragnar leapt backwards, just out of reach, but was struck with a hail of shells as a twin bolter in the war machine's shoulder opened fire. Mass-reactive rounds smashed against the young Space Wolf's breastplate, driving him to his knees.

More of the Wolves rushed forwards. The Wulfen swept around the Dreadnought's flanks, risking the deadly flames to leap in and rake their claws against the war machine's armour. Enraged, the Dreadnought lashed out wildly against its antagonists, catching one of the Wulfen in its claw and cutting him in two.

Then came a booming laugh, and Haegr strode towards the towering war machine with a berserker grin on his broad face. 'Curse your false gods for your ill fortune, traitor,' he called, hefting his thunder hammer. 'Mighty Haegr has been looking to give someone a good thrashing, and he's chosen you!'

The Dreadnought let out another savage roar and pivoted again, bringing its plasma cannon to bear, but Haegr saw the move and rushed forward with surprising speed. His hammer crackled with power as he swung it in a brutal arc, smashing the cannon's projector to pieces. Sorcerous flames lashed at the burly Wolfblade, but Haegr kept moving, spinning on one heel and smashing his hammer into the war machine's right hip. There was an earth-shaking detonation that sent pieces of torn metal spinning through the air, and the Dreadnought's right leg bent at an awkward angle. The war machine was immobilised.

However, the Dreadnought was far from finished. Howling in rage, it swung at Haegr with its power claw, striking the Wolfblade a glancing blow that hurled him through the air. Haegr hit the ground five metres away, his thunder hammer spinning across the paving stones.

'Haegr!' Ragnar shouted. The big Wolfblade slowly rose to his hands and knees, shaking his head in a daze. A burst of bolter shells blazed across Haegr's flank as the Dreadnought opened fire again. Other shells tore into the paving stones and buzzed through the air around the rest of the Wolves. The traitor Guardsmen and their daemon packs were drawing near, pressing in on the warriors from three sides. Ragnar looked back and saw Torvald, Torin, Volt and Gabriella standing back to back, blazing away at the oncoming foes.

The young Space Wolf staggered to his feet, trying to think of some way to stop the daemon-possessed war machine. Suddenly, he caught sight of a swift figure charging the Dreadnought from the right. A Wulfen dashed beneath the daemon's swinging power claw and leapt onto the machine's left leg. Flames enveloped the warrior, burning away his blond fur as the former Blood Claw climbed nimbly onto the Dreadnought's back. The war machine bellowed in fury, groping clumsily with its power claw at the bold warrior on its back, but the Wulfen crouched between the Dreadnought's twin exhaust towers and tore at the engine's power couplings with his charred hands.

Burning like a torch, Harald turned and met Ragnar's eyes. White teeth shone in a wolfish grin, framed by a blackened face. Then the Wulfen threw back his broad shoulders and heaved. Ensorcelled metal tore with a chilling shriek, and the Dreadnought's power plant exploded in a dazzling white flash.

The concussion flattened everyone within ten metres. Molten shrapnel rained down on the Wolves. The Dreadnought's power claw spun end over end across the paving stones less than a metre from where Ragnar lay.

The war machine was gone from the waist up, standing in a shallow crater melted in the stone. Beyond, the palace gates lay undefended. The young Space Wolf leapt to his feet. Shells buzzed past him as the traitor Guardsmen resumed their fire. 'Let's go!' he shouted to his stunned companions. 'Follow me!'

Ragnar charged past Haegr and the Wulfen and ran beneath the tall gateway. Beyond lay a long, rectangular courtyard, empty of life, and cloaked in deep shadow. The entrance to the palace was at the far end.

With a heavy tread, Haegr, Sigurd and the four surviving Wulfen swept through the gate. Shots chipped stone from the arch and rang from the steel gates. The burly Wolfblade had lost most of his whiskers to the searing touch of the Dreadnought's sorcerous flames, but other than that he seemed unharmed. Within moments the rest of the warband joined them, Torvald and Torin firing their bolt pistols at the daemons in their wake.

The pillar of Chaos energy overhead shone upon the Wolves with a sickly, furtive glow as they ran along the length of the courtyard. Shots whipped past them as the traitor Guardsmen boiled through the gateway and gave chase, but they could not gain much ground on the fleet-footed warriors. Ragnar felt a sense of righteous rage swelling within his breast with every step. The moment of reckoning was at hand. Madox was finally going to pay for all that he'd done. Nothing could stop them now.

Ragnar charged up the steps to the palace and put his shoulder to the doors. The dark wood smashed inward, revealing a silent, empty nave. Towering statues of daemon princes in ornate armour leered down at the Wolves as they raced inside.

Kadmus Volt pointed to the doors at the far end of the nave. 'The governor's audience chamber lies beyond,' he said over the bark of bolt pistols and the buzz of ricocheting shells. 'That was where Berek was ambushed. It must be the locus of the enemy ritual.'

The young Space Wolf nodded. His heart was racing, and his blood was afire. 'Whatever else happens, Madox must fall,' he said. 'Nothing else matters. If we die here, so be it, but Madox and his ritual must die with us.'

'Well said,' Sigurd replied solemnly. The young priest's face was blistered from the plasma blast, and the brush with death had left a grim look in his eyes.

'Enough talking,' Torvald said, hefting his axe. 'Now, go.'

Ragnar frowned at the Rune Priest. 'What about you?'

'I'm staying here,' he said. 'Someone has to hold the door and keep our pursuers off your back long enough for you to deal with Madox.' The ancient warrior studied the doorway and nodded. 'From here, I can hold those fiends at bay almost indefinitely.'

'Almost?' Ragnar said.

The Rune Priest smiled. 'Go, little brother,' he said. 'Fight well, in Leman's name.'

The young Space Wolf nodded. 'And you,' he replied.

Shots struck the doorframe and whipped around the darkened nave. With a nod of farewell, Torvald turned to face the onslaught. Ragnar and his remaining companions looked to one another and left the Rune Priest to his fate.

They crossed the nave quickly, their skin prickling at the touch of unseen energies. Ragnar heard the Wulfen growl uneasily, and felt the curse within him respond. Beyond the audience chamber's double doors, they could hear a chorus of wild, unnatural chanting.

Behind them, at the far end of the nave, Ragnar heard the first blows being struck as Torvald faced the traitor horde alone. A grim and terrible wrath came upon the young Space Wolf, like a red tide rising up behind his eyes. With a howl, he raised his boot and burst the wooden doors asunder.

Unholy light washed over Ragnar and his companions, along with a chorus of tortured shrieks from the souls of the damned. Scraps of tattered skin fluttered in on an unseen wind from the tall pillars lining the great chamber, drawn towards a whirling pillar of sorcerous energy that rose like a cyclone above the temple's black altar.

Upon the desecrated stone burned the stolen gene-seed of Madox's victims, their precious genetic material spun free in a fine, red mist that rose in twisting tendrils into the heart of the psychic whirlwind. Scores of cult sorcerers filled the great hall, standing atop the charred remains of their peers as they stretched their hands to the obsidian altar and fuelled the workings of Madox's great spell.

The foul sorcerer stood behind that same black altar, gripping the Spear of Russ in his left hand. Madox's right hand was outstretched, as though in greeting, beckoning the Wolves to their doom. His eyes burned with hate from the depths of his ornate helmet, and his baroque armour glowed with unholy power. Patterns of runes carved into the ancient armour pulsed and writhed, radiating energy like heat from a forge, and foul energies leapt in arcs of lightning from the tips of his horned helm.

Behind Madox, wreathed in the very energies of the warp itself, shone the glowing semblance of a single, terrifying eye. It glared at Ragnar with palpable malice and inhuman evil, piercing his armour and sinking invisible talons of despair into the young Space Marine's soul.

A lesser soul might have shattered before such an awful sight, but Ragnar Blackmane looked upon his old foe and felt only a savage, merciless joy. 'Madox of the Thousand Sons!' he roared. 'Your wyrd is upon you! By Russ and the Allfather, your death is at hand!'

The chanting faltered with those fierce words, and the sorcerers spun around, hissing invocations to the Ruinous Powers. Howls shook the vaulted chamber as Ragnar led his companions into battle.

Bolt pistols hammered, sending heavy shells smashing through the massed ranks of the enemy. Ragnar fired again and again into the press, scarcely marking where his rounds struck as he forced his way step by step towards his goal. Sorcerous energies flashed through the air, striking the armoured warriors, but the wards etched into Volt's Inquisitorial armour seemed to turn aside the worst of the enemy spells. Haegr and Torin stood to either side of Ragnar, wreaking a terrible slaughter with hammer and blade. On the flanks, the Wulfen pulled cultists off their feet and tore them asunder with tooth and claw. Sigurd stood among the Wulfen on the left, bellowing out the Litanies of Hate and slaying the enemy with blows from his glowing crozius. Gabriella stood on the right, moving easily among the bestial Wulfen and slashing at the cultists with her curved power sword.

The cultists fell back in disarray before the relentless assault. Scores died every moment, reaped like wheat before the Wolves' iron fury. With every step, Ragnar drew closer to the black altar, but Madox made not a single move to stop him. The master sorcerer simply waited, his eyes gleaming and his hand outstretched.

Within moments they had advanced almost two-thirds of the way across the chamber. Ragnar felt a hint of unease through the red currents of bloodlust. By then, however, it was already too late.

Swift figures emerged from the deep shadows behind the parchment covered pillars: broad, powerful figures in blue and gold armour, wielding bolt pistols and chainswords of arcane design. Their armour was decorated with grisly trophies from countless battlefields, including the burned and broken helms of Space Marine champions, and the skulls of Imperial heroes. They moved with a speed and skill beyond that of even normal Chaos Space Marines. They were veteran warriors who had slaughtered tens of thousands of foes in their time, and were the chosen men of powerful lords such as Madox.

'Look to the flanks!' Ragnar bellowed, but the veteran Chaos Space Marines were already pressing forwards, smashing the cultists out of their way in their eagerness to spill loyalist blood. Still more of the warriors were circling behind the warband, cutting off their retreat.

The only way left was to go forward. Redoubling his efforts, Ragnar threw himself at the cultists in front of him, severing limbs and splitting torsos with fearsome sweeps of his blade. He was less than three metres from the steps leading to the altar, and only about a dozen cultists stood in his path.

Ragnar heard the shriek of a chainblade biting against armour, and then heard Torin grunt in pain. A Chaos Space Marine had darted in alongside the older Wolfblade and struck him hard across his left vambrace, leaving torn armour and a deep cut above his elbow. Then Haegr let out a yell as a pair of enemy warriors attacked him from the right. The Wolfblade crushed one of the Chaos Space Marines with a downward stroke from his hammer, but the other drove his chainsword into Haegr's midsection with unnatural strength, and inflicted a bloody wound.

Anger and desperation drove Ragnar on. Madox had to die. The future of the Chapter depended upon it. He slashed left and right with his blade, killing every cultist he could reach. Then, without warning, the remaining sorcerers turned and fled from the berserk Wolf, scrambling for their lives up the stone steps.

For a fleeting instant, Ragnar felt a surge of triumph, but then a pair of Chaos Space Marines charged at him from each side, their swords flashing.

Ragnar howled in fury as he parried a blurring cut to his head, and then dodged a stop-thrust aimed at his midsection. A sword flicked out and struck his leg, the chainblade scoring the armour, but failing to penetrate. Another sword struck at his shoulder, biting deep into his right pauldron. The young Space Wolf struck back, aiming a feint at one warrior's head, and then switching to a back-handed cut that he buried deep in another Chaos Space Marine's chest. The enemy warrior staggered, and then surged upright, slashing his sword deep into Ragnar's forearm. The chosen warrior's unnatural vigour drove the Chaos Space Marine onward despite the terrible wound.

The young Space Wolf pulled his weapon free just in time to parry another blow arcing in from his left side. Suddenly he found himself entirely on the defensive, ringed by a semicircle of flashing blades at the very foot of the altar steps. He snarled with wild rage, feeling the red tide pounding in his veins as he slashed and hacked at the deadly warriors.

A bolt pistol barked just past Ragnar's shoulder. Without warning, the Chaos Space Marine to the young Space Wolf's right screamed as his body was wreathed in silver flames. Inquisitor Volt darted past the burning form and set his foot upon the stone steps, his eyes blazing with murderous hate. Raising his pistol, he fired a shot at Madox. The blessed round rang from the sorcerer's ancient armour, but the inquisitor took another step and fired again. Each time he pulled the trigger, Volt cried out a name.

'Gunter Mault. Kyr Sirenus. Mattieu Van Dorn. Yrian Kar'Doma. Issedu Orban.' Each shot struck Madox square in the chest, a relentless, punishing barrage that caused him to stagger with each hit. Volt kept coming, his face twisted into a mask of rage. 'Edwen Barone. Jedden bir Gul. The souls of my friends cry out for vengeance, you bastard. And now–'

A bolt pistol cracked from the shadows behind the altar, and Volt staggered as an armour piercing shell tore through his side. The old inquisitor reeled, blood pouring from the exit wound in his back, but he straightened and took another step. He raised his pistol, but another enemy shell tore through his left shoulder. The glowing falchion clanged onto the steps as it fell from Volt's nerveless hand.

Figures were gliding from the darkness to either side of Madox: fearsome sorcerers in ornate armour, bearing dreadblades and aiming bolt pistols at the struggling inquisitor. Their guns hammered, and Volt's body twitched as the heavy slugs riddled him from neck to hip. The old man swayed, for an instant, on his feet, his pistol still raised. With a final effort, he squeezed the trigger, gouging a crater from the front of the stone altar. Then his lifeless body crumpled, sliding in a trail of blood back down the stone steps.

Ragnar bellowed a savage curse, and cut a warrior's leg out from under him, dropping the veteran Chaos Space Marine to the ground. Cries of rage and pain echoed around him as his friends were beset from all sides. A blade bit into his hip. Ragnar growled like a wounded wolf and shot his attacker point-bank in the face. There was only one enemy warrior left, but the Thousand Son sorcerers were gliding like snakes down the bloodstained steps, their black blades poised to strike.

A wave of blinding pain speared through him as the last veteran warrior slipped past Ragnar's guard and drove his chainblade into the young Space Wolf's chest. He felt one of his hearts stop beating, and pure, animal rage took hold. Dropping his bolt pistol, he grabbed the warrior's sword wrist and hacked off the Chaos Space Marine's helm with a single swipe of his blade.

Ragnar pulled the foe's chainsword free and fell to his knees. He could feel his muscles writhing like snakes beneath his skin, and his mind was afire. The young Space Wolf looked up the steps, past the oncoming sorcerers, to the altar and the towering figure of Madox. The spear was right there, just out of reach.

A pure, wordless cry of anguish tore through Ragnar's throat, and he felt his body begin to change. His frost blade clattered to the floor as he tore madly at his gauntlets. By the time he pulled them free, the talons were already starting to grow from his fingertips.

Ragnar looked back at Torin and found the older Wolfblade on his knees as well, writhing painfully in the grip of the curse. The Wulfen continued to fight, snapping and slashing at any foe that came within reach. Sigurd was still standing, fighting two veteran Chaos Space Marines at the same time. What he lacked in skill he made up for with pure, animal ferocity. His eyes shone yellow-gold, and his curved fangs were bared.

Howls filled the air as the curse took hold. At the top of the bloodsoaked steps, Madox threw back his head and laughed, savouring his triumph.

Then a furious bellow shook the rafters, like the roar of a wounded bear. A shadow passed over Ragnar, and the ground shook beneath the tread of heavy, armoured feet. Haegr reached the foot of the stairs at a dead run, charging right at the line of sorcerers with his hammer ready to strike.

Streaming blood from half a dozen wounds, the burly Wolfblade swung his thunder hammer in a fearsome arc, smashing two of the sorcerers from his path. 'That was for Russ!' Haegr bellowed. Another sorcerer lunged in from the right, stabbing his sword into the Wolfblade's thigh. Grunting, Haegr slew the Chaos Space Marine with a swift, overhand blow. 'That was for Torin!' he said, and continued up the steps.

Another sorcerer darted in from the left, thrusting his sword deep into Haegr's side. The huge Space Wolf staggered, and then brought down his hammer and crushed the sorcerer's skull. 'That was for Gabriella,' he said grimly.

Haegr took another step. Then he drew back his hammer and swung it with all his strength, smashing the obsidian altar to bits with a deafening thunderclap. Madox reeled backwards, spitting curses as the Wolfblade reached for him with one broad hand.

'And this, you black-hearted bastard, is for my brother Ragnar!' Haegr cried, raising his fearsome hammer.

The Wolfblade closed his hand around his foe's throat, but as he pulled Madox towards him, Ragnar saw a glimmer of black metal as the sorcerer drew the hellblade at his hip.

Haegr and Madox crashed together. For a moment, neither figure moved. Metal creaked as Haegr's hand tightened around the sorcerer's throat, but then he slumped, falling to one knee as Madox pulled his sword free from Haegr's chest.

The thunder hammer fell from the Wolfblade's grasp. Still gripping the sorcerer's neck, Haegr lunged forward with the last of his strength and seized Russ's spear. Madox shouted a curse, struggling to keep hold of the relic. Desperate, he drew back his hellblade and buried it in Haegr's shoulder, right at the base of the neck. Blood fountained from the wound, but the Wolfblade would not relent. With a final, wrenching heave, Haegr tore the spear from Madox's grasp and cast it down the steps behind him.

Madox shouted with rage as the Spear of Russ plunged amid the surviving Wolves. It arced past Ragnar's head and landed, point-first, right behind Gabriella. The Navigator, fighting alongside one of the Wulfen, turned away from the Chaos sorcerer in front of her and ran for the weapon. Her xenotech pistol fell from her hand as she grabbed the haft of the ancient relic and closed her eyes, as though deep in concentration. Her pineal eye flared like a newborn star.

Abruptly, Gabriella's eyes opened again. She looked at Ragnar, just a few metres away. The Navigator's mouth opened, but no sound escaped her lips. Then her gaze fell to the black blade jutting from her abdomen and she sank slowly to the floor.

TWENTY-ONE
The Spear of Russ

HIGH ABOVE THE war-torn world of Charys, the dance of death began.

At a signal from *Holmgang*, the seven strike cruisers of the Space Wolf fleet broke away from the flagship on divergent courses, setting up orbital insertions that would carry them over their designated bombardment zones. The fleet's eight surviving escorts quickly fell behind the onrushing cruisers. Standard procedure for the *Hunter* and *Falchion* escorts was to provide a cordon in high orbit to protect the capital ships while they were locked into their attack runs.

Aboard the battle-barge, orders were passed to the helm, and *Holmgang* came about, setting up her own bombardment run. Her track would carry her over the capital city and the planet's star port. It wasn't the ideal placement for the cyclonic torpedoes, but the ship's master wanted to give the lost warriors of Berek's company the heroes' pyre that they deserved.

Across the command deck, the chief ordnance officer tapped a rune above his control station. A timer whirred and ticked, counting down the minutes remaining until launch.

THE COMMAND BUNKER was as silent as a tomb.

Sven moved through total darkness, sliding forward a step at a time, and tasting the scents in the air. He could hear the faint sounds of Gunnar and Silvertongue following a few metres behind him, and feel the pulse drumming in his temples, but little else. The Grey Hunter navigated by memory, working his way through the narrow, maze-like tunnels towards the war room at the bunker's centre.

They'd found no more bodies since entering the site, but the scent of blood hung heavy in the stale air. Sven could smell patches of it beneath his feet, the scent turning sickly sweet as it cooled and congealed. He couldn't make sense of it at first, until he realised that the spots appeared at regular intervals down the passageway. They were bloody footprints, left by whatever killed the soldier at the bunker's entrance, and they led in the direction that the Wolves needed to go.

Typical, Sven thought grimly. Never see a daemon hiding out in a supply closet or stalking the lavatories. No, they always seem to find the one place where they can cause people the most trouble, like cats, only with thumbs.

Sven grinned in the darkness and continued on.

Faint light shone around a sharp corner just ahead. The Grey Hunter paused, consulting his memory. If he remembered rightly, the war room was just around the corner, and the signals room about ten metres beyond that. *Nearly there*, he thought.

Just short of the corner, Sven paused and took a deep breath. His eyes narrowed as he tasted the charnel reek of a slaughterhouse.

The Grey Hunter swung around the corner, bolter ready. A single light strip glowed from the ceiling right outside the door to the war room, revealing a scene of carnage.

Bodies and pieces of bodies littered the ferrocrete passageway in a tremendous pool of dark blood. Broken weapons, crushed helmets and torn pieces of carapace armour were scattered among the remains, and scorch marks on the walls revealed that the victims had put up a brief but doomed fight before they'd been overwhelmed.

'Blessed Russ,' Sven whispered, studying the slaughter. There were at least six bodies lying on the ferrocrete, one of which was stretched across the threshold leading into the war room.

Gunnar and Silvertongue slipped up quietly behind Sven and took in the awful scene. 'Looks like a bomb went off,' the Long Fang said softly.

'Just claws and teeth, like the soldier at the entrance,' the Grey Hunter said. 'Those two would have been the sentries posted outside the war room,' Sven said, indicating the savaged remains of two men splayed against the wall opposite the doorway. 'The rest are logistics troops, I think.'

Silvertongue nodded thoughtfully. 'If there were still sentries here, then Athelstane hadn't left the bunker yet.'

The Grey Hunter nodded. 'See the body across the threshold? He's face-down, legs pointing into the room. He was trying to escape the war room when he died. Whatever happened,' he said, nodding at the doorway, 'started in there.'

'I agree,' the skald replied, drawing a deep breath. 'We have to check it out,' he said. 'If there's even a chance the lady commander is still alive, we need to find her.'

'I was afraid you were going to say that,' Sven replied. Stepping carefully and keeping low, he picked his way through the charnel scene and cautiously entered the room.

As bad as it was in the passageway, the war room was worse.

Blood and bits of torn flesh were everywhere, splashed on the floors and sprayed across the walls. Heavy tables had been splintered or hurled across the room, and pieces of wrecked logic engines gleamed like polished coins amid the gore. More scorch marks could be found almost everywhere Sven looked, suggesting a wild, desperate fight. Whatever it was the Guardsmen tried to stop, it was clear that they hadn't stood a chance.

Sven worked his way further into the room, peering closely at the bodies he came across. There were at least a dozen, as near as he could reckon. Gunnar and Silvertongue entered the room in the Grey Hunter's wake. Though they were veterans of scores of brutal campaigns, the sight of the vicious slaughter left them stunned. The Long Fang paused, just inside the door, while the skald picked his way carefully through the piled wreckage.

The Grey Hunter reached the far end of the chamber. 'Large group of bodies here,' he said, kneeling among the savaged corpses. He lifted a scrap of dripping cloth and studied the blood-smeared medals pinned upon it. 'Looks like senior regimental officers,' he mused. 'I guess now we know why no one got the withdrawal order.' Sven tossed the cloth aside and studied the bodies carefully. Frowning, he reached down and shifted one of the victims aside to reveal another body underneath.

'Morkai's teeth,' Sven hissed. 'Here she is. What's left of her, at least.'

Silvertongue made no reply. Worried, the Grey Hunter looked back and saw that the skald was kneeling beside a toppled table. Sven frowned. 'What is it?' he asked.

The skald reached down, pushed the table aside, and picked up a long, blood-stained power sword. 'It's Redclaw,' Silvertongue said grimly, holding the ancient blade up to the light. 'Blessed Russ,' the skald said in a bleak voice. 'Sternmark, what have you done?'

Sven felt a chill run down his spine. It was the same sensation he'd felt as a child, walking through the pine forests close to home and knowing that there was something watching him from deep within the wood. He felt his mouth go dry as he caught the same, feral scent he'd smelled at the bunker entrance. Then he saw the hulking figure just outside the war room door.

Gunnar caught the look in Sven's eye and whirled, bringing up his bolter, but the move came half a second too late. With a deep, liquid growl, the beast that had once been Mikal Sternmark lunged through the doorway and smashed the weapon from Gunnar's hand. Then it struck the Long Fang across the face with bone-crushing force. Sven heard the crunch of Gunnar's skull from clear across the room, and the old Wolf flew backwards onto a pile of broken furniture.

'Mikal Sternmark!' Silvertongue shouted. 'Stay your hand, lest you be labelled kinslayer, and forever damned.' The skald took a step forward, Redclaw held at the ready. 'Submit yourself into the keeping of your brothers, and save your tormented soul.'

The terrible beast grew still, its dripping claws poised over Gunnar's unconscious form. Sternmark had been transformed into a creature born of nightmare. His once glorious armour was drenched in dark blood and scraps of torn flesh, and his clawed hands were matted with gore. Slowly, the wolf-like head turned to regard the angry skald. Yellow-gold eyes regarded Silvertongue coldly, and then drifted to the sword in the warrior's hand. Thin lips drew back, revealing blood-stained fangs, and the Wulfen let out a predatory snarl.

Silvertongue drew a deep breath. 'I'll hold him off,' he said calmly. 'When he attacks me, you slip past and make for the signals room. Do you understand?'

Sven looked from the skald to Sternmark and back again. 'There's got to be another way,' the Grey Hunter said, feeling a cold fist of dread settle in his stomach. 'Together we could subdue him, or perhaps–'

'Do as I say!' Silvertongue snapped, taking his eyes off Sternmark just for a moment to give Sven a commanding glare.

That was all the time Sternmark needed.

The Wulfen was a blur as he charged at the skald with a bloodthirsty roar. Silvertongue's head snapped around and on pure instinct he dodged left, slicing low at the beast's right leg. The ancient power sword glanced from Sternmark's Terminator armour, but the skald's swift movement carried him beyond the reach of the Wulfen's fearsome claws.

Silvertongue fell back before the Wulfen's fierce attack, drawing the creature deeper into the room. Sven saw the skald's plan and started to move, skirting wide of the desperate battle and heading for the door. Shame stung him. Despite the skald's command, the young

Grey Hunter knew he was abandoning both of his battle-brothers to a terrible fate. Though the skald fought skilfully and with great courage, he was no match for Sternmark's prowess. Silvertongue was going to die.

Sven was well past the fight, and his path from the room was clear. Still, he hesitated, his hand tightening on the grip of his bolter. Six rounds left, he thought.

The skald feinted at the Wulfen's face, and then swung low, aiming at the beast's right knee. It was a swift, crippling blow, but the Wulfen was swifter still. The creature caught the skald's wrist and pulled Silvertongue off his feet, drawing him within reach of the beast's gaping jaws. Snarling, the Wulfen sank his teeth into the skald's throat, and then felt the cold edge of a boltgun barrel press against the side of his head.

'Let him go, brother,' Sven said quietly. 'At this range, I can't possibly miss.'

The Wulfen let the skald's unconscious form slide heavily to the floor. A fearsome growl rumbled deep in the creature's chest.

Sven let out a slow breath. 'All right, that's good,' he said. 'Now, my lord, I want you to–'

He never saw the blow. The beast's arm crashed into Sven, knocking the bolter from his hand, and then clawed fingers closed around the Grey Hunter's throat. Sven drew back his power fist, in desperation, but he knew that the blow would not land in time.

'Stay your hand, Mikal Sternmark,' a voice spoke quietly from the doorway. 'Remember yourself, and the oaths you swore to me.'

The Wulfen's fierce gaze swung from the Grey Hunter to the tall figure framed in the doorway. Sven saw the beast's eyes widen, and the hand slipped from his throat. An anguished whine escaped the creature's lips, and the beast fell to its knees amid the carnage it had caused.

Berek Thunderfist looked haggard and pale in the wan light. Decked in his resplendent armour, Sven thought at first that he was looking upon the Wolf Lord's ghost. 'My lord,' he gasped in wonder. 'When I saw you last, you stood at death's door!'

'So I did,' Berek said gravely. 'Madox wounded me sorely, and his magic trapped my soul in a realm of shadows from which I could not escape, until a lady came to me and showed me the way back to the land of the living.' A faint smile pulled at the corners of Berek's mouth. 'Our debt to House Belisarius is deeper than ever. I only hope we live long enough to repay it.'

Sven frowned in consternation. 'Forgive me, lord, but I don't understand.'

'Nor do I Sven, not entirely,' Berek said, 'and there is no time to explain. Even now the *Holmgang* is in the sky above us, preparing to bombard the planet. We have to reach them and call off the attack.'

'The *Holmgang*? Here?' Sven exclaimed. At once, the Grey Hunter bolted for the door, his scalp prickling at the thought of the doom looming high above the agri-world, but then he saw Gunnar's unconscious form and stopped in his tracks. He turned back to the slumped form of the Wulfen. 'What shall we do about him, my lord?'

Berek gazed upon the tormented face of his champion. 'He will stay here and watch over his fallen brothers,' the Wolf Lord said, in a voice like iron. 'Mikal Sternmark has been bewitched, like many of our brothers, by the sorceries of Madox and the Thousand Sons. But he is no monster,' the Wolf Lord declared. 'He has ever been true to his oaths, and he will heed me now.'

Wulfen and Wolf Lord locked eyes across the blood spattered room, and a look of comprehension shone in the creature's yellow eyes. The beast bowed low, touching its snout to the floor, and Berek turned away.

Sven followed the Wolf Lord into the hall, heading for the signals room. 'This curse, how are we going to stop it?' he asked.

'It's already begun,' Berek replied gravely. 'Once we've halted the bombardment, I'm going to turn the fleet's guns on the rebel positions while you and I rally our surviving brothers. Then we're going back into the city to finish what we started.'

GABRIELLA SEEMED TO fall in slow motion, sliding off the sorcerer's hellblade and sinking with dreadful grace to the floor. Her hands still gripped the Spear of Russ tightly, even as her life's blood poured out onto the dark stones. The Chaos sorcerer loomed above her, gripping the relic and trying to pull it free, but the Navigator held the spear's haft in a death grip. The warrior spat a hateful curse and drew back his blade, aiming a blow at Gabriella's head.

Ragnar crashed into the sorcerer at a full run, driving his shoulder into the warrior's chest. The Chaos Space Marine flew backwards with a snarl, slashing wildly with his blade and slicing open the young Space Wolf's cheek. Ragnar's hand closed around the haft of the spear, and he looked down at the stricken Navigator. Their eyes met for a single instant, and he could see the pain etched there. With a faint sigh, her hands slipped from the spear haft and she settled onto her back in a spreading pool of crimson.

He could hear her heartbeat slowing. The breath in her lungs was shallow, like a fading breeze. Horror assailed him as he looked down at the lady he had once sworn to protect.

The Wulfen called to him, beyond the red tide. It promised a simpler existence: a life without oaths or duty, living only for the moment and the red joy of the hunt. For an instant, he longed for that forgetfulness, and the feeling of power it promised.

He dimly heard the sorcerer clamber to his feet. Then came the voice of Bulveye, echoing in his head. *War within, war without.*

The Wulfen called, and Ragnar answered. *Come to me.*

With a furious hiss, the sorcerer rushed at the young Space Wolf, but Ragnar let the fury of the Wulfen drive him. He was a blur of motion, whipping the spear around and knocking the Chaos Space Marine's thrust aside. Then he brought the spear head back into line with a tight, circling motion and thrust it into the sorcerer's neck. The point of the ancient weapon punched through the ceramite plate as though it were paper, bursting from the back of the foe's neck in a gout of vile fluids. Ragnar jerked the weapon free and let the warrior's lifeless form fall to the ground.

Suddenly, Ragnar was bathed in lurid, red light, and he felt unseen hands grapple for the spear. Tendrils of energy wrapped around the haft of the relic, trailing from the foul eye floating above the ritual space. The young Space Wolf spun, glaring up at the semblance of Magnus, the foul primarch of the Thousand Sons.

He could feel the dreaded primarch channelling his energies into the spear, fighting to maintain the ritual that was corrupting the Space Wolves. Every moment the spell continued, the taint sank deeper into their souls.

Ragnar tightened his hands around the relic. He knew that he could not hope to match wills with one such as Magnus, and he did not intend to, for while he could sense the primarch's fury and his implacable hate, he could also feel the pain from a wound that had not yet healed. The spear had wounded Magnus sorely, and he was still weak.

The young Space Wolf gazed defiantly at the blazing eye and hefted the spear in his hands. With a howl of fury he drew his arm back for a murderous throw.

At once the tendrils recoiled, and a disembodied voice roared with thwarted rage. Then there was a thunderclap, and Magnus the Red, Primarch of the Thousand Sons, was gone.

Ragnar felt the echoes of the primarch's retreat reverberate across the surface of the shadow realm. The red tide began to recede in his mind, flowing back into the deep recesses from whence it had sprung.

However, the young Space Wolf wasn't ready to let it go, and he seized it by force of will, stoking the rage once more. The ritual was finally broken, but Madox, its foul architect, still remained.

The sorcerer stood above Haegr's slumped form, still clutching his bloodstained dreadblade. His left hand clenched into a trembling fist. 'Ruined!' he hissed. 'The labour of a hundred years, undone by a pack of fools.' Madox lashed out with a boot and kicked Haegr over, knocking the Wolfblade onto his back. 'But you've doomed yourself as well, Ragnar Blackmane. This world has already begun to unravel. Soon, it will return to the warp, and the things that lurk there will feast upon your soul! I shall savour your agonies like wine,' the sorcerer said, and then lowered his glowing eyes to the Navigator. 'Her, I may choose to keep as a plaything. Her spirit could entertain me for a very long time, I think.'

A chorus of hungry snarls answered Madox as the Wulfen turned from the bodies of their foes and caught the sorcerer's scent. As one, the four beasts charged at the foul sorcerer, their bloody jaws agape.

'No!' Ragnar shouted as the Wulfen charged up the stairs. Too late, the sorcerer sprang his trap.

Madox's left hand opened, and he uttered a string of blasphemous syllables. There was a rushing, wailing sound, like a merciless wind, and then a torrent of unnatural energy poured from the sorcerer's palm. The foul stream engulfed the four Wulfen, shrivelling their massive forms to smoking husks in an instant.

Ragnar was charging up the stairs as the first of the lifeless bodies fell to pieces on the stone steps. He'd sensed that Madox had been trying to bait him, and now that the sorcerer had expended his terrible spell Ragnar was determined to strike before he could ready another.

The Spear of Russ gave the young Space Wolf the advantage of reach, which he used to full effect. Madox fell back from the furious assault, his blade moving in a dark blur as he parried a flurry of lightning-fast jabs and thrusts. Though at a slight disadvantage, Madox had ten thousand years of experience on his side, and he moved with the deadly grace of a viper.

Ragnar pushed Madox relentlessly, driving him steadily backwards. The sorcerer reached the top of the steps and continued to retreat, until the young Space Wolf found himself fighting on level ground. Almost immediately, the sorcerer counter-attacked, knocking the spear aside and darting in to plunge the tip of his blade into Ragnar's thigh. Ragnar felt no pain from the blow, only a spreading coldness that sank deep into the limb.

Madox fell back, a faint hiss of laughter escaping from the depths of his ornate helm. Ragnar knew that he was being lured into playing the sorcerer's game. He remembered the fight back at the Fang, when Torin had played upon his aggression and killed him with small, precise blows. Madox was going to do the very same thing, and there was little that Ragnar could do about it.

The young Space Wolf darted forward, aiming a series of thrusts at the sorcerer's head and chest. Madox fell back, parrying them with ease. Then he lunged in and stabbed his blade into Ragnar's left hip.

'You're getting slower,' the sorcerer said, 'just a bit, perhaps, but I can tell. It's the cold, yes? You can feel it, sinking into your bones a little at a time, and each time I hit you, the feeling will get worse, until finally you're stumbling like a wounded steer.' Madox chuckled. 'I can make this last a long time, Ragnar, a very long time.'

The young Space Wolf staggered. Then, with a furious bellow, he leapt forward, stabbing at the sorcerer's sword arm. Madox expertly gauged the blow and lunged past the expected second strike, stabbing his hellsword into Ragnar's midsection.

Ragnar felt the icy coldness of the sword spread through his torso, and smiled. Madox looked up, and saw the point of Russ's spear, poised to strike.

There hadn't been a second blow. Instead, Ragnar had paused, letting the sorcerer's blade strike home. He reached out with his left hand and grabbed the sorcerer's wrist, driving the hellblade deeper into his chest and trapping it there.

Ragnar bared his teeth in a cold, wolfish grin. 'This, on the other hand, won't take very long at all.'

Madox's scream was cut short as the young Space Wolf drove the Spear of Russ through the sorcerer's faceplate.

FOR MANY YEARS to come the officers aboard the *Holmgang* would speak with pride of the part they played in the salvation of Charys. It was only in private, after several stiff glasses of amasec, that they would confess their horror at how close they'd come to unleashing their torpedoes on their lord and his men.

Berek's urgent call stopped the countdown with three seconds to spare, leaving the ordnance officers scrambling to transmit the abort code and silence the weapons' hungry spirits. Cheers erupted across the command deck as the Wolf Lord's steely voice barked orders to his fleet. The fight on the agri-world was far from over, and the guns of the great battle-barge were needed to turn the tide.

Within minutes the bombardment cannons were brought into action, unleashing a rain of devastation upon the massed rebel forces outside the planetary capital. Caught by surprise, the traitor regiments were devastated by the onslaught, and the survivors were forced to retreat in confusion back to the ruined streets of the nearby city.

But an even greater reversal was occurring invisibly across the entire world. As Madox's ritual failed and the shadow realm began to pull away from Charys, the daemon packs that had overrun the star port were forced to dissipate, drawn back to the maelstrom from whence they came. The Thousand Sons, faced with the real danger of finding themselves trapped without support on a planet so close to Fenris, chose to retreat too. They faded from sight one last time, leaving the rebel commanders screaming in vain for deliverance. Abandoned, exhausted and under fire from orbit, the rebel offensive became a panicked rout.

Berek strode out into the darkness like a vengeful god, calling his warriors to his side. The survivors of his company fell to their knees at their lord's miraculous deliverance, and soon word spread through the battered Guard regiments that the Lord of Wolves had risen from his deathbed to drive the Chaos spawn from Charys. Within hours, an armoured column of recaptured vehicles had been assembled and was making its way up the Angelus Causeway with Berek's Wolves in the lead.

Their objective was the governor's palace, and they slew every living thing that stood in their way.

RAGNAR DREW A deep breath and wrapped his hands around the hilt of the hellblade. He gritted his teeth and slowly, carefully, he pulled the vile weapon free.

The black blade clattered to the stones beside Madox's lifeless form. Ragnar peered at his bloodstained hands for a moment, noting absently that the claws were no longer there. Then he planted his boot on Madox's chest and pulled the Spear of Russ from the sorcerer's helm. There was no blood upon the adamantine spear tip, just a dark stain of dust.

Ragnar could still feel the cold spreading through his body as he turned and limped carefully down the bloodstained steps. The air felt strange. It was thin and very dry, like ozone, and he heard the ominous rumble of thunder somewhere far away. He remembered what Madox had said about the world returning to the warp.

The young Space Wolf made his way among the shrivelled bodies of the Wulfen and sank to one knee beside his fallen friend. Haegr's face was as pale as alabaster, and blood still ran freely from the terrible wound in his shoulder, staining the steps crimson beneath him. The Wolfblade's eyes fluttered, and he puffed out his singed whiskers with a short breath. 'You look awful,' he said breathlessly.

Ragnar tried to grin. 'So I'm told,' he said. He rested his hand on Haegr's breastplate, amazed that the burly Wolf hadn't already sunk into the Red Dream. 'Save your strength,' he said, looking down to where Sigurd knelt with Torin beside Gabriella's prone form. 'I'll get the Wolf Priest–'

'Are you… are you saying that the mighty Haegr is lacking in strength?' the Wolfblade smiled weakly. 'I should thrash you for that.'

The young Space Wolf felt a terrible ache in his chest that had nothing to do with his wounds. 'Get up and try, then. Torin will take bets, I'm sure.'

Haegr's grin faded. 'Some other time perhaps,' he said softly. 'Is Gabriella safe?'

Ragnar glanced again at the Navigator, and tried to sound dismissive. 'Torin's with her,' he said. 'She's resting, I think.'

'That's good,' the Wolfblade said, his voice growing faint. 'Tell her I'm sorry. I didn't want to leave her.'

'She knows, Haegr.' Ragnar said, his heart heavy with grief. 'She knows.'

The Wolfblade's eyes grew unfocused. He blinked once, and smiled. 'Don't take too long getting to the Halls of Russ,' he said, almost too faintly to hear, 'or I'll have drunk all the good ale before you get there.' He tried to laugh, but the breath escaped in a gentle sigh and the mighty warrior grew still.

Ragnar reached down and clasped his friend's broad hand in farewell. As he did, he saw the black gleam of Haegr's ale horn, lying on the steps beside him. Madox's hellblade had severed its carrying strap, but the vessel itself looked unharmed. The young Space Wolf picked it up and tied it to his belt as he stood and made his way down the steps.

A tremor shook the Chaos temple, shifting the stones beneath the young Space Wolf's feet. He slipped on something slick, and realised numbly that there was blood on his boots. But for the terrible ache in his heart, he could feel nothing from his waist to his neck. Using the spear as a walking stick, he made his way to Gabriella's side.

Sigurd was bent over the injured Navigator, pressing a bandage to the wound in her abdomen. Torin looked up as the young Space Wolf approached. His eyes were dark again, and his expression was bleak as he clutched the Navigator's hands in his own. 'She told me she tried to send a warning to Berek,' he said. 'Perhaps she saved Charys.'

Ragnar nodded dumbly. As terrible as Haegr's death had been, the sight of the wounded Navigator was more terrible still. He touched Sigurd on the arm. 'How is she?'

The young Wolf Priest shook his head. 'My unguents and salves are made for Space Wolves, not people,' he said, his voice full of regret. He caught sight of the wound in Ragnar's chest and his eyes widened. 'Your wound is still bleeding,' he said, his voice taut with concern. 'Sit down and let me see to it.'

'It's nothing,' the young Space Wolf replied. 'Save your energy for Lady Gabriella.'

Sigurd started to protest, but saw the look in Ragnar's eyes and thought better of it. He nodded his head in the direction of the steps. 'What of Haegr?'

Ragnar shook his head. Tears stung at the corners of his eyes, and he couldn't bring himself to speak.

Sigurd nodded gravely and rose to his feet. He had one last duty to perform for the burly Wolfblade. Though he had fallen in battle, his gene-seed would need to be returned to the Fang, for implantation in a new initiate. Drawing a short, curved dagger from his belt, the priest made his way to the fallen warrior.

Torin looked up at Ragnar. 'What now?' he asked. 'It sounds like the whole world is coming apart.'

'It is,' the young Space Wolf said bleakly, gazing down at Gabriella's face. Her eyes were closed, as though she were sleeping. The bandage over her chest was already stained red. Gently, he reached down and touched her cheek. 'Forgive me, my lady,' was all he could manage to say.

'Bulveye must know a way off the planet,' Torin said. 'They got here somehow, after all.'

'No doubt,' Ragnar agreed, 'but he's a day's march away. I don't think this place is going to hold together that long.'

'It won't,' a deep voice growled from the temple entrance, 'but we'll be gone long before then.'

Torvald moved with a limp as he entered the temple, and his left arm hung at an awkward angle. His armour was battered and his face bloodied, but the ancient warrior still lived. He looked at Torin and Ragnar and frowned. 'Don't act like you're looking at a ghost,' he snapped. 'It was just a horde of Guardsmen. I've fought worse in my time.'

The Rune Priest surveyed the bloodstained battlefield and then knelt by the fallen Navigator. 'This was well done, brothers,' he said solemnly. 'Leman would be proud.' Then he glanced down at Gabriella's prone form and laid a hand gently on her arm. 'Can you carry her? There's no time to waste. We have to get back to Bulveye's camp–'

Suddenly, the Navigator's eyes fluttered open. 'No,' Gabriella said weakly. 'There's another way.'

The Rune Priest's brow furrowed in concern. 'What is she talking about?'

'The co-location,' she said, 'the bridge between worlds. We can cross it.'

Torvald listened and shook his head sadly. 'No, lady. Would that I could, but crossing between the realms like that is still beyond my abilities–'

'Not for me,' she said. Gabriella pulled a hand from Torin and grabbed the Rune Priest's arm. 'Open the gate. I can guide us through.'

The Rune Priest considered this. 'What you're suggesting is fraught with risk,' he began.

'*Please*,' she said. 'Please.' Gabriella looked up at Torin and Ragnar. 'I don't want to die in this place.'

Ragnar looked into the Navigator's eyes, and nodded. 'Do it,' he told the Rune Priest.

Torvald's scowl deepened. 'Very well,' he said. 'Call the young priest. We need to be quick.'

Torin called for Sigurd, and then gently took Gabriella in his arms. Ragnar stood beside Torvald. 'We should go back to Bulveye's camp first,' he said. 'If Gabriella can guide us home, she can bring all of you with us. You can come home, after all these years.'

A strange look passed over Torvald. He looked at Ragnar, and smiled sadly. 'The thought tempts me brother,' he said, 'but our work is not finished yet. One day, when our oath has been fulfilled, we will return. You may count upon it.'

Sigurd rejoined them swiftly as pale lightning began to crackle from the Rune Priest's axe. The crackling energies reminded Ragnar of the first time he'd seen Torvald, outlined by the lightning above the shadow world. Suddenly, he glanced over at the Rune Priest. 'Torvald, when I first saw you at the agri-combine, you said you'd been looking for me, but Sigurd had no way of knowing I was on the *Fist of Russ*. How is that possible?'

The Rune Priest raised his head in the young Space Wolf's direction. His eyelids opened, revealing glowing orbs instead of eyes. '*It was foreseen,*' the Rune Priest said in an unearthly voice. '*Farewell, Ragnar Blackmane. We shall meet again.*'

Before Ragnar could reply the gate opened, and the world vanished in a haze of white light.

BRITTLE BONES SNAPPED beneath Berek Thunderfist's heels as he returned in triumph to the governor's audience chamber. Sven and several members of Gunnar's Long Fang pack followed close on the Wolf Lord's heels, and a pair of Guardsmen brought up the rear, glancing fearfully around the great chamber, and fingering the triggers of their hand flamers. Berek had brought them to finally put an end to the governor and his household, but by the time they had arrived the huge tapestry of flesh was a brown, shrivelled husk, already disintegrating in the faint breeze.

Small-arms fire crackled in the distance as Guard units began the arduous task of hunting down rebel holdouts. With the *Holmgang* in orbit, the Imperial forces were able to overcome the planetary vox jamming, and had already regained contact with several isolated packs across the planet. Charys had been won back from the brink of ruin, but at a terrible cost.

Berek surveyed the ruined chamber one last time. 'Let's go,' he told his men. 'There's nothing left to see here.'

But as the Wolf Lord turned away, Sven's eyes widened and he pointed back at the dais. 'You may want to take another look, my lord.'

The Wolf Lord glanced back. A white haze was taking shape where the governor's throne had once stood. It thickened, like mist, and he could see vague figures moving within it.

There was a clatter of bolts and a hum of power converters as the Long Fangs rushed forward, weapons at the ready. Berek held out his hand. 'Hold your fire,' he said. His nose caught a faint, familiar scent.

The figures grew more distinct, as though they were approaching from a great distance.

'Ragnar!' Sven shouted.

The young Space Wolf appeared first, the Spear of Russ held upright in his hand. Torin the Wayfarer followed, with the limp body of a Navigator in his arms. Bringing up the rear was a young Space Wolf Priest with eyes far older than his meagre years.

A vague, towering figure stood beyond the limping, battered Wolves. Berek studied the silhouette, and despite the gulf that lay between them, he knew that he was looking at one of his kin. The warrior raised a mighty axe in salute, and then vanished in the haze. In moments, the strange fog was gone.

Ragnar approached the astonished Wolf Lord, his face pale as alabaster. Blood dripped onto the stones with every step he took. He sank slowly to his knees before Berek, and with both hands he offered up Russ's spear.

'We have won back our honour, my lord,' the young Space Wolf said. 'The Spear of Russ is ours once more.'

EPILOGUE
War Within, War Without

RAGNAR STALKED DOWN the ruined passageways of the *Dominus Bellum*, feeling the ghosts of old friends loping silently in his wake.

It had taken four more months to pacify Charys, as bands of cultists and rebel Guardsmen fled the capital and took to the hills. The Chaos uprising across the subsector had virtually ended with Madox's death. When the ritual collapsed, the agents of the Thousand Sons abandoned their campaign and vanished back into the shadows. The Space Wolves and the battered Imperial Guard regiments across the region restored order swiftly and brutally, but rebuilding the damage wrought by the Chaos forces would take decades.

Victory had come at a terrible price for the Chapter. Many battle-brothers had been lost in the fighting, and many more had sunk into the Red Dream until they could recover from their injuries. Some warriors who survived the campaign bore scars on their souls that would never fully heal. Mikal Sternmark was given over to the Wolf Priests after the events on Charys, and spent many years in seclusion as he struggled with the things he'd done during the battle at the star port. He returned to serve with Berek Thunderfist during the Wolf Lord's last campaign, fighting with honour and dying beside his lord as a champion ought during the awful battle on Hadsrubal.

The Imperial authorities never learned the truth of Lady Commander Athelstane's fate. As far as anyone knew, she died as a hero of the

Imperium, which wasn't very far from the truth. It was assumed that she'd been slain fighting the daemons that had penetrated the perimeter wards, and none of Berek's warriors contradicted the official account. The Chapter looked out for its own.

Ragnar and the Spear of Russ were placed aboard a strike cruiser and despatched to Fenris as soon as the warp was safe to travel. Much of the time he spent in the Red Dream while his body recovered from the terrible wounds he'd received, but back at the Fang he was questioned at length by Ranek and the Old Wolf himself. Ragnar spoke of the Thirteenth Company to Logan Grimnar alone. After he'd told his tale, the Old Wolf had the Spear of Russ brought up from the vaults, and made Ragnar swear upon the relic never to tell another soul of what he'd seen.

For many years afterwards Ragnar tried to learn what Grimnar knew of Bulveye and his secret mission, but the wily Old Wolf claimed that such things had been lost in the mists of time. Eventually, Ragnar had stopped asking, but he remembered the last words that Torvald had said to him. Sooner or later, he'd see the Rune Priest again, and then he'd have his answers.

Six months after Ragnar placed the spear in Berek's hands on Charys, the Thunderfist's company made a solemn pilgrimage to the ancient shrine on Garm. The world still lay in ruins in the wake of the great uprising, years past, but the Chapter had spared no expense to restore the resting place of the legendary Wolf Lord to its former glory. Ragnar walked behind Berek, carrying the spear that he and his companions had won in battle. With most of the great company bearing witness, he returned the relic to its rightful place and fulfilled the oath he'd sworn. Then Berek declared to his men that by winning back the Chapter's honour, Ragnar had redeemed his own as well. The Wolf Lord declared that, by Logan Grimnar's decree, Ragnar's time among the Wolfblade was at an end.

Hours later, Gabriella and Torin found him in the shrine, standing before Garm's ivory sarcophagus. The Navigator had never fully recovered from the terrible ordeal she had suffered at Charys. She seemed weak and frail as Torin led her into the shrine, and there was a thick streak of white in her long, black hair. They said farewell to one another beside the tomb. Torin and Ragnar spoke of Haegr, and laughed once again at the memory of the burly warrior with an ale bucket on his foot. Gabriella listened, and smiled, but her eyes were haunted and her expression distant. She told Ragnar that he would always be welcome in her house on Terra, and invited him to return one day, if the Fates permitted. By then she was growing tired, and so took her leave. Torin led her gently away, her hand resting upon his arm. The next day her ship departed on the long journey to Terra. Ragnar hadn't seen either of them since.

That night, Ragnar stood vigil before the silent tomb. He left Haegr's ale horn upon the sarcophagus when he left at dawn the next day. As far as he knew, it remained there still.

A HOWL ECHOED from the darkness. Ragnar stopped in his tracks, still so deep in his reverie that he thought he was back on Charys once more. Then he heard the vile screech of a xenos beast and he was back aboard a derelict Imperial battleship, hurtling towards Corta Hydalis, and the warrior he sought was somewhere up ahead.

The Wolf Lord crouched, peering down the long, debris-strewn passageway. The sounds of battle were unmistakeable, steel ringing against bone and claws hissing across ceramite. From the sound of it, Hogun was facing off against a horde of alien horrors.

Readying his bolt pistol, Ragnar raced towards the fight.

A hundred metres ahead the passageway opened into a small, debris filled room some thirty metres across. Shafts of weak light shone down into the space through access shafts overhead, providing just enough illumination for Ragnar to see by. There, in the centre of the room stood Hogun, surrounded by a pack of genestealers.

Two of the beasts lay dead at Hogun's feet, split open by the Wolf Guard's power axe. Blood streamed from a number of minor wounds along Hogun's chest, arms and back. Four more genestealers circled Hogun warily, waiting for their prey to weaken and make a fatal mistake.

The genestealers were so intent on their prey that they didn't realise Ragnar was stealing upon them until it was too late. The Wolf Lord raised his bolt pistol and fired two quick shots. One of the creatures let out a hideous screech and collapsed, ichor streaming from wounds in its side, but Ragnar was already on the move, charging another of the genestealers before the first body hit the ground.

'For Russ and the Allfather!' he roared, hacking at the genestealer with his frost blade. The blow was swift, but the genestealer was swifter, ducking beneath the blow and lunging forward. Talons pierced the Wolf Lord's armour, digging deep into his chest. Clashing jaws snapped at Ragnar's face. He bellowed a curse, shoved his pistol under the creature's chin and pulled the trigger. Ichor and bits of chitin splashed against the far wall as the body slumped to the floor.

A heavy weight crashed against Ragnar's back, driving him to his knees. Clawed hands reached around his suit's backpack, grabbing for his neck. The Wolf Lord spun, trying to dislodge the genestealer, but the alien monster clung like a swamp tick. Talons raked across Ragnar's cheeks. Any moment those same talons would find his neck, and then he was done for.

Ragnar hurled himself backwards, smashing the genestealer against one of the walls. He heard chitin crack, but the creature refused to let go.

There was another hissing screech across the chamber as the last of the monsters fell before Hogun's axe. Then the Wolf Guard loomed in front of Ragnar, his dripping axe ready to strike. His yellow-gold eyes shone in the faint light.

Ragnar felt the genestealer's razor-sharp claws dig into his neck. Trusting to the Fates, he turned his back to Hogun.

Hogun's power axe hissed through the air, and steel rang against chitin. The genestealer let out a shriek and fell heavily to the deck.

By the time Ragnar had turned around again, Hogun was racing down a passageway on the far side of the room. 'Wait!' he called after the Wolf Guard. 'Remember your oaths to me, Hogun, and *stand fast!*'

Years of training took over, stopping the fleeing warrior in his tracks. Hogun turned like a wolf at bay, his teeth bared and his shoulders heaving. 'No oaths bind me now, my lord,' he said in a ragged voice. 'I've slain my packmates in a fit of madness. I'm wolf-bitten, and damned for all time.'

'Not true,' Ragnar said, edging slowly towards Hogun. 'Did you not just save me from certain death? What is that, if not fealty to one's lord?'

'All I wanted was to kill something,' Hogun snarled. 'If I had not run I would have tried to kill you next.'

'Is that what you think?' Ragnar said. 'Do you hold yourself in so little regard that you think you could raise your hand to your sworn lord?' He holstered his pistol and sheathed his sword. 'Very well,' the Wolf Lord said, taking another step forward. 'Strike me down, if you can.'

Hogun's eyes widened. 'What madness is this?' he said, taking a step back.

'*Stand your ground!*' Ragnar roared. He took another step closer. 'I said strike me, Hogun. Slay me with your axe if you can.'

The Wolf Guard snarled in fury. His hands tightened on the haft of his axe, but he made no move to attack. 'I cannot,' he said through clenched teeth. 'I cannot!'

'That's right,' the Wolf Lord said. 'The wolf does not rule you, Hogun. Fight it! Master the beast and make its strength your own! That is what we do. That is who we are.'

Hogun wavered, torn by shame and rage. 'Slay me then, lord,' he cried. 'I spilled the blood of my packmates. My life is forfeit.'

'So it is,' the Wolf Lord said. 'You have killed my liegemen, and so your life belongs to me, as tradition demands. Do you agree?'

The Wolf Guard straightened, accepting his fate. 'That is so, lord. Do as you will.'

'Then hear me: you are a part of my company until the Fates deem otherwise, and you will fight alongside me until there is no life left in you. You are wolf-bitten, and you have lost your honour by spilling the blood of your packmates, so from this moment forward you will fight to win it back. Do you understand?'

Hogun stared at Ragnar. 'Is such a thing possible?'

'That, and more besides,' the Wolf Lord said. 'Follow me, and serve the Allfather, Hogun. That is all I ask. Will you do this?'

The Wolf Guard fell to his knees. 'I will, my lord,' he said. 'I will follow you into Morkai's jaws if I must.'

Ragnar clapped Hogun on the shoulder. 'Let's not get ahead of ourselves,' he said with a faint smile. 'Right now, we've got to get the company back together and fight our way to the ship's reactors. Now get on your feet.'

The Wolf Lord headed back the way he'd come with Hogun following close on his heels. As they emerged into the chamber where they'd fought the genestealers, they found the Wolf Priest waiting for them.

'Petur's found Einar's pack off Jotun Three and is leading them to us,' the priest said. 'The rest of the packs are assembled back at the junction and are awaiting orders. Jurgen has checked his data-slates and believes he's found an accessway nearby that should take us right to the reactor deck.'

Ragnar took in the news with a curt nod. 'Well done,' he said, and then indicated Hogun. 'I commend this warrior into your keeping, priest. Whatever else he may be, he is still a member of my warband, and he will fight alongside us as any other warrior.'

The Wolf Priest studied Hogun for a moment, and then reached up with one hand and disengaged the clasps on his wolf skull helm. Sigurd lifted the helmet away and smiled grimly at the Wolf Guard. They fell into step behind Ragnar as the Wolf Lord rushed back to the junction, his mind already working on the tactics he would need to defeat the genestealer threat.

Behind him, the jarl's son spoke to Hogun in quiet tones. 'Listen closely, Hogun, and mark me well. I've a story to tell you of the Wulfen, and of the heroes they can become.'

ABOUT THE AUTHORS

William King was born in Stranraer, Scotland, in 1959. His short stories have appeared in *The Year's Best SF, Zenith, White Dwarf* and *Interzone.* He was the creator of the much-loved characters Gotrek & Felix and the author of four Space Wolf novels.

Lee Lightner is the penname for two authors who live in Baltimore, USA. Lifelong friends, they are both avid Space Wolf fans.

WARHAMMER
40,000

THE
SPACE WOLF
OMNIBUS

Buy this
omnibus or read
a free extract at
www.blacklibrary.com

WILLIAM KING

SPACE WOLF • RAGNAR'S CLAW • GREY HUNTER

ISBN 978-1-84416-457-8